The Editor

JAMES MCINTOSH is Professor of English and American
Culture Emeritus at the University of Michigan, Ann Arbor.
He previously taught at Tufts, Yale, and the Bread Loaf
School of English at Middlebury. He is the author of *Tho-
reau as Romantic Naturalist: His Shifting Stance toward
Nature* and *Nimble Believing: Dickinson and the Unknown*,
as well as essays on Hawthorne, Melville, Emerson, and
Goethe.

A NORTON CRITICAL EDITION

NATHANIEL HAWTHORNE'S TALES

AUTHORITATIVE TEXTS

BACKGROUNDS

CRITICISM

Second Edition

Selected and Edited by

JAMES McINTOSH
THE UNIVERSITY OF MICHIGAN

W · W · NORTON & COMPANY · *New York* · *London*

W. W. Norton & Company has been independent since its founding in 1923, when William Warder Norton and Mary D. Herter Norton first published lectures delivered at the People's Institute, the adult education division of New York City's Cooper Union. The Nortons soon expanded their program beyond the Institute, publishing books by celebrated academics from America and abroad. By midcentury, the two major pillars of Norton's publishing program—trade books and college texts—were firmly established. In the 1950s, the Norton family transferred control of the company to its employees, and today—with a staff of four hundred and a comparable number of trade, college, and professional titles published each year—W. W. Norton & Company stands as the largest and oldest publishing house owned wholly by its employees.

Composition by Westchester
Manufacturing by Maple Press
Production Manager: Sean Mintus

Library of Congress Cataloging-in-Publication Data

Hawthorne, Nathaniel, 1804–1864.
   [Selections. 2013]
   Nathaniel Hawthorne's tales : authoritative texts, backgrounds, criticism / selected and edited by James McIntosh. — 2nd ed.
       p. cm. — (A Norton critical edition)
   Includes twenty-three of Hawthorne's tales and sketches, a new preface, along with recent criticism.
   Includes bibliographical references.
   ISBN 978-0-393-93564-6 (pbk.)
   1. New England—Social life and customs—Fiction.   2. Hawthorne, Nathaniel, 1804–1864. Tales.   I. McIntosh, James, 1934–   II. Title.
   PS1853.M35 2013
   813'.3—dc22   2012015266

W. W. Norton & Company, Inc., 500 Fifth Avenue,
New York, NY 10110
wwnorton.com

W. W. Norton & Company Ltd., Castle House,
75/76 Wells Street, London W1T 3QT

1 2 3 4 5 6 7 8 9 0

Contents

Criticism

Contents

Preface

Hawthorne is one of the first and most original of all American writers of short stories. Along with *The Scarlet Letter*, his best tales are surely among his most artistically satisfying works. They may not have the adventurousness of his later romances, but they are more fully realized in themselves. As Jorge Luis Borges suggests, Hawthorne was by nature a tale writer intrigued by situations rather than a novelist infatuated with characters. He took note of situations of typical human desire, conflict, or misfortune and then worked them through with an artist's purposiveness into pointed illustrations of the human condition. As a result, "My Kinsman, Major Molineux," "Roger Malvin's Burial," "Young Goodman Brown," "The Artist of the Beautiful," "Rappaccini's Daughter," and "Feathertop"—to name a few favorites—are marvels of economy, imaginative richness, and moral and aesthetic subtlety.

The stories that follow are presented in chronological order of their publication. No division is made between "tales" and "sketches." (A tale in Hawthorne's time tended to mean a self-contained short story or miniature romance, whereas a sketch tended to mean a short essay or essayistic story.) I have selected few sketches, and the distinction seems arbitrary in any case with respect to sketchlike fictions such as "Wakefield" and "Earth's Holocaust." All Hawthorne's shorter fictions were published first in magazines or "gift-books" (sumptuous miscellanies of prose, poetry, and illustrations) before he later collected them. Hence his tales are at least "twice-told," as the title of his first collection implies. Much of his early work was published in an annual gift-book called *The Token*, which appeared in the fall before the year marked on its cover so as to be ready for the Christmas and New Year's market. Thus *The Token* dated 1831 was published in October 1830.[1] As long as Hawthorne wrote tales and sketches, he continued to publish them separately in magazines for the sake of the slender income they brought him.

---

1. Hereafter *The Token* is identified by year of publication followed by the title-page date in parentheses. When one year is listed—e.g., "the 1831 *Token*"—the year of publication is meant.

Hawthorne was born on July 4, 1804, in Salem, Massachusetts. He grew up with more leisure for the growth of his imagination than most children of his era, or of ours. Though his father died when he was only four years old, his mother's family was large and supportive, and they willingly took on the task of nurturing him and his two sisters in their households. Encouraged by his admiring sisters and his mother, Hawthorne early developed a faculty for storytelling. An injury to his foot when he was nine years old confined him at home for fourteen months; during this period he is said to have acquired the habit of constant reading. He spent much of his early adolescence in Raymond, Maine, a village then on the outskirts of New England civilization. As he later wrote, he "ran quite wild,"[2] hunting and fishing in the wilderness near Raymond. By his late teens he was already a bright, vigorous, and handsome young man. Since he was regarded by his relatives as especially promising, he was the first member of his family to be sent to college.

Soon after Hawthorne graduated in 1825 from Bowdoin College in Brunswick, Maine, he returned to his family home in Salem to make good on his ambition to become a professional writer. There he lived for over thirteen years, until after *Twice-told Tales* was published in 1837. As he ruefully remarked once he had attained a measure of fame, Hawthorne was "for a good many years, the obscurest man of letters in America."[3] Three times in the early 1830s he tried to assemble his work into books, but he was repeatedly rebuffed by editors and publishers. His first projected collection, "Seven Tales of My Native Land," he burned in a fit of exasperation. His second, "Provincial Tales," he got nowhere with. His third, "The Story Teller," a frame narrative with links of travel writing between such tales as "The Ambitious Guest" and "Wakefield," he turned over to an editor who cut it up for selections and lost some of the links. This failure to gain a hearing reinforced Hawthorne's constitutional or habitual distaste for notoriety. Meanwhile, he was persuaded to publish anonymously in out-of-the-way magazines or in *The Token,* where the curious reader might find " 'The May-Pole of Merry-Mount': By the author of 'The Gentle Boy.' " Even when he was better known, lack of money was always a problem, especially after he married in 1842. Though *Twice-told Tales* and *Mosses from an Old Manse* were critical successes and a piece like "The Celestial Rail-road" was widely read in newspaper reprintings, Hawthorne could not support his wife and children with his pen alone until he scored successes with *The Scarlet Letter, The House of the Seven Gables,* and *The Wonder Book* in

2. Quoted in Julian Hawthorne, *Nathaniel Hawthorne and His Wife* (Boston, 1884) 1:95.
3. From the preface to the 1851 edition of *Twice-told Tales,* reprinted in this edition, p. 000.

the early 1850s—and hardly then. As Hawthorne himself realized, he was never really a popular writer. Not only was he too shy, sly, and subtle for it but he worked across the biases of his own vigorous New England culture. He composed neither sermons nor nationalistic history nor inspirational essays nor poetry nor translations from the German nor genteel novels nor popular trash, all of which New England produced in abundance, but rather the slender works that suited his genius. Hawthorne was not only the first but also the only major writer of fiction to emerge from the older New England. He made his New England voice heard in all its variety, but his relation to his audience was always problematic. Indeed, communication with his reader is one of his permanently engaging themes.

The section "The Author on His Work" (p. 291 herein) includes three of his prefaces—three "letters to the world," with which he beguiles the reader into a state of curious attention—a group of his letters, and a representative selection from the American notebooks, including part of the "lost notebook" that turned up in 1976 as a family heirloom in Colorado. Hawthorne was not prone to engage in critical speculations in his letters, but they are valuable not only for the occasional light they shed on his art but also as the immediate inventions of an inveterate composer of fictions. He seldom conveys information without also imagining a role for himself in relation to his reader.

The "Criticism" section begins with key nineteenth-century assessments by Longfellow, Poe, Melville, Fuller, and James. A selection of more recent criticism dates from the late 1940s and continues to the present. The twentieth-century criticism follows more or less the chronological order of the tales: a discussion of an early tale like "My Kinsman, Major Molineux" precedes a discussion of a later tale like "Ethan Brand."

The texts of "The Old Manse," "The Celestial Rail-road," "Feather-top," and "Earth's Holocaust" are reprinted from *Mosses from an Old Manse*, volume 10 of *The Centenary Edition of the Works of Nathaniel Hawthorne.*[4] The texts of the other tales and prefaces are based on the 1837 and 1842 *Twice-told Tales*, the 1854 *Mosses from an Old Manse*, and the 1852 *Snow-Image*, with the exception of "My Kinsman, Major Molineux," which is based on *The Token* of 1831 (dated 1832). "A Note on the Text" and "Textual Variants" explain these choices and cite those few instances where I have departed from a copy-text. In addition, I have reprinted passages from the 1831 *Token* version of "The Gentle Boy" that Hawthorne dropped or revised in the 1837 *Twice-told Tales*.

4. See p. 529 for a complete citation of the *Centenary Edition*.

I am grateful to C. E. Frazer Clark Jr. for allowing me to use and peruse original editions from his remarkable Hawthorne library, to J. Donald Crowley and Nina Baym for advice concerning the text, to L. Neal Smith and Thomas Woodson for their hospitality at the Ohio State University Center for Textual Studies, and to Ellen West-brook and Connie Johnson for research assistance at critical junctures. In preparing my notes I have found Neal Frank Doubleday's *Hawthorne's Early Tales* particularly helpful.

Preface to Second Edition

For this edition I have added the early biographical sketch "Mrs. Hutchinson" and two tales, "The Wives of the Dead" and "Dr. Heidegger's Experiment." I have omitted "Main-street."

Though "Mrs. Hutchinson" was published in 1830, I have placed it after "My Kinsman, Major Molineux," "Roger Malvin's Burial," "The Gentle Boy," and "The Wives of the Dead," all published in 1831. These tales were probably composed earlier than "Mrs. Hutchinson." They provide a context for it, as well as a powerful introduction to Hawthorne.

The text of "Dr. Heidegger's Experiment" is reprinted from *Twice-told Tales*, volume 9 of *The Centenary Edition of the Works of Nathaniel Hawthorne*. The text of "The Wives of the Dead" is reprinted from *The Snow-Image and Uncollected Tales*, volume 11 of the *Centenary Edition*. The text of "Mrs. Hutchinson" is reprinted from *Miscellaneous Prose and Verse*, volume 23 of the *Centenary Edition*. When I refer to the *Centenary Edition* in my notes, I abbreviate it CE, followed by a volume number—e.g., *The Scarlet Letter* is CE 1, *Twice-told Tales* is CE 9. I am grateful to Christopher Barnes for research assistance.

The Texts of
THE TALES

[Handwritten annotations at top: "• Kinsman - male relation", "• Robin: 18, country boy arriving to Boston by ferry", "• Uncle is tarred and feathered → representation of England"]

My Kinsman, Major Molineux†

After the kings of Great Britain had assumed the right of appointing the colonial governors, the measures of the latter seldom met
with the ready and general approbation, which had been paid to
those of their predecessors, under the original charters. The people
looked with most jealous scrutiny to the exercise of power, which
did not emanate from themselves, and they usually rewarded the rulers with slender gratitude, for the compliances, by which, in softening their instructions from beyond the sea, they had incurred the
reprehension of those who gave them. The annals of Massachusetts
Bay will inform us, that of six governors, in the space of about forty
years from the surrender of the old charter, under James II, two
were imprisoned by a popular insurrection; a third, as Hutchinson[1]
inclines to believe, was driven from the province by the whizzing of
a musket ball; a fourth, in the opinion of the same historian, was
hastened to his grave by continual bickerings with the house of representatives; and the remaining two, as well as their successors, till
the Revolution, were favored with few and brief intervals of peaceful
sway. The inferior members of the court party,[2] in times of high
political excitement, led scarcely a more desirable life. These remarks
may serve as preface to the following adventures, which chanced
upon a summer night, not far from a hundred years ago. The reader,
in order to avoid a long and dry detail of colonial affairs, is requested
to dispense with an account of the train of circumstances, that had
caused much temporary inflammation of the popular mind.

It was near nine o'clock of a moonlight evening, when a boat
crossed the ferry with a single passenger, who had obtained his

[Handwritten marginal note at right: "historical context", "→ all about American independence"]

---

† First published in 1831 in *The Token* (dated 1832), then in *The Snow-Image*, 1852. We
know that a version of it was completed by late 1829 from an exchange of letters
between Hawthorne and Samuel Goodrich, the editor of *The Token*. On a historical
level, the story depicts political passions in New England during the whole period
before the American Revolution. It does not refer only to the early 1730s as the narrator seems to imply. For example, the activities of the mob closely resemble those of the
Boston Sons of Liberty during the Stamp Act crisis in 1765.
　　The name *Molineux* may ironically recall that of William Molineux, a well-to-do
Boston radical mob leader in the 1770s, said to have been present at the Boston Tea
Party and sometimes called "Major Molineux" by his compatriots. In the "Prelude" to
his *Tales of the Wayside Inn* (1863), Longfellow writes of some verses scratched in a
window of the inn by "the great Major Molineaux [*sic*], / Whom Hawthorne has immortal made." (See Hawthorne's letter thanking Longfellow for a copy of *Wayside Inn*, CE
18:627–28.)
1. Thomas Hutchinson (1711–1780), Massachusetts colonial historian and royalist official,
was the last royal governor (1771–74) before the Revolution. In the summer of 1765,
while he was lieutenant governor, Hutchinson's house was sacked by a Liberty mob. In
1684, Charles II, not James II, annulled the original Massachusetts Charter. Before
1684 governors had been elected by the colony. After that date they were appointed by
the king.
2. The party supporting royal authority.

[Handwritten note at bottom: "• parable for coming of age"]

conveyance, at that unusual hour, by the promise of an extra fare. While he stood on the landing-place, searching in either pocket for the means of fulfilling his agreement, the ferryman lifted a lantern, by the aid of which, and the newly risen moon, he took a very accurate survey of the stranger's figure. He was a youth of barely eighteen years, evidently country-bred, and now, as it should seem, upon his first visit to town. He was clad in a coarse grey coat, well worn, but in excellent repair; his under garments were durably constructed of leather, and sat tight to a pair of serviceable and well-shaped limbs; his stockings of blue yarn, were the incontrovertible handiwork of a mother or a sister; and on his head was a three-cornered hat, which in its better days had perhaps sheltered the graver brow of the lad's father. Under his left arm was a heavy cudgel, formed of an oak sapling, and retaining a part of the hardened root; and his equipment was completed by a wallet,[3] not so abundantly stocked as to incommode the vigorous shoulders on which it hung. Brown, curly hair, well-shaped features, and bright, cheerful eyes, were nature's gifts, and worth all that art could have done for his adornment.

The youth, one of whose names was Robin, finally drew from his pocket the half of a little province-bill[4] of five shillings, which, in the depreciation of that sort of currency, did but satisfy the ferryman's demand, with the surplus of a sexangular piece of parchment valued at three pence. He then walked forward into the town, with as light a step, as if his day's journey had not already exceeded thirty miles, and with as eager an eye, as if he were entering London city, instead of the little metropolis of a New England colony. Before Robin had proceeded far, however, it occurred to him, that he knew not whither to direct his steps; so he paused, and looked up and down the narrow street, scrutinizing the small and mean wooden buildings, that were scattered on either side.

'This low hovel cannot be my kinsman's dwelling,' thought he, 'nor yonder old house, where the moonlight enters at the broken casement; and truly I see none hereabouts that might be worthy of him. It would have been wise to inquire my way of the ferryman, and doubtless he would have gone with me, and earned a shilling from the Major for his pains. But the next man I meet will do as well.'

He resumed his walk, and was glad to perceive that the street now became wider, and the houses more respectable in their appearance. He soon discerned a figure moving on moderately in advance, and hastened his steps to overtake it. As Robin drew night, he saw that the passenger was a man in years, with a full periwig of grey hair, a wide-skirted coat of dark cloth, and silk stockings rolled

3. Knapsack.
4. Local paper money.

about his knees. He carried a long and polished cane, which he struck down perpendicularly before him, at every step; and at regular intervals he uttered two successive hems, of a peculiarly solemn and sepulchral intonation. Having made these observations, Robin laid hold of the skirt of the old man's coat, just when the light from the open door and windows of a barber's shop, fell upon both their figures.

'Good evening to you, honored Sir,' said he, making a low bow, and still retaining his hold of the skirt. 'I pray you to tell me whereabouts is the dwelling of my kinsman, Major Molineux?'

The youth's question was uttered very loudly; and one of the barbers, whose razor was descending on a well-soaped chin, and another who was dressing a Ramillies wig,[5] left their occupations, and came to the door. The citizen, in the meantime, turned a long favored countenance upon Robin, and answered him in a tone of excessive anger and annoyance. His two sepulchral hems, however, broke into the very centre of his rebuke, with most singular effect, like a thought of the cold grave obtruding among wrathful passions.

'Let go my garment, fellow! I tell you. I know not the man you speak of. What! I have authority, I have—hem, hem—authority; and if this be the respect you show your betters, your feet shall be brought acquainted with the stocks, by daylight, tomorrow morning!'

Robin released the old man's skirt, and hastened away, pursued by an ill-mannered roar of laughter from the barber's shop. He was at first considerably surprised by the result of his question, but, being a shrewd youth,[6] soon thought himself able to account for the mystery.

'This is some country representative,' was his conclusion, 'who has never seen the inside of my kinsman's door, and lacks the breeding to answer a stranger civilly. The man is old, or verily—I might be tempted to turn back and smite him on the nose. Ah, Robin, Robin! even the barber's boys laugh at you, for choosing such a guide! You will be wiser in time, friend Robin.'

He now became entangled in a succession of crooked and narrow streets, which crossed each other, and meandered at no great distance from the water-side. The smell of tar was obvious to his nostrils, the masts of vessels pierced the moonlight above the tops of the buildings, and the numerous signs, which Robin paused to read, informed him that he was near the centre of business. But the streets were empty, the shops were closed, and lights were visible only in the

---

5. Elaborate wig, named for a British victory over the French at Ramillies, Belgium, in 1706.
6. In Shakespeare's *Midsummer Night's Dream*, 2.1, Puck is identified as "that shrewd and knavish sprite / Call'd Robin Goodfellow."

second stories of a few dwelling-houses. At length, on the corner of a narrow lane, through which he was passing, he beheld the broad countenance of a British hero[7] swinging before the door of an inn, whence proceeded the voices of many guests. The casement of one of the lower windows was thrown back, and a very thin curtain permitted Robin to distinguish a party at supper, round a well-furnished table. The fragrance of the good cheer steamed forth into the outer air, and the youth could not fail to recollect, that the last remnant of his travelling stock of provision had yielded to his morning appetite, and that noon had found, and left him, dinnerless.

'Oh, that a parchment three-penny might give me a right to sit down at yonder table,' said Robin, with a sigh. 'But the Major will make me welcome to the best of his victuals; so I will even step boldly in, and inquire my way to his dwelling.'

He entered the tavern, and was guided by the murmur of voices, and fumes of tobacco, to the public room. It was a long and low apartment, with oaken walls, grown dark in the continual smoke, and a floor, which was thickly sanded, but of no immaculate purity. A number of persons, the larger part of whom appeared to be mariners, or in some way connected with the sea, occupied the wooden benches, or leather-bottomed chairs, conversing on various matters, and occasionally lending their attention to some topic of general interest. Three or four little groups were draining as many bowls of punch, which the great West India trade[8] had long since made a familiar drink in the colony. Others, who had the aspect of men who lived by regular and laborious handicraft, preferred the insulated bliss of an unshared potation, and became more taciturn under its influence. Nearly all, in short, evinced a predilection for the Good Creature in some of its various shapes, for this is a vice, to which, as the Fast-day[9] sermons of a hundred years ago will testify, we have a long hereditary claim. The only guests to whom Robin's sympathies inclined him, were two or three sheepish countrymen, who were using the inn somewhat after the fashion of a Turkish Caravansary; they had gotten themselves into the darkest corner of the room, and, heedless of the Nicotian[1] atmosphere, were supping on the bread of their own ovens, and the bacon cured in their own chimney-smoke. But though Robin felt a sort of brotherhood with these strangers, his eyes were attracted from them, to a person who stood near the door,

7. Picture of British soldier painted on a sign.
8. West Indian molasses was shipped in large quantities to New England and there made into rum.
9. A day set apart for public abstinence and penitence in Puritan New England. "Good Creature": rum or whiskey.
1. Heavy with tobacco smoke (from Jean Nicot, who introduced tobacco into France). "Caravansary": large inn for travelers in caravans.

holding whispered conversation with a group of ill-dressed associates. His features were separately striking almost to grotesqueness, and the whole face left a deep impression in the memory. The forehead bulged out into a double prominence, with a vale between; the nose came boldly forth in an irregular curve, and its bridge was of more than a finger's breadth; the eyebrows were deep and shaggy, and the eyes glowed beneath them like fire in a cave.

While Robin deliberated of whom to inquire respecting his kinsman's dwelling, he was accosted by the innkeeper, a little man in a stained white apron, who had come to pay his professional welcome to the stranger. Being in the second generation from a French protestant, he seemed to have inherited the courtesy of his parent nation; but no variety of circumstance was ever known to change his voice from the one shrill note in which he now addressed Robin.

'From the country, I presume, Sir?' said he, with a profound bow. 'Beg to congratulate you on your arrival, and trust you intend a long stay with us. Fine town here, Sir, beautiful buildings, and much that may interest a stranger. May I hope for the honor of your commands in respect to supper?'

'The man sees a family likeness! the rogue has guessed that I am related to the Major!' thought Robin, who had hitherto experienced little superfluous civility.

All eyes were now turned on the country lad, standing at the door, in his worn three-cornered hat, grey coat, leather breeches, and blue yarn stockings, leaning on an oaken cudgel, and bearing a wallet on his back. Robin replied to the courteous innkeeper, with such an assumption of consequence, as befitted the Major's relative.

'My honest friend,' he said, 'I shall make it a point to patronize your house on some occasion when—' here he could not help lowering his voice—'I may have more than a parchment three-pence in my pocket. My present business,' continued he, speaking with lofty confidence, 'is merely to inquire the way to the dwelling of my kinsman, Major Molineux.'

There was a sudden and general movement in the room, which Robin interpreted as expressing the eagerness of each individual to become his guide. But the innkeeper turned his eyes to a written paper on the wall, which he read, or seemed to read, with occasional recurrences to the young man's figure.

'What have we here?' said he, breaking his speech into little dry fragments. '"Left the house of the subscriber, bounden servant,[2] Hezekiah Mudge—had on when he went away, grey coat, leather breeches, master's third best hat. One pound currency reward to

---

2. A person bound by contract to servitude for a set period, usually in repayment for passage to the colonies.

whoever shall lodge him in any jail in the province." Better trudge, boy, better trudge.'

Robin had begun to draw his hand toward the lighter end of the oak cudgel, but a strange hostility in every countenance, induced him to relinquish his purpose of breaking the courteous innkeeper's head. As he turned to leave the room, he encountered a sneering glance from the bold-featured personage whom he had before noticed; and no sooner was he beyond the door, than he heard a general laugh, in which the innkeeper's voice might be distinguished, like the dropping of small stones into a kettle.

'Now is it not strange,' thought Robin, with his usual shrewdness, 'is it not strange, that the confession of an empty pocket, should outweigh the name of my kinsman, Major Molineux? Oh, if I had one of these grinning rascals in the woods, where I and my oak sapling grew up together, I would teach him that my arm is heavy, though my purse be light!'

On turning the corner of the narrow lane, Robin found himself in a spacious street, with an unbroken line of lofty houses on each side, and a steepled building at the upper end, whence the ringing of a bell announced the hour of nine. The light of the moon, and the lamps from numerous shop windows, discovered people promenading on the pavement, and amongst them, Robin hoped to recognise his hitherto inscrutable relative. The result of his former inquiries made him unwilling to hazard another, in a scene of such publicity, and he determined to walk slowly and silently up the street, thrusting his face close to that of every elderly gentleman, in search of the Major's lineaments. In his progress, Robin encountered many gay and gallant figures. Embroidered garments, of showy colors, enormous periwigs, gold-laced hats, and silver hilted swords, glided past him and dazzled his optics. Travelled youths, imitators of the European fine gentlemen of the period, trod jauntily along, half-dancing to the fashionable tunes which they hummed, and making poor Robin ashamed of his quiet and natural gait. At length, after many pauses to examine the gorgeous display of goods in the shop windows, and after suffering some rebukes for the impertinence of his scrutiny into people's faces, the Major's kinsman found himself near the steepled building, still unsuccessful in his search. As yet, however, he had seen only one side of the thronged street; so Robin crossed, and continued the same sort of inquisition down the opposite pavement, with stronger hopes than the philosopher[3] seeking an honest man, but with no better fortune. He had arrived about midway towards the lower end, from which his course began, when he

3. Diogenes, Greek philosopher (ca. 412–323 B.C.E.), carried a lantern about in daytime in his search for an honest man.

overheard the approach of some one, who struck down a cane on the flag-stones at every step, uttering, at regular intervals, two sepulchral hems.

'Mercy on us!' quoth Robin, recognising the sound.

Turning a corner, which chanced to be close at his right hand, he hastened to pursue his researches, in some other part of the town. His patience was now wearing low, and he seemed to feel more fatigue from his rambles since he crossed the ferry, than from his journey of several days on the other side. Hunger also pleaded loudly within him, and Robin began to balance the propriety of demanding, violently and with lifted cudgel, the necessary guidance from the first solitary passenger, whom he should meet. While a resolution to this effect was gaining strength, he entered a street of mean appearance, on either side of which, a row of ill-built houses was straggling towards the harbor. The moonlight fell upon no passenger along the whole extent, but in the third domicile which Robin passed, there was a half-opened door, and his keen glance detected a woman's garment within.

'My luck may be better here,' said he to himself.

Accordingly, he approached the door, and beheld it shut closer as he did so; yet an open space remained, sufficing for the fair occupant to observe the stranger, without a corresponding display on her part. All that Robin could discern was a strip of scarlet petticoat, and the occasional sparkle of an eye, as if the moonbeams were trembling on some bright thing.

'Pretty mistress,'—for I may call her so with a good conscience, thought the shrewd youth, since I know nothing to the contrary— 'my sweet pretty mistress, will you be kind enough to tell me whereabouts I must seek the dwelling of my kinsman, Major Molineux?'

Robin's voice was plaintive and winning, and the female, seeing nothing to be shunned in the handsome country youth, thrust open the door, and came forth into the moonlight. She was a dainty little figure, with a white neck, round arms, and a slender waist, at the extremity of which her scarlet petticoat jutted out over a hoop, as if she were standing in a balloon. Moreover, her face was oval and pretty, her hair dark beneath the little cap, and her bright eyes possessed a sly freedom, which triumphed over those of Robin.

'Major Molineux dwells here,' said this fair woman.

Now her voice was the sweetest Robin had heard that night, the airy counterpart of a stream of melted silver; yet he could not help doubting whether that sweet voice spoke gospel truth. He looked up and down the mean street, and then surveyed the house before which they stood. It was a small, dark edifice of two stories, the second of which projected over the lower floor; and the front apartment had the aspect of a shop for petty commodities.

'Now truly I am in luck,' replied Robin, cunningly, 'and so indeed is my kinsman, the Major, in having so pretty a housekeeper. But I prithee trouble him to step to the door; I will deliver him a message from his friends in the country, and then go back to my lodgings at the inn.'

'Nay, the Major has been a-bed this hour or more,' said the lady of the scarlet petticoat; 'and it would be to little purpose to disturb him tonight, seeing his evening draught was of the strongest. But he is a kindhearted man, and it would be as much as my life's worth, to let a kinsman of his turn away from the door. You are the good old gentleman's very picture, and I could swear that was his rainy-weather hat. Also, he has garments very much resembling those leather—But come in, I pray, for I bid you hearty welcome in his name.'

So saying, the fair and hospitable dame took our hero by the hand; and though the touch was light, and the force was gentleness, and though Robin read in her eyes what he did not hear in her words, yet the slender waisted woman, in the scarlet petticoat, proved stronger than the athletic country youth. She had drawn his half-willing footsteps nearly to the threshold, when the opening of a door in the neighborhood, startled the Major's housekeeper, and, leaving the Major's kinsman, she vanished speedily into her own domicile. A heavy yawn preceded the appearance of a man, who, like the Moonshine of Pyramus and Thisbe,[4] carried a lantern, need-lessly aiding his sister luminary in the heavens. As he walked sleepily up the street, he turned his broad, dull face on Robin, and displayed a long staff, spiked at the end.

'Home, vagabond, home!' said the watchman, in accents that seemed to fall asleep as soon as they were uttered. 'Home, or we'll set you in the stocks by peep of day!'

'This is the second hint of the kind,' thought Robin. 'I wish they would end my difficulties, by setting me there to-night.'

Nevertheless, the youth felt an instinctive antipathy towards the guardian of midnight order, which at first prevented him from asking his usual question. But just when the man was about to vanish behind the corner, Robin resolved not to lose the opportunity, and shouted lustily after him—

'I say, friend! will you guide me to the house of my kinsman, Major Molineux?'

The watchman made no reply, but turned the corner and was gone; yet Robin seemed to hear the sound of drowsy laughter steal-

---

4. "Pyramus and Thisbe" is the craftsmen's play within a play in *Midsummer Night's Dream* 5.1. The character Moonshine carries a lantern to represent the moonlight that shines on the two lovers.

ing along the solitary street. At that moment, also, a pleasant titter saluted him from the open window above his head; he looked up, and caught the sparkle of a saucy eye; a round arm beckoned to him, and next he heard light footsteps descending the staircase within. But Robin, being of the household of a New England clergyman, was a good youth, as well as a shrewd one; so he resisted temptation, and fled away.

He now roamed desperately, and at random, through the town, almost ready to believe that a spell was on him, like that, by which a wizard of his country, had once kept three pursuers wandering, a whole winter night, within twenty paces of the cottage which they sought. The streets lay before him, strange and desolate, and the lights were extinguished in almost every house. Twice, however, little parties of men, among whom Robin distinguished individuals in outlandish attire, came hurrying along, but though on both occasions they paused to address him, such intercourse did not at all enlighten his perplexity. They did but utter a few words[5] in some language of which Robin knew nothing, and perceiving his inability to answer, bestowed a curse upon him in plain English, and hastened away. Finally, the lad determined to knock at the door of every mansion that might appear worthy to be occupied by his kinsman, trusting that perseverance would overcome the fatality which had hitherto thwarted him. Firm in this resolve, he was passing beneath the walls of a church, which formed the corner of two streets, when, as he turned into the shade of its steeple, he encountered a bulky stranger, muffled in a cloak. The man was proceeding with the speed of earnest business, but Robin planted himself full before him, holding the oak cudgel with both hands across his body, as a bar to further passage.

'Halt, honest man, and answer me a question,' said he, very resolutely. 'Tell me, this instant, whereabouts is the dwelling of my kinsman, Major Molineux?'

'Keep your tongue between your teeth, fool, and let me pass,' said a deep, gruff voice, which Robin partly remembered. 'Let me pass, I say, or I'll strike you to the earth!'

'No, no, neighbor!' cried Robin, flourishing his cudgel, and then thrusting its larger end close to the man's muffled face. 'No, no, I'm not the fool you take me for, nor do you pass, till I have an answer to my question. Whereabouts is the dwelling of my kinsman, Major Molineux?'

The stranger, instead of attempting to force his passage, stept back into the moonlight, unmuffled his own face and stared full into that of Robin.

5. Passwords, like those exchanged by the Sons of Liberty.

'Watch here an hour, and Major Molineux will pass by,' said he.

Robin gazed with dismay and astonishment, on the unprecedented physiognomy of the speaker. The forehead with its double prominence, the broad-hooked nose, the shaggy eyebrows, and fiery eyes, were those which he had noticed at the inn, but the man's complexion had undergone a singular, or more properly, a two-fold change. One side of the face blazed of an intense red, while the other was black as midnight, the division line being in the broad bridge of the nose; and a mouth, which seemed to extend from ear to ear, was black or red, in contrast to the color of the cheek. The effect was as if two individual devils, a fiend of fire and a fiend of darkness, had united themselves to form this infernal visage. The stranger grinned in Robin's face, muffled his party-colored[6] features, and was out of sight in a moment.

'Strange things we travellers see' ejaculated Robin.

He seated himself, however, upon the steps of the church-door, resolving to wait the appointed time for his kinsman's appearance. A few moments were consumed in philosophical speculations, upon the species of the *genus homo*, who had just left him, but having settled this point shrewdly, rationally, and satisfactorily, he was compelled to look elsewhere for amusement. And first he threw his eyes along the street; it was of more respectable appearance than most of those into which he had wandered, and the moon, 'creating, like the imaginative power, a beautiful strangeness in familiar objects,' gave something of romance to a scene, that might not have possessed it in the light of day. The irregular, and often quaint architecture of the houses, some of whose roofs were broken into numerous little peaks; while others ascended, steep and narrow, into a single point; and others again were square; the pure milk-white of some of their complexions, the aged darkness of others, and the thousand sparklings, reflected from bright substances in the plastered walls of many; these matters engaged Robin's attention for awhile, and then began to grow wearisome. Next he endeavored to define the forms of distant objects, starting away with almost ghostly indistinctness, just as his eye appeared to grasp them; and finally he took a minute survey of an edifice, which stood on the opposite side of the street, directly in front of the church-door, where he was stationed. It was a large square mansion, distinguished from its neighbors by a balcony, which rested on tall pillars, and by an elaborate gothic window, communicating therewith.

'Perhaps this is the very house I have been seeking;' thought Robin.

Then he strove to speed away the time, by listening to a murmur, which swept continually along the street, yet was scarcely audible,

---

6. Partly of one color and partly of another, with a political pun on *party*.

except to an unaccustomed ear like his; it was a low, dull, dreamy sound, compounded of many noises, each of which was at too great a distance to be separately heard. Robin marvelled at this snore of a sleeping town, and marvelled more, whenever its continuity was broken, by now and then a distant shout, apparently loud where it originated. But altogether it was a sleep-inspiring sound, and to shake off its drowsy influence, Robin arose, and climbed a window-frame, that he might view the interior of the church. There the moonbeams came trembling in, and fell down upon the deserted pews, and extended along the quiet aisles. A fainter, yet more awful radiance, was hovering round the pulpit, and one solitary ray had dared to rest upon the opened page of the great bible. Had Nature, in that deep hour, become a worshipper in the house, which man had builded? Or was that heavenly light the visible sanctity of the place, visible because no earthly and impure feet were within the walls? The scene made Robin's heart shiver with a sensation of loneliness, stronger than he had ever felt in the remotest depths of his native woods; so he turned away, and sat down again before the door. There were graves around the church, and now an uneasy thought obtruded into Robin's breast. What if the object of his search, which had been so often and so strangely thwarted, were all the time mouldering in his shroud? What if his kinsman should glide through yonder gate, and nod and smile to him in passing dimly by?

'Oh, that any breathing thing were here with me!' said Robin.

Recalling his thoughts from this uncomfortable track, he sent them over forest, hill, and stream, and attempted to imagine how that evening of ambiguity and weariness, had been spent by his father's household. He pictured them assembled at the door, beneath the tree, the great old tree, which had been spared for its huge twisted trunk, and venerable shade, when a thousand leafy brethren fell. There, at the going down of the summer sun, it was his father's custom to perform domestic worship, that the neighbors might come and join with him like brothers of the family, and that the wayfaring man might pause to drink at that fountain, and keep his heart pure by freshening the memory of home. Robin distinguished the seat of every individual of the little audience; he saw the good man in the midst, holding the scriptures in the golden light that shone from the western clouds; he beheld him close the book, and all rise up to pray. He heard the old thanksgivings for daily mercies, the old supplications for their continuance, to which he had so often listened in weariness, but which were now among his dear remembrances. He perceived the slight inequality of his father's voice when he came to speak of the Absent One; he noted how his mother turned her face to the broad and knotted trunk; how his elder brother scorned, because the beard was rough upon his upper lip, to permit his features to be moved; how his younger sister drew down a low hanging branch before her eyes; and how the little one of all, whose sports had hitherto broken the decorum of the scene, understood the prayer for her playmate, and burst into clamorous grief. Then he saw them go in at the door; and when Robin would have entered also, the latch tinkled into its place, and he was excluded from his home.

'Am I here, or there?' cried Robin, starting; for all at once, when his thoughts had become visible and audible in a dream, the long, wide, solitary street shone out before him.

He aroused himself, and endeavored to fix his attention steadily upon the large edifice which he had surveyed before. But still his mind kept vibrating between fancy and reality; by turns, the pillars of the balcony lengthened into the tall, bare stems of pines, dwindled down to human figures, settled again in their true shape and size, and then commenced a new succession of changes. For a single moment, when he deemed himself awake, he could have sworn that a visage, one which he seemed to remember, yet could not absolutely name as his kinsman's, was looking towards him from the Gothic window. A deeper sleep wrestled with, and nearly overcame him, but fled at the sound of footsteps along the opposite pavement. Robin rubbed his eyes, discerned a man passing at the foot of the balcony, and addressed him in a loud, peevish, and lamentable cry.

'Halloo, friend! must I wait here all night for my kinsman, Major Molineux?'

The sleeping echoes awoke, and answered the voice; and the passenger, barely able to discern a figure sitting in the oblique shade of the steeple, traversed the street to obtain a nearer view. He was himself a gentleman in his prime, of open, intelligent, cheerful, and altogether prepossessing countenance. Perceiving a country youth, apparently homeless and without friends, he accosted him in a tone of real kindness, which had become strange to Robin's ears.

'Well, my good lad, why are you sitting here?' inquired he. 'Can I be of service to you in any way?'

'I am afraid not, Sir,' replied Robin, despondingly; 'yet I shall take it kindly, if you'll answer me a single question. I've been searching half the night for one Major Molineux; now, sir, is there really such a person in these parts, or am I dreaming?'

'Major Molineux! The name is not altogether strange to me,' said the gentleman, smiling. 'Have you any objection to telling me the nature of your business with him?'

Then Robin briefly related that his father was a clergyman, settled on a small salary, at a long distance back in the country, and that he and Major Molineux were brothers' children. The Major, having inherited riches, and acquired civil and military rank, had visited his cousin in great pomp a year or two before; had manifested much interest in Robin and an elder brother, and, being childless himself, had thrown out hints respecting the future establishment of one of them in life. The elder brother was destined to succeed to the farm, which his father cultivated, in the interval of sacred duties; it was therefore determined that Robin should profit by his kinsman's generous intentions, especially as he had seemed to be rather the favorite, and was thought to possess other necessary endowments.

'For I have the name of being a shrewd youth,' observed Robin, in this part of his story.

'I doubt not you deserve it,' replied his new friend, good naturedly; 'but pray proceed.'

'Well, Sir, being nearly eighteen years old, and well grown, as you see,' continued Robin, raising himself to his full height, 'I thought it high time to begin the world. So my mother and sister put me in handsome trim, and my father gave me half the remnant of his last year's salary, and five days ago I started for this place, to pay the Major a visit. But would you believe it, Sir? I crossed the ferry a little after dusk, and have yet found nobody that would show me the way to his dwelling; only an hour or two since, I was told to wait here, and Major Molineux would pass by.'

'Can you describe the man who told you this?' inquired the gentleman.

'Oh, he was a very ill-favored fellow, Sir,' replied Robin, 'with two great bumps on his forehead, a hook nose, fiery eyes, and, what struck me as the strangest, his face was of two different colors. Do you happen to know such a man, Sir?'

'Not intimately,' answered the stranger, 'but I chanced to meet him a little time previous to your stopping me. I believe you may trust his word, and that the Major will very shortly pass through this street. In the mean time, as I have a singular curiosity to witness your meeting, I will sit down here upon the steps, and bear you company.'

He seated himself accordingly, and soon engaged his companion in animated discourse. It was but of brief continuance, however, for a noise of shouting, which had long been remotely audible, drew so much nearer, that Robin inquired its cause.

'What may be the meaning of this uproar?' asked he. 'Truly, if your town be always as noisy, I shall find little sleep, while I am an inhabitant.'

'Why, indeed, friend Robin, there do appear to be three or four riotous fellows abroad to-night,' replied the gentleman. 'You must not expect all the stillness of your native woods, here in our streets. But the watch will shortly be at the heels of these lads, and—'

'Aye, and set them in the stocks by peep of day,' interrupted Robin, recollecting his own encounter with the drowsy lantern-bearer. 'But, dear Sir, if I may trust my ears, an army of watchmen would never make head against such a multitude of rioters. There were at least a thousand voices went to make up that one shout.'

'May not one man have several voices, Robin, as well as two complexions?' said his friend.

'Perhaps a man may; but heaven forbid that a woman should!' responded the shrewd youth, thinking of the seductive tones of the Major's housekeeper.

The sounds of a trumpet in some neighboring street, now became so evident and continual, that Robin's curiosity was strongly excited. In addition to the shouts, he heard frequent bursts from many instruments of discord, and a wild and confused laughter filled up the intervals. Robin rose from the steps, and looked wistfully towards a point, whither several people seemed to be hastening.

'Surely some prodigious merrymaking is going on,' exclaimed he. 'I have laughed very little since I left home, Sir, and should be sorry to lose an opportunity. Shall we just step round the corner by that darkish house, and take our share of the fun?'

'Sit down again, sit down, good Robin,' replied the gentleman, laying his hand on the skirt of the grey coat. 'You forget that we must wait here for your kinsman; and there is reason to believe that he will pass by, in the course of a very few moments.'

The near approach of the uproar had now disturbed the neighborhood; windows flew open on all sides; and many heads, in the attire of the pillow, and confused by sleep suddenly broken, were protruded to the gaze of whoever had leisure to observe them. Eager voices hailed each other from house to house, all demanding the explanation, which not a soul could give. Half-dressed men hurried towards the unknown commotion, stumbling as they went over the stone steps, that thrust themselves into the narrow foot-walk. The shouts, the laughter, and the tuneless bray, the antipodes of music, came onward with increasing din, till scattered individuals, and then denser bodies, began to appear round a corner, at the distance of a hundred yards.

'Will you recognise your kinsman, Robin, if he passes in this crowd?' inquired the gentleman.

'Indeed, I can't warrant it, Sir; but I'll take my stand here, and keep a bright look out,' answered Robin, descending to the outer edge of the pavement.

A mighty stream of people now emptied into the street, and came rolling slowly towards the church. A single horseman wheeled the corner in the midst of them, and close behind him came a band of fearful wind-instruments, sending forth a fresher discord, now that no intervening building kept it from the ear. Then a redder light disturbed the moonbeams, and a dense multitude of torches shone along the street, concealing by their glare whatever object they illuminated. The single horseman, clad in a military dress, and bearing a drawn sword, rode onward as the leader, and, by his fierce and variegated countenance, appeared like war personified; the red of one cheek was an emblem of fire and sword; the blackness of the other betokened the mourning which attends them. In his train, were wild figures in the Indian dress, and many fantastic shapes without a model, giving the whole march a visionary air, as if a dream had broken forth from some feverish brain, and were sweeping visibly through the midnight streets. A mass of people, inactive, except as applauding spectators, hemmed the procession in, and several women ran along the sidewalks, piercing the confusion of heavier sounds, with their shrill voices of mirth or terror.

'The double-faced fellow has his eye upon me,' muttered Robin, with an indefinite but uncomfortable idea, that he was himself to bear a part in the pageantry.

The leader turned himself in the saddle, and fixed his glance full upon the country youth, as the steed went slowly by. When Robin had freed his eyes from those fiery ones, the musicians were passing before him, and the torches were close at hand; but the unsteady brightness of the latter formed a veil which he could not penetrate. The rattling of wheels over the stones sometimes found its way to his ear, and confused traces of a human form appeared at intervals, and then melted into the vivid light. A moment more, and the leader thundered a command to halt; the trumpets vomited a horrid breath, and held their peace; the shouts and laughter of the people died away, and there remained only an universal hum, nearly allied to silence. Right before Robin's eyes was an uncovered cart. There the torches blazed the brightest, there the moon shone out like day, and there, in tar-and-feathery dignity, sate his kinsman, Major Molineux!

He was an elderly man, of large and majestic person, and strong, square features, betokening a steady soul; but steady as it was, his enemies had found the means to shake it. His face was pale as death, and far more ghastly; the broad forehead was contracted in his agony, so that the eyebrows formed one dark grey line; his eyes were red and wild, and the foam hung white upon his quivering lip. His whole frame was agitated by a quick, and continual tremor, which his pride strove to quell, even in those circumstances of overwhelming humiliation. But perhaps the bitterest pang of all was when his eyes met those of Robin; for he evidently knew him on the instant, as the youth stood witnessing the foul disgrace of a head that had grown grey in honor. They stared at each other in silence, and

Robin's knees shook, and his hair bristled, with a mixture of pity and terror.[7] Soon, however, a bewildering excitement began to seize upon his mind; the preceding adventures of the night, the unexpected appearance of the crowd, the torches, the confused din, and the hush that followed, the spectre of his kinsman reviled by that great multitude, all this, and more than all, a perception of tremendous ridicule in the whole scene, affected him with a sort of mental inebriety. At that moment a voice of sluggish merriment saluted Robin's ears; he turned instinctively, and just behind the corner of the church stood the lantern-bearer, rubbing his eyes, and drowsily enjoying the lad's amazement. Then he heard a peal of laughter like the ringing of silvery bells; a woman twitched his arm, a saucy eye met his, and he saw the lady of the scarlet petticoat. A sharp, dry cachinnation appealed to his memory, and, standing on tiptoe in the crowd, with his white apron over his head, he beheld the courteous little innkeeper. And lastly, there sailed over the heads of the multitude a great, broad laugh, broken in the midst by two deep sepulchral hems; thus—

'Haw, haw, haw—hem, hem—haw, haw, haw, haw!'

The sound proceeded from the balcony of the opposite edifice, and thither Robin turned his eyes. In front of the Gothic window stood the old citizen, wrapped in a wide gown, his grey periwig exchanged for a nightcap, which was thrust back from his forehead, and his silk stockings hanging down about his legs. He supported himself on his polished cane in a fit of convulsive merriment, which manifested itself on his solemn old features, like a funny inscription on a tomb-stone. Then Robin seemed to hear the voices of the barbers; of the guests of the inn; and of all who had made sport of him that night. The contagion was spreading among the multitude, when, all at once, it seized upon Robin, and he sent forth a shout of laughter that echoed through the street; every man shook his sides, every man emptied his lungs, but Robin's shout was the loudest there. The cloud-spirits peeped from their silvery islands, as the congregated mirth went roaring up the sky! The Man in the Moon heard the far bellow; 'Oho,' quoth he, 'the old Earth is frolicsome to-night!'

When there was a momentary calm in that tempestuous sea of sound, the leader gave the sign, and the procession resumed its march. On they went, like fiends that throng in mockery round some dead potentate, mighty no more, but majestic still in his agony. On they went, in counterfeited pomp, in senseless uproar, in frenzied

7. Hawthorne probably alludes here to Aristotle's account of tragic emotion in *Poetics* 14. Pity and terror, according to Aristotle, are the emotions a spectator feels in the *catharsis*, or purgative action of tragedy.

merriment, trampling all on an old man's heart. On swept the tumult, and left a silent street behind.

'Well, Robin, are you dreaming?' inquired the gentleman, laying his hand on the youth's shoulder.

Robin started, and withdrew his arm from the stone post, to which he had instinctively clung, while the living stream rolled by him. His cheek was somewhat pale, and his eye not quite so lively as in the earlier part of the evening.

'Will you be kind enough to show me the way to the Ferry?' said he, after a moment's pause.

'You have then adopted a new subject of inquiry?' observed his companion, with a smile.

'Why, yes, Sir,' replied Robin, rather dryly. 'Thanks to you, and to my other friends, I have at last met my kinsman, and he will scarce-desire to see my face again. I begin to grow weary of a town life, Sir. Will you show me the way to the Ferry?'

'No, my good friend, Robin, not to-night, at least,' said the gentleman. 'Some few days hence, if you continue to wish it, I will speed you on your journey. Or, if you prefer to remain with us, perhaps, as you are a shrewd youth, you may rise in the world, without the help of your kinsman, Major Molineux.'

Roger Malvin's Burial[†]

One of the few incidents of Indian warfare naturally susceptible of the moonlight of romance was that expedition undertaken for the defence of the frontiers in the year 1725, which resulted in the well-remembered "Lovell's Fight."[1] Imagination, by casting certain circumstances judiciously into the shade, may see much to admire in

---

† First published in 1831 in *The Token* (dated 1832), then in the *Democratic Review* for August 1843, and then in *Mosses from an Old Manse*, 1846. A version of it was completed by late 1829.

1. An episode in the long internecine struggle between New Englanders and French and Indians during the early 18th century. In May 1725, Captain John Lovewell led an expedition of forty-six men into southwestern Maine against the Pequawket Indians. Members of Lovewell's family had been surprised and murdered by Indians the previous year, and he was determined to retaliate in kind as well as to defend New England. His Massachusetts soldiers were also partly out for plunder. They had been offered a bounty of £100 for every scalp they could bring back to Boston, and on a previous expedition they had murdered and scalped ten Indian warriors whom they discovered asleep around a fire one morning (such "circumstances" were "cast in the shade" in centennial tributes to Lovewell and his men in 1825). When Lovewell's band confronted a larger band of Indians in Lovell's Fight, the frontiersmen fought valiantly for hours before they suffered a severe defeat. There was much slaughter on both sides. The English survivors were forced to retreat, leaving three wounded men in the wilderness. The "heroic" disaster was the subject of ballads, poems, and memorials for more than a century afterward.

the heroism of a little band who gave battle to twice their number
in the heart of the enemy's country. The open bravery displayed by
both parties was in accordance with civilized ideas of valor; and
chivalry itself might not blush to record the deeds of one or two
individuals. The battle, though so fatal to those who fought, was
not unfortunate in its consequences to the country; for it broke the
strength of a tribe and conduced to the peace which subsisted during several ensuing years. History and tradition are unusually minute in their memorials of this affair; and the captain of a scouting
party of frontier men has acquired as actual a military renown as
many a victorious leader of thousands. Some of the incidents contained in the following pages will be recognized, notwithstanding
the substitution of fictitious names, by such as have heard, from old
men's lips, the fate of the few combatants who were in a condition
to retreat after "Lovell's Fight."

The early sunbeams hovered cheerfully upon the tree tops, beneath
which two weary and wounded men had stretched their limbs the
night before. Their bed of withered oak leaves was strewn upon the
small level space, at the foot of a rock, situated near the summit of
one of the gentle swells by which the face of the country is there
diversified. The mass of granite, rearing its smooth, flat surface fifteen or twenty feet above their heads, was not unlike a gigantic
gravestone, upon which the veins seemed to form an inscription in
forgotten characters. On a tract of several acres around this rock,
oaks and other hard-wood trees had supplied the place of the pines,
which were the usual growth of the land; and a young and vigorous
sapling stood close beside the travellers.
    The severe wound of the elder man had probably deprived him of
sleep; for, so soon as the first ray of sunshine rested on the top of
the highest tree, he reared himself painfully from his recumbent
posture and sat erect. The deep lines of his countenance and the
scattered gray of his hair marked him as past the middle age; but his
muscular frame would, but for the effects of his wound, have been
as capable of sustaining fatigue as in the early vigor of life. Languor
and exhaustion now sat upon his haggard features; and the despairing glance which he sent forward through the depths of the forest
proved his own conviction that his pilgrimage was at an end. He
next turned his eyes to the companion who reclined by his side. The
youth—for he had scarcely attained the years of manhood—lay,
with his head upon his arm, in the embrace of an unquiet sleep,
which a thrill of pain from his wounds seemed each moment on the
point of breaking. His right hand grasped a musket; and, to judge
from the violent action of his features, his slumbers were bringing

back a vision of the conflict of which he was one of the few survivors. A shout—deep and loud in his dreaming fancy—found its way in an imperfect murmur to his lips; and, starting even at the slight sound of his own voice, he suddenly awoke. The first act of reviving recollection was to make anxious inquiries respecting the condition of his wounded fellow-traveller. The latter shook his head.

"Reuben, my boy," said he, "this rock beneath which we sit will serve for an old hunter's gravestone. There is many and many a long mile of howling wilderness before us yet; nor would it avail me any thing if the smoke of my own chimney were but on the other side of that swell of land. The Indian bullet was deadlier than I thought."

"You are weary with our three days' travel," replied the youth, "and a little longer rest will recruit you. Sit you here while I search the woods for the herbs and roots that must be our sustenance; and, having eaten, you shall lean on me, and we will turn our faces homeward. I doubt not that, with my help, you can attain to some one of the frontier garrisons."

"There is not two days' life in me, Reuben," said the other, calmly, "and I will no longer burden you with my useless body, when you can scarcely support your own. Your wounds are deep and your strength is failing fast; yet, if you hasten onward alone, you may be preserved. For me there is no hope, and I will await death here."

"If it must be so, I will remain and watch by you," said Reuben, resolutely.

"No, my son, no," rejoined his companion. "Let the wish of a dying man have weight with you; give me one grasp of your hand, and get you hence. Think you that my last moments will be eased by the thought that I leave you to die a more lingering death? I have loved you like a father, Reuben; and at a time like this I should have something of a father's authority. I charge you to be gone, that I may die in peace."

"And because you have been a father to me, should I therefore leave you to perish and to lie unburied in the wilderness?" exclaimed the youth. "No; if your end be in truth approaching, I will watch by you and receive your parting words. I will dig a grave here by the rock, in which, if my weakness overcome me, we will rest together; or, if Heaven gives me strength, I will seek my way home."

"In the cities and wherever men dwell," replied the other, "they bury their dead in the earth; they hide them from the sight of the living; but here, where no step may pass perhaps for a hundred years, wherefore should I not rest beneath the open sky, covered only by the oak leaves when the autumn winds shall strew them? And for a monument, here is this gray rock, on which my dying hand shall carve the name of Roger Malvin; and the traveller in days to come will know that here sleeps a hunter and a warrior. Tarry not, then, for a folly like this, but hasten away, if not for your own sake, for hers who will else be desolate."

Malvin spoke the last few words in a faltering voice, and their effect upon his companion was strongly visible. They reminded him that there were other and less questionable duties than that of sharing the fate of a man whom his death could not benefit. Nor can it be affirmed that no selfish feeling strove to enter Reuben's heart, though the consciousness made him more earnestly resist his companion's entreaties.

"How terrible to wait the slow approach of death in this solitude!" exclaimed he. "A brave man does not shrink in the battle; and, when friends stand round the bed, even women may die composedly; but here—"

"I shall not shrink even here, Reuben Bourne," interrupted Malvin. "I am a man of no weak heart; and, if I were, there is a surer support than that of earthly friends. You are young, and life is dear to you. Your last moments will need comfort far more than mine; and when you have laid me in the earth, and are alone, and night is settling on the forest, you will feel all the bitterness of the death that may now be escaped. But I will urge no selfish motive to your generous nature. Leave me for my sake, that, having said a prayer for your safety, I may have space to settle my account undisturbed by worldly sorrows."

"And your daughter,—how shall I dare to meet her eye?" exclaimed Reuben. "She will ask the fate of her father, whose life I vowed to defend with my own. Must I tell her that he travelled three days' march with me from the field of battle, and that then I left him to perish in the wilderness? Were it not better to lie down and die by your side than to return safe and say this to Dorcas?"

"Tell my daughter," said Roger Malvin, "that, though yourself sore wounded, and weak, and weary, you led my tottering footsteps many a mile, and left me only at my earnest entreaty, because I would not have your blood upon my soul. Tell her that through pain and danger you were faithful, and that, if your lifeblood could have saved me, it would have flowed to its last drop; and tell her that you will be something dearer than a father, and that my blessing is with you both, and that my dying eyes can see a long and pleasant path in which you will journey together."

As Malvin spoke he almost raised himself from the ground, and the energy of his concluding words seemed to fill the wild and lonely forest with a vision of happiness; but, when he sank exhausted upon his bed of oak leaves, the light which had kindled in Reuben's eye was quenched. He felt as if it were both sin and folly to think of happiness at such a moment. His companion watched his changing countenance, and sought with generous art to wile him to his own good.

"Perhaps I deceive myself in regard to the time I have to live," he resumed. "It may be that, with speedy assistance, I might recover of my wound. The foremost fugitives must, ere this, have carried tidings of our fatal battle to the frontiers, and parties will be out to succor those in like condition with ourselves. Should you meet one of these and guide them hither, who can tell but that I may sit by my own fireside again?"

A mournful smile strayed across the features of the dying man as he insinuated that unfounded hope; which, however, was not without its effect on Reuben. No merely selfish motive, nor even the desolate condition of Dorcas, could have induced him to desert his companion at such a moment—but his wishes seized upon the thought that Malvin's life might be preserved, and his sanguine nature heightened almost to certainty the remote possibility of procuring human aid.

"Surely there is reason, weighty reason, to hope that friends are not far distant," he said, half aloud. "There fled one coward, unwounded, in the beginning of the fight, and most probably he made good speed. Every true man on the frontier would shoulder his musket at the news; and, though no party may range so far into the woods as this, I shall perhaps encounter them in one day's march. Counsel me faithfully," he added, turning to Malvin, in distrust of his own motives. "Were your situation mine, would you desert me while life remained?"

"It is now twenty years," replied Roger Malvin, sighing, however, as he secretly acknowledged the wide dissimilarity between the two cases,—"it is now twenty years since I escaped with one dear friend from Indian captivity near Montreal. We journeyed many days through the woods, till at length, overcome with hunger and weariness, my friend lay down and besought me to leave him; for he knew that, if I remained, we both must perish; and, with but little hope of obtaining succor, I heaped a pillow of dry leaves beneath his head and hastened on."

"And did you return in time to save him?" asked Reuben, hanging on Malvin's words as if they were to be prophetic of his own success.

"I did," answered the other. "I came upon the camp of a hunting party before sunset of the same day. I guided them to the spot where my comrade was expecting death; and he is now a hale and hearty man upon his own farm, far within the frontiers, while I lie wounded here in the depths of the wilderness."

This example, powerful in effecting Reuben's decision, was aided, unconsciously to himself, by the hidden strength of many another motive. Roger Malvin perceived that the victory was nearly won.

"Now, go, my son, and Heaven prosper you!" he said. "Turn not back with your friends when you meet them, lest your wounds and weariness overcome you; but send hitherward two or three, that may be spared, to search for me; and believe me, Reuben, my heart will be lighter with every step you take towards home." Yet there was, perhaps, a change both in his countenance and voice as he spoke thus; for, after all, it was a ghastly fate to be left expiring in the wilderness.

Reuben Bourne, but half convinced that he was acting rightly, at length raised himself from the ground and prepared himself for his departure. And first, though contrary to Malvin's wishes, he collected a stock of roots and herbs, which had been their only food during the last two days. This useless supply he placed within reach of the dying man, for whom, also, he swept together a fresh bed of dry oak leaves. Then climbing to the summit of the rock, which on one side was rough and broken, he bent the oak sapling downward, and bound his handkerchief to the topmost branch. This precaution was not unnecessary to direct any who might come in search of Malvin; for every part of the rock, except its broad, smooth front, was concealed at a little distance by the dense undergrowth of the forest. The handkerchief had been the bandage of a wound upon Reuben's arm; and, as he bound it to the tree, he vowed by the blood that stained it that he would return, either to save his companion's life, or to lay his body in the grave. He then descended and stood, with downcast eyes, to receive Roger Malvin's parting words.

The experience of the latter suggested much and minute advice respecting the youth's journey through the trackless forest. Upon this subject he spoke with calm earnestness, as if he were sending Reuben to the battle or the chase while he himself remained secure at home, and not as if the human countenance that was about to leave him were the last he would ever behold. But his firmness was shaken before he concluded.

"Carry my blessing to Dorcas, and say that my last prayer shall be for her and you. Bid her to have no hard thoughts because you left me here,"—Reuben's heart smote him,—"for that your life would not have weighed with you if its sacrifice could have done me good. She will marry you after she has mourned a little while for her father; and Heaven grant you long and happy days, and may your children's children stand round your death bed! And, Reuben," added he, as the weakness of mortality made its way at last, "return, when your wounds are healed and your weariness refreshed,—return to this wild rock, and lay my bones in the grave, and say a prayer over them."

An almost superstitious regard, arising perhaps from the customs of the Indians, whose war was with the dead as well as the living, was paid by the frontier inhabitants to the rites of sepulture; and there are many instances of the sacrifice of life in the attempt to bury those who had fallen by the "sword of the wilderness." Reuben, therefore, felt the full importance of the promise which he most solemnly made to return and perform Roger Malvin's obsequies. It was remarkable that the latter, speaking his whole heart in his parting words, no longer endeavored to persuade the youth that even the speediest succor might avail to the preservation of his life. Reuben was internally convinced that he should see Malvin's living face no more. His generous nature would fain have delayed him, at whatever risk, till the dying scene were past; but the desire of existence and the hope of happiness had strengthened in his heart, and he was unable to resist them.

"It is enough," said Roger Malvin, having listened to Reuben's promise. "Go, and God speed you!"

The youth pressed his hand in silence, turned, and was departing. His slow and faltering steps, however, had borne him but a little way before Malvin's voice recalled him.

"Reuben, Reuben," said he, faintly; and Reuben returned and knelt down by the dying man.

"Raise me, and let me lean against the rock," was his last request. "My face will be turned towards home, and I shall see you a moment longer as you pass among the trees."

Reuben, having made the desired alteration in his companion's posture, again began his solitary pilgrimage. He walked more hastily at first than was consistent with his strength; for a sort of guilty feeling, which sometimes torments men in their most justifiable acts, caused him to seek concealment from Malvin's eyes; but after he had trodden far upon the rustling forest leaves he crept back, impelled by a wild and painful curiosity, and, sheltered by the earthy roots of an uptorn tree, gazed earnestly at the desolate man. The morning sun was unclouded, and the trees and shrubs imbibed the sweet air of the month of May; yet there seemed a gloom on Nature's face, as if she sympathized with mortal pain and sorrow. Roger Malvin's hands were uplifted in a fervent prayer, some of the words of which stole through the stillness of the woods and entered Reuben's heart, torturing it with an unutterable pang. They were the broken accents of a petition for his own happiness and that of Dorcas; and, as the youth listened, conscience, or something in its similitude, pleaded strongly with him to return and lie down again by the rock. He felt how hard was the doom of the kind and generous being whom he had deserted in his extremity. Death would come like the slow approach of a corpse, stealing gradually towards him through the forest, and showing its ghastly and motionless features from behind a nearer and yet a nearer tree. But such must have been Reuben's own fate had he tarried another sunset; and who shall impute blame to him if he shrank from so useless a sacrifice? As he gave a parting look, a breeze waved the little banner upon the sapling oak and reminded Reuben of his vow.

Many circumstances contributed to retard the wounded traveller in his way to the frontiers. On the second day the clouds, gathering densely over the sky, precluded the possibility of regulating his course by the position of the sun; and he knew not but that every effort of his almost exhausted strength was removing him farther from the home he sought. His scanty sustenance was supplied by the berries and other spontaneous products of the forest. Herds of deer, it is true, sometimes bounded past him, and partridges frequently whirred up before his footsteps; but his ammunition had been expended in the fight, and he had no means of slaying them. His wounds, irritated by the constant exertion in which lay the only hope of life, wore away his strength and at intervals confused his reason. But, even in the wanderings of intellect, Reuben's young heart clung strongly to existence; and it was only through absolute incapacity of motion that he at last sank down beneath a tree, compelled there to await death.

In this situation he was discovered by a party who, upon the first intelligence of the fight, had been despatched to the relief of the survivors. They conveyed him to the nearest settlement, which chanced to be that of his own residence.

Dorcas, in the simplicity of the olden time, watched by the bedside of her wounded lover and administered all those comforts that are in the sole gift of woman's heart and hand. During several days Reuben's recollection strayed drowsily among the perils and hardships through which he had passed, and he was incapable of returning definite answers to the inquiries with which many were eager to harass him. No authentic particulars of the battle had yet been circulated; nor could mothers, wives, and children tell whether their loved ones were detained by captivity or by the stronger chain of death. Dorcas nourished her apprehensions in silence till one afternoon when Reuben awoke from an unquiet sleep and seemed to recognize her more perfectly than at any previous time. She saw that his intellect had become composed, and she could no longer restrain her filial anxiety.

"My father, Reuben?" she began; but the change in her lover's countenance made her pause.

The youth shrank as if with a bitter pain, and the blood gushed vividly into his wan and hollow cheeks. His first impulse was to cover his face; but, apparently with a desperate effort, he half raised himself and spoke vehemently, defending himself against an imaginary accusation.

"Your father was sore wounded in the battle, Dorcas; and he bade me not burden myself with him, but only to lead him to the lakeside, that he might quench his thirst and die. But I would not desert the old man in his extremity, and, though bleeding myself, I supported him; I gave him half my strength, and led him away with me. For three days we journeyed on together, and your father was sustained beyond my hopes; but, awaking at sunrise on the fourth day, I found him faint and exhausted; he was unable to proceed; his life had ebbed away fast; and—"

"He died!" exclaimed Dorcas, faintly.

Reuben felt it impossible to acknowledge that his selfish love of life had hurried him away before her father's fate was decided. He spoke not; he only bowed his head; and, between shame and exhaustion, sank back and hid his face in the pillow. Dorcas wept when her fears were thus confirmed; but the shock, as it had been long anticipated, was on that account the less violent.

"You dug a grave for my poor father in the wilderness, Reuben?" was the question by which her filial piety manifested itself.

"My hands were weak; but I did what I could," replied the youth in a smothered tone. "There stands a noble tombstone above his head; and I would to Heaven I slept as soundly as he!"

Dorcas, perceiving the wildness of his latter words, inquired no further at the time; but her heart found ease in the thought that Roger Malvin had not lacked such funeral rites as it was possible to bestow. The tale of Reuben's courage and fidelity lost nothing when she communicated it to her friends; and the poor youth, tottering from his sick chamber to breathe the sunny air, experienced from every tongue the miserable and humiliating torture of unmerited praise. All acknowledged that he might worthily demand the hand of the fair maiden to whose father he had been "faithful unto death;" and, as my tale is not of love, it shall suffice to say that in the space of a few months Reuben became the husband of Dorcas Malvin. During the marriage ceremony the bride was covered with blushes; but the bridegroom's face was pale.

There was now in the breast of Reuben Bourne an incommunicable thought—something which he was to conceal most heedfully from her whom he most loved and trusted. He regretted, deeply and bitterly, the moral cowardice that had restrained his words when he was about to disclose the truth to Dorcas; but pride, the fear of losing her affection, the dread of universal scorn forbade him to rectify this falsehood. He felt that for leaving Roger Malvin he deserved no censure. His presence, the gratuitous sacrifice of his own life, would have added only another and a needless agony to the last moments of the dying man; but concealment had imparted to a justifiable act much of the secret effect of guilt; and Reuben, while reason told him that he had done right, experienced in no small degree the mental horrors which punish the perpetrator of undiscovered crime. By a certain association of ideas, he at times almost imagined himself a murderer. For years, also, a thought would occasionally recur, which, though he perceived all its folly and extravagance, he had not power to banish from his mind. It was a haunting and torturing fancy that his father-in-law was yet sitting at the foot of the rock, on the withered forest leaves, alive, and awaiting his pledged assistance. These mental deceptions, however, came and went, nor did he ever mistake them for realities; but in the calmest and clearest moods of his mind he was conscious that he had a deep vow unredeemed, and that an unburied corpse was calling to him out of the wilderness. Yet such was the consequence of his prevarication that he could not obey the call. It was now too late to require the assistance of Roger Malvin's friends in performing his long-deferred sepulture; and superstitious fears, of which none were more susceptible than the people of the outward settlements, forbade Reuben to go alone. Neither did he know where in the pathless and illimitable forest to seek that smooth and lettered rock at the base of which the body lay: his remembrance of every portion of his travel thence was indistinct, and the latter part had left no impression upon his mind. There was, however, a continual impulse, a voice audible only to himself, commanding him to go forth and redeem his vow; and he had a strange impression that, were he to make the trial, he would be led straight to Malvin's bones. But year after year that summons, unheard but felt, was disobeyed. His one secret thought became like a chain binding down his spirit and like a serpent gnawing into his heart; and he was transformed into a sad and downcast yet irritable man.

In the course of a few years after their marriage changes began to be visible in the external prosperity of Reuben and Dorcas. The only riches of the former had been his stout heart and strong arm; but the latter, her father's sole heiress, had made her husband master of a farm, under older cultivation, larger, and better stocked than most of the frontier establishments. Reuben Bourne, however, was a neglectful husbandman; and, while the lands of the other settlers became annually more fruitful, his deteriorated in the same proportion. The discouragements to agriculture were greatly lessened by the cessation of Indian war, during which men held the plough in one hand and the musket in the other, and were fortunate if the products of their dangerous labor were not destroyed, either in the field or in the barn, by the savage enemy. But Reuben did not profit by the altered condition of the country; nor can it be denied that his intervals of industrious attention to his affairs were but scantily rewarded with success. The irritability by which he had recently become distinguished, was another cause of his declining prosperity, as it occasioned frequent quarrels in his unavoidable intercourse with the neighboring settlers. The results of these were innumerable lawsuits; for the people of New England, in the earliest stages and wildest circumstances of the country, adopted, whenever attainable, the legal mode of deciding their differences. To be brief, the world did not go well with Reuben Bourne; and, though not till many years after his marriage, he was finally a ruined man, with but one remaining expedient against the evil fate that had pursued him. He was to throw sunlight into some deep recess of the forest, and seek subsistence from the virgin bosom of the wilderness.

The only child of Reuben and Dorcas was a son, now arrived at the age of fifteen years, beautiful in youth, and giving promise of a glorious manhood. He was peculiarly qualified for, and already began to excel in, the wild accomplishments of frontier life. His foot was fleet, his aim true, his apprehension quick, his heart glad and high; and all who anticipated the return of Indian war spoke of Cyrus[2] Bourne as a future leader in the land. The boy was loved by his father with a deep and silent strength, as if whatever was good and happy in his own nature had been transferred to his child, carrying his affections with it. Even Dorcas, though loving and beloved, was far less dear to him; for Reuben's secret thoughts and insulated emotions had gradually made him a selfish man, and he could no longer love deeply except where he saw or imagined some reflection or likeness of his own mind. In Cyrus he recognized what he had himself been in other days; and at intervals he seemed to partake of the boy's spirit and to be revived with a fresh and happy life. Reuben was accompanied by his son in the expedition, for the purpose of selecting a tract of land and felling and burning the timber, which necessarily preceded the removal of the household gods.[3] Two months of autumn were thus occupied; after which Reuben Bourne and his young hunter returned to spend their last winter in the settlements.

It was early in the month of May that the little family snapped asunder whatever tendrils of affection had clung to inanimate objects, and bade farewell to the few who, in the blight of fortune, called themselves their friends. The sadness of the parting moment

---

2. Persian emperor who is presented as the Lord's shepherd summoning the Jews to rebuild Jerusalem in Isaiah 44:28, Ezra 1–5. The biblical Reuben, by contrast, left his brother Joseph in a pit in the wilderness, though he wished to save him (see Genesis 37).
3. Cherished possessions and images symbolic of a household.

had, to each of the pilgrims, its peculiar alleviations. Reuben, a moody man, and misanthropic because unhappy, strode onward with his usual stern brow and downcast eye, feeling few regrets and disdaining to acknowledge any. Dorcas, while she wept abundantly over the broken ties by which her simple and affectionate nature had bound itself to every thing, felt that the inhabitants of her inmost heart moved on with her, and that all else would be supplied wherever she might go. And the boy dashed one teardrop from his eye, and thought of the adventurous pleasures of the untrodden forest.

O, who, in the enthusiasm of a daydream, has not wished that he were a wanderer in a world of summer wilderness, with one fair and gentle being hanging lightly on his arm? In youth his free and exulting step would know no barrier but the rolling ocean or the snow-topped mountains; calmer manhood would choose a home where Nature had strewn a double wealth in the vale of some transparent stream; and when hoary age, after long, long years of that pure life, stole on and found him there, it would find him the father of a race, the patriarch of a people, the founder of a mighty nation yet to be. When death, like the sweet sleep which we welcome after a day of happiness, came over him, his far descendants would mourn over the venerated dust. Enveloped by tradition in mysterious attributes, the men of future generations would call him godlike; and remote posterity would see him standing, dimly glorious, far up the valley of a hundred centuries.

The tangled and gloomy forest through which the personages of my tale were wandering differed widely from the dreamer's land of fantasy; yet there was something in their way of life that Nature asserted as her own, and the gnawing cares which went with them from the world were all that now obstructed their happiness. One stout and shaggy steed, the bearer of all their wealth, did not shrink from the added weight of Dorcas; although her hardy breeding sustained her, during the latter part of each day's journey, by her husband's side. Reuben and his son, their musket on their shoulders and their axes slung behind them, kept an unwearied pace, each watching with a hunter's eye for the game that supplied their food. When hunger bade, they halted and prepared their meal on the bank of some unpolluted forest brook, which, as they knelt down with thirsty lips to drink, murmured a sweet unwillingness, like a maiden at love's first kiss. They slept beneath a hut of branches, and awoke at peep of light refreshed for the toils of another day. Dorcas and the boy went on joyously, and even Reuben's spirit shone at intervals with an outward gladness; but inwardly there was a cold, cold sorrow, which he compared to the snow drifts lying deep in the glens and hollows of the rivulets while the leaves were brightly green above.

Cyrus Bourne was sufficiently skilled in the travel of the woods to observe that his father did not adhere to the course they had pursued in their expedition of the preceding autumn. They were now keeping farther to the north, striking out more directly from the settlements, and into a region of which savage beasts and savage men were as yet the sole possessors.[4] The boy sometimes hinted his opinions upon the subject, and Reuben listened attentively, and once or twice altered the direction of their march in accordance with his son's counsel; but, having so done, he seemed ill at ease. His quick and wandering glances were sent forward, apparently in search of enemies lurking behind the tree trunks; and, seeing nothing there, he would cast his eyes backwards as if in fear of some pursuer. Cyrus, perceiving that his father gradually resumed the old direction, forbore to interfere; nor, though something began to weigh upon his heart, did his adventurous nature permit him to regret the increased length and the mystery of their way.

On the afternoon of the fifth day they halted, and made their simple encampment nearly an hour before sunset. The face of the country, for the last few miles, had been diversified by swells of land resembling huge waves of a petrified sea; and in one of the corresponding hollows, a wild and romantic spot, had the family reared their hut and kindled their fire. There is something chilling, and yet heart-warming, in the thought of these three, united by strong bands of love and insulated from all that breathe beside. The dark and gloomy pines looked down upon them, and, as the wind swept through their tops, a pitying sound was heard in the forest; or did those old trees groan in fear that men were come to lay the axe to their roots at last? Reuben and his son, while Dorcas made ready their meal, proposed to wander out in search of game, of which that day's march had afforded no supply. The boy, promising not to quit the vicinity of the encampment, bounded off with a step as light and elastic as that of the deer he hoped to slay; while his father, feeling a transient happiness as he gazed after him, was about to pursue an opposite direction. Dorcas, in the meanwhile, had seated herself near their fire of fallen branches, upon the mossgrown and mouldering trunk of a tree uprooted years before. Her employment, diversified by an occasional glance at the pot, now beginning to simmer over the blaze, was the perusal of the current year's Massachusetts Almanac, which, with

4. Cf. William Bradford's description of the New England landscape that greeted the Plymouth pilgrims in 1620: "What could they see but a hideous and desolate Wilderness full of wilde Beasts and wilde Men?" Hawthorne read Bradford's description as copied in *New England's Memoriall* (1667) by Nathaniel Morton, Bradford's nephew.

the exception of an old black-letter[5] Bible, comprised all the literary wealth of the family. None pay a greater regard to arbitrary divisions of time than those who are excluded from society; and Dorcas mentioned, as if the information were of importance, that it was now the twelfth of May. Her husband started.

"The twelfth of May! I should remember it well," muttered he, while many thoughts occasioned a momentary confusion in his mind. "Where am I? Whither am I wandering? Where did I leave him?"

Dorcas, too well accustomed to her husband's wayward moods to note any peculiarity of demeanor, now laid aside the almanac and addressed him in that mournful tone which the tender hearted appropriate to griefs long cold and dead.

'It was near this time of the month, eighteen years ago, that my poor father left this world for a better. He had a kind arm to hold his head and a kind voice to cheer him, Reuben, in his last moments; and the thought of the faithful care you took of him has comforted me many a time since. O, death would have been awful to a solitary man in a wild place like this!"

"Pray Heaven, Dorcas," said Reuben, in a broken voice,—"pray Heaven that neither of us three dies solitary and lies unburied in this howling wilderness!" And he hastened away, leaving her to watch the fire beneath the gloomy pines.

Reuben Bourne's rapid pace gradually slackened as the pang, unintentionally inflicted by the words of Dorcas, became less acute. Many strange reflections, however, thronged upon him; and, straying onward rather like a sleep walker than a hunter, it was attributable to no care of his own that his devious course kept him in the vicinity of the encampment. His steps were imperceptibly led almost in a circle; nor did he observe that he was on the verge of a tract of land heavily timbered, but not with pine trees. The place of the latter was here supplied by oaks and other of the harder woods; and around their roots clustered a dense and bushy undergrowth, leaving, however, barren spaces between the trees, thick strewn with withered leaves. Whenever the rustling of the branches or the creaking of the trunks made a sound, as if the forest were waking from slumber, Reuben instinctively raised the musket that rested on his arm, and cast a quick, sharp glance on every side; but, convinced by a partial observation that no animal was near, he would again give himself up to his thoughts. He was musing on the strange influence that had led him away from his premeditated course and so far into the depths of the wilderness. Unable to penetrate to the

---

5. A heavy type with stylized ornaments often used in Bibles and religious texts. The *Massachusetts Almanac* is an ancestor of the *Farmer's Almanac*.

secret place of his soul where his motives lay hidden, he believed that a supernatural voice had called him onward and that a supernatural power had obstructed his retreat. He trusted that it was Heaven's intent to afford him an opportunity of expiating his sin; he hoped that he might find the bones so long unburied; and that, having laid the earth over them, peace would throw its sunlight into the sepulchre of his heart. From these thoughts he was aroused by a rustling in the forest at some distance from the spot to which he had wandered. Perceiving the motion of some object behind a thick veil of undergrowth, he fired, with the instinct of a hunter and the aim of a practised marksman. A low moan, which told his success, and by which even animals can express their dying agony, was unheeded by Reuben Bourne. What were the recollections now breaking upon him?

The thicket into which Reuben had fired was near the summit of a swell of land, and was clustered around the base of a rock, which, in the shape and smoothness of one of its surfaces, was not unlike a gigantic gravestone. As if reflected in a mirror, its likeness was in Reuben's memory. He even recognized the veins which seemed to form an inscription in forgotten characters: every thing remained the same, except that a thick covert of bushes shrouded the lower part of the rock, and would have hidden Roger Malvin had he still been sitting there. Yet in the next moment Reuben's eye was caught by another change that time had effected since he last stood where he was now standing again behind the earthy roots of the uptorn tree. The sapling to which he had bound the bloodstained symbol of his vow had increased and strengthened into an oak, far indeed from its maturity, but with no mean spread of shadowy branches. There was one singularity observable in this tree which made Reuben tremble. The middle and lower branches were in luxuriant life, and an excess of vegetation had fringed the trunk almost to the ground; but a blight had apparently stricken the upper part of the oak, and the very topmost bough was withered, sapless, and utterly dead. Reuben remembered how the little banner had fluttered on that topmost bough, when it was green and lovely, eighteen years before. Whose guilt had blasted it?

Dorcas, after the departure of the two hunters, continued her preparations for their evening repast. Her sylvan table was the moss-covered trunk of a large fallen tree, on the broadest part of which she had spread a snow-white cloth and arranged what were left of the bright pewter vessels that had been her pride in the settlements. It had a strange aspect, that one little spot of homely comfort in the desolate heart of Nature. The sunshine yet lingered upon the higher branches of the trees that grew on rising ground; but the shadows of evening had deepened into the hollow where the encampment was made, and the firelight began to redden as it gleamed up the tall trunks of the pines or hovered on the dense and obscure mass of foliage that circled round the spot. The heart of Dorcas was not sad; for she felt that it was better to journey in the wilderness with two whom she loved than to be a lonely woman in a crowd that cared not for her. As she busied herself in arranging seats of mould- ering wood, covered with leaves, for Reuben and her son, her voice danced through the gloomy forest in the measure of a song that she had learned in youth. The rude melody, the production of a bard who won no name, was descriptive of a winter evening in a frontier cottage, when, secured from savage inroad by the high-piled snow drifts, the family rejoiced by their own fireside. The whole song pos- sessed the nameless charm peculiar to unborrowed thought; but four continually-recurring lines shone out from the rest like the blaze of the hearth whose joys they celebrated. Into them, working magic with a few simple words, the poet had instilled the very essence of domestic love and household happiness, and they were poetry and picture joined in one. As Dorcas sang, the walls of her forsaken home seemed to encircle her; she no longer saw the gloomy pines, nor heard the wind, which still, as she began each verse, sent a heavy breath through the branches and died away in a hollow moan from the burden of the song. She was aroused by the report of a gun in the vicinity of the encampment; and either the sudden sound or her loneliness by the glowing fire caused her to tremble violently. The next moment she laughed in the pride of a mother's heart.

"My beautiful young hunter! My boy has slain a deer!" she exclaimed, recollecting that in the direction whence the shot pro- ceeded Cyrus had gone to the chase.

She waited a reasonable time to hear her son's light step bounding over the rustling leaves to tell of his success. But he did not immedi- ately appear; and she sent her cheerful voice among the trees in search of him.

"Cyrus! Cyrus!"

His coming was still delayed; and she determined, as the report had apparently been very near, to seek for him in person. Her assis- tance, also, might be necessary in bringing home the venison which she flattered herself he had obtained. She therefore set forward, directing her steps by the long-past sound, and singing as she went, in order that the boy might be aware of her approach and run to meet her. From behind the trunk of every tree and from every hiding-place in the thick foliage of the undergrowth she hoped to discover the countenance of her son, laughing with the sportive mischief that is born of affection. The sun was now beneath the horizon, and the light that came down among the trees was sufficiently dim to create many illusions in her expecting fancy. Several times she seemed indistinctly to see his face gazing out from among the leaves; and once she imagined that he stood beckoning to her at the base of a craggy rock. Keeping her eyes on this object, however, it proved to be no more than the trunk of an oak, fringed to the very ground with little branches, one of which, thrust out farther than the rest, was shaken by the breeze. Making her way round the foot of the rock, she suddenly found herself close to her husband, who had approached in another direction. Leaning upon the but of his gun, the muzzle of which rested upon the withered leaves, he was apparently absorbed in the contemplation of some object at his feet.

"How is this, Reuben? Have you slain the deer and fallen asleep over him?" exclaimed Dorcas, laughing cheerfully, on her first slight observation of his posture and appearance.

He stirred not, neither did he turn his eyes towards her; and a cold, shuddering fear, indefinite in its source and object, began to creep into her blood. She now perceived that her husband's face was ghastly pale, and his features were rigid, as if incapable of assuming any other expression than the strong despair which had hardened upon them. He gave not the slightest evidence that he was aware of her approach.

"For the love of Heaven, Reuben, speak to me!" cried Dorcas; and the strange sound of her own voice affrighted her even more than the dead silence.

Her husband started, stared into her face, drew her to the front of the rock, and pointed with his finger.

O, there lay the boy, asleep, but dreamless, upon the fallen forest leaves! His cheek rested upon his arm—his curled locks were thrown back from his brow—his limbs were slightly relaxed. Had a sudden weariness overcome the youthful hunter? Would his mother's voice arouse him? She knew that it was death.

"This broad rock is the gravestone of your near kindred, Dorcas," said her husband. "Your tears will fall at once over your father and your son."

She heard him not. With one wild shriek, that seemed to force its way from the sufferer's inmost soul, she sank insensible by the side of her dead boy. At that moment the withered topmost bough of the oak loosened itself in the stilly air, and fell in soft, light fragments upon the rock, upon the leaves, upon Reuben, upon his wife and child, and upon Roger Malvin's bones. Then Reuben's heart was stricken, and the tears gushed out like water from a rock.[6] The vow

---

6. See Isaiah 48:21, "He caused the waters to flow out of the rock for them: he clave the rock also, and the waters gushed out:" *He* is the Lord God, and *them* refers to the Israelites.

that the wounded youth had made the blighted man had come to redeem. His sin was expiated—the curse was gone from him; and in the hour when he had shed blood dearer to him than his own, a prayer, the first for years, went up to Heaven from the lips of Reuben Bourne.

The Gentle Boy[†]

In the course of the year 1656, several of the people called Quakers, led, as they professed, by the inward movement of the spirit, made their appearance in New England. Their reputation, as holders of mystic and pernicious principles, having spread before them, the Puritans early endeavored to banish, and to prevent the further intrusion of the rising sect. But the measures by which it was intended to purge the land of heresy, though more than sufficiently vigorous, were entirely unsuccessful. The Quakers, esteeming persecution as a divine call to the post of danger, laid claim to a holy courage, unknown to the Puritans themselves, who had shunned the cross,[1] by providing for the peaceable exercise of their religion in a distant wilderness. Though it was the singular fact, that every nation of the earth rejected the wandering enthusiasts who practised peace towards all men, the place of greatest uneasiness and peril, and therefore in their eyes the most eligible, was the province of Massachusetts Bay.

The fines, imprisonments, and stripes, liberally distributed by our pious forefathers; the popular antipathy, so strong that it endured nearly a hundred years after actual persecution had ceased, were attractions as powerful for the Quakers, as peace, honor, and reward, would have been for the worldly-minded. Every European vessel brought new cargoes of the sect, eager to testify against the oppression which they hoped to share; and, when ship-masters were restrained by heavy fines from affording them passage, they made long and circuitous journeys through the Indian country, and appeared in the province as if conveyed by a supernatural power.

---

† First published in 1831 in *The Token* (dated 1832). A version was completed by late 1829. Hawthorne extensively revised "The Gentle Boy" for *Twice-told Tales* in 1837, drastically pruning the narrator's expressions of opinion concerning Puritans and Quakers. (See p. 288 for omitted portions.) Hawthorne may have felt an involvement in his subject because William Hathorne, his first ancestor in the New World, was a key figure in the persecution of the Quakers. The action of the tale can be dated with some accuracy. In October 1659, two Quakers who insisted on preaching to the Puritans were hanged in Boston. One of these is presumably Ilbrahim's father in the tale. In September 1661, letters arrived from Charles II ordering a stay of executions in New England. In the tale the Quakers hear this news on a winter evening. "The Gentle Boy" was a favorite of Hawthorne's family and friends, and he reprinted it separately in 1839, with illustrations by his prospective bride, Sophia Peabody.

1. Persecution and martyrdom, which Puritans escaped by settling in New England.

Their enthusiasm, heightened almost to madness by the treatment which they received, produced actions contrary to the rules of decency, as well as of rational religion, and presented a singular contrast to the calm and staid deportment of their sectarian successors of the present day. The command of the spirit, inaudible except to the soul, and not to be controverted on grounds of human wisdom, was made a plea for most indecorous exhibitions, which, abstractedly considered, well deserved the moderate chastisement of the rod. These extravagances, and the persecution which was at once their cause and consequence, continued to increase, till, in the year 1659, the government of Massachusetts Bay indulged two members of the Quaker sect with the crown of martyrdom.

An indelible stain of blood is upon the hands of all who consented to this act, but a large share of the awful responsibility must rest upon the person then at the head of the government.[2] He was a man of narrow mind and imperfect education, and his uncompromising bigotry was made hot and mischievous by violent and hasty passions; he exerted his influence indecorously and unjustifiably to compass the death of the enthusiasts; and his whole conduct, in respect to them, was marked by brutal cruelty. The Quakers, whose revengeful feelings were not less deep because they were inactive, remembered this man and his associates, in after times. The historian of the sect[3] affirms that, by the wrath of Heaven, a blight fell upon the land in the vicinity of the 'bloody town' of Boston, so that no wheat would grow there; and he takes his stand, as it were, among the graves of the ancient persecutors, and triumphantly recounts the judgments that overtook them, in old age or at the parting hour. He tells us that they died suddenly, and violently, and in madness; but nothing can exceed the bitter mockery with which he records the loathsome disease, and 'death by rottenness,' of the fierce and cruel governor.

On the evening of the autumn day, that had witnessed the martyrdom of two men of the Quaker persuasion, a Puritan settler was returning from the metropolis to the neighboring country town in which he resided. The air was cool, the sky clear, and the lingering twilight was made brighter by the rays of a young moon, which had now nearly reached the verge of the horizon. The traveller, a man of middle age, wrapped in a grey frieze cloak, quickened his pace when he had reached the outskirts of the town, for a gloomy extent of nearly four miles lay between him and his home. The low, straw-thatched houses were scattered at considerable

2. John Endicott, governor of Massachusetts in 1659.
3. William Sewel, author of *The History of the Rise, Increase, and Progress of . . . the Christian People Called Quakers* (London, 1722). Hawthorne withdrew this text from the library of the Salem Athenaeum in 1828 and 1829.

intervals along the road, and the country having been settled but about thirty years, the tracts of original forest still bore no small proportion to the cultivated ground. The autumn wind wandered among the branches, whirling away the leaves from all except the pine-trees, and moaning as if it lamented the desolation of which it was the instrument. The road had penetrated the mass of woods that lay nearest to the town, and was just emerging into an open space, when the traveller's ears were saluted by a sound more mournful than even that of the wind. It was like the wailing of some one in distress, and it seemed to proceed from beneath a tall and lonely fir-tree, in the centre of a cleared, but unenclosed and uncultivated field. The Puritan could not but remember that this was the very spot, which had been made accursed a few hours before, by the execution of the Quakers, whose bodies had been thrown together into one hasty grave, beneath the tree on which they suffered. He struggled, however, against the superstitious fears which belonged to the age, and compelled himself to pause and listen.

'The voice is most likely mortal, nor have I cause to tremble if it be otherwise,'[4] thought he, straining his eyes through the dim moonlight. 'Methinks it is like the wailing of a child; some infant, it may be, which has strayed from its mother, and chanced upon this place of death. For the ease of mine own conscience, I must search this matter out.'

He therefore left the path, and walked somewhat fearfully across the field. Though now so desolate, its soil was pressed down and trampled by the thousand footsteps of those who had witnessed the spectacle of that day, all of whom had now retired, leaving the dead to their loneliness. The traveller at length reached the fir-tree, which from the middle upward was covered with living branches, although a scaffold had been erected beneath, and other preparations made for the work of death. Under this unhappy tree, which in after times was believed to drop poison with its dew, sat the one solitary mourner for innocent blood. It was a slender and light-clad little boy, who leaned his face upon a hillock of fresh-turned and half-frozen earth, and wailed bitterly, yet in a suppressed tone, as if his grief might receive the punishment of crime. The Puritan, whose approach had been unperceived, laid his hand upon the child's shoulder, and addressed him compassionately.

'You have chosen a dreary lodging, my poor boy, and no wonder that you weep,' said he. 'But dry your eyes, and tell me where your mother dwells. I promise you, if the journey be not too far, I will leave you in her arms to-night.'

---

4. The Puritan means that he need not tremble in the presence of evil spirits and apparitions.

The boy had hushed his wailing at once, and turned his face upward to the stranger. It was a pale, bright-eyed countenance, certainly not more than six years old, but sorrow, fear, and want, had destroyed much of its infantile expression. The Puritan, seeing the boy's frightened gaze, and feeling that he trembled under his hand, endeavored to reassure him.

'Nay, if I intended to do you harm, little lad, the readiest way were to leave you here. What! you do not fear to sit beneath the gallows on a new-made grave, and yet you tremble at a friend's touch. Take heart, child, and tell me what is your name, and where is your home?'

'Friend,' replied the little boy, in a sweet, though faltering voice, 'they call me Ilbrahim, and my home is here.'

The pale, spiritual face, the eyes that seemed to mingle with the moonlight, the sweet airy voice, and the outlandish name, almost made the Puritan believe, that the boy was in truth a being which had sprung up out of the grave on which he sat. But perceiving that the apparition stood the test of a short mental prayer, and remembering that the arm which he had touched was life-like, he adopted a more rational supposition. 'The poor child is stricken in his intellect,' thought he, 'but verily his words are fearful, in a place like this.' He then spoke soothingly, intending to humor the boy's fantasy.

'Your home will scarce be comfortable, Ilbrahim, this cold autumn night, and I fear you are ill provided with food. I am hastening to a warm supper and bed, and if you will go with me, you shall share them!'

'I thank thee, friend, but though I be hungry and shivering with cold, thou wilt not give me food nor lodging,' replied the boy, in the quiet tone which despair had taught him, even so young. 'My father was of the people whom all men hate. They have laid him under this heap of earth, and here is my home.'

The Puritan, who had laid hold of little Ilbrahim's hand, relinquished it as if he were touching a loathsome reptile. But he possessed a compassionate heart, which not even religious prejudice could harden into stone.

'God forbid that I should leave this child to perish, though he comes of the accursed sect,' said he to himself. 'Do we not all spring from an evil root? Are we not all in darkness till the light doth shine upon us? He shall not perish, neither in body, nor, if prayer and instruction may avail for him, in soul.' He then spoke aloud and kindly to Ilbrahim, who had again hid his face in the cold earth of the grave. 'Was every door in the land shut against you, my child, that you have wandered to this unhallowed spot?'

'They drove me forth from the prison when they took my father thence,' said the boy, 'and I stood afar off, watching the crowd of people, and when they were gone, I came hither, and found only this grave. I knew that my father was sleeping here, and I said, this shall be my home.'

'No, child, no; not while I have a roof over my head, or a morsel to share with you!' exclaimed the Puritan, whose sympathies were now fully excited. 'Rise up and come with me, and fear not any harm.'

The boy wept afresh, and clung to the heap of earth, as if the cold heart beneath it were warmer to him than any in a living breast. The traveller, however, continued to entreat him tenderly, and seeming to acquire some degree of confidence, he at length arose. But his slender limbs tottered with weakness, his little head grew dizzy, and he leaned against the tree of death for support.

'My poor boy, are you so feeble?' said the Puritan. 'When did you taste food last?'

'I ate of bread and water with my father in the prison,' replied Ilbrahim, 'but they brought him none neither yesterday nor to day, saying that he had eaten enough to bear him to his journey's end. Trouble not thyself for my hunger, kind friend, for I have lacked food many times ere now.'

The traveller took the child in his arms and wrapped his cloak about him, while his heart stirred with shame and anger against the gratuitous cruelty of the instruments in this persecution. In the awakened warmth of his feelings, he resolved that, at whatever risk, he would not forsake the poor little defenceless being whom Heaven had confided to his care. With this determination, he left the accursed field, and resumed the homeward path from which the wailing of the boy had called him. The light and motionless burthen scarcely impeded his progress, and he soon beheld the fire-rays from the windows of the cottage which he, a native of a distant clime, had built in the western wilderness. It was surrounded by a considerable extent of cultivated ground, and the dwelling was situated in the nook of a wood-covered hill, whither it seemed to have crept for protection.

'Look up, child,' said the Puritan to Ilbrahim, whose faint head had sunk upon his shoulder; 'there is our home.'

At the word 'home,' a thrill passed through the child's frame, but he continued silent. A few moments brought them to the cottage-door, at which the owner knocked; for at that early period, when savages were wandering everywhere among the settlers, bolt and bar were indispensable to the security of a dwelling. The summons was answered by a bond-servant,[5] a coarse-clad and dull-featured piece of humanity, who, after ascertaining that his master was the appli-

5. A person bound by contract to servitude for a set period, usually in repayment for passage to the colonies.

cant, undid the door, and held a flaring pine-knot torch to light him
in. Farther back in the passage-way, the red blaze discovered a
matronly woman, but no little crowd of children came bounding
forth to greet their father's return. As the Puritan entered, he thrust
aside his cloak, and displayed Ilbrahim's face to the female.

'Dorothy, here is a little outcast whom Providence hath put into
our hands,' observed he. 'Be kind to him, even as if he were of those
dear ones who have departed from us.'

'What pale and bright-eyed little boy is this, Tobias?' she inquired.
'Is he one whom the wilderness folk have ravished from some christian mother?'

'No, Dorothy, this poor child is no captive from the wilderness,'
he replied. 'The heathen savage would have given him to eat of his
scanty morsel, and to drink of his birchen cup; but christian men,
alas! had cast him out to die.'

Then he told her how he had found him beneath the gallows,
upon his father's grave; and how his heart had prompted him, like
the speaking of an inward voice,[6] to take the little outcast home,
and be kind unto him. He acknowledged his resolution to feed and
clothe him, as if he were his own child, and to afford him the
instruction which should counteract the pernicious errors hitherto
instilled into his infant mind. Dorothy was gifted with even a
quicker tenderness than her husband, and she approved of all his
doings and intentions.

'Have you a mother, dear child?' she inquired.

The tears burst forth from his full heart, as he attempted to
reply; but Dorothy at length understood that he had a mother, who,
like the rest of her sect, was a persecuted wanderer. She had been
taken from the prison a short time before, carried into the uninhab-
ited wilderness, and left to perish there by hunger or wild beasts.
This was no uncommon method of disposing of the Quakers, and
they were accustomed to boast, that the inhabitants of the desert
were more hospitable to them than civilized man.

'Fear not, little boy, you shall not need a mother, and a kind one,'
said Dorothy, when she had gathered this information. 'Dry your
tears, Ilbrahim, and be my child, as I will be your mother.'

The good woman prepared the little bed, from which her own children had successively been borne to another resting place. Before
Ilbrahim would consent to occupy it, he knelt down, and as Dorothy
listened to his simple and affecting prayer, she marvelled how the
parents that had taught it to him could have been judged worthy of

---

6. Quakers believe that the Holy Spirit illuminates each person by means of an "inner light"
   and speaks to him or her with an inward voice. The narrator's use of Quaker language
   foreshadows the Puritan's conversion.

death. When the boy had fallen alseep, she bent over his pale and spiritual countenance, pressed a kiss upon his white brow, drew the bedclothes up about his neck, and went away with a pensive gladness in her heart.

Tobias Pearson was not among the earliest emigrants from the old country. He had remained in England during the first years of the civil war, in which he had borne some share as a cornet of dragoons,[7] under Cromwell. But when the ambitious designs of his leader began to develop themselves,[8] he quitted the army of the parliament, and sought a refuge from the strife, which was no longer holy, among the people of his persuasion in the colony of Massachusetts. A more worldly consideration had perhaps an influence in drawing him thither; for New England offered advantages to men of unprosperous fortunes, as well as to dissatisfied religionists, and Pearson had hitherto found it difficult to provide for a wife and increasing family. To this supposed impurity of motive, the more bigoted Puritans were inclined to impute the removal by death of all the children, for whose earthly good the father had been over-thoughtful. They had left their native country blooming like roses, and like roses they had perished in a foreign soil. Those expounders of the ways of Providence, who had thus judged their brother, and attributed his domestic sorrows to his sin, were not more charitable when they saw him and Dorothy endeavoring to fill up the void in their hearts, by the adoption of an infant of the accursed sect. Nor did they fail to communicate their disapprobation to Tobias; but the latter, in reply, merely pointed at the little quiet, lovely boy, whose appearance and deportment were indeed as powerful arguments as could possibly have been adduced in his own favor. Even his beauty, however, and his winning manners, sometimes produced an effect ultimately unfavorable; for the bigots, when the outer surfaces of their iron hearts had been softened and again grew hard, affirmed that no merely natural cause could have so worked upon them.

Their antipathy to the poor infant was also increased by the ill success of divers theological discussions, in which it was attempted to convince him of the errors of his sect. Ilbrahim, it is true, was not a skilful controversialist; but the feeling of his religion was strong as instinct in him, and he could neither be enticed nor driven from the faith which his father had died for. The odium of this stubbornness was shared in a great measure by the child's protectors, insomuch that Tobias and Dorothy very shortly began to experience a most bitter species of persecution, in the cold regards

---

7. An officer in a troop of armed cavalry.
8. Oliver Cromwell dismissed Parliament in 1653, became lord protector of England, and ruled by himself.

of many a friend whom they had valued. The common people manifested their opinions more openly. Pearson was a man of some consideration, being a Representative to the General Court,[9] and an approved Lieutenant in the train-bands, yet within a week after his adoption of Ilbrahim, he had been both hissed and hooted. Once, also, when walking through a solitary piece of woods, he heard a loud voice from some invisible speaker; and it cried, 'What shall be done to the backslider? Lo! the scourge is knotted for him, even the whip of nine cords, and every cord three knots!' These insults irritated Pearson's temper for the moment; they entered also into his heart, and became imperceptible but powerful workers towards an end, which his most secret thought had not yet whispered.

On the second Sabbath after Ilbrahim became a member of their family, Pearson and his wife deemed it proper that he should appear with them at public worship. They had anticipated some opposition to this measure from the boy, but he prepared himself in silence, and at the appointed hour was clad in the new mourning suit which Dorothy had wrought for him. As the parish was then, and during many subsequent years, unprovided with a bell, the signal for the commencement of religious exercises was the beat of a drum. At the first sound of that martial call to the place of holy and quiet thoughts, Tobias and Dorothy set forth, each holding a hand of little Ilbrahim, like two parents linked together by the infant of their love. On their path through the leafless woods, they were overtaken by many persons of their acquaintance, all of whom avoided them, and passed by on the other side; but a severer trial awaited their constancy when they had descended the hill and drew near the pine-built and undecorated house of prayer. Around the door, from which the drummer still sent forth his thundering summons, was drawn up a formidable phalanx, including several of the oldest members of the congregation, many of the middle-aged, and nearly all the younger males. Pearson found it difficult to sustain their united and disapproving gaze, but Dorothy, whose mind was differently circumstanced, merely drew the boy closer to her, and faltered not in her approach. As they entered the door, they overheard the muttered sentiments of the assemblage, and when the reviling voices of the little children smote Ilbrahim's ear, he wept.

The interior aspect of the meetinghouse was rude. The low ceiling, the unplastered walls, the naked wood-work, and the undraperied pulpit, offered nothing to excite the devotion, which, without such external aids, often remains latent in the heart. The floor of the building was occupied by rows of long, cushionless benches,

9. The Massachusetts legislature.

supplying the place of pews, and the broad-aisle formed a sexual division, impassable except by children beneath a certain age.

Pearson and Dorothy separated at the door of the meetinghouse, and Ilbrahim, being within the years of infancy, was retained under the care of the latter. The wrinkled beldams involved themselves in their rusty cloaks as he passed by; even the mild-featured maidens seemed to dread contamination; and many a stern old man arose, and turned his repulsive and unheavenly countenance upon the gentle boy, as if the sanctuary were polluted by his presence. He was a sweet infant of the skies, that had strayed away from his home, and all the inhabitants of this miserable world closed up their impure hearts against him, drew back their earth-soiled garments from his touch, and said, 'We are holier than thou.'

Ilbrahim, seated by the side of his adopted mother, and retaining fast hold of her hand, assumed a grave and decorous demeanor, such as might befit a person of matured taste and understanding, who should find himself in a temple dedicated to some worship which he did not recognise, but felt himself bound to respect. The exercises had not yet commenced, however, when the boy's attention was arrested by an event, apparently of trifling interest. A woman, having her face muffled in a hood, and a cloak drawn completely about her form, advanced slowly up the broad-aisle and took place upon the foremost bench. Ilbrahim's faint color varied, his nerves fluttered, he was unable to turn his eyes from the muffled female.

When the preliminary prayer and hymn were over, the minister arose, and having turned the hour-glass which stood by the great bible, commenced his discourse. He was now well stricken in years, a man of pale, thin countenance, and his grey hairs were closely covered by a black velvet scull-cap. In his younger days he had practically learned the meaning of persecution, from Archbishop Laud,[1] and he was not now disposed to forget the lesson against which he had murmured then. Introducing the often discussed subject of the Quakers, he gave a history of that sect, and a description of their tenets, in which error predominated, and prejudice distorted the aspect of what was true. He adverted to the recent measures in the province, and cautioned his hearers of weaker parts against calling in question the just severity, which God-fearing magistrates had at length been compelled to exercise. He spoke of the danger of pity, in some cases a commendable and christian virtue, but inapplicable to this pernicious sect. He observed that such was their devilish obstinacy in error, that even the little children, the sucking babes, were hardened and desperate heretics. He affirmed that no man,

1. William Laud (1573–1645), archbishop of Canterbury, leader of the Church of England under Charles I, and a zealous opponent of the Puritans.

without Heaven's especial warrant, should attempt their conversion, lest while he lent his hand to draw them from the slough, he should himself be precipitated into its lowest depths.

The sands of the second hour were principally in the lower half of the glass, when the sermon concluded. An approving murmur followed, and the clergyman, having given out a hymn, took his seat with much self-congratulation, and endeavored to read the effect of his eloquence in the visages of the people. But while voices from all parts of the house were tuning themselves to sing, a scene occurred, which, though not very unusual at that period in the province, happened to be without precedent in this parish.

The muffled female, who had hitherto sat motionless in the front rank of the audience, now arose, and with slow, stately, and unwavering step, ascended the pulpit stairs. The quaverings of incipient harmony were hushed, and the divine[2] sat in speechless and almost terrified astonishment, while she undid the door, and stood up in the sacred desk from which his maledictions had just been thundered. She then divested herself of the cloak and hood, and appeared in a most singular array. A shapeless robe of sackcloth was girded about her waist with a knotted cord; her raven hair fell down upon her shoulders, and its blackness was defiled by pale streaks of ashes, which she had stewn upon her head. Her eyebrows, dark and strongly defined, added to the deathly whiteness of a countenance which, emaciated with want, and wild with enthusiasm and strange sorrows, retained no trace of earlier beauty. This figure stood gazing earnestly on the audience, and there was no sound, nor any movement, except a faint shuddering which every man observed in his neighbor, but was scarcely conscious of in himself. At length, when her fit of inspiration came, she spoke, for the first few moments, in a low voice, and not invariably distinct utterance. Her discourse gave evidence of an imagination hopelessly entangled with her reason; it was a vague and incomprehensible rhapsody, which, however, seemed to spread its own atmosphere round the hearer's soul, and to move his feelings by some influence unconnected with the words. As she proceeded, beautiful but shadowy images would sometimes be seen, like bright things moving in a turbid river; or a strong and singularly shaped idea leapt forth, and seized at once on the understanding or the heart. But the course of her unearthly eloquence soon led her to the persecutions of her sect, and from thence the step was short to her own peculiar sorrows. She was naturally a woman of mighty passions, and hatred and revenge now wrapped themselves in the garb of piety; the character of her speech was

2. Minister.

changed, her images became distinct though wild, and her denunciations had an almost hellish bitterness.

'The Governor and his mighty men,' she said, 'have gathered together, taking counsel among themselves and saying, "What shall we do unto this people—even unto the people that have come into this land to put our iniquity to the blush?" And lo! the devil entereth into the council-chamber, like a lame man of low stature and gravely appareled, with a dark and twisted countenance, and a bright, downcast eye. And he standeth up among the rulers; yea, he goeth to and fro, whispering to each; and every man lends his ear, for his word is "slay, slay!" But I say unto ye, Woe to them that slay! Woe to them that shed the blood of saints! Woe to them that have slain the husband, and cast forth the child, the tender infant, to wander homeless, and hungry, and cold, till he die; and have saved the mother alive, in the cruelty of their tender mercies! Woe to them in their life-time, cursed are they in the delight and pleasure of their hearts! Woe to them in their death-hour, whether it come swiftly with blood and violence, or after long and lingering pain! Woe, in the dark house, in the rottenness of the grave, when the children's children shall revile the ashes of the fathers! Woe, woe, woe, at the judgment, when all the persecuted and all the slain in this bloody land, and the father, the mother, and the child, shall await them in a day that they cannot escape! Seed of the faith, seed of the faith, ye whose hearts are moving with a power that ye know not, arise, wash your hands of this innocent blood! Lift your voices, chosen ones, cry aloud, and call down a woe and a judgment with me!'

Having thus given vent to the flood of malignity which she mistook for inspiration, the speaker was silent. Her voice was succeeded by the hysteric shrieks of several women, but the feelings of the audience generally had not been drawn onward in the current with her own. They remained stupefied, stranded as it were, in the midst of a torrent, which deafened them by its roaring, but might not move them by its violence. The clergyman, who could not hitherto have ejected the usurper of his pulpit otherwise than by bodily force, now addressed her in the tone of just indignation and legitimate authority.

'Get you down, woman, from the holy place which you profane,' he said. 'Is it to the Lord's house that you come to pour forth the foulness of your heart, and the inspiration of the devil? Get you down, and remember that the sentence of death is on you; yea, and shall be executed, were it but for this day's work?'

'I go, friend, I go, for the voice hath had its utterance,' replied she, in a depressed and even mild tone. 'I have done my mission unto thee and to thy people. Reward me with stripes, imprisonment, or death, as ye shall be permitted.'

The weakness of exhausted passion caused her steps to totter as she descended the pulpit stairs. The people, in the meanwhile, were stirring to and fro on the floor of the house, whispering among themselves, and glancing towards the intruder. Many of them now recognised her as the woman who had assaulted the Governor with frightful language, as he passed by the window of her prison; they knew, also, that she was adjudged to suffer death, and had been preserved only by an involuntary banishment into the wilderness. The new outrage, by which she had provoked her fate, seemed to render further lenity impossible; and a gentleman in military dress, with a stout man of inferior rank, drew towards the door of the meetinghouse, and awaited her approach. Scarcely did her feet press the floor, however, when an unexpected scene occurred. In that moment of her peril, when every eye frowned with death, a little timid boy pressed forth, and threw his arms round his mother.

'I am here, mother, it is I, and I will go with thee to prison,' he exclaimed.

She gazed at him with a doubtful and almost frightened expression, for she knew that the boy had been cast out to perish, and she had not hoped to see his face again. She feared, perhaps, that it was but one of the happy visions, with which her excited fancy had often deceived her, in the solitude of the desert, or in prison. But when she felt his hand warm within her own, and heard his little eloquence of childish love, she began to know that she was yet a mother.

'Blessed art thou, my son,' she sobbed. 'My heart was withered; yea, dead with thee and with thy father; and now it leaps as in the first moment when I pressed thee to my bosom.'

She knelt down, and embraced him again and again, while the joy that could find no words, expressed itself in broken accents, like the bubbles gushing up to vanish at the surface of a deep fountain. The sorrows of past years, and the darker peril that was nigh, cast not a shadow on the brightness of that fleeting moment. Soon, however, the spectators saw a change upon her face, as the consciousness of her sad estate returned, and grief supplied the fount of tears which joy had opened. By the words she uttered, it would seem that the indulgence of natural love had given her mind a momentary sense of its errors, and made her know how far she had strayed from duty, in following the dictates of a wild fanaticism.

'In a doleful hour art thou returned to me, poor boy,' she said, 'for thy mother's path has gone darkening onward, till now the end is death. Son, son, I have borne thee in my arms when my limbs were tottering, and I have fed thee with the food that I was fainting for; yet I have ill performed a mother's part by thee in life, and now I leave thee no inheritance but woe and shame. Thou wilt go seeking through the world, and find all hearts closed against thee, and their sweet affections turned to bitterness for my sake. My child, my child, how many a pang awaits thy gentle spirit, and I the cause of all!'

She hid her face on Ilbrahim's head, and her long, raven hair, discolored with the ashes of her mourning, fell down about him like a veil. A low and interrupted moan was the voice of her heart's anguish, and it did not fail to move the sympathies of many who mistook their involuntary virtue for a sin. Sobs were audible in the female section of the house, and every man who was a father, drew his hand across his eyes. Tobias Pearson was agitated and uneasy, but a certain feeling like the consciousness of guilt oppressed him, so that he could not go forth and offer himself as the protector of the child. Dorothy, however, had· watched her husband's eye. Her mind was free from the influence that had begun to work on his, and she drew near the Quaker woman, and addressed her in the hearing of all the congregation.

'Stranger, trust this boy to me, and I will be his mother,' she said, taking Ilbrahim's hand. 'Providence has signally marked out my husband to protect him, and he has fed at our table and lodged under our roof, now many days, till our hearts have grown very strongly unto him. Leave the tender child with us, and be at ease concerning his welfare.'

The Quaker rose from the ground, but drew the boy closer to her, while she gazed earnestly in Dorothy's face. Her mild, but saddened features, and neat, matronly attire, harmonized together, and were like a verse of fireside poetry. Her very aspect proved that she was blameless, so far as mortal could be so, in respect to God and man; while the enthusiast, in her robe of sackcloth and girdle of knotted cord, had as evidently violated the duties of the present life and the future, by fixing her attention wholly on the latter. The two females, as they held each a hand of Ilbrahim, formed a practical allegory; it was rational piety and unbridled fanaticism, contending for the empire of a young heart.

'Thou art not of our people,' said the Quaker, mournfully.

'No, we are not of your people,' replied Dorothy, with mildness, 'but we are Christians, looking upward to the same Heaven with you. Doubt not that your boy shall meet you there, if there be a blessing on our tender and prayerful guidance of him. Thither, I trust, my own children have gone before me, for I also have been a mother; I am no longer so,' she added, in a faltering tone, 'and your son will have all my care.'

'But will ye lead him in the path which his parents have trodden?' demanded the Quaker. 'Can ye teach him the enlightened faith which his father has died for, and for which I, even I, am soon to become an unworthy martyr? The boy has been baptized in blood; will ye keep the mark fresh and ruddy upon his forehead?'

'I will not deceive you,' answered Dorothy. 'If your child become our child, we must breed him up in the instruction which Heaven has imparted to us; we must pray for him the prayers of our own faith; we must do towards him according to the dictates of our own consciences, and not of your's. Were we to act otherwise, we should abuse your trust, even in complying with your wishes.'

The mother looked down upon her boy with a troubled countenance, and then turned her eyes upward to heaven. She seemed to pray internally, and the contention of her soul was evident.

'Friend,' she said at length to Dorothy, 'I doubt not that my son shall receive all earthly tenderness at thy hands. Nay, I will believe that even thy imperfect lights may guide him to a better world; for surely thou art on the path thither. But thou hast spoken of a husband. Doth he stand here among this multitude of people? Let him come forth, for I must know to whom I commit this most precious trust.'

She turned her face upon the male auditors, and after a momentary delay, Tobias Pearson came forth from among them. The Quaker saw the dress which marked his military rank, and shook her head; but then she noted the hesitating air, the eyes that struggled with her own, and were vanquished; the color that went and came, and could find no resting place. As she gazed, an unmirthful smile spread over her features, like sunshine that grows melancholy in some desolate spot. Her lips moved inaudibly, but at length she spake.

'I hear it, I hear it. The voice speaketh within me and saith, "Leave thy child, Catharine, for his place is here, and go hence, for I have other work for thee. Break the bonds of natural affection, martyr thy love, and know that in all these things eternal wisdom hath its ends." I go, friends, I go. Take ye my boy, my precious jewel. I go hence, trusting that all shall be well, and that even for his infant hands there is a labor in the vineyard.'

She knelt down and whispered to Ilbrahim, who at first struggled and clung to his mother, with sobs and tears, but remained passive when she had kissed his cheek and arisen from the ground. Having held her hands over his head in mental prayer, she was ready to depart.

'Farewell, friends, in mine extremity,' she said to Pearson and his wife; 'the good deed ye have done me is a treasure laid up in heaven, to be returned a thousandfold hereafter. And farewell ye, mine enemies, to whom it is not permitted to harm so much as a hair of my head, nor to stay my footsteps even for a moment. The day is coming,

when ye shall call upon me to witness for ye to this one sin uncom-
mitted, and I will rise up and answer.'

She turned her steps towards the door, and the men, who had
stationed themselves to guard it, withdrew, and suffered her to pass.
A general sentiment of pity overcame the virulence of religious
hatred. Sanctified by her love, and her affliction, she went forth, and
all the people gazed after her till she had journeyed up the hill, and
was lost behind its brow. She went, the apostle of her own unquiet
heart, to renew the wanderings of past years. For her voice had been
already heard in many lands of Christendom; and she had pined in
the cells of a Catholic Inquisition, before she felt the lash, and lay
in the dungeons of the Puritans. Her mission had extended also to
the followers of the Prophet, and from them she had received the
courtesy and kindness, which all the contending sects of our purer
religion united to deny her. Her husband and herself had resided
many months in Turkey, where even the Sultan's countenance was
gracious to them; in that pagan land, too, was Ilbrahim's[3] birthplace, and his oriental name was a mark of gratitude for the good
deeds of an unbeliever.

When Pearson and his wife had thus acquired all the rights over
Ilbrahim that could be delegated, their affection for him became,
like the memory of their native land, or their mild sorrow for the
dead, a piece of the immovable furniture of their hearts. The boy,
also, after a week or two of mental disquiet, began to gratify his
protectors, by many inadvertent proofs that he considered them as
parents, and their house as home. Before the winter snows were
melted, the persecuted infant, the little wanderer from a remote and
heathen country, seemed native in the New England cottage, and
inseparable from the warmth and security of its hearth. Under the
influence of kind treatment, and in the consciousness that he was
loved, Ilbrahim's demeanor lost a premature manliness, which had
resulted from his earlier situation; he became more childlike, and
his natural character displayed itself with freedom. It was in many
respects a beautiful one, yet the disordered imaginations of both his
father and mother had perhaps propagated a certain unhealthiness
in the mind of the boy. In his general state, Ilbrahim would derive
enjoyment from the most trifling events, and from every object about
him; he seemed to discover rich treasures of happiness, by a faculty
analogous to that of the witchhazel, which points to hidden gold
where all is barren to the eye. His airy gaiety, coming to him from a

---

3. Hawthorne's version of "Ibrahim," Arabic for *Abraham* and a common Muslim name.
   Sewel gives vivid accounts of early Quaker missionary efforts among Catholics and
   Muslims in his *History of . . . the Christian People Called Quakers.*

thousand sources, communicated itself to the family, and Ilbrahim was like a domesticated sunbeam, brightening moody countenances, and chasing away the gloom from the dark corners of the
cottage.

On the other hand, as the susceptibility of pleasure is also that of
pain, the exuberant cheerfulness of the boy's prevailing temper
sometimes yielded to moments of deep depression. His sorrows could
not always be followed up to their original source, but most frequently they appeared to flow, though Ilbrahim was young to be sad
for such a cause, from wounded love. The flightiness of his mirth
rendered him often guilty of offences against the decorum of a Puritan household, and on these occasions he did not invariably escape
rebuke. But the slightest word of real bitterness, which he was infallible in distinguishing from pretended anger, seemed to sink into his
heart and poison all his enjoyments, till he became sensible that he
was entirely forgiven. Of the malice, which generally accompanies
a superfluity of sensitiveness, Ilbrahim, was altogether destitute;
when trodden upon, he would not turn; when wounded, he could
but die. His mind was wanting in the stamina for self-support; it
was a plant that would twine beautifully round something stronger
than itself, but if repulsed, or torn away, it had no choice but to
wither on the ground. Dorothy's acuteness taught her that severity
would crush the spirit of the child, and she nurtured him with the
gentle care of one who handles a butterfly. Her husband manifested
an equal affection, although it grew daily less productive of familiar
caresses.

The feelings of the neighboring people, in regard to the Quaker
infant and his protectors, had not undergone a favorable change, in
spite of the momentary triumph which the desolate mother had
obtained over their sympathies. The scorn and bitterness, of which
he was the object, were very grievous to Ilbrahim, especially when
any circumstance made him sensible that the children, his equals
in age, partook of the enmity of their parents. His tender and social
nature had already overflowed in attachments to everything about
him, and still there was a residue of unappropriated love, which he
yearned to bestow upon the little ones who were taught to hate him.
As the warm days of spring came on, Ilbrahim was accustomed to
remain for hours, silent and inactive, within hearing of the children's voices at their play; yet, with his usual delicacy of feeling, he
avoided their notice, and would flee and hide himself from the
smallest individual among them. Chance, however, at length seemed
to open a medium of communication between his heart and theirs;
it was by means of a boy about two years older than Ilbrahim, who
was injured by a fall from a tree in the vicinity of Pearson's habitation. As the sufferer's own home was at some distance, Dorothy

willingly received him under her roof, and became his tender and careful nurse.

Ilbrahim was the unconscious possessor of much skill in physiognomy, and it would have deterred him, in other circumstances, from attempting to make a friend of this boy. The countenance of the latter immediately impressed a beholder disagreeably, but it required some examination to discover that the cause was a very slight distortion of the mouth, and the irregular, broken line, and near approach of the eyebrows. Analogous, perhaps, to these trifling deformities, was an almost imperceptible twist of every joint, and the uneven prominence of the breast; forming a body, regular in its general outline, but faulty in almost all its details. The disposition of the boy was sullen and reserved, and the village schoolmaster stigmatized him as obtuse in intellect; although, at a later period of life, he evinced ambition and very peculiar talents. But whatever might be his personal or moral irregularities, Ilbrahim's heart seized upon, and clung to him, from the moment that he was brought wounded into the cottage; the child of persecution seemed to compare his own fate with that of the sufferer, and to feel that even different modes of misfortune had created a sort of relationship between them. Food, rest, and the fresh air, for which he languished, were neglected; he nestled continually by the bed-side of the little stranger, and, with a fond jealousy, endeavored to be the medium of all the cares that were bestowed upon him. As the boy became convalescent, Ilbrahim contrived games suitable to his situation, or amused him by a faculty which he had perhaps breathed in with the air of his barbaric birthplace. It was that of reciting imaginary adventures, on the spur of the moment, and apparently in inexhaustible succession. His tales were of course monstrous, disjointed, and without aim; but they were curious on account of a vein of human tenderness, which ran through them all, and was like a sweet, familiar face, encountered in the midst of wild and unearthly scenery. The auditor paid much attention to these romances, and sometimes interrupted them by brief remarks upon the incidents, displaying shrewdness above his years, mingled with a moral obliquity which grated very harshly against Ilbrahim's instinctive rectitude. Nothing, however, could arrest the progress of the latter's affection, and there were many proofs that it met with a response from the dark and stubborn nature on which it was lavished. The boy's parents at length removed him, to complete his cure under their own roof.

Ilbrahim did not visit his new friend after his departure; but he made anxious and continual inquiries respecting him, and informed himself of the day when he was to reappear among his playmates. On a pleasant summer afternoon, the children of the neighborhood had assembled in the little forest-crowned amphitheatre behind the meetinghouse, and the recovering invalid was there, leaning on a staff. The glee of a score of untainted bosoms was heard in light and airy voices, which danced among the trees like sunshine become audible; the grown men of this weary world, as they journeyed by the spot, marvelled why life, beginning in such brightness, should proceed in gloom; and their hearts, or their imaginations, answered them and said, that the bliss of childhood gushes from its innocence. But it happened that an unexpected addition was made to the heavenly little band. It was Ilbrahim, who came towards the children, with a look of sweet confidence on his fair and spiritual face, as if, having manifested his love to one of them, he had no longer to fear a repulse from their society. A hush came over their mirth, the moment they beheld him, and they stood whispering to each other while he drew nigh; but, all at once, the devil of their fathers entered into the unbreeched fanatics, and, sending up a fierce, shrill cry, they rushed upon the poor Quaker child. In an instant, he was the centre of a brood of baby-fiends, who lifted sticks against him, pelted him with stones, and displayed an instinct of destruction, far more loathsome than the blood-thirstiness of manhood.

The invalid, in the meanwhile, stood apart from the tumult, crying out with a loud voice, 'Fear not, Ilbrahim, come hither and take my hand,' and his unhappy friend endeavored to obey him. After watching the victim's struggling approach, with a calm smile and unabashed eye, the foul-hearted little villain lifted his staff, and struck Ilbrahim on the mouth, so forcibly that the blood issued in a stream. The poor child's arms had been raised to guard his head from the storm of blows; but now he dropped them at once. His persecutors beat him down, trampled upon him, dragged him by his long, fair locks, and Ilbrahim was on the point of becoming as veritable a martyr as ever entered bleeding into heaven. The uproar, however, attracted the notice of a few neighbors, who put themselves to the trouble of rescuing the little heretic, and of conveying him to Pearson's door.

Ilbrahim's bodily harm was severe, but long and careful nursing accomplished his recovery; the injury done to his sensitive spirit was more serious, though not so visible. Its signs were principally of a negative character, and to be discovered only by those who had previously known him. His gait was thenceforth slow, even, and unvaried by the sudden bursts of sprightlier motion, which had once corresponded to his overflowing gladness; his countenance was heavier, and its former play of expression, the dance of sunshine reflected from moving water, was destroyed by the cloud over his existence; his notice was attracted in a far less degree by passing events, and he appeared to find greater difficulty in comprehending

what was new to him, than at a happier period. A stranger, founding his judgment upon these circumstances, would have said that
the dulness of the child's intellect widely contradicted the promise
of his features; but the secret was in the direction of Ilbrahim's
thoughts, which were brooding within him when they should naturally have been wandering abroad. An attempt of Dorothy to revive
his former sportiveness was the single occasion, on which his quiet
demeanor yielded to a violent display of grief; he burst into passionate weeping, and ran and hid himself, for his heart had become so
miserably sore, that even the hand of kindness tortured it like fire.
Sometimes, at night and probably in his dreams, he was heard to
cry, 'Mother! Mother!' as if her place, which a stranger had supplied
while Ilbrahim was happy, admitted of no substitute in his extreme
affliction. Perhaps, among the many life-weary wretches then upon
the earth, there was not one who combined innocence and misery
like this poor, broken-hearted infant, so soon the victim of his own
heavenly nature.

   While this melancholy change had taken place in Ilbrahim, one
of an earlier origin and of different character had come to its perfection in his adopted father. The incident with which this tale
commences found Pearson in a state of religious dulness, yet mentally disquieted, and longing for a more fervid faith than he possessed. The first effect of his kindness to Ilbrahim was to produce a
softened feeling, an incipient love for the child's whole sect; but
joined to this, and resulting perhaps from self-suspicion, was a proud
and ostentatious contempt of their tenets and practical extravagances. In the course of much thought, however, for the subject
struggled irresistibly into his mind, the foolishness of the doctrine
began to be less evident, and the points which had particularly
offended his reason assumed another aspect, or vanished entirely
away. The work within him appeared to go on even while he slept,
and that which had been a doubt, when he laid down to rest, would
often hold the place of a truth, confirmed by some forgotten demonstration, when he recalled his thoughts in the morning. But while he
was thus becoming assimilated to the enthusiasts, his contempt, in
nowise decreasing towards them, grew very fierce against himself; he
imagined, also, that every face of his acquaintance wore a sneer, and
that every word addressed to him was a gibe. Such was his state of
mind at the period of Ilbrahim's misfortune; and the emotions consequent upon that event completed the change, of which the child had
been the original instrument.

   In the mean time neither the fierceness of the persecutors, nor
the infatuation of their victims, had decreased. The dungeons were
never empty; the streets of almost every village echoed daily with
the lash; the life of a woman, whose mild and christian spirit no

cruelty could embitter, had been sacrificed;[4] and more innocent blood was yet to pollute the hands, that were so often raised in prayer. Early after the Restoration, the English Quakers represented to Charles II that a 'vein of blood was opened in his dominions;' but though the displeasure of the voluptuous king was roused, his interference was not prompt. And now the tale must stride forward over many months, leaving Pearson to encounter ignominy and misfortune; his wife to a firm endurance of a thousand sorrows; poor Ilbrahim to pine and droop like a cankered rose-bud; his mother to wander on a mistaken errand, neglectful of the holiest trust which can be committed to a woman.

A winter evening, a night of storm, had darkened over Pearson's habitation, and there were no cheerful faces to drive the gloom from his broad hearth. The fire, it is true, sent forth a glowing heat and a ruddy light, and large logs, dripping with half-melted snow, lay ready to be cast upon the embers. But the apartment was saddened in its aspect by the absence of much of the homely wealth which had once adorned it; for the exaction of repeated fines,[5] and his own neglect of temporal affairs, had greatly impoverished the owner. And with the furniture of peace, the implements of war had likewise disappeared; the sword was broken, the helm and cuirass were cast away for ever; the soldier had done with battles, and might not lift so much as his naked hand to guard his head. But the Holy Book remained, and the table on which it rested was drawn before the fire, while two of the persecuted sect sought comfort from its pages.

He who listened, while the other read, was the master of the house, now emaciated in form, and altered as to the expression and healthiness of his countenance; for his mind had dwelt too long among visionary thoughts, and his body had been worn by imprisonment and stripes. The hale and weather-beaten old man, who sat beside him, had sustained less injury from a far longer course of the same mode of life. In person he was tall and dignified, and, which alone would have made him hateful to the Puritans, his grey locks fell from beneath the broad-brimmed hat, and rested on his shoulders. As the old man read the sacred page, the snow drifted against the windows, or eddied in at the crevices of the door, while a blast kept laughing in the chimney, and the blaze leaped fiercely up to seek it. And sometimes, when the wind struck the hill at a certain angle, and swept down by the cottage across the wintry plain, its voice was the most doleful that can be conceived; it came as if the

4. Mary Dyer, Quaker martyr executed in Boston in 1660.
5. Quakers were fined in Massachusetts for not attending the established Congregational church, for failing to support the minister, and for possessing heretical literature.

Past were speaking, as if the Dead had contributed each a whisper, as if the Desolation of Ages were breathed in that one lamenting sound.

The Quaker at length closed the book, retaining however his hand between the pages which he had been reading, while he looked steadfastly at Pearson. The attitude and features of the latter might have indicated the endurance of bodily pain; he leaned his forehead on his hands, his teeth were firmly closed, and his frame was tremulous at intervals with a nervous agitation.

'Friend Tobias,' inquired the old man, compassionately, 'hast thou found no comfort in these many blessed passages of scripture?'

'Thy voice has fallen on my ear like a sound afar off and indistinct,' replied Pearson without lifting his eyes. 'Yea, and when I have harkened carefully, the words seemed cold and lifeless, and intended for another and a lesser grief than mine. Remove the book,' he added, in a tone of sullen bitterness. 'I have no part in its consolations, and they do but fret my sorrow the more.'

'Nay, feeble brother, be not as one who hath never known the light,' said the elder Quaker, earnestly, but with mildness. 'Art thou he that wouldst be content to give all, and endure all, for conscience' sake; desiring even peculiar trials, that thy faith might be purified, and thy heart weaned from worldly desires? And wilt thou sink beneath an affliction which happens alike to them that have their portion here below, and to them that lay up treasure in heaven? Faint not, for thy burthen is yet light.'

'It is heavy! It is heavier than I can bear!' exclaimed Pearson, with the impatience of a variable spirit. 'From my youth upward I have been a man marked out for wrath; and year by year, yea, day after day, I have endured sorrows such as others know not in their lifetime. And now I speak not of the love that has been turned to hatred, the honor to ignominy, the ease and plentifulness of all things to danger, want, and nakedness. All this I could have borne, and counted myself blessed. But when my heart was desolate with many losses, I fixed it upon the child of a stranger, and he became dearer to me than all my buried ones; and now he too must die, as if my love were poison. Verily, I am an accursed man, and I will lay me down in the dust, and lift up my head no more.'

'Thou sinnest, brother, but it is not for me to rebuke thee; for I also have had my hours of darkness, wherein I have murmured against the cross,' said the old Quaker. He continued, perhaps in the hope of distracting his companion's thoughts from his own sorrows. 'Even of late was the light obscured within me, when the men of blood had banished me on pain of death, and the constables led me onward from village to village, towards the wilderness. A strong and cruel hand was wielding the knotted cords; they sunk deep into the flesh, and thou mightst have tracked every reel and totter of my footsteps by the blood that followed. As we went on'—

'Have I not borne all this; and have I murmured?' interrupted Pearson, impatiently.

'Nay, friend, but hear me,' continued the other. 'As we journeyed on, night darkened on our path, so that no man could see the rage of the persecutors, or the constancy of my endurance, though Heaven forbid that I should glory therein. The lights began to glimmer in the cottage windows, and I could discern the inmates as they gathered, in comfort and security, every man with his wife and children by their own evening hearth. At length we came to a tract of fertile land; in the dim light, the forest was not visible around it; and behold! there was a straw-thatched dwelling, which bore the very aspect of my home, far over the wild ocean, far in our own England. Then came bitter thoughts upon me; yea, remembrances that were like death to my soul. The happiness of my early days was painted to me; the disquiet of my manhood, the altered faith of my declining years. I remembered how I had been moved to go forth a wanderer, when my daughter, the youngest, the dearest of my flock, lay on her dying bed, and'—

'Couldst thou obey the command at such a moment?' exclaimed Pearson, shuddering.

'Yea, yea,' replied the old man, hurriedly. 'I was kneeling by her bedside when the voice spoke loud within me; but immediately I rose, and took my staff, and gat me gone. Oh! that it were permitted me to forget her woeful look, when I thus withdrew my arm, and left her journeying through the dark valley alone! for her soul was faint, and she had leaned upon my prayers. Now in that night of horror I was assailed by the thought that I had been an erring christian and a cruel parent; yea, even my daughter, with her pale, dying features, seemed to stand by me and whisper, "Father, you are deceived; go home and shelter your grey head." Oh! thou, to whom I have looked in my farthest wanderings,' continued the Quaker, raising his agitated eyes to heaven, 'inflict not upon the bloodiest of our persecutors the unmitigated agony of my soul, when I believed that all I had done and suffered for Thee was at the instigation of a mocking fiend! But I yielded not; I knelt down and wrestled with the tempter, while the scourge bit more fiercely into the flesh. My prayer was heard, and I went on in peace and joy towards the wilderness.'

The old man, though his fanaticism had generally all the calmness of reason, was deeply moved while reciting this tale; and his unwonted emotion seemed to rebuke and keep down that of his companion. They sat in silence, with their faces to the fire, imagining, perhaps, in its red embers, new scenes of persecution yet to be encountered. The snow still drifted hard against the windows, and sometimes, as the blaze of the logs had gradually sunk, came down the spacious chimney and hissed upon the hearth. A cautious footstep might now and then be heard in a neighboring apartment, and the sound invariably drew the eyes of both Quakers to the door which led thither. When a fierce and riotous gust of wind had led his thoughts, by a natural association, to homeless travellers on such a night, Pearson resumed the conversation.

'I have well nigh sunk under my own share of this trial,' observed he, sighing heavily; 'yet I would that it might be doubled to me, if so the child's mother could be spared. Her wounds have been deep and many, but this will be the sorest of all.'

'Fear not for Catharine,' replied the old Quaker; 'for I know that valiant woman, and have seen how she can bear the cross. A mother's heart, indeed, is strong in her, and may seem to contend mightily with her faith; but soon she will stand up and give thanks that her son has been thus early an accepted sacrifice. The boy hath done his work, and she will feel that he is taken hence in kindness both to him and her. Blessed, blessed are they, that with so little suffering can enter into peace!'

The fitful rush of the wind was now disturbed by a portentous sound; it was a quick and heavy knocking at the outer door. Pearson's wan countenance grew paler, for many a visit of persecution had taught him what to dread; the old man, on the other hand, stood up erect, and his glance was firm as that of the tried soldier who awaits his enemy.

'The men of blood have come to seek me,' he observed, with calmness. 'They have heard how I was moved to return from banishment; and now am I to be led to prison, and thence to death. It is an end I have long looked for. I will open unto them, lest they say, "Lo, he feareth!"'

'Nay, I will present myself before them,' said Pearson, with recovered fortitude. 'It may be that they seek me alone, and know not that thou abidest with me.'

'Let us go boldly, both one and the other,' rejoined his companion. 'It is not fitting that thou or I should shrink.'

They therefore proceeded through the entry to the door, which they opened, bidding the applicant 'Come in, in God's name!' A furious blast of wind drove the storm into their faces, and extinguished the lamp; they had barely time to discern a figure, so white from head to foot with the drifted snow, that it seemed like Winter's self, come in human shape to seek refuge from its own desolation.

'Enter, friend, and do thy errand, be it what it may,' said Pearson. 'It must needs be pressing, since thou comest on such a bitter night.'

'Peace be with this household,' said the stranger, when they stood on the floor of the inner apartment.

Pearson started, the elder Quaker stirred the slumbering embers of the fire, till they sent up a clear and lofty blaze; it was a female voice that had spoken; it was a female form that shone out, cold and wintry, in that comfortable light.

'Catharine, blessed woman,' exclaimed the old man, 'art thou come to this darkened land again! art thou come to bear a valiant testimony as in former years? The scourge hath not prevailed against thee, and from the dungeon hast thou come forth triumphant; but strengthen, strengthen now thy heart, Catharine, for Heaven will prove thee yet this once, ere thou go to thy reward.'

'Rejoice, friends!' she replied. 'Thou who hast long been of our people, and thou whom a little child hath led to us, rejoice! Lo! I come, the messenger of glad tidings, for the day of persecution is overpast. The heart of the king, even Charles, hath been moved in gentleness towards us, and he hath sent forth his letters to stay the hands of the men of blood. A ship's company of our friends hath arrived at yonder town, and I also sailed joyfully among them.'

As Catharine spoke, her eyes were roaming about the room, in search of him for whose sake security was dear to her. Pearson made a silent appeal to the old man, nor did the latter shrink from the painful task assigned him.

'Sister,' he began, in a softened yet perfectly calm tone, 'thou tellest us of His love, manifested in temporal good; and now must we speak to thee of that self-same love, displayed in chastenings. Hitherto, Catharine, thou hast been as one journeying in a darksome and difficult path, and leading an infant by the hand; fain wouldst thou have looked heavenward continually, but still the cares of that little child have drawn thine eyes, and thy affections, to the earth. Sister! go on rejoicing, for his tottering footsteps shall impede thine own no more.'

But the unhappy mother was not thus to be consoled; she shook like a leaf, she turned white as the very snow that hung drifted into her hair. The firm old man extended his hand and held her up, keeping his eye upon her's, as if to repress any outbreak of passion.

'I am a woman, I am but a woman; will He try me above my strength?' said Catharine, very quickly, and almost in a whisper. 'I have been wounded sore; I have suffered much; many things in the body, many in the mind; crucified in myself, and in them that were dearest to me. Surely,' added she, with a long shudder, 'He hath spared me in this one thing.' She broke forth with sudden and irrepressible violence. 'Tell me, man of cold heart, what has God done to me? Hath He cast me down never to rise again? Hath He crushed my very heart in his hand? And thou, to whom I committed my child, how hast thou fulfilled thy trust? Give me back the boy, well, sound, alive, alive; or earth and heaven shall avenge me!'

The agonized shriek of Catharine was answered by the faint, the very faint voice of a child.

On this day it had become evident to Pearson, to his aged guest, and to Dorothy, that Ilbrahim's brief and troubled pilgrimage drew near its close. The two former would willingly have remained by him, to make use of the prayers and pious discourses which they deemed appropriate to the time, and which, if they be impotent as to the departing traveller's reception in the world whither he goes, may at least sustain him in bidding adieu to earth. But though Ilbrahim uttered no complaint, he was disturbed by the faces that looked upon him; so that Dorothy's entreaties, and their own conviction that the child's feet might tread heaven's pavement and not soil it, had induced the two Quakers to remove. Ilbrahim then closed his eyes and grew calm, and except for now and then, a kind and low word to his nurse, might have been thought to slumber. As night-fall came on, however, and the storm began to rise, something seemed to trouble the repose of the boy's mind, and to render his sense of hearing active and acute. If a passing wind lingered to shake the casement, he strove to turn his head towards it; if the door jarred to and fro upon its hinges, he looked long and anxiously thitherward; if the heavy voice of the old man, as he read the scriptures, rose but a little higher, the child almost held his dying breath to listen; if a snow-drift swept by the cottage, with a sound like the trailing of a garment, Ilbrahim seemed to watch that some visitant should enter.

But, after a little time, he relinquished whatever secret hope had agitated him, and, with one low, complaining whisper, turned his cheek upon the pillow. He then addressed Dorothy with his usual sweetness, and besought her to draw near him; she did so, and Ilbrahim took her hand in both of his, grasping it with a gentle pressure, as if to assure himself that he retained it. At intervals, and without disturbing the repose of his countenance, a very faint trembling passed over him from head to foot, as if a mild but somewhat cool wind had breathed upon him, and made him shiver. As the boy thus led her by the hand, in his quiet progress over the borders of eternity, Dorothy almost imagined that she could discern the near, though dim delightfulness, of the home he was about to reach; she would not have enticed the little wanderer back, though she bemoaned herself that she must leave him and return. But just when Ilbrahim's feet were pressing on the soil of Paradise, he heard a voice behind him, and it recalled him a few, few paces of the weary path which he had travelled. As Dorothy looked upon his features, she perceived that their placid expression was again disturbed; her own thoughts had been so wrapt in him, that all sounds

of the storm, and of human speech, were lost to her; but when
Catharine's shriek pierced through the room, the boy strove to raise
himself.

'Friend, she is come! Open unto her!' cried he.

In a moment, his mother was kneeling by the bedside; she drew
Ilbrahim to her bosom, and he nestled there, with no violence of joy,
but contentedly as if he were hushing himself to sleep. He looked
into her face, and reading its agony, said, with feeble earnestness;

'Mourn not, dearest mother. I am happy now.' And with these
words, the gentle boy was dead.

The king's mandate to stay the New England persecutors was effectual in preventing further martyrdoms; but the colonial authorities,
trusting in the remoteness of their situation, and perhaps in the
supposed instability of the royal government, shortly renewed their
severities in all other respects. Catharine's fanaticism had become
wilder by the sundering of all human ties; and wherever a scourge
was lifted, there was she to receive the blow; and whenever a dungeon was unbarred, thither she came, to cast herself upon the floor.
But in process of time, a more christian spirit—a spirit of forbear-
ance, though not of cordiality or approbation, began to pervade the
land in regard to the persecuted sect. And then, when the rigid old
Pilgrims eyed her rather in pity than in wrath; when the matrons fed
her with the fragments of their children's food, and offered her a
lodging on a hard and lowly bed; when no little crowd of school-boys
left their sports to cast stones after the roving enthusiast; then did
Catharine return to Pearson's dwelling, and made that her home.

As if Ilbrahim's sweetness yet lingered round his ashes; as if his
gentle spirit came down from heaven to teach his parent a true
religion, her fierce and vindictive nature was softened by the same
griefs which had once irritated it. When the course of years had
made the features of the unobtrusive mourner familiar in the settlement, she became a subject of not deep, but general interest; a being
on whom the otherwise superfluous sympathies of all might be
bestowed. Every one spoke of her with that degree of pity which it is
pleasant to experience; every one was ready to do her the little kind-
nesses, which are not costly, yet manifest good will; and when at last
she died, a long train of her once bitter persecutors followed her,
with decent sadness and tears that were not painful, to her place by
Ilbrahim's green and sunken grave.

The Wives of the Dead[†]

The following story, the simple and domestic incidents of which may be deemed scarcely worth relating, after such a lapse of time, awakened some degree of interest, a hundred years ago, in a principal seaport of the Bay Province.[1] The rainy twilight of an autumn day; a parlor on the second floor of a small house, plainly furnished, as beseemed the middling circumstances of its inhabitants, yet decorated with little curiosities from beyond the sea, and a few delicate specimens of Indian manufacture,—these are the only particulars to be premised in regard to scene and season. Two young and comely women sat together by the fireside, nursing their mutual and peculiar sorrows. They were the recent brides of two brothers, a sailor and a landsman, and two successive days had brought tidings of the death of each, by the chances of Canadian warfare,[2] and the tempestuous Atlantic. The universal sympathy excited by this bereavement, drew numerous condoling guests to the habitation of the widowed sisters. Several, among whom was the minister, had remained till the verge of evening; when one by one, whispering many comfortable passages of Scripture, that were answered by more abundant tears, they took their leave and departed to their own happier homes. The mourners, though not insensible to the kindness of their friends, had yearned to be left alone. United, as they had been, by the relationship of the living, and now more closely so by that of the dead, each felt as if whatever consolation her grief admitted, were to be found in the bosom of the other. They joined their hearts, and wept together silently. But after an hour of such indulgence, one of the sisters, all of whose emotions were influenced by her mild, quiet, yet not feeble character, began to recollect the precepts of resignation and endurance, which piety had taught her, when she did not think to need them. Her misfortune, besides, as earliest known, should earliest cease to interfere with her regular course of duties; accordingly, having placed the table before the fire, and arranged a frugal meal, she took the hand of her companion.

'Come, dearest sister; you have eaten not a morsel to-day,' she said. 'Arise, I pray you, and let us ask a blessing on that which is provided for us.'

---

† First published in 1831 in *The Token* (dated 1832). Reprinted by permission of The Ohio State University Press. Neal Frank Doubleday conjectures that Hawthorne sent it to Goodrich, editor of *The Token*, in 1829, although there is no direct evidence for this. (See Doubleday, *Hawthorne's Early Tales*, p. 215.)
1. The Province of Massachusetts, subject to the British Crown.
2. I.e., war in Canada and northern New England between the British and the French in the 1720s and 1730s, when the tale is said to take place.

Her sister-in-law was of a lively and irritable temperament, and the first pangs of her sorrow had been expressed by shrieks and passionate lamentation. She now shrunk from Mary's words, like a wounded sufferer from a hand that revives the throb.

'There is no blessing left for me, neither will I ask it,' cried Margaret, with a fresh burst of tears. 'Would it were His will that I might never taste food more.'

Yet she trembled at these rebellious expressions, almost as soon as they were uttered, and, by degrees, Mary succeeded in bringing her sister's mind nearer to the situation of her own. Time went on, and their usual hour of repose arrived. The brothers and their brides, entering the married state with no more than the slender means which then sanctioned such a step, had confederated themselves in one household, with equal rights to the parlor, and claiming exclusive privileges in two sleeping rooms contiguous to it. Thither the widowed ones retired, after heaping ashes upon the dying embers of their fire, and placing a lighted lamp upon the hearth. The doors of both chambers were left open, so that a part of the interior of each, and the beds with their unclosed curtains, were reciprocally visible. Sleep did not steal upon the sisters at one and the same time. Mary experienced the effect often consequent upon grief quietly borne, and soon sunk into temporary forgetfulness, while Margaret became more disturbed and feverish, in proportion as the night advanced with its deepest and stillest hours. She lay listening to the drops of rain, that came down in monotonous succession, unswayed by a breath of wind; and a nervous impulse continually caused her to lift her head from the pillow, and gaze into Mary's chamber and the intermediate apartment. The cold light of the lamp threw the shadows of the furniture up against the wall, stamping them immoveably there, except when they were shaken by a sudden flicker of the flame. Two vacant arm-chairs were in their old positions on opposite sides of the hearth, where the brothers had been wont to sit in young and laughing dignity, as heads of families; two humbler seats were near them, the true thrones of that little empire, where Mary and herself had exercised in love, a power that love had won. The cheerful radiance of the fire had shone upon the happy circle, and the dead glimmer of the lamp might have befitted their reunion now. While Margaret groaned in bitterness, she heard a knock at the street-door.

'How would my heart have leapt at that sound but yesterday!' thought she, remembering the anxiety with which she had long awaited tidings from her husband. 'I care not for it now; let them begone, for I will not arise.'

But even while a sort of childish fretfulness made her thus resolve, she was breathing hurriedly, and straining her ears to catch a repetition of the summons. It is difficult to be convinced of the death of one whom we have deemed another self. The knocking was now renewed in slow and regular strokes, apparently given with the soft end of a doubled fist, and was accompanied by words, faintly heard through several thicknesses of wall. Margaret looked to her sister's chamber, and beheld her still lying in the depths of sleep. She arose, placed her foot upon the floor, and slightly arrayed herself, trembling between fear and eagerness as she did so.

'Heaven help me!' sighed she. 'I have nothing left to fear, and methinks I am ten times more a coward than ever.'

Seizing the lamp from the hearth, she hastened to the window that overlooked the street-door. It was a lattice, turning upon hinges; and having thrown it back, she stretched her head a little way into the moist atmosphere. A lantern was reddening the front of the house, and melting its light in the neighboring puddles, while a deluge of darkness overwhelmed every other object. As the window grated on its hinges, a man in a broad brimmed hat and blanket-coat, stepped from under the shelter of the projecting story, and looked upward to discover whom his application had aroused. Margaret knew him as a friendly innkeeper of the town.

'What would you have, Goodman[3] Parker? cried the widow.

'Lack-a-day, is it you, Mistress Margaret?' replied the innkeeper. 'I was afraid it might be your sister Mary; for I hate to see a young woman in trouble, when I haven't a word of comfort to whisper her.'

'For Heaven's sake, what news do you bring?' screamed Margaret.

'Why, there has been an express through the town within this half hour,' said Goodman Parker, 'travelling from the eastern jurisdiction with letters from the governor and council. He tarried at my house to refresh himself with a drop and a morsel, and I asked him what tidings on the frontiers. He tells me we had the better in the skirmish you wot of, and that thirteen men reported slain are well and sound, and your husband among them. Besides, he is appointed of the escort to bring the captivated Frenchers and Indians home to the province jail. I judged you wouldn't mind being broke of your rest, and so I stept over to tell you. Good night.'

So saying, the honest man departed; and his lantern gleamed along the street, bringing to view indistinct shapes of things, and the fragments of a world, like order glimmering through chaos, or memory roaming over the past. But Margaret staid not to watch these picturesque effects. Joy flashed into her heart, and lighted it up at once, and breathless, and with winged steps, she flew to the bedside of her sister. She paused, however, at the door of the chamber, while a thought of pain broke in upon her.

3. A term of respect for a man of humble status.

'Poor Mary!' said she to herself. 'Shall I waken her, to feel her sorrow sharpened by my happiness? No; I will keep it within my own bosom till the morrow.'

She approached the bed to discover if Mary's sleep were peaceful. Her face was turned partly inward to the pillow, and had been hidden there to weep; but a look of motionless contentment was now visible upon it, as if her heart, like a deep lake, had grown calm because its dead had sunk down so far within. Happy is it, and strange, that the lighter sorrows are those from which dreams are chiefly fabricated. Margaret shrunk from disturbing her sister-in-law, and felt as if her own better fortune, had rendered her involuntarily unfaithful, and as if altered and diminished affection must be the consequence of the disclosure she had to make. With a sudden step, she turned away. But joy could not long be repressed, even by circumstances that would have excited heavy grief at another moment. Her mind was thronged with delightful thoughts, till sleep stole on and transformed them to visions, more delightful and more wild, like the breath of winter, (but what a cold comparison!) working fantastic tracery upon a window.

When the night was far advanced, Mary awoke with a sudden start. A vivid dream had latterly involved her in its unreal life, of which, however, she could only remember that it had been broken in upon at the most interesting point. For a little time, slumber hung about her like a morning mist, hindering her from perceiving the distinct outline of her situation. She listened with imperfect consciousness to two or three volleys of a rapid and eager knocking; and first she deemed the noise a matter of course, like the breath she drew; next, it appeared a thing in which she had no concern; and lastly, she became aware that it was a summons necessary to be obeyed. At the same moment, the pang of recollection darted into her mind; the pall of sleep was thrown back from the face of grief; the dim light of the chamber, and the objects therein revealed, had retained all her suspended ideas, and restored them as soon as she unclosed her eyes. Again, there was a quick peal upon the street-door. Fearing that her sister would also be disturbed, Mary wrapped herself in a cloak and hood, took the lamp from the hearth, and hastened to the window. By some accident, it had been left unhasped, and yielded easily to her hand.

'Who's there?' asked Mary, trembling as she looked forth.

The storm was over, and the moon was up; it shone upon broken clouds above, and below upon houses black with moisture, and upon little lakes of the fallen rain, curling into silver beneath the quick enchantment of a breeze. A young man in a sailor's dress, wet as if he had come out of the depths of the sea, stood alone under the window. Mary recognized him as one whose livelihood was gained by short voyages along the coast; nor did she forget, that, previous to her marriage, he had been an unsuccessful wooer of her own.

'What do you seek here, Stephen?' said she.

'Cheer up, Mary, for I seek to comfort you,' answered the rejected lover. 'You must know I got home not ten minutes ago, and the first thing my good mother told me was the news about your husband. So, without saying a word to the old woman, I clapt on my hat, and ran out of the house. I couldn't have slept a wink before speaking to you, Mary, for the sake of old times.'

'Stephen, I thought better of you!' exclaimed the widow, with gushing tears, and preparing to close the lattice; for she was no whit inclined to imitate the first wife of Zadig.[4]

'But stop, and hear my story out,' cried the young sailor. 'I tell you we spoke a brig yesterday afternoon, bound in from Old England. And who do you think I saw standing on deck, well and hearty, only a bit thinner than he was five months ago?'

Mary leaned from the window, but could not speak.

'Why, it was your husband himself,' continued the generous seaman. 'He and three others saved themselves on a spar, when the Blessing turned bottom upwards. The brig will beat into the bay by daylight, with this wind, and you'll see him here tomorrow. There's the comfort I bring you, Mary, and so good night.'

He hurried away, while Mary watched him with a doubt of waking reality, that seemed stronger or weaker as he alternately entered the shade of the houses, or emerged into the broad streaks of moonlight. Gradually, however, a blessed flood of conviction swelled into her heart, in strength enough to overwhelm her, had its increase been more abrupt. Her first impulse was to rouse her sister-in-law, and communicate the new-born gladness. She opened the chamber-door, which had been closed in the course of the night, though not latched, advanced to the bedside, and was about to lay her hand upon the slumberer's shoulder. But then she remembered that Margaret would awake to thoughts of death and woe, rendered not the less bitter by their contrast with her own felicity. She suffered the rays of the lamp to fall upon the unconscious form of the bereaved one. Margaret lay in unquiet sleep, and the drapery was displaced around her; her young cheek was rosy-tinted, and her lips half opened in a vivid smile; an expression of joy, debarred its passage by her sealed eyelids, struggled forth like incense from the whole countenance.

'My poor sister! you will waken too soon from that happy dream,' thought Mary.

4. In Voltaire's novel *Zadig* (1747) Azora is unfaithful to Zadig, her husband.

Before retiring, she set down the lamp and endeavored to arrange the bed-clothes, so that the chill air might not do harm to the feverish slumberer. But her hand trembled against Margaret's neck, a tear also fell upon her cheek, and she suddenly awoke.

Mrs. Hutchinson[†]

The character of this female suggests a train of thought which will form as natural an introduction to her story as most of the prefaces to Gay's Fables or the tales of Prior,[1] besides that the general soundness of the moral may excuse any want of present applicability. We will not look for a living resemblance of Mrs. Hutchinson, though the search might not be altogether fruitless.—But there are portentous indications, changes gradually taking place in the habits and feelings of the gentle sex, which seem to threaten our posterity with many of those public women, whereof one was a burthen too grievous for our fathers. The press, however, is now the medium through which feminine ambition chiefly manifests itself, and we will not anticipate the period, (trusting to be gone hence ere it arrive,) when fair orators shall be as numerous as the fair authors of our own day. The hastiest glance may show, how much of the texture and body of cis-atlantic literature[2] is the work of those slender fingers, from which only a light and fanciful embroidery has heretofore been required, that might sparkle upon the garment without enfeebling the web. Woman's intellect should never give the tone to that of man, and even her morality is not exactly the material for masculine virtue. A false liberality which mistakes the strong division lines of Nature for arbitrary distinctions, and a courtesy, which might polish

---

† First published in the *Salem Gazette*, December 7, 1830, then after Hawthorne's death in the first comprehensive edition of his works (Boston, 1883). Reprinted by permission of The Ohio State University Press. "Mrs. Hutchinson" displays both Hawthorne's antifeminist convictions and his tendency to sympathize intermittently with the strong women he portrays in his writings. As a dramatized personage, Ann Hutchinson foreshadows Catharine in "The Gentle Boy," Hester in *The Scarlet Letter*, and Zenobia in *The Blithedale Romance*, each in her own way a public woman who assumes a life of her own in Hawthorne's imagination, almost in the teeth of the disapproval his narrators sometimes voice toward them.

Ann Hutchinson reappears in several of Hawthorne's later writings, first in his history of early New England for children, *Grandfather's Chair*, as "a very sharp witted and well instructed lady [who] was so conscious of her own wisdom and abilities, that she thought it a pity that the world should not have the benefit of them" (CE 6:27); then briefly in "Main Street"; then again in the first chapter of *The Scarlet Letter*, where according to legend a rose bush may have "sprung up under the footsteps of the sainted Ann Hutchinson, as she entered the prison-door" (CE 1:48). Hawthorne evidently had her in mind when he created Hester Prynne.

1. Matthew Prior (1664–1721), poet and diplomat, author of popular verse tales. John Gay (1685–1732), best known for his *Beggar's Opera* (1728). His *Fables*, published in 1727, would go through more than 350 editions.
2. Literature written on this side of the Atlantic, i.e., American literature.

criticism but should never soften it, have done their best to add a girlish feebleness to the tottering infancy of our literature. The evil is likely to be a growing one. As yet, the great body of American women are a domestic race; but when a continuance of ill-judged incitements shall have turned their hearts away from the fire-side, there are obvious circumstances which will render female pens more numerous and more prolific than those of men, though but equally encouraged; and (limited of course by the scanty support of the public, but increasing indefinitely within those limits) the ink-stained Amazons will expel their rivals by actual pressure, and petticoats wave triumphant over all the field. But, allowing that such forebodings are slightly exaggerated, is it good for woman's self that the path of feverish hope, of tremulous success, of bitter and ignominious disappointment, should be left wide open to her? Is the prize worth her having if she win it? Fame does not increase the peculiar respect which men pay to female excellence, and there is a delicacy, (even in rude bosoms, where few would think to find it) that perceives, or fancies, a sort of impropriety in the display of woman's naked mind to the gaze of the world, with indications by which its inmost secrets may be searched out. In fine, criticism should examine with a stricter, instead of a more indulgent eye, the merits of females at its bar, because they are to justify themselves for an irregularity which men do not commit in appearing there; and woman, when she feels the impulse of genius like a command of Heaven within her, should be aware that she is relinquishing a part of the loveliness of her sex, and obey the inward voice with sorrowing reluctance, like the Arabian maid who bewailed the gift of Prophecy.[3] Hinting thus imperfectly at sentiments which may be developed on a future occasion, we proceed to consider the celebrated subject of this sketch.

Mrs. Hutchinson was a woman of extraordinary talent and strong imagination, whom the latter quality, following the general direction taken by the enthusiasm of the times, prompted to stand forth as a reformer in religion. In her native country, she had shown symptoms of irregular and daring thought, but, chiefly by the influence of a favorite pastor,[4] was restrained from open indiscretion. On the removal of this clergyman, becoming dissatisfied with the ministry under which she lived, she was drawn in by the great tide of Puritan emigration, and visited Massachusetts within a few years after its first settlement. But she bore trouble in her own bosom, and could find no peace in this chosen land.—She soon began to pro-

3. Possibly Sajah, who declared herself a prophet after the death of Muhammad but eventually returned to Islam.
4. John Cotton (1585–1652), Hutchinson's pastor in Boston, England. She followed Cotton to the Massachusetts Bay Colony, where both became embroiled in the Antinomian controversy of 1636–38.

mulgate strange and dangerous opinions, tending, in the peculiar situation of the colony, and from the principles which were its basis and indispensable for its temporary support, to eat into its very existence. We shall endeavor to give a more practical idea of this part of her course.

It is a summer evening. The dusk has settled heavily upon the woods, the waves, and the Trimontane peninsula,[5] increasing that dismal aspect of the embryo town which was said to have drawn tears of despondency from Mrs. Hutchinson, though she believed that her mission thither was divine. The houses, straw-thatched and lowly roofed, stand irregularly along streets that are yet roughened by the roots of the trees, as if the forest, departing at the approach of man, had left its reluctant foot prints behind. Most of the dwellings are lonely and silent; from a few we may hear the reading of some sacred text, or the quiet voice of prayer; but nearly all the sombre life of the scene is collected near the extremity of the village. A crowd of hooded women, and of men in steeple-hats and close cropt hair, are assembled at the door and open windows of a house newly built. An earnest expression glows in every face, and some press inward as if the bread of life were to be dealt forth, and they feared to lose their share, while others would fain hold them back, but enter with them since they may not be restrained. We also will go in, edging through the thronged doorway to an apartment which occupies the whole breadth of the house. At the upper end, behind a table on which are placed the Scriptures and two glimmering lamps, we see a woman, plainly attired as befits her ripened years; her hair, complexion, and eyes are dark, the latter somewhat dull and heavy, but kindling up with a gradual brightness. Let us look round upon the hearers. At her right hand, his countenance suiting well with the gloomy light which discovers it, stands Vane[6] the youthful governor, preferred by a hasty judgment of the people over all the wise and hoary heads that had preceded him to New-England. In his mysterious eyes we may read a dark enthusiasm, akin to that of the woman whose cause he has espoused, combined with a shrewd worldly foresight, which tells him that her doctrines will be productive of change and tumult, the elements of his power and delight. On her left, yet slightly drawn back so as to evince a less decided support, is Cotton, no young and hot enthusiast, but a mild, grave man in the decline of life, deep in all the learning of the

---

5. South of the Charles River, with three high hills, where Boston, Massachusetts, was founded.
6. Henry Vane (1613–1662) arrived in Boston in 1635 and served as governor of Massachusetts in 1636–37. Vane strongly supported Hutchinson and narrowly escaped being banished with her, returning to England on August 3, 1637.

age, and sanctified in heart[7] and made venerable in feature by the long exercise of his holy profession. He also is deceived by the strange fire now laid upon the altar, and he alone among his brethren is excepted in the denunciation of the new Apostle, as sealed and set apart by Heaven to the work of the ministry. Others of the priesthood stand full in front of the woman, striving to beat her down with brows of wrinkled iron, and whispering sternly and significantly among themselves, as she unfolds her seditious doctrines and grows warm in their support. Foremost is Hugh Peters, full of holy wrath, and scarce containing himself from rushing forward to convict her of damnable heresies; there also is Ward,[8] meditating a reply of empty puns, and quaint antitheses, and tinkling jests that puzzle us with nothing but a sound. The audience are variously affected, but none indifferent. On the foreheads of the aged, the mature, and strong-minded, you may generally read steadfast disapprobation, though here and there is one, whose faith seems shaken in those whom he had trusted for years; the females, on the other hand, are shuddering and weeping, and at times they cast a desolate look of fear around them; while the young men lean forward, fiery and impatient, fit instruments for whatever rash deed may be suggested. And what is the eloquence that gives rise to all these passions? The woman tells them, (and cites texts from the Holy Book to prove her words,) that they have put their trust in unregenerated and uncommissioned men, and have followed them into the wilderness for naught. Therefore their hearts are turning from those whom they had chosen to lead them to Heaven, and they feel like children who have been enticed far from home, and see the features of their guides change all at once, assuming a fiendish shape in some frightful solitude.

These proceedings of Mrs. Hutchinson could not long be endured by the provincial government. The present was a most remarkable case, in which religious freedom was wholly inconsistent with public safety, and where the principles of an illiberal age indicated the very course which must have been pursued by worldly policy and enlightened wisdom. Unity of faith was the star that had guided these people over the deep, and a diversity of sects would either have scattered them from the land to which they had as yet so few attachments, or perhaps have excited a diminutive civil war among those who had come so far to worship together. The opposition to what may be termed the established church had now lost its chief support, by the removal of Vane from office and his departure for

7. The "sanctified in heart" had received God's grace and were guaranteed salvation.
8. Nathaniel Ward (1578–1652), author of *The Simple Cobler of Aggawam*, a satire on religious toleration. Hugh Peters (1598–1660) replaced Roger Williams as minister in Salem after Williams was banished to Rhode Island.

England, and Mr. Cotton began to have that light in regard to his errors, which will sometimes break in upon the wisest and most pious men, when their opinions are unhappily discordant with those of the Powers that be. A Synod,[9] the first in New England, was speedily assembled, and pronounced its condemnation of the obnoxious doctrines. Mrs. Hutchinson was next summoned before the supreme civil tribunal, at which, however, the most eminent of the clergy were present, and appear to have taken a very active part as witnesses and advisers. We shall here resume the more picturesque style of narration.

It is a place of humble aspect where the Elders of the people are met, sitting in judgment upon the disturber of Israel.[1] The floor of the low and narrow hall is laid with planks hewn by the axe,—the beams of the roof still wear the rugged bark with which they grew up in the forest, and the hearth is formed of one broad unhammered stone, heaped with logs that roll their blaze and smoke up a chimney of wood and clay. A sleety shower beats fitfully against the windows, driven by the November blast, which comes howling onward from the northern desert, the boisterous and unwelcome herald of a New England winter. Rude benches are arranged across the apartment and along its sides, occupied by men whose piety and learning might have entitled them to seats in those high Councils of the ancient Church, whence opinions were sent forth to confirm or supersede the Gospel in the belief of the whole world and of posterity.—Here are collected all those blessed Fathers of the land, who rank in our veneration next to the Evangelists of Holy Writ, and here also are many, unpurified from the fiercest errors of the age and ready to propagate the religion of peace by violence. In the highest place sits Winthrop,[2] a man by whom the innocent and the guilty might alike desire to be judged, the first confiding in his integrity and wisdom, the latter hoping in his mildness. Next is Endicott,[3] who would stand with his drawn sword at the gate of Heaven, and resist to the death all pilgrims thither, except they travelled his own path. The infant eyes of one in this assembly beheld the faggots blazing round the martyrs, in bloody Mary's[4] time; in later life he dwelt long at Leyden, with the first who went from England for conscience sake; and now, in his weary age, it matters little where he lies down to die. There are others whose hearts were smitten in the high meridian of

9. An assembly of church officials.
1. The Puritans saw their colony as a religious community modeled on ancient Israel.
2. John Winthrop (1588–1649) succeeded Vane as governor of Massachusetts and presided over Hutchinson's trial. Winthrop was twelve times governor and deeply respected.
3. John Endicott (1588–1665) was deputy governor of Massachusetts in 1637.
4. The Catholic Queen Mary (1516–1558), or "Bloody Mary" according to Protestants, ruled England from 1553 until her death. She was succeeded by the Protestant Queen Elizabeth.

ambitious hope, and whose dreams still tempt them with the pomp of the old world and the din of its crowded cities, gleaming and echoing over the deep. In the midst, and in the centre of all eyes, we see the Woman. She stands loftily before her judges, with a determined brow, and, unknown to herself, there is a flash of carnal pride half hidden in her eye, as she surveys the many learned and famous men whom her doctrines have put in fear. They question her, and her answers are ready and acute; she reasons with them shrewdly, and brings scripture in support of every argument; the deepest controversialists of that scholastic day find here a woman, whom all their trained and sharpened intellects are inadequate to foil. But by the excitement of the contest, her heart is made to rise and swell within her, and she bursts forth into eloquence. She tells them of the long unquietness which she had endured in England, perceiving the corruption of the church, and yearning for a purer and more perfect light, and how, in a day of solitary prayer, that light was given; she claims for herself the peculiar power of distinguishing between the chosen of man and the Sealed of Heaven, and affirms that her gifted eye can see the glory round the foreheads of the Saints[5] sojourning in their mortal state.—She declares herself commissioned to separate the true shepherds from the false, and denounces present and future judgments on the land, if she be disturbed in her celestial errand. Thus the accusations are proved from her own mouth. Her judges hesitate, and some speak faintly in her defence; but, with a few dissenting voices, sentence is pronounced, bidding her go out from among them, and trouble the land no more.

Mrs. Hutchinson's adherents throughout the colony were now disarmed, and she proceeded to Rhode Island, an accustomed refuge for the exiles of Massachusetts, in all seasons of persecution. Her enemies believed that the anger of Heaven was following her, of which Governor Winthrop does not disdain to record a notable instance, very interesting in a scientific point of view, but fitter for his old and homely narrative than for modern repetition.[6] In a little time, also, she lost her husband,[7] who is mentioned in history only as attending her footsteps, and whom we may conclude to have been (like most husbands of celebrated women) a mere insignificant

---

5. For Protestants, regenerate persons whom God had saved. Hutchinson claimed to be able to distinguish those who were truly regenerate ("Sealed of Heaven") from those who were not (merely "chosen of man").

6. In his journal for 1638, Winthrop reports how after Hutchinson settled in Rhode Island, her pregnancy came to term and she "was delivered of a monstrous birth." Apparently, she had a menopausal pregnancy and her fetus aborted in a watery mass, which Winthrop describes in gruesome detail. See *The Journal of John Winthrop, 1630–49*, edited by Richard S. Dunn and Laetitia Yeandle (Cambridge, MA, 1996), 146–47.

7. William Hutchinson died in 1642, whereupon Ann Hutchinson moved the family to New Amsterdam (New York).

appendage of his mightier wife. She now grew uneasy among the Rhode-Island colonists, whose liberality towards her, at an era when liberality was not esteemed a christian virtue, probably arose from a comparative insolicitude on religious matters, more distasteful to Mrs. Hutchinson than even the uncompromising narrowness of the Puritans. Her final movement was to lead her family within the limits of the Dutch Jurisdiction, where, having felled the trees of a virgin soil, she became herself the virtual head, civil and ecclesiastical, of a little colony.

Perhaps here she found the repose, hitherto so vainly sought. Secluded from all whose faith she could not govern, surrounded by the dependents over whom she held an unlimited influence, agitated by none of the tumultuous billows which were left swelling behind her, we may suppose, that, in the stillness of Nature, her heart was stilled. But her impressive story was to have an awful close. Her last scene is as difficult to be portrayed as a shipwreck, where the shrieks of the victims die unheard along a desolate sea, and a shapeless mass of agony is all that can be brought home to the imagination. The savage foe was on the watch for blood. Sixteen persons assembled at the evening prayer; in the deep midnight, their cry rang through the forest; and daylight dawned upon the lifeless clay of all but one. It was a circumstance not to be unnoticed by our stern ancestors, in considering the fate of her who had so troubled their religion, that an infant daughter, the sole survivor amid the terrible destruction of her mother's household, was bred in a barbarous faith, and never learned the way to the Christian's Heaven. Yet we will hope, that there the mother and the child have met.[8]

The Haunted Mind[†]

What a singular moment is the first one, when you have hardly begun to recollect yourself, after starting from midnight slumber! By unclosing your eyes so suddenly, you seem to have surprised the personages of your dream in full convocation round your bed, and catch one broad glance at them before they can flit into obscurity. Or, to vary the metaphor, you find yourself, for a single instant, wide awake in that realm of illusions, whither sleep has been the passport, and behold its ghostly inhabitants and wondrous scenery, with a perception of their strangeness, such as you never attain

8. Hutchinson and all but one of the six children with her died in an Indian attack in 1643.
† First published in 1834 in The Taken (dated 1835) then in Twice-told Tales, 2nd ed., 1842.

while the dream is undisturbed. The distant sound of a church clock is borne faintly on the wind. You question with yourself half seriously, whether it has stolen to your waking ear from some gray tower, that stood within the precincts of your dream. While yet in suspense, another clock flings its heavy clang over the slumbering town, with so full and distinct a sound, and such a long murmur in the neighboring air, that you are certain it must proceed from the steeple at the nearest corner. You count the strokes—one—two, and there they cease, with a booming sound, like the gathering of a third stroke within the bell.

If you could choose an hour of wakefulness out of the whole night, it would be this. Since your sober bedtime, at eleven, you have had rest enough to take off the pressure of yesterday's fatigue; while before you, till the sun comes from 'far Cathay'[1] to brighten your window, there is almost the space of a summer night; one hour to be spent in thought, with the mind's eye half shut, and two in pleasant dreams, and two in that strangest of enjoyments, the forgetfulness alike of joy and woe. The moment of rising belongs to another period of time, and appears so distant, that the plunge out of a warm bed into the frosty air cannot yet be anticipated with dismay. Yesterday has already vanished among the shadows of the past; to-morrow has not yet emerged from the future. You have found an intermediate space, where the business of life does not intrude; where the passing moment lingers, and becomes truly the present; a spot where Father Time, when he thinks nobody is watching him, sits down by the way side to take breath. Oh, that he would fall asleep, and let mortals live on without growing older!

Hitherto you have lain perfectly still, because the slightest motion would dissipate the fragments of your slumber. Now, being irrevocably awake, you peep through the half drawn window curtain, and observe that the glass is ornamented with fanciful devices in frost work, and that each pane presents something like a frozen dream. There will be time enough to trace out the analogy, while waiting the summons to breakfast. Seen through the clear portion of the glass, where the silvery mountain peaks of the frost scenery do not ascend, the most conspicuous object is the steeple; the white spire of which directs you to the wintry lustre of the firmament. You may almost distinguish the figures on the clock that has just told the hour. Such a frosty sky; and the snow-covered roofs, and the long vista of the frozen street, all white, and the distant water hardened into rock, might make you shiver, even under four blankets and a woolen comforter. Yet look at that one glorious star! Its beams are distinguishable from all the rest, and actually cast the shadow of the

1. From the Far East, China.

casement on the bed, with a radiance of deeper hue than moonlight, though not so accurate an outline.

You sink down and muffle your head in the clothes, shivering all the while, but less from bodily chill, than the bare idea of a polar atmosphere. It is too cold even for the thoughts to venture abroad. You speculate on the luxury of wearing out a whole existence in bed, like an oyster in its shell, content with the sluggish ecstasy of inaction, and drowsily conscious of nothing but delicious warmth, such as you now feel again. Ah! that idea has brought a hideous one in its train. You think how the dead are lying in their cold shrouds and narrow coffins, through the drear winter of the grave, and cannot persuade your fancy that they neither shrink nor shiver, when the snow is drifting over their little hillocks, and the bitter blast howls against the door of the tomb. That gloomy thought will collect a gloomy multitude, and throw its complexion over your wakeful hour.

In the depths of every heart, there is a tomb and a dungeon, though the lights, the music, and revelry above may cause us to forget their existence, and the buried ones, or prisoners whom they hide. But sometimes, and oftenest at midnight, those dark receptacles are flung wide open. In an hour like this, when the mind has a passive sensibility, but no active strength; when the imagination is a mirror, imparting vividness to all ideas, without the power of selecting or controlling them; then pray that your griefs may slumber, and the brotherhood of remorse not break their chain. It is too late! A funeral train comes gliding by your bed, in which Passion and Feeling assume bodily shape, and things of the mind become dim spectres to the eye. There is your earliest Sorrow, a pale young mourner, wearing a sister's likeness to first love, sadly beautiful, with a hallowed sweetness in her melancholy features, and grace in the flow of her sable robe. Next appears a shade of ruined loveliness, with dust among her golden hair, and her bright garments all faded and defaced, stealing from your glance with drooping head, as fearful of reproach; she was your fondest Hope, but a delusive one; so call her Disappointment now. A sterner form succeeds, with a brow of wrinkles, a look and gesture of iron authority; there is no name for him unless it be Fatality, an emblem of the evil influence that rules your fortunes; a demon to whom you subjected yourself by some error at the outset of life, and were bound his slave forever, by once obeying him. See! those fiendish lineaments graven on the darkness, the writhed lip of scorn, the mockery of that living eye, the pointed finger, touching the sore place in your heart! Do you remember any act of enormous folly, at which you would blush, even in the remotest cavern of the earth? Then recognise your Shame.

Pass, wretched band! Well for the wakeful one if, riotously miserable, a fiercer tribe do not surround him, the devils of a guilty heart, that holds its hell within itself. What if Remorse should assume the features of an injured friend? What if the fiend should come in woman's garments, with a pale beauty amid sin and desolation, and lie down by your side? What if he should stand at your bed's foot, in the likeness of a corpse, with a bloody stain upon the shroud? Sufficient without such guilt, is this nightmare of the soul; this heavy, heavy sinking of the spirits; this wintry gloom about the heart; this indistinct horror of the mind, blending itself with the darkness of the chamber.

By a desperate effort, you start upright, breaking from a sort of conscious sleep, and gazing wildly round the bed, as if the fiends were any where but in your haunted mind. At the same moment, the slumbering embers on the hearth send forth a gleam which palely illuminates the whole outer room, and flickers through the door of the bed-chamber, but cannot quite dispel its obscurity. Your eye searches for whatever may remind you of the living world. With eager minuteness, you take note of the table near the fire-place, the book with an ivory knife between its leaves, the unfolded letter, the hat and the fallen glove. Soon the flame vanishes, and with it the whole scene is gone, though its image remains an instant in your mind's eye, when darkness has swallowed the reality. Throughout the chamber, there is the same obscurity as before, but not the same gloom within your breast. As your head falls back upon the pillow, you think—in a whisper be it spoken—how pleasant in these night solitudes, would be the rise and fall of a softer breathing than your own, the slight pressure of a tenderer bosom, the quiet throb of a purer heart, imparting its peacefulness to your troubled one, as if the fond sleeper were involving you in her dream.

Her influence is over you, though she have no existence but in that momentary image. You sink down in a flowery spot, on the borders of sleep and wakefulness, while your thoughts rise before you in pictures, all disconnected, yet all assimilated by a pervading gladsomeness and beauty. The wheeling of gorgeous squadrons, that glitter in the sun, is succeeded by the merriment of children round the door of a schoolhouse, beneath the glimmering shadow of old trees, at the corner of a rustic lane. You stand in the sunny rain of a summer shower, and wander among the sunny trees of an autumnal wood, and look upward at the brightest of all rainbows, overarching the unbroken sheet of snow, on the American side of Niagara. Your mind struggles pleasantly between the dancing radiance round the hearth of a young man and his recent bride, and the twittering flight of birds in spring, about their new-made nest. You feel the merry bounding of a ship before the breeze; and watch the tuneful feet of rosy girls, as they twine their last and merriest dance, in a splendid ball room; and find yourself in the brilliant

circle of a crowded theatre, as the curtain falls over a light and airy
scene.

With an involuntary start, you seize hold on consciousness, and
prove yourself but half awake, by running a doubtful parallel between
human life and the hour which has now elapsed. In both you emerge
from mystery, pass through a vicissitude that you can but imperfectly
control, and are borne onward to another mystery. Now comes the
peal of the distant clock, with fainter and fainter strokes as you
plunge farther into the wilderness of sleep. It is the knell of a temporary death. Your spirit has departed, and strays like a free citizen,
among the people of a shadowy world, beholding strange sights, yet
without wonder or dismay. So calm, perhaps, will be the final change;
so undisturbed, as if among familiar things, the entrance of the soul
to its Eternal home!

The Gray Champion†

There was once a time when New England groaned under the actual
pressure of heavier wrongs, than those threatened ones which
brought on the Revolution. James II, the bigoted successor of Charles
the Voluptuous, had annulled the charters of all the colonies,[1] and
sent a harsh and unprincipled soldier to take away our liberties and
endanger our religion. The administration of Sir Edmund Andros
lacked scarcely a single characteristic of tyranny: a Governor and
Council, holding office from the King, and wholly independent of
the country; laws made and taxes levied without concurrence of the
people, immediate or by their representatives; the rights of private
citizens violated, and the titles of all landed property declared void;

---

† First published in the *New England Magazine*, January 1835. Hawthorne chose it to lead
off *Twice-told Tales* in 1837. The action is based partly on the political upheaval in Boston in 1689. Sir Edmund Andros, appointed royal governor by James II in 1686, made
himself well hated by most Bostonians in the three years of his administration. After
the news reached Boston that William III had displaced James II on the English throne,
Andros and the chief members of his council were seized and confined by colonial rebels.
Simon Bradstreet, one of the first settlers of Massachusetts, became governor. The legend of "the gray champion," however, is drawn from another episode of colonial history.
In 1675, William Goffe, one of the Puritan judges of Charles I who had fled to New
England in 1660 upon the restoration of Charles II, came out from hiding and rallied
the white settlers of Hadley, Massachusetts, to defend themselves against an Indian
attack. Goffe then mysteriously disappeared and was known afterward as "the Angel of
Hadley." Hawthorne combines the two episodes. The "Lord of Hosts" according to
Puritan legend "provided a Champion" for the people of Hadley in the person of Goffe.
So, too, Hawthorne imagines, another gray-haired "ancient man" might have faced down
the hated royal governor and restored New England's independence during the crisis in
Boston.
1. Charles II ("the Voluptuous"), not James II, annulled the original charter of the Massachusetts Bay Colony in 1684. James II is described as "bigoted" because he ruled auto-
cratically and tried to foster Roman Catholicism.

the voice of complaint stifled by restrictions on the press; and finally, disaffection overawed by the first band of mercenary troops that ever marched on our free soil. For two years our ancestors were kept in sullen submission, by that filial love which had invariably secured their allegiance to the mother country, whether its head chanced to be a Parliament, Protector, or popish Monarch. Till these evil times, however, such allegiance had been merely nominal, and the colonists had ruled themselves, enjoying far more freedom, than is even yet the privilege of the native subjects of Great Britain.

At length, a rumor reached our shores, that the Prince of Orange[2] had ventured on an enterprise, the success of which would be the triumph of civil and religious rights and the salvation of New England. It was but a doubtful whisper; it might be false, or the attempt might fail; and, in either case, the man, that stirred against King James, would lose his head. Still the intelligence produced a marked effect. The people smiled mysteriously in the streets, and threw bold glances at their oppressors; while, far and wide, there was a subdued and silent agitation, as if the slightest signal would rouse the whole land from its sluggish despondency. Aware of their danger, the rulers resolved to avert it by an imposing display of strength, and perhaps to confirm their despotism by yet harsher measures. One afternoon in April, 1689, Sir Edmund Andros and his favorite councillors, being warm with wine, assembled the redcoats of the Governor's Guard, and made their appearance in the streets of Boston. The sun was near setting when the march commenced.

The roll of the drum, at that unquiet crisis, seemed to go through the streets, less as the martial music of the soldiers, than as a muster-call to the inhabitants themselves. A multitude, by various avenues, assembled in King-street,[3] which was destined to be the scene, nearly a century afterwards, of another encounter between the troops of Britain, and a people struggling against her tyranny. Though more than sixty years had elapsed, since the Pilgrims came, this crowd of their descendants still showed the strong and sombre features of their character, perhaps more strikingly in such a stern emergency than on happier occasions. There was the sober garb, the general severity of mien, the gloomy but undismayed expression, the scriptural forms of speech, and the confidence in Heaven's blessing on a righteous cause, which would have marked a band of the original Puritans, when threatened by some peril of the wilderness. Indeed, it was not yet time for the old spirit to be extinct; since there were men in the street, that day, who had wor-

---

2. William of Orange, ruler of the Netherlands. He was married to James II's Protestant daughter Mary and became king of England in 1689 after his successful invasion provoked the "Glorious Revolution" of 1688.
3. Renamed State Street in Boston after the American Revolution.

shiped there beneath the trees, before a house was reared to the God, for whom they had become exiles. Old soldiers of the Parliament were here too, smiling grimly at the thought, that their aged arms might strike another blow against the house of Stuart. Here also, were the veterans of King Phillip's war,[4] who had burnt villages and slaughtered young and old, with pious fierceness, while the godly souls throughout the land were helping them with prayer. Several ministers were scattered among the crowd, which, unlike all other mobs, regarded them with such reverence, as if there were sanctity in their very garments. These holy men exerted their influence to quiet the people, but not to disperse them. Meantime, the purpose of the Governor, in disturbing the peace of the town, at a period when the slightest commotion might throw the country into a ferment, was almost the universal subject of inquiry, and variously explained.

'Satan will strike his master-stroke presently,' cried some, 'because he knoweth that his time is short. All our godly pastors are to be dragged to prison! We shall see them at a Smithfield fire[5] in King-street!'

Hereupon, the people of each parish gathered closer round their minister, who looked calmly upwards and assumed a more apostolic dignity, as well befitted a candidate for the highest honor of his profession, the crown of martyrdom. It was actually fancied, at that period, that New England might have a John Rogers of her own, to take the place of that worthy in the Primer.[6]

'The Pope of Rome has given orders for a new St. Bartholomew![7] cried others. 'We are to be massacred, man and male child!'

Neither was this rumor wholly discredited, although the wiser class believed the Governor's object somewhat less atrocious. His predecessor under the old charter, Bradstreet, a venerable companion of the first settlers, was known to be in town. There were grounds for conjecturing, that Sir Edmund Andros intended, at once, to strike terror, by a parade of military force, and to confound the opposite faction, by possessing himself of their chief.

'Stand firm for the old charter Governor!' shouted the crowd, seizing upon the idea. 'The good old Governor Bradstreet!'

---

4. The life and death struggle in 1675 and 1676 between the English settlers and three Indian tribes led by Metacom, or "King Philip," chief of the Wampanoag Indians.
5. English Protestant ministers were burned at the stake in Smithfield, a district of London, in 1554 during the reign of the Catholic Queen Mary.
6. John Rogers was the first of the Protestant martyrs to be burned at Smithfield. An engraving of the scene and a poem attributed to Rogers appear in the *New England Primer*, the common spelling book of the colony.
7. On St. Bartholomew's Day, August 24, 1572, almost all the Protestants in Paris were hunted down and murdered. In the Protestant imagination, the massacre symbolized Catholic evil for centuries afterward.

While this cry was at the loudest, the people were surprised by the well known figure of Governor Bradstreet himself, a patriarch of nearly ninety, who appeared on the elevated steps of a door, and, with characteristic mildness, besought them to submit to the constituted authorities.

'My children,' concluded this venerable person, 'do nothing rashly. Cry not aloud, but pray for the welfare of New England, and expect patiently what the Lord will do in this matter!'

The event was soon to be decided. All this time, the roll of the drum had been approaching through Cornhill,[8] louder and deeper, till, with reverberations from house to house, and the regular tramp of martial footsteps, it burst into the street. A double rank of soldiers made their appearance, occupying the whole breadth of the passage, with shouldered matchlocks, and matches burning, so as to present a row of fires in the dusk. Their steady march was like the progress of a machine, that would roll irresistibly over everything in its way. Next, moving slowly, with a confused clatter of hoofs on the pavement, rode a party of mounted gentlemen, the central figure being Sir Edmund Andros, elderly, but erect and soldier-like. Those around him were his favorite councillors, and the bitterest foes of New England. At his right hand rode Edward Randolph, our arch enemy, that 'blasted wretch,' as Cotton Mather[9] calls him, who achieved the downfall of our ancient government, and was followed with a sensible curse, through life and to his grave. On the other side was Bullivant, scattering jests and mockery as he rode along. Dudley[1] came behind, with a downcast look, dreading, as well he might, to meet the indignant gaze of the people, who beheld him, their only countryman by birth, among the oppressors of his native land. The captain of a frigate in the harbor, and two or three civil officers under the Crown, were also there. But the figure which most attracted the public eye, and stirred up the deepest feeling, was the Episcopal clergyman of King's Chapel, riding haughtily among the magistrates in his priestly vestments, the fitting representative of prelacy and persecution, the union of church and state, and all those abominations which had driven the Puritans to the wilderness. Another guard of soldiers, in double rank, brought up the rear.

The whole scene was a picture of the condition of New England, and its moral, the deformity of any government that does not grow

8. A curving street leading into King Street.
9. Mather (1663–1728), a prolific and partisan historian of the Puritans. Randolph (1632–1703), British colonial agent, set himself against the Puritans after his arrival in Massachusetts in 1676. He "obtained the repeal of the first provincial charter," as Hawthorne writes in "Edward Randolph's Portrait" (1838).
1. Joseph Dudley was appointed president of part of New England after the annulment of the charter. He also served in Andros's government. Bullivant was a witty Boston apothecary who became attorney general in the Andros regime.

out of the nature of things and the character of the people. On one side the religious multitude, with their sad visages and dark attire, and on the other, the group of despotic rulers, with the high churchman in the midst, and here and there a crucifix at their bosoms, all magnificently clad, flushed with wine, proud of unjust authority, and scoffing at the universal groan. And the mercenary soldiers, waiting but the word to deluge the street with blood, showed the only means by which obedience could be secured.

'Oh! Lord of Hosts,' cried a voice among the crowd, 'provide a Champion for thy people!'

This ejaculation was loudly uttered, and served as a herald's cry, to introduce a remarkable personage. The crowd had rolled back, and were now huddled together nearly at the extremity of the street, while the soldiers had advanced no more than a third of its length. The intervening space was empty—a paved solitude, between lofty edifices, which threw almost a twilight shadow over it. Suddenly, there was seen the figure of an ancient man, who seemed to have emerged from among the people, and was walking by himself along the centre of the street, to confront the armed band. He wore the old Puritan dress, a dark cloak and a steeple-crowned hat, in the fashion of at least fifty years before, with a heavy sword upon his thigh, but a staff in his hand, to assist the tremulous gait of age.

When at some distance from the multitude, the old man turned slowly round, displaying a face of antique majesty, rendered doubly venerable by the hoary beard that descended on his breast. He made a gesture at once of encouragement and warning, then turned again, and resumed his way.

'Who is this gray patriarch!' asked the young men of their sires.

'Who is this venerable brother?' asked the old men among themselves.

But none could make reply. The fathers of the people, those of fourscore years and upwards, were disturbed, deeming it strange that they should forget one of such evident authority, whom they must have known in their early days, the associate of Winthrop[2] and all the old Councillors, giving laws, and making prayers, and leading them against the savage. The elderly men ought to have remembered him, too, with locks as gray in their youth, as their own were now. And the young! How could he have passed so utterly from their memories—that hoary sire, the relic of long-departed times, whose awful benediction had surely been bestowed on their uncovered heads, in childhood?

'Whence did he come? What is his purpose? Who can this old man be?' whispered the wondering crowd.

2. John Winthrop (1588–1649), twelve-time governor of Massachusetts.

Meanwhile, the venerable stranger, staff in hand, was pursuing his solitary walk along the centre of the street. As he drew near the advancing soldiers, and as the roll of their drum came full upon his ear, the old man raised himself to a loftier mien, while the decrepitude of age seemed to fall from his shoulders, leaving him in gray, but unbroken dignity. Now, he marched onward with a warrior's step, keeping time to the military music. Thus the aged form advanced on one side, and the whole parade of soldiers and magistrates on the other, till, when scarcely twenty yards remained between, the old man grasped his staff by the middle, and held it before him like a leader's truncheon.[3]

'Stand!' cried he.

The eye, the face, and attitude of command; the solemn, yet warlike peal of that voice, fit either to rule a host in the battle-field or be raised to God in prayer, were irresistible. At the old man's word and outstretched arm, the roll of the drum was hushed at once, and the advancing line stood still. A tremulous enthusiasm seized upon the multitude. That stately form, combining the leader and the saint,[4] so gray, so dimly seen, in such an ancient garb, could only belong to some old champion of the righteous cause, whom the oppressor's drum had summoned from his grave. They raised a shout of awe and exultation, and looked for the deliverance of New England.

The Governor, and the gentlemen of his party, perceiving themselves brought to an unexpected stand, rode hastily forward, as if they would have pressed their snorting and affrighted horses right against the hoary apparition. He, however, blenched not a step, but lancing his severe eye round the group, which half encompassed him, at last bent it sternly on Sir Edmund Andros. One would have thought that the dark old man was chief ruler there, and that the Governor and Council, with soldiers at their back, representing the whole power and authority of the Crown, had no alternative but obedience.

'What does this old fellow here?' cried Edward Randolph, fiercely. 'On, Sir Edmund! Bid the soldiers forward, and give the dotard the same choice that you give all his countrymen—to stand aside or be trampled on!'

'Nay, nay, let us show respect to the good grandsire,' said Bullivant, laughing. 'See you not, he is some old round-headed dignitary,[5] who hath lain asleep these thirty years, and knows nothing of the

---

3. A staff carried as a symbol of authority.
4. In colonial New England a person who had testified to his or her conversion and was accepted as a member in a Congregational church.
5. An official of the Puritan regime in England after 1648—like the regicide William Goffe. Puritans cut their hair short and were called "roundheads."

change of times? Doubtless, he thinks to put us down with a proclamation in Old Noll's[6] name!'

'Are you mad, old man?' demanded Sir Edmund Andros, in loud and harsh tones. 'How dare you stay the march of King James's Governor?'

'I have staid the march of a King himself, ere now,' replied the gray figure, with stern composure. 'I am here, Sir Governor, because the cry of an oppressed people hath disturbed me in my secret place; and beseeching this favor earnestly of the Lord, it was vouchsafed me to appear once again on earth, in the good old cause of his Saints. And what speak ye of James? There is no longer a popish tyrant on the throne of England, and by tomorrow noon, his name shall be a by-word in this very street, where ye would make it a word of terror. Back, thou that wast a Governor, back! With this night thy power is ended—tomorrow, the prison!—back, lest I foretel the scaffold!'[7]

The people had been drawing nearer and nearer, and drinking in the words of their champion, who spoke in accents long disused, like one unaccustomed to converse, except with the dead of many years ago. But his voice stirred their souls. They confronted the soldiers, not wholly without arms, and ready to convert the very stones of the street into deadly weapons. Sir Edmund Andros looked at the old man; then he cast his hard and cruel eye over the multitude, and beheld them burning with that lurid wrath, so difficult to kindle or to quench; and again he fixed his gaze on the aged form, which stood obscurely in an open space, where neither friend nor foe had thrust himself. What were his thoughts, he uttered no word which might discover. But whether the oppressor were overawed by the Gray Champion's look, or perceived his peril in the threatening attitude of the people, it is certain that he gave back, and ordered his soldiers to commence a slow and guarded retreat. Before another sunset, the Governor, and all that rode so proudly with him, were prisoners, and long ere it was known that James had abdicated, King William was proclaimed throughout New England.

But where was the Gray Champion? Some reported, that when the troops had gone from King-street, and the people were thronging tumultuously in their rear, Bradstreet, the aged Governor, was seen to embrace a form more aged than his own. Others soberly affirmed, that while they marveled at the venerable grandeur of his aspect, the old man had faded from their eyes, melting slowly into the hues of twilight, till, where he stood, there was an empty space.

6. I.e., Oliver Cromwell.
7. Besides Andros, Randolph, Bullivant, Dudley, and about forty-five others were also imprisoned.

But all agreed, that the hoary shape was gone. The men of that generation watched for his re-appearance, in sunshine and in twilight, but never saw him more, nor knew when his funeral passed, nor where his gravestone was.

And who was the Gray Champion? Perhaps his name might be found in the records of that stern Court of Justice, which passed a sentence, too mighty for the age, but glorious in all after times, for its humbling lesson to the monarch and its high example to the subject. I have heard, that, whenever the descendants of the Puritans are to show the spirit of their sires, the old man appears again. When eighty years had passed, he walked once more in King-street.[8] Five years later, in the twilight of an April morning, he stood on the green, beside the meeting house, at Lexington, where now the obelisk of granite, with a slab of slate inlaid, commemorates the first fallen of the Revolution. And when our fathers were toiling at the breastwork on Bunker's Hill, all through that night the old warrior walked his rounds. Long, long may it be, ere he comes again! His hour is one of darkness, and adversity, and peril. But should domestic tyranny oppress us, or the invader's step pollute our soil, still may the Gray Champion come; for he is the type of New England's hereditary spirit: and his shadowy march, on the eve of danger, must ever be the pledge, that New England's sons will vindicate their ancestry.

Young Goodman Brown[†]

Young Goodman Brown came forth at sunset into the street of Salem village,[1] but put his head back, after crossing the threshold, to exchange a parting kiss with his young wife. And Faith, as the wife was aptly named, thrust her own pretty head into the street, letting the wind play with the pink ribbons of her cap while she called to Goodman Brown.

"Dearest heart," whispered she, softly and rather sadly, when her lips were close to his ear, "prithee put off your journey until sunrise

8. The Boston Massacre took place in 1770 in King Street, where British troops fired into a rioting crowd and killed five men.
† First published in the *New England Magazine*, April 1835, then in *Mosses from an Old Manse*, 1846. Considered as a reminiscence of history, the story takes place shortly before the Salem Witch Trials of 1692. Young Goodman Brown is, among other things, a man ready to imagine that a neighbor like Goody Cloyse might be a witch. Yet the tale is much more than just a period piece about the horrors of Salem. *Goodman* and *Goody* were terms of respect for a man or a woman of humble status, and Goodman Brown's name suggests that he is an inconspicuous New England Everyman with universal problems, which he resolves in a unique manner that reflects his time and place.
1. Modern Danvers, contiguous with Salem. In the 17th century they were both settlements in the township of Salem. The witchcraft hysteria started in Salem village.

and sleep in your own bed to-night. A lone woman is troubled with such dreams and such thoughts that she's afeard of herself sometimes. Pray tarry with me this night, dear husband, of all nights in the year."

"My love and my Faith," replied young Goodman Brown, "of all nights in the year, this one night must I tarry away from thee. My journey, as thou callest it, forth and back again, must needs be done 'twixt now and sunrise. What, my sweet, pretty wife, dost thou doubt me already, and we but three months married?"

"Then God bless you!" said Faith, with the pink ribbons; "and may you find all well when you come back."

"Amen!" cried Goodman Brown. "Say thy prayers, dear Faith, and go to bed at dusk, and no harm will come to thee."

So they parted; and the young man pursued his way until, being about to turn the corner by the meeting house, he looked back and saw the head of Faith still peeping after him with a melancholy air, in spite of her pink ribbons.

"Poor little Faith!" thought he, for his heart smote him. "What a wretch am I to leave her on such an errand! She talks of dreams, too. Methought as she spoke there was trouble in her face, as if a dream had warned her what work is to be done to-night. But no, no; 'twould kill her to think it. Well, she's a blessed angel on earth; and after this one night I'll cling to her skirts and follow her to heaven."

With this excellent resolve for the future, Goodman Brown felt himself justified in making more haste on his present evil purpose. He had taken a dreary road, darkened by all the gloomiest trees of the forest, which barely stood aside to let the narrow path creep through, and closed immediately behind. It was all as lonely as could be; and there is this peculiarity in such a solitude, that the traveller knows not who may be concealed by the innumerable trunks and the thick boughs overhead; so that with lonely footsteps he may yet be passing through an unseen multitude.

"There may be a devilish Indian behind every tree," said Goodman Brown to himself; and he glanced fearfully behind him as he added, "What if the devil himself should be at my very elbow!"

His head being turned back, he passed a crook of the road, and, looking forward again, beheld the figure of a man, in grave and decent attire, seated at the foot of an old tree. He arose at Goodman Brown's approach and walked onward side by side with him.

"You are late, Goodman Brown," said he. "The clock of the Old South[2] was striking as I came through Boston; and that is full fifteen minutes agone."

2. The Old South Meeting House was built in 1670, on the site of the later Old South Church. Salem village was sixteen or more miles from colonial Boston.

"Faith kept me back a while," replied the young man, with a tremor in his voice, caused by the sudden appearance of his companion, though not wholly unexpected.

It was now deep dusk in the forest, and deepest in that part of it where these two were journeying. As nearly as could be discerned, the second traveller was about fifty years old, apparently in the same rank of life as Goodman Brown, and bearing a considerable resemblance to him, though perhaps more in expression than features. Still they might have been taken for father and son. And yet, though the elder person was as simply clad as the younger and as simple in manner too, he had an indescribable air of one who knew the world, and who would not have felt abashed at the governor's dinner table or in King William's[3] court, were it possible that his affairs should call him thither. But the only thing about him that could be fixed upon as remarkable was his staff, which bore the likeness of a great black snake, so curiously wrought that it might almost be seen to twist and wriggle itself like a living serpent. This, of course, must have been an ocular deception, assisted by the uncertain light.

"Come, Goodman Brown," cried his fellow-traveller, "this is a dull pace for the beginning of a journey. Take my staff, if you are so soon weary."

"Friend," said the other, exchanging his slow pace for a full stop, "having kept covenant[4] by meeting thee here, it is my purpose now to return whence I came. I have scruples touching the matter thou wot'st[5] of."

"Sayest thou so?" replied he of the serpent, smiling apart. "Let us walk on, nevertheless, reasoning as we go; and if I convince thee not thou shalt turn back. We are but a little way in the forest yet."

"Too far! too far!" exclaimed the goodman, unconsciously resuming his walk. "My father never went into the woods on such an errand, nor his father before him. We have been a race of honest men and good Christians since the days of the martyrs;[6] and shall I be the first of the name of Brown that ever took this path and kept—"

"Such company, thou wouldst say," observed the elder person, interpreting his pause. "Well said, Goodman Brown! I have been as well acquainted with your family as with ever a one among the Puritans; and that's no trifle to say. I helped your grandfather, the constable, when he lashed the Quaker woman so smartly through the streets of Salem; and it was I that brought your father a pitch-pine

3. William III, king of England from 1689 to 1702.
4. Agreement, with the implicit meaning of religious commitment to a contract with God (or, in Brown's case, the devil).
5. Knowest.
6. The Protestant martyrs, executed in England under Queen Mary in the 1550s.

knot, kindled at my own hearth, to set fire to an Indian village, in King Philip's war.[7] They were my good friends, both; and many a pleasant walk have we had along this path, and returned merrily after midnight. I would fain be friends with you for their sake."

"If it be as thou sayest," replied Goodman Brown, "I marvel they never spoke of these matters; or, verily, I marvel not, seeing that the least rumor of the sort would have driven them from New England. We are a people of prayer, and good works to boot, and abide no such wickedness."

"Wickedness or not," said the traveller with the twisted staff, "I have a very general acquaintance here in New England. The deacons of many a church have drunk the communion wine with me; the selectmen of divers towns make me their chairman; and a majority of the Great and General Court[8] are firm supporters of my interest. The governor and I, too—But these are state secrets."

"Can this be so?" cried Goodman Brown, with a stare of amazement at his undisturbed companion. "Howbeit, I have nothing to do with the governor and council; they have their own ways, and are no rule for a simple husbandman like me. But, were I to go on with thee, how should I meet the eye of that good old man, our minister, at Salem village? O, his voice would make me tremble both Sabbath day and lecture day."[9]

Thus far the elder traveller had listened with due gravity; but now burst into a fit of irrepressible mirth, shaking himself so violently that his snakelike staff actually seemed to wriggle in sympathy.

"Ha! ha! ha!" shouted he again and again; then composing himself. "Well, go on, Goodman Brown, go on; but, prithee, don't kill me with laughing."

"Well, then, to end the matter at once," said Goodman Brown, considerably nettled, "there is my wife, Faith. It would break her dear little heart; and I'd rather break my own."

"Nay, if that be the case," answered the other, "e'en go thy ways, Goodman Brown. I would not for twenty old women like the one hobbling before us that Faith should come to any harm."

As he spoke, he pointed his staff at a female figure on the path, in whom Goodman Brown recognized a very pious and exemplary dame,

---

7. "He lashed": in 1659, five wandering Quakers, including the woman Ann Coleman, were whipped through Salem, Boston, and Dedham by order of William Hathorne (1607–1681), a magistrate in Salem and Hawthorne's first male ancestor in the New World. Captain William Hathorne, eldest son of the magistrate, led a Salem company of militia in the war and helped burn an Indian village. For "King Philip's War," see "The Gray Champion," n. 4, p. 79.
8. The Massachusetts legislature.
9. A day in midweek, usually Thursday, on which there were public lectures on the Scriptures.

who had taught him his catechism in youth, and was still his moral and spiritual adviser, jointly with the minister and Deacon Gookin.[1]

"A marvel, truly, that Goody Cloyse[2] should be so far in the wilderness at nightfall," said he. "But, with your leave, friend, I shall take a cut through the woods until we have left this Christian woman behind. Being a stranger to you, she might ask whom I was consorting with and whither I was going."

"Be it so," said his fellow-traveller. "Betake you to the woods, and let me keep the path."

Accordingly the young man turned aside, but took care to watch his companion, who advanced softly along the road until he had come within a staff's length of the old dame. She, meanwhile, was making the best of her way, with singular speed for so aged a woman, and mumbling some indistinct words—a prayer, doubtless—as she went. The traveller put forth his staff and touched her withered neck with what seemed the serpent's tail.

"The devil!" screamed the pious old lady.

"Then Goody Cloyse knows her old friend?" observed the traveller, confronting her and leaning on his writhing stick.

"Ah, forsooth, and is it your worship indeed?" cried the good dame. "Yea, truly is it, and in the very image of my old gossip,[3] Goodman Brown, the grandfather of the silly fellow that now is. But—would your worship believe it?—my broomstick hath strangely disappeared, stolen; as I suspect, by that unhanged witch, Goody Cory, and that, too, when I was all anointed with the juice of smallage, and cinque-foil, and wolf's bane—"[4]

"Mingled with fine wheat and the fat of a new-born babe," said the shape of old Goodman Brown.

"Ah, your worship knows the recipe," cried the old lady, cackling aloud. "So, as I was saying, being all ready for the meeting, and no horse to ride on, I made up my mind to foot it; for they tell me there is a nice young man to be taken into communion to-night. But now your good worship will lend me your arm, and we shall be there in a twinkling."

"That can hardly be," answered her friend. "I may not spare you my arm, Goody Cloyse; but here is my staff, if you will."

1. Daniel Gookin (1612–1687), colonial magistrate, and superintendent of the Christian Indians. Along with William Hathorne, he looked after the affairs of Captain William Hathorne's widow in the 1670s.
2. Sarah Cloyse was accused as a witch and was in prison awaiting sentence in 1692 when the witchcraft persecutions ended. She was examined by Judge John Hathorne, son of William Hathorne and a central figure in the Salem trials.
3. Friend.
4. A kind of aconite. "Smallage": a wild celery. "Cinquefoil": a member of the rose family. Plants with supposedly magical powers; Hawthorne found the recipe in Cervantes's novella *The Conversation of the Dogs*. Martha Cory was hanged as a witch in 1692.

So saying, he threw it down at her feet, where, perhaps, it assumed life, being one of the rods which its owner had formerly lent to the Egyptian magi.[5] Of this fact, however, Goodman Brown could not take cognizance. He had cast up his eyes in astonishment, and, looking down again, beheld neither Goody Cloyse nor the serpentine staff, but his fellow-traveller alone, who waited for him as calmly as if nothing had happened.

"That old woman taught me my catechism," said the young man; and there was a world of meaning in this simple comment.

They continued to walk onward, while the elder traveller exhorted his companion to make good speed and persevere in the path, discoursing so aptly that his arguments seemed rather to spring up in the bosom of his auditor than to be suggested by himself. As they went, he plucked a branch of maple to serve for a walking stick, and began to strip it of the twigs and little boughs, which were wet with evening dew. The moment his fingers touched them they became strangely withered and dried up as with a week's sunshine. Thus the pair proceeded, at a good free pace, until suddenly, in a gloomy hollow of the road, Goodman Brown sat himself down on the stump of a tree and refused to go any farther."

"Friend," said he, stubbornly, "my mind is made up. Not another step will I budge on this errand. What if a wretched old woman do choose to go to the devil when I thought she was going to heaven: is that any reason why I should quit my dear Faith and go after her?"

"You will think better of this by and by," said his acquaintance, composedly. "Sit here and rest yourself a while; and when you feel like moving again, there is my staff to help you along."

Without more words, he threw his companion the maple stick, and was as speedily out of sight as if he had vanished into the deepening gloom. The young man sat a few moments by the roadside, applauding himself greatly, and thinking with how clear a conscience he should meet the minister in his morning walk, nor shrink from the eye of good old Deacon Gookin. And what calm sleep would be his that very night, which was to have been spent so wickedly, but so purely and sweetly now, in the arms of Faith! Amidst these pleasant and praiseworthy meditations, Goodman Brown heard the tramp of horses along the road, and deemed it advisable to conceal himself within the verge of the forest, conscious of the guilty purpose that had brought him thither, though now so happily turned from it.

On came the hoof tramps and the voices of the riders, two grave old voices, conversing soberly as they drew near. These mingled sounds appeared to pass along the road, within a few yards of the

5. See Exodus 7:9–12. The Egyptian wise men and sorcerers of Pharaoh threw rods on the ground, which then became serpents.

young man's hiding-place; but, owing doubtless to the depth of the gloom at that particular spot, neither the travellers nor their steeds were visible. Though their figures brushed the small boughs by the wayside, it could not be seen that they intercepted, even for a moment, the faint gleam from the strip of bright sky athwart which they must have passed. Goodman Brown alternately crouched and stood on tiptoe, pulling aside the branches and thrusting forth his head as far as he durst without discerning so much as a shadow. It vexed him the more, because he could have sworn, were such a thing possible, that he recognized the voices of the minister and Deacon Gookin, jogging along quietly, as they were wont to do, when bound to some ordination or ecclesiastical council. While yet within hearing, one of the riders stopped to pluck a switch.

"Of the two, reverend sir," said the voice like the deacon's, "I had rather miss an ordination dinner than to-night's meeting. They tell me that some of our community are to be here from Falmouth[6] and beyond, and others from Connecticut and Rhode Island, besides several of the Indian powwows, who, after their fashion, know almost as much deviltry as the best of us. Moreover, there is a goodly young woman to be taken into communion."

"Mighty well, Deacon Gookin!" replied the solemn old tones of the minister. "Spur up, or we shall be late. Nothing can be done, you know, until I get on the ground."

The hoofs clattered again; and the voices, talking so strangely in the empty air, passed on through the forest, where no church had ever been gathered or solitary Christian prayed. Whither, then, could these holy men be journeying so deep into the heathen wilderness? Young Goodman Brown caught hold of a tree for support, being ready to sink down on the ground, faint and overburdened with the heavy sickness of his heart. He looked up to the sky, doubting whether there really was a heaven above him. Yet there was the blue arch, and the stars brightening in it.

"With heaven above and Faith below, I will yet stand firm against the devil!" cried Goodman Brown.

While he still gazed upward into the deep arch of the firmament and had lifted his hands to pray, a cloud, though no wind was stirring, hurried across the zenith and hid the brightening stars. The blue sky was still visible except directly overhead, where this black mass of cloud was sweeping swiftly northward. Aloft in the air, as if from the depths of the cloud, came a confused and doubtful sound of voices. Once the listener fancied that he could distinguish the accents of townspeople of his own, men and women, both pious and ungodly, many of whom he had met at the communion table, and

6. On the southern coast of Massachusetts, seventy miles from Salem.

had seen others rioting at the tavern. The next moment, so indistinct were the sounds, he doubted whether he had heard aught but the murmur of the old forest, whispering without a wind. Then came a stronger swell of those familiar tones, heard daily in the sunshine at Salem village, but never until now from a cloud of night. There was one voice, of a young woman, uttering lamentations, yet with an uncertain sorrow, and entreating for some favor, which, perhaps, it would grieve her to obtain; and all the unseen multitude, both saints and sinners, seemed to encourage her onward.

"Faith!" shouted Goodman Brown, in a voice of agony and desperation; and the echoes of the forest mocked him, crying, "Faith! Faith!" as if bewildered wretches were seeking her all through the wilderness.

The cry of grief, rage, and terror was yet piercing the night, when the unhappy husband held his breath for a response. There was a scream, drowned immediately in a louder murmur of voices, fading into far-off laughter, as the dark cloud swept away, leaving the clear and silent sky above Goodman Brown. But something fluttered lightly down through the air and caught on the branch of a tree. The young man seized it, and beheld a pink ribbon.

"My Faith is gone!" cried he, after one stupefied moment. "There is no good on earth; and sin is but a name. Come, devil; for to thee is this world given."

And, maddened with despair, so that he laughed loud and long, did Goodman Brown grasp his staff and set forth again, at such a rate that he seemed to fly along the forest path rather than to walk or run. The road grew wilder and drearier and more faintly traced, and vanished at length, leaving him in the heart of the dark wilderness, still rushing onward with the instinct that guides mortal man to evil. The whole forest was peopled with frightful sounds—the creaking of the trees, the howling of wild beasts, and the yell of Indians; while sometimes the wind tolled like a distant church bell, and sometimes gave a broad roar around the traveller, as if all Nature were laughing him to scorn. But he was himself the chief horror of the scene, and shrank not from its other horrors.

"Ha! ha! ha!" roared Goodman Brown when the wind laughed at him. "Let us hear which will laugh loudest. Think not to frighten me with your deviltry. Come witch, come wizard, come Indian powwow, come devil himself, and here comes Goodman Brown. You may as well fear him as he fear you."

In truth, all through the haunted forest there could be nothing more frightful than the figure of Goodman Brown. On he flew among the black pines, brandishing his staff with frenzied gestures, now giving vent to an inspiration of horrid blasphemy, and now shouting forth such laughter as set all the echoes of the forest laughing like demons around him. The fiend in his own shape is less hideous than when he rages in the breast of man. Thus sped the demoniac on his course, until, quivering among the trees, he saw a red light before him, as when the felled trunks and branches of a clearing have been set on fire, and throw up their lurid blaze against the sky, at the hour of midnight. He paused, in a lull of the tempest that had driven him onward, and heard the swell of what seemed a hymn, rolling solemnly from a distance with the weight of many voices. He knew the tune; it was a familiar one in the choir of the village meeting house. The verse died heavily away, and was lengthened by a chorus, not of human voices, but of all the sounds of the benighted wilderness pealing in awful harmony together. Goodman Brown cried out; and his cry was lost to his own ear by its unison with the cry of the desert.

In the interval of silence he stole forward until the light glared full upon his eyes. At one extremity of an open space, hemmed in by the dark wall of the forest, arose a rock, bearing some rude, natural resemblance either to an altar or a pulpit, and surrounded by four blazing pines, their tops aflame, their stems untouched, like candles at an evening meeting. The mass of foliage that had overgrown the summit of the rock was all on fire, blazing high into the night and fitfully illuminating the whole field. Each pendent twig and leafy festoon was in a blaze. As the red light arose and fell, a numerous congregation alternately shone forth, then disappeared in shadow, and again grew, as it were, out of the darkness, peopling the heart of the solitary woods at once.

"A grave and dark-clad company," quoth Goodman Brown.

In truth they were such. Among them, quivering to and fro between gloom and splendor, appeared faces that would be seen next day at the council board of the province, and others which, Sabbath after Sabbath, looked devoutly heavenward, and benignantly over the crowded pews, from the holiest pulpits in the land. Some affirm that the lady of the governor was there. At least there were high dames well known to her, and wives of honored husbands, and widows, a great multitude, and ancient maidens, all of excellent repute, and fair young girls, who trembled lest their mothers should espy them. Either the sudden gleams of light flashing over the obscure field bedazzled Goodman Brown, or he recognized a score of the church members of Salem village famous for their especial sanctity. Good old Deacon Gookin had arrived, and waited at the skirts of that venerable saint, his revered pastor. But, irreverently consorting with these grave, reputable, and pious people, these elders of the church, these chaste dames and dewy virgins, there were men of dissolute lives and women of spotted fame, wretches given over to all mean and filthy vice, and suspected even of horrid crimes. It was strange to see that the good shrank not from the wicked, nor were the sinners abashed by the saints. Scattered also among their palefaced enemies were the Indian priests, or powwows, who had often scared their native forest with more hideous incantations than any known to English witchcraft.

"But where is Faith?" thought Goodman Brown, and, as hope came into his heart, he trembled.

Another verse of the hymn arose, a slow and mournful strain, such as the pious love, but joined to words which expressed all that our nature can conceive of sin, and darkly hinted at far more. Unfathomable to mere mortals is the lore of fiends. Verse after verse was sung; and still the chorus of the desert swelled between like the deepest tone of a mighty organ; and with the final peal of that dreadful anthem there came a sound, as if the roaring wind, the rushing streams, the howling beasts, and every other voice of the unconverted wilderness was mingling and according with the voice of guilty man in homage to the prince of all. The four blazing pines threw up a loftier flame, and obscurely discovered shapes and visages of horror on the smoke wreaths above the impious assembly. At the same moment the fire on the rock shot redly forth and formed a glowing arch above its base, where now appeared a figure. With reverence be it spoken, the figure bore no slight similitude, both in garb and manner, to some grave divine of the New England churches.

"Bring forth the converts!" cried a voice that echoed through the field and rolled into the forest.

At the word, Goodman Brown stepped forth from the shadow of the trees and approached the congregation, with whom he felt a loathful brotherhood by the sympathy of all that was wicked in his heart. He could have well nigh sworn that the shape of his own dead father beckoned him to advance, looking downward from a smoke wreath, while a woman, with dim features of despair, threw out her hand to warn him back. Was it his mother? But he had no power to retreat one step, nor to resist, even in thought, when the minister and good old Deacon Gookin seized his arms and led him to the blazing rock. Thither came also the slender form of a veiled female, led between Goody Cloyse, that pious teacher of the catechism, and Martha Carrier,[7] who had received the devil's promise to be queen of hell. A rampant hag was she. And there stood the proselytes beneath the canopy of fire.

"Welcome, my children," said the dark figure, "to the communion of your race. Ye have found thus young your nature and your destiny. My children, look behind you!"

7. Hanged as a witch in 1692. Cotton Mather cried out at the hanging, "This is the hag whom the devil promised to make Queen of Hell."

They turned; and flashing forth, as it were, in a sheet of flame, the fiend worshippers were seen; the smile of welcome gleamed darkly on every visage.

"There," resumed the sable form, "are all whom ye have reverenced from youth. Ye deemed them holier than yourselves, and shrank from your own sin, contrasting it with their lives of righteousness and prayerful aspirations heavenward. Yet here are they all in my worshipping assembly. This night it shall be granted you to know their secret deeds; how hoary-bearded elders of the church have whispered wanton words to the young maids of their households; how many a woman, eager for widow's weeds, has given her husband a drink at bedtime and let him sleep his last sleep in her bosom; how beardless youths have made haste to inherit their fathers' wealth; and how fair damsels—blush not, sweet ones—have dug little graves in the garden, and bidden me, the sole guest, to an infant's funeral. By the sympathy of your human hearts for sin ye shall scent out all the places—whether in church, bed chamber, street, field, or forest—where crime has been committed, and shall exult to behold the whole earth one stain of guilt, one mighty blood spot. Far more than this. It shall be yours to penetrate, in every bosom, the deep mystery of sin, the fountain of all wicked arts, and which inexhaustibly supplies more evil impulses than human power—than my power at its utmost—can make manifest in deeds. And now, my children, look upon each other."

They did so; and, by the blaze of the hell-kindled torches, the wretched man beheld his Faith, and the wife her husband, trembling before that unhallowed altar.

"Lo, there ye stand, my children," said the figure, in a deep and solemn tone, almost sad with its despairing awfulness, as if his once angelic nature[8] could yet mourn for our miserable race. "Depending upon one another's hearts, ye had still hoped that virtue were not all a dream. Now are ye undeceived. Evil is the nature of mankind. Evil must be your only happiness. Welcome again, my children, to the communion of your race."

"Welcome," repeated the fiend worshippers, in one cry of despair and triumph.

And there they stood, the only pair, as it seemed, who were yet hesitating on the verge of wickedness in this dark world. A basin was hollowed, naturally, in the rock. Did it contain water, reddened by the lurid light? or was it blood? or, perchance, a liquid flame? Herein did the shape of evil dip his hand and prepare to lay the mark of baptism upon their foreheads, that they might be partakers of the mystery of sin, more conscious of the secret guilt of others, both in

8. The devil was one of the most exalted angels before he was expelled from heaven.

deed and thought, than they could now be of their own. The husband cast one look at his pale wife, and Faith at him. What polluted wretches would the next glance show them to each other, shuddering alike at what they disclosed and what they saw!

"Faith! Faith!" cried the husband, "look up to heaven, and resist the wicked one."

Whether Faith obeyed, he knew not. Hardly had he spoken when he found himself amid calm night and solitude, listening to a roar of the wind which died heavily away through the forest. He staggered against the rock, and felt it chill and damp; while a hanging twig, that had been all on fire, besprinkled his cheek with the coldest dew.

The next morning young Goodman Brown came slowly into the street of Salem village, staring around him like a bewildered man. The good old minister was taking a walk along the graveyard to get an appetite for breakfast and meditate his sermon, and bestowed a blessing, as he passed, on Goodman Brown. He shrank from the venerable saint as if to avoid an anathema. Old Deacon Gookin was at domestic worship, and the holy words of his prayer were heard through the open window. "What God doth the wizard pray to?" quoth Goodman Brown. Goody Cloyse, that excellent old Christian, stood in the early sunshine at her own lattice, catechizing a little girl who had brought her a pint of morning's milk. Goodman Brown snatched away the child as from the grasp of the fiend himself. Turning the corner by the meeting house, he spied the head of Faith, with the pink ribbons, gazing anxiously forth, and bursting into such joy at sight of him that she skipped along the street and almost kissed her husband before the whole village. But Goodman Brown looked sternly and sadly into her face, and passed on without a greeting.

Had Goodman Brown fallen asleep in the forest and only dreamed a wild dream of a witch meeting?

Be it so, if you will; but, alas! it was a dream of evil omen for young Goodman Brown. A stern, a sad, a darkly meditative, a distrustful, if not a desperate, man did he become from the night of that fearful dream. On the Sabbath day, when the congregation were singing a holy psalm, he could not listen, because an anthem of sin rushed loudly upon his ear and drowned all the blessed strain. When the minister spoke from the pulpit, with power and fervid eloquence and with his hand on the open Bible, of the sacred truths of our religion, and of saintlike lives and triumphant deaths, and of future bliss or misery unutterable, then did Goodman Brown turn pale, dreading lest the roof should thunder down upon the gray blasphemer and his hearers. Often, awaking suddenly at midnight, he shrank from the bosom of Faith; and at morning or eventide, when the family knelt down at prayer, he scowled, and muttered to himself, and gazed

lives the rest of his life in fear

sternly at his wife, and turned away. And when he had lived long, and was borne to his grave, a hoary corpse, followed by Faith, an aged woman, and children and grandchildren, a goodly procession, besides neighbors not a few, they carved no hopeful verse upon his tombstone; for his dying hour was gloom.

Wakefield[†]

In some old magazine or newspaper, I recollect a story, told as truth, of a man—let us call him Wakefield—who absented himself for a long time from his wife. The fact, thus abstractedly stated, is not very uncommon, nor—without a proper distinction of circumstances—to be condemned either as naughty or nonsensical. Howbeit, this, though far from the most aggravated, is perhaps the strangest instance, on record, of marital delinquency; and, moreover, as remarkable a freak as may be found in the whole list of human oddities. The wedded couple lived in London. The man, under pretence of going a journey, took lodgings in the next street to his own house, and there, unheard of by his wife or friends, and without the shadow of a reason for such self-banishment, dwelt upwards of twenty years. During that period, he beheld his home every day, and frequently the forlorn Mrs. Wakefield. And after so great a gap in his matrimonial felicity—when his death was reckoned certain, his estate settled, his name dismissed from memory, and his wife, long, long ago, resigned to her autumnal widowhood—he entered the door one evening, quietly, as from a day's absence, and became a loving spouse till death.

This outline is all that I remember. But the incident, though of the purest originality, unexampled, and probably never to be repeated, is one, I think, which appeals to the general sympathies of mankind. We know, each for himself, that none of us would perpetrate such a folly, yet feel as if some other might. To my own contemplations, at least, it has often recurred, always exciting wonder, but with a sense that the story must be true, and a conception of its hero's character. Whenever any subject so forcibly affects the mind, time is well spent in thinking of it. If the reader choose, let him do his own meditation; or if he prefer to ramble with me through the twenty years of Wakefield's vagary, I bid him welcome; trusting that there will be a pervading spirit and a moral, even should we fail to find them, done up neatly, and condensed into the final sentence.

† First published in the *New England Magazine*, May 1835, then in *Twice-told Tales*, 1837. The idea for "Wakefield" seems to have come to Hawthorne from Dr. William King's *Anecdotes of His Own Times* (1818). King tells of a certain Howe who left his wife for seventeen years and then returned to her without explaining his conduct.

Thought has always its efficacy, and every striking incident its moral.

What sort of a man was Wakefield? We are free to shape out our own idea, and call it by his name. He was now in the meridian of life; his matrimonial affections, never violent, were sobered into a calm habitual sentiment; of all husbands, he was likely to be the most constant, because a certain sluggishness would keep his heart at rest, wherever it might be placed. He was intellectual, but not actively so; his mind occupied itself in long and lazy musings, that tended to no purpose, or had not vigor to attain it; his thoughts were seldom so energetic as to seize hold of words. Imagination, in the proper meaning of the term, made no part of Wakefield's gifts. With a cold, but not depraved nor wandering heart, and a mind never feverish with riotous thoughts, nor perplexed with originality, who could have anticipated, that our friend would entitle himself to a foremost place among the doers of eccentric deeds? Had his acquaintances been asked, who was the man in London, the surest to perform nothing today which should be remembered on the morrow, they would have thought of Wakefield. Only the wife of his bosom might have hesitated. She, without having analyzed his character, was partly aware of a quiet selfishness, that had rusted into his inactive mind—of a peculiar sort of vanity, the most uneasy attribute about him—of a disposition to craft, which had seldom produced more positive effects than the keeping of petty secrets, hardly worth revealing—and, lastly, of what she called a little strangeness, sometimes, in the good man. This latter quality is indefinable, and perhaps non-existent.

Let us now imagine Wakefield bidding adieu to his wife. It is the dusk of an October evening. His equipment is a drab greatcoat, a hat covered with an oilcloth, top-boots, an umbrella in one hand and a small portmanteau[1] in the other. He has informed Mrs. Wakefield that he is to take the night-coach into the country. She would fain inquire the length of his journey, its object, and the probable time of his return; but, indulgent to his harmless love of mystery, interrogates him only by a look. He tells her not to expect him positively by the return coach, nor to be alarmed should he tarry three or four days; but, at all events, to look for him at supper on Friday evening. Wakefield himself, be it considered, has no suspicion of what is before him. He holds out his hand; she gives her own, and meets his parting kiss, in the matter-of-course way of a ten years' matrimony; and forth goes the middle-aged Mr. Wakefield, almost

1. Traveling bag. "Greatcoat": heavy overcoat. "Top-boots": high boots. Hawthorne uses English idioms in "Wakefield," just as he uses the language of colonial Salem in "Young Goodman Brown."

resolved to perplex his good lady by a whole week's absence. After the door has closed behind him, she perceives it thrust partly open, and a vision of her husband's face, through the aperture, smiling on her, and gone in a moment. For the time, this little incident is dismissed without a thought. But, long afterwards, when she has been more years a widow than a wife, that smile recurs, and flickers across all her reminiscences of Wakefield's visage. In her many musings, she surrounds the original smile with a multitude of fantasies, which make it strange and awful; as, for instance, if she imagines him in a coffin, that parting look is frozen on his pale features; or, if she dreams of him in Heaven, still his blessed spirit wears a quiet and crafty smile. Yet, for its sake, when all others have given him up for dead, she sometimes doubts whether she is a widow.

But, our business is with the husband. We must hurry after him, along the street, ere he lose his individuality, and melt into the great mass of London life. It would be vain searching for him there. Let us follow close at his heels, therefore, until, after several superfluous turns and doublings, we find him comfortably established by the fireside of a small apartment, previously bespoken. He is in the next street to his own, and at his journey's end. He can scarcely trust his good fortune, in having got thither unperceived—recollecting that, at one time, he was delayed by the throng, in the very focus of a lighted lantern; and, again, there were footsteps, that seemed to tread behind his own, distinct from the multitudinous tramp around him; and, anon, he heard a voice shouting afar, and fancied that it called his name. Doubtless, a dozen busybodies had been watching him, and told his wife the whole affair. Poor Wakefield! Little knowest thou thine own insignificance in this great world! No mortal eye but mine has traced thee. Go quietly to thy bed, foolish man; and, on the morrow, if thou wilt be wise, get thee home to good Mrs. Wakefield, and tell her the truth. Remove not thyself, even for a little week, from thy place in her chaste bosom. Were she, for a single moment, to deem thee dead, or lost, or lastingly divided from her, thou wouldst be wofully conscious of a change in thy true wife, for ever after. It is perilous to make a chasm in human affections; not that they gape so long and wide—but so quickly close again!

Almost repenting of his frolic, or whatever it may be termed, Wakefield lies down betimes, and starting from his first nap, spreads forth his arms into the wide and solitary waste of the unaccustomed bed. 'No'—thinks he, gathering the bed-clothes about him—'I will not sleep alone another night.'

In the morning, he rises earlier than usual, and sets himself to consider what he really means to do. Such are his loose and rambling modes of thought, that he has taken this very singular step, with the consciousness of a purpose, indeed, but without being able to define it sufficiently for his own contemplation. The vagueness of the project, and the convulsive effort with which he plunges into the execution of it, are equally characteristic of a feeble-minded man. Wakefield sifts his ideas, however, as minutely as he may, and finds himself curious to know the progress of matters at home— how his exemplary wife will endure her widowhood, of a week; and, briefly, how the little sphere of creatures and circumstances, in which he was a central object, will be affected by his removal. A morbid vanity, therefore, lies nearest the bottom of the affair. But, how is he to attain his ends? Not, certainly, by keeping close in this comfortable lodging, where, though he slept and awoke in the next street to his home, he is as effectually abroad, as if the stage-coach had been whirling him away all night. Yet, should he reappear, the whole project is knocked in the head. His poor brains being hopelessly puzzled with this dilemma, he at length ventures out, partly resolving to cross the head of the street, and send one hasty glance towards his forsaken domicile. Habit—for he is a man of habits—takes him by the hand, and guides him, wholly unaware, to his own door, where, just at the critical moment, he is aroused by the scraping of his foot upon the step. Wakefield! whither are you going?

At that instant, his fate was turning on the pivot. Little dreaming of the doom to which his first backward step devotes him, he hurries away, breathless with agitation hitherto unfelt, and hardly dares turn his head, at the distant corner. Can it be, that nobody caught sight of him? Will not the whole household—the decent Mrs. Wakefield, the smart maidservant, and the dirty little footboy—raise a hue-and-cry, through London streets, in pursuit of their fugitive lord and master? Wonderful escape! He gathers courage to pause and look homeward, but is perplexed with a sense of change about the familiar edifice, such as affects us all, when, after a separation of months or years, we again see some hill or lake, or work of art, with which we were friends, of old. In ordinary cases, this indescribable impression is caused by the comparison and contrast between our imperfect reminiscences and the reality. In Wakefield, the magic of a single night has wrought a similar transformation, because, in that brief period, a great moral change has been effected. But this is a secret from himself. Before leaving the spot, he catches a far and momentary glimpse of his wife, passing athwart the front window, with her face turned towards the head of the street. The crafty nincompoop takes to his heels, scared with the idea, that, among a thousand such atoms of mortality, her eye must have detected him. Right glad is his heart, though his brain be somewhat dizzy, when he finds himself by the coal-fire of his lodgings.

So much for the commencement of this long whim-wham. After the initial conception, and the stirring up of the man's sluggish temperament to put it in practice, the whole matter evolves itself in a natural train. We may suppose him, as the result of deep deliberation, buying a new wig, of reddish hair, and selecting sundry garments, in a fashion unlike his customary suit of brown, from a Jew's old-clothes bag.[2] It is accomplished. Wakefield is another man. The new system being now established, a retrograde movement to the old would be almost as difficult as the step that placed him in his unparalleled position. Furthermore, he is rendered obstinate by a sulkiness, occasionally incident to his temper, and brought on, at present, by the inadequate sensation which he conceives to have been produced in the bosom of Mrs. Wakefield. He will not go back until she be frightened half to death. Well; twice or thrice has she passed before his sight, each time with a heavier step, a paler cheek, and more anxious brow; and in the third week of his non-appearance, he detects a portent of evil entering the house, in the guise of an apothecary. Next day, the knocker is muffled. Towards nightfall, comes the chariot of a physician, and deposits its big-wigged and solemn burthen at Wakefield's door, whence, after a quarter of an hour's visit, he emerges, perchance the herald of a funeral. Dear woman! Will she die? By this time, Wakefield is excited to something like energy of feeling, but still lingers away from his wife's bed-side, pleading with his conscience, that she must not be disturbed at such a juncture. If aught else restrains him, he does not know it. In the course of a few weeks, she gradually recovers; the crisis is over; her heart is sad, perhaps, but quiet; and, let him return soon or late, it will never be feverish for him again. Such ideas glimmer through the mist of Wakefield's mind, and render him indistinctly conscious, that an almost impassable gulf divides his hired apartment from his former home. 'It is but in the next street!' he sometimes says. Fool! it is in another world. Hitherto, he has put off his return from one particular day to another; henceforward, he leaves the precise time undetermined. Not tomorrow—probably next week—pretty soon. Poor man! The dead have nearly as much chance of revisiting their earthly homes, as the self-banished Wakefield.

Would that I had a folio[3] to write, instead of an article of a dozen pages! Then might I exemplify how an influence, beyond our control, lays its strong hand on every deed which we do, and weaves its consequences into an iron tissue of necessity. Wakefield is spellbound. We must leave him, for ten years or so, to haunt around his house, without once crossing the threshold, and to be faithful to his wife, with all the affection of which his heart is capable, while he

---

2. Jews, restricted in employment in England and elsewhere, were allowed to buy and sell clothes and were the usual old-clothes peddlers in London.
3. A volume with pages of the largest size.

is slowly fading out of hers. Long since, it must be remarked, he has lost the perception of singularity in his conduct.

Now for a scene! Amid the throng of a London street, we distinguish a man, now waxing elderly, with few characteristics to attract careless observers, yet bearing, in his whole aspect, the hand-writing of no common fate, for such as have the skill to read it. He is meagre; his low and narrow forehead is deeply wrinkled; his eyes, small and lustreless, sometimes wander apprehensively about him, but oftener seem to look inward. He bends his head, and moves with an indescribable obliquity of gait, as if unwilling to display his full front to the world. Watch him, long enough to see what we have described, and you will allow, that circumstances—which often produce remarkable men from nature's ordinary handiwork—have produced one such here. Next, leaving him to sidle along the footwalk, cast your eyes in the opposite direction, where a portly female, considerably in the wane of life, with a prayer-book in her hand, is proceeding to yonder church. She has the placid mien of settled widowhood. Her regrets have either died away, or have become so essential to her heart, that they would be poorly exchanged for joy. Just as the lean man and well-conditioned woman are passing, a slight obstruction occurs, and brings these two figures directly in contact. Their hands touch; the pressure of the crowd forces her bosom against his shoulder; they stand, face to face, staring into each other's eyes. After a ten years' separation, thus Wakefield meets his wife!

The throng eddies away, and carries them asunder. The sober widow, resuming her former pace, proceeds to church, but pauses in the portal, and throws a perplexed glance along the street. She passes in, however, opening her prayer-book as she goes. And the man? With so wild a face, that busy and selfish London stands to gaze after him, he hurries to his lodgings, bolts the door, and throws himself upon the bed. The latent feelings of years break out; his feeble mind acquires a brief energy from their strength; all the miserable strangeness of his life is revealed to him at a glance: and he cries out, passionately—'Wakefield! Wakefield! You are mad!'

Perhaps he was so. The singularity of his situation must have so moulded him to itself, that, considered in regard to his fellow-creatures and the business of life, he could not be said to possess his right mind. He had contrived, or rather he had happened, to dissever himself from the world—to vanish—to give up his place and privileges with living men, without being admitted among the dead. The life of a hermit is nowise parallel to his. He was in the bustle of the city, as of old; but the crowd swept by, and saw him not; he was, we may figuratively say, always beside his wife, and at his hearth, yet must never feel the warmth of the one, nor the affection of the other. It was Wakefield's unprecedented fate, to retain his original share of human sympathies, and to be still involved in human interests, while he had lost his reciprocal influence on them. It would be a most curious speculation, to trace out the effect of such circumstances on his heart and intellect, separately, and in unison. Yet, changed as he was, he would seldom be conscious of it, but deem himself the same man as ever; glimpses of the truth, indeed, would come, but only for the moment; and still he would keep saying—'I shall soon go back!'—nor reflect, that he had been saying so for twenty years.

I conceive, also, that these twenty years would appear, in the retrospect, scarcely longer than the week to which Wakefield had at first limited his absence. He would look on the affair as no more than an interlude in the main business of his life. When, after a little while more, he should deem it time to re-enter his parlor, his wife would clap her hands for joy, on beholding the middle-aged Mr. Wakefield. Alas, what a mistake! Would Time but await the close of our favorite follies, we should be young men, all of us, and till Doomsday.

One evening, in the twentieth year since he vanished, Wakefield is taking his customary walk towards the dwelling which he still calls his own. It is a gusty night of autumn, with frequent showers, that patter down upon the pavement, and are gone, before a man can put up his umbrella. Pausing near the house, Wakefield discerns, through the parlor-windows of the second floor, the red glow, and the glimmer and fitful flash, of a comfortable fire. On the ceiling appears a grotesque shadow of good Mrs. Wakefield. The cap, the nose and chin, and the broad waist, form an admirable caricature, which dances, moreover, with the up-flickering and down-sinking blaze, almost too merrily for the shade of an elderly widow. At this instant, a shower chances to fall, and is driven, by the unmannerly gust, full into Wakefield's face and bosom. He is quite penetrated with its autumnal chill. Shall he stand, wet and shivering here, when his own hearth has a good fire to warm him, and his own wife will run to fetch the gray coat and small-clothes,[4] which, doubtless, she has kept carefully in the closet of their bedchamber? No! Wakefield is no such fool. He ascends the steps—heavily!—for twenty years have stiffened his legs, since he came down—but he knows it not. Stay, Wakefield! Would you go to the sole home that is left you? Then step into your grave! The door opens. As he passes in, we have a parting glimpse of his visage, and recognise the crafty smile, which was the precursor of the little joke, that he has ever since been playing off

4. Breeches.

at his wife's expense. How unmercifully has he quizzed[5] the poor woman! Well; a good night's rest to Wakefield!

This happy event—supposing it to be such—could only have occurred at an unpremeditated moment. We will not follow our friend across the threshold. He has left us much food for thought, a portion of which shall lend its wisdom to a moral, and be shaped into a figure. Amid the seeming confusion of our mysterious world, individuals are so nicely adjusted to a system, and systems to one another, and to a whole, that, by stepping aside for a moment, a man exposes himself to a fearful risk of losing his place for ever. Like Wakefield, he may become, as it were, the Outcast of the Universe.

specific to general

The Ambitious Guest[†]

One September night, a family had gathered round their hearth, and piled it high with the drift-wood of mountain-streams, the dry cones of the pine, and the splintered ruins of great trees, that had come crashing down the precipice. Up the chimney roared the fire, and brightened the room with its broad blaze. The faces of the father and mother had a sober gladness; the children laughed; the eldest daughter was the image of Happiness at seventeen; and the aged grandmother, who sat knitting in the warmest place, was the image of Happiness grown old. They had found the 'herb, heart's ease,'[1] in the bleakest spot of all New England. This family were situated in the Notch of the White Hills, where the wind was sharp throughout the year, and pitilessly cold in the winter—giving their cottage all its fresh inclemency, before it descended on the valley of the Saco.[2] They dwelt in a cold spot and a dangerous one; for a mountain towered above their heads, so steep, that the stones would often rumble down its sides, and startle them at midnight.

---

5. Made fun of.

† First published in the *New England Magazine*, June 1835, then in *Twice-told Tales*, 2nd edition, 1842. The tale is based on an actual event. On August 28, 1826, Samuel Willey and his family were annihilated by a landslide in the White Mountains of New Hampshire. Their house served as an inn on the east–west road through the mountains, and a guest might well have perished with them. The Willeys were thought by some to have taken refuge in a stable better protected than the house itself. Yet the house survived the avalanche intact, as in "The Ambitious Guest."

1. The pansy. Hawthorne probably remembers the boy who wears "that Herb called Hearts-ease in his Bosom" from Bunyan's *Pilgrim's Progress*.

2. A river running from the mountainous country of north-central New Hampshire through southwestern Maine to the Atlantic. "The Notch": now Crawford's Notch, after Ethan Crawford, who kept an inn for travelers in the heart of the mountains. Hawthorne visited the area in 1832 and stayed at Crawford's inn. He gives a lively account of his excursion in "Sketches from Memory," first published in the *New England Magazine*, November 1835.

The daughter had just uttered some simple jest, that filled them all with mirth, when the wind came through the Notch and seemed to pause before their cottage—rattling the door, with a sound of wailing and lamentation, before it passed into the valley. For a moment, it saddened them, though there was nothing unusual in the tones. But the family were glad again, when they perceived that the latch was lifted by some traveller, whose footsteps had been unheard amid the dreary blast, which heralded his approach, and wailed as he was entering, and went moaning away from the door.

Though they dwelt in such a solitude, these people held daily converse with the world. The romantic pass of the Notch is a great artery, through which the life-blood of internal commerce is continually throbbing, between Maine, on one side, and the Green Mountains and the shores of the St. Lawrence on the other. The stage-coach always drew up before the door of the cottage. The wayfarer, with no companion but his staff, paused here to exchange a word, that the sense of loneliness might not utterly overcome him, ere he could pass through the cleft of the mountain, or reach the first house in the valley. And here the teamster, on his way to Portland market, would put up for the night—and, if a bachelor, might sit an hour beyond the usual bed-time, and steal a kiss from the mountain maid, at parting. It was one of those primitive taverns, where the traveller pays only for food and lodging, but meets with a homely kindness, beyond all price. When the footsteps were heard, therefore, between the outer door and the inner one, the whole family rose up, grandmother, children, and all, as if about to welcome some one who belonged to them, and whose fate was linked with theirs.

The door was opened by a young man. His face at first wore the melancholy expression, almost despondency, of one who travels a wild and bleak road, at night-fall and alone, but soon brightened up, when he saw the kindly warmth of his reception. He felt his heart spring forward to meet them all, from the old woman, who wiped a chair with her apron, to the little child that held out its arms to him. One glance and smile placed the stranger on a footing of innocent familiarity with the eldest daughter.

'Ah, this fire is the right thing!' cried he; 'especially when there is such a pleasant circle round it. I am quite benumbed; for the Notch is just like the pipe of a great pair of bellows; it has blown a terrible blast in my face, all the way from Bartlett.'

'Then you are going towards Vermont?' said the master of the house, as he helped to take a light knapsack off the young man's shoulders.

'Yes; to Burlington, and far enough beyond,' replied he. 'I meant to have been at Ethan Crawford's to-night; but a pedestrian lingers along such a road as this. It is no matter; for, when I saw this good fire, and all your cheerful faces, I felt as if you had kindled it on purpose for me, and were waiting my arrival. So I shall sit down among you, and make myself at home.'

The frank-hearted stranger had just drawn his chair to the fire, when something like a heavy footstep was heard without, rushing down the steep side of the mountain, as with long and rapid strides, and taking such a leap, in passing the cottage, as to strike the opposite precipice. The family held their breath, because they knew the sound, and their guest held his, by instinct.

'The old Mountain has thrown a stone at us, for fear we should forget him,' said the landlord, recovering himself. 'He sometimes nods his head, and threatens to come down; but we are old neighbors, and agree together pretty well, upon the whole. Besides, we have a sure place of refuge, hard by, if he should be coming in good earnest.'

Let us now suppose the stranger to have finished his supper of bear's meat; and, by his natural felicity of manner, to have placed himself on a footing of kindness with the whole family—so that they talked as freely together, as if he belonged to their mountain brood. He was of a proud, yet gentle spirit—haughty and reserved among the rich and great; but ever ready to stoop his head to the lowly cottage door, and be like a brother or a son at the poor man's fireside. In the household of the Notch, he found warmth and simplicity of feeling, the pervading intelligence of New England, and a poetry of native growth, which they had gathered, when they little thought of it, from the mountain-peaks and chasms, and at the very threshold of their romantic and dangerous abode. He had travelled far and alone; his whole life, indeed, had been a solitary path; for, with the lofty caution of his nature, he had kept himself apart from those who might otherwise have been his companions. The family, too, though so kind and hospitable, had that consciousness of unity among themselves, and separation from the world at large, which, in every domestic circle, should still keep a holy place, where no stranger may intrude. But, this evening, a prophetic sympathy impelled the refined and educated youth to pour out his heart before the simple mountaineers, and constrained them to answer him with the same free confidence. And thus it should have been. Is not the kindred of a common fate a closer tie than that of birth?

The secret of the young man's character was, a high and abstracted ambition. He could have borne to live an undistinguished life, but not to be forgotten in the grave. Yearning desire had been transformed to hope; and hope, long cherished, had become like certainty, that, obscurely as he journeyed now, a glory was to beam on all his path-way—though not, perhaps, while he was treading it. But, when posterity should gaze back into the gloom of what was now the present, they would trace the brightness of his footsteps, brightening as meaner glories faded, and confess, that a gifted one had passed from his cradle to his tomb, with none to recognise him.

'As yet,' cried the stranger—his cheek glowing and his eye flashing with enthusiasm—'as yet, I have done nothing. Were I to vanish from the earth tomorrow, none would know so much of me as you; that a nameless youth came up, at night-fall, from the valley of the Saco, and opened his heart to you in the evening, and passed through the Notch, by sunrise, and was seen no more. Not a soul would ask— "Who was he?—Whither did the wanderer go?" But, I cannot die till I have achieved my destiny. Then, let Death come! I shall have built my monument!'

There was a continual flow of natural emotion, gushing forth amid abstracted reverie, which enabled the family to understand this young man's sentiments, though so foreign from their own. With quick sensibility of the ludicrous, he blushed at the ardor into which he had been betrayed.

'You laugh at me,' said he, taking the eldest daughter's hand, and laughing himself. 'You think my ambition as nonsensical as if I were to freeze myself to death on the top of Mount Washington, only that people might spy at me from the country roundabout. And truly, that would be a noble pedestal for a man's statue!'

'It is better to sit here by this fire,' answered the girl, blushing, 'and be comfortable and contented, though nobody thinks about us.'

'I suppose,' said her father, after a fit of musing, 'there is something natural in what the young man says; and if my mind had been turned that way, I might have felt just the same. It is strange, wife, how his talk has set my head running on things, that are pretty certain never to come to pass.'

'Perhaps they may,' observed the wife. 'Is the man thinking what he will do when he is a widower?'

'No, no!' cried he, repelling the idea with reproachful kindness. 'When I think of your death, Esther, I think of mine, too. But I was wishing we had a good farm, in Bartlett, or Bethlehem, or Littleton, or some other township round the White Mountains; but not where they could tumble on our heads. I should want to stand well with my neighbors, and be called 'Squire, and sent to General Court,[3] for a term or two; for a plain, honest man may do as much good there as a lawyer. And when I should be grown quite an old man, and you an old woman, so as not to be long apart, I might die happy enough in my bed, and leave you all crying around me. A slate grave-stone would suit me as well as a marble one—with just my name and age,

3. The state legislature.

and a verse of a hymn, and something to let people know, that I lived an honest man and died a Christian.'

'There now!' exclaimed the stranger; 'it is our nature to desire a monument, be it slate, or marble, or a pillar of granite, or a glorious memory in the universal heart of man.'

'We're in a strange way, to-night,' said the wife, with tears in her eyes. 'They say it's a sign of something, when folks' minds go a wandering so. Hark to the children!'

They listened accordingly. The younger children had been put to bed in another room, but with an open door between, so that they could be heard talking busily among themselves. One and all seemed to have caught the infection from the fireside circle, and were outvying each other, in wild wishes, and childish projects of what they would do, when they came to be men and women. At length, a little boy, instead of addressing his brothers and sisters, called out to his mother.

"I'll tell you what I wish, mother,' cried he. 'I want you and father and grandma'm, and all of us, and the stranger too, to start right away, and go and take a drink out of the basin of the Flume!'

Nobody could help laughing at the child's notion of leaving a warm bed, and dragging them from a cheerful fire, to visit the basin of the Flume—a brook, which tumbles over the precipice, deep within the Notch. The boy had hardly spoken, when a wagon rattled along the road, and stopped a moment before the door. It appeared to contain two or three men, who were cheering their hearts with the rough chorus of a song, which resounded, in broken notes, between the cliffs, while the singers hesitated whether to continue their journey, or put up here for the night.

'Father,' said the girl, 'they are calling you by name.'

But the good man doubted whether they had really called him, and was unwilling to show himself too solicitous of gain, by inviting people to patronize his house. He therefore did not hurry to the door; and the lash being soon applied, the travellers plunged into the Notch, still singing and laughing, though their music and mirth came back drearily from the heart of the mountain.

'There, mother!' cried the boy, again. 'They'd have given us a ride to the Flume.'

Again they laughed at the child's pertinacious fancy for a nightramble. But it happened, that a light cloud passed over the daughter's spirit; she looked gravely into the fire, and drew a breath that was almost a sigh. It forced its way, in spite of a little struggle to repress it. Then starting and blushing, she looked quickly round the circle, as if they had caught a glimpse into her bosom. The stranger asked what she had been thinking of.

'Nothing,' answered she, with a downcast smile. 'Only I felt lone-some just then.'

'Oh, I have always had a gift of feeling what is in other people's hearts,' said he, half seriously. 'Shall I tell the secrets of yours? For I know what to think, when a young girl shivers by a warm hearth, and complains of lonesomeness at her mother's side. Shall I put these feelings into words?'

'They would not be a girl's feelings any longer, if they could be put into words,' replied the mountain nymph, laughing, but avoid-ing his eye.

All this was said apart. Perhaps a germ of love was springing in their hearts, so pure that it might blossom in Paradise, since it could not be matured on earth; for women worship such gentle dignity as his; and the proud, contemplative, yet kindly soul is oftenest capti-vated by simplicity like hers. But, while they spoke softly, and he was watching the happy sadness, the lightsome shadows, the shy yearnings of a maiden's nature, the wind, through the Notch, took a deeper and drearier sound. It seemed, as the fanciful stranger said, like the choral strain of the spirits of the blast, who, in old Indian times, had their dwelling among these mountains, and made their heights and recesses a sacred region.[4] There was a wail, along the road, as if a funeral were passing. To chase away the gloom, the fam-ily threw pine branches on their fire, till the dry leaves crackled and the flame arose, discovering once again a scene of peace and humble happiness. The light hovered about them fondly, and caressed them all. There were the little faces of the children, peeping from their bed apart, and here the father's frame of strength, the mother's sub-dued and careful mien, the high-browed youth, the budding girl, and the good old grandam, still knitting in the warmest place. The aged woman looked up from her task, and, with fingers ever busy, was the next to speak.

'Old folks have their notions,' said she, 'as well as young ones. You've been wishing and planning; and letting your heads run on one thing and another, till you've set my mind a wandering too. Now what should an old woman wish for, when she can go but a step or two before she comes to her grave? Children, it will haunt me night and day, till I tell you.'

'What is it, mother?' cried the husband and wife, at once.

Then the old woman, with an air of mystery, which drew the cir-cle closer round the fire, informed them that she had provided her

---

4. In "Sketches from Memory," Hawthorne tells how he and his fellow travelers recounted Indian myths of the mountains by Ethan Crawford's fireplace: "In the mythology of the savage, these mountains were . . . considered sacred and inaccessible, full of unearthly wonders . . . and inhabited by deities, who sometimes shrouded themselves in the snow-storm, and came down on the lower world."

grave-clothes some years before—a nice linen shroud, a cap with a muslin ruff, and every thing of a finer sort than she had worn since her wedding-day. But, this evening, an old superstition had strangely recurred to her. It used to be said, in her younger days, that, if any thing were amiss with a corpse, if only the ruff were not smooth, or the cap did not set right, the corpse, in the coffin and beneath the clods, would strive to put up its cold hands and arrange it. The bare thought made her nervous.

'Don't talk so, grandmother!' said the girl, shuddering.

'Now,'—continued the old woman, with singular earnestness, yet smiling strangely at her own folly,—'I want one of you, my children— when your mother is drest, and in the coffin—I want one of you to hold a looking-glass over my face. Who knows but I may take a glimpse at myself, and see whether all's right?'

'Old and young, we dream of graves and monuments,' murmured the stranger youth. 'I wonder how mariners feel, when the ship is sinking, and they, unknown and undistinguished, are to be buried together in the ocean—that wide and nameless sepulchre!'

For a moment, the old woman's ghastly conception so engrossed the minds of her hearers, that a sound, abroad in the night, rising like the roar of a blast, had grown broad, deep, and terrible, before the fated group were conscious of it. The house, and all within it, trembled; the foundations of the earth seemed to be shaken, as if this awful sound were the peal of the last trump. Young and old exchanged one wild glance, and remained an instant, pale, affrighted, without utterance, or power to move. Then the same shriek burst simultaneously from all their lips.

'The Slide! The Slide!'

The simplest words must intimate, but not portray, the unutterable horror of the catastrophe. The victims rushed from their cottage, and sought refuge in what they deemed a safer spot—where, in contemplation of such an emergency, a sort of barrier had been reared. Alas! they had quitted their security, and fled right into the pathway of destruction. Down came the whole side of the mountain, in a cataract of ruin. Just before it reached the house, the stream broke into two branches—shivered not a window there, but overwhelmed the whole vicinity, blocked up the road, and annihilated every thing in its dreadful course. Long ere the thunder of that great Slide had ceased to roar among the mountains, the mortal agony had been endured, and the victims were at peace. Their bodies were never found.

The next morning, the light smoke was seen stealing from the cottage chimney, up the mountain-side. Within, the fire was yet smouldering on the hearth, and the chairs in a circle round it, as if the inhabitants had but gone forth to view the devastation of the Slide, and would shortly return, to thank Heaven for their miraculous escape. All had left separate tokens, by which those, who had known the family, were made to shed a tear for each. Who has not heard their name? The story has been told far and wide, and will for ever be a legend of these mountains. Poets have sung their fate.

There were circumstances, which led some to suppose that a stranger had been received into the cottage on this awful night, and had shared the catastrophe of all its inmates. Others denied that there were sufficient grounds for such a conjecture. Wo, for the high-souled youth, with his dream of Earthly Immortality! His name and person utterly unknown; his history, his way of life, his plans, a mystery never to be solved; his death and his existence, equally a doubt! Whose was the agony of that death-moment?

Puritanism = 1620

The May-Pole of Merry Mount[†]

There is an admirable foundation for a philosophic romance, in the curious history of the early settlement of Mount Wollaston, or Merry Mount. In the slight sketch here attempted, the facts, recorded on the grave pages of our New England annalists, have wrought themselves, almost spontaneously, into a sort of allegory. The masques, mummeries, and festive customs, described in the text, are in accordance with the manners of the age. Authority, on these points may be found in Strutt's Book of English Sports and Pastimes.[1]

Symbol

Bright were the days at Merry Mount, when the May-Pole was the banner-staff of that gay colony! They who reared it, should their banner be triumphant, were to pour sun-shine over New England's rugged hills, and scatter flower-seeds throughout the soil. Jollity and

---

[†] First published in 1835 in *The Token* (dated 1836), then in *Twice-told Tales*, 1837. From 1625 to 1630, a colony of English fur traders existed at Mount Wollaston, now Quincy, Massachusetts, between the religiously minded settlers in Plymouth to the south and Salem to the north. By 1627, Thomas Morton, a hedonistic lawyer and adventurer, had become the chief man in Mount Wollaston. He renamed it Merry Mount and set out to make it as high-living a place as he could in wilderness circumstances. He adopted the maypole, the traditional center for dancing on May Day in England, as the permanent symbol of his enterprise. The Merrymounters decorated a forest tree with flowers and engaged in "revels and merriment after the old English custom" round about it. These pagan activities scandalized their neighbors, who several times invaded Morton's settlement. In 1628, Morton was arrested for trafficking in firearms with the Indians and deported to England. While Morton was absent, John Endicott of Salem led an expedition to Merry Mount, cut down the maypole, and warned the settlers to behave more decently. Endicott was then governor of the nascent Massachusetts Bay Colony. Little is known of Endicott's visit, and Hawthorne's tale is not a strictly historical account but a fictional presentation of a historical conflict of values. Merry Mount disappeared when the next governor, John Winthrop, had it burned to the ground in 1630.

1. Joseph Strutt, *The Sports and Pastimes of the People of England* (London, 1801).

gloom were contending for an empire. Midsummer eve[2] had come, bringing deep verdure to the forest, and roses in her lap, of a more vivid hue than the tender buds of Spring. But May, or her mirthful spirit, dwelt all the year round at Merry Mount, sporting with the Summer months, and revelling with Autumn, and basking in the glow of Winter's fireside. Through a world of toil and care, she flitted with a dreamlike smile, and came hither to find a home among the lightsome hearts of Merry Mount.

Never had the May-Pole been so gaily decked as at sunset on midsummer eve. This venerated emblem was a pine tree, which had preserved the slender grace of youth, while it equalled the loftiest height of the old wood monarchs. From its top streamed a silken banner, colored like the rainbow. Down nearly to the ground, the pole was dressed with birchen boughs, and others of the liveliest green, and some with silvery leaves, fastened by ribbons that fluttered in fantastic knots of twenty different colors, but no sad[3] ones. Garden flowers, and blossoms of the wilderness, laughed gladly forth amid the verdure, so fresh and dewy, that they must have grown by magic on that happy pine tree. Where this green and flowery splendor terminated, the shaft of the May-Pole[4] was stained with the seven brilliant hues of the banner at its top. On the lowest green bough hung an abundant wreath of roses, some that had been gathered in the sunniest spots of the forest, and others, of still richer blush, which the colonists had reared from English seed. Oh, people of the Golden Age, the chief of your husbandry, was to raise flowers!

But what was the wild throng that stood hand in hand about the May-Pole? It could not be, that the Fauns and Nymphs, when driven from their classic groves and homes of ancient fable, had sought refuge, as all the persecuted did, in the fresh woods of the West. These were Gothic monsters, though perhaps of Grecian ancestry. On the shoulders of a comely youth, uprose the head and branching antlers of a stag; a second, human in all other points, had the grim visage of a wolf; a third, still with the trunk and limbs of a mortal man, showed the beard and horns of a venerable he-goat. There was the likeness of a bear erect, brute in all but his hind legs, which were adorned with pink silk stockings. And here again, almost as wondrous, stood a real bear of the dark forest, lending each of his fore paws to the grasp of a human hand, and as ready for the dance

---

2. The evening before midsummer day, June 24. Midsummer eve was a traditional occasion for gaiety and sometimes for lovemaking in English festivals.
3. Dark, gloomy.
4. Traditionally, the maypole was decorated for May Day, a folk festival at which a May Queen was crowned and persons dressed in animal masks and outlandish costumes danced around the pole. May games might continue to be celebrated later in May but not throughout the year as imagined in the tale. No May Day festival was occurring on the occasion of Endicott's visit to Merry Mount.

as any in that circle. His inferior nature rose half-way, to meet his companions as they stooped. Other faces wore the similitude of man or woman, but distorted or extravagant, with red noses pendulous before their mouths, which seemed of awful depth, and stretched from ear to ear in an eternal fit of laughter. Here might be seen the Salvage Man,[5] well known in heraldry, hairy as a baboon, and girdled with green leaves. By his side, a nobler figure, but still a counterfeit, appeared an Indian hunter, with feathery crest and wampum belt. Many of this strange company wore fools-caps, and had little bells appended to their garments, tinkling with a silvery sound, responsive to the inaudible music of their gleesome spirits. Some youths and maidens were of soberer garb, yet well maintained their places in the irregular throng, by the expression of wild revelry upon their features. Such were the colonists of Merry Mount, as they stood in the broad smile of sunset, round their venerated May-Pole.

Had a wanderer, bewildered in the melancholy forest, heard their mirth, and stolen a half-affrighted glance, he might have fancied them the crew of Comus,[6] some already transformed to brutes, some midway between man and beast, and the others rioting in the flow of tipsy jollity that foreran the change. But a band of Puritans, who watched the scene, invisible themselves, compared the masques to those devils and ruined souls, with whom their superstition peopled the black wilderness.

Within the ring of monsters, appeared the two airiest forms, that had ever trodden on any more solid footing than a purple and golden cloud. One was a youth, in glistening apparel, with a scarf of the rainbow pattern crosswise on his breast. His right hand held a gilded staff, the ensign[7] of high dignity among the revellers, and his left grasped the slender fingers of a fair maiden, not less gaily decorated than himself. Bright roses glowed in contrast with the dark and glossy curls of each, and were scattered round their feet, or had sprung up spontaneously there. Behind this lightsome couple, so close to the May-Pole that its boughs shaded his jovial face, stood the figure of an English priest, canonically dressed, yet decked with flowers, in Heathen fashion, and wearing a chaplet of the native vine leaves. By the riot of his rolling eye, and the pagan decorations of his holy garb, he seemed the wildest monster there, and the very Comus of the crew.

---

5. A figure dressed in leaves, skins, or ivy, representing a savage of the woods. The figure often appears in heraldic coats of arms.
6. In Milton's *Comus*, a sorcerer and reveler who offers travelers in the woods a refreshment that turns them into monsters, with heads of wild beasts and bodies of men, whereupon they are conscripted into his "crew."
7. Sign, emblem.

'Votaries of the May-Pole,' cried the flower-decked priest, 'merrily, all day long, have the woods echoed to your mirth. But be this your merriest hour, my hearts! Lo, here stand the Lord and Lady of the May, whom I, a clerk of Oxford,[8] and high-priest of Merry Mount, am presently to join in holy matrimony. Up with your nimble spirits, ye morrice-dancers, green men, and glee-maidens,[9] bears and wolves, and horned gentlemen! Come; a chorus now, rich with the old mirth of Merry England, and the wilder glee of this fresh forest; and then a dance, to show the youthful pair what life is made of, and how airily they should go through it! All ye that love the May-Pole, lend your voices to the nuptial song of the Lord and Lady of the May!"

This wedlock was more serious than most affairs of Merry Mount, where jest and delusion, trick and fantasy, kept up a continual carnival. The Lord and Lady of the May, though their titles must be laid down at sunset, were really and truly to be partners for the dance of life, beginning the measure that same bright eve. The wreath of roses, that hung from the lowest green bough of the May-Pole, had been twined for them, and would be thrown over both their heads, in symbol of their flowery union. When the priest had spoken, therefore, a riotous uproar burst from the rout of monstrous figures.

'Begin you the stave,[1] reverend Sir,' cried they all; 'and never did the woods ring to such a merry peal, as we of the May-Pole shall send up!'

Immediately a prelude of pipe, cittern,[2] and viol, touched with practised ministrelsy, began to play from a neighboring thicket, in such a mirthful cadence, that the boughs of the May-Pole quivered to the sound. But the May Lord, he of the gilded staff, chancing to look into his Lady's eyes, was wonderstruck at the almost pensive glance that met his own.

'Edith, sweet Lady of the May,' whispered he, reproachfully, 'is yon wreath of roses a garland to hang above our graves, that you look so sad? Oh, Edith, this is our golden time! Tarnish it not by any pensive shadow of the mind; for it may be, that nothing of futurity will be brighter than the mere remembrance of what is now passing.'

'That was the very thought that saddened me! How came it in your mind too?' said Edith, in a still lower tone than he; for it was high treason to be sad at Merry Mount. 'Therefore do I sigh amid this festive music. And besides, dear Edgar, I struggle as with a dream, and fancy that these shapes of our jovial friends are visionary, and their

8. Clergyman and graduate of Oxford University.
9. Girl singers. "Morrice-dancers": costumed dancers in a traditional English folk dance. "Green men": men dressed in the greenery of the woods.
1. Verse or stanza.
2. Guitar with a pear-shaped body.

mirth unreal, and that we are no true Lord and Lady of the May. What is the mystery in my heart?'

Just then, as if a spell had loosened them, down came a little shower of withering rose leaves from the May-Pole. Alas, for the young lovers! No sooner had their hearts glowed with real passion, than they were sensible of something vague and unsubstantial in their former pleasures, and felt a dreary presentiment of inevitable change. From the moment that they truly loved, they had subjected themselves to earth's doom of care, and sorrow, and troubled joy, and had no more a home at Merry Mount. That was Edith's mystery. Now leave we the priest to marry them, and the masquers to sport round the May-Pole, till the last sunbeam be withdrawn from its summit, and the shadows of the forest mingle gloomily in the dance. Meanwhile, we may discover who these gay people were.

Two hundred years ago, and more, the old world and its inhabitants became mutually weary of each other. Men voyaged by thousands to the West; some to barter glass beads, and such like jewels, for the furs of the Indian hunter; some to conquer virgin empires; and one stern band to pray. But none of these motives had much weight with the colonists of Merry Mount. Their leaders were men who had sported so long with life, that when Thought and Wisdom came, even these unwelcome guests were led astray, by the crowd of vanities which they should have put to flight. Erring Thought and perverted Wisdom were made to put on masques, and play the fool. The men of whom we speak, after losing the heart's fresh gaiety, imagined a wild philosophy of pleasure, and came hither to act out their latest day-dream. They gathered followers from all that giddy tribe, whose whole life is like the festal days of soberer men. In their train were minstrels, not unknown in London streets; wandering players, whose theatres had been the halls of noblemen; mummers, rope-dancers, and mountebanks,[3] who would long be missed at wakes, church-ales, and fairs; in a word, mirth-makers of every sort, such as abounded in that age, but now began to be discountenanced by the rapid growth of Puritanism. Light had their footsteps been on land, and as lightly they came across the sea. Many had been maddened by their previous troubles into a gay despair; others were as madly gay in the flush of youth, like the May Lord and his Lady; but whatever might be the quality of their mirth, old and young were gay at Merry Mount. The young deemed themselves happy. The elder spirits, if they knew that mirth was but the counterfeit of happiness, yet followed the false shadow wilfully, because at least her garments glittered brightest. Sworn triflers of

---

3. Showmen who mount on benches to hawk wares or tell stories. "Mummers": masked merrymakers.

a life-time, they would not venture among the sober truths of life, not even to be truly blest.

All the hereditary pastimes of Old England were transplanted hither. The King of Christmas was duly crowned, and the Lord of Misrule[4] bore potent sway. On the eve of Saint John,[5] they felled whole acres of the forest to make bonfires, and danced by the blaze all night, crowned with garlands, and throwing flowers into the flame. At harvest time, though their crop was of the smallest, they made an image with the sheaves of Indian corn, and wreathed it with autumnal garlands, and bore it home triumphantly. But what chiefly characterized the colonists of Merry Mount, was their veneration for the May-Pole. It has made their true history a poet's tale. Spring decked the hallowed emblem with young blossoms and fresh green boughs; Summer brought roses of the deepest blush, and the perfected foliage of the forest; Autumn enriched it with that red and yellow gorgeousness, which converts each wild-wood leaf into a painted flower; and Winter silvered it with sleet, and hung it round with icicles, till it flashed in the cold sunshine, itself a frozen sunbeam. Thus each alternate season did homage to the May-Pole, and paid it a tribute of its own richest splendor. Its votaries danced round it, once, at least, in every month; sometimes they called it their religion, or their altar; but always, it was the banner-staff of Merry Mount.

Unfortunately, there were men in the new world, of a sterner faith than these May-Pole worshipers. Not far from Merry Mount was a settlement of Puritans, most dismal wretches, who said their prayers before daylight, and then wrought in the forest or the cornfield, till evening made it prayer time again. Their weapons were always at hand, to shoot down the straggling savage. When they met in conclave, it was never to keep up the old English mirth, but to hear sermons three hours long, or to proclaim bounties on the heads of wolves and the scalps of Indians. Their festivals were fast-days, and their chief pastime the singing of psalms. Woe to the youth or maiden, who did but dream of a dance! The selectman nodded to the constable; and there sat the light-heeled reprobate in the stocks; or if he danced, it was round the whipping-post, which might be termed the Puritan May-Pole.

A party of these grim Puritans, toiling through the difficult woods, each with a horse-load of iron armor to burthen his footsteps, would sometimes draw near the sunny precincts of Merry Mount. There were the silken colonists, sporting round their May-Pole; perhaps

Paradox

---

4. Mock official appointed by the royal court who presided over Christmas revels at the end of the 15th and the beginning of the 16th centuries. "King of Christmas": an officer in a royal or noble household, in charge of Christmas revels in November and December.
5. Midsummer eve.

teaching a bear to dance, or striving to communicate their mirth to the grave Indian; or masquerading in the skins of deer and wolves, which they had hunted for that especial purpose. Often, the whole colony were playing at blind-man's buff, magistrates and all with their eyes bandaged, except a single scape-goat, whom the blinded sinners pursued by the tinkling of the bells at his garments. Once, it is said, they were seen following a flower-decked corpse, with merriment and festive music, to his grave. But did the dead man laugh? In their quietest times, they sang ballads and told tales, for the edification of their pious visiters; or perplexed them with juggling tricks; or grinned at them through horse-collars; and when sport itself grew wearisome, they made game of their own stupidity, and began a yawning match. At the very least of these enormities, the men of iron shook their heads and frowned so darkly, that the revellers looked up, imagining that a momentary cloud had overcast the sunshine, which was to be perpetual there. On the other hand, the Puritans affirmed, that, when a psalm was pealing from their place of worship, the echo, which the forest sent them back, seemed often like the chorus of a jolly catch, closing with a roar of laughter. Who but the fiend, and his bond-slaves, the crew of Merry Mount, had thus disturbed them! In due time, a feud arose, stern and bitter on one side, and as serious on the other as any thing could be, among such light spirits as had sworn allegiance to the May-Pole. The future complexion of New England was involved in this important quarrel. Should the grisly saints establish their jurisdiction over the gay sinners, then would their spirits darken all the clime, and make it a land of clouded visages, of hard toil, of sermon and psalm, for ever. But should the banner-staff of Merry Mount be fortunate, sunshine would break upon the hills, and flowers would beautify the forest, and late posterity do homage to the May-Pole!

After these authentic passages from history, we return to the nuptials of the Lord and Lady of the May. Alas! we have delayed too long, and must darken our tale too suddenly. As we glance again at the May-Pole, a solitary sun-beam is fading from the summit, and leaves only a faint golden tinge, blended with the hues of the rainbow banner. Even that dim light is now withdrawn, relinquishing the whole domain of Merry Mount to the evening gloom, which has rushed so instantaneously from the black surrounding woods. But some of these black shadows have rushed forth in human shape.

Yes: with the setting sun, the last day of mirth had passed from Merry Mount. The ring of gay masquers was disordered and broken; the stag lowered his antlers in dismay; the wolf grew weaker than a lamb; the bells of the morrice-dancers tinkled with tremulous affright. The Puritans had played a characteristic part in the May-

Pole mummeries. Their darksome figures were intermixed with the wild shapes of their foes, and made the scene a picture of the moment, when waking thoughts start up amid the scattered fantasies of a dream. The leader of the hostile party stood in the centre of the circle, while the rout of monsters cowered around him, like evil spirits in the presence of a dread magician. No fantastic foolery could look him in the face. So stern was the energy of his aspect, that the whole man, visage, frame, and soul, seemed wrought of iron, gifted with life and thought, yet all of one substance with his head-piece and breast-plate. It was the Puritan of Puritans; it was Endicott himself!

'Stand off, priest of Baal![6] said he, with a grim frown, and laying no reverent hand upon the surplice, 'I know thee, Blackstone![7] Thou art the man, who couldst not abide the rule even of thine own corrupted church, and hast come hither to preach iniquity, and to give example of it in thy life. But now shall it be seen that the Lord hath sanctified this wilderness for his peculiar people. Woe unto them that would defile it! And first, for this flower-decked abomination, the altar of thy worship!'

And with his keen sword, Endicott assaulted the hallowed May-Pole. Nor long did it resist his arm. It groaned with a dismal sound; it showered leaves and rose-buds upon the remorseless enthusiast; and finally, with all its green boughs, and ribbons, and flowers, symbolic of departed pleasures, down fell the banner-staff of Merry Mount. As it sank, tradition says, the evening sky grew darker, and the woods threw forth a more sombre shadow.

'There,' cried Endicott, looking triumphantly on his work, 'there lies the only May-Pole in New-England! The thought is strong within me, that, by its fall, is shadowed forth the fate of light and idle mirth-makers, amongst us and our posterity. Amen, saith John Endicott!'

'Amen!' echoed his followers.

But the votaries of the May-Pole gave one groan for their idol. At the sound, the Puritan leader glanced at the crew of Comus, each a figure of broad mirth, yet, at this moment, strangely expressive of sorrow and dismay.

6. Ancient god of fertility, the empty god of idol-worshipers according to the Old Testament.
7. "Did Governor Endicott speak less positively, we should suspect a mistake here. The Rev. Mr. Blackstone, though an eccentric, is not known to have been an immoral man. We rather doubt his identity with the priest of Merry Mount" (*Hawthorne's note*). William Blackstone was an individualistic clergyman—a graduate of Cambridge, not Oxford—who settled in 1625 near what would become Boston. Instead of presiding over divine services at Merry Mount, he contributed to a fund for its suppression. Yet, though he left England because he "did not like the LORD BISHOPS," he also quarreled with the Puritans of the Bay Colony. He continued to wear a canonical surplice while living on his farm, which scandalized his Puritan neighbors.

'Valiant captain,' quoth Peter Palfrey, the Ancient[8] of the band, 'what order shall be taken with the prisoners?'

'I thought not to repent me of cutting down a May-Pole,' replied Endicott, 'yet now I could find in my heart to plant it again, and give each of these bestial pagans one other dance round their idol. It would have served rarely for a whipping-post!'

'But there are pine trees enow,' suggested the lieutenant.

'True, good Ancient,' said the leader. 'Wherefore, bind the heathen crew, and bestow on them a small matter of stripes apiece, as earnest[9] of our future justice. Set some of the rogues in the stocks to rest themselves, so soon as Providence shall bring us to one of our own well-ordered settlements, where such accommodations may be found. Further penalties, such as branding and cropping of ears, shall be thought of hereafter.'

'How many stripes for the priest?' inquired Ancient Palfrey.

'None as yet,' answered Endicott, bending his iron frown upon the culprit. 'It must be for the Great and General Court to determine, whether stripes and long imprisonment, and other grievous penalty, may atone for his transgressions. Let him look to himself! For such as violate our civil order, it may be permitted us to show mercy. But woe to the wretch that troubleth our religion!'

'And this dancing bear,' resumed the officer. 'Must he share the stripes of his fellows?'

'Shoot him through the head!' said the energetic Puritan. 'I suspect witchcraft in the beast.'

'Here be a couple of shining ones,' continued Peter Palfrey, pointing his weapon at the Lord and Lady of the May. 'They seem to be of high station among these misdoers. Methinks their dignity will not be fitted with less than a double share of stripes.'

Endicott rested on his sword, and closely surveyed the dress and aspect of the hapless pair. There they stood, pale, downcast, and apprehensive. Yet there was an air of mutual support, and of pure affection, seeking aid and giving it, that showed them to be man and wife, with the sanction of a priest upon their love. The youth, in the peril of the moment, had dropped his gilded staff, and thrown his arm about the Lady of the May, who leaned against his breast, too lightly to burthen him, but with weight enough to express that their destinies were linked together, for good or evil. They looked first at each other, and then into the grim captain's face. There they stood, in the first hour of wedlock, while the idle pleasures, of which their companions were the emblems, had given place to the sternest cares of life, personified by the dark Puritans. But never

8. Standard bearer. Peter Palfrey was one of the first settlers in Salem.
9. Pledge.

had their youthful beauty seemed so pure and high, as when its glow was chastened by adversity.

'Youth,' said Endicott, 'ye stand in an evil case, thou and thy maiden wife. Make ready presently; for I am minded that ye shall both have a token to remember your wedding-day!'

'Stern man,' cried the May Lord, 'how can I move thee? Were the means at hand, I would resist to the death. Being powerless, I entreat! Do with me as thou wilt; but let Edith go untouched!'

'Not so,' replied the immitigable zealot. 'We are not wont to show an idle courtesy to that sex, which requireth the stricter discipline. What sayest thou, maid? Shall thy silken bridegroom suffer thy share of the penalty, besides his own?'

'Be it death,' said Edith, 'and lay it all on me!'

Truly, as Endicott had said, the poor lovers stood in a woeful case. Their foes were triumphant, their friends captive and abased, their home desolate, the benighted wilderness around them, and a rigorous destiny, in the shape of the Puritan leader, their only guide. Yet the deepening twilight could not altogether conceal, that the iron man was softened; he smiled, at the fair spectacle of early love; he almost sighed, for the inevitable blight of early hopes.

'The troubles of life have come hastily on this young couple,' observed Endicott. 'We will see how they comport themselves under their present trials, ere we burthen them with greater. If, among the spoil, there be any garments of a more decent fashion, let them be put upon this May Lord and his Lady, instead of their glistening vanities. Look to it, some of you.'

'And shall not the youth's hair be cut?' asked Peter Palfrey, looking with abhorrence at the love-lock and long glossy curls of the young man.

'Crop it forthwith, and that in the true pumpkin-shell fashion,'[1] answered the captain. 'Then bring them along with us, but more gently than their fellows. There be qualities in the youth, which may make him valiant to fight, and sober to toil, and pious to pray; and in the maiden, that may fit her to become a mother in our Israel,[2] bringing up babes in better nurture than her own hath been. Nor think ye, young ones, that they are the happiest, even in our lifetime of a moment, who misspend it in dancing round a May-Pole!'

And Endicott, the severest Puritan of all who laid the rock-foundation of New England, lifted the wreath of roses from the ruin of the MayPole, and threw it, with his own gauntleted hand, over the heads of the Lord and Lady of the May. It was a deed of

1. Roundhead style, close-cropped in the Puritan fashion. Puritans were called "pumpkin-shells" by their longer-haired opponents.
2. I.e., Our New English Israel, a figural name some Puritans in the Bay Colony adopted for their struggling settlement.

prophecy. As the moral gloom of the world overpowers all systematic gaiety, even so was their home of wild mirth made desolate amid
the sad forest. They returned to it no more. But, as their flowery
garland was wreathed of the brightest roses that had grown there, so,
in the tie that united them, were intertwined all the purest and best
of their early joys. They went heavenward, supporting each other
along the difficult path which it was their lot to tread[3] and never
wasted one regretful thought on the vanities of Merry Mount.

The Minister's Black Veil[†]

A Parable[1]

The sexton stood in the porch of Milford meeting-house, pulling
lustily at the bell-rope. The old people of the village came stooping
along the street. Children, with bright faces, tript merrily beside
their parents, or mimicked a graver gait, in the conscious dignity of
their Sunday clothes. Spruce bachelors looked sidelong at the pretty
maidens, and fancied that the sabbath sunshine made them prettier
than on week-days. When the throng had mostly streamed into the
porch, the sexton began to toll the bell, keeping his eye on the Reverend Mr. Hooper's door. The first glimpse of the clergyman's figure was the signal for the bell to cease its summons.

'But what has good Parson Hooper got upon his face?' cried the
sexton in astonishment.

All within hearing immediately turned about, and beheld the
semblance of Mr. Hooper, pacing slowly his meditative way towards
the meeting-house. With one accord they started, expressing more
wonder than if some strange minister were coming to dust the cushions of Mr. Hooper's pulpit.

---

3. See Milton's last lines on Adam and Eve as they leave the Garden of Eden at the end of
   Paradise Lost 12:646–49: "The World was all before them, where to choose / Their place
   of rest, and Providence their guide: / They hand in hand, with wand'ring steps and slow,
   / Through Eden took their solitary way." Four paragraphs earlier, Hawthorne also alludes
   to this passage. Of Edith and Edgar he writes, "their home [was] desolate . . . and a rigorous destiny, in the shape of the Puritan leader, their only guide."
† First published in 1835 in *The Token* (dated 1836), then in *Twice-told Tales*, 1837. The
   story takes place early in the 18th century. During Parson Hooper's lifetime, the New
   England Congregationalist community, which had grown worldly and complacent, was
   agitated by a series of religious revivals known as the Great Awakening (ca. 1734–43).
   Probably Hawthorne conceives Hooper as a minister who seeks to awaken the torpid
   spirit of his town, though as usual his treatment of Hooper is psychological as well as
   historical.
1. 'Another clergyman in New England, Mr. Joseph Moody, of York, Maine, who died
   about eighty years since, made himself remarkable by the same eccentricity that is here
   related of the Reverend Mr. Hooper. In his case, however, the symbol had a different
   import. In early life he had accidentally killed a beloved friend; and from that day till
   the hour of his own death, he hid his face from men' [*Hawthorne's note.*]

'Are you sure it is our parson?' inquired Goodman Gray of the sexton.

'Of a certainty it is good Mr. Hooper,' replied the sexton. 'He was to have exchanged pulpits with Parson Shute of Westbury; but Parson Shute sent to excuse himself yesterday, being to preach a funeral sermon.'

The cause of so much amazement may appear sufficiently slight. Mr. Hooper, a gentlemanly person of about thirty, though still a bachelor, was dressed with due clerical neatness, as if a careful wife had starched his band, and brushed the weekly dust from his Sunday's garb. There was but one thing remarkable in his appearance. Swathed about his forehead, and hanging down over his face, so low as to be shaken by his breath, Mr. Hooper had on a black veil. On a nearer view, it seemed to consist of two folds of crape, which entirely concealed his features, except the mouth and chin, but probably did not intercept his sight, farther than to give a darkened aspect to all living and inanimate things. With this gloomy shade before him, good Mr. Hooper walked onward, at a slow and quiet pace, stooping somewhat and looking on the ground, as is customary with abstracted men, yet nodding kindly to those of his parishioners who still waited on the meeting-house steps. But so wonder-struck were they, that his greeting hardly met with a return.

'I can't really feel as if good Mr. Hooper's face was behind that piece of crape,' said the sexton.

'I don't like it,' muttered an old woman, as she hobbled into the meeting-house. 'He has changed himself into something awful, only by hiding his face.'

'Our parson has gone mad!" cried Goodman Gray, following him across the threshold.

A rumor of some unaccountable phenomenon had preceded Mr. Hooper into the meeting-house, and set all the congregation astir. Few could refrain from twisting their heads towards the door; many stood upright, and turned directly about; while several little boys clambered upon the seats, and came down again with a terrible racket. There was a general bustle, a rustling of the women's gowns and shuffling of the men's feet, greatly at variance with that hushed repose which should attend the entrance of the minister. But Mr. Hooper appeared not to notice the perturbation of his people. He entered with an almost noiseless step, bent his head mildly to the pews on each side, and bowed as he passed his oldest parishioner, a white-haired great-grandsire, who occupied an arm-chair in the centre of the aisle. It was strange to observe, how slowly this venerable man became conscious of something singular in the appearance of his pastor. He seemed not fully to partake of the prevailing wonder, till Mr. Hooper had ascended the stairs, and showed himself in the pulpit, face to face with his congregation, except for the black veil. That mysterious emblem was never once withdrawn. It shook with his measured breath as he gave out the psalm; it threw its obscurity between him and the holy page, as he read the Scriptures; and while he prayed, the veil lay heavily on his uplifted countenance. Did he seek to hide it from the dread Being whom he was addressing?

Such was the effect of this simple piece of crape, that more than one woman of delicate nerves was forced to leave the meetinghouse. Yet perhaps the pale-faced congregation was almost as fearful a sight to the minister, as his black veil to them.

Mr. Hooper had the reputation of a good preacher, but not an energetic one: he strove to win his people heavenward, by mild persuasive influences, rather than to drive them thither, by the thunders of the Word. The sermon which he now delivered, was marked by the same characteristics of style and manner, as the general series of his pulpit oratory. But there was something, either in the sentiment of the discourse itself, or in the imagination of the auditors, which made it greatly the most powerful effort that they had ever heard from their pastor's lips. It was tinged, rather more darkly than usual, with the gentle gloom of Mr. Hooper's temperament. The subject had reference to secret sin, and those sad mysteries which we hide from our nearest and dearest, and would fain conceal from our own consciousness, even forgetting that the Omniscient can detect them. A subtle power was breathed into his words. Each member of the congregation, the most innocent girl, and the man of hardened breast, felt as if the preacher had crept upon them, behind his awful veil, and discovered their hoarded iniquity of deed or thought. Many spread their clasped hands on their bosoms. There was nothing terrible in what Mr. Hooper said; at least, no violence; and yet, with every tremor of his melancholy voice, the hearers quaked. An unsought pathos came hand in hand with awe. So sensible were the audience of some unwonted attribute in their minister, that they longed for a breath of wind to blow aside the veil, almost believing that a stranger's visage would be discovered, though the form, gesture, and voice were those of Mr. Hooper.

At the close of the services, the people hurried out with indecorous confusion, eager to communicate their pent-up amazement, and conscious of lighter spirits, the moment they lost sight of the black veil. Some gathered in little circles, huddled closely together, with their mouths all whispering in the centre; some went homeward alone, wrapt in silent meditation; some talked loudly, and profaned the Sabbath-day with ostentatious laughter. A few shook their sagacious heads, intimating that they could penetrate the mystery;

while one or two affirmed that there was no mystery at all, but only that Mr. Hooper's eyes were so weakened by the midnight lamp, as to require a shade. After a brief interval, forth came good Mr. Hooper also, in the rear of his flock. Turning his veiled face from one group to another, he paid due reverence to the hoary heads, saluted the middle-aged with kind dignity, as their friend and spiritual guide, greeted the young with mingled authority and love, and laid his hands on the little children's heads to bless them. Such was always his custom on the Sabbath-day. Strange and bewildered looks repaid him for his courtesy. None, as on former occasions, aspired to the honor of walking by their pastor's side. Old Squire Saunders, doubtless by an accidental lapse of memory, neglected to invite Mr. Hooper to his table, where the good clergyman had been wont to bless the food, almost every Sunday since his settlement. He returned, therefore, to the parsonage, and, at the moment of closing the door, was observed to look back upon the people, all of whom had their eyes fixed upon the minister. A sad smile gleamed faintly from beneath the black veil, and flickered about his mouth, glimmering as he disappeared.

'How strange,' said a lady, 'that a simple black veil, such as any woman might wear on her bonnet, should become such a terrible thing on Mr. Hooper's face!'

'Something must surely be amiss with Mr. Hooper's intellects,' observed her husband, the physician of the village. 'But the strangest part of the affair is the effect of this vagary, even on a sober-minded man like myself. The black veil, though it covers only our pastor's face, throws its influence over his whole person, and makes him ghost-like from head to foot. Do you not feel it so?'

'Truly do I,' replied the lady; 'and I would not be alone with him for the world. I wonder he is not afraid to be alone with himself!'

'Men sometimes are so,' said her husband.

The afternoon service was attended with similar circumstances. At its conclusion, the bell tolled for the funeral of a young lady. The relatives and friends were assembled in the house, and the more distant acquaintances stood about the door, speaking of the good qualities of the deceased, when their talk was interrupted by the appearance of Mr. Hooper, still covered with his black veil. It was now an appropriate emblem. The clergyman stepped into the room where the corpse was laid, and bent over the coffin, to take a last farewell of his deceased parishioner. As he stooped, the veil hung straight down from his forehead, so that, if her eye-lids had not been closed for ever, the dead maiden might have seen his face. Could Mr. Hooper be fearful of her glance, that he so hastily caught back the black veil? A person, who watched the interview between the dead and living, scrupled not to affirm, that, at the instant when the clergyman's features were disclosed, the corpse had slightly shuddered, rustling the shroud and muslin cap, though the countenance retained the composure of death. A superstitious old woman was the only witness of this prodigy. From the coffin, Mr. Hooper passed into the chamber of the mourners, and thence to the head of the staircase, to make the funeral prayer. It was a tender and heart-dissolving prayer, full of sorrow, yet so imbued with celestial hopes, that the music of a heavenly harp, swept by the fingers of the dead, seemed faintly to be heard among the saddest accents of the minister. The people trembled, though they but darkly understood him, when he prayed that they, and himself, and all of mortal race, might be ready, as he trusted this young maiden had been, for the dreadful hour that should snatch the veil from their faces. The bearers went heavily forth, and the mourners followed, saddening all the street, with the dead before them, and Mr. Hooper in his black veil behind.

'Why do you look back?' said one in the procession to his partner.

'I had a fancy,' replied she, 'that the minister and the maiden's spirit were walking hand in hand.'

'And so had I, at the same moment,' said the other.

That night, the handsomest couple in Milford village were to be joined in wedlock. Though reckoned a melancholy man, Mr. Hooper had a placid cheerfulness for such occasions, which often excited a sympathetic smile, where livelier merriment would have been thrown away. There was no quality of his disposition which made him more beloved than this. The company at the wedding awaited his arrival with impatience trusting that the strange awe, which had gathered over him throughout the day, would now be dispelled. But such was not the result. When Mr. Hooper came, the first thing that their eyes rested on was the same horrible black veil, which had added deeper gloom to the funeral, and could portend nothing but evil to the wedding. Such was its immediate effect on the guests, that a cloud seemed to have rolled duskily from beneath the black crape, and dimmed the light of the candles. The bridal pair stood up before the minister. But the bride's cold fingers quivered in the tremulous hand of the bridegroom, and her death-like paleness caused a whisper, that the maiden who had been buried a few hours before, was come from her grave to be married. If ever another wedding were so dismal, it was that famous one, where they tolled the wedding-knell.[2] After performing the ceremony, Mr. Hooper raised a glass of wine to his lips, wishing happiness to the new-married couple, in a strain of mild pleasantry that ought to have brightened the features of the

2. An allusion to Hawthorne's own "The Wedding-Knell," published along with this tale in *The Token* of 1835 and in *Twice-told Tales*, 1837.

guests, like a cheerful gleam from the hearth. At that instant, catching a glimpse of his figure in the looking-glass, the black veil involved his own spirit in the horror with which it overwhelmed all others. His frame shuddered—his lips grew white—he spilt the untasted wine upon the carpet—and rushed forth into the darkness. For the Earth, too, had on her Black Veil.

The next day, the whole village of Milford talked of little else than Parson Hooper's black veil. That, and the mystery concealed behind it, supplied a topic for discussion between acquaintances meeting in the street, and good women gossiping at their open windows. It was the first item of news that the tavern-keeper told to his guests. The children babbled of it on their way to school. One imitative little imp covered his face with an old black handkerchief, thereby so affrighting his playmates, that the panic seized himself, and he well nigh lost his wits by his own waggery.

It was remarkable, that, of all the busy-bodies and impertinent people in the parish, not one ventured to put the plain question to Mr. Hooper, wherefore he did this thing. Hitherto, whenever there appeared the slightest call for such interference, he had never lacked advisers, nor shown himself averse to be guided by their judgment. If he erred at all, it was by so painful a degree of self-distrust, that even the mildest censure would lead him to consider an indifferent action as a crime. Yet, though so well acquainted with this amiable weakness, no individual among his parishioners chose to make the black veil a subject of friendly remonstrance. There was a feeling of dread, neither plainly confessed nor carefully concealed, which caused each to shift the responsibility upon another, till at length it was found expedient to send a deputation of the church, in order to deal with Mr. Hooper about the mystery, before it should grow into a scandal. Never did an embassy so ill discharge its duties. The minister received them with friendly courtesy, but became silent, after they were seated, leaving to his visiters the whole burthen of introducing their important business. The topic, it might be supposed, was obvious enough. There was the black veil, swathed round Mr. Hooper's forehead, and concealing every feature above his placid mouth, on which, at times, they could perceive the glimmering of a melancholy smile. But that piece of crape, to their imagination, seemed to hang down before his heart, the symbol of a fearful secret between him and them. Were the veil but cast aside, they might speak freely of it, but not till then. Thus they sat a considerable time, speechless, confused, and shrinking uneasily from Mr. Hooper's eye, which they felt to be fixed upon them with an invisible glance. Finally, the deputies returned abashed to their constituents, pronouncing the matter too weighty to be handled, except by a council of the churches, if, indeed, it might not require a general synod.

But there was one person in the village, unappalled by the awe with which the black veil had impressed all beside herself. When the deputies returned without an explanation, or even venturing to demand one, she, with the calm energy of her character, determined to chase away the strange cloud that appeared to be settling round Mr. Hooper, every moment more darkly than before. As his plighted wife, it should be her privilege to know what the black veil concealed. At the minister's first visit, therefore, she entered upon the subject, with a direct simplicity, which made the task easier both for him and her. After he had seated himself, she fixed her eyes steadfastly upon the veil, but could discern nothing of the dreadful gloom that had so overawed the multitude: it was but a double fold of crape, hanging down from his forehead to his mouth, and slightly stirring with his breath.

'No,' said she aloud, and smiling, 'there is nothing terrible in this piece of crape, except that it hides a face which I am always glad to look upon. Come, good sir, let the sun shine from behind the cloud. First lay aside your black veil: then tell me why you put it on.'

Mr. Hooper's smile glimmered faintly.

'There is an hour to come,' said he, 'when all of us shall cast aside our veils. Take it not amiss, beloved friend, if I wear this piece of crape till then.'

'Your words are a mystery too,' returned the young lady. 'Take away the veil from them, at least.'

'Elizabeth, I will,' said he, 'so far as my vow may suffer me. Know, then, this veil is a type[3] and a symbol, and I am bound to wear it ever, both in light and darkness, in solitude and before the gaze of multitudes, and as with strangers, so with my familiar friends. No mortal eye will see it withdrawn. This dismal shade must separate me from the world: even you, Elizabeth, can never come behind it!'

'What grievous affliction hath befallen you,' she earnestly inquired, 'that you should thus darken your eyes for ever?'

'If it be a sign of mourning,' replied Mr. Hooper, 'I, perhaps, like most other mortals, have sorrows dark enough to be typified by a black veil.'

'But what if the world will not believe that it is the type of an innocent sorrow?' urged Elizabeth. 'Beloved and respected as you are, there may be whispers, that you hide your face under the consciousness of secret sin. For the sake of your holy office, do away this scandal!'

The color rose into her cheeks, as she intimated the nature of the rumors that were already abroad in the village. But Mr. Hooper's mildness did not forsake him. He even smiled again—that same

3. Object that typifies a religious or spiritual idea.

sad smile, which always appeared like a faint glimmering of light, proceeding from the obscurity beneath the veil.

'If I hide my face for sorrow, there is cause enough,' he merely replied; 'and if I cover it for secret sin, what mortal might not do the same?'

And with this gentle, but unconquerable obstinacy, did he resist all her entreaties. At length Elizabeth sat silent. For a few moments she appeared lost in thought, considering, probably, what new methods might be tried, to withdraw her lover from so dark a fantasy, which, if it had no other meaning, was perhaps a symptom of mental disease. Though of a firmer character than his own, the tears rolled down her cheeks. But, in an instant, as it were, a new feeling took the place of sorrow: her eyes were fixed insensibly on the black veil, when, like a sudden twilight in the air, its terrors fell around her. She arose, and stood trembling before him.

'And do you feel it then at last?' said he mournfully.

She made no reply, but covered her eyes with her hand, and turned to leave the room. He rushed forward and caught her arm.

'Have patience with me, Elizabeth!' cried he passionately. 'Do not desert me, though this veil must be between us here on earth. Be mine, and hereafter there shall be no veil over my face, no darkness between our souls! It is but a mortal veil—it is not for eternity! Oh! you know not how lonely I am, and how frightened, to be alone behind my black veil. Do not leave me in this miserable obscurity for ever!'

'Lift the veil but once, and look me in the face,' said she.

'Never! It cannot be!' replied Mr. Hooper.

'Then, farewell!' said Elizabeth.

She withdraw her arm from his grasp, and slowly departed, pausing at the door, to give one long, shuddering gaze, that seemed almost to penetrate the mystery of the black veil. But, even amid his grief, Mr. Hooper smiled to think that only a material emblem had separated him from happiness, though the horrors which it shadowed forth, must be drawn darkly between the fondest of lovers.

From that time no attempts were made to remove Mr. Hooper's black veil, or, by a direct appeal, to discover the secret which it was supposed to hide. By persons who claimed a superiority to popular prejudice, it was reckoned merely an eccentric whim, such as often mingles with the sober actions of men otherwise rational, and tinges them all with its own semblance of insanity. But with the multitude, good Mr. Hooper was irreparably a bugbear.[4] He could not walk the street with any peace of mind, so conscious was he that the gentle and timid would turn aside to avoid him, and that others would

4. Frightening creature.

make it a point of hardihood to throw themselves in his way. The impertinence of the latter class compelled him to give up his customary walk, at sunset, to the burial ground; for when he leaned pensively over the gate, there would always be faces behind the grave-stones, peeping at his black veil. A fable went the rounds, that the stare of the dead people drove him thence. It grieved him, to the very depth of his kind heart, to observe how the children fled from his approach, breaking up their merriest sports, while his melancholy figure was yet afar off. Their instinctive dread caused him to feel, more strongly than aught else, that a preternatural horror was interwoven with the threads of the black crape. In truth, his own antipathy to the veil was known to be so great, that he never willingly passed before a mirror, nor stooped to drink at a still fountain, lest, in its peaceful bosom, he should be affrighted by himself. This was what gave plausibility to the whispers, that Mr. Hooper's conscience tortured him for some great crime, too horrible to be entirely concealed, or otherwise than so obscurely intimated. Thus, from beneath the black veil, there rolled a cloud into the sunshine, an ambiguity of sin or sorrow, which enveloped the poor minister, so that love or sympathy could never reach him. It was said, that ghost and fiend consorted with him there. With self-shudderings and outward terrors, he walked continually in its shadow, groping darkly within his own soul, or gazing through a medium that saddened the whole world. Even the lawless wind, it was believed, respected his dreadful secret, and never blew aside the veil. But still good Mr. Hooper sadly smiled, at the pale visages of the worldly throng as he passed by.

Among all its bad influences, the black veil had the one desirable effect, of making its wearer a very efficient clergyman. By the aid of his mysterious emblem—for there was no other apparent cause—he became a man of awful power, over souls that were in agony for sin. His converts always regarded him with a dread peculiar to themselves, affirming, though but figuratively, that, before he brought them to celestial light, they had been with him behind the black veil. Its gloom, indeed, enabled him to sympathize with all dark affections. Dying sinners cried aloud for Mr. Hooper, and would not yield their breath till he appeared; though ever, as he stooped to whisper consolation, they shuddered at the veiled face so near their own. Such were the terrors of the black veil, even when death had bared his visage! Strangers came long distances to attend service at his church, with the mere idle purpose of gazing at his figure, because it was forbidden them to behold his face. But many were made to quake ere they departed! Once, during Governor Belcher's administration, Mr. Hooper was appointed to preach the election

sermon.[5] Covered with his black veil, he stood before the chief magistrate, the council, and the representatives, and wrought so deep an
impression, that the legislative measures of that year, were characterized by all the gloom and piety of our earliest ancestral sway.

In this manner Mr. Hooper spent a long life, irreproachable in
outward act, yet shrouded in dismal suspicions; kind and loving,
though unloved, and dimly feared; a man apart from men, shunned
in their health and joy, but ever summoned to their aid in mortal
anguish. As years wore on, shedding their snows above his sable veil,
he acquired a name throughout the New England churches, and
they called him Father Hooper. Nearly all his parishioners, who were
of mature age when he was settled, had been borne away by many a
funeral: he had one congregation in the church, and a more crowded
one in the church-yard; and having wrought so late into the evening,
and done his work so well, it was now good Father Hooper's turn to
rest.

Several persons were visible by the shaded candlelight, in the
death-chamber of the old clergyman. Natural connexions he had
none. But there was the decorously grave, though unmoved physician, seeking only to mitigate the last pangs of the patient whom he
could not save. There were the deacons, and other eminently pious
members of his church. There, also, was the Reverend Mr. Clark, of
Westbury, a young and zealous divine, who had ridden in haste to
pray by the bed-side of the expiring minister. There was the nurse,
no hired handmaiden of death, but one whose calm affection had
endured thus long, in secrecy, in solitude, amid the chill of age,
and would not perish, even at the dying hour. Who, but Elizabeth!
And there lay the hoary head of good Father Hooper upon the
death-pillow, with the black veil still swathed about his brow and
reaching down over his face, so that each more difficult gasp of his
faint breath caused it to stir. All through life that piece of crape had
hung between him and the world: it had separated him from cheerful brotherhood and woman's love, and kept him in that saddest of
all prisons, his own heart; and still it lay upon his face, as if to
deepen the gloom of his darksome chamber, and shade him from
the sunshine of eternity.

For some time previous, his mind had been confused, wavering
doubtfully between the past and the present, and hovering forward,
as it were, at intervals, into the indistinctness of the world to come.
There had been feverish turns, which tossed him from side to side,

---

5. Delivered at the installation of the province's governmental officials. To be chosen to
   preach the sermon was a signal honor for a minister. Jonathan Belcher (1681–1775),
   governor of Massachusetts (1730–41).

and wore away what little strength he had. But in his most convulsive struggles, and in the wildest vagaries of his intellect, when no other thought retained its sober influence, he still showed an awful solicitude lest the black veil should slip aside. Even if his bewildered soul could have forgotten, there was a faithful woman at his pillow, who, with averted eyes, would have covered that aged face, which she had last beheld in the comeliness of manhood. At length the death-stricken old man lay quietly in the torpor of mental and bodily exhaustion, with an imperceptible pulse, and breath that grew fainter and fainter, except when a long, deep, and irregular inspiration seemed to prelude the flight of his spirit.

The minister of Westbury approached the bedside.

'Venerable Father Hooper,' said he, 'the moment of your release is at hand. Are you ready for the lifting of the veil, that shuts in time from eternity?'

Father Hooper at first replied merely by a feeble motion of his hand; then, apprehensive, perhaps, that his meaning might be doubtful, he exerted himself to speak.

'Yea,' said he, in faint accents, 'my soul hath a patient weariness until that veil be lifted.'

'And is it fitting,' resumed the Reverend Mr. Clark, 'that a man so given to prayer, of such a blameless example, holy in deed and thought, so far as mortal judgment may pronounce; is it fitting that a father in the church should leave a shadow on his memory, that may seem to blacken a life so pure? I pray you, my venerable brother, let not this thing be! Suffer us to be gladdened by your triumphant aspect, as you go to your reward. Before the veil of eternity be lifted, let me cast aside this black veil from your face!'

And thus speaking, the Reverend Mr. Clark bent forward to reveal the mystery of so many years. But, exerting a sudden energy, that made all the beholders stand aghast, Father Hooper snatched both his hands from beneath the bed-clothes, and pressed them strongly on the black veil, resolute to struggle, if the minister of Westbury would contend with a dying man.

'Never!' cried the veiled clergyman. 'On earth, never!'

'Dark old man!' exclaimed the affrighted minister, 'with what horrible crime upon your soul are you now passing to the judgment?'

Father Hooper's breath heaved; it rattled in his throat; but, with a mighty effort, grasping forward with his hands, he caught hold of life, and held it back till he should speak. He even raised himself in bed; and there he sat, shivering with the arms of death around him, while the black veil hung down, awful, at that last moment, in the gathered terrors of a life-time. And yet the faint, sad smile, so often there, now seemed to glimmer from its obscurity, and linger on Father Hooper's lips.

'Why do you tremble at me alone?' cried he, turning his veiled face round the circle of pale spectators. 'Tremble also at each other! Have men avoided me, and women shown no pity, and children screamed and fled, only for my black veil? What, but the mystery which it obscurely typifies, has made this piece of crape so awful? When the friend shows his inmost heart to his friend; the lover to his best-beloved; when man does not vainly shrink from the eye of his Creator, loathsomely treasuring up the secret of his sin; then deem me a monster, for the symbol beneath which I have lived, and die! I look around me, and, lo! on every visage a Black Veil!'

While his auditors shrank from one another, in mutual affright, Father Hooper fell back upon his pillow, a veiled corpse, with a faint smile lingering on the lips. Still veiled, they laid him in his coffin, and a veiled corpse they bore him to the grave. The grass of many years has sprung up and withered on that grave, the burial-stone is moss-grown, and good Mr. Hooper's face is dust; but awful is still the thought, that it mouldered beneath the Black Veil!

The Man of Adamant[†]

An Apologue[1]

In the old times of religious gloom and intolerance, lived Richard Digby, the gloomiest and most intolerant of a stern brotherhood. His plan of salvation was so narrow, that, like a plank in a tempestuous sea, it could avail no sinner but himself, who bestrode it triumphantly, and hurled anathemas against the wretches whom he saw struggling with the billows of eternal death. In his view of the matter, it was a most abominable crime—as, indeed, it is a great folly—for men to trust to their own strength, or even to grapple to any other fragment of the wreck, save this narrow plank, which, moreover, he took special care to keep out of their reach. In other words, as his creed was like no man's else, and being well pleased that Providence had intrusted him alone, of mortals, with the treasure of a true faith, Richard Digby determined to seclude himself to the sole and constant enjoyment of his happy fortune.

"And verily," thought he, "I deem it a chief condition of Heaven's mercy to myself, that I hold no communion with those abominable

---

† First published in 1836 in *The Token* (dated 1837), then in *The Snow-Image*, 1852. Richard Digby is an extreme example of those aberrant 17th-century Separatist Puritans who sanctified themselves according to exclusive doctrines of their own. The tale, however, is not known to have a historical basis.
1. "An allegorical story intended to convey a useful lesson" (*Oxford English Dictionary*). But the narrative technique in "The Man of Adamant" is more playful than one might expect to find in a didactic story.

myriads which it hath cast off to perish. Peradventure, were I to tarry longer in the tents of Kedar,[2] the gracious boon would be revoked, and I also be swallowed up in the deluge of wrath, or consumed in the storm of fire and brimstone, or involved in whatever new kind of ruin is ordained for the horrible perversity of this generation."

So Richard Digby took an axe, to hew space enough for a tabernacle in the wilderness, and some few other necessaries, especially a sword and gun, to smite and slay any intruder upon his hallowed seclusion; and plunged into the dreariest depths of the forest. On its verge, however, he paused a moment, to shake off the dust of his feet against the village where he had dwelt, and to invoke a curse on the meeting-house, which he regarded as a temple of heathen idolatry. He felt a curiosity, also, to see whether the fire and brimstone would not rush down from Heaven at once, now that the one righteous man had provided for his own safety. But, as the sunshine continued to fall peacefully on the cottages and fields, and the husbandmen labored and children played, and as there were many tokens of present happiness, and nothing ominous of a speedy judgment, he turned away, somewhat disappointed. The further he went, however, and the lonelier he felt himself, and the thicker the trees stood along his path, and the darker the shadow overhead, so much the more did Richard Digby exult. He talked to himself, as he strode onward; he read his Bible to himself, as he sat beneath the trees; and, as the gloom of the forest hid the blessed sky, I had almost added, that, at morning, noon, and eventide, he prayed to himself. So congenial was this mode of life to his disposition, that he often laughed to himself, but was displeased when an echo tossed him back the long, loud roar.

In this manner, he journeyed onward three days and two nights, and came, on the third evening, to the mouth of a cave, which, at first sight, reminded him of Elijah's cave at Horeb, though perhaps it more resembled Abraham's sepulchral cave, at Machpelah.[3] It entered into the heart of a rocky hill. There was so dense a veil of tangled foliage about it, that none but a sworn lover of gloomy recesses would have discovered the low arch of its entrance, or have dared to step within its vaulted chamber, where the burning eyes of a panther might encounter him. If Nature meant this remote and dismal cavern for the use of man, it could only be to bury in its gloom

---

2. East of Palestine, a dwelling place of Ishmaelites and alien to the Children of Israel. Digby remembers Psalms 120:5, "Woe is me, that I sojourn in Mesech, that I dwell in the tents of Kedar!"

3. Where Abraham and his family were buried. Elijah fled for refuge to a cave in Horeb, where the Lord spoke to him, and Elijah complained that he alone was left among the prophets—see 1 Kings 19:8–12.

the victims of a pestilence, and then to block up its mouth with stones, and avoid the spot forever after. There was nothing bright nor cheerful near it, except a bubbling fountain, some twenty paces off, at which Richard Digby hardly threw away a glance. But he thrust his head into the cave, shivered, and congratulated himself.

"The finger of Providence hath pointed my way!" cried he, aloud, while the tomb-like den returned a strange echo, as if some one within were mocking him. "Here my soul will be at peace; for the wicked will not find me, Here I can read the Scriptures, and be no more provoked with lying interpretations. Here I can offer up acceptable prayers, because my voice will not be mingled with the sinful supplications of the multitude. Of a truth, the only way to heaven leadeth through the narrow entrance of this cave,—and I alone have found it!"[4]

In regard to this cave, it was observable that the roof, so far as the imperfect light permitted it to be seen, was hung with substances resembling opaque icicles; for the damps of unknown centuries, dripping down continually, had become as hard as adamant; and wherever that moisture fell, it seemed to possess the power of converting what it bathed to stone. The fallen leaves and sprigs of foliage, which the wind had swept into the cave, and the little feathery shrubs, rooted near the threshold, were not wet with a natural dew, but had been embalmed by this wondrous process. And here I am put in mind that Richard Digby, before he withdrew himself from the world, was supposed by skilful physicians to have contracted a disease for which no remedy was written in their medical books. It was a deposition of calculous particles within his heart, caused by an obstructed circulation of the blood; and, unless a miracle should be wrought for him, there was danger that the malady might act on the entire substance of the organ, and change his fleshly heart to stone. Many, indeed, affirmed that the process was already near its consummation. Richard Digby, however, could never be convinced that any such direful work was going on within him; nor when he saw the sprigs of marble foliage, did his heart even throb the quicker, at the similitude suggested by these once tender herbs. It may be that this same insensibility was a symptom of the disease.

Be that as it might, Richard Digby was well contented with his sepulchral cave. So dearly did he love this congenial spot, that, instead of going a few paces to the bubbling spring for water, he allayed his thirst with now and then a drop of moisture from the roof, which, had it fallen anywhere but on his tongue, would have been congealed into a pebble. For a man predisposed to stoniness of

---

4. Digby perverts Matthew 7:14, "Strait is the gate, and narrow is the way, which leadeth unto life, and few there be that find it."

the heart, this surely was unwholesome liquor. But there he dwelt, for three days more, eating herbs and roots, drinking his own destruction, sleeping, as it were, in a tomb, and awaking to the solitude of death, yet esteeming this horrible mode of life as hardly inferior to celestial bliss. Perhaps superior; for, above the sky, there would be angels to disturb him. At the close of the third day, he sat in the portal of his mansion, reading the Bible aloud, because no other ear could profit by it, and reading it amiss, because the rays of the setting sun did not penetrate the dismal depth of shadow round about him, nor fall upon the sacred page. Suddenly, however, a faint gleam of light was thrown over the volume, and, raising his eyes, Richard Digby saw that a young woman stood before the mouth of the cave, and that the sunbeams bathed her white garment, which thus seemed to possess a radiance of its own.

"Good-evening, Richard," said the girl; "I have come from afar to find thee."

The slender grace and gentle loveliness of this young woman were at once recognized by Richard Digby. Her name was Mary Goffe. She had been a convert to his preaching of the word in England, before he yielded himself to that exclusive bigotry which now enfolded him with such an iron grasp that no other sentiment could reach his bosom. When he came a pilgrim to America, she had remained in her father's hall; but now, as it appeared, had crossed the ocean after him, impelled by the same faith that led other exiles hither, and perhaps by love almost as holy. What else but faith and love united could have sustained so delicate a creature, wandering thus far into the forest, with her golden hair dishevelled by the boughs, and her feet wounded by the thorns? Yet, weary and faint though she must have been, and affrighted at the dreariness of the cave, she looked on the lonely man with a mild and pitying expression, such as might beam from an angel's eyes, towards an afflicted mortal. But the recluse, frowning sternly upon her, and keeping his finger between the leaves of his half-closed Bible, motioned her away with his hand.

"Off!" cried he. "I am sanctified,[5] and thou art sinful. Away!"

"O, Richard," said she, earnestly, "I have come this weary way because I heard that a grievous distemper had seized upon thy heart; and a great Physician hath given me the skill to cure it. There is no other remedy than this which I have brought thee. Turn me not away,

---

5. According to the Shorter Catechism, the most familiar summary of Puritan doctrine throughout the colonial period, sanctified persons "are renewed in the whole Man, after the Image of God, & are enabled more & more to die unto Sin, & live unto Righteousness." Those who are not sanctified still live in sin.

therefore, nor refuse my medicine; for then must this dismal cave be thy sepulchre."

"Away!" replied Richard Digby, still with a dark frown. "My heart is in better condition than thine own. Leave me, earthly one; for the sun is almost set; and when no light reaches the door of the cave, then is my prayer-time."

Now, great as was her need, Mary Goffe did not plead with this stony-hearted man for shelter and protection, nor ask anything whatever for her own sake. All her zeal was for his welfare.

"Come back with me!" she exclaimed, clasping her hands,—"come back to thy fellow-men; for they need thee, Richard, and thou hast tenfold need of them. Stay not in this evil den; for the air is chill, and the damps are fatal; nor will any that perish within it ever find the path to heaven. Hasten hence, I entreat thee, for thine own soul's sake; for either the roof will fall upon thy head, or some other speedy destruction is at hand."

"Perverse woman!" answered Richard Digby, laughing aloud,— for he was moved to bitter mirth by her foolish vehemence,—"I tell thee that the path to heaven leadeth straight through this narrow portal where I sit. And, moreover, the destruction thou speakest of is ordained, not for this blessed cave, but for all other habitations of mankind, throughout the earth. Get thee hence speedily, that thou mayst have thy share!"

So saying, he opened his Bible again, and fixed his eyes intently on the page, being resolved to withdraw his thoughts from this child of sin and wrath, and to waste no more of his holy breath upon her. The shadow had now grown so deep, where he was sitting, that he made continual mistakes in what he read, converting all that was gracious and merciful to denunciations of vengeance and unutterable woe on every created being but himself. Mary Goffe, meanwhile, was leaning against a tree, beside the sepulchral cave, very sad, yet with something heavenly and ethereal in her unselfish sorrow. The light from the setting sun still glorified her form, and was reflected a little way within the darksome den, discovering so terrible a gloom that the maiden shuddered for its self-doomed inhabitant. Espying the bright fountain near at hand, she hastened thither, and scooped up a portion of its water, in a cup of birchen bark. A few tears mingled with the draught, and perhaps gave it all its efficacy. She then returned to the mouth of the cave, and knelt down at Richard Digby's feet.

"Richard," she said, with passionate fervor, yet a gentleness in all her passion, "I pray thee, by thy hope of heaven, and as thou wouldst not dwell in this tomb forever, drink of this hallowed water, be it but a single drop! Then, make room for me by thy side, and let us read together one page of that blessed volume,—and, lastly, kneel down with me and pray! Do this, and thy stony heart shall become softer than a babe's, and all be well."[6]

But Richard Digby, in utter abhorrence of the proposal, cast the Bible at his feet, and eyed her with such a fixed and evil frown, that he looked less like a living man than a marble statue, wrought by some dark-imagined sculptor to express the most repulsive mood that human features could assume. And, as his look grew even devilish, so, with an equal change, did Mary Goffe become more sad, more mild, more pitiful, more like a sorrowing angel. But, the more heavenly she was, the more hateful did she seem to Richard Digby, who at length raised his hand, and smote down the cup of hallowed water upon the threshold of the cave, thus rejecting the only medicine that could have cured his stony heart. A sweet perfume lingered in the air for a moment, and then was gone.

"Tempt me no more, accursed woman," exclaimed he, still with his marble frown, "lest I smite thee down also! What hast thou to do with my Bible?—what with my prayers?—what with my heaven?"

No sooner had he spoken these dreadful words, than Richard Digby's heart ceased to beat; while—so the legend says—the form of Mary Goffe melted into the last sunbeams, and returned from the sepulchral cave to heaven. For Mary Goffe had been buried in an English church-yard, months before; and either it was her ghost that haunted the wild forest, or else a dreamlike spirit, typifying pure Religion.

Above a century afterwards, when the trackless forest of Richard Digby's day had long been interspersed with settlements, the children of a neighboring farmer were playing at the foot of a hill. The trees, on account of the rude and broken surface of this acclivity, had never been felled, and were crowded so densely together as to hide all but a few rocky prominences, wherever their roots could grapple with the soil. A little boy and girl, to conceal themselves from their playmates, had crept into the deepest shade, where not only the darksome pines, but a thick veil of creeping plants suspended from an overhanging rock, combined to make a twilight at noonday, and almost a midnight at all other seasons. There the children hid themselves, and shouted, repeating the cry at intervals, till the whole party of pursuers were drawn thither, and pulling aside the matted foliage, let in a doubtful glimpse of daylight. But scarcely was this accomplished, when the little group uttered a simultaneous shriek, and tumbled headlong down the hill, making the best of their way homeward, without a second glance into the gloomy

---

6. Mary reminds Richard of the Lord's assurance to Israel in Ezekiel 36:26, "I will take away the stony heart out of your flesh, and I will give you an heart of flesh."

recess. Their father, unable to comprehend what had so startled them, took his axe, and, by felling one or two trees, and tearing away the creeping plants, laid the mystery open to the day. He had discovered the entrance of a cave, closely resembling the mouth of a sepulchre, within which sat the figure of a man, whose gesture and attitude warned the father and children to stand back, while his visage wore a most forbidding frown. This repulsive personage seemed to have been carved in the same gray stone that formed the walls and portal of the cave. On minuter inspection, indeed, such blemishes were observed, as made it doubtful whether the figure were really a statue, chiselled by human art, and somewhat worn and defaced by the lapse of ages, or a freak of Nature, who might have chosen to imitate, in stone, her usual handiwork of flesh. Perhaps it was the least unreasonable idea, suggested by this strange spectacle, that the moisture of the cave possessed a petrifying quality, which had thus awfully embalmed a human corpse.

There was something so frightful in the aspect of this Man of Adamant, that the farmer, the moment that he recovered from the fascination of his first gaze, began to heap stones into the mouth of the cavern. His wife, who had followed him to the hill, assisted her husband's efforts. The children, also, approached as near as they durst, with their little hands full of pebbles, and cast them on the pile. Earth was then thrown into the crevices, and the whole fabric overlaid with sods. Thus all traces of the discovery were obliterated, leaving only a marvellous legend, which grew wilder from one generation to another, as the children told it to their grandchildren, and they to their posterity, till few believed that there had ever been a cavern or a statue, where now they saw but a grassy patch on the shadowy hill-side. Yet, grown people avoid the spot, nor do children play there. Friendship, and Love, and Piety, all human and celestial sympathies, should keep aloof from that hidden cave; for there still sits, and, unless an earthquake crumble down the roof upon his head, shall sit forever, the shape of Richard Digby, in the attitude of repelling the whole race of mortals—not from heaven—but from the horrible loneliness of his dark, cold sepulchre!

Dr. Heidegger's Experiment[†]

That very singular man, old Dr. Heidegger, once invited four venerable friends to meet him in his study. There were three white-bearded

† First published in the *Knickerbocker, or New-York Monthly Magazine*, January 1837, then in *Twice-told Tales*, 1837. In the *Knickerbocker* it was called "The Fountain of Youth." Reprinted by permission of The Ohio State University Press.

gentlemen, Mr. Medbourne, Colonel Killigrew, and Mr. Gascoigne, and a withered gentlewoman, whose name was the Widow Wycherly. They were all melancholy old creatures, who had been unfortunate in life, and whose greatest misfortune it was, that they were not long ago in their graves. Mr. Medbourne, in the vigor of his age, had been a prosperous merchant, but had lost his all by a frantic speculation, and was now little better than a mendicant. Colonel Killigrew had wasted his best years, and his health and substance, in the pursuit of sinful pleasures, which had given birth to a brood of pains, such as the gout, and divers other torments of soul and body. Mr. Gascoigne was a ruined politician, a man of evil fame, or at least had been so, till time had buried him from the knowledge of the present generation, and made him obscure instead of infamous. As for the Widow Wycherly, tradition tells us that she was a great beauty in her day; but, for a long while past, she had lived in deep seclusion, on account of certain scandalous stories, which had prejudiced the gentry of the town against her. It is a circumstance worth mentioning, that each of these three old gentlemen, Mr. Medbourne, Colonel Killigrew, and Mr. Gascoigne, were early lovers of the Widow Wycherly, and had once been on the point of cutting each other's throats for her sake. And, before proceeding farther, I will merely hint, that Dr. Heidegger and all his four guests were sometimes thought to be a little beside themselves; as is not unfrequently the case with old people, when worried either by present troubles or woful recollections.

'My dear old friends,' said Dr. Heidegger, motioning them to be seated, 'I am desirous of your assistance in one of those little experiments with which I amuse myself here in my study.'

If all stories were true, Dr. Heidegger's study must have been a very curious place. It was a dim, old-fashioned chamber, festooned with cobwebs, and besprinkled with antique dust. Around the walls stood several oaken book-cases, the lower shelves of which were filled with rows of gigantic folios, and black-letter quartos, and the upper with little parchment covered duodecimos. Over the central book-case was a bronze bust of Hippocrates,[1] with which, according to some authorities, Dr. Heidegger was accustomed to hold consultations, in all difficult cases of his practice. In the obscurest corner of the room stood a tall and narrow oaken closet, with its door ajar, within which doubtfully appeared a skeleton. Between two of the book-cases hung a looking-glass, presenting its high and dusty plate within a tarnished gilt frame. Among many wonderful stories related of this mirror, it was fabled that the spirits of all the doctor's deceased patients dwelt within its verge, and would stare him in the face whenever he looked thitherward. The opposite side of the chamber

---

1. Greek physician (ca. 460–ca. 370 B.C.E.), recognized as the Father of Medicine.

was ornamented with the full length portrait of a young lady, arrayed in the faded magnificence of silk, satin, and brocade, and with a visage as faded as her dress. Above half a century ago, Dr. Heidegger had been on the point of marriage with this young lady; but, being affected with some slight disorder, she had swallowed one of her lover's prescriptions, and died on the bridal evening. The greatest curiosity of the study remains to be mentioned: it was a ponderous folio volume, bound in black leather, with massive silver clasps. There were no letters on the back, and nobody could tell the title of the book. But it was well known to be a book of magic; and once, when a chambermaid had lifted it, merely to brush away the dust, the skeleton had rattled in its closet, the picture of the young lady had stepped one foot upon the floor, and several ghastly faces had peeped forth from the mirror; while the brazen head of Hippocrates frowned, and said—'Forbear!'

Such was Dr. Heidegger's study. On the summer afternoon of our tale, a small round table, as black as ebony, stood in the centre of the room, sustaining a cut-glass vase, of beautiful form and elaborate workmanship. The sunshine came through the window, between the heavy festoons of two faded damask curtains, and fell directly across this vase; so that a mild splendor was reflected from it on the ashen visages of the five old people who sat around. Four champaigne glasses were also on the table.

'My dear old friends,' repeated Dr. Heidegger, 'may I reckon on your aid in performing an exceedingly curious experiment?'

Now Dr. Heidegger was a very strange old gentleman, whose eccentricity had become the nucleus for a thousand fantastic stories. Some of these fables, to my shame be it spoken, might possibly be traced back to mine own veracious self; and if any passages of the present tale should startle the reader's faith, I must be content to bear the stigma of a fiction-monger.

When the doctor's four guests heard him talk of his proposed experiment, they anticipated nothing more wonderful than the murder of a mouse in an air-pump, or the examination of a cobweb by the microscope, or some similar nonsense, with which he was constantly in the habit of pestering his intimates. But without waiting for a reply, Dr. Heidegger hobbled across the chamber, and returned with the same ponderous folio, bound in black leather, which common report affirmed to be a book of magic. Undoing the silver clasps, he opened the volume, and took from among its black-letter pages a rose, or what was once a rose, though now the green leaves and crimson petals had assumed one brownish hue, and the ancient flower seemed ready to crumble to dust in the doctor's hands.

'This rose,' said Dr. Heidegger, with a sigh, 'this same withered and crumbling flower, blossomed five-and-fifty years ago. It was given me by Sylvia Ward, whose portrait hangs yonder; and I meant to wear it in my bosom at our wedding. Five-and-fifty years it has been treasured between the leaves of this old volume. Now, would you deem it possible that this rose of half a century could ever bloom again?'

'Nonsense!' said the Widow Wycherly, with a peevish toss of her head. 'You might as well ask whether an old woman's wrinkled face could ever bloom again.'

'See!' answered Dr. Heidegger.

He uncovered the vase, and threw the faded rose into the water which it contained. At first, it lay lightly on the surface of the fluid, appearing to imbibe none of its moisture. Soon, however, a singular change began to be visible. The crushed and dried petals stirred, and assumed a deepening tinge of crimson, as if the flower were reviving from a deathlike slumber; the slender stalk and twigs of foliage became green; and there was the rose of half a century, looking as fresh as when Sylvia Ward had first given it to her lover. It was scarcely full-blown; for some of its delicate red leaves curled modestly around its moist bosom, within which two or three dew-drops were sparkling.

'That is certainly a very pretty deception,' said the doctor's friends; carelessly, however, for they had witnessed greater miracles at a conjurer's show: 'pray how was it effected?'

'Did you never hear of the "Fountain of Youth,"' asked Dr. Heidegger, 'which Ponce De Leon, the Spanish adventurer, went in search of, two or three centuries ago?'

'But did Ponce De Leon ever find it?' said the Widow Wycherly.

'No,' answered Dr. Heidegger, 'for he never sought it in the right place. The famous Fountain of Youth, if I am rightly informed, is situated in the southern part of the Floridian peninsula, not far from Lake Macaco.[2] Its source is overshadowed by several gigantic magnolias, which, though numberless centuries old, have been kept as fresh as violets, by the virtues of this wonderful water. An acquaintance of mine, knowing my curiosity in such matters, has sent me what you see in the vase.'

'Ahem!' said Colonel Killigrew, who believed not a word of the doctor's story: 'and what may be the effect of this fluid on the human frame?'

'You shall judge for yourself, my dear colonel,' replied Dr. Heidegger; 'and all of you, my respected friends, are welcome to so much of this admirable fluid, as may restore to you the bloom of youth. For

---

2. I.e., Lake Okeechobee, a large lake in south Florida bordering the Everglades. It was sometimes called Lake Macaco during the early 19th century.

my own part, having had much trouble in growing old, I am in no hurry to grow young again. With your permission, therefore, I will merely watch the progress of the experiment.'

While he spoke, Dr. Heidegger had been filling the four champaigne glasses with the water of the Fountain of Youth. It was apparently impregnated with an effervescent gas, for little bubbles were continually ascending from the depths of the glasses, and bursting in silvery spray at the surface. As the liquor diffused a pleasant perfume, the old people doubted not that it possessed cordial and comfortable properties; and, though utter skeptics as to its rejuvenescent power, they were inclined to swallow it at once. But Dr. Heidegger besought them to stay a moment.

'Before you drink, my respectable old friends,' said he, 'it would be well that, with the experience of a life-time to direct you, you should draw up a few general rules for your guidance, in passing a second time through the perils of youth. Think what a sin and shame it would be, if, with your peculiar advantages, you should not become patterns of virtue and wisdom to all the young people of the age!'

The doctor's four venerable friends made him no answer, except by a feeble and tremulous laugh; so very ridiculous was the idea, that, knowing how closely repentance treads behind the steps of error, they should ever go astray again.

'Drink, then,' said the doctor, bowing: 'I rejoice that I have so well selected the subjects of my experiment.'

With palsied hands, they raised the glasses to their lips. The liquor, if it really possessed such virtues as Dr. Heidegger imputed to it, could not have been bestowed on four human beings who needed it more wofully. They looked as if they had never known what youth or pleasure was, but had been the offspring of Nature's dotage, and always the gray, decrepit, sapless, miserable creatures, who now sat stooping round the doctor's table, without life enough in their souls or bodies to be animated even by the prospect of growing young again. They drank off the water, and replaced their glasses on the table.

Assuredly there was an almost immediate improvement in the aspect of the party, not unlike what might have been produced by a glass of generous wine, together with a sudden glow of cheerful sunshine, brightening over all their visages at once. There was a healthful suffusion on their cheeks, instead of the ashen hue that had made them look so corpselike. They gazed at one another, and fancied that some magic power had really begun to smooth away the deep and sad inscriptions which Father Time had been so long engraving on their brows. The Widow Wycherly adjusted her cap, for she felt almost like a woman again.

'Give us more of this wondrous water!' cried they, eagerly. 'We are younger—but we are still too old! Quick!—give us more!'

'Patience, patience!' quoth Dr. Heidegger, who sat watching the experiment, with philosophic coolness. 'You have been a long time growing old. Surely, you might be content to grow young in half an hour! But the water is at your service.'

Again he filled their glasses with the liquor of youth, enough of which still remained in the vase to turn half the old people in the city to the age of their own grand-children. While the bubbles were yet sparkling on the brim, the doctor's four guests snatched their glasses from the table, and swallowed the contents at a single gulp. Was it delusion! Even while the draught was passing down their throats, it seemed to have wrought a change on their whole systems. Their eyes grew clear and bright; a dark shade deepened among their silvery locks; they sat around the table, three gentlemen of middle age, and a woman, hardly beyond her buxom prime.

'My dear widow, you are charming!' cried Colonel Killigrew, whose eyes had been fixed upon her face, while the shadows of age were flitting from it like darkness from the crimson day-break.

The fair widow knew, of old, that Colonel Killigrew's compliments were not always measured by sober truth; so she started up and ran to the mirror, still dreading that the ugly visage of an old woman would meet her gaze. Meanwhile, the three gentlemen behaved in such a manner, as proved that the water of the Fountain of Youth possessed some intoxicating qualities; unless, indeed, their exhilaration of spirits were merely a lightsome dizziness, caused by the sudden removal of the weight of years. Mr. Gascoigne's mind seemed to run on political topics, but whether relating to the past, present, or future, could not easily be determined, since the same ideas and phrases have been in vogue these fifty years. Now he rattled forth full-throated sentences about patriotism, national glory, and the people's right; now he muttered some perilous stuff or other, in a sly and doubtful whisper, so cautiously that even his own conscience could scarcely catch the secret; and now, again, he spoke in measured accents, and a deeply deferential tone, as if a royal ear were listening to his well-turned periods. Colonel Killigrew all this time had been trolling forth a jolly bottle-song, and ringing his glass in symphony with the chorus, while his eyes wandered towards the buxom figure of the Widow Wycherly. On the other side of the table, Mr. Medbourne was involved in a calculation of dollars and cents, with which was strangely intermingled a project for supplying the East Indies with ice, by harnessing a team of whales to the polar icebergs.

As for the Widow Wycherly, she stood before the mirror, curtsey-
ing and simpering to her own image, and greeting it as the friend
whom she loved better than all the world beside. She thrust her
face close to the glass, to see whether some long-remembered wrin-
kle or crow's-foot had indeed vanished. She examined whether the
snow had so entirely melted from her hair, that the venerable cap
could be safely thrown aside. At last, turning briskly away, she came
with a sort of dancing step to the table.

'My dear old doctor,' cried she, 'pray favor me with another glass!'

'Certainly, my dear madam, certainly!' replied the complaisant
doctor; 'see! I have already filled the glasses.'

There, in fact, stood the four glasses, brim full of this wonderful
water, the delicate spray of which, as it effervesced from the surface, resembled the tremulous glitter of diamonds. It was now so
nearly sunset, that the chamber had grown duskier than ever; but
a mild and moon-like splendor gleamed from within the vase, and
rested alike on the four guests, and on the doctor's venerable figure. He sat in a high-backed, elaborately-carved, oaken arm-chair,
with a gray dignity of aspect that might have well befitted that very
Father Time, whose power had never been disputed, save by this
fortunate company. Even while quaffing the third draught of the
Fountain of Youth, they were almost awed by the expression of his
mysterious visage.

But, the next moment, the exhilarating gush of young life shot
through their veins. They were now in the happy prime of youth.
Age, with its miserable train of cares, and sorrows, and diseases,
was remembered only as the trouble of a dream, from which they
had joyously awoke. The fresh gloss of the soul, so early lost, and
without which the world's successive scenes had been but a gal-
lery of faded pictures, again threw its enchantment over all their
prospects. They felt like new-created beings, in a new-created
universe.

'We are young! We are young!' they cried, exultingly.

Youth, like the extremity of age, had effaced the strongly marked
characteristics of middle life, and mutually assimilated them all.
They were a group of merry youngsters, almost maddened with the
exuberant frolicksomeness of their years. The most singular effect
of their gayety was an impulse to mock the infirmity and decrepitude of which they had so lately been the victims. They laughed
loudly at their old-fashioned attire, the wide-skirted coats and
flapped waistcoats of the young men, and the ancient cap and gown
of the blooming girl. One limped across the floor, like a gouty grandfather; one set a pair of spectacles astride of his nose, and pretended
to pore over the black-letter pages of the book of magic; a third

seated himself in an arm-chair, and strove to imitate the venerable dignity of Dr. Heidegger. Then all shouted mirthfully, and leaped about the room. The Widow Wycherly—if so fresh a damsel could be called a widow—tripped up to the doctor's chair, with a mischievous merriment in her rosy face.

'Doctor, you dear old soul,' cried she, 'get up and dance with me!' And then the four young people laughed louder than ever, to think what a queer figure the poor old doctor would cut.

'Pray excuse me,' answered the doctor, quietly. 'I am old and rheumatic, and my dancing days were over long ago. But either of these gay young gentlemen will be glad of so pretty a partner.'

'Dance with me, Clara!' cried Colonel Killigrew.

'No, no, I will be her partner!' shouted Mr. Gascoigne.

'She promised me her hand, fifty years ago!' exclaimed Mr. Medbourne.

They all gathered round her. One caught both her hands in his passionate grasp—another threw his arm about her waist—the third buried his hand among the glossy curls that clustered beneath the widow's cap. Blushing, panting, struggling, chiding, laughing, her warm breath fanning each of their faces by turns, she strove to disengage herself, yet still remained in their triple embrace. Never was there a livelier picture of youthful rivalship, with bewitching beauty for the prize. Yet, by a strange deception, owing to the duskiness of the chamber, and the antique dresses which they still wore, the tall mirror is said to have reflected the figures of the three old, gray, withered grand-sires, ridiculously contending for the skinny ugliness of a shrivelled grand-dam.

But they were young: their burning passions proved them so. Inflamed to madness by the coquetry of the girl-widow, who neither granted nor quite withheld her favors, the three rivals began to interchange threatening glances. Still keeping hold of the fair prize, they grappled fiercely at one another's throats. As they struggled to and fro, the table was overturned, and the vase dashed into a thousand fragments. The precious Water of Youth flowed in a bright stream across the floor, moistening the wings of a butterfly, which, grown old in the decline of summer, had alighted there to die. The insect fluttered lightly through the chamber, and settled on the snowy head of Dr. Heidegger.

'Come, come, gentlemen!—come, Madam Wycherly,' exclaimed the doctor, 'I really must protest against this riot.'

They stood still, and shivered; for it seemed as if gray Time were calling them back from their sunny youth, far down into the chill and darksome vale of years. They looked at old Dr. Heidegger, who sat in his carved arm-chair, holding the rose of half a century, which he had rescued from among the fragments of the shattered vase. At the motion of his hand, the four rioters resumed their seats; the more readily, because their violent exertions had wearied them, youthful though they were.

'My poor Sylvia's rose!' ejaculated Dr. Heidegger, holding it in the light of the sunset clouds: 'it appears to be fading again.'

And so it was. Even while the party were looking at it, the flower continued to shrivel up, till it became as dry and fragile as when the doctor had first thrown it into the vase. He shook off the few drops of moisture which clung to its petals.

'I love it as well thus, as in its dewy freshness,' observed he, pressing the withered rose to his withered lips. While he spoke, the butterfly fluttered down from the doctor's snowy head, and fell upon the floor.

His guests shivered again. A strange chillness, whether of the body or spirit they could not tell, was creeping gradually over them all. They gazed at one another, and fancied that each fleeting moment snatched away a charm, and left a deepening furrow where none had been before. Was it an illusion? Had the changes of a life-time been crowded into so brief a space, and were they now four aged people, sitting with their old friend, Dr. Heidegger?

'Are we grown old again, so soon!' cried they, dolefully.

In truth, they had. The Water of Youth possessed merely a virtue more transient than that of wine. The delirium which it created had effervesced away. Yes! they were old again. With a shuddering impulse, that showed her a woman still, the widow clasped her skinny hands before her face, and wished that the coffin-lid were over it, since it could be no longer beautiful.

'Yes, friends, ye are old again,' said Dr. Heidegger; 'and lo! the Water of Youth is all lavished on the ground. Well—I bemoan it not; for if the fountain gushed at my very doorstep, I would not stoop to bathe my lips in it—no, though its delirium were for years instead of moments. Such is the lesson ye have taught me!'

But the doctor's four friends had taught no such lesson to themselves. They resolved forthwith to make a pilgrimage to Florida, and quaff at morning, noon, and night, from the Fountain of Youth.

Endicott and the Red Cross†

At noon of an autumnal day, more than two centuries ago, the English colors were displayed by the standard-bearer of the Salem trainband,[1] which had mustered for martial exercise under the orders of John Endicott. It was a period, when the religious exiles were accustomed often to buckle on their armor, and practise the handling of their weapons of war. Since the first settlement of New England, its prospects had never been so dismal. The dissensions between Charles the First and his subjects were then, and for several years afterwards, confined to the floor of Parliament. The measures of the King and ministry were rendered more tyrannically violent by an opposition, which had not yet acquired sufficient confidence in its own strength, to resist royal injustice with the sword. The bigoted and haughty primate, Laud, Archbishop of Canterbury, controlled the religious affairs of the realm, and was consequently invested with powers which might have wrought the utter ruin of the two Puritan colonies, Plymouth and Massachusetts. There is evidence on record, that our forefathers perceived their danger, but were resolved that their infant country should not fall without a struggle, even beneath the giant strength of the King's right arm.

Such was the aspect of the times, when the folds of the English banner, with the Red Cross in its field, were flung out over a company of Puritans. Their leader, the famous Endicott, was a man of stern and resolute countenance, the effect of which was heightened by a grizzled beard that swept the upper portion of his breastplate. This piece of armor was so highly polished, that the whole surrounding scene had its image in the glittering steel. The central object in the mirrored picture, was an edifice of humble architecture, with neither steeple nor bell to proclaim it,—what nevertheless it was,— the house of prayer. A token of the perils of the wilderness was seen in the grim head of a wolf, which had just been slain within the precincts of the town, and, according to the regular mode of claiming the bounty, was nailed on the porch of the meetinghouse. The blood

---

† First published in 1837 in *The Token* (dated 1838), then in *Twice-told Tales*, 2nd edition, 1842. The tale dramatizes an incident in the career of John Endicott, first governor of Massachusetts and "the Puritan of Puritans," as Hawthorne calls him in "The May-Pole of Merry Mount." One day in the autumn of 1634, Endicott, then a deputy official in the colonial government and in charge of the militia in Salem, cut the red cross out of the English banner belonging to the company of militia mustered before him. The English flag of the company was composed of the red cross of St. George on a white field. Though the rending of the cross was a rash deed and got Endicott in trouble with Boston authorities, many Puritans along with him regarded the ceremonial use of the cross as idolatrous and associated it with the Roman Catholic Church. Hawthorne altered the historical facts to point up Endicott's severity of temper. In 1634 Roger Williams was thirty, not sixty, and a Protestant zealot, not a mild-mannered compromiser. Rather than restraining Endicott, he influenced him to cut the cross out of the flag.
1. Militia.

was still plashing on the doorstep. There happened to be visible, at the same noontide hour, so many other characteristics of the times and manners of the Puritans, that we must endeavor to represent them in a sketch, though far less vividly than they were reflected in the polished breastplate of John Endicott.

In close vicinity to the sacred edifice appeared that important engine of Puritanic authority, the whipping-post,—with the soil around it well trodden by the feet of evil-doers, who had there been disciplined. At one corner of the meetinghouse was the pillory,[2] and at the other the stocks; and, by a singular good fortune for our sketch, the head of an Episcopalian and suspected Catholic was grotesquely encased in the former machine; while a fellow-criminal, who had boisterously quaffed a health to the King, was confined by the legs in the latter. Side by side, on the meetinghouse steps, stood a male and a female figure. The man was a tall, lean, haggard personification of fanaticism, bearing on his breast this label,—A WANTON GOSPELLER,—which betokened that he had dared to give interpretations of Holy Writ, unsanctioned by the infallible judgment of the civil and religious rulers. His aspect showed no lack of zeal to maintain his heterodoxies, even at the stake. The woman wore a cleft stick on her tongue, in appropriate retribution for having wagged that unruly member against the elders of the church; and her countenance and gestures gave much cause to apprehend, that, the moment the stick should be removed, a repetition of the offence would demand new ingenuity in chastising it.

The above-mentioned individuals had been sentenced to undergo their various modes of ignominy, for the space of one hour at noonday. But among the crowd were several, whose punishment would be life-long; some, whose ears had been cropt, like those of puppy-dogs; others, whose cheeks had been branded with the initials of their misdemeanors; one, with his nostrils slit and seared; and another, with a halter about his neck, which he was forbidden ever to take off, or to conceal beneath his garments. Methinks he must have been grievously tempted to affix the other end of the rope to some convenient beam or bough. There was likewise a young woman, with no mean share of beauty, whose doom it was to wear the letter A on the breast of her gown, in the eyes of all the world and her own children. And even her own children knew what that initial signified. Sporting with her infamy, the lost and desperate creature had embroidered the fatal token in scarlet cloth, with golden thread and the nicest art of needle-work; so that the capital A might have been thought to mean Admirable, or any thing rather than Adulteress.

2. Wooden framework on a post, with holes for head and hands, in which offenders were locked and exposed for public punishment.

Let not the reader argue, from any of these evidences of iniquity, that the times of the Puritans were more vicious than our own, when, as we pass along the very street of this sketch, we discern no badge of infamy on man or woman. It was the policy of our ancestors to search out even the most secret sins, and expose them to shame, without fear or favor, in the broadest light of the noonday sun. Were such the custom now, perchance we might find materials for a no less piquant sketch than the above.

Except the malefactors whom we have described, and the diseased or infirm persons, the whole male population of the town, between sixteen years and sixty, were seen in the ranks of the trainband. A few stately savages, in all the pomp and dignity of the primeval Indian, stood gazing at the spectacle. Their flint-headed arrows were but childish weapons, compared with the matchlocks of the Puritans, and would have rattled harmlessly against the steel caps and hammered iron breastplates, which enclosed each soldier in an individual fortress. The valiant John Endicott glanced with an eye of pride at his sturdy followers, and prepared to renew the martial toils of the day.

'Come, my stout hearts!' quoth he, drawing his sword. 'Let us show these poor heathen that we can handle our weapons like men of might. Well for them, if they put us not to prove it in earnest!'

The iron-breasted company straightened their line, and each man drew the heavy butt of his matchlock close to his left foot, thus awaiting the orders of the captain. But, as Endicott glanced right and left along the front, he discovered a personage at some little distance, with whom it behoved him to hold a parley. It was an elderly gentleman, wearing a black cloak and band, and a high-crowned hat, beneath which was a velvet skull-cap, the whole being the garb of a Puritan minister. This reverend person bore a staff, which seemed to have been recently cut in the forest, and his shoes were bemired, as if he had been travelling on foot through the swamps of the wilderness. His aspect was perfectly that of a pilgrim, heightened also by an apostolic dignity. Just as Endicott perceived him, he laid aside his staff, and stooped to drink at a bubbling fountain, which gushed into the sunshine about a score of yards from the corner of the meetinghouse. But, ere the good man drank, he turned his face heavenward in thankfulness, and then, holding back his gray beard with one hand, he scooped up his simple draught in the hollow of the other.

'What, ho! good Mr. Williams,' shouted Endicott. 'You are welcome back again to our town of peace. How does our worthy Governor Winthrop? And what news from Boston?'

'The Governor hath his health, worshipful Sir,' answered Roger Williams, now resuming his staff, and drawing near. 'And, for the news, here is a letter, which, knowing I was to travel hitherward today, his Excellency committed to my charge. Belike it contains tidings of much import; for a ship arrived yesterday from England.'

Mr. Williams, the minister of Salem, and of course known to all the spectators, had now reached the spot where Endicott was standing under the banner of his company, and put the Governor's epistle into his hand. The broad seal was impressed with Winthrop's coat of arms. Endicott hastily unclosed the letter, and began to read; while, as his eye passed down the page, a wrathful change came over his manly countenance. The blood glowed through it, till it seemed to be kindling with an internal heat; nor was it unnatural to suppose that his breastplate would likewise become red hot, with the angry fire of the bosom which it covered. Arriving at the conclusion, he shook the letter fiercely in his hand, so that it rustled as loud as the flag above his head.

'Black tidings these, Mr. Williams,' said he; 'blacker never came to New England. Doubtless you know their purport?'

'Yea, truly,' replied Roger Williams; 'for the Governor consulted, respecting this matter, with my brethren in the ministry at Boston; and my opinion was likewise asked. And his Excellency entreats you by me, that the news be not suddenly noised abroad, lest the people be stirred up unto some outbreak, and thereby give the King and the Archbishop a handle against us.'

'The Governor is a wise man,—a wise man, and a meek and moderate,' said Endicott, setting his teeth grimly. 'Nevertheless, I must do according to my own best judgment. There is neither man, woman, nor child in New England, but has a concern as dear as life in these tidings; and, if John Endicott's voice be loud enough, man, woman, and child shall hear them. Soldiers, wheel into a hollow square! Ho, good people! Here are news for one and all of you.'

The soldiers closed in around their captain; and he and Roger Williams stood together under the banner of the Red Cross; while the women and the aged men pressed forward, and the mothers held up their children to look Endicott in the face. A few taps of the drum gave signal for silence and attention.

'Fellow-soldiers,—fellow-exiles,' began Endicott, speaking under strong excitement, yet powerfully restraining it, 'wherefore did ye leave your native country? Wherefore, I say, have we left the green and fertile fields, the cottages, or, perchance, the old gray halls, where we were born and bred, the churchyards where our forefathers lie buried? Wherefore have we come hither to set up our own tombstones in a wilderness? A howling wilderness it is! The wolf and the bear meet us within halloo of our dwellings. The savage lieth in wait for us in the dismal shadow of the woods. The stubborn roots of the trees break our ploughshares, when we would till the earth.

Our children cry for bread, and we must dig in the sands of the sea-
shore to satisfy them. Wherefore, I say again, have we sought this
country of a rugged soil and wintry sky? Was it not for the enjoyment
of our civil rights? Was it not for liberty to worship God according to
our conscience?'

'Call you this liberty of conscience?' interrupted a voice on the
steps of the meetinghouse.

It was the Wanton Gospeller. A sad and quiet smile flitted across
the mild visage of Roger Williams.[3] But Endicott, in the excitement
of the moment, shook his sword wrathfully at the culprit,—an ominous gesture from a man like him.

'What hast thou to do with conscience, thou knave?' cried he. 'I
said, liberty to worship God, not license to profane and ridicule
him. Break not in upon my speech; or I will lay thee neck and heels
till this time tomorrow! Hearken to me, friends, nor heed that
accursed rhapsodist. As I was saying, we have sacrificed all things,
and have come to a land whereof the old world hath scarcely heard,
that we might make a new world unto ourselves, and painfully seek a
path from hence to Heaven. But what think ye now? This son of a
Scotch tyrant,—this grandson of a papistical and adulterous Scotch
woman,[4] whose death proved that a golden crown doth not always
save an anointed head from the block—'

'Nay, brother, nay,' interposed Mr. Williams; 'thy words are not
meet for a secret chamber, far less for a public street.'

'Hold thy peace, Roger Williams!' answered Endicott, imperi-
ously. 'My spirit is wiser than thine, for the business now in hand. I
tell ye, fellow-exiles, that Charles of England, and Laud, our bitterest persecutor, arch-priest of Canterbury, are resolute to pursue us
even hither. They are taking counsel, saith this letter, to send over a
governor-general, in whose breast shall be deposited all the law and
equity of the land. They are minded, also, to establish the idolatrous
forms of English Episcopacy; so that, when Laud shall kiss the
Pope's toe, as cardinal of Rome, he may deliver New England, bound
hand and foot, into the power of his master!'

3. Williams, though neither quiet nor mild, would have agreed with the Wanton Gospeller,
   not with Endicott. He held that "to punish a man for any matters of his conscience is
   persecution." When Endicott later turned against the banished Williams as a heretic,
   Williams wrote, "Are all the thousands and millions of consciences . . . fuell only for a
   prison, for a *whip*, for a *stake*, for a *Gallowes*? *Endicot, Endicot*, why huntest thou me?"
   (quoted in Sacvan Bercovitch, "Endicott's Breastplate," *Studies in Short Fiction* 4
   [1967]: 294).
4. Mary Stuart, Queen of Scots (1542–87), mother of James VI of Scotland, who later
   became James I of England. Mary Stuart lost her authority in Scotland because she
   alienated the Protestants and also married the supposed murderer of her husband. She
   escaped to England in 1567 but was made a royal prisoner and was executed in 1587
   after she had been for many years the center of Catholic intrigues to depose the Protestant Queen Elizabeth.

A deep groan from the auditors,—a sound of wrath, as well as fear and sorrow,—responded to this intelligence.

'Look ye to it, brethren,' resumed Endicott, with increasing energy. 'If this king and this arch-prelate have their will, we shall briefly behold a cross on the spire of this tabernacle which we have builded, and a high altar within its walls, with wax tapers burning round it at noonday. We shall hear the sacring-bell, and the voices of the Romish priests saying the mass. But think ye, Christian men, that these abominations may be suffered without a sword drawn? without a shot fired? without blood spilt, yea, on the very stairs of the pulpit? No,—be ye strong of hand, and stout of heart! Here we stand on our own soil, which we have bought with our goods, which we have won with our swords, which we have cleared with our axes, which we have tilled with the sweat of our brows, which we have sanctified with our prayers to the God that brought us hither! Who shall enslave us here? What have we to do with this mitred prelate,[5]—with this crowned king? What have we to do with England?'

Endicott gazed round at the excited countenances of the people, now full of his own spirit, and then turned suddenly to the standard-bearer, who stood close behind him.

'Officer, lower your banner!' said he.

The officer obeyed; and, brandishing his sword, Endicott thrust it through the cloth, and, with his left hand, rent the Red Cross completely out of the banner. He then waved the tattered ensign above his head.

'Sacrilegious wretch!' cried the high-churchman in the pillory, unable longer to restrain himself; 'thou hast rejected the symbol of our holy religion!'

'Treason, treason!' roared the royalist in the stocks. 'He hath defaced the King's banner!'

'Before God and man, I will avouch the deed,' answered Endicott. 'Beat a flourish, drummer!—shout, soldiers and people!—in honor of the ensign of New England. Neither Pope nor Tyrant hath part in it now!'

With a cry of triumph, the people gave their sanction to one of the boldest exploits which our history records. And, for ever honored be the name of Endicott! We look back through the mist of ages, and recognise, in the rending of the Red Cross from New England's banner, the first omen of that deliverance which our fathers consummated, after the bones of the stern Puritan had lain more than a century in the dust.

5. Archbishop Laud.

The Birthmark[†]

In the latter part of the last century there lived a man of science, an eminent proficient in every branch of natural philosophy, who not long before our story opens had made experience of a spiritual affinity more attractive than any chemical one. He had left his laboratory to the care of an assistant, cleared his fine countenance from the furnace smoke, washed the stain of acids from his fingers, and persuaded a beautiful woman to become his wife. In those days, when the comparatively recent discovery of electricity and other kindred mysteries of Nature seemed to open paths into the region of miracle, it was not unusual for the love of science to rival the love of woman in its depth and absorbing energy. The higher intellect, the imagination, the spirit, and even the heart might all find their congenial aliment in pursuits which, as some of their ardent votaries believed, would ascend from one step of powerful intelligence to another, until the philosopher should lay his hand on the secret of creative force and perhaps make new worlds for himself. We know not whether Aylmer possessed this degree of faith in man's ultimate control over Nature. He had devoted himself, however, too unreservedly to scientific studies ever to be weaned from them by any second passion. His love for his young wife might prove the stronger of the two; but it could only be by intertwining itself with his love of science and uniting the strength of the latter to his own.

Such a union accordingly took place, and was attended with truly remarkable consequences and a deeply impressive moral. One day, very soon after their marriage, Aylmer sat gazing at his wife with a trouble in his countenance that grew stronger until he spoke.

"Georgiana," said he, "has it never occurred to you that the mark upon your cheek might be removed?"

"No, indeed," said she, smiling; but, perceiving the seriousness of his manner, she blushed deeply. "To tell you the truth, it has been so often called a charm that I was simple enough to imagine it might be so."

"Ah, upon another face perhaps it might," replied her husband; "but never on yours. No, dearest Georgiana, you came so nearly perfect from the hand of Nature that this slightest possible defect, which we hesitate whether to term a defect or a beauty, shocks me, as being the visible mark of earthly imperfection."

"Shocks you, my husband!" cried Georgiana, deeply hurt; at first reddening with momentary anger, but then bursting into tears.

[†] First published in *The Pioneer*, March 1843, then in *Mosses from an Old Manse*, 1846.

"Then why did you take me from my mother's side? You cannot love what shocks you!"

To explain this conversation, it must be mentioned that in the centre of Georgiana's left cheek there was a singular mark, deeply interwoven, as it were, with the texture and substance of her face. In the usual state of her complexion—a healthy though delicate bloom—the mark wore a tint of deeper crimson, which imperfectly defined its shape amid the surrounding rosiness. When she blushed it gradually became more indistinct, and finally vanished amid the triumphant rush of blood that bathed the whole cheek with its brilliant glow. But if any shifting motion caused her to turn pale there was the mark again, a crimson stain upon the snow, in what Aylmer sometimes deemed an almost fearful distinctness. Its shape bore not a little similarity to the human hand, though of the smallest pygmy size. Georgiana's lovers were wont to say that some fairy at her birth hour had laid her tiny hand upon the infant's cheek, and left this impress there in token of the magic endowments that were to give her such sway over all hearts. Many a desperate swain would have risked life for the privilege of pressing his lips to the mysterious hand. It must not be concealed, however, that the impression wrought by this fairy sign manual varied exceedingly according to the difference of temperament in the beholders. Some fastidious persons—but they were exclusively of her own sex—affirmed that the bloody hand, as they chose to call it, quite destroyed the effect of Georgiana's beauty and rendered her countenance even hideous. But it would be as reasonable to say that one of those small blue stains which sometimes occur in the purest statuary marble would convert the Eve of Powers[1] to a monster. Masculine observers, if the birthmark did not heighten their admiration, contented themselves with wishing it away, that the world might possess one living specimen of ideal loveliness without the semblance of a flaw. After his marriage,—for he thought little or nothing of the matter before,—Aylmer discovered that this was the case with himself.

Had she been less beautiful,—if Envy's self could have found aught else to sneer at,—he might have felt his affection heightened by the prettiness of this mimic hand, now vaguely portrayed, now lost, now stealing forth again and glimmering to and fro with every pulse of emotion that throbbed within her heart; but, seeing her otherwise so perfect, he found this one defect grow more and more intolerable with every moment of their united lives. It was the fatal flaw of humanity which Nature, in one shape or another, stamps ineffaceably on all her productions, either to imply that they are temporary and finite, or that their perfection must be wrought by toil

---

1. Statue of Eve by Hiram Powers (1805–1873), American sculptor.

and pain. The crimson hand expressed the ineludible gripe in which mortality clutches the highest and purest of earthly mould, degrading them into kindred with the lowest, and even with the very brutes, like whom their visible frames return to dust. In this manner, selecting it as the symbol of his wife's liability to sin, sorrow, decay, and death, Aylmer's sombre imagination was not long in rendering the birthmark a frightful object, causing him more trouble and horror than ever Georgiana's beauty, whether of soul or sense, had given him delight.

At all the seasons which should have been their happiest he invariably, and without intending it, nay, in spite of a purpose to the contrary, reverted to this one disastrous topic. Trifling as it at first appeared, it so connected itself with innumerable trains of thought and modes of feeling that it became the central point of all. With the morning twilight Aylmer opened his eyes upon his wife's face and recognized the symbol of imperfection; and when they sat together at the evening hearth his eyes wandered stealthily to her cheek, and beheld, flickering with the blaze of the wood fire, the spectral hand that wrote mortality where he would fain have worshipped. Georgiana soon learned to shudder at his gaze. It needed but a glance with the peculiar expression that his face often wore to change the roses of her cheek into a deathlike paleness, amid which the crimson hand was brought strongly out, like a bas-relief of ruby on the whitest marble.[2]

Late one night, when the lights were growing dim so as hardly to betray the stain on the poor wife's cheek, she herself, for the first time, voluntarily took up the subject.

"Do you remember, my dear Aylmer," said she, with a feeble attempt at a smile, "have you any recollection, of a dream last night about this odious hand?"

"None! none whatever!" replied Aylmer, starting; but then he added, in a dry, cold tone, affected for the sake of concealing the real depth of his emotion, "I might well dream of it; for, before I fell asleep, it had taken a pretty firm hold of my fancy."

"And you did dream of it?" continued Georgiana, hastily; for she dreaded lest a gush of tears should interrupt what she had to say. "A terrible dream! I wonder that you can forget it. Is it possible to forget this one expression?—'It is in her heart now; we must have it out!' Reflect, my husband; for by all means I would have you recall that dream."

---

2. Sculpture in which a ruby figure projects slightly in "low relief" from a white marble background.

The mind is in a sad state when Sleep, the all-involving, cannot confine her spectres within the dim region of her sway, but suffers them to break forth, affrighting this actual life with secrets that perchance belong to a deeper one. Aylmer now remembered his dream. He had fancied himself with his servant Aminadab, attempting an operation for the removal of the birthmark; but the deeper went the knife, the deeper sank the hand, until at length its tiny grasp appeared to have caught hold of Georgiana's heart; whence, however, her husband was inexorably resolved to cut or wrench it away.

When the dream had shaped itself perfectly in his memory Aylmer sat in his wife's presence with a guilty feeling. Truth often finds its way to the mind close muffled in robes of sleep, and then speaks with uncompromising directness of matters in regard to which we practise an unconscious self-deception during our waking moments. Until now he had not been aware of the tyrannizing influence acquired by one idea over his mind, and of the lengths which he might find in his heart to go for the sake of giving himself peace.

"Aylmer," resumed Georgiana, solemnly, "I know not what may be the cost to both of us to rid me of this fatal birthmark. Perhaps its removal may cause cureless deformity; or it may be the stain goes as deep as life itself. Again: do we know that there is a possibility, on any terms, of unclasping the firm gripe of this little hand which was laid upon me before I came into the world?"

"Dearest Georgiana, I have spent much thought upon the subject," hastily interrupted Aylmer. "I am convinced of the perfect practicability of its removal."

"If there be the remotest possibility of it," continued Georgiana, "let the attempt be made, at whatever risk. Danger is nothing to me; for life, while this hateful mark makes me the object of your horror and disgust,—life is a burden which I would fling down with joy. Either remove this dreadful hand, or take my wretched life! You have deep science. All the world bears witness of it. You have achieved great wonders. Cannot you remove this little, little mark, which I cover with the tips of two small fingers? Is this beyond your power, for the sake of your own peace, and to save your poor wife from madness?"

"Noblest, dearest, tenderest wife," cried Aylmer, rapturously, "doubt not my power. I have already given this matter the deepest thought—thought which might almost have enlightened me to create a being less perfect than yourself. Georgiana, you have led me deeper than ever into the heart of science. I feel myself fully competent to render this dear cheek as faultless as its fellow; and then, most beloved, what will be my triumph when I shall have corrected what Nature left imperfect in her fairest work! Even Pygmalion,[3] when his sculptured woman assumed life, felt not greater ecstasy than mine will be."

"It is resolved, then," said Georgiana, faintly smiling. "And, Aylmer, spare me not, though you should find the birthmark take refuge in my heart at last."

Her husband tenderly kissed her cheek—her right cheek—not that which bore the impress of the crimson hand.

The next day Aylmer apprised his wife of a plan that he had formed whereby he might have opportunity for the intense thought and constant watchfulness which the proposed operation would require; while Georgiana, likewise, would enjoy the perfect repose essential to its success. They were to seclude themselves in the extensive apartments occupied by Aylmer as a laboratory, and where, during his toilsome youth, he had made discoveries in the elemental powers of Nature that had roused the admiration of all the learned societies in Europe. Seated calmly in this laboratory, the pale philosopher had investigated the secrets of the highest cloud region and of the profoundest mines; he had satisfied himself of the causes that kindled and kept alive the fires of the volcano; and had explained the mystery of fountains, and how it is that they gush forth, some so bright and pure, and others with such rich medicinal virtues, from the dark bosom of the earth. Here, too, at an earlier period, he had studied the wonders of the human frame, and attempted to fathom the very process by which Nature assimilates all her precious influences from earth and air, and from the spiritual world, to create and foster man, her masterpiece. The latter pursuit, however, Aylmer had long laid aside in unwilling recognition of the truth—against which all seekers sooner or later stumble—that our great creative Mother, while she amuses us with apparently working in the broadest sunshine, is yet severely careful to keep her own secrets, and, in spite of her pretended openness, shows us nothing but results. She permits us, indeed, to mar, but seldom to mend, and, like a jealous patentee, on no account to make. Now, however, Aylmer resumed these half-forgotten investigations; not, of course, with such hopes or wishes as first suggested them; but because they involved much physiological truth and lay in the path of his proposed scheme for the treatment of Georgiana.

As he led her over the threshold of the laboratory, Georgiana was cold and tremulous. Aylmer looked cheerfully into her face, with intent to reassure her, but was so startled with the intense glow of

---

3. Legendary Greek sculptor who carved an ivory statue of a maiden, fell in love with it, and prayed successfully to Aphrodite to bring it to life. See Ovid, *Metamorphoses* 10.

the birthmark upon the whiteness of her cheek that he could not restrain a strong convulsive shudder. His wife fainted.

"Aminadab![4] Aminadab! shouted Aylmer, stamping violently on the floor.

Forthwith there issued from an inner apartment a man of low stature, but bulky frame, with shaggy hair hanging about his visage, which was grimed with the vapors of the furnace. This personage had been Aylmer's underworker during his whole scientific career, and was admirably fitted for that office by his great mechanical readiness, and the skill with which, while incapable of comprehending a single principle, he executed all the details of his master's experiments. With his vast strength, his shaggy hair, his smoky aspect, and the indescribable earthiness that incrusted him, he seemed to represent man's physical nature; while Aylmer's slender figure, and pale, intellectual face, were no less apt a type of the spiritual element.

"Throw open the door of the boudoir, Aminadab," said Aylmer, "and burn a pastil."[5]

"Yes, master," answered Aminadab, looking intently at the lifeless form of Georgiana; and then he muttered to himself, "If she were my wife, I'd never part with that birthmark."

When Georgiana recovered consciousness she found herself breathing an atmosphere of penetrating fragrance, the gentle potency of which had recalled her from her deathlike faintness. The scene around her looked like enchantment. Aylmer had converted those smoky, dingy, sombre rooms, where he had spent his brightest years in recondite pursuits, into a series of beautiful apartments not unfit to be the secluded abode of a lovely woman. The walls were hung with gorgeous curtains, which imparted the combination of grandeur and grace that no other species of adornment can achieve; and, as they fell from the ceiling to the floor, their rich and ponderous folds, concealing all angles and straight lines, appeared to shut in the scene from infinite space. For aught Georgiana knew, it might be a pavilion among the clouds. And Aylmer, excluding the sunshine, which would have interfered with his chemical processes, had supplied its place with perfumed lamps, emitting flames of various hue, but all uniting in a soft, impurpled radiance. He now knelt by his wife's side, watching her earnestly, but without alarm; for he was confident in his science, and felt that he could draw a magic circle round her within which no evil might intrude.

---

4. A common biblical name, that of a descendant of David in Matthew 1:4, for example. But also "bad anima" spelled backward.
5. Paste containing aromatic substances used as a disinfectant.

"Where am I? Ah, I remember," said Georgiana, faintly; and she placed her hand over her cheek to hide the terrible mark from her husband's eyes.

"Fear not, dearest!" exclaimed he. "Do not shrink from me! Believe me, Georgiana, I even rejoice in this single imperfection, since it will be such a rapture to remove it."

"O, spare me!" sadly replied his wife. "Pray do not look at it again. I never can forget that convulsive shudder."

In order to soothe Georgiana, and, as it were, to release her mind from the burden of actual things, Aylmer now put in practice some of the light and playful secrets which science had taught him among its profounder lore. Airy figures, absolutely bodiless ideas, and forms of unsubstantial beauty came and danced before her, imprinting their momentary footsteps on beams of light. Though she had some indistinct idea of the method of these optical phenomena, still the illusion was almost perfect enough to warrant the belief that her husband possessed sway over the spiritual world. Then again, when she felt a wish to look forth from her seclusion, immediately, as if her thoughts were answered, the procession of external existence flitted across a screen. The scenery and the figures of actual life were perfectly represented, but with that bewitching yet indescribable difference which always makes a picture, an image, or a shadow so much more attractive than the original. When wearied of this, Aylmer bade her cast her eyes upon a vessel containing a quantity of earth. She did so, with little interest at first; but was soon startled to perceive the germ of a plant shooting upward from the soil. Then came the slender stalk; the leaves gradually unfolded themselves; and amid them was a perfect and lovely flower.

"It is magical!" cried Georgiana. "I dare not touch it."

"Nay, pluck it," answered Aylmer,—"pluck it, and inhale its brief perfume while you may. The flower will wither in a few moments and leave nothing save its brown seed vessels; but thence may be perpetuated a race as ephemeral as itself."

But Georgiana had no sooner touched the flower than the whole plant suffered a blight, its leaves turning coal-black as if by the agency of fire.

"There was too powerful a stimulus," said Aylmer, thoughtfully.

To make up for this abortive experiment, he proposed to take her portrait by a scientific process of his own invention. It was to be effected by rays of light striking upon a polished plate of metal. Georgiana assented; but, on looking at the result, was affrighted to find the features of the portrait blurred and indefinable; while the minute figure of a hand appeared where the cheek should have been. Aylmer snatched the metallic plate and threw it into a jar of corrosive acid.

Soon, however, he forgot these mortifying failures. In the intervals of study and chemical experiment he came to her flushed and exhausted, but seemed invigorated by her presence, and spoke in glowing language of the resources of his art. He gave a history of the long dynasty of the alchemists, who spent so many ages in quest of the universal solvent by which the golden principle might be elicited from all things vile and base. Aylmer appeared to believe that, by the plainest scientific logic, it was altogether within the limits of possibility to discover this long-sought medium; "but," he added, "a philosopher who should go deep enough to acquire the power would attain too lofty a wisdom to stoop to the exercise of it." Not less singular were his opinions in regard to the elixir vitae. He more than intimated that it was at his option to concoct a liquid that should prolong life for years, perhaps interminably; but that it would produce a discord in Nature which all the world, and chiefly the quaffer of the immortal nostrum, would find cause to curse.

"Aylmer, are you in earnest?" asked Georgiana, looking at him with amazement and fear. "It is terrible to possess such power, or even to dream of possessing it."

"O, do not tremble, my love," said her husband. "I would not wrong either you or myself by working such inharmonious effects upon our lives; but I would have you consider how trifling, in comparison, is the skill requisite to remove this little hand."

At the mention of the birthmark, Georgiana, as usual, shrank as if a redhot iron had touched her cheek.

Again Aylmer applied himself to his labors. She could hear his voice in the distant furnace room giving directions to Aminadab, whose harsh, uncouth, misshapen tones were audible in response, more like the grunt or growl of a brute than human speech. After hours of absence, Aylmer reappeared and proposed that she should now examine his cabinet of chemical products and natural treasures of the earth. Among the former he showed her a small vial, in which, he remarked, was contained a gentle yet most powerful fragrance, capable of impregnating all the breezes that blow across a kingdom. They were of inestimable value, the contents of that little vial; and, as he said so, he threw some of the perfume into the air and filled the room with piercing and invigorating delight.

"And what is this?" asked Georgiana, pointing to a small crystal globe containing a gold-colored liquid. "It is so beautiful to the eye that I could imagine it the elixir of life."

"In one sense it is," replied Aylmer; "or rather, the elixir of immortality. It is the most precious poison that ever was concocted in this world. By its aid I could apportion the lifetime of any mortal at whom you might point your finger. The strength of the dose would determine whether he were to linger out years, or drop dead in the midst of a breath. No king on his guarded throne could keep his life if I, in my private station, should deem that the welfare of millions justified me in depriving him of it."

"Why do you keep such a terrific drug?" inquired Georgiana in horror.

"Do not mistrust me, dearest," said her husband, smiling; "its virtuous potency is yet greater than its harmful one. But see! here is a powerful cosmetic. With a few drops of this in a vase of water, freckles may be washed away as easily as the hands are cleansed. A stronger infusion would take the blood out of the cheek, and leave the rosiest beauty a pale ghost."

"Is it with this lotion that you intend to bathe my cheek?" asked Georgiana, anxiously.

"O, no," hastily replied her husband; "this is merely superficial. Your case demands a remedy that shall go deeper."

In his interviews with Georgiana, Aylmer generally made minute inquiries as to her sensations, and whether the confinement of the rooms and the temperature of the atmosphere agreed with her. These questions had such a particular drift that Georgiana began to conjecture that she was already subjected to certain physical influences, either breathed in with the fragrant air or taken with her food. She fancied likewise, but it might be altogether fancy, that there was a stirring up of her system—a strange, indefinite sensation creeping through her veins, and tingling, half painfully, half pleasurably, at her heart. Still, whenever she dared to look into the mirror, there she beheld herself pale as a white rose and with the crimson birthmark stamped upon her cheek. Not even Aylmer now hated it so much as she.

To dispel the tedium of the hours which her husband found it necessary to devote to the processes of combination and analysis, Georgiana turned over the volumes of his scientific library. In many dark old tomes she met with chapters full of romance and poetry. They were the works of the philosophers of the middle ages, such as Albertus Magnus, Cornelius Agrippa, Paracelsus, and the famous friar who created the prophetic Brazen Head.[6] All these antique naturalists stood in advance of their centuries, yet were imbued with some of their credulity, and therefore were believed, and perhaps imagined themselves to have acquired from the investigation of Nature a power above Nature, and from physics a sway over the spiritual world. Hardly less curious and imaginative were the early

---

6. I.e., Roger Bacon (ca. 1214–1294), English scientist, alchemist, and theologian. He was said to have constructed a brazen head that uttered mysterious prophecies. Albertus Magnus (ca. 1206–1280), teacher of Thomas Aquinas and investigator of the combination of metals. Cornelius Agrippa (ca. 1486–1535), German apologist for magic. Paracelsus (ca. 1493–1541), Swiss physician and alchemist.

volumes of the Transactions of the Royal Society,[7] in which the members, knowing little of the limits of natural possibility, were continually recording wonders or proposing methods whereby wonders might be wrought.

But, to Georgiana, the most engrossing volume was a large folio from her husband's own hand, in which he had recorded every experiment of his scientific career, its original aim, the methods adopted for its development, and its final success or failure, with the circumstances to which either event was attributable. The book, in truth, was both the history and emblem of his ardent, ambitious, imaginative, yet practical and laborious life. He handled physical details as if there were nothing beyond them; yet spiritualized them all and redeemed himself from materialism by his strong and eager aspiration towards the infinite. In his grasp the veriest clod of earth assumed a soul. Georgiana, as she read, reverenced Aylmer and loved him more profoundly than ever, but with a less entire dependence on his judgment than heretofore. Much as he had accomplished, she could not but observe that his most splendid successes were almost invariably failures, if compared with the ideal at which he aimed. His brightest diamonds were the merest pebbles, and felt to be so by himself, in comparison with the inestimable gems which lay hidden beyond his reach. The volume, rich with achievements that had won renown for its author, was yet as melancholy a record as ever mortal hand had penned. It was the sad confession and continual exemplification of the shortcomings of the composite man, the spirit burdened with clay and working in matter, and of the despair that assails the higher nature at finding itself so miserably thwarted by the earthly part. Perhaps every man of genius, in whatever sphere, might recognize the image of his own experience in Aylmer's journal.

So deeply did these reflections affect Georgiana that she laid her face upon the open volume and burst into tears. In this situation she was found by her husband.

"It is dangerous to read in a sorcerer's books," said he with a smile, though his countenance was uneasy and displeased. "Georgiana, there are pages in that volume which I can scarcely glance over and keep my senses. Take heed lest it prove as detrimental to you."

"It has made me worship you more than ever," said she.

"Ah, wait for this one success," rejoined he, "then worship me if you will. I shall deem myself hardly unworthy of it. But come, I have sought you for the luxury of your voice. Sing to me, dearest."

.

---

7. Society founded in England in the 1660s. In its early years it stimulated research into all manner of scientific subjects and fostered experiments both useful and eccentric.

So she poured out the liquid music of her voice to quench the thirst of his spirit. He then took his leave with a boyish exuberance of gayety, assuring her that her seclusion would endure but a little longer, and that the result was already certain. Scarcely had he departed when Georgiana felt irresistibly impelled to follow him. She had forgotten to inform Aylmer of a symptom which for two or three hours past had begun to excite her attention. It was a sensation in the fatal birthmark, not painful, but which induced a restlessness throughout her system. Hastening after her husband, she intruded for the first time into the laboratory.

The first thing that struck her eye was the furnace, that hot and feverish worker, with the intense glow of its fire, which by the quantities of soot clustered above it seemed to have been burning for ages. There was a distilling apparatus in full operation. Around the room were retorts, tubes, cylinders, crucibles, and other apparatus of chemical research. An electrical machine stood ready for immediate use. The atmosphere felt oppressively close, and was tainted with gaseous odors which had been tormented forth by the processes of science. The severe and homely simplicity of the apartment, with its naked walls and brick pavement, looked strange, accustomed as Georgiana had become to the fantastic elegance of her boudoir. But what chiefly, indeed almost solely, drew her attention, was the aspect of Aylmer himself.

He was pale as death, anxious and absorbed, and hung over the furnace as if it depended upon his utmost watchfulness whether the liquid which it was distilling should be the draught of immortal happiness or misery. How different from the sanguine and joyous mien that he had assumed for Georgiana's encouragement!

"Carefully now, Aminadab; carefully, thou human machine; carefully, thou man of clay," muttered Aylmer, more to himself than his assistant. "Now, if there be a thought too much or too little, it is all over."

"Ho! ho!" mumbled Aminadab. "Look, master! look!"

Aylmer raised his eyes hastily, and at first reddened, then grew paler than ever, on beholding Georgiana. He rushed towards her and seized her arm with a gripe that left the print of his fingers upon it.

"Why do you come hither? Have you no trust in your husband?" cried he, impetuously. "Would you throw the blight of that fatal birthmark over my labors? It is not well done. Go, prying woman! go!"

"Nay, Aylmer," said Georgiana with the firmness of which she possessed no stinted endowment, "it is not you that have a right to complain. You mistrust your wife; you have concealed the anxiety with which you watch the development of this experiment. Think not so unworthily of me, my husband. Tell me all the risk we run, and fear not that I shall shrink; for my share in it is far less than your own."

"No, no, Georgiana!" said Aylmer, impatiently; "it must not be."

"I submit," replied she, calmly. "And, Aylmer, I shall quaff whatever draught you bring me; but it will be on the same principle that would induce me to take a dose of poison if offered by your hand."

"My noble wife," said Aylmer, deeply moved, "I knew not the height and depth of your nature until now. Nothing shall be concealed. Know, then, that this crimson hand, superficial as it seems, has clutched its grasp into your being with a strength of which I had no previous conception. I have already administered agents powerful enough to do aught except to change your entire physical system. Only one thing remains to be tried. If that fail us we are ruined."

"Why did you hesitate to tell me this?" asked she.

"Because, Georgiana," said Aylmer, in a low voice, "there is danger."

"Danger? There is but one danger—that this horrible stigma shall be left upon my cheek!" cried Georgiana. "Remove it, remove it, whatever be the cost, or we shall both go mad!"

"Heaven knows your words are too true," said Aylmer, sadly. "And now, dearest, return to your boudoir. In a little while all will be tested."

He conducted her back and took leave of her with a solemn tenderness which spoke far more than his words how much was now at stake. After his departure Georgiana became rapt in musings. She considered the character of Aylmer and did it completer justice than at any previous moment. Her heart exulted, while it trembled, at his honorable love—so pure and lofty that it would accept nothing less than perfection nor miserably make itself contented with an earthlier nature than he had dreamed of. She felt how much more precious was such a sentiment than that meaner kind which would have borne with the imperfection for her sake, and have been guilty of treason to holy love by degrading its perfect idea to the level of the actual; and with her whole spirit she prayed that, for a single moment, she might satisfy his highest and deepest conception. Longer than one moment she well knew it could not be; for his spirit was ever on the march, ever ascending, and each instant required something that was beyond the scope of the instant before.

The sound of her husband's footsteps aroused her. He bore a crystal goblet containing a liquor colorless as water, but bright enough to be the draught of immortality. Aylmer was pale; but it seemed rather the consequence of a highly-wrought state of mind and tension of spirit than of fear or doubt.

"The concoction of the draught has been perfect," said he, in answer to Georgiana's look. "Unless all my science have deceived me, it cannot fail."

"Save on your account, my dearest Aylmer," observed his wife, "I might wish to put off this birthmark of mortality by relinquishing mortality itself in preference to any other mode. Life is but a sad possession to those who have attained precisely the degree of moral advancement at which I stand. Were I weaker and blinder, it might be happiness. Were I stronger, it might be endured hopefully. But, being what I find myself, methinks I am of all mortals the most fit to die."

"You are fit for heaven without tasting death!" replied her husband. "But why do we speak of dying? The draught cannot fail. Behold its effect upon this plant."

On the window seat there stood a geranium diseased with yellow blotches which had overspread all its leaves. Aylmer poured a small quantity of the liquid upon the soil in which it grew. In a little time, when the roots of the plant had taken up the moisture, the unsightly blotches began to be extinguished in a living verdure.

"There needed no proof," said Georgiana, quietly. "Give me the goblet. I joyfully stake all upon your word."

"Drink, then, thou lofty creature!" exclaimed Aylmer, with fervid admiration. "There is no taint of imperfection on thy spirit. Thy sensible frame, too, shall soon be all perfect."

She quaffed the liquid and returned the goblet to his hand.

"It is grateful," said she, with a placid smile. "Methinks it is like water from a heavenly fountain; for it contains I know not what of unobtrusive fragrance and deliciousness. It allays a feverish thirst that had parched me for many days. Now, dearest, let me sleep. My earthly senses are closing over my spirit like the leaves around the heart of a rose at sunset."

She spoke the last words with a gentle reluctance, as if it required almost more energy than she could command to pronounce the faint and lingering syllables. Scarcely had they loitered through her lips ere she was lost in slumber. Aylmer sat by her side, watching her aspect with the emotions proper to a man the whole value of whose existence was involved in the process now to be tested. Mingled with this mood, however, was the philosophic investigation characteristic of the man of science. Not the minutest symptom escaped him. A heightened flush of the cheek, a slight irregularity of breath, a quiver of the eyelid, a hardly perceptible tremor through the frame,—such were the details which, as the moments passed, he wrote down in his folio volume. Intense thought had set its stamp upon every previous page of that volume; but the thoughts of years were all concentrated upon the last.

While thus employed, he failed not to gaze often at the fatal hand, and not without a shudder. Yet once, by a strange and unaccountable impulse, he pressed it with his lips. His spirit recoiled, however, in the very act; and Georgiana, out of the midst of her deep sleep, moved uneasily and murmured as if in remonstrance. Again Aylmer resumed his watch. Nor was it without avail. The crimson hand, which at first had been strongly visible upon the marble paleness of Georgiana's cheek, now grew more faintly outlined. She remained not less pale than ever; but the birthmark, with every breath that came and went, lost somewhat of its former distinctness. Its presence had been awful; its departure was more awful still. Watch the stain of the rainbow fading out of the sky, and you will know how that mysterious symbol passed away. *metaphor*

"By Heaven! it is well nigh gone!" said Aylmer to himself, in almost irrepressible ecstasy. "I can scarcely trace it now. Success! success! And now it is like the faintest rose color. The slightest flush of blood across her cheek would overcome it. But she is so pale!"

He drew aside the window curtain and suffered the light of natural day to fall into the room and rest upon her cheek. At the same time he heard a gross, hoarse chuckle, which he had long known as his servant Aminadab's expression of delight.

"Ah, clod! ah, earthly mass!" cried Aylmer, laughing in a sort of frenzy, "you have served me well! Matter and spirit—earth and heaven—have both done their part in this! Laugh, thing of the senses! You have earned the right to laugh."

These exclamations broke Georgiana's sleep. She slowly unclosed her eyes and gazed into the mirror which her husband had arranged for that purpose. A faint smile flitted over her lips when she recognized how barely perceptible was now that crimson hand which had once blazed forth with such disastrous brilliancy as to scare away all their happiness. But then her eyes sought Aylmer's face with a trouble and anxiety that he could by no means account for.

"My poor Aylmer!" murmured she.

"Poor? Nay, richest, happiest, most favored!" exclaimed he. "My peerless bride, it is successful! You are perfect!"

"My poor Aylmer," she repeated, with a more than human tenderness, "you have aimed loftily; you have done nobly. Do not repent that, with so high and pure a feeling, you have rejected the best that earth could offer. Aylmer, dearest Aylmer, I am dying!"

Alas! it was too true! The fatal hand had grappled with the mystery of life, and was the bond by which an angelic spirit kept itself in union with a mortal frame. As the last crimson tint of the birth-mark—that sole token of human imperfection—faded from her cheek, the parting breath of the now perfect woman passed into the atmosphere, and her soul, lingering a moment near her husband, took its heavenward flight. Then a hoarse, chuckling laugh was heard again! Thus ever does the gross fatality of earth exult in its invariable triumph over the immortal essence which, in this dim sphere of half development, demands the completeness of a higher state. Yet, had Aylmer reached a profounder wisdom, he need not thus have flung away the happiness which would have woven his mortal life of the selfsame texture with the celestial. The momentary circumstance was too strong for him; he failed to look beyond the shadowy scope of time, and, living once for all in eternity, to find the perfect future in the present.

The Celestial Rail-road†

Not a great while ago, passing through the gate of dreams, I visited that region of the earth in which lies the famous city of Destruction. It interested me much to learn, that, by the public spirit of some of the inhabitants, a rail-road has recently been established between this populous and flourishing town, and the Celestial City.[1] Having a little time upon my hands, I resolved to gratify a liberal curiosity by making a trip thither. Accordingly, one fine morning, after paying my bill at the hotel, and directing the porter to stow my luggage behind a coach, I took my seat in the vehicle, and set out for the Station House. It was my good fortune to enjoy the company of a gentleman— one Mr. Smooth-it-away—who, though he had never actually visited the Celestial City, yet seemed as well acquainted with its laws, customs, policy, and statistics, as with those of the city of Destruction, of which he was a native townsman. Being, moreover, a director of the rail-road corporation, and one of its largest stockholders, he had it in his power to give me all desirable information respecting that praiseworthy enterprise.

Our coach rattled out of the city, and, at a short distance from its outskirts, passed over a bridge, of elegant construction, but somewhat too slight, as I imagined, to sustain any considerable weight. On both sides lay an extensive quagmire, which could not have been more disagreeable either to sight or smell, had all the kennels of the earth emptied their pollution there.

---

† First published in the *Democratic Review*, May 1843, then in *Mosses from an Old Manse*, 1846; reprinted often in newspapers after first publication. Reprinted by permission of The Ohio State University Press. For his satirical sketch, Hawthorne reworks and speeds up the plot of John Bunyan's *Pilgrim's Progress* (1678), a book familiar to most American and British readers in the 19th century.
1. In *The Pilgrim's Progress*, Bunyan's pilgrim-hero Christian leaves his home in the City of Destruction, meets many difficulties and temptations on his arduous journey, and finally arrives at the Celestial City, where he and his companion Hopeful "enter into the joy of our Lord."

"This," remarked Mr. Smooth-it-away, "is the famous Slough of Despond[2]—a disgrace to all the neighborhood; and the greater, that it might so easily be converted into firm ground."

"I have understood," said I, "that efforts have been made for that purpose, from time immemorial. Bunyan mentions that above twenty thousand cart-loads of wholesome instructions had been thrown in here, without effect."

"Very probably!—and what effect could be anticipated from such unsubstantial stuff?" cried Mr. Smooth-it-away. "You observe this convenient bridge. We obtained a sufficient foundation for it by throwing into the slough some editions of books of morality, volumes of French philosophy and German rationalism, tracts, sermons, and essays of modern clergymen, extracts from Plato, Confucius, and various Hindoo sages, together with a few ingenious commentaries upon texts of Scripture—all of which, by some scientific process, have been converted into a mass like granite. The whole bog might be filled up with similar matter."

It really seemed to me, however, that the bridge vibrated and heaved up and down, in a very formidable manner; and, spite of Mr. Smooth-it-away's testimony to the solidity of its foundation, I should be loth to cross it in a crowded omnibus; especially if each passenger were encumbered with as heavy luggage as that gentleman and myself. Nevertheless, we got over without accident, and soon found ourselves at the Station House. This very neat and spacious edifice is erected on the site of the little Wicket-Gate,[3] which formerly, as all old pilgrims will recollect, stood directly across the highway, and, by its inconvenient narrowness, was a great obstruction to the traveller of liberal mind and expansive stomach. The reader of John Bunyan will be glad to know, that Christian's old friend Evangelist, who was accustomed to supply each pilgrim with a mystic roll, now presides at the ticket-office. Some malicious persons, it is true, deny the identity of this reputable character with the Evangelist[4] of old times, and even pretend to bring competent evidence of an imposture. Without involving myself in the dispute, I shall merely observe, that, so far as my experience goes, the square pieces of pasteboard, now delivered to passengers, are much more convenient and useful along the road, than the antique roll of parchment. Whether they

2. Christian falls into the Slough of Despond soon after leaving the City of Destruction, but a man "whose name was Help . . . set him upon sound ground, and bid him go on his way."
3. Christian passes through this narrow gate early in his journey. Cf. Matthew 7:14, "strait is the gate, and narrow is the way, which leadeth unto life, and few there be that find it."
4. At the beginning of The Pilgrim's Progress, Evangelist gives Christian a parchment roll on which is written "Fly from the wrath to come."

will be as readily received at the gate of the Celestial City, I decline giving an opinion.

A large number of passengers were already at the Station House, awaiting the departure of the cars. By the aspect and demeanor of these persons, it was easy to judge that the feelings of the community had undergone a very favorable change, in reference to the Celestial pilgrimage. It would have done Bunyan's heart good to see it. Instead of a lonely and ragged man, with a huge burthen on his back,[5] plodding along sorrowfully on foot, while the whole city hooted after him, here were parties of the first gentry and most respectable people in the neighborhood, setting forth towards the Celestial City, as cheerfully as if the pilgrimage were merely a summer tour. Among the gentlemen were characters of deserved eminence, magistrates, politicians, and men of wealth, by whose example religion could not but be greatly recommended to their meaner brethren. In the ladies' apartment, too, I rejoiced to distinguish some of those flowers of fashionable society, who are so well fitted to adorn the most elevated circles of the Celestial City. There was much pleasant conversation about the news of the day, topics of business, politics, or the lighter matters of amusement; while religion, though indubitably the main thing at heart, was thrown tastefully into the back-ground. Even an infidel would have heard little or nothing to shock his sensibility.

One great convenience of the new method of going on pilgrimage, I must not forget to mention. Our enormous burthens, instead of being carried on our shoulders, as had been the custom of old, were all snugly deposited in the baggage-car, and, as I was assured, would be delivered to their respective owners, at the journey's end. Another thing, likewise, the benevolent reader will be delighted to understand. It may be remembered that there was an ancient feud between Prince Beelzebub and the keeper of the Wicket-Gate,[6] and that the adherents of the former distinguished personage were accustomed to shoot deadly arrows at honest pilgrims, while knocking at the door. This dispute, much to the credit as well of the illustrious potentate above-mentioned as of the worthy and enlightened Directors of the rail-road, has been pacifically arranged, on the principle of mutual compromise. The prince's subjects are now pretty numerously employed about the Station House, some in taking care of the baggage, others in collecting fuel, feeding the engines, and such congenial occupations; and I can conscientiously affirm, that persons more attentive to their business, more willing to accommodate,

---

5. Christian bears the burden of sin on his back until it falls from him when he comes to the place of the Cross. Hawthorne's travelers have stowed their burdens (their luggage) in the baggage car, where they can ignore them.
6. Good-will, who pulls Christian forward through the gate to protect him from the arrows of Beelzebub (the devil).

or more generally agreeable to the passengers, are not to be found on any rail-road. Every good heart must surely exult at so satisfactory an arrangement of an immemorial difficulty.

"Where is Mr. Greatheart?"[7] inquired I. "Beyond a doubt, the Directors have engaged that famous old champion to be chief engineer on the rail-road?"

"Why, no," said Mr. Smooth-it-away, with a dry cough. "He was offered the situation of brake-man; but, to tell you the truth, our friend Greatheart has grown preposterously stiff and narrow, in his old age. He has so often guided pilgrims over the road, on foot, that he considers it a sin to travel in any other fashion. Besides, the old fellow had entered so heartily into the ancient feud with Prince Beelzebub, that he would have been perpetually at blows or ill language with some of the prince's subjects, and thus have embroiled us anew. So, on the whole, we were not sorry when honest Greatheart went off to the Celestial City in a huff, and left us at liberty to choose a more suitable and accommodating man. Yonder comes the engineer of the train. You will probably recognize him at once."

The engine at this moment took its station in advance of the cars, looking, I must confess, much more like a sort of mechanical demon, that would hurry us to the infernal regions, than a laudable contrivance for smoothing our way to the Celestial City. On its top sat a personage almost enveloped in smoke and flame, which—not to startle the reader—appeared to gush from his own mouth and stomach, as well as from the engine's brazen abdomen.

"Do my eyes deceive me?" cried I. "What on earth is this! A living creature?—if so, he is own brother to the engine that he rides upon!"

"Poh, poh; you are obtuse!" said Mr. Smooth-it-away, with a hearty laugh. "Don't you know Apollyon, Christian's old enemy, with whom he fought so fierce a battle in the Valley of Humiliation?[8] He was the very fellow to manage the engine; and so we have reconciled him to the custom of going on pilgrimage, and engaged him as chief engineer."

"Bravo, bravo!" exclaimed I, with irrepressible enthusiasm, "This shows the liberality of the age; this proves, if anything can, that all musty prejudices are in a fair way to be obliterated. And how will Christian rejoice to hear of this happy transformation of his old antagonist! I promise myself great pleasure in informing him of it, when we reach the Celestial City."

The passengers being all comfortably seated, we now rattled away merrily, accomplishing a greater distance in ten minutes, than

7. Greatheart guides, counsels, and defends Christian's wife on her journey to the Celestial City in *The Pilgrim's Progress, The Second Part* (1685).
8. In the Valley of Humiliation, Christian overcomes Apollyon, who spits fire and roars like a dragon. Apollyon is "the angel of the bottomless pit" in Revelation 9:11.

Christian probably trudged over, in a day. It was laughable, while we glanced along, as it were, at the tail of a thunder-bolt, to observe two dusty foot-travellers, in the old pilgrim-guise, with cockle-shell and staff,[9] their mystic rolls of parchment in their hands, and their intolerable burthens on their backs. The preposterous obstinacy of these honest people, in persisting to groan and stumble along the difficult pathway, rather than take advantage of modern improvements, excited great mirth among our wiser brotherhood. We greeted the two pilgrims with many pleasant gibes and a roar of laughter; whereupon, they gazed at us with such woeful and absurdly compassionate visages, that our merriment grew tenfold more obstreperous. Apollyon, also, entered heartily into the fun, and contrived to flirt the smoke and flame of the engine, or of his own breath, into their faces, and enveloped them in an atmosphere of scalding steam. These little practical jokes amused us mightily, and doubtless afforded the pilgrims the gratification of considering themselves martyrs.

At some distance from the rail-road, Mr. Smooth-it-away pointed to a large, antique edifice, which, he observed, was a tavern of long standing, and had formerly been a noted stopping-place for pilgrims. In Bunyan's road-book, it is mentioned as the Interpreter's House.[1]

"I have long had a curiosity to visit that old mansion," remarked I.

"It is not one of our stations, as you perceive," said my companion. "The keeper was violently opposed to the rail-road; and well he might be, as the track left his house of entertainment on one side, and thus was pretty certain to deprive him of all his reputable customers. But the foot-path still passes his door; and the old gentleman now and then receives a call from some simple traveller, and entertains him with fare as old-fashioned as himself."

Before our talk on this subject came to a conclusion, we were rushing by the place where Christian's burthen fell from his shoulders, at the sight of the cross. This served as a theme for Mr. Smooth-it-away, Mr. Live-for-the-world, Mr. Hide-sin-in-the-heart, Mr. Scaly Conscience, and a knot of gentlemen from the town of Shun Repentance, to descant upon the inestimable advantages resulting from the safety of our baggage. Myself, and all the passengers indeed, joined with great unanimity in this view of the matter; for our burthens were rich in many things, esteemed precious throughout the world; and, especially, we each of us possessed a great variety of favorite Habits, which we trusted would not be out of fashion, even in the polite circles of the Celestial City. It would have been a sad spectacle, to see such an assortment of valuable articles tumbling into

9. Pilgrims traditionally wore hats with cockleshells and carried wooden staffs.
1. Christian stops for religious instruction at the Interpreter's House.

the sepulchre. Thus pleasantly conversing on the favorable circumstances of our position, as compared with those of past pilgrims,
and of narrow-minded ones at the present day, we soon found ourselves at the foot of the Hill Difficulty.[2] Through the very heart of
this rocky mountain a tunnel has been constructed, of most admirable architecture, with a lofty arch and a spacious double-track; so
that, unless the earth and rocks should chance to crumble down, it
will remain an eternal monument of the builder's skill and enterprise. It is a great, though incidental advantage, that the materials
from the heart of the Hill Difficulty have been employed in filling up
the Valley of Humiliation;[3] thus obviating the necessity of descending into that disagreeable and unwholesome hollow.

"This is a wonderful improvement, indeed," said I. "Yet I should
have been glad of an opportunity to visit the Palace Beautiful,[4] and
be introduced to the charming young ladies—Miss Prudence, Miss
Piety, Miss Charity, and the rest—who have the kindness to entertain pilgrims there."

"Young ladies!" cried Mr. Smooth-it-away, as soon as he could
speak for laughing. "And charming young ladies! Why, my dear fellow, they are old maids, every soul of them—prim, starched, dry,
and angular—and not one of them, I will venture to say, has altered
so much as the fashion of her gown, since the days of Christian's
pilgrimage."

"Ah, well," said I, much comforted. "Then I can very readily
dispense with their acquaintance."

The respectable Apollyon was now putting on the steam at a
prodigious rate, anxious, perhaps, to get rid of the unpleasant reminiscences, connected with the spot where he had so disastrously
encountered Christian. Consulting Mr. Bunyan's road-book, I perceived that we must now be within a few miles of the Valley of the
Shadow of Death;[5] into which doleful region, at our present speed,
we should plunge much sooner than seemed at all desirable. In truth,
I expected nothing better than to find myself in the ditch on one
side, or the quag on the other. But, on communicating my apprehensions to Mr. Smooth-it-away, he assured me that the difficulties of
this passage, even in its worst condition, had been vastly exaggerated, and that, in its present state of improvement, I might consider
myself as safe as on any rail-road in Christendom.

2. Christian's narrow path lies right up this hill.
3. On the other side of the Hill Difficulty.
4. A house on the Hill Difficulty where pilgrims stop for rest and refreshment. There
   Prudence, Piety, and Charity converse with Christian.
5. Beyond the Valley of Humiliation. In the Valley of the Shadow of Death, Christian is
   beset by darkness, flames, and dreadful noises.

Even while we were speaking, the train shot into the entrance of this dreaded Valley. Though I plead guilty to some foolish palpitations of the heart, during our headlong rush over the causeway here constructed, yet it were unjust to withhold the highest encomiums on the boldness of its original conception, and the ingenuity of those who executed it. It was gratifying, likewise, to observe how much care had been taken to dispel the everlasting gloom, and supply the defect of cheerful sunshine; not a ray of which has ever penetrated among these awful shadows. For this purpose, the inflammable gas, which exudes plentifully from the soil, is collected by means of pipes, and thence communicated to a quadruple row of lamps, along the whole extent of the passage. Thus a radiance has been created, even out of the fiery and sulphurous curse that rests forever upon the Valley; a radiance hurtful, however, to the eyes, and somewhat bewildering, as I discovered by the changes which it wrought in the visages of my companions. In this respect, as compared with natural daylight, there is the same difference as between truth and falsehood; but, if the reader have ever travelled through the Dark Valley, he will have learned to be thankful for any light that he could get; if not from the sky above, then from the blasted soil beneath. Such was the red brilliancy of these lamps, that they appeared to build walls of fire on both sides of the track, between which we held our course at lightning-speed, while a reverberating thunder filled the Valley with its echoes. Had the engine run off the track—a catastrophe, it is whispered, by no means unprecedented— the bottomless pit, if there be any such place, would undoubtedly have received us. Just as some dismal fooleries of this nature had made my heart quake, there came a tremendous shriek, careering along the Valley as if a thousand devils had burst their lungs to utter it, but which proved to be merely the whistle of the engine, on arriving at a stopping-place.

The spot, where we had now paused, is the same that our friend Bunyan—a truthful man, but infected with many fantastic notions— has designated, in terms plainer than I like to repeat, as the mouth of the infernal region.[6] This, however, must be a mistake; inasmuch as Mr. Smooth-it-away, while we remained in the smoky and lurid cavern, took occasion to prove that Tophet[7] has not even a metaphorical existence. The place, he assured us, is no other than the crater of a half-extinct volcano, in which the Directors had caused forges to be set up, for the manufacture of rail-road iron. Hence, also, is obtained a plentiful supply of fuel for the use of the engines.

---

6. "The mouth of hell" is in the midst of the Valley of the Shadow of Death. Hawthorne's narrator is too genteel to mention "hell."
7. A place of human sacrifice in the Old Testament (see Jeremiah 7:31), is here another genteelism for hell.

Whoever had gazed into the dismal obscurity of the broad cavern-mouth, whence, ever and anon, darted huge tongues of dusky flame,—and had seen the strange, half-shaped monsters, and visions of faces horribly grotesque, into which the smoke seemed to wreathe itself,—and had heard the awful murmurs, and shrieks, and deep shuddering whispers of the blast, sometimes forming itself into words almost articulate,—he would have seized upon Mr. Smooth-it-away's comfortable explanation, as greedily as we did. The inhab-itants of the cavern, moreover, were unlovely personages, dark, smoke-begrimed, generally deformed, with misshapen feet, and a glow of dusky redness in their eyes; as if their hearts had caught fire, and were blazing out of the upper windows. It struck me as a peculiarity, that the laborers at the forge, and those who brought fuel to the engine, when they began to draw short breath, positively emitted smoke from their mouth and nostrils.

Among the idlers about the train, most of whom were puffing cigars which they had lighted at the flame of the crater, I was per-plexed to notice several, who, to my certain knowledge, had hereto-fore set forth by rail-road for the Celestial City. They looked dark, wild, and smoky, with a singular resemblance, indeed, to the native inhabitants; like whom, also, they had a disagreeable propensity to ill-natured gibes and sneers; the habit of which had wrought a settled contortion of their visages. Having been on speaking terms with one of these persons—an indolent, good-for-nothing fellow, who went by the name of Take-it-easy—I called to him, and inquired what was his business there.

"Did you not start," said I, "for the Celestial City?"

"That's a fact," said Mr. Take-it-easy, carelessly puffing some smoke into my eyes. "But I heard such bad accounts, that I never took pains to climb the hill, on which the city stands. No business doing—no fun going on—nothing to drink, and no smoking allowed—and a thrumming of church-music from morning till night! I would not stay in such a place, if they offered me house-room and living free."

"But, my good Mr. Take-it-easy," cried I, "why take up your resi-dence here, of all places in the world?"

"Oh," said the loafer, with a grin, "it is very warm hereabouts, and I meet with plenty of old acquaintance, and altogether the place suits me. I hope to see you back again, some day soon. A pleasant journey to you!"

While he was speaking, the bell of the engine rang, and we dashed away, after dropping a few passengers, but receiving no new ones. Rattling onward through the Valley, we were dazzled with the fiercely gleaming gas-lamps, as before. But sometimes, in the dark of intense brightness, grim faces, that bore the aspect and expression of individual sins, or evil passions, seemed to thrust themselves through the veil of light, glaring upon us, and stretching forth a great dusky hand, as if to impede our progress. I almost thought, that they were my own sins that appalled me there. These were freaks of imagination—nothing more, certainly,—mere delusions, which I ought to be heartily ashamed of—but, all through the Dark Valley, I was tormented, and pestered, and dolefully bewildered, with the same kind of waking dreams. The mephitic gasses of that region intoxicate the brain. As the light of natural day, however, began to struggle with the glow of the lanterns, these vain imaginations lost their vividness, and finally vanished with the first ray of sunshine that greeted our escape from the Valley of the Shadow of Death. Ere we had gone a mile beyond it, I could well nigh have taken my oath that this whole gloomy passage was a dream.

At the end of the Valley, as John Bunyan mentions, is a cavern, where, in his days, dwelt two cruel giants, Pope and Pagan, who had strewn the ground about their residence with the bones of slaughtered pilgrims.[8] These vile old troglodytes are no longer there; but into their deserted cave another terrible giant has thrust himself, and makes it his business to seize upon honest travellers, and fat them for his table with plentiful meals of smoke, mist, moonshine, raw potatoes, and saw-dust. He is a German by birth, and is called Giant Transcendentalist; but as to his form, his features, his substance, and his nature generally, it is the chief peculiarity of this huge miscreant, that neither he for himself, nor anybody for him, has ever been able to describe them. As we rushed by the cavern's mouth, we caught a hasty glimpse of him, looking somewhat like an ill-proportioned figure, but considerably more like a heap of fog and duskiness. He shouted after us, but in so strange a phraseology that we knew not what he meant, nor whether to be encouraged or affrighted.

It was late in the day, when the train thundered into the ancient city of Vanity, where Vanity Fair[9] is still at the height of prosperity, and exhibits an epitome of whatever is brilliant, gay, and fascinating, beneath the sun. As I purposed to make a considerable stay here, it gratified me to learn that there is no longer the want of harmony between the townspeople and pilgrims, which impelled the former to such lamentably mistaken measures as the persecution of Christian, and the fiery martyrdom of Faithful.[1] On the contrary, as

8. Christian passes by this cavern easily because Pagan has long been dead and Pope is powerless to hurt him.
9. The pilgrims' way to the Celestial City lies through the town of Vanity, where a fair is kept all the year long.
1. Christian's fellow pilgrim on part of his journey. Faithful is tried, tortured, and burned at the stake in Vanity Fair.

the new rail-road brings with it great trade and a constant influx of strangers, the lord of Vanity Fair is its chief patron, and the capitalists of the city are among the largest stockholders. Many passengers stop to take their pleasure or make their profit in the Fair, instead of going onward to the Celestial City. Indeed, such are the charms of the place, that people often affirm it to be the true and only heaven; stoutly contending that there is no other, that those who seek further are mere dreamers, and that, if the fabled brightness of the Celestial City lay but a bare mile beyond the gates of Vanity, they would not be fools enough to go thither. Without subscribing to these, perhaps, exaggerated encomiums, I can truly say, that my abode in the city was mainly agreeable, and my intercourse with the inhabitants productive of much amusement and instruction.

Being naturally of a serious turn, my attention was directed to the solid advantages derivable from a residence here, rather than to the effervescent pleasures, which are the grand object with too many visitants. The Christian reader, if he have had no accounts of the city later than Bunyan's time, will be surprised to hear that almost every street has its church, and that the reverend clergy are nowhere held in higher respect than at Vanity Fair. And well do they deserve such honorable estimation; for the maxims of wisdom and virtue, which fall from their lips, come from as deep a spiritual source, and tend to us as lofty a religious aim, as those of the sagest philosophers of old. In justification of this high praise, I need only mention the names of the Rev. Mr. Shallow-deep; the Rev. Mr. Stumble-at-truth; that fine old clerical character, the Rev. Mr. This-to-day, who expects shortly to resign his pulpit to the Rev. Mr. That-to-morrow; together with the Rev. Mr. Bewilderment; the Rev. Mr. Clog-the-spirit; and, last and greatest, the Rev. Dr. Wind-of-doctrine. The labors of these eminent divines are aided by those of innumerable lecturers,[2] who diffuse such a various profundity, in all subjects of human or celestial science, that any man may acquire an omnigenous erudition, without the trouble of even learning to read. Thus literature is etherealized by assuming for its medium the human voice; and knowledge, depositing all its heavier particles—except, doubtless, its gold—becomes exhaled into a sound, which forthwith steals into the ever-open ear of the community. These ingenious methods constitute a sort of machinery, by which thought and study are done to every person's hand, without his putting himself to the slightest inconvenience in the matter. There is another species of machine for the wholesale manufacture of individual morality. This excellent result is effected by societies for all manner of virtuous

---

2. Traveling lecturers provided popular entertainment and instruction in Hawthorne's day.

purposes; with which a man has merely to connect himself, throwing, as it were, his quota of virtue into the common stock; and the president and directors will take care that the aggregate amount be well applied. All these, and other wonderful improvements in ethics, religion, and literature, being made plain to my comprehension by the ingenious Mr. Smooth-it-away, inspired me with a vast admiration of Vanity Fair.

It would fill a volume, in an age of pamphlets, were I to record all my observations in this great capital of human business and pleasure. There was an unlimited range of society—the powerful, the wise, the witty, and the famous in every walk of life—princes, presidents, poets, generals, artists, actors, and philanthropists, all making their own market at the Fair, and deeming no price too exorbitant for such commodities as hit their fancy. It was well worth one's while, even if he had no idea of buying or selling, to loiter through the bazaars, and observe the various sorts of traffic that were going forward.

Some of the purchasers, I thought, made very foolish bargains. For instance, a young man, having inherited a splendid fortune, laid out a considerable portion of it in the purchase of diseases, and finally spent all the rest for a heavy lot of repentance and a suit of rags. A very pretty girl bartered a heart as clear as crystal, and which seemed her most valuable possession, for another jewel of the same kind, but so worn and defaced as to be utterly worthless. In one shop, there were a great many crowns of laurel and myrtle, which soldiers, authors, statesmen, and various other people, pressed eagerly to buy; some purchased these paltry wreaths with their lives; others by a toilsome servitude of years; and many sacrificed whatever was most valuable, yet finally slunk away without the crown. There was a sort of stock or scrip, called Conscience, which seemed to be in great demand, and would purchase almost anything. Indeed, few rich commodities were to be obtained without paying a heavy sum in this particular stock; and a man's business was seldom very lucrative, unless he knew precisely when and how to throw his hoard of Conscience into the market. Yet, as this stock was the only thing of permanent value, whoever parted with it was sure to find himself a loser, in the long run. Several of the speculations were of a questionable character. Occasionally, a member of congress recruited his pocket by the sale of his constituents; and I was assured that public officers have often sold their country, at very moderate prices. Thousands sold their happiness for a whim. Gilded chains were in great demand, and purchased with almost any sacrifice. In truth, those who desired, according to the old adage, to sell anything valuable for a song, might find customers all over the Fair; and there were innumerable messes of pottage, piping hot, for such as chose to buy them with their birth-rights.[3] A few articles, however, could not be found genuine, at Vanity Fair. If a customer wished to renew his stock of youth, the dealers offered him a set of false teeth and an auburn wig; if he demanded peace of mind, they recommended opium or a brandy-bottle.

Tracts of land and golden mansions, situate in the Celestial City, were often exchanged, at very disadvantageous rates, for a few years lease of small, dismal, inconvenient tenements in Vanity Fair. Prince Beelzebub himself took great interest in this sort of traffic, and sometimes condescended to meddle with smaller matters. I once had the pleasure to see him bargaining with a miser for his soul, which, after much ingenious skirmishing on both sides, his Highness succeeded in obtaining at about the value of sixpence. The prince remarked, with a smile, that he was a loser by the transaction.

Day after day, as I walked the streets of Vanity, my manners and deportment became more and more like those of the inhabitants. The place began to seem like home; the idea of pursuing my travels to the Celestial City was almost obliterated from my mind. I was reminded of it, however, by the sight of the same pair of simple pilgrims at whom we had laughed so heartily, when Apollyon puffed smoke and steam into their faces, at the commencement of our journey. There they stood amid the densest bustle of Vanity—the dealers offering them their purple, and fine linen, and jewels; the men of wit and humor gibing at them; a pair of buxom ladies ogling them askance; while the benevolent Mr. Smooth-it-away whispered some of his wisdom at their elbows, and pointed to a newly erected temple—but there were these worthy simpletons, making the scene look wild and monstrous, merely by their sturdy repudiation of all part in its business or pleasures.

One of them—his name was Stick-to-the-right—perceived in my face, I suppose, a species of sympathy and almost admiration, which, to my own great surprise, I could not help feeling for this pragmatic couple. It prompted him to address me.

"Sir," inquired he, with a sad, yet mild and kindly voice, "do you call yourself a pilgrim?"

"Yes," I replied. "My right to that appellation is indubitable. I am merely a sojourner here in Vanity Fair, being bound for the Celestial City, by the new rail-road."

"Alas, friend," rejoined Mr. Stick-to-the-right, "I do assure you, and beseech you to receive the truth of my words, that that whole concern is a bubble. You may travel on it all your life-time, were you to live thousands of years, and yet never get beyond the limits of

---

3. Esau sells Jacob his birthright for a "mess of pottage"—a bowl of red lentil broth—in Genesis 25:27–34.

Vanity Fair! Yea; though you should deem yourself entering the gates of the Blessed City, it will be nothing but a miserable delusion."

"The Lord of the Celestial City," began the other pilgrim, whose name was Mr. Foot-it-to-Heaven, "has refused, and will ever refuse, to grant an act of incorporation for this rail-road; and unless that be obtained, no passenger can ever hope to enter his dominions. Wherefore, every man, who buys a ticket, must lay his account with losing the purchase-money—which is the value of his own soul."

"Poh, nonsense!" said Mr. Smooth-it-away, taking my arm and leading me off. "These fellows ought to be indicted for a libel. If the law stood as it once did in Vanity Fair, we should see them grinning through the iron-bars of the prison-window."

This incident made a considerable impression on my mind, and contributed with other circumstances to indispose me to a permanent residence in the city of Vanity; although, of course, I was not simple enough to give up my original plan of gliding along easily and commodiously by rail-road. Still, I grew anxious to be gone. There was one strange thing that troubled me; amid the occupations or amusements of the Fair, nothing was more common than for a person—whether at a feast, theatre, or church, or trafficking for wealth and honors, or whatever he might be doing, and however unseasonable the interruption—suddenly to vanish like a soap-bubble, and be never more seen of his fellows; and so accustomed were the latter to such little accidents, that they went on with their business, as quietly as if nothing had happened. But it was otherwise with me.

Finally, after a pretty long residence at the Fair, I resumed my journey towards the Celestial City, still with Mr. Smooth-it-away at my side. At a short distance beyond the suburbs of Vanity, we passed the ancient silver-mine, of which Demas[4] was the first discoverer, and which is now wrought to great advantage, supplying nearly all the coined currency of the world. A little further onward was the spot where Lot's wife had stood for ages, under the semblance of a pillar of salt.[5] Curious travellers have long since carried it away piece-meal. Had all regrets been punished as rigorously as this poor dame's were, my yearning for the relinquished delights of Vanity Fair might have produced a similar change in my own corporeal substance, and left me a warning to future pilgrims.

---

4. An inconstant Christian who forsook the Apostle Paul (see 2 Timothy 4:10). In *The Pilgrim's Progress*, Demas presides over a silver mine near the Hill Lucre.
5. Christian and Hopeful observe this pillar of salt, on which is written "Remember Lot's wife," who looked back at Sodom and was turned into a pillar of salt. See Genesis 19:17–26.

The next remarkable object was a large edifice, constructed of moss-grown stone, but in a modern and airy style of architecture. The engine came to a pause in its vicinity, with the usual tremendous shriek.

"This was formerly the castle of the redoubted giant Despair,"[6] observed Mr. Smooth-it-away; "but, since his death, Mr. Flimsy-faith has repaired it, and now keeps an excellent house of entertainment here. It is one of our stopping-places."

"It seems but slightly put together," remarked I, looking at the frail, yet ponderous walls. "I do not envy Mr. Flimsy-faith his habitation. Some day, it will thunder down upon the heads of the occupants."

"We shall escape, at all events," said Mr. Smooth-it-away; "for Apollyon is putting on the steam again."

The road now plunged into a gorge of the Delectable Mountains,[7] and traversed the field where, in former ages, the blind men wandered and stumbled among the tombs. One of these ancient tombstones had been thrust across the track, by some malicious person, and gave the train of cars a terrible jolt. Far up the rugged side of a mountain, I perceived a rusty iron-door, half-overgrown with bushes and creeping-plants, but with smoke issuing from its crevices.

"Is that," inquired I, "the very door in the hill-side, which the shepherds assured Christian was a by-way to hell?"[8]

"That was a joke on the part of the shepherds," said Mr. Smooth-it-away, with a smile. "It is neither more nor less than the door of a cavern, which they use as a smoke-house for the preparation of mutton-hams."

My recollections of the journey are now, for a little space, dim and confused; inasmuch as a singular drowsiness here overcame me, owing to the fact that we were passing over the Enchanted Ground, the air of which encourages a disposition to sleep.[9] I awoke, however, as soon as we crossed the borders of the pleasant land of Beulah.[1] All the passengers were rubbing their eyes, comparing watches, and congratulating one another on the prospect of arriving so seasonably at the journey's end. The sweet breezes of this happy clime came refreshingly to our nostrils; we beheld the glimmering gush of silver fountains, overhung by trees of beautiful foliage and delicious fruit, which were propagated by grafts from

6. Christian and Hopeful are tempted to leave the narrow way and are caught by Despair, who imprisons them in his castle.
7. The pilgrims pass through these mountains in the last stage of their journey.
8. Good shepherds guide the pilgrims through the mountains and warn them about this door.
9. Warned by the shepherds of the dangers of the Enchanted Ground, Christian and Hopeful keep awake by discoursing on religion.
1. From Beulah the pilgrims have their first clear view of the Celestial City.

the Celestial gardens. Once, as we dashed onward like a hurricane, there was a flutter of wings, and the bright appearance of an angel in the air, speeding forth on some heavenly mission. The engine now announced the close vicinity of the final Station House, by one last and horrible scream, in which there seemed to be distinguishable every kind of wailing and woe, and bitter fierceness of wrath, all mixed up with the wild laughter of a devil or a madman. Throughout our journey, at every stopping-place, Apollyon had exercised his ingenuity in screwing the most abominable sounds out of the whistle of the steam-engine; but, in this closing effort, he outdid himself, and created an infernal uproar, which, besides disturbing the peaceful inhabitants of Beulah, must have sent its discord even through the Celestial gates.

While the horrid clamor was still ringing in our ears, we heard an exulting strain, as if a thousand instruments of music, with height, and depth, and sweetness in their tones, at once tender and triumphant, were struck in unison, to greet the approach of some illustrious hero, who had fought the good fight, and won a glorious victory, and was come to lay aside his battered arms forever. Looking to ascertain what might be the occasion of this glad harmony, I perceived, on alighting from the cars, that a multitude of Shining Ones had assembled on the other side of the river, to welcome two poor pilgrims,[2] who were just emerging from its depths. They were the same whom Apollyon and ourselves had persecuted with taunts and gibes, and scalding steam, at the commencement of our journey; the same whose unworldly aspect and impressive words had stirred my conscience, amid the wild revellers of Vanity Fair.

"How amazingly well those men have got on!" cried I to Mr. Smooth-it-away. "I wish we were secure of as good a reception."

"Never fear—never fear!" answered my friend. "Come!—make haste!—the ferry-boat will be off directly; and in three minutes you will be on the other side of the river. No doubt you will find coaches to carry you up to the city-gates."

A steam ferry-boat, the last improvement on this important route, lay at the river-side, puffing, snorting, and emitting all those other disagreeable utterances, which betoken the departure to be immediate. I hurried on board, with the rest of the passengers, most of whom were in great perturbation; some bawling out for their baggage; some tearing their hair, and exclaiming that the boat would explode or sink; some already pale with the heaving of the stream; some gazing affrighted at the ugly aspect of the steersman; and some still dizzy with the slumberous influences of the Enchanted Ground.

2. Christian and Hopeful are welcomed by the Shining Ones after they pass through the river of Death.

Looking back to the shore, I was amazed to discern Mr. Smooth-it-away, waving his hand in token of farewell!

"Don't you go over to the Celestial City?" exclaimed I.

"Oh, no!" answered he with a queer smile, and that same disagreeable contortion of visage, which I had remarked in the inhabitants of the Dark Valley. "Oh, no! I have come thus far only for the sake of your pleasant company. Good bye! We shall meet again."

And then did my excellent friend, Mr. Smooth-it-away, laugh outright; in the midst of which cachination, a smoke-wreath issued from his mouth and nostrils; while a twinkle of lurid flame darted out of either eye, proving indubitably that his heart was all of a red blaze. The impudent Fiend! To deny the existence of Tophet, when he felt its fiery tortures raging within his breast! I rushed to the side of the boat, intending to fling myself on shore. But the wheels, as they began their revolutions, threw a dash of spray over me, so cold—so deadly cold, with the chill that will never leave those waters, until Death be drowned in his own river[3]—that, with a shiver and a heart-quake, I awoke. Thank Heaven, it was a Dream!

Earth's Holocaust[†]

Once upon a time—but whether in time past or time to come, is a matter of little or no moment—this wide world had become so over-burthened with an accumulation of worn-out trumpery, that the inhabitants determined to rid themselves of it by a general bonfire. The site fixed upon, at the representation of the Insurance Companies, and as being as central a spot as any other on the globe, was one of the broadest prairies of the West, where no human habitation would be endangered by the flames, and where a vast assemblage of spectators might commodiously admire the show. Having a taste for sights of this kind, and imagining, likewise, that the illumination of the bonfire might reveal some profundity of moral truth, heretofore hidden in mist or darkness, I made it convenient to journey thither and be present. At my arrival, although the heap of condemned rubbish was as yet comparatively small, the torch had already been applied. Amid that boundless plain, in the dusk of evening, like a far-off star alone in the firmament, there was merely visible one tremulous gleam, whence none could have anticipated so fierce a blaze as was destined to ensue. With every moment, however, there came foot-travellers, women holding up their aprons,

---

3. Death itself will die at the resurrection of the just according to Christian eschatology.
† First published in *Graham's Magazine*, March 1844, then in *Mosses from an Old Manse*, 1846. Reprinted by permission of The Ohio State University Press.

men on horseback, wheelbarrows, lumbering baggage-wagons, and other vehicles great and small, and from far and near, laden with articles that were judged fit for nothing but to be burnt.

"What materials have been used to kindle the flames?" inquired I of a bystander; for I was desirous of knowing the whole process of the affair, from beginning to end.

The person whom I addressed was a grave man, fifty years old or thereabout, who had evidently come thither as a looker-on; he struck me immediately as having weighed for himself the true value of life and its circumstances, and therefore as feeling little personal interest in whatever judgment the world might form of them. Before answering my question, he looked me in the face, by the kindling light of the fire.

"Oh, some very dry combustibles," replied he, "and extremely suitable to the purpose—no other, in fact, than yesterday's newspapers, last month's magazines, and last year's withered leaves. Here, now, comes some antiquated trash, that will take fire like a handfull of shavings."

As he spoke, some rough-looking men advanced to the verge of the bonfire, and threw in, as it appeared, all the rubbish of the Herald's Office; the blazonry of coat-armor; the crests and devices of illustrious families; pedigrees that extended back, like lines of light, into the mist of the dark ages; together with stars, garters, and embroidered collars; each of which, as paltry a bauble as it might appear to the uninstructed eye, had once possessed vast significance, and was still, in truth, reckoned among the most precious of moral or material facts, by the worshippers of the gorgeous past. Mingled with this confused heap, which was tossed into the flames by armsfull at once, were innumerable badges of knighthood; comprising those of all the European sovereignties, and Napoleon's decoration of the Legion of Honor, the ribands of which were entangled with those of the ancient order of St. Louis.[1] There, too, were the medals of our own society of Cincinnati,[2] by means of which, as history tells us, an order of hereditary knights came near being constituted out of the king-quellers of the Revolution. And, besides, there were the patents of nobility of German counts and barons, Spanish grandees, and English peers, from the worm-eaten instrument signed by William the Conqueror, down to the bran-new parchment of the latest lord, who has received his honors from the fair hand of Victoria.

---

1. Feudal order of knighthood founded by Louis IX of France (1226–1270). "Legion of Honor": high French civilian and military decoration, instituted in 1802.
2. Founded in 1783 by officers of the Revolutionary Army. Membership descended through the eldest sons.

At sight of the dense volumes of smoke, mingled with vivid jets of flame, that gushed and eddied forth from this immense pile of earthly distinctions, the multitude of plebeian spectators set up a joyous shout, and clapt their hands with an emphasis that made the welkin echo. That was their moment of triumph, achieved after long ages, over creatures of the same clay and same spiritual infirmities, who had dared to assume the privileges due only to Heaven's better workmanship. But now there rushed towards the blazing heap a gray-haired man, of stately presence, wearing a coat from the breast of which some star, or other badge of rank, seemed to have been forcibly wrenched away. He had not the tokens of intellectual power in his face; but still there was the demeanor—the habitual, and almost native dignity—of one who had been born to the idea of his own social superiority, and had never felt it questioned, till that moment.

"People," cried he, gazing at the ruin of what was dearest in his eyes, with grief and wonder, but, nevertheless, with a degree of stateliness—"people, what have you done! This fire is consuming all that marked your advance from barbarism, or that could have prevented your relapse thither. We—the men of the privileged orders—were those who kept alive, from age to age, the old chivalrous spirit; the gentle and generous thought; the higher, the purer, the more refined and delicate life! With the nobles, too, you cast off the poet, the painter, the sculptor—all the beautiful arts;—for we were their patrons, and created the atmosphere in which they flourish. In abolishing the majestic distinctions of rank, society loses not only its grace, but its steadfastness "

More he would doubtless have spoken; but here there arose an outcry, sportive, contemptuous, and indignant, that altogether drowned the appeal of the fallen nobleman; insomuch that, casting one look of despair at his own half-burnt pedigree, he shrunk back into the crowd, glad to shelter himself under his new-found insignificance.

"Let him thank his stars that we have not flung him into the same fire!" shouted a rude figure, spurning the embers with his foot. "And, henceforth, let no man dare to show a piece of musty parchment, as his warrant for lording it over his fellows! If he have strength of arm, well and good; it is one species of superiority. If he have wit, wisdom, courage, force of character, let these attributes do for him what they may. But, from this day forward, no mortal must hope for place and consideration, by reckoning up the mouldy bones of his ancestors! That nonsense is done away."

"And in good time," remarked the grave observer by my side—in a low voice however—"if no worse nonsense come in its place. But at all events, this species of nonsense has fairly lived out its life."

There was little space to muse or moralize over the embers of this time-honored rubbish; for, before it was half burnt out, there came another multitude from beyond the sea, bearing the purple robes of royalty, and the crowns, globes, and sceptres of emperors and kings. All these had been condemned as useless baubles; playthings, at best, fit only for the infancy of the world, or rods to govern and chastise it in its nonage; but with which universal manhood, at its full-grown stature, could no longer brook to be insulted. Into such contempt had these regal insignia now fallen, that the gilded crown and tinselled robes of the player-king,[3] from Drury Lane Theatre, had been thrown in among the rest, doubtless as a mockery of his brother-monarchs, on the great stage of the world. It was a strange sight, to discern the crown-jewels of England, glowing and flashing in the midst of the fire. Some of them had been delivered down from the times of the Saxon princes; others were purchased with vast revenues, or, perchance, ravished from the dead brows of the native potentates of Hindostan;[4] and the whole now blazed with a dazzling lustre, as if a star had fallen in that spot, and been shattered into fragments. The splendor of the ruined monarchy had no reflection, save in those inestimable precious-stones. But, enough on this subject! It were but tedious to describe how the Emperor of Austria's mantle was converted to tinder, and how the posts and pillars of the French throne became a heap of coals, which it was impossible to distinguish from those of any other wood. Let me add, however, that I noticed one of the exiled Poles, stirring up the bonfire with the Czar of Russia's sceptre, which he afterwards flung into the flames.[5]

"The smell of singed garments is quite intolerable here," observed my new acquaintance, as the breeze enveloped us in the smoke of a royal wardrobe. "Let us get to windward, and see what they are doing on the other side of the bonfire."

We accordingly passed round, and were just in time to witness the arrival of a vast procession of Washingtonians—as the votaries of temperance call themselves now-a-days—accompanied by thousands of the Irish disciples of Father Mathew,[6] with that great apostle at their head. They brought a rich contribution to the bonfire; being nothing less than all the hogsheads and barrels of liquor in the world, which they rolled before them across the prairie.

"Now, my children," cried Father Mathew, when they reached the verge of the fire—"one shove more, and the work is done! And now let us stand off, and see Satan deal with his own liquor!"

3. Costumes worn by stage kings in plays at the Drury Lane Theatre in London.
4. Here the Indian subcontinent, largely under English domination by 1844.
5. Czar Nicholas I brutally suppressed Polish rebellions against Russian rule in the 1830s.
6. Theobald Mathew (1790–1856), Irish priest, social worker, and "apostle of temperance."

Accordingly, having placed their wooden vessels within reach of the flames, the procession stood off at a safe distance, and soon beheld them burst into a blaze that reached the clouds, and threatened to set the sky itself on fire. And well it might. For here was the whole world's stock of spirituous liquors, which, instead of kindling a frenzied light in the eyes of individual topers as of yore, soared upward with a bewildering gleam that startled all mankind. It was the aggregate of that fierce fire, which would otherwise have scorched the hearts of millions. Meantime, numberless bottles of precious wine were flung into the blaze; which lapped up the contents as if it loved them, and grew, like other drunkards, the merrier and fiercer for what it quaffed. Never again will the insatiable thirst of the fire-fiend be so pampered! Here were the treasures of famous bon-vivants—liquors that had been tossed on ocean, and mellowed in the sun, and hoarded long in the recesses of the earth—the pale, the gold, the ruddy juice of whatever vineyards were most delicate—the entire vintage of Tokay[7]—all mingling in one stream with the vile fluids of the common pot-house, and contributing to heighten the self-same blaze. And while it rose in a gigantic spire, that seemed to wave against the arch of the firmament, and combine itself with the light of stars, the multitude gave a shout, as if the broad earth were exulting in its deliverance from the curse of ages.

But the joy was not universal. Many deemed that human life would be gloomier than ever, when that brief illumination should sink down. While the reformers were at work, I had overheard muttered expostulations from several respectable gentlemen with red noses, and wearing gouty shoes; and a ragged worthy, whose face looked like a hearth where the fire is burnt out, now expressed his discontent more openly and boldly.

"What is this world good for," said the Last Toper, "now that we can never be jolly any more? What is to comfort the poor man in sorrow and perplexity?—how is he to keep his heart warm against the cold winds of this cheerless earth?—and what do you propose to give him, in exchange for the solace that you take away? How are old friends to sit together by the fireside, without a cheerful glass between them? A plague upon your reformation! It is a sad world, a cold world, a selfish world, a low world, not worth an honest fellow's living in, now that good-fellowship is gone forever!"

This harangue excited great mirth among the bystanders. But, preposterous as was the sentiment, I could not help commiserating the forlorn condition of the Last Toper, whose boon-companions had dwindled away from his side, leaving the poor fellow without a soul to countenance him in sipping his liquor, nor, indeed, any liquor to

7. A sweet wine from Tokay, Hungary.

sip. Not that this was quite the true state of the case; for I had
observed him, at a critical moment, filch a bottle of fourth-proof[8]
brandy that fell beside the bonfire, and hide it in his pocket.

The spirituous and fermented liquors being thus disposed of, the
zeal of the reformers next induced them to replenish the fire with
all the boxes of tea and bags of coffee in the world. And now came
the planters of Virginia, bringing their crops of tobacco. These,
being cast upon the heap of inutility, aggregated it to the size of a
mountain, and incensed the atmosphere with such potent fragrance,
that methought we should never draw pure breath again. The present sacrifice seemed to startle the lovers of the weed, more than
any that they had hitherto witnessed.

"Well;—they've put my pipe out," said an old gentleman, flinging
it into the flames in a pet. "What is this world coming to? Everything
rich and racy—all the spice of life—is to be condemned as useless.
Now that they have kindled the bonfire, if these nonsensical reformers would fling themselves into it, all would be well enough!"

"Be patient," responded a staunch conservative;—"it will come to
that in the end. They will first fling us in, and finally themselves."

From the general and systematic measures of reform, I now turned
to consider the individual contributions to this memorable bonfire.
In many instances, these were of a very amusing character. One poor
fellow threw in his empty purse, and another, a bundle of counterfeit
or insolvable bank-notes. Fashionable ladies threw in their last season's bonnets, together with heaps of ribbon, yellow lace, and much
other half-worn milliner's ware; all of which proved even more evanescent in the fire, than it had been in the fashion. A multitude of
lovers, of both sexes—discarded maids or bachelors, and couples,
mutually weary of one another—tossed in bundles of perfumed letters and enamored sonnets. A hack-politician, being deprived of
bread by the loss of office, threw in his teeth, which happened to be
false ones. The Rev. Sydney Smith[9]—having voyaged across the
Atlantic for that sole purpose—came up to the bonfire, with a bitter
grin, and threw in certain repudiated bonds, fortified though they
were with the broad seal of a sovereign state. A little boy of five years
old, in the premature manliness of the present epoch, threw in his
playthings; a college-graduate, his diploma; an apothecary, ruined by
the spread of homoeopathy, his whole stock of drugs and medicines; a physician, his library; a parson, his old sermons; and a fine
gentleman of the old school, his code of manners, which he had formerly written down for the benefit of the next generation. A widow,

8. Refined several times, of excellent quality.
9. Sydney Smith (1771–1845). English clergyman, writer, and wit. In an article in the *Edinburgh Review* he exposed Pennsylvania for its unethical repudiation of debts. He had lost
   his own money in a loan to the state—hence his "bitter grin."

resolving on a second marriage, slily threw in her dead husband's miniature. A young man, jilted by his mistress, would willingly have flung his own desperate heart into the flames, but could find no means to wrench it out of his bosom. An American author, whose works were neglected by the public, threw his pen and paper into the bonfire,[1] and betook himself to some less discouraging occupation. It somewhat startled me to overhear a number of ladies, highly respectable in appearance, proposing to fling their gowns and petticoats into the flames, and assume the garb, together with the manners, duties, offices, and responsibilities, of the opposite sex.

What favor was accorded to this scheme, I am unable to say; my attention being suddenly drawn to a poor, deceived, and half-delirious girl, who, exclaiming that she was the most worthless thing alive or dead, attempted to cast herself into the fire, amid all that wrecked and broken trumpery of the world. A good man, however, ran to her rescue.

"Patience, my poor girl!" said he, as he drew her back from the fierce embrace of the destroying angel. "Be patient, and abide Heaven's will. So long as you possess a living soul, all may be restored to its first freshness. These things of matter, and creations of human fantasy, are fit for nothing but to be burnt, when once they have had their day. But your day is Eternity!"

"Yes," said the wretched girl, whose frenzy seemed now to have sunk down into deep despondency;—"yes; and the sunshine is blotted out of it!"

It was now rumored among the spectators, that all the weapons and munitions of war were to be thrown into the bonfire; with the exception of the world's stock of gunpowder, which, as the safest mode of disposing of it, had already been drowned in the sea. This intelligence seemed to awaken great diversity of opinion. The hopeful philanthropist esteemed it a token that the millenium was already come; while persons of another stamp, in whose view mankind was a breed of bull-dogs, prophesied that all the old stoutness, fervor, nobleness, generosity, and magnanimity of the race, would disappear; these qualities, as they affirmed, requiring blood for their nourishment. They comforted themselves, however, in the belief that the proposed abolition of war was impracticable, for any length of time together.

Be that as it might, numberless great guns, whose thunder had long been the voice of battle—the artillery of the Armada, the battering-trains of Marlborough, and the adverse cannon of

---

1. Cf. Hawthorne's "The Devil in Manuscript" (1835). Around 1830, Hawthorne burned a number of his youthful works.

Napoleon and Wellington[2]—were trundled into the midst of the fire. By the continual addition of dry combustibles, it had now waxed so intense, that neither brass nor iron could withstand it. It was wonderful to behold, how those terrible instruments of slaughter melted away like playthings of wax. Then the armies of the earth wheeled around the mighty furnace, with their military music playing triumphant marches, and flung in their muskets and swords. The standard-bearers, likewise, cast one look upward at their banners, all tattered with shot-holes, and inscribed with the names of victorious fields; and giving them a last flourish on the breeze, they lowered them into the flame, which snatched them upward in its rush towards the clouds. This ceremony being over, the world was left without a single weapon in its hands, except, possibly, a few old King's arms and rusty swords, and other trophies of the Revolution, in some of our state-armories. And now the drums were beaten and the trumpets brayed all together, as a prelude to the proclamation of universal and eternal peace, and the announcement that glory was no longer to be won by blood; but that it would henceforth be the contention of the human race, to work out the greatest mutual good; and that beneficence, in the future annals of the earth, would claim the praise of valor. The blessed tidings were accordingly promulgated, and caused infinite rejoicings among those who had stood aghast at the horror and absurdity of war.

But I saw a grim smile pass over the scarred visage of a stately old commander—by his war-worn figure and rich military dress, he might have been one of Napoleon's famous marshals—who, with the rest of the world's soldiery, had just flung away the sword, that had been familiar to his right hand for half-a-century.

"Aye, aye!" grumbled he. "Let them proclaim what they please; but, in the end, we shall find that all this foolery has only made more work for the armorers and cannon-founderies."

"Why, Sir," exclaimed I, in astonishment, "do you imagine that the human race will ever so far return on the steps of its past madness, as to weld another sword, or cast another cannon?"

"There will be no need," observed, with a sneer, one who neither felt benevolence, nor had faith in it. "When Cain wished to slay his brother, he was at no loss for a weapon."

"We shall see," replied the veteran commander.—"If I am mistaken, so much the better; but, in my opinion—without pretending to philosophize about the matter—the necessity of war lies far deeper than these honest gentlemen suppose. What! Is there a field for all the petty disputes of individuals, and shall there be no great

---

2. Wellington defeated Napoleon in the battle of Waterloo, 1815. The duke of Marlborough was England's foremost general early in the 18th century.

law-court for the settlement of national difficulties? The battle-field is the only court where such suits can be tried!"

"You forget, General," rejoined I, "that, in this advanced stage of civilization, Reason and Philanthropy combined will constitute just such a tribunal as is requisite."

"Ah, I had forgotten that, indeed!" said the old warrior, as he limped away.

The fire was now to be replenished with materials that had hitherto been considered of even greater importance to the well-being of society, than the warlike munitions which we had already seen consumed. A body of reformers had travelled all over the earth, in quest of the machinery by which the different nations were accustomed to inflict the punishment of death. A shudder passed through the multitude, as these ghastly emblems were dragged forward. Even the flames seemed at first to shrink away, displaying the shape and murderous contrivance of each in a full blaze of light, which, of itself, was sufficient to convince mankind of the long and deadly error of human law. Those old implements of cruelty—those horrible monsters of mechanism—those inventions which it seemed to demand something worse than man's natural heart to contrive, and which had lurked in the dusky nooks of ancient prisons, the subject of terror-stricken legends—were now brought forth to view. Headsmen's axes, with the rust of noble and royal blood upon them, and a vast collection of halters that had choked the breath of plebeian victims, were thrown in together. A shout greeted the arrival of the guillotine, which was thrust forward on the same wheels that had borne it from one to another of the blood-stained streets of Paris. But the loudest roar of applause went up, telling the distant sky of the triumph of the earth's redemption, when the gallows made its appearance. An ill-looking fellow, however, rushed forward, and putting himself in the path of the reformers, bellowed hoarsely, and fought with brute fury to stay their progress.

It was little matter of surprise, perhaps, that the executioner should thus do his best to vindicate and uphold the machinery by which he himself had his livelihood, and worthier individuals their death. But it deserved special note, that men of a far different sphere—even of that consecrated class in whose guardianship the world is apt to trust its benevolence—were found to take the hangman's view of the question.

"Stay, my brethren!" cried one of them. "You are misled by a false philanthropy!—you know not what you do. The gallows is a heaven-oriented instrument! Bear it back, then, reverently, and set it up in its old place; else the world will fall to speedy ruin and desolation!"

"Onward, onward!" shouted a leader in the reform. "Into the flames with the accursed instrument of man's bloody policy! How can human law inculcate benevolence and love, while it persists in setting up the gallows as its chief symbol? One heave more, good friends; and the world will be redeemed from its greatest error!"

A thousand hands, that, nevertheless, loathed the touch, now lent their assistance, and thrust the ominous burthen far, far, into the centre of the raging furnace. There its fatal and abhorred image was beheld, first black, then a red coal, then ashes.

"That was well done!" exclaimed I.

"Yes; it was well done," replied—but with less enthusiasm than I expected—the thoughtful observer who was still at my side; "well done, if the world be good enough for the measure. Death, however, is an idea that cannot easily be dispensed with, in any condition between the primal innocence and that other purity and perfection, which, perchance, we are destined to attain, after travelling round the full circle. But, at all events, it is well that the experiment should now be tried."

"Too cold!—too cold!" impatiently exclaimed the young and ardent leader in this triumph. "Let the heart have its voice here, as well as the intellect. And as for ripeness—and as for progress—let mankind always do the highest, kindest, noblest thing, that, at any given period, it has attained to the perception of; and surely that thing cannot be wrong, nor wrongly timed!"

I know not whether it were the excitement of the scene, or whether the good people around the bonfire were really growing more enlightened, every instant; but they now proceeded to measures, in the full length of which I was hardly prepared to keep them company. For instance, some threw their marriage-certificates into the flames, and declared themselves candidates for a higher, holier, and more comprehensive union than that which had subsisted from the birth of time, under the form of the connubial tie. Others hastened to the vaults of banks, and to the coffers of the rich—all of which were open to the first-comer, on this fated occasion—and brought entire bales of paper-money to enliven the blaze, and tons of coin to be melted down by its intensity. Henceforth, they said, universal benevolence, uncoined and exhaustless, was to be the golden currency of the world. At this intelligence, the bankers, and speculators in the stocks, grew pale; and a pick-pocket, who had reaped a rich harvest among the crowd, fell down in a deadly fainting-fit. A few men of business burnt their day-books and legers, the notes and obligations of their creditors, and all other evidences of debts due to themselves; while perhaps a somewhat larger number satisfied their zeal for reform with the sacrifice of any uncomfortable recollection of their own indebtment. There was then a cry, that the period was arrived, when the title-deeds of landed property should be given to the flames, and the whole soil of the earth revert to the public, from whom it had been wrongfully abstracted, and most unequally distributed among individuals. Another party demanded, that all written constitutions, set forms of government, legislative acts, statute-books, and everything else on which human invention had endeavored to stamp its arbitrary laws, should at once be destroyed, leaving the consummated world as free as the man first created.

Whether any ultimate action was taken with regard to these propositions, is beyond my knowledge; for, just then, some matters were in progress that concerned my sympathies more nearly.

"See!—see!—what heaps of books and pamphlets," cried a fellow, who did not seem to be a lover of literature. "Now we shall have a glorious blaze!"

"That's just the thing," said a modern philosopher. "Now we shall get rid of the weight of dead men's thought, which has hitherto pressed so heavily on the living intellect, that it has been incompetent to any effectual self-exertion. Well done, my lads! Into the fire with them! Now you are enlightening the world, indeed!"

"But what is to become of the Trade?" cried a frantic bookseller.

"Oh, by all means, let them accompany their merchandise," coolly observed an author. "It will be a noble funeral-pile!"

The truth was, that the human race had now reached a stage of progress, so far beyond what the wisest and wittiest men of former ages had ever dreamed of, that it would have been a manifest absurdity to allow the earth to be any longer encumbered with their poor achievements in the literary line. Accordingly, a thorough and searching investigation had swept the booksellers' shops, hawkers' stands, public and private libraries, and even the little book-shelf by the country fireside, and had brought the world's entire mass of printed paper, bound or in sheets, to swell the already mountain-bulk of our illustrious bonfire. Thick, heavy folios, containing the labors of lexicographers, commentators, and encyclopediasts, were flung in, and, falling among the embers with a leaden thump, smouldered away to ashes, like rotten wood. The small, richly-gilt, French tomes, of the last age, with the hundred volumes of Voltaire among them, went off in a brilliant shower of sparkles, and little jets of flame; while the current literature of the same nation burnt red and blue,[3] and threw an infernal light over the visages of the spectators, converting them all to the aspect of parti-colored fiends. A collection of German stories emitted a scent of brimstone. The English standard authors made excellent fuel, generally exhibiting the properties of sound oak logs. Milton's works, in particular, sent up a powerful blaze, gradually reddening into a coal, which promised to endure longer than almost any other material of the pile. From Shakspeare

3. The municipal colors of Paris, associated with the French Revolution.

there gushed a flame of such marvellous splendor, that men shaded their eyes as against the sun's meridian glory; nor, even when the works of his own elucidators were flung upon him, did he cease to flash forth a dazzling radiance, from beneath the ponderous heap. It is my belief, that he is still blazing as fervidly as ever.

"Could a poet but light a lamp at that glorious flame," remarked I, "he might then consume the midnight oil to some good purpose."

"That is the very thing which modern poets have been too apt to do—or, at least, to attempt," answered a critic. "The chief benefit to be expected from this conflagration of past literature, undoubtedly is, that writers will henceforth be compelled to light their lamps at the sun or stars."

"If they can reach so high," said I. "But that task requires a giant, who may afterwards distribute the light among inferior men. It is not every one that can steal the fire from Heaven, like Prometheus; but when once he had done the deed, a thousand hearths were kindled by it."

It amazed me much to observe, how indefinite was the proportion between the physical mass of any given author, and the property of brilliant and long-continued combustion. For instance, there was not a quarto volume of the last century—nor, indeed, of the present— that could compete, in that particular, with a child's little gilt-covered book, containing Mother Goose's Melodies. The Life and Death of Tom Thumb outlasted the biography of Marlborough.[4] An epic— indeed, a dozen of them—was converted to white ashes, before the single sheet of an old ballad was half-consumed. In more than one case, too, when volumes of applauded verse proved incapable of any- thing better than a stifling smoke, an unregarded ditty of some nameless bard—perchance, in the corner of a newspaper—soared up among the stars, with a flame as brilliant as their own. Speaking of the properties of flame, methought Shelley's poetry emitted a purer light than almost any other productions of his day; contrasting beautifully with the fitful and lurid gleams, and gushes of black vapor, that flashed and eddied from the volumes of Lord Byron.[5] As for Tom Moore, some of his songs diffused an odor like a burning pastille.[6]

I felt particular interest in watching the combustion of American authors, and scrupulously noted, by my watch, the precise number

4. William Coxe's Life of Marlborough (1820) comes to some thirteen hundred pages. The Life and Death of Tom Thumb the Great (1731), a short, uproarious burlesque tragedy by Henry Fielding.
5. Percy Bysshe Shelley (1792–1822) and George Gordon, Lord Byron (1788–1824). English Romantic poets. While Byron was universally notorious and widely read, a taste for Shelley was unusual in the United States in 1843.
6. A paste containing aromatic substances, used as a disinfectant. Tom Moore (1779– 1852), Irish lyrical poet and satirist.

of moments that changed most of them from shabbily-printed books to indistinguishable ashes. It would be invidious, however, if not perilous, to betray these awful secrets; so that I shall content myself with observing, that it was not invariably the writer most frequent in the public mouth, that made the most splendid appearance in the bonfire. I especially remember, that a great deal of excellent inflammability was exhibited in a thin volume of poems by Ellery Channing;[7] although, to speak the truth, there were certain portions that hissed and spluttered in a very disagreeable fashion. A curious phenomenon occurred, in reference to several writers, native as well as foreign. Their books, though of highly respectable figure, instead of bursting into a blaze, or even smouldering out their substance in smoke, suddenly melted away, in a manner that proved them to be ice.

If it be no lack of modesty to mention my own works, it must here be confessed, that I looked for them with fatherly interest, but in vain. Too probably, they were changed to vapor by the first action of the heat; at best, I can only hope, that, in their quiet way, they contributed a glimmering spark or two to the splendor of the evening.

"Alas, and woe is me!" thus bemoaned himself a heavy-looking gentleman in green spectacles. "The world is utterly ruined, and there is nothing to live for any longer! The business of my life is snatched from me. Not a volume to be had for love or money!"

"This," remarked the sedate observer beside me, "is a book-worm—one of those men who are born to gnaw dead thoughts. His clothes, you see, are covered with the dust of libraries. He has no inward fountain of ideas; and, in good earnest, now that the old stock is abolished, I do not see what is to become of the poor fellow. Have you no word of comfort for him?"

"My dear Sir," said I to the desperate book-worm, "is not Nature better than a book?—is not the human heart deeper than any system of philosophy?—is not life replete with more instruction than past observers have found it possible to write down in maxims? Be of good cheer! The great book of Time is still spread wide open before us; and, if we read it aright, it will be to us a volume of eternal Truth."

"Oh, my books, my books, my precious, printed books!" reiterated the forlorn book-worm. "My only reality was a bound volume; and now they will not leave me even a shadowy pamphlet!"

In fact, the last remnant of the literature of all the ages was now descending upon the blazing heap, in the shape of a cloud of pamphlets from the press of the New World. These, likewise, were

---

7. William Ellery Channing (1818–1901), Concord poet. Hawthorne gives an affectionate portrait of Channing in "The Old Manse." Even Channing's friends enjoyed poking fun at the fitful irregularity of his style.

consumed in the twinkling of an eye, leaving the earth, for the first time since the days of Cadmus,[8] free from the plague of letters—an enviable field for the authors of the next generation!

"Well!—and does anything remain to be done?" inquired I, somewhat anxiously. "Unless we set fire to the earth itself, and then leap boldly off into infinite space, I know not that we can carry reform to any further point."

"You are vastly mistaken, my good friend," said the observer. "Believe me, the fire will not be allowed to settle down, without the addition of fuel that will startle many persons, who have lent a willing hand thus far."

Nevertheless, there appeared to be a relaxation of effort, for a little time, during which, probably, the leaders of the movement were considering what should be done next. In the interval, a philosopher threw his theory into the flames; a sacrifice, which, by those who knew how to estimate it, was pronounced the most remarkable that had yet been made. The combustion, however, was by no means brilliant. Some indefatigable people, scorning to take a moment's ease, now employed themselves in collecting all the withered leaves and fallen boughs of the forest, and thereby recruited the bonfire to a greater height than ever. But this was mere by-play.

"Here comes the fresh fuel that I spoke of," said my companion.

To my astonishment, the persons who now advanced into the vacant space, around the mountain of fire, bore surplices and other priestly garments, mitres, crosiers, and a confusion of popish and protestant emblems, with which it seemed their purpose to consummate this great Act of Faith. Crosses, from the spires of old cathedrals, were cast upon the heap, with as little remorse as if the reverence of centuries, passing in long array beneath the lofty towers, had not looked up to them as the holiest of symbols. The font, in which infants were consecrated to God; the sacramental vessels,[9] whence Piety had received the hallowed draught; were given to the same destruction. Perhaps it most nearly touched my heart, to see, among these devoted relics, fragments of the humble communion-tables and undecorated pulpits, which I recognized as having been torn from the meeting-houses of New-England. Those simple edifices might have been permitted to retain all of sacred embellishment that their Puritan founders had bestowed, even though the mighty structure of St. Peter's had sent its spoils to the fire of this terrible sacrifice. Yet I felt that these were but the externals of

8. Legendary founder of Thebes, said to have introduced the Phoenician alphabet into Greece.
9. Communion cups.

religion, and might most safely be relinquished by spirits that best knew their deep significance.

"All is well," said I, cheerfully. "The wood-paths shall be the aisles of our cathedral—the firmament itself shall be its ceiling! What needs an earthly roof between the Deity and his worshipper? Our faith can well afford to lose all the drapery that even the holiest men have thrown around it, and be only the more sublime in its simplicity."

"True," said my companion. "But will they pause here?"

The doubt, implied in his question, was well-founded. In the general destruction of books, already described, a holy volume—that stood apart from the catalogue of human literature, and yet, in one sense, was at its head—had been spared. But the Titan[1] of innovation—angel or fiend, double in his nature, and capable of deeds befitting both characters—at first shaking down only the old and rotten shapes of things, had now, as it appeared, laid his terrible hand upon the main pillars, which supported the whole edifice of our moral and spiritual state. The inhabitants of the earth had grown too enlightened to define their faith within a form of words, or to limit the spiritual by any analogy to our material existence. Truths, which the Heavens trembled at, were now but a fable of the world's infancy. Therefore, as the final sacrifice of human error, what else remained, to be thrown upon the embers of that awful pile, except the Book, which, though a celestial revelation to past ages, was but a voice from a lower sphere, as regarded the present race of man? It was done! Upon the blazing heap of falsehood and worn-out truth—things that the earth had never needed, or had ceased to need, or had grown childishly weary of—fell the ponderous church-Bible, the great old volume, that had lain so long on the cushions of the pulpit, and whence the pastor's solemn voice had given holy utterances, on so many a Sabbath-day. There, likewise, fell the family-Bible, which the long-buried patriarch had read to his children—in prosperity or sorrow, by the fireside, and in the summer-shade of trees—and had bequeathed downward, as the heirloom of generations. There fell the bosom-Bible, the little volume that had been the soul's friend of some sorely tried Child of Dust, who thence took courage, whether his trial were for life or death, steadfastly confronting both, in the strong assurance of Immortality.

All these were flung into the fierce and riotous blaze; and then a mighty wind came roaring across the plain, with a desolate howl, as if it were the angry lamentation of the Earth for the loss of Heaven's sunshine; and it shook the gigantic pyramid of flame, and scattered

---

1. The Titans were giant gods who lost control of the universe to Zeus and his Olympians in a violent struggle.

the cinders of half-consumed abominations around upon the spectators.

"This is terrible!" said I, feeling that my cheek grew pale, and seeing a like change in the visages about me.

"Be of good courage yet," answered the man with whom I had so often spoken. He continued to gaze steadily at the spectacle, with a singular calmness, as if it concerned him merely as an observer.— "Be of good courage—nor yet exult too much; for there is far less both of good and evil, in the effect of this bonfire, than the world might be willing to believe."

"How can that be?" exclaimed I, impatiently.—"Has it not consumed everything? Has it not swallowed up, or melted down, every human or divine appendage of our mortal state, that had substance enough to be acted on by fire? Will there be anything left us, tomorrow morning, better or worse than a heap of embers and ashes?"

"Assuredly there will," said my grave friend. "Come hither tomorrow morning—or whenever the combustible portion of the pile shall be quite burnt out—and you will find among the ashes everything really valuable that you have seen cast into the flames. Trust me; the world of tomorrow will again enrich itself with the gold and diamonds, which have been cast off by the world of to-day. Not a truth is destroyed—nor buried so deep among the ashes, but it will be raked up at last."

This was a strange assurance. Yet I felt inclined to credit it; the more especially as I beheld, among the wallowing flames, a copy of the Holy Scriptures, the pages of which, instead of being blackened into tinder, only assumed a more dazzling whiteness, as the finger-marks of human imperfection were purified away. Certain marginal notes and commentaries, it is true, yielded to the intensity of the fiery test, but without detriment to the smallest syllable that had flamed from the pen of inspiration.

"Yes;—there is the proof of what you say," answered I, turning to the observer. "But, if only what is evil can feel the action of the fire, then, surely, the conflagration has been of inestimable utility. Yet, if I understand aright, you intimate a doubt whether the world's expectation of benefit will be realized by it."

"Listen to the talk of these worthies," said he, pointing to a group in front of the blazing pile.—"Possibly, they may teach you something useful, without intending it."

The persons, whom he indicated, consisted of that brutal and most earthy figure, who had stood forth so furiously in defence of the gallows—the hangman, in short—together with the Last Thief and the Last Murderer; all three of whom were clustered about the Last Toper. The latter was liberally passing the brandy-bottle, which he had rescued from the general destruction of wines and spirits. This little convivial party seemed at the lowest pitch of despondency; as considering that the purified world must needs be utterly unlike, the sphere that they had hitherto known, and therefore but a strange and desolate abode for gentlemen of their kidney.

"The best counsel for all of us, is," remarked the hangman, "that—as soon as we have finished the last drop of liquor—I help you, my three friends, to a comfortable end upon the nearest tree, and then hang myself on the same bough. This is no world for us, any longer."

"Poh, poh, my good fellows!" said a dark-complexioned personage, who now joined the group—his complexion was indeed fearfully dark; and his eyes glowed with a redder light than that of the bonfire—"Be not so cast down, my dear friends; you shall see good days yet. There is one thing that these wiseacres have forgotten to throw into the fire, and without which all the rest of the conflagration is just nothing at all—yes; though they had burnt the earth itself to a cinder!"

"And what may that be?" eagerly demanded the Last Murderer.

"What, but the human heart itself!" said the dark-visaged stranger, with a portentous grin. "And, unless they hit upon some method of purifying that foul cavern, forth from it will re-issue all the shapes of wrong and misery—the same old shapes, or worse ones—which they have taken such a vast deal of trouble to consume to ashes. I have stood by, this live-long night, and laughed in my sleeve at the whole business. Oh, take my word for it, it will be the old world yet!"

This brief conversation supplied me with a theme for lengthened thought. How sad a truth—if true it were—that Man's age-long endeavor for perfection had served only to render him the mockery of the Evil Principle, from the fatal circumstance of an error at the very root of the matter! The Heart—the Heart—there was the little, yet boundless sphere, wherein existed the original wrong, of which the crime and misery of this outward world were merely types. Purify that inner sphere; and the many shapes of evil that haunt the outward, and which now seem almost our only realities, will turn to shadowy phantoms, and vanish of their own accord. But, if we go no deeper than the Intellect, and strive, with merely that feeble instrument, to discern and rectify what is wrong, our whole accomplishment will be a dream; so unsubstantial, that it matters little whether the bonfire, which I have so faithfully described, were what we choose to call a real event, and a flame that would scorch the finger—or only a phosphoric radiance, and a parable of my own brain!

The Artist of the Beautiful[†]

An elderly man, with his pretty daughter on his arm, was passing along the street, and emerged from the gloom of the cloudy evening into the light that fell across the pavement from the window of a small shop. It was a projecting window; and on the inside were suspended a variety of watches, pinchbecks,[1] silver, and one or two of gold, all with their faces turned from the street, as if churlishly disinclined to inform the wayfarers what o'clock it was. Seated within the shop, sidelong to the window, with his pale face bent earnestly over some delicate piece of mechanism on which was thrown the concentrated lustre of a shade lamp, appeared a young man.

"What can Owen Warland[2] be about?" muttered old Peter Hovenden, himself a retired watchmaker and the former master of this same young man whose occupation he was now wondering at. "What can the fellow be about? These six months past I have never come by his shop without seeing him just as steadily at work as now. It would be a flight beyond his usual foolery to seek for the perpetual motion; and yet I know enough of my old business to be certain that what he is now so busy with is no part of the machinery of a watch."

"Perhaps, father," said Annie, without showing much interest in the question, "Owen is inventing a new kind of timekeeper. I am sure he has ingenuity enough."

"Poh, child! He has not the sort of ingenuity to invent any thing better than a Dutch toy," answered her father, who had formerly been put to much vexation by Owen Warland's irregular genius. "A plague on such ingenuity! All the effect that ever I knew of it was, to spoil the accuracy of some of the best watches in my shop. He would turn the sun out of its orbit and derange the whole course of time, if, as I said before, his ingenuity could grasp any thing bigger than a child's toy!"

"Hush, father! He hears you!" whispered Annie, pressing the old man's arm. "His ears are as delicate as his feelings; and you know how easily disturbed they are. Do let us move on."

So Peter Hovenden and his daughter Annie plodded on without further conversation, until in a by-street of the town they found themselves passing the open door of a blacksmith's shop. Within was seen the forge, now blazing up and illuminating the high and dusky

---

[†] First published in the *Democratic Review*, June 1844, then in *Mosses from an Old Manse*, 1846.

1. An alloy of zinc and copper used as imitation gold.

2. The name "Owen" is Celtic; according to 19th-century convention, Celts are artistic, irregular, and sometimes prone to magic. "Warland" suggests "war against land."

roof, and now confining its lustre to a narrow precinct of the coal-strewn floor, according as the breath of the bellows was pulled forth or again inhaled into its vast leathern lungs. In the intervals of brightness it was easy to distinguish objects in remote corners of the shop and the horseshoes that hung upon the wall; in the momentary gloom the fire seemed to be glimmering amidst the vagueness of unenclosed space. Moving about in this red glare and alternate dusk was the figure of the blacksmith, well worthy to be viewed in so picturesque an aspect of light and shade, where the bright blaze struggled with the black night, as if each would have snatched his comely strength from the other. Anon he drew a whitehot bar of iron from the coals, laid it on the anvil, uplifted his arm of might, and was soon enveloped in the myriads of sparks which the strokes of his hammer scattered into the surrounding gloom.

"Now, that is a pleasant sight," said the old watchmaker. "I know what it is to work in gold; but give me the worker in iron after all is said and done. He spends his labor upon a reality. What say you, daughter Annie?"

"Pray don't speak so loud, father," whispered Annie. "Robert Danforth[3] will hear you."

"And what if he should hear me?" said Peter Hovenden. "I say again, it is a good and a wholesome thing to depend upon main strength and reality, and to earn one's bread with the bare and brawny arm of a blacksmith. A watchmaker gets his brain puzzled by his wheels within a wheel, or loses his health or the nicety of his eyesight, as was my case, and finds himself at middle age, or a little after, past labor at his own trade, and fit for nothing else, yet too poor to live at his ease. So I say once again, give me main strength for my money. And then, how it takes the nonsense out of a man! Did you ever hear of a blacksmith being such a fool as Owen Warland yonder?"

"Well said, uncle Hovenden!" shouted Robert Danforth from the forge, in a full, deep, merry voice, that made the roof reecho. "And what says Miss Annie to that doctrine? She, I suppose, will think it a genteeler business to tinker up a lady's watch than to forge a horseshoe or make a gridiron."

Annie drew her father onward without giving him time for reply.

But we must return to Owen Warland's shop, and spend more meditation upon his history and character than either Peter Hovenden, or probably his daughter Annie, or Owen's old schoolfellow, Robert Danforth, would have thought due to so slight a subject. From the time that his little fingers could grasp a penknife, Owen had been remarkable for a delicate ingenuity, which sometimes

3. The name of a sturdy Saxon.

produced pretty shapes in wood, principally figures of flowers and birds, and sometimes seemed to aim at the hidden mysteries of mechanism. But it was always for purposes of grace, and never with any mockery of the useful. He did not, like the crowd of schoolboy artisans, construct little windmills on the angle of a barn or water-mills across the neighboring brook. Those who discovered such peculiarity in the boy as to think it worth their while to observe him closely, sometimes saw reason to suppose that he was attempting to imitate the beautiful movements of Nature as exemplified in the flight of birds or the activity of little animals. It seemed, in fact, a new development of the love of the beautiful, such as might have made him a poet, a painter, or a sculptor, and which was as com-pletely refined from all utilitarian coarseness as it could have been in either of the fine arts. He looked with singular distaste at the stiff and regular processes of ordinary machinery. Being once car-ried to see a steam engine, in the expectation that his intuitive com-prehension of mechanical principles would be gratified, he turned pale and grew sick, as if something monstrous and unnatural had been presented to him. This horror was partly owing to the size and terrible energy of the iron laborer; for the character of Owen's mind was microscopic, and tended naturally to the minute, in accor-dance with his diminutive frame and the marvellous smallness and delicate power of his fingers. Not that his sense of beauty was thereby diminished into a sense of prettiness. The beautiful idea has no relation to size, and may be as perfectly developed in a space too minute for any but microscopic investigation as within the ample verge that is measured by the arc of the rainbow. But, at all events, this characteristic minuteness in his objects and accomplishments made the world even more incapable than it might otherwise have been of appreciating Owen Warland's genius. The boy's relatives saw nothing better to be done—as perhaps there was not—than to bind him apprentice to a watchmaker, hoping that his strange inge-nuity might thus be regulated and put to utilitarian purposes.

Peter Hovenden's opinion of his apprentice has already been expressed. He could make nothing of the lad. Owen's apprehension of the professional mysteries, it is true, was inconceivably quick; but he altogether forgot or despised the grand object of a watchmaker's business, and cared no more for the measurement of time than if it had been merged into eternity. So long, however, as he remained under his old master's care, Owen's lack of sturdiness made it possible, by strict injunctions and sharp oversight, to restrain his creative eccentricity within bounds; but when his apprenticeship was served out, and he had taken the little shop which Peter Hov-enden's failing eyesight compelled him to relinquish, then did peo-ple recognize how unfit a person was Owen Warland to lead old blind Father Time along his daily course. One of his most rational projects was to connect a musical operation with the machinery of his watches, so that all the harsh dissonances of life might be rendered tuneful, and each flitting moment fall into the abyss of the past in golden drops of harmony. If a family clock was intrusted to him for repair,—one of those tall, ancient clocks that have grown nearly allied to human nature by measuring out the lifetime of many generations,—he would take upon himself to arrange a dance or funeral procession of figures across its venerable face, representing twelve mirthful or melancholy hours. Several freaks of this kind quite destroyed the young watchmaker's credit with that steady and matter-of-fact class of people who hold the opinion that time is not to be trifled with, whether considered as the medium of advancement and prosperity in this world or preparation for the next. His custom rapidly diminished—a misfortune, however, that was probably reckoned among his better accidents by Owen Warland, who was becoming more and more absorbed in a secret occupation which drew all his science and manual dexterity into itself, and likewise gave full employment to the characteristic tendencies of his genius. This pursuit had already consumed many months.

After the old watchmaker and his pretty daughter had gazed at him out of the obscurity of the street, Owen Warland was seized with a fluttering of the nerves, which made his hand tremble too violently to proceed with such delicate labor as he was now engaged upon.

"It was Annie herself!" murmured he. "I should have known it, by this throbbing of my heart, before I heard her father's voice. Ah, how it throbs! I shall scarcely be able to work again on this exquisite mechanism to-night. Annie! dearest Annie! thou shouldst give firmness to my heart and hand, and not shake them thus; for, if I strive to put the very spirit of beauty into form and give it motion, it is for thy sake alone. O throbbing heart, be quiet! If my labor be thus thwarted, there will come vague and unsatisfied dreams, which will leave me spiritless to-morrow."

As he was endeavoring to settle himself again to his task, the shop door opened and gave admittance to no other than the stalwart figure which Peter Hovenden had paused to admire, as seen amid the light and shadow of the blacksmith's shop. Robert Danforth had brought a little anvil of his own manufacture, and peculiarly constructed, which the young artist had recently bespoken. Owen examined the article, and pronounced it fashioned according to his wish.

"Why, yes," said Robert Danforth, his strong voice filling the shop as with the sound of a bass viol, "I consider myself equal to any thing in the way of my own trade; though I should have made but a poor figure at yours with such a fist as this," added he, laughing, as he laid his vast hand beside the delicate one of Owen. "But what then? I put more main strength into one blow of my sledge hammer than all that you have expended since you were a 'prentice. Is not that the truth?"

"Very probably," answered the low and slender voice of Owen. "Strength is an earthly monster. I make no pretensions to it. My force, whatever there may be of it, is altogether spiritual."

"Well, but, Owen, what are you about?" asked his old school-fellow, still in such a hearty volume of tone that it made the artist shrink, especially as the question related to a subject so sacred as the absorbing dream of his imagination. "Folks do say that you are trying to discover the perpetual motion."

"The perpetual motion? Nonsense!" replied Owen Warland, with a movement of disgust; for he was full of little petulances. "It can never be discovered. It is a dream that may delude men whose brains are mystified with matter, but not me. Besides, if such a discovery were possible, it would not be worth my while to make it only to have the secret turned to such purposes as are now effected by steam and water power. I am not ambitious to be honored with the paternity of a new kind of cotton machine."

"That would be droll enough!" cried the blacksmith, breaking out into such an uproar of laughter that Owen himself and the bell glasses on his workboard quivered in unison. "No, no, Owen! No child of yours will have iron joints and sinews. Well, I won't hinder you any more. Good night, Owen, and success; and if you need any assistance, so far as a downright blow of hammer upon anvil will answer the purpose, I'm your man."

And with another laugh the man of main strength left the shop.

"How strange it is," whispered Owen Warland to himself, leaning his head upon his hand, "that all my musings, my purposes, my passion for the beautiful, my consciousness of power to create it—a finer, more ethereal power, of which this earthly giant can have no conception,—all, all, look so vain and idle whenever my path is crossed by Robert Danforth! He would drive me mad were I to meet him often. His hard, brute force darkens and confuses the spiritual element within me; but I, too, will be strong in my own way. I will not yield to him."

He took from beneath a glass a piece of minute machinery, which he set in the condensed light of his lamp, and, looking intently at it through a magnifying glass, proceeded to operate with a delicate instrument of steel. In an instant, however, he fell back in his chair and clasped his hands, with a look of horror on his face that made its small features as impressive as those of a giant would have been.

"Heaven! What have I done?" exclaimed he. "The vapor, the influence of that brute force,—it has bewildered me and obscured my perception. I have made the very stroke—the fatal stroke—that I have dreaded from the first. It is all over—the toil of months, the object of my life. I am ruined!"

And there he sat, in strange despair, until his lamp flickered in the socket and left the Artist of the Beautiful in darkness.

Thus it is that ideas, which grow up within the imagination and appear so lovely to it and of a value beyond whatever men call valuable, are exposed to be shattered and annihilated by contact with the practical. It is requisite for the ideal artist[4] to possess a force of character that seems hardly compatible with its delicacy; he must keep his faith in himself while the incredulous world assails him with its utter disbelief; he must stand up against mankind and be his own sole disciple, both as respects his genius and the objects to which it is directed.

For a time Owen Warland succumbed to this severe but inevitable test. He spent a few sluggish weeks with his head so continually resting in his hands that the townspeople had scarcely an opportunity to see his countenance. When at last it was again uplifted to the light of day, a cold, dull, nameless change was perceptible upon it. In the opinion of Peter Hovenden, however, and that order of sagacious understandings who think that life should be regulated, like clockwork, with leaden weights, the alteration was entirely for the better. Owen now, indeed, applied himself to business with dogged industry. It was marvellous to witness the obtuse gravity with which he would inspect the wheels of a great, old silver watch; thereby delighting the owner, in whose fob it had been worn till he deemed it a portion of his own life, and was accordingly jealous of its treatment. In consequence of the good report thus acquired, Owen Warland was invited by the proper authorities to regulate the clock in the church steeple. He succeeded so admirably in this matter of public interest that the merchants gruffly acknowledged his merits on 'Change;[5] the nurse whispered his praises as she gave the potion in the sick chamber; the lover blessed him at the hour of appointed interview; and the town in general thanked Owen for the punctuality of dinner time. In a word, the heavy weight upon his spirits kept every thing in order, not merely within his own system, but wheresoever the iron accents of the church clock were audible. It was a circumstance, though minute yet characteristic of his present state, that, when employed to engrave names or initials on silver spoons, he now wrote the requisite letters in the plainest possible style, omitting a variety of fanciful flourishes that had heretofore distinguished his work in this kind.

---

4. The artist who strives to represent an idea.
5. The Exchange, a building where the merchants of a town transact business.

One day, during the era of this happy transformation, old Peter Hovenden came to visit his former apprentice.

"Well, Owen," said he, "I am glad to hear such good accounts of you from all quarters, and especially from the town clock yonder, which speaks in your commendation every hour of the twenty-four. Only get rid altogether of your nonsensical trash about the beautiful, which I nor nobody else, nor yourself to boot, could ever understand,—only free yourself of that, and your success in life is as sure as daylight. Why, if you go on in this way, I should even venture to let you doctor this precious old watch of mine; though, except my daughter Annie, I have nothing else so valuable in the world."

"I should hardly dare touch it, sir," replied Owen, in a depressed tone; for he was weighed down by his old master's presence.

"In time," said the latter,—"in time, you will be capable of it."

The old watchmaker, with the freedom naturally consequent on his former authority, went on inspecting the work which Owen had in hand at the moment, together with other matters that were in progress. The artist, meanwhile, could scarcely lift his head. There was nothing so antipodal to his nature as this man's cold, unimaginative sagacity, by contact with which every thing was converted into a dream except the densest matter of the physical world. Owen groaned in spirit and prayed fervently to be delivered from him.

"But what is this?" cried Peter Hovenden abruptly, taking up a dusty bell glass, beneath which appeared a mechanical something, as delicate and minute as the system of a butterfly's anatomy. "What have we here? Owen! Owen! there is a witchcraft in these little chains, and wheels, and paddles. See! with one pinch of my finger and thumb I am going to deliver you from all future peril."

"For Heaven's sake," screamed Owen Warland, springing up with wonderful energy, "as you would not drive me mad, do not touch it! The slightest pressure of your finger would ruin me forever."

"Aha, young man! And is it so?" said the old watchmaker, looking at him with just enough of penetration to torture Owen's soul with the bitterness of worldly criticism. "Well, take your own course; but I warn you again that in this small piece of mechanism lives your evil spirit. Shall I exorcise him?"

"You are my evil spirit," answered Owen, much excited,—"you and the hard, coarse world! The leaden thoughts and the despondency that you fling upon me are my clogs, else I should long ago have achieved the task that I was created for."

Peter Hovenden shook his head, with the mixture of contempt and indignation which mankind, of whom he was partly a representative, deem themselves entitled to feel towards all simpletons who seek other prizes than the dusty ones along the highway. He then took his leave, with an uplifted finger and a sneer upon his face that haunted the artist's dreams for many a night afterwards. At the time of his old master's visit, Owen was probably on the point of taking up the relinquished task; but, by this sinister event, he was thrown back into the state whence he had been slowly emerging.

But the innate tendency of his soul had only been accumulating fresh vigor during its apparent sluggishness. As the summer advanced he almost totally relinquished his business, and permitted Father Time, so far as the old gentleman was represented by the clocks and watches under his control, to stray at random through human life, making infinite confusion among the train of bewildered hours. He wasted the sunshine, as people said, in wandering through the woods and fields and along the banks of streams. There, like a child, he found amusement in chasing butterflies or watching the motions of water insects. There was something truly mysterious in the intentness with which he contemplated these living playthings as they sported on the breeze or examined the structure of an imperial insect whom he had imprisoned. The chase of butterflies was an apt emblem of the ideal pursuit in which he had spent so many golden hours; but would the beautiful idea ever be yielded to his hand like the butterfly[6] that symbolized it? Sweet, doubtless, were these days, and congenial to the artist's soul. They were full of bright conceptions, which gleamed through his intellectual world as the butterflies gleamed through the outward atmosphere, and were real to him, for the instant, without the toil, and perplexity, and many disappointments of attempting to make them visible to the sensual eye. Alas that the artist, whether in poetry or whatever other material, may not content himself with the inward enjoyment of the beautiful, but must chase the flitting mystery beyond the verge of his ethereal domain, and crush its frail being in seizing it with a material grasp. Owen Warland felt the impulse to give external reality to his ideas as irresistibly as any of the poets or painters who have arrayed the world in a dimmer and fainter beauty, imperfectly copied from the richness of their visions.

The night was now his time for the slow process of re-creating the one idea to which all his intellectual activity referred itself. Always at the approach of dusk he stole into the town, locked himself within his shop, and wrought with patient delicacy of touch for many hours. Sometimes he was startled by the rap of the watchman, who, when all the world should be asleep, had caught the gleam of lamplight through the crevices of Owen Warland's shutters. Daylight, to the morbid sensibility of his mind, seemed to have an intrusiveness that interfered with his pursuits. On cloudy and inclement

6. Traditionally a symbol of the spiritual; the goddess Psyche (soul) has the wings of a butterfly in some Greek myth.

days, therefore, he sat with his head upon his hands, muffling, as it were, his sensitive brain in a mist of indefinite musings; for it was a relief to escape from the sharp distinctness with which he was compelled to shape out his thoughts during his nightly toil.

From one of these fits of torpor he was aroused by the entrance of Annie Hovenden, who came into the shop with the freedom of a customer and also with something of the familiarity of a childish friend. She had worn a hole through her silver thimble, and wanted Owen to repair it.

"But I don't know whether you will condescend to such a task," said she, laughing, "now that you are so taken up with the notion of putting spirit into machinery."

"Where did you get that idea, Annie?" said Owen, starting in surprise.

"O, out of my own head," answered she, "and from something that I heard you say, long ago, when you were but a boy and I a little child. But come; will you mend this poor thimble of mine?"

"Any thing for your sake, Annie," said Owen Warland,—"any thing, even were it to work at Robert Danforth's forge."

"And that would be a pretty sight!" retorted Annie, glancing with imperceptible slightness[7] at the artist's small and slender frame. "Well; here is the thimble."

"But that is a strange idea of yours," said Owen, "about the spiritualization of matter."

And then the thought stole into his mind that this young girl possessed the gift to comprehend him better than all the world besides. And what a help and strength would it be to him in his lonely toil if he could gain the sympathy of the only being whom he loved! To persons whose pursuits are insulated from the common business of life—who are either in advance of mankind or apart from it—there often comes a sensation of moral cold that makes the spirit shiver as if it had reached the frozen solitudes around the pole. What the prophet, the poet, the reformer, the criminal, or any other man with human yearnings, but separated from the multitude by a peculiar lot, might feel, poor Owen Warland felt.

"Annie," cried he, growing pale as death at the thought, "how gladly would I tell you the secret of my pursuit! You, methinks, would estimate it rightly. You, I know, would hear it with a reverence that I must not expect from the harsh, material world."

"Would I not? to be sure I would!" replied Annie Hovenden, lightly laughing. "Come; explain to me quickly what is the meaning of this

7. Slighting, contempt.

little whirligig, so delicately wrought that it might be a plaything for Queen Mab.[8] See! I will put it in motion."

"Hold!" exclaimed Owen, "hold!"

Annie had but given the slightest possible touch, with the point of a needle, to the same minute portion of complicated machinery which has been more than once mentioned, when the artist seized her by the wrist with a force that made her scream aloud. She was affrighted at the convulsion of intense rage and anguish that writhed across his features. The next instant he let his head sink upon his hands.

"Go, Annie," murmured he; "I have deceived myself, and must suffer for it. I yearned for sympathy, and thought, and fancied, and dreamed that you might give it me; but you lack the talisman,[9] Annie, that should admit you into my secrets. That touch has undone the toil of months and the thought of a lifetime! It was not your fault, Annie; but you have ruined me!"

Poor Owen Warland! He had indeed erred, yet pardonably; for if any human spirit could have sufficiently reverenced the processes so sacred in his eyes, it must have been a woman's. Even Annie Hovenden, possibly, might not have disappointed him had she been enlightened by the deep intelligence of love.

The artist spent the ensuing winter in a way that satisfied any persons who had hitherto retained a hopeful opinion of him that he was, in truth, irrevocably doomed to inutility as regarded the world, and to an evil destiny on his own part. The decease of a relative had put him in possession of a small inheritance. Thus freed from the necessity of toil, and having lost the steadfast influence of a great purpose,—great, at least, to him,—he abandoned himself to habits from which it might have been supposed the mere delicacy of his organization would have availed to secure him. But, when the ethereal portion of a man of genius is obscured, the earthly part assumes an influence the more uncontrollable, because the character is now thrown off the balance to which Providence had so nicely adjusted it, and which, in coarser natures, is adjusted by some other method. Owen Warland made proof[1] of whatever show of bliss may be found in riot. He looked at the world through the golden medium of wine, and contemplated the visions that bubble up so gayly around the brim of the glass, and that people the air with shapes of pleasant madness, which so soon grow ghostly and forlorn. Even when this dismal and inevitable change had taken place, the young man might

---

8. Miniature fairy queen, with "a whip of cricket's bone" and a chariot made of "an empty hazelnut," who visits men in dreams. See *Romeo and Juliet* 1.4.53ff.
9. Magical sign or word.
1. Tested by experience.

still have continued to quaff the cup of enchantments, though its vapor did but shroud life in gloom and fill the gloom with spectres that mocked at him. There was a certain irksomeness of spirit, which, being real, and the deepest sensation of which the artist was now conscious, was more intolerable than any fantastic miseries and horrors that the abuse of wine could summon up. In the latter case he could remember, even out of the midst of his trouble, that all was but a delusion; in the former, the heavy anguish was his actual life.

From this perilous state he was redeemed by an incident which more than one person witnessed, but of which the shrewdest could not explain or conjecture the operation on Owen Warland's mind. It was very simple. On a warm afternoon of spring, as the artist sat among his riotous companions with a glass of wine before him, a splendid butterfly flew in at the open window and fluttered about his head.

"Ah," exclaimed Owen, who had drank freely, "are you alive again, child of the sun and playmate of the summer breeze, after your dismal winter's nap? Then it is time for me to be at work!"

And, leaving his unemptied glass upon the table, he departed, and was never known to sip another drop of wine.

And now, again, he resumed his wanderings in the woods and fields. It might be fancied that the bright butterfly, which had come so spirit-like into the window as Owen sat with the rude revellers, was indeed a spirit commissioned to recall him to the pure, ideal life that had so etherealized him among men. It might be fancied that he went forth to seek this spirit in its sunny haunts; for still, as in the summer time gone by, he was seen to steal gently up wherever a butterfly had alighted, and lose himself in contemplation of it. When it took flight his eyes followed the winged vision, as if its airy track would show the path to heaven. But what could be the purpose of the unseasonable toil, which was again resumed, as the watchman knew by the lines of lamplight through the crevices of Owen Warland's shutters? The townspeople had one comprehensive explanation of all these singularities. Owen Warland had gone mad! How universally efficacious—how satisfactory, too, and soothing to the injured sensibility of narrowness and dullness—is this easy method of accounting for whatever lies beyond the world's most ordinary scope! From St. Paul's days down to our poor little Artist of the Beautiful, the same talisman has been applied to the elucidation of all mysteries in the words or deeds of men who spoke or acted too wisely or too well. In Owen Warland's case the judgment of his townspeople may have been correct. Perhaps he was mad. The lack of sympathy—that contrast between himself and his neighbors which took away the restraint of example—was enough to make him so. Or possibly he had caught just so much of ethereal radiance as served to bewilder him, in an earthly sense, by its intermixture with the common daylight.

One evening, when the artist had returned from a customary ramble and had just thrown the lustre of his lamp on the delicate piece of work so often interrupted, but still taken up again, as if his fate were imbodied in its mechanism, he was surprised by the entrance of old Peter Hovenden. Owen never met this man without a shrinking of the heart. Of all the world he was most terrible, by reason of a keen understanding which saw so distinctly what it did see, and disbelieved so uncompromisingly in what it could not see. On this occasion the old watchmaker had merely a gracious word or two to say.

"Owen, my lad," said he, "we must see you at my house to-morrow night."

The artist began to mutter some excuse.

"O, but it must be so," quoth Peter Hovenden, "for the sake of the days when you were one of the household. What, my boy! don't you know that my daughter Annie is engaged to Robert Danforth? We are making an entertainment, in our humble way, to celebrate the event."

"Ah!" said Owen.

That little monosyllable was all he uttered; its tone seemed cold and unconcerned to an ear like Peter Hovenden's; and yet there was in it the stifled outcry of the poor artist's heart, which he compressed within him like a man holding down an evil spirit. One slight outbreak, however, imperceptible to the old watchmaker, he allowed himself. Raising the instrument with which he was about to begin his work, he let it fall upon the little system of machinery that had, anew, cost him months of thought and toil. It was shattered by the stroke!

Owen Warland's story would have been no tolerable representation of the troubled life of those who strive to create the beautiful, if, amid all other thwarting influences, love had not interposed to steal the cunning from his hand. Outwardly he had been no ardent or enterprising lover; the career of his passion had confined its tumults and vicissitudes so entirely within the artist's imagination that Annie herself had scarcely more than a woman's intuitive perception of it; but, in Owen's view, it covered the whole field of his life. Forgetful of the time when she had shown herself incapable of any deep response, he had persisted in connecting all his dreams of artistical success with Annie's image; she was the visible shape in which the spiritual power that he worshipped, and on whose altar he hoped to lay a not unworthy offering, was made manifest to him. Of course he had deceived himself; there were no such attributes in Annie Hovenden as his imagination had endowed her with. She, in the aspect which she wore to his inward vision, was as much a creature of his own as the mysterious piece of mechanism would be were it ever realized. Had he become convinced of his mistake through the medium of successful love,—had he won Annie to his bosom, and there beheld her fade from angel into ordinary woman,— the disappointment might have driven him back, with concentrated energy, upon his sole remaining object. On the other hand, had he found Annie what he fancied, his lot would have been so rich in beauty that out of its mere redundancy he might have wrought the beautiful into many a worthier type[2] than he had toiled for; but the guise in which his sorrow came to him, the sense that the angel of his life had been snatched away and given to a rude man of earth and iron, who could neither need nor appreciate her ministrations,— this was the very perversity of fate that makes human existence appear too absurd and contradictory to be the scene of one other hope or one other fear. There was nothing left for Owen Warland but to sit down like a man that had been stunned.

He went through a fit of illness. After his recovery his small and slender frame assumed an obtuser garniture of flesh than it had ever before worn. His thin cheeks became round; his delicate little hand, so spiritually fashioned to achieve fairy taskwork, grew plumper than the hand of a thriving infant. His aspect had a childishness such as might have induced a stranger to pat him on the head—pausing, however, in the act, to wonder what manner of child was here. It was as if the spirit had gone out of him, leaving the body to flourish in a sort of vegetable existence. Not that Owen Warland was idiotic. He could talk, and not irrationally. Somewhat of a babbler, indeed, did people begin to think him; for he was apt to discourse at wearisome length of marvels of mechanism that he had read about in books, but which he had learned to consider as absolutely fabulous. Among them he enumerated the Man of Brass, constructed by Albertus Magnus, and the Brazen Head of Friar Bacon;[3] and, coming down to later times, the automata of a little coach and horses, which it was pretended had been manufactured for the Dauphin of France; together with an insect that buzzed about the ear like a living fly, and yet was but a contrivance of minute steel springs. There was a story, too, of a duck that waddled, and quacked, and ate; though, had any honest citizen purchased it for dinner, he would have found himself cheated with the mere mechanical apparition of a duck.

"But all these accounts," said Owen Warland, "I am now satisfied are mere impositions."

2. Symbol, example.
3. See n. 6, p. 160.

Then, in a mysterious way, he would confess that he once thought differently. In his idle and dreamy days he had considered it possible, in a certain sense, to spiritualize machinery, and to combine with the new species of life and motion thus produced a beauty that should attain to the ideal which Nature has proposed to herself in all her creatures, but has never taken pains to realize. He seemed, however, to retain no very distinct perception either of the process of achieving this object or of the design itself.

"I have thrown it all aside now," he would say. "It was a dream such as young men are always mystifying themselves with. Now that I have acquired a little common sense, it makes me laugh to think of it."

Poor, poor and fallen Owen Warland! These were the symptoms that he had ceased to be an inhabitant of the better sphere that lies unseen around us. He had lost his faith in the invisible, and now prided himself, as such unfortunates invariably do, in the wisdom which rejected much that even his eye could see, and trusted confidently in nothing but what his hand could touch. This is the calamity of men whose spiritual part dies out of them and leaves the grosser understanding to assimilate them more and more to the things of which alone it can take cognizance; but in Owen Warland the spirit was not dead nor passed away; it only slept.

How it awoke again is not recorded. Perhaps the torpid slumber was broken by a convulsive pain. Perhaps, as in a former instance, the butterfly came and hovered about his head and reinspired him,—as indeed this creature of the sunshine had always a mysterious mission for the artist,—reinspired him with the former purpose of his life. Whether it were pain or happiness that thrilled through his veins, his first impulse was to thank Heaven for rendering him again the being of thought, imagination, and keenest sensibility that he had long ceased to be.

"Now for my task," said he. "Never did I feel such strength for it as now."

Yet, strong as he felt himself, he was incited to toil the more diligently by an anxiety lest death should surprise him in the midst of his labors. This anxiety, perhaps, is common to all men who set their hearts upon anything so high, in their own view of it, that life becomes of importance only as conditional to its accomplishment. So long as we love life for itself, we seldom dread the losing it. When we desire life for the attainment of an object, we recognize the frailty of its texture. But, side by side with this sense of insecurity, there is a vital faith in our invulnerability to the shaft of death while engaged in any task that seems assigned by Providence as our proper thing to do, and which the world would have cause to mourn for should we leave it unaccomplished. Can the philosopher, big with the inspiration of an idea that is to reform mankind, believe that he is to be beckoned from this sensible existence at the very instant when he is mustering his breath to speak the word of light? Should he perish so, the weary ages may pass away—the world's whole life sand may fall, drop by drop—before another intellect is prepared to develop the truth that might have been uttered then. But history affords many an example where the most precious spirit, at any particular epoch manifested in human shape, has gone hence untimely, without space allowed him, so far as mortal judgment could discern, to perform his mission on the earth. The prophet dies, and the man of torpid heart and sluggish brain lives on. The poet leaves his song half sung, or finishes it beyond the scope of mortal ears, in a celestial choir. The painter—as Allston[4] did—leaves half his conception on the canvas to sadden us with its imperfect beauty, and goes to picture forth the whole, if it be no irreverence to say so, in the hues of heaven. But rather such incomplete designs of this life will be perfected nowhere. This so frequent abortion of man's dearest projects must be taken as a proof that the deeds of earth, however etherealized by piety or genius, are without value, except as exercises and manifestations of the spirit. In heaven, all ordinary thought is higher and more melodious than Milton's song. Then, would he add another verse to any strain that he had left unfinished here?

But to return to Owen Warland. It was his fortune, good or ill, to achieve the purpose of his life. Pass we over a long space of intense thought, yearning effort, minute toil, and wasting anxiety, succeeded by an instant of solitary triumph: let all this be imagined; and then behold the artist, on a winter evening, seeking admittance to Robert Danforth's fireside circle. There he found the man of iron, with his massive substance, thoroughly warmed and attempered by domestic influences. And there was Annie, too, now transformed into a matron, with much of her husband's plain and sturdy nature, but imbued, as Owen Warland still believed, with a finer grace, that might enable her to be the interpreter between strength and beauty. It happened, likewise, that old Peter Hovenden was a guest this evening at his daughter's fireside; and it was his well-remembered expression of keen, cold criticism that first encountered the artist's glance.

"My old friend Owen!" cried Robert Danforth, starting up, and compressing the artist's delicate fingers with a hand that was accustomed to gripe bars of iron. "This is kind and neighborly to come to

4. Washington Allston (1779–1843), American painter, who spent much effort in his later years on a never-completed painting, *Belshazzar's Feast*, now in the Detroit Institute of Arts.

us at last. I was afraid your perpetual motion had bewitched you
out of the remembrance of old times."

"We are glad to see you," said Annie, while a blush reddened her
matronly cheek. "It was not like a friend to stay from us so long."

"Well, Owen," inquired the old watchmaker, as his first greeting,
"how comes on the beautiful? Have you created it at last?"

The artist did not immediately reply, being startled by the apparition of a young child of strength that was tumbling about on the
carpet—a little personage who had come mysteriously out of the
infinite, but with something so sturdy and real in his composition
that he seemed moulded out of the densest substance which earth
could supply. This hopeful infant crawled towards the new comer,
and setting himself on end, as Robert Danforth expressed the posture, stared at Owen with a look of such sagacious observation that
the mother could not help exchanging a proud glance with her husband. But the artist was disturbed by the child's look, as imagining
a resemblance between it and Peter Hovenden's habitual expression.
He could have fancied that the old watchmaker was compressed into
this baby shape, and looking out of those baby eyes, and repeating, as
he now did, the malicious question:—

"The beautiful, Owen! How comes on the beautiful? Have you
succeeded in creating the beautiful?"

"I have succeeded," replied the artist, with a momentary light of
triumph in his eyes and a smile of sunshine, yet steeped in such
depth of thought that it was almost sadness. "Yes, my friends, it is the
truth. I have succeeded."

"Indeed!" cried Annie, a look of maiden mirthfulness peeping
out of her face again. "And is it lawful, now, to inquire what the
secret is?"

"Surely; it is to disclose it that I have come," answered Owen Warland. "You shall know, and see, and touch, and possess the secret!
For, Annie,—if by that name I may still address the friend of my
boyish years,—Annie, it is for your bridal gift that I have wrought
this spiritualized mechanism, this harmony of motion, this mystery
of beauty. It comes late indeed; but it is as we go onward in life,
when objects begin to lose their freshness of hue and our souls their
delicacy of perception, that the spirit of beauty is most needed. If,—
forgive me, Annie,—if you know how to value this gift, it can never
come too late."

He produced, as he spoke, what seemed a jewel box. It was carved
richly out of ebony by his own hand, and inlaid with a fanciful tracery of pearl, representing a boy in pursuit of a butterfly, which, elsewhere, had become a winged spirit, and was flying heavenward;
while the boy, or youth, had found such efficacy in his strong desire
that he ascended from earth to cloud, and from cloud to celestial

atmosphere, to win the beautiful. This case of ebony the artist opened, and bade Annie place her finger on its edge. She did so, but almost screamed as a butterfly fluttered forth, and, alighting on her finger's tip, sat waving the ample magnificence of its purple and gold-speckled wings, as if in prelude to a flight. It is impossible to express by words the glory, the splendor, the delicate gorgeousness which were softened into the beauty of this object. Nature's ideal butterfly was here realized in all its perfection; not in the pattern of such faded insects as flit among earthly flowers, but of those which hover across the meads of paradise for child-angels and the spirits of departed infants to disport themselves with. The rich down was visible upon its wings; the lustre of its eyes seemed instinct with spirit. The firelight glimmered around this wonder—the candles gleamed upon it; but it glistened apparently by its own radiance, and illuminated the finger and outstretched hand on which it rested with a white gleam like that of precious stones. In its perfect beauty, the consideration of size was entirely lost. Had its wings overarched the firmament, the mind could not have been more filled or satisfied.

"Beautiful! Beautiful!" exclaimed Annie. "Is it alive? Is it alive?"

"Alive? To be sure it is," answered her husband. "Do you suppose any mortal has skill enough to make a butterfly, or would put himself to the trouble of making one, when any child may catch a score of them in a summer's afternoon? Alive? Certainly! But this pretty box is undoubtedly of our friend Owen's manufacture; and really it does him credit."

At this moment the butterfly waved its wings anew, with a motion so absolutely lifelike that Annie was startled, and even awestricken; for, in spite of her husband's opinion, she could not satisfy herself whether it was indeed a living creature or a piece of wondrous mechanism.

"Is it alive?" she repeated, more earnestly than before.

"Judge for yourself," said Owen Warland, who stood gazing in her face with fixed attention.

The butterfly now flung itself upon the air, fluttered round Annie's head, and soared into a distant region of the parlor, still making itself perceptible to sight by the starry gleam in which the motion of its wings enveloped it. The infant on the floor followed its course with his sagacious little eyes. After flying about the room, it returned in a spiral curve and settled again on Annie's finger.

"But is it alive?" exclaimed she again; and the finger on which the gorgeous mystery had alighted was so tremulous that the butterfly was forced to balance himself with his wings. "Tell me if it be alive, or whether you created it."

"Wherefore ask who created it, so it be beautiful?" replied Owen Warland. "Alive? Yes, Annie; it may well be said to possess life, for it has absorbed my own being into itself; and in the secret of that butterfly, and in its beauty,—which is not merely outward, but deep as its whole system,—is represented the intellect, the imagination, the sensibility, the soul of an Artist of the Beautiful! Yes; I created it. But"—and here his countenance somewhat changed—"this butterfly is not now to me what it was when I beheld it afar off in the daydreams of my youth."

"Be it what it may, it is a pretty plaything," said the blacksmith, grinning with childlike delight. "I wonder whether it would condescend to alight on such a great clumsy finger as mine? Hold it hither, Annie."

By the artist's direction, Annie touched her finger's tip to that of her husband; and, after a momentary delay, the butterfly fluttered from one to the other. It preluded a second flight by a similar, yet not precisely the same, waving of wings as in the first experiment; then, ascending from the blacksmith's stalwart finger, it rose in a gradually enlarging curve to the ceiling, made one wide sweep around the room, and returned with an undulating movement to the point whence it had started.

"Well, that does beat all nature!" cried Robert Danforth, bestowing the heartiest praise that he could find expression for; and, indeed, had he paused there, a man of finer words and nicer perception could not easily have said more. "That goes beyond me, I confess. But what then? There is more real use in one downright blow of my sledge hammer than in the whole five years' labor that our friend Owen has wasted on this butterfly."

Here the child clapped his hands and made a great babble of indistinct utterance, apparently demanding that the butterfly should be given him for a plaything.

Owen Warland, meanwhile, glanced sidelong at Annie, to discover whether she sympathized in her husband's estimate of the comparative value of the beautiful and the practical. There was, amid all her kindness towards himself, amid all the wonder and admiration with which she contemplated the marvellous work of his hands and incarnation of his idea, a secret scorn—too secret, perhaps, for her own consciousness, and perceptible only to such intuitive discernment as that of the artist. But Owen, in the latter stages of his pursuit, had risen out of the region in which such a discovery might have been torture. He knew that the world, and Annie as the representative of the world, whatever praise might be bestowed, could never say the fitting word nor feel the fitting sentiment which should be the perfect recompense of an artist who, symbolizing a lofty moral by a material trifle,—converting what was earthly to spiritual gold,—had won the beautiful into his handiwork. Not at this latest moment was he to learn that the reward of all high performance must be sought within itself, or sought in vain. There was, however, a view of the matter which Annie and her husband, and even Peter Hovenden, might fully have understood, and which would have satisfied them that the toil of years had here been worthily bestowed. Owen Warland might have told them that this butterfly, this plaything, this bridal gift of a poor watchmaker to a blacksmith's wife, was, in truth, a gem of art that a monarch would have purchased with honors and abundant wealth, and have treasured it among the jewels of his kingdom as the most unique and wondrous of them all. But the artist smiled and kept the secret to himself.

"Father," said Annie, thinking that a word of praise from the old watchmaker might gratify his former apprentice, "do come and admire this pretty butterfly."

"Let us see," said Peter Hovenden, rising from his chair, with a sneer upon his face that always made people doubt, as he himself did, in everything but a material existence. "Here is my finger for it to alight upon. I shall understand it better when once I have touched it."

But, to the increased astonishment of Annie, when the tip of her father's finger was pressed against that of her husband, on which the butterfly still rested, the insect drooped its wings and seemed on the point of falling to the floor. Even the bright spots of gold upon its wings and body, unless her eyes deceived her, grew dim, and the glowing purple took a dusky hue, and the starry lustre that gleamed around the blacksmith's hand became faint and vanished.

"It is dying! it is dying!" cried Annie, in alarm.

"It has been delicately wrought," said the artist calmly. "As I told you, it has imbibed a spiritual essence—call it magnetism,[5] or what you will. In an atmosphere of doubt and mockery its exquisite susceptibility suffers torture, as does the soul of him who instilled his own life into it. It has already lost its beauty; in a few moments more its mechanism would be irreparably injured."

"Take away your hand, father!" entreated Annie, turning pale. "Here is my child; let it rest on his innocent hand. There, perhaps, its life will revive and its colors grow brighter than ever."

Her father, with an acrid smile, withdrew his finger. The butterfly then appeared to recover the power of voluntary motion, while its hues assumed much of their original lustre, and the gleam of starlight, which was its most ethereal attribute, again formed a halo round about it. At first, when transferred from Robert Danforth's hand to the small finger of the child, this radiance grew so powerful that it positively threw the little fellow's shadow back against the

5. I.e., animal magnetism, or hypnotism.

wall. He, meanwhile, extended his plump hand as he had seen his
father and mother do, and watched the waving of the insect's wings
with infantine delight. Nevertheless, there was a certain odd expression of sagacity that made Owen Warland feel as if here were old
Peter Hovenden, partially, and but partially, redeemed from his hard
scepticism into childish faith.

"How wise the little monkey looks!" whispered Robert Danforth
to his wife.

"I never saw such a look on a child's face," answered Annie, admiring her own infant, and with good reason, far more than the artistic
butterfly. "The darling knows more of the mystery than we do."

As if the butterfly, like the artist, were conscious of something not
entirely congenial in the child's nature, it alternately sparkled and
grew dim. At length it arose from the small hand of the infant with
an airy motion that seemed to bear it upward without an effort, as if
the ethereal instincts with which its master's spirit had endowed it
impelled this fair vision involuntarily to a higher sphere. Had there
been no obstruction, it might have soared into the sky and grown
immortal. But its lustre gleamed upon the ceiling; the exquisite texture of its wings brushed against that earthly medium; and a sparkle
or two, as of stardust, floated downward and lay glimmering on the
carpet. Then the butterfly came fluttering down, and, instead of
returning to the infant, was apparently attracted towards the artist's
hand.

"Not so! not so!" murmured Owen Warland, as if his handiwork
could have understood him. "Thou hast gone forth out of thy master's heart. There is no return for thee."

With a wavering movement, and emitting a tremulous radiance,
the butterfly struggled, as it were, towards the infant, and was about
to alight upon his finger; but, while it still hovered in the air, the
little child of strength, with his grandsire's sharp and shrewd expression in his face, made a snatch at the marvellous insect and compressed it in his hand. Annie screamed. Old Peter Hovenden burst
into a cold and scornful laugh. The blacksmith, by main force,
unclosed the infant's hand, and found within the palm a small heap
of glittering fragments, whence the mystery of beauty had fled forever. And as for Owen Warland, he looked placidly at what seemed
the ruin of his life's labor, and which was yet no ruin. He had caught
a far other butterfly than this. When the artist rose high enough to
achieve the beautiful, the symbol by which he made it perceptible to
mortal senses became of little value in his eyes while his spirit possessed itself in the enjoyment of the reality.

Drowne's Wooden Image[†]

One sunshiny morning, in the good old times of the town of Boston, a young carver in wood, well known by the name of Drowne, stood contemplating a large oaken log, which it was his purpose to convert into the figure head of a vessel. And while he discussed within his own mind what sort of shape or similitude it were well to bestow upon this excellent piece of timber, there came into Drowne's workshop a certain Captain Hunnewell, owner and commander of the good brig called the Cynosure, which had just returned from her first voyage to Fayal.[1]

"Ah! that will do, Drowne, that will do!" cried the jolly captain, tapping the log with his ratan. "I bespeak this very piece of oak for the figure head of the Cynosure. She has shown herself the sweetest craft that ever floated, and I mean to decorate her prow with the handsomest image that the skill of man can cut out of timber. And, Drowne, you are the fellow to execute it."

"You give me more credit than I deserve, Captain Hunnewell," said the carver, modestly, yet as one conscious of eminence in his art. "But, for the sake of the good brig, I stand ready to do my best. And which of these designs do you prefer? Here"—pointing to a staring, half-length figure, in a white wig and scarlet coat—"here is an excellent model, the likeness of our gracious king. Here is the valiant Admiral Vernon.[2] Or, if you prefer a female figure, what say you to Britannia with the trident?"

"All very fine, Drowne; all very fine," answered the mariner. "But as nothing like the brig ever swam the ocean, so I am determined she shall have such a figure head as old Neptune never saw in his life. And what is more, as there is a secret in the matter, you must pledge your credit not to betray it."

"Certainly," said Drowne, marvelling, however, what possible mystery there could be in reference to an affair so open, of necessity, to the inspection of all the world as the figure head of a vessel. "You may depend, captain, on my being as secret as the nature of the case will permit."

[†] First published July 1844, in *Godey's Lady's Book*, then in *Mosses from an Old Manse*, 1846. The story apparently takes place in Boston in the early 1770s. The painter John Singleton Copley, who comments sympathetically on Drowne's creation, left Boston permanently for England in 1774. The historical Deacon Shem Drowne (1684–1774) was the coppersmith who made the weathervanes on Faneuil Hall and the Old Province House. He was not a wood carver, nor could he have been a young man while Copley lived in Boston. Yet he might well have stood for the typical untutored artisan to Hawthorne's early readers.

1. An island in the Azores.
2. Edward Vernon (1684–1757), British admiral. Washington's half-brother Lawrence served under him and named Mount Vernon after him.

Captain Hunnewell then took Drowne by the button, and communicated his wishes in so low a tone that it would be unmannerly to repeat what was evidently intended for the carver's private ear. We shall, therefore, take the opportunity to give the reader a few desirable particulars about Drowne himself.

He was the first American who is known to have attempted—in a very humble line, it is true—that art in which we can now reckon so many names already distinguished, or rising to distinction. From his earliest boyhood he had exhibited a knack—for it would be too proud a word to call it genius—a knack, therefore, for the imitation of the human figure in whatever material came most readily to hand. The snows of a New England winter had often supplied him with a species of marble as dazzlingly white, at least, as the Parian or the Carrara,[3] and if less durable, yet sufficiently so to correspond with any claims to permanent existence possessed by the boy's frozen statues. Yet they won admiration from maturer judges than his schoolfellows, and were, indeed, remarkably clever, though destitute of the native warmth that might have made the snow melt beneath his hand. As he advanced in life, the young man adopted pine and oak as eligible materials for the display of his skill, which now began to bring him a return of solid silver as well as the empty praise that had been an apt reward enough for his productions of evanescent snow. He became noted for carving ornamental pump heads, and wooden urns for gate posts, and decorations, more grotesque than fanciful, for mantelpieces. No apothecary would have deemed himself in the way of obtaining custom without setting up a gilded mortar, if not a head of Galen or Hippocrates,[4] from the skilful hand of Drowne.

But the great scope of his business lay in the manufacture of figure heads for vessels. Whether it were the monarch himself, or some famous British admiral or general, or the governor of the province, or perchance the favorite daughter of the ship owner, there the image stood above the prow, decked out in gorgeous colors, magnificently gilded, and staring the whole world out of countenance, as if from an innate consciousness of its own superiority. These specimens of native sculpture had crossed the sea in all directions, and been not ignobly noticed among the crowded shipping of the Thames, and wherever else the hardy mariners of New England had pushed their adventures. It must be confessed that a family likeness pervaded these respectable progeny of Drowne's skill; that the benign countenance of the king resembled those of his subjects,

3. Marble from the Aegean island of Paros and from Tuscany, respectively.
4. Apothecary shops or pharmacies typically had identifying symbols hanging outside their doors, such as a mortar for grinding medicinal powders or an image of a famous doctor. Galen (ca. 130–201 C.E.) and Hippocrates (ca. 460–377 B.C.E.) were distinguished physicians of antiquity.

and that Miss Peggy Hobart, the merchant's daughter, bore a remarkable similitude to Britannia, Victory, and other ladies of the allegoric sisterhood; and, finally, that they all had a kind of wooden aspect, which proved an intimate relationship with the unshaped blocks of timber in the carver's workshop. But at least there was no inconsiderable skill of hand, nor a deficiency of any attribute to render them really works of art, except that deep quality, be it of soul or intellect, which bestows life upon the lifeless and warmth upon the cold, and which, had it been present, would have made Drowne's wooden image instinct with spirit.

The captain of the Cynosure had now finished his instructions.

"And Drowne," said he, impressively, "you must lay aside all other business and set about this forthwith. And as to the price, only do the job in first rate style, and you shall settle that point yourself."

"Very well, captain," answered the carver, who looked grave and somewhat perplexed, yet had a sort of smile upon his visage; "depend upon it, I'll do my utmost to satisfy you."

From that moment the men of taste about Long Wharf and the Town Dock who were wont to show their love for the arts by frequent visits to Drowne's workshop, and admiration of his wooden images, began to be sensible of a mystery in the carver's conduct. Often he was absent in the daytime. Sometimes, as might be judged by gleams of light from the shop windows, he was at work until a late hour of the evening; although neither knock nor voice, on such occasions, could gain admittance for a visitor, or elicit any word of response. Nothing remarkable, however, was observed in the shop at those hours when it was thrown open. A fine piece of timber, indeed, which Drowne was known to have reserved for some work of especial dignity, was seen to be gradually assuming shape. What shape it was destined ultimately to take was a problem to his friends and a point on which the carver himself preserved a rigid silence. But day after day, though Drowne was seldom noticed in the act of working upon it, this rude form began to be developed until it became evident to all observers that a female figure was growing into mimic life. At each new visit they beheld a larger pile of wooden chips and a nearer approximation to something beautiful. It seemed as if the hamadryad[5] of the oak had sheltered herself from the unimaginative world within the heart of her native tree, and that it was only necessary to remove the strange shapelessness that had incrusted her, and reveal the grace and loveliness of a divinity. Imperfect as the design, the attitude, the costume, and especially the face of the image still remained, there was already an effect that drew the eye from the

5. Wood nymph, the indwelling spirit of a tree, who dies with the tree's death.

wooden cleverness of Drowne's earlier productions and fixed it upon the tantalizing mystery of this new project.

Copley, the celebrated painter, then a young man and a resident of Boston, came one day to visit Drowne; for he had recognized so much of moderate ability in the carver as to induce him, in the dearth of professional sympathy, to cultivate his acquaintance. On entering the shop the artist glanced at the inflexible image of king, commander, dame, and allegory that stood around, on the best of which might have been bestowed the questionable praise that it looked as if a living man had here been changed to wood, and that not only the physical, but the intellectual and spiritual part, partook of the stolid transformation. But in not a single instance did it seem as if the wood were imbibing the ethereal essence of humanity. What a wide distinction is here! and how far would the slightest portion of the latter merit have outvalued the utmost degree of the former!

"My friend Drowne," said Copley, smiling to himself, but alluding to the mechanical and wooden cleverness that so invariably distinguished the images, "you are really a remarkable person! I have seldom met with a man in your line of business that could do so much; for one other touch might make this figure of General Wolfe,[6] for instance, a breathing and intelligent human creature."

"You would have me think that you are praising me highly, Mr. Copley," answered Drowne, turning his back upon Wolfe's image in apparent disgust. "But there has come a light into my mind. I know, what you know as well, that the one touch which you speak of as deficient is the only one that would be truly valuable, and that without it these works of mine are no better than worthless abortions. There is the same difference between them and the works of an inspired artist as between a sign-post daub and one of your best pictures."

"This is strange," cried Copley, looking him in the face, which now, as the painter fancied, had a singular depth of intelligence, though hitherto it had not given him greatly the advantage over his own family of wooden images. "What has come over you? How is it that, possessing the idea which you have now uttered, you should produce only such works as these?"

The carver smiled, but made no reply. Copley turned again to the images, conceiving that the sense of deficiency which Drowne had just expressed, and which is so rare in a merely mechanical character, must surely imply a genius, the tokens of which had heretofore been overlooked. But no; there was not a trace of it. He was about to withdraw when his eyes chanced to fall upon a half-developed

---

6. General James Wolfe (1727–1759), killed during the British victory in the battle of Quebec and a great hero to the colonials.

figure which lay in a corner of the workshop, surrounded by scattered chips of oak. It arrested him at once.

"What is here? Who has done this?" he broke out, after contemplating it in speechless astonishment for an instant. "Here is the divine, the life-giving touch. What inspired hand is beckoning this wood to arise and live? Whose work is this?"

"No man's work," replied Drowne. "The figure lies within that block of oak, and it is my business to find it."

"Drowne," said the true artist, grasping the carver fervently by the hand, "you are a man of genius!"

As Copley departed, happening to glance backward from the threshold, he beheld Drowne bending over the half-created shape, and stretching forth his arms as if he would have embraced and drawn it to his heart; while, had such a miracle been possible, his countenance expressed passion enough to communicate warmth and sensibility to the lifeless oak.

"Strange enough!" said the artist to himself. "Who would have looked for a modern Pygmalion in the person of a Yankee mechanic!"[7]

As yet, the image was but vague in its outward presentment; so that, as in the cloud shapes around the western sun, the observer rather felt, or was led to imagine, than really saw what was intended by it. Day by day, however, the work assumed greater precision, and settled its irregular and misty outline into distincter grace and beauty. The general design was now obvious to the common eye. It was a female figure, in what appeared to be a foreign dress; the gown being laced over the bosom, and opening in front so as to disclose a skirt or petticoat, the folds and inequalities of which were admirably represented in the oaken substance. She wore a hat of singular gracefulness, and abundantly laden with flowers, such as never grew in the rude soil of New England, but which, with all their fanciful luxuriance, had a natural truth that it seemed impossible for the most fertile imagination to have attained without copying from real prototypes. There were several little appendages to this dress, such as a fan, a pair of earrings, a chain about the neck, a watch in the bosom, and a ring upon the finger, all of which would have been deemed beneath the dignity of sculpture.[8] They were put on, however, with as much taste as a lovely woman might have shown in her

---

7. A man employed in manual labor. Pygmalion, legendary Greek sculptor, carved an ivory statue of a maiden, fell in love with it, and prayed successfully to Aphrodite to bring it to life.
8. For details of the dress and ornaments on Drowne's statue, Hawthorne drew on Sophia Peabody's description of a "Spanish beauty" in her 1834 "Cuba Journal." He copied numerous passages from the Cuba Journal into his own notebook in 1838, soon after he met Sophia (see CE 23:198, 535).

attire, and could therefore have shocked none but a judgment spoiled by artistic rules.

The face was still imperfect; but gradually, by a magic touch, intelligence and sensibility brightened through the features, with all the effect of light gleaming forth from within the solid oak. The face became alive. It was a beautiful, though not precisely regular, and somewhat haughty aspect, but with a certain piquancy about the eyes and mouth, which, of all expressions, would have seemed the most impossible to throw over a wooden countenance. And now, so far as carving went, this wonderful production was complete.

"Drowne," said Copley, who had hardly missed a single day in his visits to the carver's workshop, "if this work were in marble it would make you famous at once; nay, I would almost affirm that it would make an era in the art. It is as ideal as an antique statue, and yet as real as any lovely woman whom one meets at a fireside or in the street. But I trust you do not mean to desecrate this exquisite crea-ture with paint, like those staring kings and admirals yonder?"

"Not paint her!" exclaimed Captain Hunnewell, who stood by; "not paint the figure head of the Cynosure! And what sort of a figure should I cut in a foreign port with such an unpainted oaken stick as this over my prow! She must, and she shall, be painted to the life, from the topmost flower in her hat down to the silver spangles on her slippers."

"Mr. Copley," said Drowne, quietly, "I know nothing of marble statuary, and nothing of the sculptor's rules of art; but of this wooden image, this work of my hands, this creature of my heart,"—and here his voice faltered and choked in a very singular manner,—"of this—of her—I may say that I know something. A wellspring of inward wis-dom gushed within me as I wrought upon the oak with my whole strength, and soul, and faith. Let others do what they may with marble, and adopt what rules they choose. If I can produce my desired effect by painted wood, those rules are not for me, and I have a right to disregard them."

"The very spirit of genuis," muttered Copley to himself. "How otherwise should this carver feel himself entitled to transcend all rules, and make me ashamed of quoting them?"

He looked earnestly at Drowne, and again saw that expression of human love which, in a spiritual sense, as the artist could not help imagining, was the secret of the life that had been breathed into this block of wood.

The carver, still in the same secresy that marked all his opera-tions upon this mysterious image, proceeded to paint the habili-ments in their proper colors, and the countenance with Nature's red and white. When all was finished he threw open his workshop, and admitted the townspeople to behold what he had done. Most persons, at their first entrance, felt impelled to remove their hats, and pay such reverence as was due to the richly-dressed and beautiful young lady who seemed to stand in a corner of the room, with oaken chips and shavings scattered at her feet. Then came a sensation of fear; as if, not being actually human, yet so like humanity, she must therefore be something preternatural. There was, in truth, an indefinable air and expression that might reasonably induce the query. Who and from what sphere this daughter of the oak should be? The strange, rich flowers of Eden on her head; the complexion, so much deeper and more brilliant than those of our native beauties; the foreign, as it seemed, and fantastic garb, yet not too fantastic to be worn decorously in the street; the delicately-wrought embroidery of the skirt; the broad gold chain about her neck; the curious ring upon her finger; the fan, so exquisitely sculptured in open work, and painted to resemble pearl and ebony;—where could Drowne, in his sober walk of life, have beheld the vision here so matchlessly imbodied! And then her face! In the dark eyes and around the voluptuous mouth there played a look made up of pride, coquetry, and a gleam of mirthfulness, which impressed Copley with the idea that the image was secretly enjoying the perplexed admiration of himself and all other beholders.

"And will you," said he to the carver, "permit this masterpiece to become the figure head of a vessel? Give the honest captain yonder figure of Britannia—it will answer his purpose far better—and send this fairy queen to England, where, for aught I know, it may bring you a thousand pounds."

"I have not wrought it for money," said Drowne.

"What sort of a fellow is this!" thought Copley. "A Yankee, and throw away the chance of making his fortune! He has gone mad; and thence has come this gleam of genius."

There was still further proof of Drowne's lunacy, if credit were due to the rumor that he had been seen kneeling at the feet of the oaken lady, and gazing with a lover's passionate ardor into the face that his own hands had created. The bigots of the day hinted that it would be no matter of surprise if an evil spirit were allowed to enter this beautiful form, and seduce the carver to destruction.

The fame of the image spread far and wide. The inhabitants visited it so universally, that after a few days of exhibition there was hardly an old man or a child who had not become minutely familiar with its aspect. Even had the story of Drowne's wooden image ended here, its celebrity might have been prolonged for many years by the reminiscences of those who looked upon it in their childhood, and saw nothing else so beautiful in after life. But the town was now astounded by an event the narrative of which has formed itself into one of the most singular legends that are yet to be met with in the traditionary chimney corners of the New England metropolis, where old men and women sit dreaming of the past, and wag their heads at the dreamers of the present and the future.

One fine morning, just before the departure of the Cynosure on her second voyage to Fayal, the commander of that gallant vessel was seen to issue from his residence in Hanover Street.[9] He was stylishly dressed in a blue broadcloth coat, with gold lace at the seams and button holes, an embroidered scarlet waistcoat, a triangular hat, with a loop and broad binding of gold, and wore a silver-hilted hanger[1] at his side. But the good captain might have been arrayed in the robes of a prince or the rags of a beggar, without in either case attracting notice, while obscured by such a companion as now leaned on his arm. The people in the street started, rubbed their eyes, and either leaped aside from their path, or stood as if transfixed to wood or marble in astonishment.

"Do you see it?—do you see it?" cried one, with tremulous eagerness. "It is the very same!"

"The same?" answered another, who had arrived in town only the night before. "Who do you mean? I see only a sea captain in his shore-going clothes, and a young lady in a foreign habit, with a bunch of beautiful flowers in her hat. On my word, she is as fair and bright a damsel as my eyes have looked on this many a day!"

"Yes; the same!—the very same!" repeated the other. "Drowne's wooden image has come to life!"

Here was a miracle indeed! Yet, illuminated by the sunshine, or darkened by the alternate shade of the houses, and with its garments fluttering lightly in the morning breeze, there passed the image along the street. It was exactly and minutely the shape, the garb, and the face which the townspeople had so recently thronged to see and admire. Not a rich flower upon her head, not a single leaf, but had had its prototype in Drowne's wooden workmanship, although now their fragile grace had become flexible, and was shaken by every footstep that the wearer made. The broad gold chain upon the neck was identical with the one represented on the image, and glistened with the motion imparted by the rise and fall of the bosom which it decorated. A real diamond sparkled on her finger. In her right hand she bore a pearl and ebony fan, which she flourished with a fantastic and bewitching coquetry, that was likewise expressed in all her movements as well as in the style of her beauty and the attire that so well harmonized with it. The face, with its brilliant depth of complexion, had the same piquancy of mirthful mischief that was

9. Street close to Boston Harbor. Hawthorne's indications of Boston streets are precise in the tale.
1. Light sword.

fixed upon the countenance of the image, but which was here varied and continually shifting, yet always essentially the same, like
the sunny gleam upon a bubbling fountain. On the whole, there was
something so airy and yet so real in the figure, and withal so perfectly did it represent Drowne's image, that people knew not whether
to suppose the magic wood etherealized into a spirit or warmed and
softened into an actual woman.

"One thing is certain," muttered a Puritan of the old stamp,
"Drowne has sold himself to the devil; and doubtless this gay Captain Hunnewell is a party to the bargain."

"And I," said a young man who overheard him, "would almost
consent to be the third victim, for the liberty of saluting those lovely
lips."

"And so would I," said Copley, the painter, "for the privilege of taking her picture."

The image, or the apparition, whichever it might be, still escorted
by the bold captain, proceeded from Hanover Street through some
of the cross lanes that make this portion of the town so intricate, to
Ann Street, thence into Dock Square, and so downward to Drowne's
shop, which stood just on the water's edge. The crowd still followed,
gathering volume as it rolled along. Never had a modern miracle
occurred in such broad daylight, nor in the presence of such a multitude of witnesses. The airy image, as if conscious that she was the
object of the murmurs and disturbance that swelled behind her,
appeared slightly vexed and flustered, yet still in a manner consistent
with the light vivacity and sportive mischief that were written in her
countenance. She was observed to flutter her fan with such vehement rapidity that the elaborate delicacy of its workmanship gave
way, and it remained broken in her hand.

Arriving at Drowne's door, while the captain threw it open, the
marvellous apparition paused an instant on the threshold, assuming the very attitude of the image, and casting over the crowd that
glance of sunny coquetry which all remembered on the face of the
oaken lady. She and her cavalier then disappeared.

"Ah!" murmured the crowd, drawing a deep breath, as with one
vast pair of lungs.

"The world looks darker now that she has vanished," said some of
the young men.

But the aged, whose recollections dated as far back as witch
times, shook their heads, and hinted that our forefathers would have
thought it a pious deed to burn the daughter of the oak with fire.

"If she be other than a bubble of the elements," exclaimed Copley, "I must look upon her face again."

He accordingly entered the shop; and there, in her usual corner,
stood the image, gazing at him, as it might seem, with the very same

expression of mirthful mischief that had been the farewell look of the apparition when, but a moment before, she turned her face towards the crowd. The carver stood beside his creation mending the beautiful fan, which by some accident was broken in her hand. But there was no longer any motion in the lifelike image, nor any real woman in the workshop, nor even the witchcraft of a sunny shadow, that might have deluded people's eyes as it flitted along the street. Captain Hunnewell, too, had vanished. His hoarse, sea-breezy tones, however, were audible on the other side of a door that opened upon the water.

"Sit down in the stern sheets, my lady," said the gallant captain. "Come, bear a hand, you lubbers, and set us on board in the turning of a minute glass."

And then was heard the stroke of oars.

"Drowne," said Copley, with a smile of intelligence, "you have been a truly fortunate man. What painter or statuary ever had such a subject! No wonder that she inspired a genius into you, and first created the artist who afterwards created her image."

Drowne looked at him with a visage that bore the traces of tears, but from which the light of imagination and sensibility, so recently illuminating it, had departed. He was again the mechanical carver that he had been known to be all his lifetime.

"I hardly understand what you mean, Mr. Copley," said he, putting his hand to his brow. "This image! Can it have been my work? Well, I have wrought it in a kind of dream; and now that I am broad awake I must set about finishing yonder figure of Admiral Vernon."

And forthwith he employed himself on the stolid countenance of one of his wooden progeny, and completed it in his own mechanical style, from which he was never known afterwards to deviate. He followed his business industriously for many years, acquired a competence, and in the latter part of his life attained to a dignified station in the church, being remembered in records and traditions as Deacon Drowne, the carver. One of his productions, an Indian chief, gilded all over, stood during the better part of a century on the cupola of the Province House, bedazzling the eyes of those who looked upward, like an angel of the sun. Another work of the good deacon's hand—a reduced likeness of his friend Captain Hunnewell, holding a telescope and quadrant—may be seen to this day, at the corner of Broad and State Streets, serving in the useful capacity of sign to the shop of a nautical instrument maker. We know not how to account for the inferiority of this quaint old figure, as compared with the recorded excellence of the Oaken Lady, unless on the supposition that in every human spirit there is imagination, sensibility, creative power, genius, which, according to circumstances, may either be developed in this world, or shrouded in a mask of dulness until another state of being. To our friend Drowne there came a brief season of excitement, kindled by love. It rendered him a genius for that one occasion, but, quenched in disappointment, left him again the mechanical carver in wood, without the power even of appreciating the work that his own hands had wrought. Yet who can doubt that the very highest state to which a human spirit can attain, in its loftiest aspirations, is its truest and most natural state, and that Drowne was more consistent with himself when he wrought the admirable figure of the mysterious lady, than when he perpetrated a whole progeny of blockheads?

There was a rumor in Boston, about this period, that a young Portuguese lady of rank, on some occasion of political or domestic disquietude, had fled from her home in Fayal and put herself under the protection of Captain Hunnewell, on board of whose vessel, and at whose residence, she was sheltered until a change of affairs. This fair stranger must have been the original of Drowne's Wooden Image.

Rappaccini's Daughter[†]

Writings of Aubépine

We do not remember to have seen any translated specimens of the productions of M. de l'Aubépine[1]—a fact the less to be wondered at, as his very name is unknown to many of his own countrymen as well as to the student of foreign literature. As a writer, he seems to occupy an unfortunate position between the Transcendentalists (who, under one name or another, have their share in all the current literature of the world) and the great body of pen-and-ink men who address the intellect and sympathies of the multitude. If not too refined, at all events too remote, too shadowy, and unsubstantial in his modes of development to suit the taste of the latter class, and yet too popular to satisfy the spiritual or metaphysical requisitions of the former, he must necessarily find himself without an audience, except here and there an individual or possibly an isolated clique. His writings, to do them justice, are not altogether destitute of fancy and originality; they might have won him greater reputation but for an inveterate love of allegory, which is apt to invest his plots and charac-

---

† First published in the *Democratic Review*, December 1844, then in *Mosses from an Old Manse*, 1846. The preface, "Writings of Aubépine," appeared before the tale proper, in the *Democratic Review*.

1. French for "Hawthorne." A young French acquaintance bestowed the name on Hawthorne on a holiday in Maine in 1837, and he sometimes used it afterward to sign letters to his fiancée, Sophia Peabody. This preface is a whimsical account of Hawthorne's career, with hints on how to attend to the special aesthetic qualities of his tales.

[handwritten marginalia: "references other great works. Dante's Divine Comedies", "Milton: Paradise Lost"]

ters with the aspect of scenery and people in the clouds and to steal away the human warmth out of his conceptions. His fictions are sometimes historical, sometimes of the present day, and sometimes, so far as can be discovered, have little or no reference either to time or space. In any case, he generally contents himself with a very slight embroidery of outward manners,—the faintest possible counterfeit of real life,—and endeavors to create an interest by some less obvious peculiarity of the subject. Occasionally a breath of Nature, a rain-drop of pathos and tenderness, or a gleam of humor will find its way into the midst of his fantastic imagery, and make us feel as if, after all, we were yet within the limits of our native earth. We will only add to this very cursory notice that M. de l'Aubépine's productions, if the reader chance to take them in precisely the proper point of view, may amuse a leisure hour as well as those of a brighter man; if otherwise, they can hardly fail to look excessively like nonsense.

Our author is voluminous; he continues to write and publish with as much praiseworthy and indefatigable prolixity as if his efforts were crowned with the brilliant success that so justly attends those of Eugène Sue.[2] His first appearance was by a collection of stories in a long series of volumes entitled *Contes deux fois racontées.*[3] The titles of some of his more recent works (we quote from memory) are as follows: *Le Voyage Céleste à Chemin de Fer*, 3 tom., 1838. *Le nou-veau Père Adam et la nouvelle Mère Eve*, 2 tom., 1839. *Roderic; ou le Serpent à l'estomac*, 2 tom., 1840. *Le Culte du Feu*, a folio volume of ponderous research into the religion and ritual of the old Persian Ghebers, published in 1841. *La Soirée du Chateau en Espagne*, 1 tom. 8vo., 1842; and *L'Artiste du Beau; ou le Papillon Mécanique* 5 tom. 4to., 1843.[4] Our somewhat wearisome perusal of this startling catalogue of volumes has left behind it a certain personal affection and sympathy, though by no means admiration, for M. de l'Aubépine; and we would fain do the little in our power towards introducing him favorably to the American public. The ensuing tale is a transla-tion of his *Béatrice; ou la Belle Empoisonneuse*, recently published in *La Revue Anti-Aristocratique.*[5] This journal, edited by the Comte de Bearhaven,[6] has for some years past led the defence of liberal

---

2. French popular novelist (1804–1857).
3. *Twice-told Tales* (1837), Hawthorne's first book except for the anonymous *Fanshawe* (1828), from which he dissociated himself.
4. In this mock list, "tom." (an abbreviation for *tome*, French for "volume"), "folio," "8vo," and "4to" (octavo and quarto) are jokes: Hawthorne's tales each took up only a few magazine pages. Except for the imaginary *Evening in a Castle in Spain*, the titles refer to tales or sketches by Hawthorne: "The Celestial Rail-Road," "The New Adam and Eve," "Egotism; or, The Bosom-Serpent," "Fire-Worship," and "The Artist of the Beautiful."
5. The *Democratic Review*.
6. John O'Sullivan, editor of the *Democratic Review* and Hawthorne's friend.

principles and popular rights with a faithfulness and ability worthy of all praise.

Rappaccini's Daughter

A young man, named Giovanni Guasconti, came, very long ago, from the more southern region of Italy, to pursue his studies at the University of Padua. Giovanni, who had but a scanty supply of gold ducats in his pocket, took lodgings in a high and gloomy chamber of an old edifice which looked not unworthy to have been the palace of a Paduan noble, and which, in fact exhibited over its entrance the armorial bearings of a family long since extinct. The young stranger, who was not unstudied in the great poem of his country recollected that one of the ancestors of this family, and perhaps an occupant of this very mansion, had been pictured by Dante as a partaker of the immortal agonies of his Inferno.[7] These reminiscences and associations, together with the tendency to heartbreak natural to a young man for the first time out of his native sphere, caused Giovanni to sigh heavily as he looked around the desolate and ill-furnished apartment.

"Holy Virgin, signor!" cried old Dame Lisabetta, who, won by the youth's remarkable beauty of person was kindly endeavoring to give the chamber a habitable air, "what a sigh was that to come out of a young man's heart! Do you find this old mansion gloomy? For the love of Heaven, then, put your head out of the window, and you will see as bright sunshine as you have left in Naples."

Guasconti mechanically did as the old woman advised, but could not quite agree with her that the Paduan sunshine was as cheerful as that of southern Italy. Such as it was, however, it fell upon a garden beneath the window and expended its fostering influences on a variety of plants, which seemed to have been cultivated with exceeding care.

"Does this garden belong to the house?" asked Giovanni.

"Heaven forbid, signor, unless it were fruitful of better pot herbs than any that grow there now," answered old Lisabetta. "No; that garden is cultivated by the own hands of Signor Giacomo Rappaccini, the famous doctor, who, I warrant him, has been heard of as far as Naples. It is said that he distils these plants into medicines that are as potent as a charm. Oftentimes you may see the signor doctor at work, and perchance the signora, his daughter, too, gathering the strange flowers that grow in the garden."

---

7. In *Inferno* 17.64–75, Dante observes an unnamed Paduan nobleman and usurer among those who have committed crimes against Nature.

The old woman had now done what she could for the aspect of the chamber; and, commending the young man to the protection of the saints, took her departure.

Giovanni still found no better occupation than to look down into the garden beneath his window. From its appearance, he judged it to be one of those botanic gardens which were of earlier date in Padua than elsewhere in Italy or in the world. Or, not improbably, it might once have been the pleasure-place of an opulent family; for there was the ruin of a marble fountain in the centre, sculptured with rare art, but so wofully shattered that it was impossible to trace the original design from the chaos of remaining fragments. The water, however, continued to gush and sparkle into the sunbeams as cheerfully as ever. A little gurgling sound ascended to the young man's window and made him feel as if the fountain were an immortal spirit, that sung its song unceasingly and without heeding the vicissitudes around it, while one century imbodied it in marble and another scattered the perishable garniture on the soil. All about the pool into which the water subsided grew various plants, that seemed to require a plentiful supply of moisture for the nourishment of gigantic leaves, and, in some instances, flowers gorgeously magnificent. There was one shrub in particular, set in a marble vase in the midst of the pool, that bore a profusion of purple blossoms, each of which had the lustre and richness of a gem; and the whole together made a show so resplendent that it seemed enough to illuminate the garden, even had there been no sunshine. Every portion of the soil was peopled with plants and herbs, which, if less beautiful, still bore tokens of assiduous care, as if all had their individual virtues, known to the scientific mind that fostered them. Some were placed in urns, rich with old carving, and others in common garden pots; some crept serpent-like along the ground or climbed on high, using whatever means of ascent was offered them. One plant had wreathed itself round a statue of Vertumnus,[8] which was thus quite veiled and shrouded in a drapery of hanging foliage, so happily arranged that it might have served a sculptor for a study.

While Giovanni stood at the window he heard a rustling behind a screen of leaves, and became aware that a person was at work in the garden. His figure soon emerged into view, and showed itself to be that of no common laborer, but a tall, emaciated, sallow, and sickly-looking man, dressed in a scholar's garb of black. He was beyond the middle term of life, with gray hair, a thin, gray beard, and a face singularly marked with intellect and cultivation, but which

---

8. The Roman god of the seasons. In Ovid's *Metamorphoses* 14, Vertumnus woos and wins the modest Pomona in her secluded garden.

could never, even in his more youthful days, have expressed much warmth of heart.

Nothing could exceed the intentness with which this scientific gardener examined every shrub which grew in his path: it seemed as if he was looking into their inmost nature, making observations in regard to their creative essence, and discovering why one leaf grew in this shape and another in that, and wherefore such and such flowers differed among themselves in hue and perfume. Nevertheless, in spite of this deep intelligence on his part, there was no approach to intimacy between himself and these vegetable existences. On the contrary, he avoided their actual touch or the direct inhaling of their odors with a caution that impressed Giovanni most disagreeably; for the man's demeanor was that of one walking among malignant influences, such as savage beasts, or deadly snakes, or evil spirits, which, should he allow them one moment of license, would wreak upon him some terrible fatality. It was strangely frightful to the young man's imagination to see this air of insecurity in a person cultivating a garden, that most simple and innocent of human toils, and which had been alike the joy and labor of the unfallen parents of the race. Was this garden, then, the Eden of the present world? And this man, with such a perception of harm in what his own hands caused to grow,—was he the Adam?

The distrustful gardener, while plucking away the dead leaves or pruning the too luxuriant growth of the shrubs, defended his hands with a pair of thick gloves. Nor were these his only armor. When, in his walk through the garden, he came to the magnificent plant that hung its purple gems beside the marble fountain, he placed a kind of mask over his mouth and nostrils, as if all this beauty did but conceal a deadlier malice; but, finding his task still too dangerous, he drew back, removed the mask, and called loudly, but in the infirm voice of a person affected with inward disease,—

"Beatrice! Beatrice!"

"Here am I, my father. What would you?" cried a rich and youthful voice from the window of the opposite house—a voice as rich as a tropical sunset, and which made Giovanni, though he knew not why, think of deep hues of purple or crimson and of perfumes heavily delectable. "Are you in the garden?"

"Yes, Beatrice," answered the gardener; "and I need your help."

Soon there emerged from under a sculptured portal the figure of a young girl, arrayed with as much richness of taste as the most splendid of the flowers, beautiful as the day, and with a bloom so deep and vivid that one shade more would have been too much. She looked redundant with life, health, and energy; all of which attributes were bound down and compressed, as it were, and girdled tensely, in their luxuriance, by her virgin zone.[9] Yet Giovanni's fancy must have grown morbid while he looked down into the garden; for the impression which the fair stranger made upon him was as if here were another flower, the human sister of those vegetable ones, as beautiful as they, more beautiful than the richest of them, but still to be touched only with a glove, nor to be approached without a mask. As Beatrice came down the garden path, it was observable that she handled and inhaled the odor of several of the plants which her father had most sedulously avoided.

"Here, Beatrice," said the latter, "see how many needful offices require to be done to our chief treasure. Yet, shattered as I am, my life might pay the penalty of approaching it so closely as circumstances demand. Henceforth, I fear, this plant must be consigned to your sole charge."

"And gladly will I undertake it," cried again the rich tones of the young lady, as she bent towards the magnificent plant and opened her arms as if to embrace it. "Yes, my sister, my splendor, it shall be Beatrice's task to nurse and serve thee; and thou shalt reward her with thy kisses and perfumed breath, which to her is as the breath of life."

Then, with all the tenderness in her manner that was so strikingly expressed in her words, she busied herself with such attentions as the plant seemed to require; and Giovanni, at his lofty window, rubbed his eyes, and almost doubted whether it were a girl tending her favorite flower, or one sister performing the duties of affection to another. The scene soon terminated. Whether Dr. Rappaccini had finished his labors in the garden, or that his watchful eye had caught the stranger's face, he now took his daughter's arm and retired. Night was already closing in; oppressive exhalations seemed to proceed from the plants and steal upward past the open window; and Giovanni, closing the lattice, went to his couch and dreamed of a rich flower and beautiful girl. Flower and maiden were different, and yet the same, and fraught with some strange peril in either shape.

But there is an influence in the light of morning that tends to rectify whatever errors of fancy, or even of judgment, we may have incurred during the sun's decline, or among the shadows of the night, or in the less wholesome glow of moonshine. Giovanni's first movement, on starting from sleep, was to throw open the window and gaze down into the garden which his dreams had made so fertile of mysteries. He was surprised, and a little ashamed, to find how real and matter-of-fact an affair it proved to be, in the first rays of

9. Her belt, "virgin" because Beatrice appears to be an unmarried girl.

the sun which gilded the dewdrops that hung upon leaf and blossom, and, while giving a brighter beauty to each rare flower, brought
every thing within the limits of ordinary experience. The young man
rejoiced that, in the heart of the barren city, he had the privilege of
overlooking this spot of lovely and luxuriant vegetation. It would
serve, he said to himself, as a symbolic language to keep him in
communion with Nature. Neither the sickly and thoughtworn Dr.
Giacomo Rappaccini, it is true, nor his brilliant daughter, were now
visible; so that Giovanni could not determine how much of the singularity which he attributed to both was due to their own qualities
and how much to his wonder-working fancy; but he was inclined to
take a most rational view of the whole matter.

In the course of the day he paid his respects to Signor Pietro
Baglioni, professor of medicine in the university, a physician of eminent repute, to whom Giovanni had brought a letter of introduction.
The professor was an elderly personage, apparently of genial nature
and habits that might almost be called jovial. He kept the young
man to dinner, and made himself very agreeable by the freedom and
liveliness of his conversation, especially when warmed by a flask or
two of Tuscan wine. Giovanni, conceiving that men of science,
inhabitants of the same city, must needs be on familiar terms with
one another, took an opportunity to mention the name of Dr. Rappaccini. But the professor did not respond with so much cordiality as
he had anticipated.

"Ill would it become a teacher of the divine art of medicine," said
Professor Pietro Baglioni, in answer to a question of Giovanni, "to
withhold due and well-considered praise of a physician so eminently
skilled as Rappaccini; but, on the other hand, I should answer it
but scantily to my conscience were I to permit a worthy youth like
yourself, Signor Giovanni, the son of an ancient friend, to imbibe
erroneous ideas respecting a man who might hereafter chance to
hold your life and death in his hands. The truth is, our worshipful
Dr. Rappaccini has as much science as any member of the faculty—
with perhaps one single exception—in Padua, or all Italy; but there
are certain grave objections to his professional character."

"And what are they?" asked the young man.

"Has my friend Giovanni any disease of body or heart, that he is
so inquisitive about physicians?" said the professor, with a smile.
"But as for Rappaccini, it is said of him—and I, who know the man
well, can answer for its truth—that he cares infinitely more for science than for mankind. His patients are interesting to him only as
subjects for some new experiment. He would sacrifice human life,
his own among the rest, or whatever else was dearest to him, for the
sake of adding so much as a grain of mustard seed to the great heap
of his accumulated knowledge."

"Methinks he is an awful[1] man indeed," remarked Guasconti, mentally recalling the cold and purely intellectual aspect of Rappaccini. "And yet, worshipful professor, is it not a noble spirit? Are there many men capable of so spiritual a love or science?"

"God forbid," answered the professor, somewhat testily; "at least, unless they take sounder views of the healing art than those adopted by Rappaccini. It is his theory that all medicinal virtues are comprised within those substances which we term vegetable poisons. These he cultivates with his own hands, and is said even to have produced new varieties of poison, more horribly deleterious than Nature, without the assistance of this learned person, would ever have plagued the world withal. That the signor doctor does less mischief than might be expected with such dangerous substances, is undeniable. Now and then, it must be owned, he has effected, or seemed to effect, a marvellous cure; but, to tell you my private mind, Signor Giovanni, he should receive little credit for such instances of success,—they being probably the work of chance,—but should be held strictly accountable for his failures, which may justly be considered his own work."

The youth might have taken Baglioni's opinions with many grains of allowance had he known that there was a professional warfare of long continuance between him and Dr. Rappaccini, in which the latter was generally thought to have gained the advantage. If the reader be inclined to judge for himself, we refer him to certain black-letter tracts on both sides, preserved in the medical department of the University of Padua.

"I know not, most learned professor," returned Giovanni, after musing on what had been said of Rappaccini's exclusive zeal for science,—"I know not how dearly this physician may love his art; but surely there is one object more dear to him. He has a daughter."

"Aha!" cried the professor, with a laugh. "So now our friend Giovanni's secret is out. You have heard of this daughter, whom all the young men in Padua are wild about, though not half a dozen have ever had the good hap to see her face. I know little of the Signora Beatrice save that Rappaccini is said to have instructed her deeply in his science, and that, young and beautiful as fame reports her, she is already qualified to fill a professor's chair. Perchance her father destines her for mine! Other absurd rumors there be, not worth talking about or listening to. So now, Signor Giovanni, drink off your glass of lachryma."[2]

Guasconti returned to his lodgings somewhat heated with the wine he had quaffed, and which caused his brain to swim with

1. Frightful.
2. Lacrima Christi, an Italian wine.

strange fantasies in reference to Dr. Rappaccini and the beautiful
Beatrice. On his way, happening to pass by a florist's, he bought a
fresh bouquet of flowers.

Ascending to his chamber, he seated himself near the window,
but within the shadow thrown by the depth of the wall, so that he
could look down into the garden with little risk of being discovered.
All beneath his eye was a solitude. The strange plants were basking
in the sunshine, and now and then nodding gently to one another,
as if in acknowledgment of sympathy and kindred. In the midst, by
the shattered fountain, grew the magnificent shrub, with its purple
gems clustering all over it; they glowed in the air, and gleamed back
again out of the depths of the pool, which thus seemed to overflow
with colored radiance from the rich reflection that was steeped
in it. At first, as we have said, the garden was a solitude. Soon,
however,—as Giovanni had half hoped, half feared, would be the
case,—a figure appeared beneath the antique sculptured portal,
and came down between the rows of plants, inhaling their various
perfumes as if she were one of those beings of old classic fable that
lived upon sweet odors. On again beholding Beatrice, the young
man was even startled to perceive how much her beauty exceeded
his recollection of it; so brilliant, so vivid, was its character, that she
glowed amid the sunlight, and, as Giovanni whispered to himself,
positively illuminated the more shadowy intervals of the garden
path. Her face being now more revealed than on the former occasion, he was struck by its expression of simplicity and sweetness—
qualities that had not entered into his idea of her character, and
which made him ask anew what manner of mortal she might be. Nor
did he fail again to observe, or imagine, an analogy between the
beautiful girl and the gorgeous shrub that hung its gemlike flowers
over the fountain—a resemblance which Beatrice seemed to have
indulged a fantastic humor in heightening, both by the arrangement of her dress and the selection of its hues.

Approaching the shrub, she threw open her arms, as with a passionate ardor, and drew its branches into an intimate embrace—so
intimate that her features were hidden in its leafy bosom and her
glistening ringlets all intermingled with the flowers.

"Give me thy breath, my sister," exclaimed Beatrice; "for I am
faint with common air. And give me this flower of thine, which I
separate with gentlest fingers from the stem and place it close beside
my heart."

With these words the beautiful daughter of Rappaccini plucked
one of the richest blossoms of the shrub, and was about to fasten it
in her bosom. But now, unless Giovanni's draughts of wine had
bewildered his senses, a singular incident occurred. A small orange-
colored reptile, of the lizard or chameleon species, chanced to be

creeping along the path, just at the feet of Beatrice. It appeared to
Giovanni,—but, at the distance from which he gazed, he could
scarcely have seen any thing so minute,—it appeared to him, however, that a drop or two of moisture from the broken stem of the
flower descended upon the lizard's head. For an instant the reptile
contorted itself violently, and then lay motionless in the sunshine.
Beatrice observed this remarkable phenomenon, and crossed herself, sadly, but without surprise; nor did she therefore hesitate to
arrange the fatal flower in her bosom. There it blushed, and almost
glimmered with the dazzling effect of a precious stone, adding to
her dress and aspect the one appropriate charm which nothing else
in the world could have supplied. But Giovanni, out of the shadow
of his window, bent forward and shrank back, and murmured and
trembled.

"Am I awake? Have I my senses?" said he to himself. "What is
this being? Beautiful shall I call her, or inexpressibly terrible?"

Beatrice now strayed carelessly through the garden, approaching
closer beneath Giovanni's window, so that he was compelled to
thrust his head quite out of its concealment in order to gratify the
intense and painful curiosity which she excited. At this moment
there came a beautiful insect over the garden wall: it had, perhaps,
wandered through the city, and found no flowers or verdure among
those antique haunts of men until the heavy perfumes of Dr. Rappaccini's shrubs had lured it from afar. Without alighting on the
flowers, this winged brightness seemed to be attracted by Beatrice,
and lingered in the air and fluttered about her head. Now, here it
could not be but that Giovanni Guasconti's eyes deceived him. Be
that as it might, he fancied that, while Beatrice was gazing at the
insect with childish delight, it grew faint and fell at her feet; its
bright wings shivered; it was dead—from no cause that he could
discern, unless it were the atmosphere of her breath. Again Beatrice
crossed herself and sighed heavily as she bent over the dead insect.

An impulsive movement of Giovanni drew her eyes to the window.
There she beheld the beautiful head of the young man—rather a
Grecian than an Italian head, with fair, regular features, and a glistening of gold among his ringlets—gazing down upon her like a
being that hovered in mid air. Scarcely knowing what he did,
Giovanni threw down the bouquet which he had hitherto held in his
hand.

"Signora," said he, "there are pure and healthful flowers. Wear
them for the sake of Giovanni Guasconti."

"Thanks, signor," replied Beatrice, with her rich voice, that came
forth as it were like a gush of music, and with a mirthful expression
half childish and half womanlike. "I accept your gift, and would
fain recompense it with this precious purple flower; but, if I toss it

into the air, it will not reach you. So Signor Guasconti must even content himself with my thanks."

She lifted the bouquet from the ground, and then, as if inwardly ashamed at having stepped aside from her maidenly reserve to respond to a stranger's greeting, passed swiftly homeward through the garden. But, few as the moments were, it seemed to Giovanni, when she was on the point of vanishing beneath the sculptured portal, that his beautiful bouquet was already beginning to wither in her grasp. It was an idle thought; there could be no possibility of distinguishing a faded flower from a fresh one at so great a distance.

For many days after this incident the young man avoided the window that looked into Dr. Rappaccini's garden, as if something ugly and monstrous would have blasted his eyesight had he been betrayed into a glance. He felt conscious of having put himself, to a certain extent, within the influence of an unintelligible power by the communication which he had opened with Beatrice. The wisest course would have been, if his heart were in any real danger, to quit his lodgings and Padua itself at once; the next wiser, to have accustomed himself, as far as possible, to the familiar and daylight view of Beatrice—thus bringing her rigidly and systematically within the limits of ordinary experience. Least of all, while avoiding her sight, ought Giovanni to have remained so near this extraordinary being that the proximity and possibility even of intercourse should give a kind of substance and reality to the wild vagaries which his imagination ran riot continually in producing. Guasconti had not a deep heart—or, at all events, its depths were not sounded now; but he had a quick fancy, and an ardent southern temperament, which rose every instant to a higher fever pitch. Whether or no Beatrice possessed those terrible attributes, that fatal breath, the affinity with those so beautiful and deadly flowers which were indicated by what Giovanni had witnessed, she had at least instilled a fierce and subtle poison into his system! It was not love, although her rich beauty was a madness to him; nor horror, even while he fancied her spirit to be imbued with the same baneful essence that seemed to pervade her physical frame; but a wild offspring of both love and horror that had each parent in it, and burned like one and shivered like the other. Giovanni knew not what to dread; still less did he know what to hope; yet hope and dread kept a continual warfare in his breast, alternately vanquishing one another and starting up afresh to renew the contest. Blessed are all simple emotions, be they dark or bright! It is the lurid intermixture of the two that produces the illuminating blaze of the infernal regions.

Sometimes he endeavored to assuage the fever of his spirit by a rapid walk through the streets of Padua or beyond its gates: his footsteps kept time with the throbbings of his brain, so that the walk was apt to accelerate itself to a race. One day he found himself arrested; his arm was seized by a portly personage, who had turned back on recognizing the young man and expended much breath in overtaking him.

"Signor Giovanni! Stay, my young friend!" cried he. "Have you forgotten me? That might well be the case if I were as much altered as yourself."

It was Baglioni, whom Giovanni had avoided ever since their first meeting, from a doubt that the professor's sagacity would look too deeply into his secrets. Endeavoring to recover himself, he stared forth wildly from his inner world into the outer one and spoke like a man in a dream.

"Yes; I am Giovanni Guasconti. You are Professor Pietro Baglioni. Now let me pass!"

"Not yet, not yet, Signor Giovanni Guasconti," said the professor, smiling, but at the same time scrutinizing the youth with an earnest glance. "What! did I grow up side by side with your father? and shall his son pass me like a stranger in these old streets of Padua? Stand still, Signor Giovanni; for we must have a word or two before we part."

"Speedily, then, most worshipful professor, speedily," said Giovanni, with feverish impatience. "Does not your worship see that I am in haste?"

Now, while he was speaking there came a man in black along the street, stooping and moving feebly like a person in inferior health. His face was all overspread with a most sickly and sallow hue, but yet so pervaded with an expression of piercing and active intellect that an observer might easily have overlooked the merely physical attributes and have seen only this wonderful energy. As he passed, this person exchanged a cold and distant salutation with Baglioni, but fixed his eyes upon Giovanni with an intentness that seemed to bring out whatever was within him worthy of notice. Nevertheless, there was a peculiar quietness in the look, as if taking merely a speculative, not a human, interest in the young man.

"It is Dr. Rappaccini!" whispered the professor when the stranger had passed. "Has he ever seen your face before?"

"Not that I know," answered Giovanni, starting at the name.

"He *has* seen you! he must have seen you!" said Baglioni, hastily. "For some purpose or other, this man of science is making a study of you. I know that look of his! It is the same that coldly illuminates his face as he bends over a bird, a mouse, or a butterfly; which, in pursuance of some experiment, he has killed by the perfume of a flower; a look as deep as Nature itself, but without Nature's warmth of love. Signor Giovanni, I will stake my life upon it, you are the subject of one of Rappaccini's experiments!"

"Will you make a fool of me?" cried Giovanni, passionately. "*That,* signor professor, were an untoward experiment."

"Patience! patience!" replied the imperturbable professor. "I tell thee, my poor Giovanni, that Rappaccini has a scientific interest in thee. Thou hast fallen into fearful hands! And the Signora Beatrice,— what part does she act in this mystery?"

But Guasconti, finding Baglioni's pertinacity intolerable, here broke away, and was gone before the professor could again seize his arm. He looked after the young man intently and shook his head.

"This must not be," said Baglioni to himself. "The youth is the son of my old friend, and shall not come to any harm from which the arcana[3] of medical science can preserve him. Besides, it is too insufferable an impertinence in Rappaccini thus to snatch the lad out of my own hands, as I may say, and make use of him for his infernal experiments. This daughter of his! It shall be looked to. Perchance, most learned Rappaccini, I may foil you where you little dream of it!"

Meanwhile Giovanni had pursued a circuitous route, and at length found himself at the door of his lodgings. As he crossed the threshold he was met by old Lisabetta, who smirked and smiled, and was evidently desirous to attract his attention; vainly, however, as the ebullition of his feelings had momentarily subsided into a cold and dull vacuity. He turned his eyes full upon the withered face that was puckering itself into a smile, but seemed to behold it not. The old dame, therefore, laid her grasp upon his cloak.

"Signor! signor!" whispered she, still with a smile over the whole breadth of her visage, so that it looked not unlike a grotesque carving in wood, darkened by centuries. "Listen, signor! There is a private entrance into the garden!"

"What do you say?" exclaimed Giovanni, turning quickly about, as if an inanimate thing should start into feverish life. "A private entrance into Dr. Rappaccini's garden?"

"Hush! hush! not so loud!" whispered Lisabetta, putting her hand over his mouth. "Yes; into the worshipful doctor's garden, where you may see all his fine shrubbery. Many a young man in Padua would give gold to be admitted among those flowers."

Giovanni put a piece of gold into her hand.

"Show me the way," said he.

A surmise, probably excited by his conversation with Baglioni, crossed his mind, that this interposition of old Lisabetta might perchance be connected with the intrigue, whatever were its nature, in which the professor seemed to suppose that Dr. Rappaccini was involving him. But such a suspicion, though it disturbed Giovanni, was inadequate to restrain him. The instant that he was aware of

3. Secrets.

the possibility of approaching Beatrice, it seemed an absolute necessity of his existence to do so. It mattered not whether she were angel or demon; he was irrevocably within her sphere, and must obey the law that whirled him onward, in ever-lessening circles, towards a result which he did not attempt to foreshadow; and yet, strange to say, there came across him a sudden doubt whether this intense interest on his part were not delusory; whether it were really of so deep and positive a nature as to justify him in now thrusting himself into an incalculable position; whether it were not merely the fantasy of a young man's brain, only slightly or not at all connected with his heart.

He paused, hesitated, turned half about, but again went on. His withered guide led him along several obscure passages, and finally undid a door, through which, as it was opened, there came the sight and sound of rustling leaves, with the broken sunshine glimmering among them. Giovanni stepped forth, and, forcing himself through the entanglement of a shrub that wreathed its tendrils over the hidden entrance, stood beneath his own window in the open area of Dr. Rappaccini's garden.

How often is it the case that, when impossibilities have come to pass and dreams have condensed their misty substance into tangible realities, we find ourselves calm, and even coldly self-possessed, amid circumstances which it would have been a delirium of joy or agony to anticipate! Fate delights to thwart us thus. Passion will choose his own time to rush upon the scene, and lingers sluggishly behind when an appropriate adjustment of events would seem to summon his appearance. So was it now with Giovanni. Day after day his pulses had throbbed with feverish blood at the improbable idea of an interview with Beatrice, and of standing with her, face to face, in this very garden, basking in the Oriental sunshine of her beauty, and snatching from her full gaze the mystery which he deemed the riddle of his own existence. But now there was a singular and untimely equanimity within his breast. He threw a glance around the garden to discover if Beatrice or her father were present, and, perceiving that he was alone, began a critical observation of the plants.

The aspect of one and all of them dissatisfied him; their gorgeousness seemed fierce, passionate, and even unnatural. There was hardly an individual shrub which a wanderer, straying by himself through a forest, would not have been startled to find growing wild, as if an unearthly face had glared at him out of the thicket. Several also would have shocked a delicate instinct by an appearance of artificialness indicating that there had been such commixture, and, as it were, adultery of various vegetable species, that the production was no longer of God's making, but the monstrous offspring of man's depraved fancy, glowing with only an evil mockery of beauty. They were probably the result of experiment, which in one or two cases had succeeded in mingling plants individually lovely into a compound possessing the questionable and ominous character that distinguished the whole growth of the garden. In fine, Giovanni recognized but two or three plants in the collection, and those of a kind that he well knew to be poisonous. While busy with these contemplations he heard the rustling of a silken garment, and, turning, beheld Beatrice emerging from beneath the sculptured portal.

Giovanni had not considered with himself what should be his deportment; whether he should apologize for his intrusion into the garden, or assume that he was there with the privity at least, if not by the desire, of Dr. Rappaccini or his daughter; but Beatrice's manner placed him at his ease, though leaving him still in doubt by what agency he had gained admittance. She came lightly along the path and met him near the broken fountain. There was surprise in her face, but brightened by a simple and kind expression of pleasure.

"You are a connoisseur in flowers, signor," said Beatrice, with a smile, alluding to the bouquet which he had flung her from the window. "It is no marvel, therefore, if the sight of my father's rare collection has tempted you to take a nearer view. If he were here, he could tell you many strange and interesting facts as to the nature and habits of these shrubs; for he has spent a lifetime in such studies, and this garden is his world."

"And yourself, lady," observed Giovanni, "if fame says true,—you likewise are deeply skilled in the virtues indicated by these rich blossoms and these spicy perfumes. Would you deign to be my instructress, I should prove an apter scholar than if taught by Signor Rappaccini himself."

"Are there such idle rumors?" asked Beatrice, with the music of a pleasant laugh. "Do people say that I am skilled in my father's science of plants? What a jest is there! No; though I have grown up among these flowers, I know no more of them than their hues and perfume; and sometimes methinks I would fain rid myself of even that small knowledge. There are many flowers here, and those not the least brilliant, that shock and offend me when they meet my eye. But pray, signor, do not believe these stories about my science. Believe nothing of me save what you see with your own eyes."

"And must I believe all that I have seen with my own eyes?" asked Giovanni, pointedly, while the recollection of former scenes made him shrink. "No, signora; you demand too little of me. Bid me believe nothing save what comes from your own lips."

It would appear that Beatrice understood him. There came a deep flush to her cheek; but she looked full into Giovanni's eyes, and responded to his gaze of uneasy suspicion with a queenlike haughtiness.

"I do so bid you, signor," she replied. "Forget whatever you may have fancied in regard to me. If true to the outward senses, still it may be false in its essence; but the words of Beatrice Rappaccini's lips are true from the depths of the heart outward. Those you may believe."

A fervor glowed in her whole aspect and beamed upon Giovanni's consciousness like the light of truth itself; but while she spoke there was a fragrance in the atmosphere around her, rich and delightful, though evanescent, yet which the young man, from an indefinable reluctance, scarcely dared to draw into his lungs. It might be the odor of the flowers. Could it be Beatrice's breath which thus embalmed her words with a strange richness, as if by steeping them in her heart? A faintness passed like a shadow over Giovanni and flitted away; he seemed to gaze through the beautiful girl's eyes into her transparent soul, and felt no more doubt or fear.

The tinge of passion that had colored Beatrice's manner vanished; she became gay, and appeared to derive a pure delight from her communion with the youth not unlike what the maiden of a lonely island might have felt conversing with a voyager from the civilized world. Evidently her experience of life had been confined within the limits of that garden. She talked now about matters as simple as the daylight or summer clouds, and now asked questions in reference to the city, or Giovanni's distant home, his friends, his mother, and his sisters—questions indicating such seclusion, and such lack of familiarity with modes and forms, that Giovanni responded as if to an infant. Her spirit gushed out before him like a fresh rill that was just catching its first glimpse of the sunlight and wondering at the reflections of earth and sky which were flung into its bosom. There came thoughts, too, from a deep source, and fantasies of a gemlike brilliancy, as if diamonds and rubies sparkled upward among the bubbles of the fountain. Ever and anon there gleamed across the young man's mind a sense of wonder that he should be walking side by side with the being who had so wrought upon his imagination, whom he had idealized in such hues of terror, in whom he had positively witnessed such manifestations of dreadful attributes—that he should be conversing with Beatrice like a brother, and should find her so human and so maidenlike. But such reflections were only momentary; the effect of her character was too real not to make itself familiar at once.

In this free intercourse they had strayed through the garden, and now, after many turns among its avenues, were come to the shattered fountain, beside which grew the magnificent shrub, with its treasury of glowing blossoms. A fragrance was diffused from it which Giovanni recognized as identical with that which he had attributed to Beatrice's breath, but incomparably more powerful. As her eyes fell upon it, Giovanni beheld her press her hand to her bosom as if her heart were throbbing suddenly and painfully.

"For the first time in my life," murmured she, addressing the shrub, "I had forgotten thee."

"I remember, signora," said Giovanni, "that you once promised to reward me with one of these living gems for the bouquet which I had the happy boldness to fling to your feet. Permit me now to pluck it as a memorial of this interview."

He made a step towards the shrub with extended hand; but Beatrice darted forward, uttering a shriek that went through his heart like a dagger. She caught his hand and drew it back with the whole force of her slender figure. Giovanni felt her touch thrilling through his fibres.

"Touch it not!" exclaimed she, in a voice of agony. "Not for thy life! It is fatal!"

Then, hiding her face, she fled from him and vanished beneath the sculptured portal. As Giovanni followed her with his eyes, he beheld the emaciated figure and pale intelligence of Dr. Rappaccini, who had been watching the scene, he knew not how long, within the shadow of the entrance.

No sooner was Guasconti alone in his chamber than the image of Beatrice came back to his passionate musings, invested with all the witchery that had been gathering around it ever since his first glimpse of her, and now likewise imbued with a tender warmth of girlish womanhood. She was human; her nature was endowed with all gentle and feminine qualities; she was worthiest to be worshipped; she was capable, surely, on her part, of the height and heroism of love. Those tokens which he had hitherto considered as proofs of a frightful peculiarity in her physical and moral system were now either forgotten or by the subtle sophistry of passion transmitted into a golden crown of enchantment, rendering Beatrice the more admirable by so much as she was the more unique. Whatever had looked ugly was now beautiful; or, if incapable of such a change, it stole away and hid itself among those shapeless half ideas which throng the dim region beyond the daylight of our perfect consciousness. Thus did he spend the night, nor fell asleep until the dawn had begun to awake the slumbering flowers in Dr. Rappaccini's garden, whither Giovanni's dreams doubtless led him. Up rose the sun in his due season, and, flinging his beams upon the young man's eyelids, awoke him to a sense of pain. When thoroughly aroused, he became sensible of a burning and tingling agony in his hand—in his right hand—the very hand which Beatrice had grasped in her own when he was on the point of plucking one of the gemlike flowers. On the back of that hand there was now a purple print like that of four small fingers, and the likeness of a slender thumb upon his wrist.

O, how stubbornly does love,—or even that cunning semblance
of love which flourishes in the imagination, but strikes no depth
of root into the heart,—how stubbornly does it hold its faith until
the moment comes when it is doomed to vanish into thin mist!
Giovanni wrapped a handkerchief about his hand and wondered
what evil thing had stung him, and soon forgot his pain in a revery
of Beatrice.

After the first interview, a second was in the inevitable course of
what we call fate. A third; a fourth; and a meeting with Beatrice in
the garden was no longer an incident in Giovanni's daily life, but the
whole space in which he might be said to live; for the anticipation
and memory of that ecstatic hour made up the remainder. Nor was
it otherwise with the daughter of Rappaccini. She watched for the
youth's appearance and flew to his side with confidence as unreserved as if they had been playmates from early infancy—as if they
were such playmates still. If, by any unwonted chance, he failed to
come at the appointed moment, she stood beneath the window and
sent up the rich sweetness of her tones to float around him in his
chamber and echo and reverberate throughout his heart? "Giovanni!
Giovanni! Why tarriest thou? Come down!" And down he hastened
into that Eden of poisonous flowers.

But, with all this intimate familiarity, there was still a reserve in
Beatrice's demeanor, so rigidly and invariably sustained that the idea
of infringing it scarcely occurred to his imagination. By all appreciable signs, they loved; they had looked love with eyes that conveyed
the holy secret from the depths of one soul into the depths of the
other, as if it were too sacred to be whispered by the way; they had
even spoken love in those gushes of passion when their spirits darted
forth in articulated breath like tongues of long hidden flame; and yet
there had been no seal of lips, no clasp of hands, nor any slightest
caress such as love claims and hallows. He had never touched one
of the gleaming ringlets of her hair; her garment—so marked was the
physical barrier between them—had never been waved against
him by a breeze. On the few occasions when Giovanni had seemed
tempted to overstep the limit, Beatrice grew so sad, so stern, and
withal wore such a look of desolate separation, shuddering at itself,
that not a spoken word was requisite to repel him. At such times he
was startled at the horrible suspicions that rose, monster-like, out of
the caverns of his heart and stared him in the face; his love grew thin
and faint as the morning mist; his doubts alone had substance. But,
when Beatrice's face brightened again after the momentary shadow,
she was transformed at once from the mysterious, questionable being
whom he had watched with so much awe and horror; she was now
the beautiful and unsophisticated girl whom he felt that his spirit
knew with a certainty beyond all other knowledge.

A considerable time had now passed since Giovanni's last meeting with Baglioni. One morning, however, he was disagreeably surprised by a visit from the professor, whom he had scarcely thought of for whole weeks, and would willingly have forgotten still longer. Given up as he had long been to a pervading excitement, he could tolerate no companions except upon condition of their perfect sympathy with his present state of feeling. Such sympathy was not to be expected from Professor Baglioni.

The visitor chatted carelessly for a few moments about the gossip of the city and the university, and then took up another topic.

"I have been reading an old classic author lately," said he, "and met with a story that strangely interested me.[4] Possibly you may remember it. It is of an Indian prince, who sent a beautiful woman as a present to Alexander the Great. She was as lovely as the dawn and gorgeous as the sunset; but what especially distinguished her was a certain rich perfume in her breath—richer than a garden of Persian roses. Alexander, as was natural to a youthful conqueror, fell in love at first sight with this magnificent stranger; but a certain sage physician, happening to be present, discovered a terrible secret in regard to her."

"And what was that?" asked Giovanni, turning his eyes downward to avoid those of the professor.

"That this lovely woman," continued Baglioni, with emphasis, "had been nourished with poisons from her birth upward, until her whole nature was so imbued with them that she herself had become the deadliest poison in existence. Poison was her element of life. With that rich perfume of her breath she blasted the very air. Her love would have been poison—her embrace death. Is not this a marvellous tale?"

"A childish fable," answered Giovanni, nervously starting from his chair. "I marvel how your worship finds time to read such nonsense among your graver studies."

"By the by," said the professor, looking uneasily about him, "what singular fragrance is this in your apartment? Is it the perfume of your gloves? It is faint, but delicious; and yet, after all, by no means agreeable. Were I to breathe it long, methinks it would make me ill. It is like the breath of a flower; but I see no flowers in the chamber."

"Nor are there any," replied Giovanni, who had turned pale as the professor spoke; "nor, I think, is there any fragrance except in your worship's imagination. Odors, being a sort of element combined of the sensual and the spiritual, are apt to deceive us in this manner.

---

4. Hawthorne met with the story in Sir Thomas Browne's *Vulgar Errors* (1646), an "old classic" for New England readers.

The recollection of a perfume, the bare idea of it, may easily be mistaken for a present reality."

"Ay; but my sober imagination does not often play such tricks," said Baglioni; "and, were I to fancy any kind of odor, it would be that of some vile apothecary drug, wherewith my fingers are likely enough to be imbued. Our worshipful friend Rappaccini, as I have heard, tinctures his medicaments with odors richer than those of Araby. Doubtless, likewise, the fair and learned Signora Beatrice would minister to her patients with draughts as sweet as a maiden's breath; but woe to him that sips them!"

Giovanni's face evinced many contending emotions. The tone in which the professor alluded to the pure and lovely daughter of Rappaccini was a torture to his soul; and yet the intimation of a view of her character, opposite to his own, gave instantaneous distinctness to a thousand dim suspicions, which now grinned at him like so many demons. But he strove hard to quell them and to respond to Baglioni with a true lover's perfect faith.

"Signor professor," said he, "you were my father's friend; perchance, too, it is your purpose to act a friendly part towards his son. I would fain feel nothing towards you save respect and deference; but I pray you to observe, signor, that there is one subject on which we must not speak. You know not the Signora Beatrice. You cannot, therefore, estimate the wrong—the blasphemy, I may even say—that is offered to her character by a light or injurious word."

"Giovanni! my poor Giovanni!" answered the professor, with a calm expression of pity, "I know this wretched girl far better than yourself. You shall hear the truth in respect to the poisoner Rappaccini and his poisonous daughter; yes, poisonous as she is beautiful. Listen; for, even should you do violence to my gray hairs, it shall not silence me. That old fable of the Indian woman has become a truth by the deep and deadly science of Rappaccini and in the person of the lovely Beatrice."

Giovanni groaned and hid his face.

"Her father," continued Baglioni, "was not restrained by natural affection from offering up his child in this horrible manner as the victim of his insane zeal for science; for, let us do him justice, he is as true a man of science as ever distilled his own heart in an alembic. What, then, will be your fate? Beyond a doubt you are selected as the material of some new experiment. Perhaps the result is to be death; perhaps a fate more awful still. Rappaccini, with what he calls the interest of science before his eyes, will hesitate at nothing."

"It is a dream," muttered Giovanni to himself; "surely it is a dream."

"But," resumed the professor, "be of good cheer, son of my friend. It is not yet too late for the rescue. Possibly we may even succeed in bringing back this miserable child within the limits of ordinary nature, from which her father's madness has estranged her. Behold this little silver vase! It was wrought by the hands of the renowned Benvenuto Cellini,[5] and is well worthy to be a love gift to the fairest dame in Italy. But its contents are invaluable. One little sip of this antidote would have rendered the most virulent poisons of the Borgias[6] innocuous. Doubt not that it will be as efficacious against those of Rappaccini. Bestow the vase, and the precious liquid within it, on your Beatrice, and hopefully await the result."

Baglioni laid a small, exquisitely wrought silver vial on the table and withdrew, leaving what he had said to produce its effect upon the young man's mind.

"We will thwart Rappaccini yet," thought he, chuckling to himself, as he descended the stairs; "but, let us confess the truth of him, he is a wonderful man—a wonderful man indeed; a vile empiric,[7] however, in his practice, and therefore not to be tolerated by those who respect the good old rules of the medical profession."

Throughout Giovanni's whole acquaintance with Beatrice, he had occasionally, as we have said, been haunted by dark surmises as to her character; yet so thoroughly had she made herself felt by him as a simple, natural, most affectionate, and guileless creature, that the image now held up by Professor Baglioni looked as strange and incredible as if it were not in accordance with his own original conception. True, there were ugly recollections connected with his first glimpses of the beautiful girl; he could not quite forget the bouquet that withered in her grasp, and the insect that perished amid the sunny air, by no ostensible agency save the fragrance of her breath. These incidents, however, dissolving in the pure light of her character, had no longer the efficacy of facts, but were acknowledged as mistaken fantasies, by whatever testimony of the senses they might appear to be substantiated. There is something truer and more real than what we can see with the eyes and touch with the finger. On such better evidence had Giovanni founded his confidence in Beatrice, though rather by the necessary force of her high attributes than by any deep and generous faith on his part. But now his spirit was incapable of sustaining itself at the height to which the early enthusiasm of passion had exalted it; he fell down, grovelling among earthly doubts, and defiled therewith the pure whiteness of Beatrice's image. Not that he gave her up; he did but distrust. He resolved to institute some decisive test that should satisfy him, once for all, whether there were those dreadful peculiarities in her physical nature which could not be supposed to exist

---

5. Benvenuto Cellini (1500–1571), Italian sculptor and metalworker.
6. Powerful Italian Renaissance family, notorious for its cruelty and intrigue.
7. Charlatan.

without some corresponding monstrosity of soul. His eyes, gazing down afar, might have deceived him as to the lizard, the insect, and the flowers; but if he could witness, at the distance of a few paces, the sudden blight of one fresh and healthful flower in Beatrice's hand, there would be room for no further question. With this idea he hastened to the florist's and purchased a bouquet that was still gemmed with the morning dewdrops.

It was now the customary hour of his daily interview with Beatrice. Before descending into the garden, Giovanni failed not to look at his figure in the mirror—a vanity to be expected in a beautiful young man, yet, as displaying itself at that troubled and feverish moment, the token of a certain shallowness of feeling and insincerity of character. He did gaze, however, and said to himself that his features had never before possessed so rich a grace, nor his eyes such vivacity, nor his cheeks so warm a hue of superabundant life.

"At least," thought he, "her poison has not yet insinuated itself into my system. I am no flower to perish in her grasp."

With that thought he turned his eyes on the bouquet, which he had never once laid aside from his hand. A thrill of indefinable horror shot through his frame on perceiving that those dewy flowers were already beginning to droop; they wore the aspect of things that had been fresh and lovely yesterday. Giovanni grew white as marble, and stood motionless before the mirror, staring at his own reflection there as at the likeness of something frightful. He remembered Baglioni's remark about the fragrance that seemed to pervade the chamber. It must have been the poison in his breath! Then he shuddered—shuddered at himself. Recovering from his stupor, he began to watch with curious eye a spider that was busily at work hanging its web from the antique cornice of the apartment, crossing and recrossing the artful system of interwoven lines—as vigorous and active a spider as ever dangled from an old ceiling. Giovanni bent towards the insect, and emitted a deep, long breath. The spider suddenly ceased its toil; the web vibrated with a tremor orginating in the body of the small artisan. Again Giovanni sent forth a breath, deeper, longer, and imbued with a venomous feeling out of his heart: he knew not whether he were wicked, or only desperate. The spider made a convulsive gripe with his limbs and hung dead across the window.

"Accursed! accursed!" muttered Giovanni, addressing himself. "Hast thou grown so poisonous that this deadly insect perishes by thy breath?"

At that moment a rich, sweet voice came floating up from the garden.

"Giovanni! Giovanni! It is past the hour! Why tarriest thou? Come down!"

"Yes," muttered Giovanni again. "She is the only being whom my breath may not slay! Would that it might!"

He rushed down, and in an instant was standing before the bright and loving eyes of Beatrice. A moment ago his wrath and despair had been so fierce that he could have desired nothing so much as to wither her by a glance; but with her actual presence there came influences which had too real an existence to be at once shaken off; recollections of the delicate and benign power of her feminine nature, which had so often enveloped him in a religious calm; recollections of many a holy and passionate outgush of her heart, when the pure fountain had been unsealed from its depths and made visible in its transparency to his mental eye; recollections which, had Giovanni known how to estimate them, would have assured him that all this ugly mystery was but an earthly illusion, and that, whatever mist of evil might seem to have gathered over her, the real Beatrice was a heavenly angel. Incapable as he was of such high faith, still her presence had not utterly lost its magic. Giovanni's rage was quelled into an aspect of sullen insensibility. Beatrice, with a quick spiritual sense, immediately felt that there was a gulf of blackness between them which neither he nor she could pass. They walked on together, sad and silent, and came thus to the marble fountain and to its pool of water on the ground, in the midst of which grew the shrub that bore gemlike blossoms. Giovanni was affrighted at the eager enjoyment—the appetite, as it were—with which he found himself inhaling the fragrance of the flowers.

"Beatrice," asked he, abruptly, "whence came this shrub?"

"My father created it," answered she, with simplicity.

"Created it! created it!" repeated Giovanni. "What mean you, Beatrice?"

"He is a man fearfully acquainted with the secrets of Nature," replied Beatrice; "and, at the hour when I first drew breath, this plant sprang from the soil, the offspring of his science, of his intellect, while I was but his earthly child. Approach it not!" continued she, observing with terror that Giovanni was drawing nearer to the shrub. "It has qualities that you little dream of. But I, dearest Giovanni,—I grew up and blossomed with the plant and was nourished with its breath. It was my sister, and I loved it with a human affection; for, alas!—hast thou not suspected it?—there was an awful doom."

Here Giovanni frowned so darkly upon her that Beatrice paused and trembled. But her faith in his tenderness reassured her, and made her blush that she had doubted for an instant.

"There was an awful doom," she continued, "The effect of my father's fatal love of science, which estranged me from all society of my kind. Until Heaven sent thee, dearest Giovanni, O, how lonely was thy poor Beatrice!"

"Was it a hard doom?" asked Giovanni, fixing his eyes upon her.

"Only of late have I known how hard it was," answered she, tenderly. "O, yes; but my heart was torpid, and therefore quiet."

Giovanni's rage broke forth from his sullen gloom like a lightning flash out of a dark cloud.

"Accursed one!" cried he, with venomous scorn and anger. "And, finding thy solitude wearisome, thou hast severed me likewise from all the warmth of life and enticed me into thy region of unspeakable horror!"

"Giovanni!" exclaimed Beatrice, turning her large bright eyes upon his face. The force of his words had not found its way into her mind; she was merely thunderstruck.

"Yes, poisonous thing!" repeated Giovanni, beside himself with passion. "Thou hast done it! Thou hast blasted me! Thou hast filled my veins with poison! Thou hast made me as hateful, as ugly, as loathsome and deadly a creature as thyself—a world's wonder of hideous monstrosity! Now, if our breath be happily as fatal to ourselves as to all others, let us join our lips in one kiss of unutterable hatred, and so die!"

"What has befallen me?" murmured Beatrice, with a low moan out of her heart. "Holy Virgin, pity me, a poor heart-broken child!"

"Thou,—dost thou pray?" cried Giovanni, still with the same fiendish scorn. "Thy very prayers, as they come from thy lips, taint the atmosphere with death. Yes, yes; let us pray! Let us to church and dip our fingers in the holy water at the portal! They that come after us will perish as by a pestilence! Let us sign crosses in the air! It will be scattering curses abroad in the likeness of holy symbols!"

"Giovanni," said Beatrice, calmly, for her grief was beyond passion, "why dost thou join thyself with me thus in those terrible words? I, it is true, am the horrible thing thou namest me. But thou,—what hast thou to do, save with one other shudder at my hideous misery to go forth out of the garden and mingle with thy race, and forget that there ever crawled on earth such a monster as poor Beatrice?"

"Dost thou pretend ignorance?" asked Giovanni, scowling upon her. "Behold! this power have I gained from the pure daughter of Rappaccini."

There was a swarm of summer insects flitting through the air in search of the food promised by the flower odors of the fatal garden. They circled round Giovanni's head, and were evidently attracted towards him by the same influence which had drawn them for an instant within the sphere of several of the shrubs. He sent forth a breath among them, and smiled bitterly at Beatrice as at least a score of the insects fell dead upon the ground.

"I see it! I see it!" shrieked Beatrice. "It is my father's fatal science! No, no, Giovanni; it was not I! Never! never! I dreamed only to love thee and be with thee a little time, and so to let thee pass away, leaving but thine image in mine heart; for, Giovanni, believe it, though my body be nourished with poison, my spirit is God's creature, and craves love as its daily food. But my father,—he has united us in this fearful sympathy. Yes; spurn me, tread upon me, kill me! O, what is death after such words as thine? But it was not I. Not for a world of bliss would I have done it."

Giovanni's passion had exhausted itself in its outburst from his lips. There now came across him a sense, mournful, and not without tenderness, of the intimate and peculiar relationship between Beatrice and himself. They stood, as it were, in an utter solitude, which would be made none the less solitary by the densest throng of human life. Ought not, then, the desert of humanity around them to press this insulated pair closer together? If they should be cruel to one another, who was there to be kind to them? Besides, thought Giovanni, might there not still be a hope of his returning within the limits of ordinary nature, and leading Beatrice, the redeemed Beatrice, by the hand? O, weak, and selfish, and unworthy spirit, that could dream of an earthly union and earthly happiness as possible, after such deep love had been so bitterly wronged as was Beatrice's love by Giovanni's blighting words! No, no; there could be no such hope. She must pass heavily, with that broken heart, across the borders of Time—she must bathe her hurts in some fount of paradise, and forget her grief in the light of immortality, and *there* be well.

But Giovanni did not know it.

"Dear Beatrice," said he, approaching her, while she shrank away as always at his approach, but now with a different impulse, "dearest Beatrice, our fate is not yet so desperate. Behold! there is a medicine, potent, as a wise physician has assured me, and almost divine in its efficacy. It is composed of ingredients the most opposite to those by which thy awful father has brought this calamity upon thee and me. It is distilled of blessed herbs. Shall we not quaff it together, and thus be purified from evil?"

"Give it me!" said Beatrice, extending her hand to receive the little silver vial which Giovanni took from his bosom. She added, with a peculiar emphasis, "I will drink; but do thou await the result."

She put Baglioni's antidote to her lips; and, at the same moment, the figure of Rappaccini emerged from the portal and came slowly towards the marble fountain. As he drew near, the pale man of science seemed to gaze with a triumphant expression at the beautiful youth and maiden, as might an artist who should spend his life in achieving a picture or a group of statuary and finally be satisfied with his success. He paused; his bent form grew erect with conscious power; he spread out his hands over them in the attitude of a father imploring a blessing upon his children; but those were the same hands that had thrown poison into the stream of their lives. Giovanni trembled. Beatrice shuddered nervously, and pressed her hand upon her heart.

"My daughter," said Rappaccini, "thou art no longer lonely in the world. Pluck one of those precious gems from thy sister shrub and bid thy bridegroom wear it in his bosom. It will not harm him now. My science and the sympathy between thee and him have so wrought within his system that he now stands apart from common men, as thou dost, daughter of my pride and triumph, from ordinary women. Pass on, then, through the world, most dear to one another and dreadful to all besides!"

"My father," said Beatrice, feebly—and still as she spoke she kept her hand upon her heart,—"wherefore didst thou inflict this miserable doom upon thy child?"

"Miserable!" exclaimed Rappaccini. "What mean you, foolish girl? Dost thou deem it misery to be endowed with marvellous gifts against which no power nor strength could avail an enemy—misery, to be able to quell the mightiest with a breath—misery, to be as terrible as thou art beautiful? Wouldst thou, then, have preferred the condition of a weak woman, exposed to all evil and capable of none?"

"I would fain have been loved, not feared," murmured Beatrice, sinking down upon the ground. "But now it matters not. I am going, father, where the evil which thou hast striven to mingle with my being will pass away like a dream—like the fragrance of these poisonous flowers, which will no longer taint my breath among the flowers of Eden. Farewell, Giovanni! Thy words of hatred are like lead within my heart; but they, too, will fall away as I ascend. O, was there not, from the first, more poison in thy nature than in mine?"

To Beatrice,—so radically had her earthly part been wrought upon by Rappaccini's skill,—as poison had been life, so the powerful antidote was death; and thus the poor victim of man's ingenuity and of thwarted nature, and of the fatality that attends all such efforts of perverted wisdom, perished there, at the feet of her father and Giovanni. Just at that moment Professor Pietro Baglioni looked forth from the window, and called loudly, in a tone of triumph mixed with horror, to the thunder-stricken man of science,—

"Rappaccini! Rappaccini! and is *this* the upshot of your experiment?"

Ethan Brand†

A Chapter from an Abortive Romance

Bartram the lime-burner,[1] a rough, heavy-looking man, begrimed with charcoal, sat watching his kiln, at nightfall, while his little son played at building houses with the scattered fragments of marble, when, on the hill-side below them, they heard a roar of laughter, not mirthful, but slow, and even solemn, like a wind shaking the boughs of the forest.

"Father, what is that?" asked the little boy, leaving his play, and pressing betwixt his father's knees.

"O, some drunken man, I suppose," answered the lime-burner; "some merry fellow from the bar-room in the village, who dared not laugh loud enough within doors, lest he should blow the roof of the house off. So here he is, shaking his jolly sides at the foot of Graylock."[2]

"But, father," said the child, more sensitive than the obtuse, middle-aged clown,[3] "he does not laugh like a man that is glad. So the noise frightens me!"

"Don't be a fool, child!" cried his father, gruffly. "You will never make a man, I do believe; there is too much of your mother in you. I have known the rustling of a leaf startle you. Hark! Here comes the merry fellow, now. You shall see that there is no harm in him."

Bartram and his little son, while they were talking thus, sat watching the same lime-kiln that had been the scene of Ethan Brand's solitary and meditative life, before he began his search for the Unpardonable Sin. Many years, as we have seen, had now elapsed, since that portentous night when the IDEA was first developed. The kiln, however, on the mountain-side, stood unimpaired, and was in nothing changed since he had thrown his dark thoughts into the intense glow of its furnace, and melted them, as it were into the one thought that took possession of his life. It was a rude, round, tower-like structure, about twenty feet high, heavily built of rough stones, and with a hillock of earth heaped about the larger part of its circumference; so that the blocks and fragments of marble might be drawn by cart-loads, and thrown in at the top. There was an opening at the bottom of the tower, like an oven-mouth, but large

---

† First published in the *Boston Weekly Museum*, January 1850, then in the *Dollar Magazine*, May 1851, then in *The Snow-Image*, 1852. Its title in the *Museum* was "The Unpardonable Sin. From an Unpublished Work," and it may have been planned as the last chapter of a longer romance Hawthorne worked on but never finished.

1. Limestone or marble heated in a kiln is converted to lime, used in making cement, porcelain, and glass.
2. Highest mountain in the Berkshires, in western Massachusetts.
3. Countryman, boor.

enough to admit a man in a stooping posture, and provided with a massive iron door. With the smoke and jets of flame issuing from the chinks and crevices of this door, which seemed to give admittance into the hill-side, it resembled nothing so much as the private entrance to the infernal regions, which the shepherds of the Delectable Mountains were accustomed to show to pilgrims.[4]

There are many such lime-kilns in that tract of country, for the purpose of burning the white marble which composes a large part of the substance of the hills. Some of them, built years ago, and long deserted, with weeds growing in the vacant round of the interior, which is open to the sky, and grass and wild-flowers rooting themselves into the chinks of the stones, look already like relics of antiquity, and may yet be overspread with the lichens of centuries to come. Others, where the lime-burner still feeds his daily and nightlong fire, afford points of interest to the wanderer among the hills, who seats himself on a log of wood or a fragment of marble, to hold a chat with the solitary man. It is a lonesome, and, when the character is inclined to thought, may be an intensely thoughtful occupation; as it proved in the case of Ethan Brand, who had mused to such strange purpose, in days gone by, while the fire in this very kiln was burning.

The man who now watched the fire was of a different order, and troubled himself with no thoughts save the very few that were requisite to his business. At frequent intervals, he flung back the clashing weight of the iron door, and, turning his face from the insufferable glare, thrust in huge logs of oak, or stirred the immense brands with a long pole. Within the furnace were seen the curling and riotous flames, and the burning marble, almost molten with the intensity of heat; while without, the reflection of the fire quivered on the dark intricacy of the surrounding forest, and showed in the foreground a bright and ruddy little picture of the hut, the spring beside its door, the athletic and coal-begrimed figure of the lime-burner, and the half-frightened child, shrinking into the protection of his father's shadow. And when again the iron door was closed, then reäppeared the tender light of the half-full moon, which vainly strove to trace out the indistinct shapes of the neighboring mountains; and, in the upper sky, there was a flitting congregation of clouds, still faintly tinged with the rosy sunset, though thus far down into the valley the sunshine had vanished long and long ago.

The little boy now crept still closer to his father, as footsteps were heard ascending the hill-side, and a human form thrust aside the bushes that clustered beneath the trees.

---

4. In Bunyan's *Pilgrim's Progress*, good shepherds warn the pilgrim Christian about this entrance to hell even while he views the Celestial City from the Delectable Mountains.

"Halloo! who is it?" cried the lime-burner, vexed at his son's timidity, yet half infected by it. "Come forward, and show yourself, like a man, or I'll fling this chunk of marble at your head!"

"You offer me a rough welcome," said a gloomy voice, as the unknown man drew nigh. "Yet I neither claim nor desire a kinder one, even at my own fireside."

To obtain a distincter view, Bartram threw open the iron door of the kiln, whence immediately issued a gush of fierce light, that smote full upon the stranger's face and figure. To a careless eye there appeared nothing very remarkable in his aspect, which was that of a man in a coarse, brown, country-made suit of clothes, tall and thin, with the staff and heavy shoes of a wayfarer. As he advanced, he fixed his eyes—which were very bright—intently upon the brightness of the furnace, as if he beheld, or expected to behold, some object worthy of note within it.

"Good-evening, stranger," said the lime-burner; "whence come you, so late in the day?"

"I come from my search," answered the wayfarer; "for, at last, it is finished."

"Drunk!—or crazy!" muttered Bartram to himself. "I shall have trouble with the fellow. The sooner I drive him away, the better."

The little boy, all in a tremble, whispered to his father, and begged him to shut the door of the kiln, so that there might not be so much light; for that there was something in the man's face which he was afraid to look at, yet could not look away from. And, indeed, even the lime-burner's dull and torpid sense began to be impressed by an indescribable something in that thin, rugged, thoughtful visage, with the grizzled hair hanging wildly about it, and those deeply-sunken eyes, which gleamed like fires within the entrance of a mysterious cavern. But, as he closed the door, the stranger turned towards him, and spoke in a quiet, familiar way, that made Bartram feel as if he were a sane and sensible man, after all.

"Your task draws to an end, I see," said he. "This marble has already been burning three days. A few hours more will convert the stone to lime."

"Why, who are you?" exclaimed the lime-burner. "You seem as well acquainted with my business as I am myself."

"And well I may be," said the stranger; "for I followed the same craft many a long year, and here, too, on this very spot. But you are a new comer in these parts. Did you never hear of Ethan Brand?"

"The man that went in search of the Unpardonable Sin?" asked Bartram, with a laugh.

"The same," answered the stranger. "He has found what he sought, and therefore he comes back again."

"What! then you are Ethan Brand himself?" cried the lime-burner, in amazement. "I am a new comer here, as you say, and they call it eighteen years since you left the foot of Graylock. But, I can tell you, the good folks still talk about Ethan Brand, in the village yonder, and what a strange errand took him away from his lime-kiln. Well, and so you have found the Unpardonable Sin?"

"Even so!" said the stranger, calmly.

"If the question is a fair one," proceeded Bartram, "where might it be?"

Ethan Brand laid his finger on his own heart.

"Here!" replied he.

And then, without mirth in his countenance, but as if moved by an involuntary recognition of the infinite absurdity of seeking throughout the world for what was the closest of all things to himself, and looking into every heart, save his own, for what was hidden in no other breast, he broke into a laugh of scorn. It was the same slow, heavy laugh, that had almost appalled the lime-burner when it heralded the wayfarer's approach.

The solitary mountain-side was made dismal by it. Laughter, when out of place, mistimed, or bursting forth from a disordered state of feeling, may be the most terrible modulation of the human voice. The laughter of one asleep, even if it be a little child,—the madman's laugh,—the wild, screaming laugh of a born idiot, are sounds that we sometimes tremble to hear, and would always willingly forget. Poets have imagined no utterance of fiends or hobgoblins so fearfully appropriate as a laugh. And even the obtuse lime-burner felt his nerves shaken, as this strange man looked inward at his own heart, and burst into laughter that rolled away into the night, and was indistinctly reverberated among the hills.

"Joe," said he to his little son, "scamper down to the tavern in the village, and tell the jolly fellows there that Ethan Brand has come back, and that he has found the Unpardonable Sin!"

The boy darted away on his errand, to which Ethan Brand made no objection, nor seemed hardly to notice it. He sat on a log of wood, looking steadfastly at the iron door of the kiln. When the child was out of sight and his swift and light footsteps ceased to be heard treading first on the fallen leaves and then on the rocky mountain-path, the lime-burner began to regret his departure. He felt that the little fellow's presence had been a barrier between his guest and himself, and that he must now deal, heart to heart, with a man who, on his own confession, had committed the one only crime for which Heaven could afford no mercy. That crime, in its indistinct blackness, seemed to overshadow him. The lime-burner's own sins rose up within him, and made his memory riotous with a throng of evil shapes that asserted their kindred with the Master Sin, whatever it might be, which it was within the scope of man's corrupted nature to conceive and cherish. They were all of one family; they went to and fro between his breast and Ethan Brand's, and carried dark greetings from one to the other.

Then Bartram remembered the stories which had grown tradition-ary in reference to this strange man, who had come upon him like a shadow of the night, and was making himself at home in his old place, after so long absence that the dead people, dead and buried for years, would have had more right to be at home, in any familiar spot, than he. Ethan Brand, it was said, had conversed with Satan himself in the lurid blaze of this very kiln. The legend had been matter of mirth heretofore, but looked grisly now. According to this tale, before Ethan Brand departed on his search, he had been accustomed to evoke a fiend from the hot furnace of the lime-kiln, night after night, in order to confer with him about the Unpardonable Sin; the man and the fiend each laboring to frame the image of some mode of guilt which could neither be atoned for nor forgiven. And with the first gleam of light upon the mountaintop, the fiend crept in at the iron door, there to abide the intensest element of fire, until again sum-moned forth to share in the dreadful task of extending man's possible guilt beyond the scope of Heaven's else infinite mercy.

While the lime-burner was struggling with the horror of these thoughts, Ethan Brand rose from the log, and flung open the door of the kiln. The action was in such accordance with the idea in Bartram's mind, that he almost expected to see the Evil One issue forth, red-hot from the raging furnace.

"Hold! hold!" cried he, with a tremulous attempt to laugh; for he was ashamed of his fears, although they overmastered him. "Don't, for mercy's sake, bring out your devil now!"

"Man!" sternly replied Ethan Brand, "what need have I of the devil? I have left him behind me, on my track. It is with such half-way sinners as you that he busies himself. Fear not, because I open the door. I do but act by old custom, and am going to trim your fire, like a lime-burner, as I was once."

He stirred the vast coals, thrust in more wood, and bent forward to gaze into the hollow prison-house of the fire, regardless of the fierce glow that reddened upon his face. The lime-burner sat watch-ing him, and half suspected his strange guest of a purpose, if not to evoke a fiend, at least to plunge bodily into the flames, and thus vanish from the sight of man. Ethan Brand, however, drew quietly back, and closed the door of the kiln.

"I have looked," said he, "into many a human heart that was seven times hotter with sinful passions than yonder furnace is with fire. But I found not there what I sought. No, not the Unpardonable Sin!"

"What is the Unpardonable Sin?" asked the lime-burner; and then he shrank further from his companion, trembling lest his question should be answered.

"It is a sin that grew within my own breast," replied Ethan Brand, standing erect, with a pride that distinguishes all enthusiasts of his stamp. "A sin that grew nowhere else! The sin of an intellect that triumphed over the sense of brotherhood with man and reverence for God, and sacrificed everything to its own mighty claims! The only sin that deserves a recompense of immortal agony! Freely, were it to do again, would I incur the guilt. Unshrinkingly I accept the retribution!"

"The man's head is turned," muttered the lime-burner to himself. "He may be a sinner, like the rest of us,—nothing more likely,— but, I'll be sworn, he is a madman too."

Nevertheless he felt uncomfortable at his situation, alone with Ethan Brand on the wild mountain-side, and was right glad to hear the rough murmur of tongues, and the footsteps of what seemed a pretty numerous party, stumbling over the stones and rustling through the underbrush. Soon appeared the whole lazy regiment that was wont to infest the village tavern, comprehending three or four individuals who had drunk flip[5] beside the bar-room fire through all the winters, and smoked their pipes beneath the stoop through all the summers, since Ethan Brand's departure. Laughing boisterously, and mingling all their voices together in unceremonious talk, they now burst into the moonshine and narrow streaks of fire-light that illuminated the open space before the lime-kiln. Bartram set the door ajar again, flooding the spot with light, that the whole company might get a fair view of Ethan Brand, and he of them.

There, among other old acquaintances, was a once ubiquitous man, now almost extinct, but whom we were formerly sure to encounter at the hotel of every thriving village throughout the country. It was the stage-agent.[6] The present specimen of the genus was a wilted and smoke-dried man, wrinkled and red-nosed, in a smartly-cut, brown, bob-tailed coat, with brass buttons, who, for a length of time unknown, had kept his desk and corner in the bar-room, and was still puffing what seemed to be the same cigar that he had lighted twenty years before. He had great fame as a dry joker, though, perhaps, less on account of any intrinsic humor than from a certain flavor of brandy-toddy and tobacco-smoke, which impregnated all his ideas and expressions, as well as his person. Another well-remembered though strangely-altered face was that of Lawyer Giles, as people still called him in courtesy; an elderly ragamuffin, in his soiled

---

5. Mixture of beer and hard liquor, sweetened with sugar and heated with a hot iron.
6. Commercial agent who directs passengers to stagecoaches.

shirt-sleeves and tow-cloth[7] trousers. This poor fellow had been an attorney, in what he called his better days, a sharp practitioner, and in great vogue among the village litigants; but flip, and sling,[8] and toddy, and cocktails, imbibed at all hours, morning, noon and night, had caused him to slide from intellectual to various kinds and degrees of bodily labor, till, at last, to adopt his own phrase, he slid into a soap-vat. In other words, Giles was now a soap-boiler, in a small way. He had come to be but the fragment of a human being, a part of one foot having been chopped off by an axe, and an entire hand torn away by the devilish grip of a steam-engine. Yet, though the corporeal hand was gone, a spiritual member remained; for, stretching forth the stump, Giles steadfastly averred that he felt an invisible thumb and fingers with as vivid a sensation as before the real ones were amputated. A maimed and miserable wretch he was; but one, nevertheless, whom the world could not trample on, and had no right to scorn, either in this or any previous stage of his misfortunes, since he had still kept up the courage and spirit of a man, asked nothing in charity, and with his one hand—and that the left one—fought a stern battle against want and hostile circumstances.

Among the throng, too, came another personage, who, with certain points of similarity to Lawyer Giles, had many more of difference. It was the village doctor; a man of some fifty years, whom, at an earlier period of his life, we introduced as paying a professional visit to Ethan Brand during the latter's supposed insanity. He was now a purple-visaged, rude, and brutal, yet half-gentlemanly figure, with something wild, ruined, and desperate in his talk, and in all the details of his gesture and manners. Brandy possessed this man like an evil spirit, and made him as surly and savage as a wild beast, and as miserable as a lost soul; but there was supposed to be in him such wonderful skill, such native gifts of healing, beyond any which medical science could impart, that society caught hold of him, and would not let him sink out of its reach. So swaying to and fro upon his horse, and grumbling thick accents at the bedside, he visited all the sick chambers for miles about among the mountain towns, and sometimes raised a dying man, as it were, by miracle, or quite as often, no doubt, sent his patient to a grave that was dug many a year too soon. The doctor had an everlasting pipe in his mouth, and, as somebody said, in allusion to his habit of swearing, it was always alight with hell-fire.

These three worthies pressed forward, and greeted Ethan Brand each after his own fashion, earnestly inviting him to partake of the contents of a certain black bottle, in which, as they averred, he

7. Light coarse cloth of flax or hemp.
8. I.e., gin-sling; gin, sugar, water, and lemon.

would find something far better worth seeking for than the Unpardonable Sin. No mind, which has wrought itself by intense and solitary meditation into a high state of enthusiasm, can endure the kind of contact with low and vulgar modes of thought and feeling to which Ethan Brand was now subjected. It made him doubt—and, strange to say, it was a painful doubt—whether he had indeed found the Unpardonable Sin, and found it within himself. The whole question on which he had exhausted life, and more than life, looked like a delusion.

"Leave me," he said, bitterly, "ye brute beasts, that have made yourselves so, shrivelling up your souls with fiery liquors! I have done with you. Years and years ago, I groped into your hearts, and found nothing there for my purpose. Get ye gone!"

"Why, you uncivil scoundrel," cried the fierce doctor, "is that the way you respond to the kindness of your best friends? Then let me tell you the truth. You have no more found the Unpardonable Sin than yonder boy Joe has. You are but a crazy fellow,—I told you so twenty years ago,—neither better nor worse than a crazy fellow, and the fit companion of old Humphrey, here!"

He pointed to an old man, shabbily dressed, with long white hair, thin visage, and unsteady eyes. For some years past this aged person had been wandering about among the hills, inquiring of all travellers whom he met for his daughter. The girl, it seemed, had gone off with a company of circus-performers; and occasionally tidings of her came to the village, and fine stories were told of her glittering appearance as she rode on horseback in the ring, or performed marvellous feats on the tightrope.

The white-haired father now approached Ethan Brand, and gazed unsteadily into his face.

"They tell me you have been all over the earth," said he, wringing his hands with earnestness. "You must have seen my daughter, for she makes a grand figure in the world, and everybody goes to see her. Did she send any word to her old father, or say when she was coming back?"

Ethan Brand's eye quailed beneath the old man's. That daughter, from whom he so earnestly desired a word of greeting, was the Esther of our tale, the very girl whom, with such cold and remorseless purpose, Ethan Brand had made the subject of a psychological experiment, and wasted, absorbed, and perhaps annihilated her soul, in the process.

"Yes," murmured he, turning away from the hoary wanderer; "it is no delusion. There is an Unpardonable Sin!"

While these things were passing, a merry scene was going forward in the area of cheerful light, beside the spring and before the door of the hut. A number of the youth of the village, young men and girls, had hurried up the hill-side, impelled by curiosity to see Ethan Brand, the hero of so many a legend familiar to their child-hood. Finding nothing, however, very remarkable in his aspect,—nothing but a sun-burnt wayfarer, in plain garb and dusty shoes, who sat looking into the fire, as if he fancied pictures among the coals,—these young people speedily grew tired of observing him. As it happened, there was other amusement at hand. An old German Jew, travelling with a diorama[9] on his back, was passing down the mountain-road towards the village just as the party turned aside from it, and, in hopes of eking out the profits of the day, the show-man had kept them company to the lime-kiln.

"Come, old Dutchman,"[1] cried one of the young men, "let us see your pictures, if you can swear they are worth looking at!"

"O, yes, Captain," answered the Jew,—whether as a matter of courtesy or craft, he styled everybody Captain,—"I shall show you, indeed, some very superb pictures!"

So, placing his box in a proper position, he invited the young men and girls to look through the glass orifices of the machine, and proceeded to exhibit a series of the most outrageous scratchings and daubings, as specimens of the fine arts, that ever an itinerant showman had the face to impose upon his circle of spectators. The pictures were worn out, moreover, tattered, full of cracks and wrinkles, dingy with tobacco-smoke, and otherwise in a most piti-able condition. Some purported to be cities, public edifices, and ruined castles in Europe; others represented Napoleon's battles and Nelson's sea-fights; and in the midst of these would be seen a gigan-tic, brown, hairy hand,—which might have been mistaken for the Hand of Destiny, though, in truth, it was only the showman's—pointing its forefinger to various scenes of the conflict, while its owner gave historical illustrations. When, with much merriment at its abominable deficiency of merit, the exhibition was concluded, the German bade little Joe put his head into the box. Viewed through the magnifying glasses, the boy's round, rosy visage assumed the strangest imaginable aspect of an immense Titanic child, the mouth grinning broadly, and the eyes and every other feature overflowing with fun at the joke. Suddenly, however, that merry face turned pale, and its expression changed to horror, for this easily impressed and excitable child had become sensible that the eye of Ethan Brand was fixed upon him through the glass.

"You make the little man to be afraid, Captain," said the German Jew, turning up the dark and strong outline of his visage, from his

9. Box with a small opening containing a lens for viewing inserted pictures.
1. German.

stooping posture. "But look again, and, by chance, I shall cause you to see somewhat that is very fine, upon my word!"

Ethan Brand gazed into the box for an instant, and then starting back, looked fixedly at the German. What had he seen? Nothing, apparently; for a curious youth, who had peeped in almost at the same moment, beheld only a vacant space of canvas.

"I remember you now," muttered Ethan Brand to the showman.

"Ah, Captain," whispered the Jew of Nuremburg, with a dark smile, "I find it to be a heavy matter in my show-box,—this Unpardonable Sin! By my faith, Captain, it has wearied my shoulders, this long day, to carry it over the mountain."

"Peace," answered Ethan Brand, sternly, "or get thee into the furnace yonder!"

The Jew's exhibition had scarcely concluded, when a great, elderly dog,—who seemed to be his own master, as no person in the company laid claim to him,—saw fit to render himself the object of public notice. Hitherto, he had shown himself a very quiet, well-disposed old dog, going round from one to another, and, by way of being sociable, offering his rough head to be patted by any kindly hand that would take so much trouble. But now, all of a sudden, this grave and venerable quadruped, of his own mere motion, and without the slightest suggestion from anybody else, began to run round after his tail, which, to heighten the absurdity of the proceeding, was a great deal shorter than it should have been. Never was seen such headlong eagerness in pursuit of an object that could not possibly be attained; never was heard such a tremendous outbreak of growling, snarling, barking, and snapping,—as if one end of the ridiculous brute's body were at deadly and most unforgivable enmity with the other. Faster and faster, round about went the cur; and faster and still faster fled the unapproachable brevity of his tail; and louder and fiercer grew his yells of rage and animosity; until, utterly exhausted, and as far from the goal as ever, the foolish old dog ceased his performance as suddenly as he had begun it. The next moment he was as mild, quiet, sensible, and respectable in his deportment, as when he first scraped acquaintance with the company.

As may be supposed, the exhibition was greeted with universal laughter, clapping of hands, and shouts of encore, to which the canine performer responded by wagging all that there was to wag of his tail, but appeared totally unable to repeat his very successful effort to amuse the spectators.

Meanwhile, Ethan Brand had resumed his seat upon the log, and moved, it might be, by a perception of some remote analogy between his own case and that of this self-pursuing cur, he broke into the awful laugh, which, more than any other token, expressed the condition of his inward being. From that moment, the merriment of the party was at an end; they stood aghast, dreading lest the inauspicious sound should be reverberated around the horizon, and that mountain would thunder it to mountain, and so the horror be prolonged upon their ears. Then, whispering one to another that it was late,—that the moon was almost down,—that the August night was growing chill,—they hurried homewards, leaving the lime-burner and little Joe to deal as they might with their unwelcome guest. Save for these three human beings, the open space on the hill-side was a solitude, set in a vast gloom of forest. Beyond that darksome verge, the fire-light glimmered on the stately trunks and almost black foliage of pines, intermixed with the lighter verdure of sapling oaks, maples, and poplars, while here and there lay the gigantic corpses of dead trees, decaying on the leaf-strewn soil. And it seemed to little Joe—a timorous and imaginative child—that the silent forest was holding its breath, until some fearful thing should happen.

Ethan Brand thrust more wood into the fire, and closed the door of the kiln; then looking over his shoulder at the lime-burner and his son, he bade, rather than advised, them to retire to rest.

"For myself, I cannot sleep," said he. "I have matters that it concerns me to meditate upon. I will watch the fire, as I used to do in the old time."

"And call the devil out of the furnace to keep you company, I suppose," muttered Bartram, who had been making intimate acquaintance with the black bottle above-mentioned, "but watch, if you like, and call as many devils as you like! For my part, I shall be all the better for a snooze. Come, Joe!"

As the boy followed his father into the hut, he looked back at the wayfarer, and the tears came into his eyes, for his tender spirit had an intuition of the bleak and terrible loneliness in which this man had enveloped himself.

When they had gone, Ethan Brand sat listening to the crackling of the kindled wood, and looking at the little spirts of fire that issued through the chinks of the door. These trifles, however, once so familiar, had but the slightest hold of his attention, while deep within his mind he was reviewing the gradual but marvellous change that had been wrought upon him by the search to which he had devoted himself. He remembered how the night dew had fallen upon him,—how the dark forest had whispered to him,—how the stars had gleamed upon him,—a simple and loving man, watching his fire in the years gone by, and ever musing as it burned. He remembered with what tenderness, with what love and sympathy for mankind, and what pity for human guilt and woe, he had first begun to contemplate those ideas which afterwards became the inspiration of his life; with what reverence he had then looked into the heart of man, viewing it as a temple originally divine, and, however desecrated, still to be held sacred by a brother; with what awful fear he had deprecated the success of his pursuit, and prayed that the Unpardonable Sin might never be revealed to him. Then ensued that vast intellectual development, which, in its progress, disturbed the counterpoise between his mind and heart. The Idea that possessed his life had operated as a means of education; it had gone on cultivating his powers to the highest point of which they were susceptible; it had raised him from the level of an unlettered laborer to stand on a star-light eminence, whither the philosophers of the earth, laden with the lore of universities, might vainly strive to clamber after him. So much for the intellect! But where was the heart? That, indeed, had withered—had contracted—had hardened—had perished! It had ceased to partake of the universal throb. He had lost his hold of the magnetic chain of humanity. He was no longer a brother-man, opening the chambers or the dungeons of our common nature by the key of holy sympathy, which gave him a right to share in all its secrets; he was now a cold observer, looking on mankind as the subject of his experiment, and, at length, converting man and woman to be his puppets, and pulling the wires that moved them to such degrees of crime as were demanded for his study.

Thus Ethan Brand became a fiend. He began to be so from the moment that his moral nature had ceased to keep the pace of improvement with his intellect. And now, as his highest effort and inevitable development,—as the bright and gorgeous flower, and rich, delicious fruit of his life's labor,—he had produced the Unpardonable Sin!

"What more have I to seek? What more to achieve?" said Ethan Brand to himself. "My task is done, and well done!"

Starting from the log with a certain alacrity in his gait, and ascending the hillock of earth that was raised against the stone circumference of the lime-kiln, he thus reached the top of the structure. It was a space of perhaps ten feet across, from edge to edge, presenting a view of the upper surface of the immense mass of broken marble with which the kiln was heaped. All these innumerable blocks and fragments of marble were red-hot and vividly on fire, sending up great spouts of blue flame, which quivered aloft and danced madly, as within a magic circle, and sank and rose again, with continual and multitudinous activity. As the lonely man bent forward over this terrible body of fire, the blasting heat smote up against his person with a breath that, it might be supposed, would have scorched and shrivelled him up in a moment.

Ethan Brand stood erect, and raised his arms on high. The blue flames played upon his face, and imparted the wild and ghastly light which alone could have suited its expression; it was that of a fiend on the verge of plunging into his gulf of intensest torment.

"O Mother Earth," cried he, "who art no more my Mother, and into whose bosom this frame shall never be resolved! O mankind, whose brotherhood I have cast off, and trampled thy great heart beneath my feet! O stars of heaven, that shone on me of old, as if to light me onward and upward!—farewell all, and forever. Come, deadly element of Fire,—henceforth my familiar friend! Embrace me, as I do thee!"

That night the sound of a fearful peal of laughter rolled heavily through the sleep of the lime-burner and his little son; dim shapes of horror and anguish haunted their dreams, and seemed still present in the rude hovel, when they opened their eyes to the daylight.

"Up, boy, up!" cried the lime-burner, staring about him. "Thank Heaven, the night is gone, at last; and rather than pass such another, I would watch my lime-kiln, wide awake, for a twelvemonth. This Ethan Brand, with his humbug of an Unpardonable Sin, has done me no such mighty favor, in taking my place!"

He issued from the hut, followed by little Joe, who kept fast hold of his father's hand. The early sunshine was already pouring its gold upon the mountain-tops; and though the valleys were still in shadow, they smiled cheerfully in the promise of the bright day that was hastening onward. The village, completely shut in by hills, which swelled away gently about it, looked as if it had rested peacefully in the hollow of the great hand of Providence. Every dwelling was distinctly visible; the little spires of the two churches pointed upwards, and caught a fore-glimmering of brightness from the sun-gilt skies upon their gilded weather-cocks. The tavern was astir, and the figure of the old, smoke-dried stage-agent, cigar in mouth, was seen beneath the stoop. Old Graylock was glorified with a golden cloud upon his head. Scattered likewise over the breasts of the surrounding mountains, there were heaps of hoary mist, in fantastic shapes, some of them far down into the valley, others high up towards the summits, and still others, of the same family of mist or cloud, hovering in the gold radiance of the upper atmosphere. Stepping from one to another of the clouds that rested on the hills, and thence to the loftier brotherhood that sailed in air, it seemed almost as if a mortal man might thus ascend into the heavenly regions. Earth was so mingled with sky that it was a day-dream to look at it.

To supply that charm of the familiar and homely, which Nature so readily adopts into a scene like this, the stage-coach was rattling down the mountain-road, and the driver sounded his horn, while echo[2] caught up the notes, and intertwined them into a rich and varied and elaborate harmony, of which the original performer could lay claim to little share. The great hills played a concert among themselves, each contributing a strain of airy sweetness.

Little Joe's face brightened at once.

"Dear father," cried he, skipping cheerily to and fro, "that strange man is gone, and the sky and the mountains all seem glad of it!"

"Yes," growled the lime-burner, with an oath, "but he has let the fire go down, and no thanks to him if five hundred bushels of lime are not spoiled. If I catch the fellow hereabouts again, I shall feel like tossing him into the furnace!"

With his long pole in his hand, he ascended to the top of the kiln. After a moment's pause, he called to his son.

"Come up here, Joe!" said he.

So little Joe ran up the hillock, and stood by his father's side. The marble was all burnt into perfect, snow-white lime. But on its surface, in the midst of the circle,—snow-white too, and thoroughly converted into lime,—lay a human skeleton, in the attitude of a person who, after long toil, lies down to long repose. Within the ribs— strange to say—was the shape of a human heart.

"Was the fellow's heart made of marble?" cried Bartram, in some perplexity at this phenomenon. "At any rate, it is burnt into what looks like special good lime; and, taking all the bones together, my kiln is half a bushel the richer for him."

So saying, the rude lime-burner lifted his pole, and, letting it fall upon the skeleton, the relics of Ethan Brand were crumbled into fragments.

Feathertop[†]

A Moralized Legend

"Dickon,"[1] cried Mother Rigby, "a coal for my pipe!"

The pipe was in the old dame's mouth, when she said these words. She had thrust it there after filling it with tobacco, but without stooping to light it at the hearth; where, indeed, there was no appearance of a fire having been kindled, that morning. Forthwith,

---

2. In Ovid, Echo is a nymph who when she dies becomes a voice in woods and mountains answering back what she hears.

† Hawthorne's last story, written in the early autumn of 1851. First published in two installments in the *International Monthly Magazine*, February and March 1852, then in *Mosses from an Old Manse*, 2nd edition, 1854. Reprinted by permission of The Ohio State University Press.

1. Like "dickens" (in a phrase like "What the dickens!"), it appears to be slang for "devil."

however, as soon as the order was given, there was an intense red glow out of the bowl of the pipe, and a whiff of smoke from Mother Rigby's lips. Whence the coal came, and how brought thither by an invisible hand, I have never been able to discover.

"Good!" quoth Mother Rigby, with a nod of her head. "Thank ye, Dickon! And now for making this scarecrow. Be within call, Dickon, in case I need you again."

The good woman had risen thus early, (for, as yet, it was scarcely sunrise,) in order to set about making a scarecrow, which she intended to put in the middle of her cornpatch. It was now the latter week of May, and the crows and blackbirds had already discovered the little green, rolled-up leaf of the Indian corn, just peeping out of the soil. She was determined, therefore, to contrive as lifelike a scarecrow as ever was seen, and to finish it immediately, from top to toe, so that it should begin its sentinel's duty that very morning. Now, Mother Rigby (as everybody must have heard) was one of the most cunning and potent witches in New England, and might, with very little trouble, have made a scarecrow ugly enough to frighten the minister himself. But, on this occasion, as she had awakened in an uncommonly pleasant humor, and was further dulcified by her pipe of tobacco, she resolved to produce something fine, beautiful, and splendid, rather than hideous and horrible.

"I don't want to set up a hobgoblin in my own corn-patch and almost at my own door-step," said Mother Rigby to herself, puffing out a whiff of smoke. "I could do it if I pleased; but I'm tired of doing marvellous things, and so I'll keep within the bounds of every-day business, just for variety's sake. Besides, there's no use in scaring the little children, for a mile roundabout, though 'tis true I'm a witch!"

It was settled, therefore, in her own mind, that the scarecrow should represent a fine gentleman of the period, so far as the materials at hand would allow. Perhaps it may be as well to enumerate the chief of the articles that went to the composition of this figure.

The most important item of all, probably, although it made so little show, was a certain broomstick, on which Mother Rigby had taken many an airy gallop at midnight, and which now served the scarecrow by way of a spinal column, or, as the unlearned phrase it, a backbone. One of its arms was a disabled flail, which used to be wielded by Goodman Rigby, before his spouse worried him out of this troublesome world; the other, if I mistake not, was composed of the pudding-stick and a broken rung of a chair, tied loosely together at the elbow. As for its legs, the right was a hoe-handle, and the left, an undistinguished and miscellaneous stick from the wood-pile. Its lungs, stomach, and other affairs of that kind, were nothing better than a meal-bag stuffed with straw. Thus, we have made out the

skeleton and entire corporosity[2] of the scarecrow, with the exception of its head; and this was admirably supplied by a somewhat
withered and shrivelled pumpkin in which Mother Rigby cut two
holes for the eyes and a slit for the mouth, leaving a bluish-colored
knob, in the middle, to pass for a nose. It was really quite a respectable face.

"I've seen worse ones on human shoulders, at any rate," said
Mother Rigby. "And many a fine gentleman has a pumpkin-head, as
well as my scarecrow!"

But the clothes, in this case, were to be the making of the man.
So the good old woman took down from a peg an ancient plum-
colored coat, of London make, and with relics of embroidery on its
seams, cuffs, pocket-flaps, and button-holes, but lamentably worn
and faded, patched at the elbows, tattered at the skirts,[3] and thread-
bare all over. On the left breast was a round hole, whence either a
star of nobility had been rent away, or else the hot heart of some
former wearer had scorched it through and through. The neighbors
said, that this rich garment belonged to the Black Man's[4] wardrobe,
and that he kept it at Mother Rigby's cottage for the convenience
of slipping it on, whenever he wished to make a grand appearance at
the governor's table. To match the coat, there was a velvet waistcoat
of very ample size, and formerly embroidered with foliage, that had
been as brightly golden as the maple-leaves in October, but which
had now quite vanished out of the substance of the velvet. Next came
a pair of scarlet breeches, once worn by the French governor of Louisbourg, and the knees of which had touched the lower step of the
throne of Louis le Grand.[5] The Frenchman had given these small-
clothes to an Indian powwow, who parted with them to the old
witch for a gill of strong-waters, at one of their dances in the forest.
Furthermore, Mother Rigby produced a pair of silk stockings and
put them on the figure's legs, where they showed as unsubstantial as
a dream, with the wooden reality of the two sticks making itself
miserably apparent through the holes. Lastly, she put her dead husband's wig on the bare scalp of the pumpkin, and surmounted the
whole with a rusty three-cornered hat, in which was stuck the longest tail-feather of a rooster.

Then the old dame stood the figure up in a corner of her cottage,
and chuckled to behold its yellow semblance of a visage, with its
knobby little nose thrust into the air. It had a strangely self-satisfied
aspect, and seemed to say—"Come look at me!"

2. Bodily bulk.
3. Outer edges.
4. Devil's.
5. Louis XIV (1638–1715), king of France. The French built a fort at Louisbourg, Cape
Breton Island, in the early 18th century.

"And you are well worth looking at—that's a fact!" quoth Mother Rigby, in admiration at her own handiwork. "I've made many a puppet, since I've been a witch; but methinks this is the finest of them all. 'Tis almost too good for a scarecrow. And, by the by, I'll just fill a fresh pipe of tobacco, and then take him out to the corn-patch."

While filling her pipe, the old woman continued to gaze with almost motherly affection at the figure in the corner. To say the truth—whether it were chance, or skill, or downright witchcraft—there was something wonderfully human in this ridiculous shape, bedizened with its tattered finery; and as for the countenance, it appeared to shrivel its yellow surface into a grin—a funny kind of expression, betwixt scorn and merriment, as if it understood itself to be a jest at mankind. The more Mother Rigby looked, the better she was pleased.

"Dickon," cried she, sharply, "another coal for my pipe!"

Hardly had she spoken, than, just as before, there was a red glowing coal on the top of the tobacco. She drew in a long whiff, and puffed it forth again into the bar of morning sunshine, which struggled through the one dusty pane of her cottage window. Mother Rigby always liked to flavor her pipe with a coal of fire from the particular chimney-corner, whence this had been brought. But where that chimney-corner might be, or who brought the coal from it—further than that the invisible messenger seemed to respond to the name of Dickon—I cannot tell.

"That puppet yonder," thought Mother Rigby, still with her eyes fixed on the scarecrow, "is too good a piece of work to stand all summer in a corn-patch, frightening away the crows and blackbirds. He's capable of better things. Why, I've danced with a worse one, when partners happened to be scarce, at our witch meetings in the forest! What if I should let him take his chance among the other men of straw and empty fellows, who go bustling about the world?"

The old witch took three or four more whiffs of her pipe, and smiled.

"He'll meet plenty of his brethren, at every street-corner!" continued she. "Well; I didn't mean to dabble in witchcraft to-day, further than the lighting of my pipe; but a witch I am, and a witch I'm likely to be, and there's no use trying to shirk it. I'll make a man of my scarecrow, were it only for the joke's sake!"

While muttering these words, Mother Rigby took the pipe from her own mouth, and thrust it into the crevice which represented the same feature in the pumpkin-visage of the scarecrow.

"Puff, darling, puff!" said she. "Puff away, my fine fellow! Your life depends on it!"

This was a strange exhortation, undoubtedly, to be addressed to a mere thing of sticks, straw, and old clothes, with nothing better than a shrivelled pumpkin for a head; as we know to have been the scarecrow's case. Nevertheless, as we must carefully hold in remembrance, Mother Rigby was a witch of singular power and dexterity; and, keeping this fact duly before our minds, we shall see nothing beyond credibility in the remarkable incidents of our story. Indeed, the great difficulty will be at once got over, if we can only bring ourselves to believe, that, as soon as the old dame bade him puff, there came a whiff of smoke from the scarecrow's mouth. It was the very feeblest of whiffs, to be sure; but it was followed by another and another, each more decided than the preceding one.

"Puff away, my pet! Puff away, pretty one!" Mother Rigby kept repeating, with her pleasantest smile. "It is the breath of life to ye; and that you may take my word for!"

Beyond all question, the pipe was bewitched. There must have been a spell, either in the tobacco, or in the fiercely glowing coal that so mysteriously burned on top of it, or in the pungently aromatic smoke, which exhaled from the kindled weed. The figure, after a few doubtful attempts, at length blew forth a volley of smoke, extending all the way from the obscure corner into the bar of sunshine. There it eddied and melted away among the motes of dust. It seemed a convulsive effort; for the two or three next whiffs were fainter, although the coal still glowed, and threw a gleam over the scarecrow's visage. The old witch clapt her skinny palms together, and smiled encouragingly upon her handiwork. She saw that the charm worked well. The shrivelled, yellow face, which heretofore had been no face at all, had already a thin, fantastic haze, as it were, of human likeness, shifting to-and-fro across it; sometimes vanishing entirely, but growing more perceptible than ever, with the next whiff from the pipe. The whole figure, in like manner, assumed a show of life, such as we impart to ill-defined shapes among the clouds, and half-deceive ourselves with the pastime of our own fancy.

If we must needs pry closely into the matter, it may be doubted whether there was any real change, after all, in the sordid, worn-out, worthless, and ill-joined substance of the scarecrow; but merely a spectral illusion, and a cunning effect of light and shade, so colored and contrived as to delude the eyes of most men. The miracles of witchcraft seem always to have had a very shallow subtlety; and, at least, if the above explanation do not hit the truth of the process, I can suggest no better.

"Well puffed, my pretty lad!" still cried old Mother Rigby. "Come; another good, stout whiff; and let it be with might and main! Puff for thy life, I tell thee! Puff out of the very bottom of thy heart; if any heart thou hast, or any bottom to it! Well done, again! Thou didst suck in that mouthfull, as if for the pure love of it."

And then the witch beckoned to the scarecrow, throwing so much magnetic potency into her gesture, that it seemed as if it must inevitably be obeyed, like the mystic call of the loadstone, when it summons the iron.

"Why lurkest thou in the corner, lazy one?" said she. "Step forth! Thou has the world before thee!"

Upon my word, if the legend were not one which I heard on my grandmother's knee, and which had established its place among things credible before my childish judgment could analyze its probability, I question whether I should have the face to tell it now!

In obedience to Mother Rigby's word, and extending its arm as if to reach her outstretched hand, the figure made a step forward—a kind of hitch and jerk, however, rather than a step—then tottered, and almost lost its balance. What could the witch expect? It was nothing, after all, but a scarecrow, stuck upon two sticks. But the strong-willed old beldam scowled, and beckoned, and flung the energy of her purpose so forcibly at this poor combination of rotten wood, and musty straw, and ragged garments, that it was compelled to show itself a man, in spite of the reality of things. So it stept into the bar of sunshine. There it stood—poor devil of a contrivance that it was!—with only the thinnest vesture of human similitude about it, through which was evident the stiff, ricketty, incongruous, faded, tattered, good-for-nothing patchwork of its substance, ready to sink in a heap upon the floor, as conscious of its own unworthiness to be erect. Shall I confess the truth? At its present point of vivification, the scarecrow reminds me of some of the lukewarm and abortive characters, composed of heterogeneous materials, used for the thousandth time, and never worth using, with which romance-writers (and myself, no doubt, among the rest) have so overpeopled the world of fiction.

But the fierce old hag began to get angry and show a glimpse of her diabolic nature, (like a snake's head peeping with a hiss out of her bosom,)[6] at this pusillanimous behavior of the thing, which she had taken the trouble to put together.

"Puff away, wretch!" cried she wrathfully. "Puff, puff, puff, thou thing of straw and emptiness!—thou rag or two!—thou meal bag!—thou pumpkin-head!—thou nothing!—where shall I find a name vile enough to call thee by! Puff, I say, and suck in thy fantastic life along with the smoke; else I snatch the pipe from thy mouth, and hurl thee where that red coal came from!"

Thus threatened, the unhappy scarecrow had nothing for it, but to puff away for dear life. As need was, therefore, it applied itself

---

6. A whimsical allusion to Hawthorne's own highly moralized story "Egotism; or, The Bosom-Serpent" (1843).

lustily to the pipe, and sent forth such abundant vollies of tobacco-smoke that the small cottage-kitchen became all vaporous. The one sunbeam struggled mistily through, and could but imperfectly define the image of the cracked and dusty window-pane on the opposite wall. Mother Rigby, meanwhile, with one brown arm akimbo and the other stretched towards the figure, loomed grimly amid the obscurity, with such port and expression as when she was wont to heave a ponderous nightmare on her victims, and stand at the bedside to enjoy their agony. In fear and trembling did this poor scarecrow puff. But its efforts, it must be acknowledged, served an excellent purpose; for, with each successive whiff, the figure lost more and more of its dizzy and perplexing tenuity, and seemed to take denser substance. Its very garments, moreover, partook of the magical change, and shone with the gloss of novelty, and glistened with the skilfully embroidered gold that had long ago been rent away. And, half-revealed among the smoke, a yellow visage bent its lustreless eyes on Mother Rigby.

At last, the old witch clenched her fist, and shook it at the figure. Not that she was positively angry, but merely acting on the principle—perhaps untrue, or not the only truth, though as high a one as Mother Rigby could be expected to attain—that feeble and torpid natures, being incapable of better inspiration, must be stirred up by fear. But, here was the crisis. Should she fail in what she now sought to effect, it was her ruthless purpose to scatter the miserable simulacre into its original elements.

"Thou hast a man's aspect," said she sternly. "Have also the echo and mockery of a voice! I bid thee speak!"

The scarecrow gasped, struggled, and at length emitted a murmur, which was so incorporated with its smoky breath that you could scarcely tell whether it were indeed a voice, or only a whiff of tobacco. Some narrators of this legend hold the opinion, that Mother Rigby's conjurations, and the fierceness of her will, had compelled a familiar spirit into the figure, and that the voice was his.

"Mother," mumbled the poor, stifled voice, "be not so awful with me! I would fain speak; but being without wits, what can I say?"

"Thou canst speak, darling, canst thou?" cried Mother Rigby, relaxing her grim countenance into a smile. "And what shalt thou say, quotha! Say, indeed! Art thou of the brotherhood of the empty skull, and demandest of me what thou shalt say? Thou shalt say a thousand things, and saying them a thousand times over, thou shalt still have said nothing! Be not afraid, I tell thee! When thou comest into the world, (whither I purpose sending thee, forthwith,) thou shalt not lack the wherewithal to talk. Talk! Why, thou shalt babble like a mill-stream, if thou wilt. Thou hast brains enough for that, I trow!"

"At your service, mother," responded the figure.

"And that was well said, my pretty one!" answered Mother Rigby. "Then thou spakest like thyself, and meant nothing. Thou shalt have a hundred such set phrases, and five hundred to the boot of them.[7] And now, darling, I have taken so much pains with thee, and thou art so beautiful, that, by my troth, I love thee better than any witch's puppet in the world; and I've made them of all sorts—clay, wax, straw, sticks, night-fog, morning-mist; sea-foam, and chimney-smoke! But thou art the very best. So give heed to what I say!"

"Yes, kind mother," said the figure, "with all my heart!"

"With all thy heart!" cried the old witch, setting her hands to her sides, and laughing loudly. "Thou hast such a pretty way of speaking! With all thy heart! And thou didst put thy hand to the left side of thy waistcoat, as if thou really hadst one!"

So now, in high good-humor with this fantastic contrivance of hers, Mother Rigby told the scarecrow that it must go and play its part in the great world, where not one man in a hundred, she affirmed, was gifted with more real substance than itself. And, that he might hold up his head with the best of them, she endowed him, on the spot, with an unreckonable amount of wealth. It consisted partly of a gold mine in Eldorado, and of ten thousand shares in a broken bubble, and of half a million acres of vineyard at the North pole, and of a castle in the air and a chateau in Spain, together with all the rents and income therefrom accruing. She further made over to him the cargo of a certain ship, laden with salt of Cadiz,[8] which she herself, by her necromantic arts, had caused to founder, ten years before, in the deepest of mid-ocean. If the salt were not dissolved, and could be brought to market, it would fetch a pretty penny among the fishermen. That he might not lack ready money, she gave him a copper farthing, of Birmingham manufacture being all the coin she had about her, and likewise a great deal of brass,[9] which she applied to his forehead, thus making it yellower than ever.

"With that brass alone," quoth Mother Rigby, "thou canst pay thy way all over the earth. Kiss me, pretty darling! I have done my best for thee."

Furthermore, that the adventurer might lack no possible advantage towards a fair start in life, this excellent old dame gave him a token, by which he was to introduce himself to a certain magistrate, member of the council, merchant, and elder of the church, (the four capacities constituting but one man,) who stood at the head of society in the neighboring metropolis. The token was neither more nor

---

7. In addition to them.
8. Chief Spanish port for exports to Spain's American colonies in the 18th century.
9. Effrontery. "Farthing": British coin worth one fourth of a penny.

less than a single word, which Mother Rigby whispered to the scarecrow, and which the scarecrow was to whisper to the merchant.

"Gouty as the old fellow is, he'll run thy errands for thee, when
once thou hast given him that word in his ear," said the old witch.
"Mother Rigby knows the worshipful Justice Gookin,[1] and the worshipful justice knows Mother Rigby!"

Here the witch thrust her wrinkled face close to the puppet's,
chuckling irrepressibly, and fidgetting all though her system, with
delight at the idea which she meant to communicate.

"The worshipful Master Gookin," whispered she, "hath a comely
maiden to his daughter! And hark ye, my pet! Thou hast a fair outside, and a pretty wit enough of thine own. Yea; a pretty wit enough!
Thou wilt think better of it, when thou hast seen more of other
people's wits. Now, with thy outside and thy inside, thou art the very
man to win a young girl's heart. Never doubt it! I tell thee it shall be
so. Put but a bold face on the matter, sigh, smile, flourish thy hat,
thrust forth thy leg like a dancing-master, put thy right hand to the
left side of thy waistcoat—and pretty Polly Gookin is thine own!"

All this while, the new creature had been sucking in and exhaling
the vapory fragrance of his pipe, and seemed now to continue this
occupation as much for the enjoyment which it afforded, as because
it was an essential condition of his existence. It was wonderful to
see how exceedingly like a human being it behaved. Its eyes (for it
appeared to possess a pair) were bent on Mother Rigby, and at suitable junctures, it nodded or shook its head. Neither did it lack words
proper for the occasion—'Really! Indeed! Pray tell me! Is it possible!
Upon my word! By no means! Oh! Ah! Hem!'—and other such
weighty utterances as imply attention, inquiry, acquiescence, or dissent, on the part of the auditor. Even had you stood by, and seen the
scarecrow made, you could scarcely have resisted the conviction that
it perfectly understood the cunning counsels, which the old witch
poured into its counterfeit of an ear. The more earnestly it applied its
lips to the pipe, the more distinctly was its human likeness stamped
among visible realities; the more sagacious grew its expression; the
more lifelike its gestures and movements, and the more intelligibly
audible its voice. Its garments, too, glistened so much the brighter
with an illusory magnificence. The very pipe, in which burned the
spell of all this wonderwork, ceased to appear as a smoke-blackened
earthen stump, and became a meerschaum, with painted bowl and
amber mouth-piece.

---

1. Apparently a reminder of "Young Goodman Brown," another witch story, in which the
respectable Deacon Gookin appears at the devil's black mass in the forest. The historical
Daniel Gookin (1612–1687) was a Massachusetts judge.

It might be apprehended, however, that, as the life of the illusion seemed identical with the vapor of the pipe, it would terminate simultaneously with the reduction of the tobacco to ashes. But the beldam foresaw the difficulty.

"Hold thou the pipe, my precious one," said she, "while I fill it for thee again."

It was sorrowful to behold how the fine gentleman began to fade back into a scarecrow, while Mother Rigby shook the ashes out of the pipe, and proceeded to replenish it from her tobacco-box.

"Dickon," cried she, in her high, sharp tone, "another coal for this pipe!"

No sooner said than the intensely red speck of fire was glowing within the pipe-bowl; and the scarecrow, without waiting for the witch's bidding, applied the tube to its lips, and drew in a few short, convulsive whiffs, which soon, however, became regular and equable.

"Now, mine own heart's darling," quoth Mother Rigby, "whatever may happen to thee, thou must stick to thy pipe. Thy life is in it; and that, at least, thou knowest well, if thou knowest naught besides. Stick to thy pipe, I say! Smoke, puff, blow thy cloud; and tell the people, if any question be made, that it is for thy health, and that so the physician orders thee to do. And, sweet one, when thou shalt find thy pipe getting low, go apart into some corner, and (first filling thyself with smoke) cry sharply—'Dickon, a fresh pipe of tobacco!' and—'Dickon, another coal for my pipe!'—and have it into thy pretty mouth, as speedily as may be. Else, instead of a gallant gentleman in a gold-laced coat, thou wilt be but a jumble of sticks, and tattered clothes, and a bag of straw, and a withered pumpkin! Now depart, my treasure, and good luck go with thee!"

"Never fear, mother!" said the figure, in a stout voice, and sending forth a courageous whiff of smoke. "I will thrive, if an honest man and a gentleman may!"

"Oh, thou wilt be the death of me!" cried the old witch, convulsed with laughter. "That was well said! If an honest man and a gentleman may! Thou playest thy part to perfection. Get along with thee for a smart fellow; and I will wager on thy head, as a man of pith and substance, with a brain, and what they call a heart, and all else that a man should have, against any other thing on two legs. I hold myself a better witch than yesterday, for thy sake. Did not I make thee? And I defy any witch in New England to make such another! Here; take my staff along with thee!"

The staff, though it was but a plain oaken stick, immediately took the aspect of a gold-headed cane.

"That gold-head has as much sense in it as thine own," said Mother Rigby, "and it will guide thee straight to worshipful Master

Gookin's door. Get thee gone, my pretty pet, my darling, my precious one, my treasure; and if any ask thy name, it is Feathertop.[2]
For thou hast a feather in thy hat, and I have thrust a handfull of
feathers into the hollow of thy head,[3] and thy wig, too, is of the fashion they call Feathertop—so be Feathertop thy name!"

And, issuing from the cottage, Feathertop strode manfully towards
town. Mother Rigby stood at the threshold, well pleased to see how
the sunbeams glistened on him, as if all his magnificence were real,
and how diligently and lovingly he smoked his pipe, and how hand-
somely he walked, in spite of a little stiffness of his legs. She watched
him, until out of sight, and threw a witch-benediction after her darling, when a turn of the road snatched him from her view.

Betimes in the forenoon, when the principal street of the neighboring town was just at its acme of life and bustle, a stranger of very
distinguished figure was seen on the sidewalk. His port, as well as
his garments, betokened nothing short of nobility. He wore a richly
embroidered plum-colored coat, a waistcoat of costly velvet, magnificently adorned with golden foliage, a pair of splendid scarlet breeches,
and the finest and glossiest of white silk stockings. His head was
covered with a peruque, so daintily powdered and adjusted that it
would have been a sacrilege to disorder it with a hat; which, therefore, (and it was a gold-laced hat, set off with a snowy feather,) he
carried beneath his arm. On the breast of his coat glistened a star.
He managed his gold-headed cane with an airy grace, peculiar to the
fine gentleman of the period; and, to give the highest possible finish
to his equipment, he had lace ruffles at his wrists, of a most ethereal
delicacy, sufficiently avouching how idle and aristocratic must be
the hands which they half concealed.

It was a remarkable point in the accoutrement of this brilliant personage, that he held in his left hand a fantastic kind of a pipe, with
an exquisitely painted bowl, and an amber mouth-piece. This he
applied to his lips, as often as every five or six paces, and inhaled a
deep whiff of smoke, which, after being retained a moment in his
lungs, might be seen to eddy gracefully from his mouth and nostrils.

As may well be supposed, the street was all a-stir to find out the
stranger's name.

"It is some great nobleman, beyond question," said one of the
townspeople, "Do you see the star at his breast?"

"Nay; it is too bright to be seen," said another. "Yes; he must needs
be a nobleman, as you say. But, by what conveyance, think you, can
his lordship have voyaged or travelled hither? There has been no

---

2. A type of wig, "the giddy Feathertop," as Hawthorne calls it in "Old News" (1835).
3. A "feather-head" is an empty-headed person, one who has feathers in the hollow of his
head. A "feather in the hat" is a mark of honor.

vessel from the old country for a month past; and if he have arrived overland from the southward, pray where are his attendants and equipage?"

"He needs no equipage to set off his rank," remarked a third. "If he came among us in rags, nobility would shine through a hole in his elbow. I never saw such dignity of aspect. He has the old Norman blood in his veins, I warrant him!"

"I rather take him to be a Dutchman, or one of your High Germans,"[4] said another citizen. "The men of those countries have always the pipe at their mouths."

"And so has a Turk," answered his companion. "But, in my judgment, this stranger hath been bred at the French court, and hath there learned politeness and grace of manner, which none understand so well as the nobility of France. That gait, now! A vulgar spectator might deem it stiff—he might call it a hitch and jerk—but, to my eye, it hath an unspeakable majesty, and must have been acquired by constant observation of the deportment of the Grand Monarque.[5] The stranger's character and office are evident enough. He is a French ambassador, come to treat with our rulers about the cession of Canada."

"More probably a Spaniard," said another, "and hence his yellow complexion. Or, most likely, he is from the Havana, or from some port on the Spanish Main, and comes to make investigation about the piracies which our Governor is thought to connive at. Those settlers in Peru and Mexico have skins as yellow as the gold which they dig out of their mines."

"Yellow or not," cried a lady, "he is a beautiful man!—so tall—so slender!—such a fine, noble face, with so well-shaped a nose, and all that delicacy of expression about the mouth! And, bless me, how bright his star is! It positively shoots out flames!"

"So do your eyes, fair lady!" said the stranger, with a bow, and a flourish of his pipe; for he was just passing at the instant. "Upon my honor, they have quite dazzled me!"

"Was ever so original and exquisite a compliment?" murmured the lady, in an ecstasy of delight.

Amid the general admiration, excited by the stranger's appearance, there were only two dissenting voices. One was that of an impertinent cur, which, after snuffing at the heels of the glistening figure, put its tail between its legs and skulked into its master's backyard, vociferating an execrable howl. The other dissentient was a

---

4. There was no such thing as a "High German," in Hawthorne's time at least, but he tried with indifferent success to learn Hochdeutsch or High German, the literary language of Germany, in 1838 and afterward.
5. Louis XIV.

young child, who squalled at the fullest stretch of his lungs, and babbled some unintelligible nonsense about a pumpkin.

Feathertop, meanwhile, pursued his way along the street. Except for the few complimentary words to the lady, and, now and then, a slight inclination of the head, in requital of the profound reverences of the bystanders, he seemed wholly absorbed in his pipe. There needed no other proof of his rank and consequence, than the perfect equanimity with which he comported himself, while the curiosity and admiration of the town swelled almost into clamor around him. With a crowd still gathering behind his footsteps, he finally reached the mansion-house of the worshipful Justice Gookin, entered the gate, ascended the steps of the front-door, and knocked. In the interim, before his summons was answered, the stranger was observed to shake the ashes out of his pipe.

"What did he say, in that sharp voice?" inquired one of the spectators.

"Nay, I know not," answered his friend. "But the sun dazzles my eyes strangely! How dim and faded his lordship looks, all of a sudden! Bless my wits, what is the matter with me!"

"The wonder is," said the other, "that his pipe, (which was out only an instant ago,) should be all a-light again, and with the reddest coal I ever saw! There is something mysterious about this stranger. What a whiff of smoke was that! Dim and faded, do you call him? Why, as he turns about, the star on his breast is all a-blaze."

"It is, indeed," said his companion; "and it will go near to dazzle pretty Polly Gookin, whom I see peeping at it out of the chamber-window."

The door being now opened, Feathertop turned to the crowd, made a stately bend of his body, like a great man acknowledging the reverence of the meaner sort, and vanished into the house. There was a mysterious kind of a smile, if it might not better be called a grin or grimace, upon his visage; but of all the throng that beheld him, not an individual appears to have possessed insight enough to detect the illusive character of the stranger, except a little child and a cur-dog.

Our legend here loses somewhat of its continuity, and, passing over the preliminary explanation between Feathertop and the merchant, goes in quest of the pretty Polly Gookin. She was a damsel of a soft, round figure, with light hair and blue eyes, and a fair rosy face, which seemed neither very shrewd nor very simple. This young lady had caught a glimpse of the glistening stranger, while standing at the threshold, and had forthwith put on a laced cap, a string of beads, her finest kerchief, and her stiffest damask petticoat, in preparation for the interview. Hurrying from her chamber to the parlor, she had ever since been viewing herself in the large looking-glass, and practising pretty airs—now a smile, now a ceremonious dignity of aspect, and now a softer smile than the former—kissing her hand, likewise, tossing her head, and managing her fan; while, within the mirror, an unsubstantial little maid repeated every gesture, and did all the foolish things that Polly did, but without making her ashamed of them. In short, it was the fault of pretty Polly's ability, rather than her will, if she failed to be as complete an artifice as the illustrious Feathertop himself; and when she thus tampered with her own simplicity, the witch's phantom might well hope to win her.

No sooner did Polly hear her father's gouty footsteps approaching the parlor-door, accompanied with the stiff clatter of Feathertop's high-heeled shoes, than she seated herself bolt upright, and innocently began warbling a song.

"Polly! Daughter Polly!" cried the old merchant. "Come hither, child!"

Master Gookin's aspect, as he opened the door, was doubtful and troubled.

"This gentleman," continued he, presenting the stranger, "is the Chevalier Feathertop—nay, I beg his pardon, my Lord Feathertop!— who hath brought me a token of remembrance from an ancient friend of mine. Pay your duty to his lordship, child, and honor him as his quality deserves."

After these few words of introduction, the worshipful magistrate immediately quitted the room. But, even in that brief moment, (had the fair Polly glanced aside at her father, instead of devoting herself wholly to the brilliant guest,) she might have taken warning of some mischief nigh at hand. The old man was nervous, fidgetty, and very pale. Purposing a smile of courtesy, he had deformed his face with a sort of galvanic[6] grin, which when Feathertop's back was turned, he exchanged for a scowl; at the same time shaking his fist, and stamping his gouty foot—an incivility which brought its retribution along with it. The truth appears to have been, that Mother Rigby's word of introduction, whatever it might be, had operated far more on the rich merchant's fears, than on his good-will. Moreover, being a man of wonderfully acute observation, he had noticed that the painted figures, on the bowl of Feathertop's pipe, were in motion. Looking more closely, he became convinced, that these figures were a party of little demons, each duly provided with horns and a tail, and dancing hand in hand, with gestures of diabolical merriment, round the circumference of the pipe-bowl. As if to confirm his suspicions, while Master Gookin ushered his guest along a dusky passage, from his private room to the parlor, the star on Feathertop's breast had

6. As if produced by electric shock.

scintillated actual flames, and threw a flickering gleam upon the wall, the ceiling, and the floor.

With such sinister prognostics manifesting themselves on all hands, it is not to be marvelled at that the merchant should have felt that he was committing his daughter to a very questionable acquaintance. He cursed, in his secret soul, the insinuating elegance of Feathertop's manners, as this brilliant personage bowed, smiled, put his hand on his heart, inhaled a long whiff from his pipe, and enriched the atmosphere with the smoky vapor of a fragrant and visible sigh. Gladly would poor Master Gookin have thrust his dangerous guest into the street. But there was a constraint and terror within him. This respectable old gentleman, we fear, at an earlier period of life, had given some pledge or other to the Evil Principle, and perhaps was now to redeem it by the sacrifice of his daughter.

It so happened that the parlor-door was partly of glass, shaded by a silken curtain, the folds of which hung a little awry. So strong was the merchant's interest in witnessing what was to ensue between the fair Polly and the gallant Feathertop, that, after quitting the room, he could by no means refrain from peeping through the crevice of the curtain.

But there was nothing very miraculous to be seen; nothing— except the trifles previously noticed—to confirm the idea of a supernatural peril, environing the pretty Polly. The stranger, it is true, was evidently a thorough and practised man of the world, systematic and self-possessed, and therefore the sort of person to whom a parent ought not to confide a simple young girl, without due watchfulness for the result. The worthy magistrate, who had been conversant with all degrees and qualities of mankind, could not but perceive that every motion and gesture of the distinguished Feathertop came in its proper place; nothing had been left rude or native in him; a well-digested conventionalism had incorporated itself thoroughly with his substance, and transformed him into a work of art. Perhaps it was this peculiarity that invested him with a species of ghastliness and awe. It is the effect of anything completely and consummately artificial, in human shape, that the person impresses us as an unreality, and as having hardly pith enough to cast a shadow upon the floor. As regarded Feathertop, all this resulted in a wild, extravagant, and fantastical impression, as if his life and being were akin to the smoke that curled upward from his pipe.

But pretty Polly Gookin felt not thus. The pair were now promenading the room; Feathertop with his dainty stride, and no less dainty grimace; the girl with a native maidenly grace, just touched, not spoiled, by a slightly affected manner, which seemed caught from the perfect artifice of her companion. The longer the interview continued, the more charmed was pretty Polly, until, within the first quarter of an hour, (as the old magistrate noted by his watch,) she was evidently beginning to be in love. Nor need it have been witchcraft that subdued her in such a hurry; the poor child's heart, it may be, was so very fervent, that it melted her with its own warmth, as reflected from the hollow semblance of a lover. No matter what Feathertop said, his words found depth and reverberation in her ear; no matter what he did, his action was heroic to her eye. And, by this time, it is to be supposed, there was a blush on Polly's cheek, a tender smile about her mouth, and a liquid softness in her glance; while the star kept coruscating on Feathertop's breast, and the little demons careered, with more frantic merriment than ever, about the circumference of his pipe-bowl. Oh, pretty Polly Gookin, why should these imps rejoice so madly that a silly maiden's heart was about to be given to a shadow! Is it so unusual a misfortune?—so rare a triumph?

By and by, Feathertop paused, and throwing himself into an imposing attitude, seemed to summon the fair girl to survey his figure, and resist him longer, if she could. His star, his embroidery, his buckles, glowed, at that instant, with unutterable splendor; the picturesque hues of his attire took a richer depth of coloring; there was a gleam and polish over his whole presence, betokening the perfect witchery of well-ordered manners. The maiden raised her eyes, and suffered them to linger upon her companion with a bashful and admiring gaze. Then, as if desirous of judging what value her own simple comeliness might have, side by side with so much brilliancy, she cast a glance towards the full-length looking-glass, in front of which they happened to be standing. It was one of the truest plates in the world, and incapable of flattery. No sooner did the images, therein reflected, meet Polly's eye, than she shrieked, shrank from the stranger's side, gazed at him, for a moment, in the wildest dismay, and sank insensible upon the floor. Feathertop, likewise, had looked towards the mirror, and there beheld, not the glittering mockery of his outside show, but a picture of the sordid patchwork of his real composition, stript of all witchcraft.

The wretched simulacrum! We almost pity him. He threw up his arms, with an expression of despair, that went farther than any of his previous manifestations, towards vindicating his claims to be reckoned human. For perchance the only time, since this so often empty and deceptive life of mortals began its course, an Illusion had seen and fully recognized itself.

Mother Rigby was seated by her kitchen-hearth, in the twilight of this eventful day, and had just shaken the ashes out of a new pipe, when she heard a hurried tramp along the road. Yet it did not seem so much the tramp of human footsteps, as the clatter of sticks or the rattling of dry bones.

"Ha!" thought the old witch. "What step is that? Whose skeleton is out of its grave now, I wonder!"

A figure burst headlong into the cottage-door. It was Feathertop! His pipe was still a-light; the star still flamed upon his breast; the embroidery still glowed upon his garments; nor had he lost, in any degree or manner that could be estimated, the aspect that assimilated him with our mortal-brotherhood. But yet, in some indescribable way, (as is the case with all that has deluded us, when once found out,) the poor reality was felt beneath the cunning artifice.

"What has gone wrong?" demanded the witch. "Did yonder snuffling hypocrite thrust my darling from his door? The villain! I'll set twenty fiends to torment him, till he offer thee his daughter on his bended knees!"

"No, mother," said Feathertop despondingly, "it was not that!"

"Did the girl scorn my precious one?" asked Mother Rigby, her fierce eyes glowing like two coals of Tophet.[7] "I'll cover her face with pimples! Her nose shall be as red as the coal in thy pipe! Her front teeth shall drop out! In a week hence, she shall not be worth thy having!"

"Let her alone, mother!" answered poor Feathertop. "The girl was half-won; and methinks a kiss from her sweet lips might have made me altogether human! But," he added, after a brief pause, and then a howl of self-contempt, "I've seen myself, mother!—I've seen myself for the wretched, ragged, empty thing I am! I'll exist no longer!"

Snatching the pipe from his mouth, he flung it with all his might against the chimney, and, at the same instant, sank upon the floor, a medley of straw and tattered garments, with some sticks protruding from the heap; and a shrivelled pumpkin in the midst. The eye-holes were now lustreless; but the rudely-carved gap, that just before had been a mouth, still seemed to twist itself into a despairing grin, and was so far human.

"Poor fellow!" quoth Mother Rigby, with a rueful glance at the relics of her ill-fated contrivance. "My poor, dear, pretty Feathertop! There are thousands upon thousands of coxcombs and charlatans in the world, made up of just such a jumble of worn-out, forgotten, and good-for-nothing trash, as he was! Yet they live in fair repute, and never see themselves for what they are! And why should my poor puppet be the only one to know himself, and perish for it?"

While thus muttering, the witch had filled a fresh pipe of tobacco, and held the stem between her fingers, as doubtful whether to thrust it into her own mouth or Feathertop's.

"Poor Feathertop!" she continued. "I could easily give him another chance, and send him forth again to-morrow. But, no! his feelings

7. Hell.

are too tender; his sensibilities too deep. He seems to have too much heart to bustle for his own advantage, in such an empty and heartless world. Well, well! I'll make a scarecrow of him, after all. 'Tis an innocent and a useful vocation, and will suit my darling well; and if each of his human brethren had as fit a one, 'twould be the better for mankind; and as for this pipe of tobacco, I need it more than he!"

So saying, Mother Rigby put the stem between her lips. "Dickon!" cried she, in her high, sharp tone, "another coal for my pipe!"

A NOTE ON THE TEXT

Any edition of Hawthorne's tales must be based largely on printed texts that appeared in books, magazines, and gift-books during his lifetime. Of the tales and prefaces included in this Norton Critical Edition, manuscripts survive for only "The Old Manse," "The Celestial Rail-road," "Earth's Holocaust," and "Feathertop" and for the prefaces to *Twice-told Tales* and *The Snow-Image, and Other Twice-told Tales.* Otherwise, we are dependent on books and magazines, and our task is to reprint them faithfully, correcting only when corrections seem clearly warranted.

The texts of the two short prefaces in the first published editions do not vary substantively from the manuscripts, and these texts from the first editions are reprinted in the Norton edition. In the case of "The Old Manse" and the three tales for which there are manuscripts, we reprint the texts from *The Centenary Edition of the Works of Nathaniel Hawthorne.* The Centenary editors have reproduced the manuscripts of these four pieces far more precisely than Hawthorne's nineteenth-century editors managed to do, and the Centenary text has definitive authority.[1]

All but one of the other texts of the tales in the Norton Critical Edition are based on the most authoritative book printings. I have preferred to use books rather than magazines or gift-books for copytexts because Hawthorne took the occasions his books offered him to make some revisions and also because the collection texts are generally freer of mechanical error than are earlier printings. Haw-

---

1. I have also used CE texts for the two tales and the biographical sketch I added to the second edition: "The Wives of the Dead," "Dr. Heidegger's Experiment," and "Mrs. Hutchinson." I omitted a note Hawthorne added to "Dr Heidegger's Experiment" in 1860, published in the 1865 edition of *Twice-told Tales.* He asserts in the note that he did not plagiarize the idea of the story from a chapter in one of the novels of Alexandre Dumas, as claimed in "an English Review," since Dumas's novel was published more than twenty years after Hawthorne wrote "Dr. Heidegger." On the contrary, Hawthorne suggests that Dumas might have copied from him.

thorne gave acute attention to the first edition of *Twice-told Tales* (1837) and to the new tales in the second edition (1842). *Mosses from an Old Manse* presents more difficult problems. The first edition (1846) is carelessly printed in places. Recalling that it had "several errors,"[2] Hawthorne chose to examine this edition before having the book reissued—not his usual practice with a second edition. He made, as he wrote, "a careful revision"[3] of the first edition while he was American consul in Liverpool, England, and his corrected copy was used in the preparation of the second edition (1854). The 1854 edition, published by Hawthorne's trusted Boston firm of Ticknor and Fields, was carefully printed. It is sometimes argued that the 1854 *Mosses* is suspect because Hawthorne was by then estranged from the spirit of his earlier tales. In a notorious letter to his publisher, he wrote, "I am not quite sure that I entirely comprehend my own meaning in some of these blasted allegories. . . . I am a good deal changed since those times."[4] Though I feel the force of this complaint, I have nevertheless chosen the 1854 *Mosses* as the copy text for the tales in *Mosses* for which there is no manuscript. Hawthorne's 1854 revisions, as I read them, reflect neither his bafflement nor any desire to revamp the work of an inadequate earlier self. They are studied clarifications, not obscuring transformations. He performed the "disagreeable task"[5] of reviewing his own writings with his characteristic scrupulousness and gave us, whether he was disposed to or not, the best collection text of the *Mosses*.

The 1852 *Snow-Image*, from which we reprint "The Wives of the Dead," "Ethan Brand," and "The Man of Adamant," has an adequate text for the most part. Hawthorne appears not to have exercised himself greatly about the collection. Yet we know that he read proof, made a few corrections, and authorized the book as published by Ticknor and Fields. I have, however, deviated from my usual practice in that I use the 1831 *Token* printing of "My Kinsman, Major Molineux" as copy-text. I accept the Centenary editors' argument that a copyist, not Hawthorne, made all or nearly all the revisions that appear in *The Snow-Image* version of the tale.[6] Hawthorne evidently let these changes stand when he read them in proof, but he does not seem either to have had access to the *Token* text himself or to have shown a renewed interest in the tale. The *Token* text probably represents his engaged intentions better than that in *The Snow-Image*.

2. Letter to Fields, August 6, 1853.
3. Letter to Fields, April 13, 1854 (see p. 339 herein).
4. Ibid.
5. Ibid.
6. See Fredson Bowers, Textual Commentary, *The Snow-Image and Uncollected Tales*, CE 11:413–14.

TEXTUAL VARIANTS

The following list records all departures from copy-texts. On rare occasions editorial sophistications seem to have crept into the texts of the collections, though because we have no manuscripts for most of the tales we can posit such sophistications only conjecturally. When, in my judgment, Hawthorne's sense or syntax has been obscured in the collections by an editor, I have restored earlier readings from original publications in those few instances where they seem to have clear authority. I have made these changes sparingly and cautiously in order to maintain the integrity of the collection texts. I have also corrected a few obvious printing errors. The editors of the Centenary Edition, volumes 9, 10, and 11, give all substantive variants in appendices and include discussions of some of their choices. I have found these appendices extremely helpful. I have, however, checked my departures from copy-texts by referring to original printings.

Each story that has one or more variant readings is cited below, with its copy-text and any alternative texts used in preparing the edition. The stories appear in the order in which they occur in the Norton edition. In the list of variants, the word or words in boldface, preceded by page/line number from this Norton Critical Edition, give the reading of the Norton text. Copy-text readings that have been emended are given in regular type following a boldface entry. The sources of both the Norton reading and the copy-text reading are presented after each variant listed. The following abbreviations are used to designate these sources:

BW	*Boston Weekly Museum*
DM	*Dollar Magazine*
DR	*United States Magazine and Democratic Review*
GL	*Godey's Magazine and Lady's Book*
NE	*New-England Magazine*
NCE	Norton Critical Edition
P	*Pioneer*
T	*The Token*
37	*Twice-told Tales*, 1837
42	*Twice-told Tales*, 1842
46	*Mosses from an Old Manse*, 1846
54	*Mosses from an Old Manse*, 1854
52	*The Snow-Image, and Other Twice-told Tales*, 1852

List of Variants

"My Kinsman, Major Molineux"—copy-text, *Token* of 1831; later printing, *The Snow-Image*, 1852.
3 NCE omits *Token* ascription BY THE AUTHOR OF 'SIGHTS FROM A STEEPLE']
3.1 **James II NCE**] James II. T
7.13 '**"Left 52**] "Left T
7.16 **Better 52**] 'Better T
7.17 **begun 52**] began T
9.13 **more,' 52**] more, T
9.14 **to-52**] to T
12.34 **trunk; 52**] trunk, T
15.27 **kept 52**] keep T

"Roger Malvin's Burial"—copy-test, 1854 *Mosses*; earlier printings, *Token* of 1831, 1843 *Democratic Review*, 1846 *Mosses*.
18.2 **judiciously T, DR, 46**] judicially 54
23.27 **shrank T, DR**] shrink 46, 54
27.2 **affection T**] affections DR, 46, 54

"The Gentle Boy"—copy-text, 1837 *Twice-told Tales*; earlier printing, *Token* of 1831.
48.39 **than T**] then 37
49.16 **Charles II NCE**] Charles II. 37
49.17 **opened T**] open 37
52.8 **heavily; 'yet T**] heavily;' yet 37

"The Gray Chamption"—copy-text, 1837 *Twice-told Tales*; earlier printing, *New-England Magazine* of 1835.
59.1 **James II, NCE**] James II., 37

"Young Goodman Brown"—copy-text, 1854 *Mosses*; earlier printings, *New-England Magazine* of 1835, 1846 *Mosses*.
73.42 **widow's NE, 46**] widows' 54

"The Ambitious Guest"—copy-text, 1842 *Twice-told Tales*; earlier printing, *New-England Magazine* of 1835.
88.9 **has NE**] had 42

"The May-Pole of Merry Mount"—copy-text, 1837 *Twice-told Tales*; earlier printing, *Token* of 1835.
96.2 **were T**] where 37

"The Man of Adamant"—copy-text, 1852 *Snow-Image*; earlier printing, *Token* of 1836.
109.11 **fleshly T**] fleshy 52
111.30 **Richard T**] Richard's 52

"Endicott and the Red Cross"—copy-text, 1842 *Twice-told Tales*; earlier printing, *Token* of 1838.
117.10 **block—'NCE**] block—" T

"The Birthmark"—copy-text, 1854 *Mosses*; earlier printings, *Pioneer* of 1843, 1846 *Mosses*.
120.32 **bas-relief P, 46**] bass relief 54
130.15 **slightest P, 46**] lightest 54
130.37 **that earth P**] the earth 46. 54

"The Artist of the Beautiful"—copy-text, 1854 *Mosses*; earlier printings, *Democratic Review* of 1844, 1846 *Mosses*.
165.38 **ones DR**] one 46, 54

166.24 **process DR**] progress 46, 54
169.12 **has DR**] had 46, 54
169.35 **event." DR**] event. 54
174.5 **overarched DR**] overreached 46, 54

"Drowne's Wooden Image"—copy-text, 1854 *Mosses*; earlier printings, *Godey's* of 1844, 1846 *Mosses*.
183.2 **the perplexed admiration of himself and all other GL**] the perplexing admiration of himself and other 46, 54

"Rappaccini's Daughter"—copy-text, 1854 *Mosses*; earlier printings, *Democratic Review* of 1844, 1846 *Mosses*.
186.29 **Writings of Aubépine DR**] [From the writings of Aubépine.] 54 (Aubépine preface omitted 46)

"Ethan Brand"—copy-text, 1852 *Snow-image*; earlier printings, *Boston Museum* of 1850, *Dollar Magazine* of 1851.
241.6 **star-light BW, DM**] star-lit 52

HAWTHORNE'S REVISIONS OF "THE GENTLE BOY"

"The Gentle Boy" is the only tale that Hawthorne radically revised for publication in book form. The version he settled on for the 1837 *Twice-told Tales* (reprinted in this edition) differs significantly from the version that appeared in *The Token* of 1831. Hawthorne cut several long passages of editorializing or description, removed a few obviously opinionated clauses and sentences, and made a number of other small changes. The narrative voice is thus more muted, less obtrusive in the revised version in *Twice-told Tales*. A more careful balance is maintained in judging the quarrels of Puritans and Quakers.[1] By 1837, Hawthorne had learned the nuances of narrative manipulation as well as any fiction writer of his period, and he was evidently uncomfortable with his straightforward, didactic pronouncements in a tale of such importance to him. Yet the opinions expressed in the earlier *Token* version are fascinating traces of Hawthorne's thinking at the start of his career. Moreover, a good deal of the local detail Hawthorne sacrificed in the revision is worth preserving. In some of these passages, he dwells with absorbed interest on the minute circumstances of life in seventeenth-century New England.

We present below all passages cut from the *Token* "Gentle Boy," along with all changes of wording except for Hawthorne's corrections of obvious errors. We have not included changes in punctua-

---

1. See Seymour Gross, "Hawthorne's Revisions of 'The Gentle Boy,'" *American Literature* 26 (1954): 196–208, *passim*. This is a full and useful study of the revisions.

tion, paragraphing, grammar, or spelling. For a fuller record of the differences between the two versions, the reader should consult *Twice-told Tales*, CE 9:613–19.

The word or words in boldface, preceded by page / line numbers from this Norton Critical Edition, give the readings of the Norton text, identical except for one emendation to the text of the 1837 *Twice-told Tales*. The rejected readings from the *Token* text are given in regular type, and are followed by the symbol "T."

33.20 **abstractedly**] abstractly T
33.25–6 **crown of martyrdom. ¶An indelible stain**] crown of martyrdom. ¶That those who were active in, or consenting to, this measure, made themselves responsible for innocent blood, is not to be denied: yet the extenuating circumstances of their conduct are more numerous than can generally be pleaded by persecutors. The inhabitants of New England were a people, whose original bond of union was their peculiar religious principles. For the peaceful exercise of their own mode of worship, an object, the very reverse of universal liberty of conscience, they had hewn themselves a home in the wilderness; they had made vast sacrifices of whatever is dear to man; they had exposed themselves to the peril of death, and to a life which rendered the accomplishment of that peril almost a blessing. They had found no city of refuge prepared for them, but, with Heaven's assistance, they had created one; and it would be hard to say whether justice did not authorize their determination, to guard its gate against all who were destitute of the prescribed title to admittance. The principle of their foundation was such, that to destroy the unity of religion, might have been to subvert the government, and break up the colony, especially at a period when the state of affairs in England had stopped the tide of emigration, and drawn back many of the pilgrims to their native homes. The magistrates of Massachusetts Bay were, moreover, most imperfectly informed respecting the real tenets and character of the Quaker sect. They had heard of them, from various parts of the earth, as opposers of every known opinion, and enemies of all established governments; they had beheld extravagances which seemed to justify these accusations; and the idea suggested by their own wisdom may be gathered from the fact, that the persons of many individuals were searched, in the expectation of discovering witch-marks. But after all allowances, it is to be feared that the death of the Quakers was principally owing to the polemic fierceness, that distinct passion of human nature, which has so often produced frightful guilt in the most sincere and zealous advocates of virtue and religion. An indelible stain T
34.9 **home**] house T
34.31 **walked**] continued T
35.16 **spiritual**] spirited T
37.3 **from us.' ¶'What pale**] from us.' ¶The wife's eyes filled with tears; she inquired neither who little Ilbrahim was, nor whence he came, but kissed his cheek and led the way into the dwelling. The sitting-room, which was also the kitchen, was lighted by a cheerful fire upon the large stone-laid hearth, and a confused variety of objects shone out and disappeared in the unsteady blaze. There were the household articles, the many wooden trenchers, the one large pewter dish, and the copper kettle whose inner surface was glittering like gold. There were the lighter implements of husbandry, the spade, the sickle, and the scythe, all hanging by the door, and the axe before which a thousand trees had bowed themselves. On another part of the wall were the steel cap and iron breast-plate, the sword and the matchlock gun. There, in a corner, was a little chair, the memorial of a brood of children whose place by the fire-side was vacant forever. And there, on a table near the window, among all those tokens of labor, war, and mourning, was the Holy Bible, the book of life, an emblem of the blessed comforts which it offers to those who can receive them, amidst the toil, the strife, and sorrow of this world. Dorothy hastened to bring the little chair from its corner; she placed it on the hearth, and, seating the poor orphan there, addressed him in words of tenderness, such as only a mother's experience could have taught her. At length, when he had timidly begun to taste his warm bread and milk, she drew her husband apart. ¶'What pale T
37.17 **intentions. ¶'Have**] intentions. She drew near to Ilbrahim, who, having finished his repast, sat with the tears hanging upon his long eye-lashes, but with a singular and unchildlike composure on his little face. ¶'Have T
39.5 **drum. At**] drum; in connexion with which peculiarity it may be mentioned, that an apartment of the meetinghouse served the purposes of a powder-magazine and armory. At T

39.28 **certain age.** ¶**Pearson and Dorothy**] certain age. On one side of the house sat the women, generally in sad-colored and most unfanciful apparel, although there were a few high headdresses, on which the 'Cobler of Agawam' would have lavished his empty wit of words. There was no veil to be seen among them all, and it must be allowed that the November sun, shining brightly through the windows, fell upon many a demure but pretty set of features, which no barbarity of art could spoil. The masculine department of the house presented somewhat more variety than that of the women. Most of the men, it is true, were clad in black or dark-grey broadcloth, and all coincided in the short, ungraceful, and ear-displaying cut of their hair. But those who were in martial author-ity, having arrayed themselves in their embroidered buff-coats, contrasted strikingly with the remainder of the congregation, and attracted many youthful thoughts which should have been otherwise employed. Pearson and Dorothy T

40.6–7 **a man of pale, thin countenance**] a man of pale, thin, yet not intellectual coun-tenance T

40.23 **depths.** ¶**The sands**] depths. Into this discourse was worked much learning, both sacred and profane, which, however, came forth not digested into its original elements, but in short quotations, as if the preacher were unable to amalgamate his own mind with that of the author. His own language was generally plain, even to affectation, but there were frequent specimens of a dull man's efforts to be witty—little ripples fretting the surface of a stagnant pool. ¶The sands T

40.37 **thundered. She then divested**] thundered. Having thus usurped a station to which her sex can plead no title, she divested T

45.4 **lay in the dungeons**] ate the bread, T

45.29 **rich treasures**] precious views T

45.30 **gold**] treasure T

48.3 **but now he dropped them at once. His**] but now he dropped them at once, for he was stricken in a tender part. His T

49.7–10 **gibe. Such was his state of mind at the period of Ilbrahim's misfortune; and the emotions consequent upon that event completed the change, of which the child had been the original instrument.** ¶**In the mean time**] gibe. At length, when the change in his belief was fully accomplished, the contest grew very terrible between the love of the world, in its thousand shapes, and the power which moved him to sacri-fice all for the one pure faith; to quote his own words, subsequently uttered at a meeting of Friends, it was as if 'Earth and Hell had garrisoned the fortress of his miserable soul, and Heaven came battering against it to storm the walls.' Such was his state of warfare at the period of Ilbrahim's misfortune; and the emotions consequent upon that event enlisted with the besieging army, and decided the victory. There was a triumphant shout within him, and from that moment all was peace. Dorothy had not been the sub-ject of a similar process, for her reason was as clear as her heart was tender. ¶In the mean time T

49.17 **opened**] T open 37

49.19–20 **encounter ignominy**] exult in the midst of ignominy T

49.44 **life. In person**] life. His features were strong and well connected, and seemed to express firmness of purpose and sober understanding, although his actions had fre-quently been at variance with this last attribute. In person T

51.45 **imagining**] imaging T

53.23 **Sister!**] Favorite sister! T

55.24 **green and sunken grave.**] green and sunken grave. My heart is glad of this triumph of our better nature; it gives me a kindlier feeling for the fathers of my native land; and with it I will close the tale. T

THE AUTHOR ON HIS WORK

PREFACES

Hawthorne's prefaces not only provide clues to his work but also make good reading in themselves. All of them are written for occasions and should be understood in their contexts. They are performances, not confessions or definitive pronouncements on Hawthorne as man and author. Hawthorne's early readers, like Longfellow and even Melville, read his work in part for personality. The first reviews of his tales were full of speculation as to what sort of man he was, and Hawthorne obliged this impulse on the part of his readers by introducing himself at the start of his books. In fact, he had been in the habit of projecting himself in various guises even before he was reviewed. Like Irving and some of his English precursors, he tends to strike up a relation with his reader in the act of writing a tale. In the stories included in this edition, "Wakefield" extends to the reader an especially genial invitation, while "Rappaccini's Daughter" has a whimsical headnote about the author as a prolific Frenchman. Hawthorne repeatedly and knowingly imagined a personality for himself, to be treated by the discerning reader as partly a fiction. As Arlin Turner writes, "In his notebooks and prefaces, and even in his letters, Hawthorne must be read with the same alertness to indirection, understatement, symbol and irony we have learned to exert in reading his tales and romances."[1]

"The Old Manse" is an elaborate invitation to the reader. It offers not just a pleasant picture of Hawthorne's life and his friends but a graceful performance that makes one comfortable with a civilized author idealizing his domestic affairs in the pastoral-transcendental village of Concord. After such an introduction, the reader may well feel receptive to the tales that follow it. The preface to the 1851 *Twice-told Tales* gives a succinct, complex impression of the writer. Before he composed it, Hawthorne wrote his publisher in October 1850, "as it seems to be the fashion now-adays for authors to write prefaces to their new editions, I will write a very pretty one,"[2] implying that he meant to write it with a measure of irony. However, the irony of the finished preface is hard to pin down. By late 1850 Hawthorne was disposed to look back critically at his years in a Salem garret, and the preface is in part a decorous dismissal of his earlier writings and earlier projected self. Yet it distills so many attitudes—bitterness at the public for not taking him up in his "most effervescent" years, self-deprecation for the gentlemanly reserve and slightness of his stories, cheerful thankfulness for what his stories have brought him in life—that the reader ends it intrigued by Hawthorne and his writing. It works as an invitation in spite of what it ostensibly says. The preface to *The Snow-Image* is a relatively direct indication of Hawthorne's literary intentions and his views as a writer in late 1851. He defines his artistic self as clearly as

1. Arlin Turner, "Needs in Hawthorne Biography," *Nathaniel Hawthorne Journal* 2 (1972): 44.
2. Hawthorne, *The Letters, 1843–1853*, CE 16:369.

he ever will, as "a person, who has been burrowing, to his utmost ability, into the depths of our common nature, for the purposes of psychological romance,—and who pursues his researches in that dusky region, as he needs must, as well by the tact of sympathy as by the light of observation." Thus he reveals his curious gift, his necessary mission, and his balance of mind.

Hawthorne's tendency toward self-deprecation is not entirely an ironic pose. He had a faculty for sharp-eyed censure. Few of his fictional characters escape it; their pretensions are exposed without their realizing it, especially if they are men. Fortunately his authorial sense of justice is tempered with mercy—"the light of observation" is softened by "the tact of sympathy." We can assume he applied his power of censure to himself and his writings, but as a child of New England gave himself due sympathy only grudgingly. Moreover, the career of writing seems not to have been an easy fate. He waited for inspiration and was vexed when it failed to come. When he had finished major work, he was afterward detached from what he had made. Edwin P. Whipple, one of Hawthorne's favorite contemporary critics, wrote of "the seeming separation of his genius from his will. . . . His great books appear not so much created by him as through him. They have the character of revelations,—he, the instrument, being often troubled with the burden they impose on his mind."[3] His self-deprecations may be understood in part as expressions of impatience with this burden of revelation.

Yet Hawthorne also speaks conspicuously in the prefaces and elsewhere of "the pleasure of composition" and of his happiness when he worked among his fantasies. He knew that "Providence"—to use his favorite word of belief—made him a writer. And he wanted to know that he was a good and serious one. He was eager, especially as a tale writer, for fame. When the New York journalist Evert Duyckinck wrote an article in 1841 praising Hawthorne's "fanciful pathos delighting in sepulchral images" and comparing his character to Hamlet's, Hawthorne was gratified. He thanked Duyckinck: "I would far rather receive earnest praise from a single individual, than to be claimed a tolerably pleasant writer by a thousand, or a million."[4] Though Hawthorne did not usually profess to think of his work in such grand terms, a man who is pleased to see himself compared to Hamlet does not regard himself as insignificant.

The text of "The Old Manse" is from *Mosses from an Old Manse*, volume 10 of the Centenary Edition. The texts of the prefaces to *Twicetold Tales* and *The Snow-Image* are from the 1851 edition of *Twice-told Tales* and the 1852 edition of *The Snow-Image*, the first printings of the two prefaces

3. Edwin P. Whipple, *Character and Characteristic Men* (Boston, 1866), 234, 235–36.
4. Hawthorne, *The Letters, 1813–1843,* CE 15:599.

The Old Manse[†]

The Author Makes the Reader Acquainted with His Abode

Between two tall gate-posts of rough-hewn stone, (the gate itself having fallen from its hinges, at some unknown epoch,) we beheld the gray front of the old parsonage, terminating the vista of an avenue of black-ash trees. It was now a twelvemonth since the funeral procession of the venerable clergyman,[1] its last inhabitant, had turned from that gate-way towards the village burying-ground. The wheel-track, leading to the door, as well as the whole breadth of the avenue, was almost overgrown with grass, affording dainty mouthfuls to two or three vagrant cows, and an old white horse, who had his own living to pick up along the roadside. The glimmering shadows, that lay half-asleep between the door of the house and the public highway, were a kind of spiritual medium, seen through which, the edifice had not quite the aspect of belonging to the material world. Certainly it had little in common with those ordinary abodes, which stand so imminent upon the road that every passer-by can thrust his head, as it were, into the domestic circle. From these quiet windows, the figures of passing travellers looked too remote and dim to disturb the sense of privacy. In its near retirement, and accessible seclusion, it was the very spot for the residence of a clergy man; a man not estranged from human life, yet enveloped, in the midst of it, with a veil woven of intermingled gloom and brightness. It was worthy to have been one of the time-honored parsonages of England, in which, through many generations, a succession of holy occupants pass from youth to age, and bequeath each an inheritance of sanctity to pervade the house and hover over it, as with an atmosphere.

Nor, in truth, had the old Manse ever been prophaned by a lay occupant, until that memorable summer-afternoon when I entered it as my home. A priest had built it; a priest had succeeded to it; other priestly men, from time to time, had dwelt in it; and children, born in its chambers, had grown up to assume the priestly character. It was awful to reflect how many sermons must have been written there. The latest inhabitant alone—he, by whose translation to Paradise

† First published as the preface to *Mosses from an Old Manse* (1846). Reprinted by permission of The Ohio State University Press. A "manse" is the house of a minister, and Hawthorne and his new wife, Sophia, rented what he called "the old Manse" in Concord from July 1842 to October 1845. It was built in 1765 for the Reverend William Emerson, Ralph Waldo Emerson's grandfather. After Reverend Emerson's death as a chaplain in the Revolutionary Army in 1776, his widow married Dr. Ezra Ripley, another clergyman, who occupied the Manse for fifty years till his death in 1841. "The Old Manse" not only initiates Hawthorne's second collection of tales, but it is also the first of his extended autobiographical prefaces, to be followed by "The Custom-House" in *The Scarlet Letter*.
1. Dr. Ezra Ripley.

the dwelling was left vacant—had penned nearly three thousand discourses, besides the better, if not the greater number, that gushed living from his lips. How often, no doubt, had he paced to-and-fro along the avenue, attuning his meditations, to the sighs and gentle murmurs, and deep and solemn peals of the wind, among the lofty tops of the trees! In that variety of natural utterances, he could find something accordant with every passage of his sermon, were it of tenderness or reverential fear. The boughs over my head seemed shadowy with solemn thoughts, as well as with rustling leaves. I took shame to myself for having been so long a writer of idle stories, and ventured to hope that wisdom would descend upon me with the falling leaves of the avenue; and that I should light upon an intellectual treasure in the old Manse, well worth those hoards of long-hidden gold, which people seek for in moss-grown houses. Profound treatises of morality;—a layman's unprofessional, and therefore unprejudiced views of religion;—histories, (such as Bancroft[2] might have written, had he taken up his abode here, as he once purposed,) bright with picture, gleaming over a depth of philosophic thought;—these were the works that might fitly have flowed from such a retirement. In the humblest event, I resolved at least to achieve a novel, that should evolve some deep lesson, and should possess physical substance enough to stand alone.

In furtherance of my design, and as if to leave me no pretext for not fulfilling it, there was, in the rear of the house, the most delightful little nook of a study that ever afforded its snug seclusion to a scholar. It was here that Emerson wrote 'Nature'; for he was then an inhabitant of the Manse, and used to watch the Assyrian dawn and the Paphian sunset and moonrise, from the summit of our eastern hill.[3] When I first saw the room, its walls were blackened with the smoke of unnumbered years, and made still blacker by the grim prints of Puritan ministers that hung around. These worthies looked strangely like bad angels, or, at least, like men who had wrestled so continually and so sternly with the devil, that somewhat of his sooty fierceness had been imparted to their own visages. They had all vanished now. A cheerful coat of paint, and golden-tinted paper-hangings, lighted up the small apartment; while the shadow of a willow-tree, that swept against the overhanging eaves, attempered the cheery western sunshine. In place of the grim prints,

---

2. George Bancroft (1800–1891), author of *History of the United States* (10 vols., 1834–74).
3. Hawthorne paraphrases a passage from chapter 3 of *Nature:* "Give me health and a day, and I will make the pomp of emperors ridiculous. The dawn is my Assyria; the sun-set and moon-rise my Paphos, and unimaginable realms of faerie; broad noon shall be my England of the senses and the understanding; the night shall be my Germany of mystic philosophy and dreams." Emerson lived in the Old Manse in 1834–35 and there partly composed his early philosophical treatise *Nature* (1836).

there was the sweet and lovely head of one of Raphael's Madonnas, and two pleasant little pictures of the Lake of Como. The only other decorations were a purple vase of flowers, always fresh, and a bronze one containing graceful ferns. My books (few, and by no means choice; for they were chiefly such waifs as chance had thrown in my way) stood in order about the room, seldom to be disturbed.

The study had three windows, set with little, old-fashioned panes of glass, each with a crack across it. The two on the western side looked, or rather peeped, between the willow-branches, down into the orchard, with glimpses of the river through the trees. The third, facing northward, commanded a broader view of the river, at a spot where its hitherto obscure waters gleam forth into the light of history. It was at this window that the clergyman, who then dwelt in the Manse, stood watching the outbreak of a long and deadly struggle between two nations;[4] he saw the irregular array of his parishioners on the farther side of the river, and the glittering line of the British, on the hither bank. He awaited, in an agony of suspense, the rattle of the musketry. It came—and there needed but a gentle wind to sweep the battle-smoke around this quiet house.

Perhaps the reader—whom I cannot help considering as my guest in the old Manse, and entitled to all courtesy in the way of sight-showing—perhaps he will choose to take a nearer view of the memorable spot. We stand now on the river's brink. It may well be called the Concord—the river of peace and quietness—for it is certainly the most unexcitable and sluggish stream that ever loitered, imperceptibly, towards its eternity, the sea. Positively, I had lived three weeks beside it, before it grew quite clear to my perception which way the current flowed. It never has a vivacious aspect, except when a north-western breeze is vexing its surface, on a sunshiny day. From the incurable indolence of its nature, the stream is happily incapable of becoming the slave of human ingenuity, as is the fate of so many a wild, free mountain-torrent. While all things else are compelled to subserve some useful purpose, it idles its sluggish life away, in lazy liberty, without turning a solitary spindle, or affording even water-power enough to grind the corn that grows upon its banks. The torpor of its movement allows it nowhere a bright pebbly shore, nor so much as a narrow strip of glistening sand, in any part of its course. It slumbers between broad prairies, kissing the long meadow-grass, and bathes the overhanging boughs of elder-bushes and willows, or the roots of elms and ash-trees, and clumps of maples. Flags and rushes grow along its plashy shore; the yellow water-lily spreads its broad, flat leaves on the margin; and the fragrant white

---

4. Reverend William Emerson watched the battle of Concord from the Manse on April 19, 1775.

pond-lily abounds, generally selecting a position just so far from the river's brink, that it cannot be grasped, save at the hazard of plunging in.

It is a marvel whence this perfect flower derives its loveliness and perfume, springing, as it does, from the black mud over which the river sleeps, and where lurk the slimy eel, and speckled frog, and the mud turtle, whom continual washing cannot cleanse. It is the very same black mud out of which the yellow lily sucks its obscene life and noisome odor. Thus we see, too, in the world, that some persons assimilate only what is ugly and evil from the same moral circumstances which supply good and beautiful results—the fragrance of celestial flowers—to the daily life of others.

The reader must not, from any testimony of mine, contract a dislike towards our slumberous stream. In the light of a calm and golden sunset, it becomes lovely beyond expression; the more lovely for the quietude that so well accords with the hour, when even the wind, after blustering all day long, usually hushes itself to rest. Each tree and rock, and every blade of grass, is distinctly imaged, and, however unsightly in reality, assumes ideal beauty in the reflection. The minutest things of earth, and the broad aspect of the firmament, are pictured equally without effort, and with the same felicity of success. All the sky glows downward at our feet; the rich clouds float through the unruffled bosom of the stream, like heavenly thoughts through a peaceful heart. We will not, then, malign our river as gross and impure, while it can glorify itself with so adequate a picture of the heaven that broods above it; or, if we remember its tawny hue and the muddiness of its bed, let it be a symbol that the earthliest human soul has an infinite spiritual capacity, and may contain the better world within its depths. But, indeed, the same lesson might be drawn out of any mud-puddle in the streets of a city—and, being taught us everywhere, it must be true.

Come; we have pursued a somewhat devious track, in our walk to the battle-ground. Here we are, at the point where the river was crossed by the old bridge, the possession of which was the immediate object of the contest. On the hither side, grow two or three elms, throwing a wide circumference of shade, but which must have been planted at some period within the threescore years and ten, that have passed since the battle-day. On the farther shore, overhung by a clump of elder-bushes, we discern the stone abutment of the bridge. Looking down into the river, I once discovered some heavy fragments of the timbers, all green with half-a-century's growth of water-moss; for, during that length of time, the tramp of horses and human footsteps have ceased, along this ancient highway. The stream has here about the breadth of twenty strokes of a swimmer's arm; a space not too wide, when the bullets were whistling across.

Old people, who dwell hereabouts, will point out the very spots, on the western bank, where our countrymen fell down and died; and, on this side of the river, an obelisk of granite has grown up from the soil that was fertilized with British blood. The monument, not more than twenty feet in height, is such as it befitted the inhabitants of a village to erect, in illustration of a matter of local interest, rather than what was suitable to commemorate an epoch of national history. Still, by the fathers of the village this famous deed was done; and their descendants might rightfully claim the privilege of building a memorial.

A humbler token of the fight, yet a more interesting one than the granite obelisk, may be seen close under the stone-wall, which separates the battle-ground from the precincts of the parsonage. It is the grave—marked by a small, moss-grown fragment of stone at the head, and another at the foot—the grave of two British soldiers, who were slain in the skirmish, and have ever since slept peacefully where Zechariah Brown and Thomas Davis buried them. Soon was their warfare ended;—a weary night-march from Boston—a rattling volley of musketry across the river;—and then these many years of rest! In the long procession of slain invaders, who passed into eternity from the battle-fields of the Revolution, these two nameless soldiers led the way.

Lowell,[5] the poet, as we were once standing over this grave, told me a tradition in reference to one of the inhabitants below. The story has something deeply impressive, though its circumstances cannot altogether be reconciled with probability. A youth, in the service of the clergyman, happened to be chopping wood, that April morning, at the back door of the Manse; and when the noise of battle rang from side to side of the bridge, he hastened across the intervening field, to see what might be going forward. It is rather strange, by the way, that this lad should have been so diligently at work, when the whole population of town and county were startled out of their customary business, by the advance of the British troops. Be that as it might, the tradition says that the lad now left his task, and hurried to the battle-field, with the axe still in his hand. The British had by this time retreated—the Americans were in pursuit— and the late scene of strife was thus deserted by both parties. Two soldiers lay on the ground; one was a corpse; but, as the young New-Englander drew nigh, the other Briton raised himself painfully upon his hands and knees, and gave a ghastly stare into his face. The boy—it must have been a nervous impulse, without purpose, without thought, and betokening a sensitive and impressible nature, rather

---

5. James Russell Lowell (1819–1891), Cambridge poet and one of Hawthorne's editors.

than a hardened one—the boy uplifted his axe, and dealt the wounded soldier a fierce and fatal blow upon the head.

I could wish that the grave might be opened; for I would fain know whether either of the skeleton soldiers have the mark of an axe in his skull. The story comes home to me like truth. Oftentimes, as an intellectual and moral exercise, I have sought to follow that poor youth through his subsequent career, and observe how his soul was tortured by the blood-stain, contracted, as it had been, before the long custom of war had robbed human life of its sanctity, and while it still seemed murderous to slay a brother man. This one circumstance has borne more fruit for me, than all that history tells us of the fight.

Many strangers come, in the summer-time, to view the battle-ground. For my own part, I have never found my imagination much excited by this, or any other scene of historic celebrity; nor would the placid margin of the river have lost any of its charm for me, had men never fought and died there. There is a wilder interest in the tract of land—perhaps a hundred yards in breadth—which extends between the battle-field and the northern face of our old Manse, with its contiguous avenue and orchard. Here, in some unknown age, before the white man came, stood an Indian village, convenient to the river, whence its inhabitants must have drawn so large a part of their subsistence. The site is identified by the spear and arrow-heads, the chisels, and other implements of war, labor, and the chase, which the plough turns up from the soil. You see a splinter of stone, half hidden beneath a sod; it looks like nothing worthy of note; but, if you have faith enough to pick it up—behold a relic! Thoreau,[6] who has a strange faculty of finding what the Indians have left behind them, first set me on the search; and I afterwards enriched myself with some very perfect specimens, so rudely wrought that it seemed almost as if chance had fashioned them. Their great charm consists in this rudeness, and in the individuality of each article, so different from the productions of civilized machinery, which shapes everything on one pattern. There is an exquisite delight, too, in picking up, for one's self, an arrow-head that was dropt centuries ago, and has never been handled since, and which we thus receive directly from the hand of the red hunter, who purposed to shoot it at his game, or at an enemy. Such an incident builds up again the Indian village, amid its encircling forest, and recalls to life the painted chiefs and warriors, the squaws at their household toil, and the children sporting among the wigwams; while the little wind-rocked papoose swings from the branch of a tree. It can hardly be

6. While at the Manse, Hawthorne met and grew to like Henry David Thoreau (1817–1862), still an aspiring young man of Concord and not yet a well-known writer.

told whether it is a joy or a pain, after such a momentary vision, to gaze around in the broad daylight of reality, and see stone-fences, white houses, potatoe-fields, and men doggedly hoeing, in their shirt-sleeves and homespun pantaloons. But this is nonsense. The old Manse is better than a thousand wigwams.

The old Manse! We had almost forgotten it, but will return thither through the orchard. This was set out by the last clergyman, in the decline of his life, when the neighbors laughed at the hoary-headed man for planting trees, from which he could have no prospect of gathering fruit. Even had that been the case, there was only so much the better motive for planting them, in the pure and unselfish hope of benefitting his successors—an end so seldom achieved by more ambitious efforts. But the old minister, before reaching his patriarchal age of ninety, ate the apples from this orchard during many years, and added silver and gold to his annual stipend, by disposing of the superfluity. It is pleasant to think of him, walking among the trees in the quiet afternoons of early autumn, and picking up here and there a windfall; while he observes how heavily the branches are weighed down, and computes the number of empty flour-barrels that will be filled by their burthen. He loved each tree, doubtless, as if it had been his own child. An orchard has a relation to mankind, and readily connects itself with matters of the heart. The trees possess a domestic character; they have lost the wild nature of their forest-kindred, and have grown humanized by receiving the care of man, as well as by contributing to his wants. There is so much individuality of character, too, among apple-trees, that it gives them an additional claim to be the objects of human interest. One is harsh and crabbed in its manifestations; another gives us fruit as mild as charity. One is churlish and illiberal, evidently grudging the few apples that it bears; another exhausts itself in free-hearted benevolence. The variety of grotesque shapes, into which apple-trees contort themselves, has its effect on those who get acquainted with them; they stretch out their crooked branches, and take such hold of the imagination that we remember them as humorists and odd fellows. And what is more melancholy than the old apple-trees, that linger about the spot where once stood a homestead, but where there is now only a ruined chimney, rising out of a grassy and weed-grown cellar? They offer their fruit to every wayfarer—apples that are bitter-sweet with the moral of time's vicissitude.

I have met with no other such pleasant trouble in the world, as that of finding myself, with only the two or three mouths which it was my privilege to feed, the sole inheritor of the old clergyman's wealth of fruits. Throughout the summer, there were cherries and currants; and then came Autumn, with this immense burthen of apples, dropping them continually from his over-laden shoulders, as he trudged along. In the stillest afternoon, if I listened, the thump of a great apple was audible, falling without a breath of wind, from the mere necessity of perfect ripeness. And, besides, there were pear-trees, that flung down bushels upon bushels of heavy pears, and peach-trees, which, in a good year, tormented me with peaches, neither to be eaten nor kept, nor, without labor and perplexity, to be given away. The idea of an infinite generosity and exhaustless bounty, on the part of our Mother Nature, was well worth obtaining through such cares as these. That feeling can be enjoyed in perfection only by the natives of the summer islands, where the breadfruit, the cocoa, the palm, and the orange, grow spontaneously, and hold forth the ever-ready meal; but, likewise, almost as well, by a man long habituated to city-life, who plunges into such a solitude as that of the old Manse, where he plucks the fruit of trees that he did not plant, and which therefore, to my heterodox taste, bear the closest resemblance to those that grew in Eden. It has been an apophthegm, these five thousand years, that toil sweetens the bread it earns. For my part, (speaking from hard experience, acquired while belaboring the rugged furrows of Brook Farm,) I relish best the free gifts of Providence.

Not that it can be disputed, that the light toil, requisite to cultivate a moderately sized garden, imparts such zest to kitchen-vegetables as is never found in those of the market-gardener. Childless men, if they would know something of the bliss of paternity, should plant a seed—be it squash, bean, Indian corn, or perhaps a mere flower, or worthless weed—should plant it with their own hands, and nurse it from infancy to maturity, altogether by their own care. If there be not too many of them, each individual plant becomes an object of separate interest. My garden, that skirted the avenue of the Manse, was of precisely the right extent. An hour or two of morning labor was all that it required. But I used to visit and re-visit it, a dozen times a day, and stand in deep contemplation over my vegetable progeny, with a love that nobody could share nor conceive of, who had never taken part in the process of creation. It was one of the most bewitching sights in the world, to observe a hill of beans thrusting aside the soil, or a row of early peas, just peeping forth sufficiently to trace a line of delicate green. Later in the season, the humming-birds were attracted by the blossoms of a peculiar variety of bean; and they were a joy to me, those little spiritual visitants, for deigning to sip airy food out of my nectar-cups. Multitudes of bees used to bury themselves in the yellow blossoms of the summer-squashes. This, too, was a deep satisfaction; although, when they had laden themselves with sweets, they flew away to some unknown hive, which would give back nothing in requital of what my garden had contributed. But I was glad thus to fling a benefaction upon the passing breeze, with the certainty that somebody must profit by it, and that there would be a little more honey in the world, to allay the sourness and bitterness which mankind is always complaining of. Yes, indeed; my life was the sweeter for that honey.

Speaking of summer-squashes, I must say a word of their beautiful and varied forms. They presented an endless diversity of urns and vases, shallow or deep, scalloped or plain, moulded in patterns which a sculptor would do well to copy, since Art has never invented anything more graceful. A hundred squashes in the garden were worthy—in my eyes, at least—of being rendered indestructible in marble. If ever Providence (but I know it never will) should assign me a superfluity of gold, part of it shall be expended for a service of plate, or most delicate porcelain, to be wrought into the shapes of summer-squashes, gathered from vines which I will plant with my own hands. As dishes for containing vegetables, they would be peculiarly appropriate.

But, not merely the squeamish love of the Beautiful was gratified by my toil in the kitchen-garden. There was a hearty enjoyment, likewise, in observing the growth of the crook-necked winter squashes, from the first little bulb, with the withered blossom adhering to it, until they lay strewn upon the soil, big, round fellows, hiding their heads beneath the leaves, but turning up their great yellow rotundities to the noontide sun. Gazing at them, I felt that, by my agency, something worth living for had been done. A new substance was borne into the world. They were real and tangible existences, which the mind could seize hold of and rejoice in. A cabbage, too,— especially the early Dutch cabbage, which swells to a monstrous circumference, until its ambitious heart often bursts asunder,—is a matter to be proud of, when we can claim a share with the earth and sky in producing it. But, after all, the hugest pleasure is reserved, until these vegetable children of ours are smoking on the table, and we, like Saturn,[7] make a meal of them.

What with the river, the battle-field, the orchard, and the garden, the reader begins to despair of finding his way back into the old Manse. But, in agreeable weather, it is the truest hospitality to keep him out of doors. I never grew quite acquainted with my habitation, till a long spell of sulky rain had confined me beneath its roof. There could not be a more sombre aspect of external Nature, than as then seen from the windows of my study. The great willow-tree had caught, and retained among its leaves, a whole cataract of water, to be shaken down, at intervals, by the frequent gusts of wind. All day long, and for a week together, the rain was drip-drip-dripping and splash-splash-splashing from the eaves, and bubbling and foaming

---

7. Saturn devoured his children in order to continue his rule over the universe.

into the tubs beneath the spouts. The old, unpainted shingles of the house and outbuildings were black with moisture; and the mosses, of ancient growth upon the walls, looked green and fresh, as if they were the newest things and after-thought of Time. The usually mirrored surface of the river was blurred by an infinity of rain-drops; the whole landscape had a completely water-soaked appearance, conveying the impression that the earth was wet through, like a sponge; while the summit of a wooded hill, about a mile distant, was enveloped in a dense mist, where the demon of the tempest seemed to have his abiding-place, and to be plotting still direr inclemencies.

Nature has no kindness—no hospitality—during rain. In the fiercest heat of sunny days, she retains a secret mercy, and welcomes the wayfarer to shady nooks of the woods, whither the sun cannot penetrate; but she provides no shelter against her storms. It makes us shiver to think of those deep, umbrageous, recesses—those overshadowing banks—where we found such enjoyment during the sultry afternoons. Not a twig of foliage there, but would dash a little shower into our faces. Looking reproachfully towards the impenetrable sky—if sky there be, above that dismal uniformity of cloud—we are apt to murmur against the whole system of the universe, since it involves the extinction of so many summer days, in so short a life, by the hissing and spluttering rain. In such spells of weather—and, it is to be supposed, such weather came—Eve's bower in Paradise must have been but a cheerless and aguish kind of shelter, nowise comparable to the old parsonage, which had resources of its own, to beguile the week's imprisonment. The idea of sleeping on a couch of wet roses!

Happy the man who, in a rainy day, can betake himself to a huge garret, stored, like that of the Manse, with lumber that each generation has left behind it, from a period before the Revolution. Our garret was an arched hall, dimly illuminated through small and dusty windows; it was but a twilight at the best; and there were nooks, or rather caverns of deep obscurity, the secrets of which I never learned, being too reverent of their dust and cobwebs. The beams and rafters, roughly hewn, and with strips of bark still on them, and the rude masonry of the chimneys, made the garret look wild and uncivilized; an aspect unlike what was seen elsewhere, in the quiet and decorous old house. But, on one side, there was a little white-washed apartment, which bore the traditionary title of the Saints' Chamber, because holy men, in their youth, had slept, and studied, and prayed there. With its elevated retirement, its one window, its small fireplace, and its closet, convenient for an oratory, it was the very spot where a young man might inspire himself with solemn enthusiasm, and cherish saintly dreams. The occupants, at various epochs, had left brief records and ejaculations, inscribed upon the walls, There, too, hung a tattered and shrivelled roll of canvass, which, on inspection, proved to be the forcibly wrought picture of a clergyman, in wig, band, and gown, holding a Bible in his hand. As I turned his face towards the light, he eyed me with an air of authority such as men of his profession seldom assume, in our days. The original had been pastor of the parish, more than a century ago, a friend of Whitefield,[8] and almost his equal in fervid eloquence. I bowed before the effigy of the dignified divine, and felt as if I had now met face to face with the ghost, by whom, as there was reason to apprehend, the Manse was haunted.

Houses of any antiquity, in New England, are so invariably possessed with spirits, that the matter seems hardly worth alluding to. Our ghost used to heave deep sighs in a particular corner of the parlor; and sometimes rustled paper, as if he were turning over a sermon, in the long upper entry;—where, nevertheless, he was invisible, in spite of the bright moon-shine that fell through the eastern window. Not improbably, he wished me to edit and publish a selection from a chest full of manuscript discourses, that stood in the garret. Once, while Hillard[9] and other friends sat talking with us in the twilight, there came a rustling noise, as of a minister's silk gown, sweeping through the very midst of the company, so closely as almost to brush against the chairs. Still, there was nothing visible. A yet stranger business was that of a ghostly servant-maid, who used to be heard in the kitchen, at deepest midnight, grinding coffee, cooking, ironing—performing, in short, all kinds of domestic labor—although no traces of anything accomplished could be detected, the next morning. Some neglected duty of her servitude—some ill-starched ministerial band—disturbed the poor damsel in her grave, and kept her at work without any wages.

But, to return from this digression. A part of my predecessor's library was stored in the garret; no unfit receptacle, indeed, for such dreary trash as comprised the greater number of volumes. The old books would have been worth nothing at an auction. In this venerable garret, however, they possessed an interest quite apart from their literary value, as heirlooms, many of which had been transmitted down through a series of consecrated hands, from the days of the mighty Puritan divines. Autographs of famous names were to be seen, in faded ink, on some of their fly-leaves; and there were marginal observations, or interpolated pages closely covered with manuscript, in illegible short-hand, perhaps concealing matter of profound truth and wisdom. The world will never be the better for it. A few of

8. George Whitefield (1714–1770), the English evangelist who converted thousands in the colonies during the Great Awakening of the 1740s. His Concord friend was Daniel Bliss, Emerson's great-grandfather and a minister in Concord, 1739–64.
9. George S. Hillard (1808–1879), Boston attorney and Hawthorne's lawyer.

the books were Latin folios, written by Catholic authors; others demolished Papistry as with a sledge-hammer, in plain English. A dissertation on the book of Job—which only Job himself could have had patience to read—filled at least a score of small, thickset quartos, at the rate of two or three volumes to a chapter. Then there was a vast folio Body of Divinity; too corpulent a body, it might be feared, to comprehend the spiritual element of religion. Volumes of this form dated back two hundred years, or more, and were generally bound in black leather, exhibiting precisely such an appearance as we should attribute to books of enchantment. Others, equally antique, were of a size proper to be carried in the large waistcoat-pockets of old times; diminutive, but as black as their bulkier brethren, and abundantly interfused with Greek and Latin quotations. These little old volumes impressed me as if they had been intended for very large ones, but had been unfortunately blighted, at an early stage of their growth.

The rain pattered upon the roof, and the sky gloomed through the dusty garret-windows; while I burrowed among these venerable books, in search of any living thought, which should burn like a coal of fire, or glow like an inextinguishable gem, beneath the dead trumpery that had long hidden it. But I found no such treasure; all was dead alike; and I could not but muse deeply and wonderingly upon the humiliating fact, that the works of man's intellect decay like those of his hands. Thought grows mouldy. What was good and nourishing food for the spirits of one generation, affords no sustenance for the next. Books of religion, however, cannot be considered a fair test of the enduring and vivacious properties of human thought; because such books so seldom really touch upon their ostensible subject, and have therefore so little business to be written at all. So long as an unlettered soul can attain to saving grace, there would seem to be no deadly error in holding theological libraries to be accumulations of, for the most part, stupendous impertinence.

Many of the books had accrued in the latter years of the last clergyman's lifetime. These threatened to be of even less interest than the elder works, a century hence, to any curious inquirer who should then rummage among them, as I was doing now. Volumes of the Liberal Preacher and Christian Examiner,[1] occasional sermons, controversial pamphlets, tracts, and other productions of a like fugitive nature, took the place of the thick and heavy volumes of past time. In a physical point of view, there was much the same difference as between a feather and a lump of lead; but, intellectually regarded, the specific gravity of old and new was about upon a par. Both, also,

---

1. A bimonthly Unitarian review (1824–69). The *Liberal Preacher* (1827–43), a monthly that published contemporary sermons.

were alike frigid. The elder books, nevertheless, seemed to have been earnestly written, and might be conceived to have possessed warmth, at some former period; although, with the lapse of time, the heated masses had cooled down even to the freezing point. The frigidity of the modern productions, on the other hand, was characteristic and inherent, and evidently had little to do with the writer's qualities of mind and heart. In fine, of this whole dusty heap of literature, I tossed aside all the sacred part, and felt myself none the less a Christian for eschewing it. There appeared no hope of either mounting to the better world on a Gothic staircase of ancient folios, or of flying thither on the wings of a modern tract.

Nothing, strange to say, retained any sap, except what had been written for the passing day and year, without the remotest pretension or idea of permanence. There were a few old newspapers, and still older almanacs, which reproduced, to my mental eye, the epochs when they had issued from the press, with a distinctness that was altogether unaccountable. It was as if I had found bits of magic looking-glass among the books, with the images of a vanished century in them. I turned my eyes towards the tattered picture, above-mentioned, and asked of the austere divine, wherefore it was that he and his brethren, after the most painful rummaging and groping into their minds, had been able to produce nothing half so real, as these newspaper scribblers and almanac-makers had thrown off, in the effervescence of a moment. The portrait responded not; so I sought an answer for myself. It is the Age itself that writes newspapers and almanacs, which therefore have a distinct purpose and meaning, at the time, and a kind of intelligible truth for all times; whereas, most other works—being written by men who, in the very act, set themselves apart from their age—are likely to possess little significance when new, and none at all, when old. Genius, indeed, melts many ages into one, and thus effects something permanent, yet still with a similarity of office to that of the more ephemeral writer. A work of genius is but the newspaper of a century, or perchance of a hundred centuries.

Lightly as I have spoken of these old books, there yet lingers with me a superstitious reverence for literature of all kinds. A bound volume has a charm in my eyes, similar to what scraps of manuscript possess, for the good Mussulman. He imagines, that those wind-wafted records are perhaps hallowed by some sacred verse; and I, that every new book, or antique one, may contain the 'Open Sesame'—the spell to disclose treasures, hidden in some unsuspected cave of Truth. Thus, it was not without sadness, that I turned away from the library of the old Manse.

Blessed was the sunshine when it came again, at the close of another stormy day, beaming from the edge of the western horizon;

while the massive firmament of clouds threw down all the gloom it could, but served only to kindle the golden light into a more brilliant glow, by the strongly contrasted shadows. Heaven smiled at the earth, so long unseen, from beneath its heavy eyelid. Tomorrow for the hill-tops and the wood-paths!

Or it might be that Ellery Channing[2] came up the avenue, to join me in a fishing-excursion on the river. Strange and happy times were those, when we cast aside all irksome forms and straight-laced habitudes, and delivered ourselves up to the free air, to live like the Indians or any less conventional race, during one bright semi-circle of the sun. Rowing our boat against the current, between wide meadows, we turned aside into the Assabeth. A more lovely stream than this, for a mile above its junction with the Concord, has never flowed on earth—nowhere, indeed, except to lave the interior regions of a poet's imagination. It is sheltered from the breeze by woods and a hill-side; so that elsewhere there might be a hurricane, and here scarcely a ripple across the shaded water. The current lingers along so gently, that the mere force of the boatman's will seems sufficient to propel his craft against it. It comes flowing softly through the midmost privacy and deepest heart of a wood, which whispers it to be quiet, while the stream whispers back again from its sedgy borders, as if river and wood were hushing one another to sleep. Yes; the river sleeps along its course, and dreams of the sky, and of the clustering foliage, amid which fall showers of broken sunlight, imparting specks of vivid cheerfulness, in contrast with the quiet depth of the prevailing tint. Of all this scene, the slumbering river has a dream-picture in its bosom. Which, after all, was the most real—the picture, or the original?—the objects palpable to our grosser senses, or their apotheosis in the stream beneath? Surely, the disembodied images stand in closer relation to the soul. But, both the original and the reflection had here an ideal charm; and, had it been a thought more wild, I could have fancied that this river had strayed forth out of the rich scenery of my companion's inner world;—only the vegetation along its banks should then have had an Oriental character.

Gentle and unobtrusive as the river is, yet the tranquil woods seem hardly satisfied to allow it passage. The trees are rooted on the very verge of the water, and dip their pendent branches into it. At one spot, there is a lofty bank, on the slope of which grow some hemlocks, declining across the stream, with outstretched arms, as if resolute to take the plunge. In other places, the banks are almost on a level with the water; so that the quiet congregation of trees set

---

2. William Ellery Channing (1815–1901), Concord poet and friend and walking companion to Emerson and Thoreau as well as Hawthorne.

their feet in the flood, and are fringed with foliage down to the surface. Cardinal-flowers kindle their spiral flames, and illuminate the
dark nooks among the shrubbery. The pond-lily grows abundantly
along the margin; that delicious flower which, as Thoreau tells me,
opens its virgin bosom to the first sunlight, and perfects its being
through the magic of that genial kiss. He has beheld beds of them
unfolding in due succession, as the sunrise stole gradually from
flower to flower; a sight not to be hoped for, unless when a poet
adjusts his inward eye to a proper focus with the outward organ.[3]
Grape-vines, here and there, twine themselves around shrub and
tree, and hang their clusters over the water, within reach of the
boatman's hand. Oftentimes, they unite two trees of alien race in an
inextricable twine, marrying the hemlock and the maple against
their will, and enriching them with a purple offspring, of which
neither is the parent. One of these ambitious parasites has climbed
into the upper branches of a tall white-pine, and is still ascending
from bough to bough, unsatisfied, till it shall crown the tree's airy
summit with a wreath of its broad foliage and a cluster of its grapes.

The winding course of the stream continually shut out the scene
behind us, and revealed as calm and lovely a one before. We glided
from depth to depth, and breathed new seclusion at every turn. The
shy kingfisher flew from the withered branch, close at hand, to
another at a distance, uttering a shrill cry of anger or alarm. Ducks—
that had been floating there, since the preceding eve—were startled
at our approach, and skimmed along the glassy river, breaking its
dark surface with a bright streak. The pickerel leaped from among
the lily-pads. The turtle, sunning itself upon a rock, or at the root of
a tree, slid suddenly into the water with a plunge. The painted
Indian, who paddled his canoe along the Assabeth, three hundred
years ago, could hardly have seen a wilder gentleness, displayed upon
its banks and reflected in its bosom, than we did. Nor could the same
Indian have prepared his noontide meal with more simplicity. We
drew up our skiff at some point where the overarching shade formed
a natural bower, and there kindled a fire with the pine-cones and
decayed branches that lay strewn plentifully around. Soon the smoke
ascended among the trees, impregnated with a savory incense, not
heavy, dull, and surfeiting, like the steam of cookery within doors,
but sprightly and piquant. The smell of our feast was akin to the
woodland odors with which it mingled; there was no sacrilege committed by our intrusion there; the sacred solitude was hospitable,
and granted us free leave to cook and eat, in the recess that was at

---

3. Cf. Emerson's *Nature*, chapter 1: "The lover of nature is he whose inward and outward
senses are still truly adjusted to each other; who has retained the spirit of infancy even
into the era of manhood."

once our kitchen and banquetting-hall. It is strange what humble offices may be performed, in a beautiful scene, without destroying its poetry. Our fire, red-gleaming among the trees, and we beside it, busied with culinary rites and spreading out our meal on a moss-grown log, all seemed in unison with the river gliding by, and the foliage rustling over us. And, what was strangest, neither did our mirth seem to disturb the propriety of the solemn woods; although the hobgoblins of the old wilderness, and the will-of-the-whisps that glimmered in the marshy places, might have come trooping to share our table-talk, and have added their shrill laughter to our merriment. It was the very spot in which to utter the extremest nonsense, or the profoundest wisdom—or that ethereal product of the mind which partakes of both, and may become one or the other, in correspondence with the faith and insight of the auditor.

So, amid sunshine and shadow, rustling leaves, and sighing waters, up-gushed our talk, like the babble of a fountain. The evanescent spray was Ellery's; and his, too, the lumps of golden thought, that lay glimmering in the fountain's bed, and brightened both our faces by the reflection. Could he have drawn out that virgin gold, and stamped it with the mint-mark that alone gives currency, the world might have had the profit, and he the fame. My mind was the richer, merely by the knowledge that it was there. But the chief profit of those wild days, to him and me, lay—not in any definite idea—not in any angular or rounded truth, which we dug out of the shapeless mass of problematical stuff—but in the freedom which we thereby won from all custom and conventionalism, and fettering influences of man on man. We were so free today, that it was impossible to be slaves again tomorrow. When we crossed the threshold of a house, or trod the thronged pavements of a city, still the leaves of the trees, that overhung the Assabeth, were whispering to us—'Be free! Be free!' Therefore, along that shady river-bank, there are spots, marked with a heap of ashes and half-consumed brands, only less sacred in my remembrance than the hearth of a household-fire.

And yet how sweet—as we floated homeward adown the golden river, at sunset—how sweet was it to return within the system of human society, not as to a dungeon and a chain, but as to a stately edifice, whence we could go forth at will into statelier simplicity! How gently, too, did the sight of the old Manse—best seen from the river, overshadowed with its willow, and all environed about with the foliage of its orchard and avenue—how gently did its gray, homely aspect rebuke the speculative extravagances of the day! It had grown sacred, in connection with the artificial life against which we inveighed; it had been a home, for many years, in spite of all; it was my home, too;—and, with these thoughts, it seemed to me that all the artifice and conventionalism of life was but an impalpable thinness upon its surface, and that the depth below was none the worse for it. Once, as we turned our boat to the bank, there was a cloud in the shape of an immensely gigantic figure of a hound, couched above the house, as if keeping guard over it. Gazing at this symbol, I prayed that the upper influences might long protect the institutions that had grown out of the heart of mankind.

If ever my readers should decide to give up civilized life, cities, houses, and whatever moral or material enormities, in addition to these, the perverted ingenuity of our race has contrived,—let it be in the early autumn. Then, Nature will love him better than at any other season, and will take him to her bosom with a more motherly tenderness. I could scarcely endure the roof of the old house above me, in those first autumnal days. How early in the summer, too, the prophecy of autumn comes!—earlier in some years than in others,— sometimes, even in the first weeks of July. There is no other feeling like what is caused by this faint, doubtful, yet real perception, if it be not rather a foreboding, of the year's decay—so blessedly sweet and sad, in the same breath.

Did I say that there was no feeling like it? Ah, but there is a half-acknowledged melancholy, like to this, when we stand in the perfected vigor of our life, and feel that Time has now given us all his flowers, and that the next work of his never idle fingers must be—to steal them, one by one, away!

I have forgotten whether the song of the cricket be not as early a token of autumn's approach, as any other;—that song, which may be called an audible stillness; for, though very loud and heard afar, yet the mind does not take note of it as a sound; so completely is its individual existence merged among the accompanying characteristics of the season. Alas, for the pleasant summer-time! In August, the grass is still verdant on the hills and in the vallies; the foliage of the trees is as dense as ever, and as green; the flowers gleam forth in richer abundance along the margin of the river, and by the stone-walls, and deep among the woods; the days, too, are as fervid now as they were a month ago;—and yet, in every breath of wind, and in every beam of sunshine, we hear the whispered farewell, and behold the parting smile, of a dear friend. There is a coolness amid all the heat; a mildness in the blazing noon. Not a breeze can stir, but it thrills us with the breath of autumn. A pensive glory is seen in the far, golden gleams, among the shadows of the trees. The flowers— even the brightest of them, and they are the most gorgeous of the year—have this gentle sadness wedded to their pomp, and typify the character of the delicious time, each within itself. The brilliant cardinal-flower has never seemed gay to me.

Still later in the season, Nature's tenderness waxes stronger. It is impossible not to be fond of our Mother now; for she is so fond of us! At other periods, she does not make this impression on me, or only at rare intervals; but, in these genial days of autumn, when she has perfected her harvests, and accomplished every needful thing that was given her to do, then she overflows with a blessed superfluity of love. She has leisure to caress her children now.

It is good to be alive, at such times. Thank heaven for breath!—yes, for mere breath!—when it is made up of a heavenly breeze like this! It comes with a real kiss upon our cheeks; it would linger fondly around us, if it might; but, since it must be gone, it embraces us with its whole kindly heart, and passes onward, to embrace likewise the next thing that it meets. A blessing is flung abroad, and scattered far and wide over the earth, to be gathered up by all who choose. I recline upon the still unwithered grass, and whisper to myself:—'Oh, perfect day!—Oh, beautiful world!—Oh, beneficent God!' And it is the promise of a blissful Eternity; for our Creator would never have made such lovely days, and have given us the deep hearts to enjoy them, above and beyond all thought, unless we were meant to be immortal. This sunshine is the golden pledge thereof. It beams through the gates of Paradise, and shows us glimpses far inward.

By-and-by—in a little time—the outward world puts on a drear austerity. On some October morning, there is a heavy hoar-frost on the grass, and along the tops of the fences; and, at sunrise, the leaves fall from the trees of our avenue without a breath of wind, quietly descending by their own weight. All summer long, they have murmured like the noise of waters; they have roared loudly, while the branches were wrestling with the thunder-gust; they have made music, both glad and solemn; they have attuned my thoughts by their quiet sound, as I paced to-and-fro beneath the arch of intermingling boughs. Now, they can only rustle under my feet. Henceforth, the gray parsonage begins to assume a larger importance, and draws to its fireside—for the abomination of the air-tight stove is reserved till wintry weather—draws closer and closer to its fireside the vagrant impulses, that had gone wandering about, through the summer.

When summer was dead and buried, the old Manse became as lonely as a hermitage. Not that ever—in my time, at least—it had been thronged with company; but, at no rare intervals, we welcomed some friend out of the dusty glare and tumult of the world, and rejoiced to share with him the transparent obscurity that was flung over us. In one respect, our precincts were like the Enchanted Ground,[4] through which the pilgrim travelled on his way to the Celestial City. The guests, each and all, felt a slumberous influence upon them; they fell asleep in chairs, or took a more deliberate siesta on the sofa, or were seen stretched among the shadows of the

4. See n. 9, p. 179.

orchard, looking up dreamily through the boughs. They could not have paid a more acceptable compliment to my abode, nor to my own qualities as a host. I held it as a proof, that they left their cares behind them, as they passed between the stone gate-posts, at the entrance of our avenue; and that the so powerful opiate was the abundance of peace and quiet, within and all around us. Others could give them pleasure and amusement, or instruction—these could be picked up anywhere—but it was for me to give them rest— rest, in a life of trouble. What better could be done for those weary and world-worn spirits?—for him, whose career of perpetual action was impeded and harassed by the rarest of his powers, and the richest of his acquirements?—for another, who had thrown his ardent heart, from earliest youth, into the strife of politics, and now, perchance, began to suspect that one lifetime is too brief for the accomplishment of any lofty aim?—for her,[5] on whose feminine nature had been imposed the heavy gift of intellectual power, such as a strong man might have staggered under, and with it the necessity to act upon the world?—in a word, not to multiply instances, what better could be done for anybody, who came within our magic circle, than to throw the spell of a tranquil spirit over him? And when it had wrought its full effect, then we dismissed him, with but misty reminiscences, as if he had been dreaming of us.

Were I to adopt a pet idea, as so many people do, and fondle it in my embraces to the exclusion of all others, it would be, that the great want which mankind labors under, at this present period, is— sleep! The world should recline its vast head on the first convenient pillow, and take an age-long nap. It has gone distracted, through a morbid activity, and, while preternaturally wide-awake, is nevertheless tormented by visions, that seem real to it now, but would assume their true aspect and character, were all things once set right by an interval of sound repose. This is the only method of getting rid of old delusions, and avoiding new ones—of regenerating our race, so that it might in due time awake, as an infant out of dewy slumber—of restoring to us the simple perception of what is right, and the single-hearted desire to achieve it; both of which have long been lost, in consequence of this weary activity of brain, and torpor or passion of the heart, that now afflicts the universe. Stimulants, the only mode of treatment hitherto attempted, cannot quell the disease; they do but heighten the delirium.

---

5. Margaret Fuller (1810–1850), first editor of the Transcendentalist *Dial* and an eminent New England intellectual. She was one of the Hawthornes' earliest visitors at the Old Manse. "For him": Horatio Bridge (1806–1893), perhaps Hawthorne's closest friend from Bowdoin days. "For another": Franklin Pierce (1804–1869), another Bowdoin classmate, later fourteenth president of the United States.

Let not the above paragraph ever be quoted against the author; for, though tinctured with its modicum of truth, it is the result and expression of what he knew, while he was writing, to be but a distorted survey of the state and prospects of mankind. There were circumstances around me, which made it difficult to view the world precisely as it exists; for, serene and sober as was the old Manse, it was necessary to go but a little way beyond its threshold, before meeting with stranger moral shapes of men than might have been encountered elsewhere, in a circuit of a thousand miles.

These hobgoblins of flesh and blood were attracted thither by the wide-spreading influence of a great original Thinker, who had his earthly abode at the opposite extremity of our village.[6] His mind acted upon other minds, of a certain constitution, with wonderful magnetism, and drew many men upon long pilgrimages, to speak with him face to face. Young visionaries—to whom just so much of insight had been imparted, as to make life all a labyrinth around them—came to seek the clue that should guide them out of their self-involved bewilderment. Gray-headed theorists—whose systems, at first air, had finally imprisoned them in an iron frame work—travelled painfully to his door, not to ask deliverance, but to invite this free spirit into their own thraldom. People that had lighted on a new thought, or a thought that they fancied new, came to Emerson, as the finder of a glittering gem hastens to a lapidary, to ascertain its quality and value. Uncertain, troubled, earnest wanderers, through the midnight of the moral world, beheld his intellectual fire, as a beacon burning on a hill-top, and, climbing the difficult ascent, looked forth into the surrounding obscurity, more hopefully than hitherto. The light revealed objects unseen before—mountains, gleaming lakes, glimpses of a creation among the chaos—but also, as was unavoidable, it attracted bats and owls, and the whole host of night-birds, which flapped their dusky wings against the gazer's eyes, and sometimes were mistaken for fowls of angelic feather. Such delusions always hover nigh, whenever a beacon-fire of truth is kindled.

For myself, there had been epochs of my life, when I, too, might have asked of this prophet the master-word, that should solve me the riddle of the universe; but now, being happy, I felt as if there were no question to be put, and therefore admired Emerson as a poet of deep beauty and austere tenderness, but sought nothing from him as a philosopher. It was good, nevertheless, to meet him in the wood-paths, or sometimes in our avenue, with that pure, intellectual

6. Hawthorne pokes fun at reformers and philanthropists who were attracted to Concord by the presence of Emerson. Emerson's house was two miles away, beyond the center of Concord.

gleam diffused about his presence, like the garment of a shining-
one; and he so quiet, so simple, so without pretension, encountering
each man alive as if expecting to receive more than he could impart.
And, in truth, the heart of many an ordinary man had, perchance,
inscriptions which he could not read. But it was impossible to dwell
in his vicinity, without inhaling, more or less, the mountain-
atmosphere of his lofty thought, which, in the brains of some people,
wrought a singular giddiness—new truth being as heady as new
wine. Never was a poor little country village infested with such a
variety of queer, strangely dressed, oddly behaved mortals, most of
whom took upon themselves to be important agents of the world's
destiny, yet were simply bores of a very intense water. Such, I imagine, is the invariable character of persons who crowd so closely about
an original thinker, as to draw in his unuttered breath, and thus
become imbued with a false originality. This triteness of novelty is
enough to make any man, of common sense, blaspheme at all ideas
of less than a century's standing; and pray that the world may be
petrified and rendered immovable, in precisely the worst moral and
physical state that it ever yet arrived at, rather than be benefited by
such schemes of such philosophers.

And now, I begin to feel—and perhaps should have sooner felt—
that we have talked enough of the old Manse. Mine honored reader,
it may be, will vilify the poor author as an egotist, for babbling
through so many pages about a moss-grown country parsonage, and
his life within its walls, and on the river, and in the woods,—and the
influences that wrought upon him, from all these sources. My conscience, however, does not reproach me with betraying anything too
sacredly individual to be revealed by a human spirit, to its brother
or sister spirit. How narrow—how shallow and scanty too—is the
stream of thought that has been flowing from my pen, compared
with the broad tide of dim emotions, ideas, and associations, which
swell around me from that portion of my existence! How little have
I told!—and, of that little, how almost nothing is even tinctured
with any quality that makes it exclusively my own! Has the reader
gone wandering, hand in hand with me, through the inner passages
of my being, and have we groped together into all its chambers, and
examined their treasures or their rubbish? Not so. We have been
standing on the green sward, but just within the cavern's mouth,
where the common sunshine is free to penetrate, and where every
footstep is therefore free to come. I have appealed to no sentiment
or sensibilities, save such as are diffused among us all. So far as I
am a man of really individual attributes, I veil my face; nor am I, nor
have ever been, one of those supremely hospitable people, who serve
up their own hearts delicately fried, with brain-sauce, as a tidbit for
their beloved public.

Glancing back over what I have written, it seems but the scattered reminiscences of a single summer. In fairy-land, there is no measurement of time; and, in a spot so sheltered from the turmoil of life's ocean, three years hastened away with a noiseless flight, as the breezy sunshine chases the cloud-shadows across the depths of a still valley. Now came hints, growing more and more distinct, that the owner of the old house was pining for his native air. Carpenters next appeared, making a tremendous racket among the outbuildings, strewing the green grass with pine-shavings and chips of chestnut joists, and vexing the whole antiquity of the place with their discordant renovations. Soon, moreover, they divested our abode of the veil of woodbine, which had crept over a large portion of its southern face. All the aged mosses were cleaned unsparingly away; and there were horrible whispers about brushing up the external walls with a coat of paint—a purpose as little to my taste, as might be that of rouging the venerable cheeks of one's grandmother. But the hand that renovates is always more sacrilegious than that which destroys. In fine, we gathered up our household goods, drank a farewell cup of tea in our pleasant little breakfast-room—delicately fragrant tea, an unpurchaseable luxury, one of the many angel-gifts that had fallen like dew upon us—and passed forth between the tall stone gate-posts, as uncertain as the wandering Arabs where our tent might next be pitched. Providence took me by the hand, and—an oddity of dispensation which, I trust, there is no irreverence in smiling at—has led me, as the newspapers announce while I am writing, from the Old Manse into a Custom-House![7] As a storyteller, I have often contrived strange vicissitudes for my imaginary personages, but none like this.

The treasure of intellectual gold, which I hoped to find in our secluded dwelling, had never come to light. No profound treatise of ethics—no philosophic history—no novel, even, that could stand, unsupported, on its edges. All that I had to show, as a man of letters, were these few tales and essays, which had blossomed out like flowers in the calm summer of my heart and mind. Save editing (an easy task) the journal of my friend of many years, the African Cruiser,[8] I had done nothing else. With these idle weeds and withering blossoms, I have intermixed some that were produced long ago—old, faded things, reminding me of flowers pressed between the leaves of a book—and now offer the bouquet, such as it is, to any

---

7. The Salem Custom-House, where Hawthorne was surveyor and inspector of revenue from 1846 to 1849, before writing *The Scarlet Letter*.
8. In 1845, Hawthorne edited Horatio Bridge's *Journal of an African Cruiser* for Wiley and Putnam of New York, the publisher of *Mosses from an Old Manse*. Hawthorne's name appeared on the title page of the *Journal* as editor. He is quietly puffing his and his friend's recent book here.

whom it may please. These fitful sketches, with so little of external life about them, yet claiming no profundity of purpose,—so reserved, even while they sometimes seem so frank,—often but half in earnest, and, never, even when most so, expressing satisfactorily the thoughts which they profess to image—such trifles, I truly feel, afford no solid basis for a literary reputation. Nevertheless, the public—if my limited number of readers, whom I venture to regard rather as a circle of friends, may be termed a public—will receive them the more kindly, as the last offering, the last collection of this nature, which it is my purpose ever to put forth. Unless I could do better, I have done enough in this kind. For myself, the book will always retain one charm, as reminding me of the river, with it delightful solitudes, and of the avenue, the garden, and the orchard, and especially the dear old Manse, with the little study on its western side, and the sunshine glimmering through the willow-branches while I wrote.

Let the reader, if he will do me so much honor, imagine himself my guest, and that, having seen whatever may be worthy of notice, within and about the old Manse, he has finally been ushered into my study. There, after seating him in an antique elbow-chair, an heirloom of the house, I take forth a roll of manuscript, and intreat his attention to the following tales:—an act of personal inhospitality, however, which I never was guilty of, nor ever will be, even to my worst enemy.

Preface to the 1851 Edition of *Twice-told Tales*[†]

The Author of Twice-told Tales has a claim to one distinction, which, as none of his literary brethren will care about disputing it with him, he need not be afraid to mention. He was, for a good many years, the obscurest man of letters in America.

These stories were published in Magazines and Annuals,[1] extending over a period of ten or twelve years, and comprising the whole of the writer's young manhood, without making (so far as he has ever been aware) the slightest impression on the Public. One or two among them,—The Rill from the Town-Pump, in perhaps a greater degree than any other,—had a pretty wide newspaper circulation; as for the rest, he has no grounds for supposing, that, on their first appearance, they met with the good or evil fortune to be read by any body. Throughout the time above specified, he had no incitement to

---

† First published with the 3rd edition of *Twice-told Tales*, in 1851.
1. Especially in the annual gift-book *The Token*, in which Hawthorne published much of his fiction before 1838.

literary effort in a reasonable prospect of reputation or profit; nothing but the pleasure itself of composition—an enjoyment not at all amiss in its way, and perhaps essential to the merit of the work in hand, but which, in the long run, will hardly keep the chill out of a writer's heart, or the numbness out of his fingers. To this total lack of sympathy, at the age when his mind would naturally have been most effervescent, the Public owe it, (and it is certainly an effect not to be regretted, on either part,) that the Author can show nothing for the thought and industry of that portion of his life, save the forty sketches, or thereabouts, included in these volumes.

Much more, indeed, he wrote; and some very small part of it might yet be rummaged out, (but it would not be worth the trouble,) among the dingy pages of fifteen-or-twenty-year-old periodicals, or within the shabby morocco covers of faded Souvenirs.[2] The remainder of the works, alluded to, had a very brief existence, but, on the score of brilliancy, enjoyed a fate vastly superior to that of their brotherhood, which succeeded in getting through the press. In a word, the Author burned them without mercy or remorse, and, moreover, without any subsequent regret, and had more than one occasion to marvel that such very dull stuff, as he knew his condemned manuscripts to be, should yet have possessed inflammability enough to set the chimney on fire![3]

After a long while, the first collected volume of the Tales was published. By this time, if the Author had ever been greatly tormented by literary ambition, (which he does not remember or believe to have been the case,) it must have perished, beyond resuscitation, in the dearth of nutriment. This was fortunate; for the success of the volume was not such as would have gratified a craving desire for notoriety. A moderate edition was "got rid of" (to use the Publisher's very significant phrase) within a reasonable time, but apparently without rendering the writer or his productions much more generally known than before. The great bulk of the reading Public probably ignored the book altogether. A few persons read it, and liked it better than it deserved. At an interval of three or four years, the second volume was published, and encountered much the same sort of kindly, but calm, and very limited reception. The circulation of the two volumes was chiefly confined to New England; nor was it until long after this period, if it even yet be the case, that the Author could regard him-

2. By 1851, old volumes of *The Token* were "faded Souvenirs" with "shabby morocco covers."
3. Hawthorne burned some of his early manuscripts around 1830. There is no clear evidence that he burned so "much" as he implies here, but he refers to the event several times, suggesting that it was a momentous occasion for him. He presents a lively fictional version of the incident in "The Devil in Manuscript" (1835).

self as addressing the American Public, or, indeed, any Public at all. He was merely writing to his known or unknown friends.

As he glances over these long forgotten pages, and considers his way of life, while composing them, the Author can very clearly discern why all this was so. After so many sober years, he would have reason to be ashamed if he could not criticise his own work as fairly as another man's; and, though it is little his business, and perhaps still less his interest, he can hardly resist a temptation to achieve something of the sort. If writers were allowed to do so, and would perform the task with perfect sincerity and unreserve, their opinions of their own productions would often be more valuable and instructive than the works themselves.

At all events, there can be no harm in the Author's remarking, that he rather wonders how the TWICE-TOLD TALES should have gained what vogue they did, than that it was so little and so gradual. They have the pale tint of flowers that blossomed in too retired a shade—the coolness of a meditative habit, which diffuses itself through the feeling and observation of every sketch. Instead of passion, there is sentiment; and, even in what purport to be pictures of actual life, we have allegory, not always so warmly dressed in its habiliments of flesh and blood, as to be taken into the reader's mind without a shiver. Whether from lack of power, or an unconquerable reserve, the Author's touches have often an effect of tameness; the merriest man can hardly contrive to laugh at his broadest humor; the tenderest woman, one would suppose, will hardly shed warm tears at his deepest pathos. The book, if you would see any thing in it, requires to be read in the clear, brown, twilight atmosphere in which it was written; if opened in the sunshine, it is apt to look exceedingly like a volume of blank pages.

With the foregoing characteristics, proper to the productions of a person in retirement, (which happened to be the Author's category at the time,) the book is devoid of others that we should quite as naturally look for. The sketches are not, it is hardly necessary to say, profound; but it is rather more remarkable that they so seldom, if ever, show any design on the writer's part to make them so. They have none of the abstruseness of idea, or obscurity of expression, which mark the written communications of a solitary mind with itself. They never need translation. It is, in fact, the style of a man of society. Every sentence, so far as it embodies thought or sensibility, may be understood and felt by any body, who will give himself the trouble to read it, and will take up the book in a proper mood.

This statement of apparently opposite peculiarities leads us to a perception of what the sketches truly are. They are not the talk of a secluded man with his own mind and heart, (had it been so, they

could hardly have failed to be more deeply and permanently valuable,) but his attempts, and very imperfectly successful ones, to open
an intercourse with the world.

The Author would regret to be understood as speaking sourly or
querulously of the slight mark, made by his earlier literary efforts, on
the Public at large. It is so far the contrary, that he has been moved to
write this Preface, chiefly as affording him an opportunity to express
how much enjoyment he has owed to these volumes, both before and
since their publication. They are the memorials of very tranquil and
not unhappy years. They failed, it is true—nor could it have been
otherwise—in winning an extensive popularity. Occasionally, however, when he deemed them entirely forgotten, a paragraph or an
article, from a native or foreign critic, would gratify his instincts of
authorship with unexpected praise,—too generous praise, indeed,
and too little alloyed with censure, which, therefore, he learned the
better to inflict upon himself. And, by-the-by, it is a very suspicious
symptom of a deficiency of the popular element in a book, when it
calls forth no harsh criticism. This has been particularly the fortune
of the TWICE-TOLD TALES. They made no enemies, and were so little
known and talked about, that those who read, and chanced to like
them, were apt to conceive the sort of kindness for the book, which
a person naturally feels for a discovery of his own.

This kindly feeling, (in some cases, at least,) extended to the
Author, who, on the internal evidence of his sketches, came to be
regarded as a mild, shy, gentle, melancholic, exceedingly sensitive,
and not very forcible man, hiding his blushes under an assumed
name, the quaintness of which was supposed, somehow or other, to
symbolize his personal and literary traits. He is by no means certain, that some of his subsequent productions have not been influenced and modified by a natural desire to fill up so amiable an
outline, and to act in consonance with the character assigned to him;
nor, even now, could he forfeit it without a few tears of tender sensibility. To conclude, however,—these volumes have opened the way
to most agreeable associations, and to the formation of imperishable
friendships; and there are many golden threads, interwoven with his
present happiness, which he can follow up more or less directly,
until he finds their commencement here; so that his pleasant pathway among realities seems to proceed out of the Dream-Land of his
youth, and to be bordered with just enough of its shadowy foliage to
shelter him from the heat of the day. He is therefore satisfied with
what the TWICE-TOLD TALES have done for him, and feels it to be far
better than fame.

LENOX, January 11, 1851.

Preface to *The Snow-Image*[†]

TO HORATIO BRIDGE, ESQ., U.S.N[1]

MY DEAR BRIDGE:

Some of the more crabbed of my critics, I understand, have pronounced your friend egotistical, indiscreet, and even impertinent, on account of the Prefaces and Introductions with which, on several occasions, he has seen fit to pave the reader's way into the interior edifice of a book. In the justice of this censure I do not exactly concur, for the reasons, on the one hand, that the public generally has negatived the idea of undue freedom on the author's part, by evincing, it seems to me, rather more interest in these aforesaid Introductions than in the stories which followed,—and that, on the other hand, with whatever appearance of confidential intimacy, I have been especially careful to make no disclosures respecting myself which the most indifferent observer might not have been acquainted with, and which I was not perfectly willing that my worst enemy should know. I might further justify myself, on the plea that, ever since my youth, I have been addressing a very limited circle of friendly readers, without much danger of being overheard by the public at large; and that the habits thus acquired might pardonably continue, although strangers may have begun to mingle with my audience.

But the charge, I am bold to say, is not a reasonable one, in any view which we can fairly take of it. There is no harm, but, on the contrary, good, in arraying some of the ordinary facts of life in a slightly idealized and artistic guise. I have taken facts which relate to myself, because they chance to be nearest at hand, and likewise are my own property. And, as for egotism, a person, who has been burrowing, to his utmost ability, into the depths of our common nature, for the purposes of psychological romance,—and who pursues his researches in that dusky region, as he needs must, as well by the tact of sympathy as by the light of observation,—will smile at incurring such an imputation in virtue of a little preliminary talk about his external habits, his abode, his casual associates, and other matters entirely upon the surface. These things hide the man, instead of displaying him. You must make quite another kind of inquest, and look through the whole range of his fictitious characters, good and evil, in order to detect any of his essential traits.

[†] First published with *The Snow-Image, and Other Twice-told Tales*, in 1852.

1. Horatio Bridge (1806–1893) was Hawthorne's lifelong friend from the time they were classmates at Bowdoin together in the 1820s. In 1837, without Hawthorne's knowledge, Bridge underwrote the publication of *Twice-told Tales* by guaranteeing the publisher against loss. Bridge in effect launched Hawthorne on his career. Bridge became an officer in the U.S. Navy in 1838.

Be all this as it may, there can be no question as to the propriety of my inscribing this volume of earlier and later sketches[2] to you, and pausing here, a few moments, to speak of them, as friend speaks to friend; still being cautious, however, that the public and the critics shall overhear nothing which we care about concealing. On you, if on no other person, I am entitled to rely, to sustain the position of my Dedicatee. If anybody is responsible for my being at this day an author, it is yourself. I know not whence your faith came; but, while we were lads together at a country college,—gathering blue-berries, in study-hours, under those tall academic pines; or watching the great logs, as they tumbled along the current of the Androscoggin; or shooting pigeons and gray squirrels in the woods; or bat-fowling[3] in the summer twilight; or catching trouts in that shadowy little stream which, I suppose, is still wandering river-ward through the forest,— though you and I will never cast a line in it again,—two idle lads, in short (as we need not fear to acknowledge now), doing a hundred things that the Faculty never heard of, or else it had been the worse for us,—still it was your prognostic of your friend's destiny, that he was to be a writer of fiction.

And a fiction-monger, in due season, he became. But, was there ever such a weary delay in obtaining the slightest recognition from the public, as in my case? I sat down by the wayside of life, like a man under enchantment, and a shrubbery sprung up around me, and the bushes grew to be saplings, and the saplings became trees, until no exit appeared possible, through the entangling depths of my obscurity. And there, perhaps, I should be sitting at this moment, with the moss on the imprisoning tree-trunks, and the yellow leaves of more than a score of autumns piled above me, if it had not been for you. For it was through your interposition,—and that, moreover, unknown to himself,—that your early friend was brought before the public, somewhat more prominently than theretofore, in the first volume of Twice-told Tales. Not a publisher in America, I presume, would have thought well enough of my forgotten or never noticed stories, to risk the expense of print and paper; nor do I say this with any purpose of casting odium on the respectable fraternity of book-sellers, for their blindness to my wonderful merit. To confess the truth, I doubted of the public recognition quite as much as they could do. So much the more generous was your confidence; and knowing, as I do, that it was founded on old friendship rather than cold criticism, I value it only the more for that.

So, now, when I turn back upon my path, lighted by a transitory gleam of public favor, to pick up a few articles which were left out of

---

2. *The Snow-Image* contains both early work previously uncollected, such as "My Kinsman, Major Molineux" (1831), and recent tales and sketches written after *Mosses from an Old Manse*, such as "Ethan Brand" (1849).
3. Trapping bats. The Androscoggin is a river in Maine and New Hampshire where lumber comes down from the north woods.

my former collections, I take pleasure in making them the memorial of our very long and unbroken connection. Some of these sketches were among the earliest that I wrote, and, after lying for years in manuscript, they at last skulked into the Annuals or Magazines, and have hidden themselves there ever since. Others were the productions of a later period; others, again, were written recently. The comparison of these various trifles—the indices of intellectual condition at far separated epochs—affects me with a singular complexity of regrets. I am disposed to quarrel with the earlier sketches, both because a mature judgment discerns so many faults, and still more because they come so nearly up to the standard of the best that I can achieve now. The ripened autumnal fruit tastes but little better than the early windfalls. It would, indeed, be mortifying to believe that the summer-time of life has passed away, without any greater progress and improvement than is indicated here. But,—at least, so I would fain hope,—these things are scarcely to be depended upon, as measures of the intellectual and moral man. In youth, men are apt to write more wisely than they really know or feel; and the remainder of life may be not idly spent in realizing and convincing themselves of the wisdom which they uttered long ago. The truth that was only in the fancy then may have since become a substance in the mind and heart.

I have nothing further, I think, to say; unless it be that the public need not dread my again trespassing on its kindness, with any more of these musty and mouse-nibbled leaves of old periodicals, trans-formed, by the magic arts of my friendly publishers, into a new book. These are the last. Or, if a few still remain, they are either such as no paternal partiality could induce the author to think worth preserv-ing, or else they have got into some very dark and dusty hiding-place, quite out of my own remembrance and whence no researches can avail to unearth them. So there let them rest.

Very sincerely yours,

N.H

Lenox, November 1st, 1851.

LETTERS

Hawthorne's letters, now published as a complete collection in the Centenary Edition, should change the public image of the man and writer. The few letters I have selected constitute but a small sample of the many hundreds he wrote. Yet even in these few one can sense the variety in his personality. By turns he is whimsical, sententious, high-spirited, low-spirited, businesslike, impractical, modest, and self-promoting. He was adept at tactfully changing his manner of address to suit a particular occasion. We may notice, for example, how differently he relates to Longfellow in three letters included here, or how guarded yet gracious he is to Margaret Fuller in explaining his wishes to protect his wife from too many guests. Not many of his letters suggest that he is preoccupied with his own fiction; generally he preferred to let his fictive imagination work its will in a sphere apart. Only in the two letters to Evert Duyckinck concerning "The Old Manse" does he dwell on his plans or his accomplishments. Yet the letters as a group reveal something of Hawthorne the artist even when he is not posing as such. They reflect his moral sentiments—his distrust of isolation, his fondness for privacy, his idealized conception of married love. They give some indication of the growth and change of his sensibility during his career as a writer of tales and sketches. Above all, they register his agility and clarity of mind. He takes the measure of his correspondents, and responds to them generously, but with controlled intelligence.

The texts of the letters are from volumes 15, 16, and 17 of the Centenary Edition. I am extremely grateful to Neal Smith and Thomas Woodson of the Center for Textual Studies for allowing me to read many of the letters well before publication and to draw on Professor Woodson's research in my notes.

To Elizabeth C. Hathorne, Raymond†

Salem. March 13th. 1821

Dear Mother,

* * * I am quite reconciled to going to College, since I am to spend the Vacations with you. Yet four years of the best part of my Life is a great deal to throw away. I have not yet concluded what profession I shall have. The being a Minister is of course out of the Question. I should not think that even you could desire me to choose so dull a way of life. Oh no Mother, I was not born to vegetate forever in one place, and to live and die as calm and tranquil as—A Puddle of Water. As to Lawyers there are so many of them already that one half of them (upon a moderate calculation) are in a state of actual starvation. A Physician then seems to be "Hobson's Choice."[1] but yet I should not like to live by the diseases and Infirmities of my fellow

---

† Reprinted by permission of The Ohio State University Press. Mrs. Hathorne and her daughter Elizabeth were living in a family house in Raymond, a village in extreme southern Maine, while Nathaniel and his sister Louisa stayed in their uncle Robert Manning's house in Salem and Nathaniel prepared for Bowdoin College.

1. A choice one must make, as there is no real alternative.

Creatures. And it would weigh very heavily on my Conscience if in the course of my practice, I should chance to send any unlucky Patient "Ad inferum," which being interpreted, is "to the realms below." Oh that I was rich enough to live without a profession. What do you think of my becoming an Author, and relying for support upon my pen. Indeed I think the illegibility of my handwriting is very authorlike. How proud you would feel to see my works praised by the reviewers, as equal to proudest productions of the scribbling sons of John Bull. But Authors are always poor Devils, and therefore Satan may take them. I am in the same predicament as the honest gentleman in Espriella's Letters.

> "I am an Englishman and naked I
>   stand here
> A musing in my mind what
>   garment I shall wear"[2]

But as the Mail closes soon I must stop the career of my pen. I will only inform you that I now write no Poetry, or anything else. I hope that either Elizabeth[3] or you will write to me next week.

I remain,
Your Affectionate Son,
Nath Hathorne[4]

Do not show this Letter

To H. W. Longfellow, Cambridge[†]

Salem, June 4th. 1837.

Dear Sir,

Not to burthen you with my correspondence, I have delayed a rejoinder to your very kind and cordial letter, until now.[1] It gratifies me to find that you have occasionally felt an interest in my situation; but your quotation from Jean Paul, about the 'lark-nest,' makes

2. Hawthorne quotes a bit inaccurately from Robert Southey, *Letters from England: by Don Manuel Alvarez Espriella* (1807), letter 49.
3. Elizabeth Manning Hathorne, Nathaniel's older sister.
4. Hawthorne added the "w" in the spelling of his name not long after he graduated from college.
† Reprinted by permission of The Ohio State University Press. After several years in Europe and a stint of teaching at Bowdoin, Longfellow moved to Cambridge in 1836 to take up duties as professor of foreign languages at Harvard.
1. Longfellow wrote Hawthorne a generous letter on March 9, 1837, after Hawthorne had written Longfellow to let him know that he was having a copy of *Twice-told Tales* sent to him.

me smile.[2] You would have been much nearer the truth, if you had pictured me as dwelling in an owl's nest; for mine is about as dismal, and, like the owl, I seldom venture abroad till after dusk. By some witchcraft or other—for I really cannot assign any reasonable why and wherefore—I have been carried apart from the main current of life, and find it impossible to get back again. Since we last met—which, I remember, was in Sawtell's[3] room, where you read a farewell poem to the relics of the class—ever since that time, I have secluded myself from society; and yet I never meant any such thing, nor dreamed what sort of life I was going to lead. I have made a captive of myself and put me into a dungeon; and now I cannot find the key to let myself out—and if the door were open, I should be almost afraid to come out. You tell me that you have met with troubles and changes. I know not what they may have been; but I can assure you that trouble is the next best thing to enjoyment, and that there is no fate in this world so horrible as to have no share in either its joys or sorrows. For the last ten years, I have not lived, but only dreamed about living. It may be true that there have been some unsubstantial pleasures here in the shade, which I should have missed in the sunshine; but you cannot conceive how utterly devoid of satisfaction all my retrospects are. I have laid up no treasure of pleasant remembrances, against old age; but there is some comfort in thinking that my future years can hardly fail to be more varied, and therefore more tolerable, than the past.

You give me more credit than I deserve, in supposing that I have led a studious life. I have, indeed, turned over a good many books, but in so desultory a way that it cannot be called study, nor has it left me the fruits of study. As to my literary efforts, I do not think much of them—neither is it worth while to be ashamed of them. They would have been better, I trust, if written under more favorable circumstances. I have had no external excitement—no consciousness that the public would like what I wrote, nor much hope nor a very passionate desire that they should do so. Nevertheless, having nothing else to be ambitious of, I have felt considerably interested in literature; and if my writings had made any decided impression, I should probably have been stimulated to greater exertions; but there has been no warmth of approbation, so that I have always written

2. In his letter of March 9, Longfellow wrote, "I have always thought of you, as of one who had realized Jean Paul's idea of happiness.—'to nestle yourself so snugly . . . that in looking out from your warm lark-nest you likewise can discover no wolf-dens, charnel-houses or thunder-rods, but only blades and ears, every one of which for the nest-bird is a tree, and a parasol and an umbrella.' Is it so? For your sake I hope it may be" (quoted in CE 15: 253). Jean Paul Friedrich Richter (1763–1825) was a popular and prolific German novelist and a favorite of Longfellow's. Longfellow quotes from Jean Paul's preface to *The Life of Quintus Fixlein* (1795), in a modified version of Carlyle's translation.
3. Cullen Sawtelle (1805–1887), classmate of Hawthorne's and Longfellow's at Bowdoin College, later a Maine lawyer and congressman.

with benumbed fingers. I have another great difficulty, in the lack of materials; for I have seen so little of the world, that I have nothing but thin air to concoct my stories of, and it is not easy to give a life-like semblance to such shadowy stuff. Sometimes, through a peep-hole, I have caught a glimpse of the real world; and the two or three articles, in which I have portrayed such glimpses, please me better than the others.

I have now, or soon shall have, one sharp spur to exertion, which I lacked at an earlier period; for I see little prospect but that I must scribble for a living. But this troubles me much less than you would suppose. I can turn my pen to all sorts of drudgery, such as children's books &c, and by and bye, I shall get some editorship that will answer my purpose. Frank Pierce, who was with us at college, offered me his influence to obtain an office in the Exploring Expedition;[4] but I believe that he was mistaken in supposing that a vacancy existed. If such a post were attainable, I should certainly accept it; for, though fixed so long to one spot, I have always had a desire to run round the world.

The copy of my Tales was sent to Mr. Owen's, the book-seller's in Cambridge.[5] I am glad to find that you had read and liked some of the stories. To be sure, you could not well help flattering me a little, but I value your praise too highly not to have faith in its sincerity. When I last heard from the publishers—which was not very recently—the book was doing pretty well. Six or seven hundred copies had been sold. I suppose, however, these awful times have now stopped the sale.[6]

I intend, in a week or two, to come out of my owl's nest, and not return to it till late in the summer—employing the interval in making a tour somewhere in New-England.[7] You, who have the dust of distant countries on your "sandal-shoon,"[8] cannot imagine how much enjoyment I shall have in this little excursion. Whenever I get abroad, I feel just as young as I did ten years ago. What a letter am I inflicting on you! I trust you will answer it.

Yours sincerely,
Nath Hawthorne

---

4. The United States Exploring Expedition of 1838–42 to the South Seas and Antarctica. Along with Horatio Bridge, Franklin Pierce (1804–1867), Hawthorne's friend and later fourteenth president of the United States, tried without success to have Hawthorne appointed historian of the expedition.
5. *Twice-told Tales* was published on March 6, 1837. John Owen (1805–1872) was a Cambridge bookseller and one of Longfellow's publishers.
6. The economic depression of 1837.
7. Hawthorne visited Horatio Bridge in Augusta, Maine, in July and August—see the lively journal of the trip in *The American Notebooks*, ed. Claude M. Simpson, CE 8:32–70.
8. *Hamlet* 4.5.26.

To H. W. Longfellow, Cambridge[†]

Salem, June 19th. 1837

Dear Longfellow,

I have to-day received, and read with huge delight, your review of 'Hawthorne's Twice-told Tales.'[1] I frankly own that I was not without hopes that you would do this kind office for the book; though I could not have anticipated how very kindly it would be done. Whether or no the public will agree to the praise which you bestow on me, there are at least five persons who think you the most sagacious critic on earth—viz. my mother and two sisters, my old maiden aunt,[2] and finally, the sturdiest believer of the whole five, my own self. If I doubt the sincerity and correctness of any of my critics, it shall be of those who censure me. Hard would be the lot of a poor scribbler, if he may not have this privilege.

I intend to set out on my travels early next week—probably on Monday or Tuesday—and as I must come first to Boston, I will, if possible, ride out to Cambridge; for I am anxious to hold a talk.

Very sincerely yours,
Nath. Hawthorne.

To H. W. Longfellow, Cambridge[‡]

Salem, Jan[y] 12th. 1839

My dear Longfellow,

I was nowise to blame for going down the steps of the Tremont, almost at the moment that you were coming up; inasmuch as I did not receive your letter, appointing the rendezvous, till I reached Salem that evening.[1] Those little devils in your hollow teeth had made you oblivious,[2] and caused you to carry the epistle in your pocket at least a week, before putting it into the Post-Office. But never mind; for, please God, we will meet in future often enough to make up for lost time. It has pleased Mr. Bancroft (knowing that what little ability I have is altogether adapted for active life) to offer me the post of

---

† Reprinted by permission of The Ohio State University Press.
1. See p. 359 for an excerpt from the review.
2. Mary Manning, Hawthorne's mother's sister.
‡ Reprinted by permission of The Ohio State University Press.
1. Hawthorne and Longfellow missed each other at the Tremont House, a hotel in Boston, on October 24, 1838.
2. Longfellow suffered drastically from toothache for two weeks in October.

Inspector in the Boston Custom-House; and I am going to accept it, with as much confidence in my suitableness for it, as Sancho Panza had in his gubernatorial qualifications.[3] I have no reason to doubt my capacity to fulfil the duties; for I don't know what they are; but, as nearly as I can understand, I shall be a sort of Port-Admiral, and take command of vessels after they enter the harbor, and have control of their cargoes. Pray heaven I may have opportunities to make defalcation! They tell me that a considerable portion of my time will be unoccupied; the which I mean to employ in sketches of my new experience, under some such titles as follow:—"Passages in the life of a Custom-House Officer"—"Scenes in Dock"—"Voyages at Anchor"—"Nibblings of a Wharf-Rat"—"Trials of a Tide-Waiter"—"Romance of the Revenue Service"—together with an ethical work in two volumes on the subject of Duties—the first volume to treat of moral and religious Duties; and the second, of the Duties imposed by the Revenue Laws, which I already begin to consider as much the most important class.

Thus you see I have abundance of literary labor in prospect; and this makes it more tolerable that you refuse to let me blow a blast upon the "Wonder-Horn."[4] Assuredly, you have a right to make all the music on your own instrument; but I should serve you right were I to set up an opposition—for instance, with a corn-stalk fiddle, or a pumpkin vine trumpet. Really I do mean to turn my attention to writing for children, either on my own hook, or for the series of works projected by the Board of Education—to which I have been requested to contribute. It appears to me that there is a very fair chance of profit.

I received a letter, the other day, from Bridge, dated at Rome, November 3[d.] He speaks of the Consul, Mr. Greene—"an old friend of Longfellow's."[5] Bridge seems to be leading a very happy life. I wish some one of the vessels, which are to be put under my command, would mutiny, and run away with the worshipful Inspector to the Mediterranean. Well—I have a presentiment that I shall be there one day.

I shall remove to Boston in the course of a fortnight; and, most sincerely, I do not know that I have any pleasanter anticipation than that of frequently meeting you. I saw Mr. Sparks[6] at Miss Silsbee's,

3. See *Don Quixote*, part 2, chapters 33, 43, 45, 47, 49, 51. George Bancroft (1800–1891), historian, Democratic politician, and Collector of the Port of Boston in 1839.
4. Longfellow and Hawthorne considered collaborating on a book of fairy tales for children, "A Boy's Wonder-Horn." (Longfellow took the name from Arnim and Brentano's fine German collection of folk poetry, *Des Knaben Wunderhorn* [1818]). They then agreed that Longfellow would work on the book alone, but publishers were reluctant; he eventually gave up the project.
5. George Washington Greene (1811–1893), U.S. consul at Rome, 1837–45. For Horatio Bridge, n. 1, p. 321.
6. Jared Sparks (1789–1866), professor of history at Harvard. On May 21, 1839, he married Mary Sillsbee, an old flame of Hawthorne's.

some time since; and he said you were thinking of a literary paper. Why not? Your name would go a great way towards insuring its success; and it is intolerable that there should not be a single belles-lettres journal in New-England. And whatever aid a Custom-House officer could afford, should always be forthcoming. By the way, "The Inspector" would be as good a title for a paper as "The Spectator."[7]

If you mean to see me in Salem, you must come pretty quick.[8]

Yours truly,
Nath. Hawthorne.

To Sophia Peabody, Boston

Salem, October 4th 1840—½ past 10. A.M.

Mine ownest,[1]

Here sits thy husband in his old accustomed chamber,[2] where he used to sit in years gone by, before his soul became acquainted with thine. Here I have written many tales—many that have been burned to ashes—many that doubtless deserved the same fate. This deserves to be called a haunted chamber; for thousands upon thousands of visions have appeared to me in it; and some few of them have become visible to the world. If ever I should have a biographer, he ought to make great mention of this chamber in my memoirs, because so much of my lonely youth was wasted here; and here my mind and character were formed; and here I have been glad and hopeful, and here I have been despondent; and here I sat a long, long time, waiting patiently for the world to know me, and sometimes wondering why it did not know me sooner, or whether it would ever know me at all—at least, till I were in my grave. And sometimes (for I had no wife then to keep my heart warm) it seemed as if I were already in the grave, with only life enough to be chilled and benumbed. But oftener I was happy—at least, as happy as I then knew how to be, or was aware of the possibility of being. By and bye, the world found me out in my lonely chamber, and called me forth—not, indeed, with a loud roar of acclamation, but rather with a still,

---

7. *The Spectator* (1711–12) was a famous and much-imitated English periodical edited by Joseph Addison and Richard Steele.
8. Hawthorne moved from Salem to Boston on January 17 to take up his duties as inspector in the Custom-House.
1. The extravagance of Hawthorne's amatory language to his prospective bride is conventional, but he seems to have taken pleasure in it as a private idiom for his intimacy with Sophia Peabody. Hawthorne met Peabody in November 1837. He wrote more than a hundred letters to her between 1839 and 1842, when they married. They were not yet married when he wrote this letter, though he already assumes the name of "husband."
2. Hawthorne's room in his mother's house, where he lived from July 1825 until January 1839.

small voice, and forth I went, but found nothing in the world that I thought preferable to my old solitude, till at length a certain Dove was revealed to me, in the shadow of a seclusion as deep as my own had been.[3] And I drew nearer and nearer to the Dove, and opened my bosom to her, and she flitted into it, and closed her wings there—and there she nestles now and forever, keeping my heart warm, and renewing my life with her own. So now I begin to understand why I was imprisoned so many years in this lonely chamber, and why I could never break through the viewless bolts and bars; for if I had sooner made my escape into the world, I should have grown hard and rough, and been covered with earthly dust, and my heart would have become callous by rude encounters with the multitude; so that I should have been all unfit to shelter a heavenly Dove in my arms. But living in solitude till the fulness of time was come, I still kept the dew of my youth and the freshness of my heart, and had these to offer to my Dove.

Well, dearest, I had no notion what I was going to write, when I began; and indeed I doubted whether I should write anything at all; for after such intimate communion as that of our last blissful evening, it seems as if a sheet of paper could only be a veil betwixt us. Ownest, in the times that I have been speaking of, I used to think that I could imagine all passions, all feelings, all states of the heart and mind; but how little did I know what it is to be mingled with another's being! Thou only hast taught me that I have a heart—thou only hast thrown a light deep downward, and upward, into my soul. Thou only hast revealed me to myself; for without thy aid, my best knowledge of myself would have been merely to know my own shadow—to watch it flickering on the wall, and mistake its fantasies for my own real actions. Indeed, we are but shadows—we are not endowed with real life, and all that seems most real about us is but the thinnest substance of a dream—till the heart is touched. That touch creates us—then we begin to be—thereby we are beings of reality, and inheritors of eternity. Now, dearest, dost thou comprehend what thou hast done for me? And is it not a somewhat fearful thought, that a few slight circumstances might have prevented us from meeting, and then I should have returned to my solitude, sooner or later (probably now, when I have thrown down my burthen of coal and salt)[4] and never should have been created at all! But this is an idle speculation. If the whole world had stood between us, we must have met—if we had been born in different ages, we could not have been sundered.

* * *

3. Sophia Peabody Hawthorne (1811–1871) was living quietly with her family in Salem when Hawthorne met her in 1837. Her health was delicate.
4. Hawthorne worked as an inspector at the Boston Custom-House in 1840, but he chafed at the burden and resigned on January 1, 1841.

To G. S. Hillard, Boston[†]

Brook Farm, July 16th. 1841.

Dear Hillard,

I have not written that infernal story.[1] The thought of it has tormented me ever since I came here, and has deprived me of all the comfort I might otherwise have had, in my few moments of leisure. Thank God, it is now too late—so I disburthen my mind of it, now and forever.

You cannot think how exceedingly I regret the necessity of disappointing you; but what could be done? An engagement to write a story must in its nature be conditional; because stories grow like vegetables, and are not manufactured, like a pine table. My former stories all sprung up of their own accord, out of a quiet life. Now, I have no quiet at all; for when my outward man is at rest—which is seldom, and for short intervals—my mind is bothered with a sort of dull excitement, which makes it impossible to think continuously of any subject. You cannot make a silk purse out of a sow's ear; nor must you expect pretty stories from a man who feeds pigs.

My hands are covered with a new crop of blisters—the effect of raking hay; so excuse this scrawl.

Yours truly,
Nath. Hawthorne

To Margaret Fuller, Concord[‡]

Concord, August 25th, 1842.

Dear Margaret,

Sophia has told me of her conversation with you, about our receiving Mr. Ellery Channing and your sister as inmates of our household.[1] I found that my wife's ideas were not altogether unfavorable to the

---

† Reprinted by permission of The Ohio State University Press.
1. Hawthorne had agreed to try to write something for the *Token* of 1841 (dated 1842), edited now by his friend George Hillard.
‡ Reprinted by permission of The Ohio State University Press.
1. Margaret Fuller visited the newlywed Hawthornes in the Old Manse on August 20. Her sister Ellen Fuller was engaged to be married to Ellery Channing. Margaret Fuller was well known in New England for her prodigious learning and her willingness to put herself forward as an intellectual woman. Sophia Peabody Hawthorne admired Fuller as one of her unofficial teachers. Fuller presided over a series of "conversations" for interested women in Sophia's sister Elizabeth Peabody's house in Boston in 1840. Hawthorne also knew Fuller from Brook Farm, where she was a frequent visitor. In August 1842, she was visiting the Emersons in Concord.

plan—which, together with your own implied opinion in its favor, has led me to consider it with a good deal of attention; and my conclusion is, that the comfort of both parties would be put in great jeopardy. In saying this, I would not be understood to mean anything against the social qualities of Mr. and Mrs. Channing[2]—my objection being wholly independent of such considerations. Had it been proposed to Adam and Eve to receive two angels into their Paradise, as *boarders*, I doubt whether they would have been altogether pleased to consent. Certain I am, that, whatever might be the tact, and the sympathies of the heavenly guests, the boundless freedom of Paradise would at once have become finite and limited by their presence. The host and hostess would no longer have lived their own natural life, but would have had a constant reference to the two angels; and thus the whole four would have been involved in an unnatural relation—which the whole system of boarding out essentially and inevitably is.

One of my strongest objections is the weight of domestic care which would be thrown upon Sophia's shoulders by the proposed arrangement. She is so little acquainted with it, that she cannot estimate how much she would have to bear. I do not fear any burthen that may accrue from our own exclusive relation, because skill and strength will come with the natural necessity; but I should not feel myself justified in adding one scruple to the weight. I wish to remove everything that may impede her full growth and development—which, in her case, it seems to me, is not to be brought about by care and toil, but by perfect repose and happiness. Perhaps she ought not to have any earthly care whatever—certainly none which is not wholly pervaded with love, as a cloud is with warm light. Besides, she has many visions of great deeds to be wrought on canvass and in marble,[3] during the coming autumn and winter; and none of these can be accomplished, unless she can retain quite as much freedom from household drudgery as she enjoys at present. In short, it is my faith and religion not wilfully to mix her up with any earthly annoyance.

You will not consider it impertinent, if I express an opinion about the most advisable course for your young relatives, should they retain their purpose of boarding out. I think that they ought not to seek for delicacy of character, and nice tact, and sensitive feelings, in their hosts. In such a relation as they propose, these characteristics should never exist on more than one side; nor should there be any idea of personal friendship, where the real condition of the bond is, to supply food and lodging for a pecuniary compensation. They will be able to keep their own delicacy and sensitiveness much more inviolate, if they make themselves inmates of the rudest farmer's

---

2. The Channings were in fact not married until September 23.
3. Sophia was an amateur artist. The breakfast room in the Old Manse served as her studio.

household in Concord, where there will be no nice sensibilities to manage, and where their own feelings will be no more susceptible of damage from the farmer's family than from the cattle in his barn-yard. There will be a freedom in this sort of life, which is not other-wise attainable, except under a roof of their own. They can then say explicitly what they want, and can battle for it, if necessary; and such a contest would leave no wound on either side. Now, where four sen-sitive people were living together, united by any tie save that of entire affection and confidence, it would take but a trifle to render their whole common life diseased and intolerable.

* * *

This epistle has grown to greater length than I expected, and yet it is but a very imperfect expression of my ideas upon the subject. Sophia wished me to write; and, as it was myself that made the objec-tions, it seemed no more than just that I should assume the office of stating them to you. There is nobody to whom I would more willingly speak my mind, because I can be certain of being thoroughly under-stood. I would say more,—but here is the bottom of the page.

Sincerely your friend,
Nath. Hawthorne.

To Margaret Fuller, Cambridge[†]

Concord. Feby 1st. 1843.

Dear Margaret.

I ought to have answered your letter a great while ago; but I have an immense deal of scribbling to do—being a monthly contributor to three or four periodicals,[1] so that I find it necessary to keep writing without any period at all.

* * *

We have been very happy this winter; we go on continually learn-ing to be happy, and should consider ourselves perfectly so now, only that we find ourselves making advances all the time. I do sup-pose that nobody ever lived, in one sense, quite so selfish a life as we do. Not a footstep, except our own, comes up the avenue for weeks and weeks; and we let the world alone as much as the world does us. During the greater part of the day, we are separately engaged at our respective avocations; but we meet in my study in the evening, which

---

† Reprinted by permission of The Ohio State University Press.
1. *Sargent's*, the *Pioneer*, and the *Democratic Review* at the time. Hawthorne was trying to be a good provider.

we spend without any set rule, and in a considerable diversity of method—but on looking back, I do not find anything to tell of or describe. The essence would flit away out of the description, and leave a very common-place residuum; whereas the real thing has a delicate pungency. We have read through Milton's Paradise Lost, and other famous books; and it somewhat startles me to think how we, in some cases, annul the verdict of applauding centuries, and compel poets and prosers to stand another trial, and receive condemnatory sentence at our bar. It is a pity that there is no period after which an author may be safe. Forever and ever, he is to be tried again and again, and by everybody that chooses to be his Judge; so that, even if he be honorably acquitted at every trial, his ghost must be in everlasting torment.

I have skated like a very schoolboy, this winter. Indeed, since my marriage, the circle of my life seems to have come round, and brought back many of my school-day enjoyments; and I find a deeper pleasure in them now than when I first went over them. I pause upon them, and taste them with a sort of epicurism, and am boy and man together. As for Sophia, I keep her as tranquil as a summer-sunset. As regards both of us, the time that we spend together seems to spread over all the time that we are apart; and consequently we have the idea of being in each other's society a good deal more than we are. I wonder, sometimes, how she is able to dispense with all society but mine. In my own case, there is no wonder—indeed, in neither of our cases; and it is only when I get apart from myself, and take another person's view of the matter, that I think so.

I have missed Ellery Channing very much in my skating expeditions. Has he quite deserted us for good and all?[2] How few people in this world know how to be idle!—it is a much higher faculty than any sort of usefulness or ability. Such rare persons, if the world knew what was due to them or good for itself, would have food and raiment as free as air, for the sake of their inestimable example. I do not mean to deny Ellery's ability for any sort of vulgar usefulness; but he certainly *can* lie in the sun.

I wish you might begin at the end of this scrawl instead of at the usual extremity; because then you would profit by the advice which I here give—not to attempt to decypher it. Sophia wants to read it, but I have too much regard for her to consent. She sends her love. Of course, you will be in Concord when the pleasant weather comes, for a month, or a week, or a day; and you must spend a proportionable part of the time at our house.

Your friend,
Nath Hawthorne.

---

2. Ellery and Ellen Channing spent part of the winter in Cambridge with Margaret Fuller and her mother. They moved to Concord in April 1843.

To E. A. Duyckinck, New York[†]

Concord, July 1st, 1845.

Dear Sir,

My story makes no good progress.[1] There are many matters that thrust themselves between, and hinder my mind from any close approximation to the subject; and for days and weeks together, sometimes, I forget that there is any story to be forthcoming—and am sorry to remember it at last. I am fit for nothing, at present, higher or finer than such another piece of book-manufacture as the Journals.[2] My health is not so good, this summer, as it always has been hitherto. I feel no physical vigor; and my inner man droops in sympathy. It was my purpose to construct a sort of frame-work, in this new story, for the series of stories already published, and to make the scene an idealization of our old parsonage, and of the river close at hand, with glimmerings of my actual life—yet so transmogrified that the reader should not know what was reality and what fancy. Perhaps such sketches would be more easily written after I have pitched my tent elsewhere. That will be in a few months, now. It grieves me to keep you waiting for this story, if it be important that you should have it; but if I were to attempt writing it now, the result would be most pitiable.

* * *

To E. A. Duyckinck, New York[‡]

Salem, April 15th. 1846.

My dear Duyckinck,

I send you the initial article,[1] promised so many thousand years ago. The delay has really not been my fault—only my misfortune. Nothing that I tried to write would flow out of my pen, till a very little while ago—when forth came this sketch, of its own accord, and

---

† Reprinted by permission of The Ohio State University Press.
1. "The Old Manse." In early 1845, Evert Duyckinck, as an editor for the publishers Wiley and Putnam of New York, persuaded Hawthorne to make a collection of his more recent tales and sketches, and Hawthorne proposed to write an introductory sketch for it.
2. Hawthorne edited the manuscript of Horatio Bridge's *Journal of an African Cruiser* (New York: Wiley and Putnam, 1845). He also arranged for publication of the *Journal* and received a royalty.
‡ Reprinted by permission of The Ohio State University Press.
1. "The Old Manse."

much unlike what I had purposed. I like it pretty well, at this present writing; and my wife better than I. It is truth, as you will perceive, with perhaps a gleam or two of ideal light thrown over it—yet hardly the less true for that. I have written it as impersonally as I could, considering the nature of the thing, and do not feel as if there were any indelicacy in it, towards myself or anybody else.

I shall feel anxious about the accuracy of the press, in relation to this article, and therefore beg you to send me the proof-sheets of it.

*   *   *

I suppose you know that I have just become an office-holder.[2] Nevertheless, my emoluments not having yet commenced, I am dismally in want of money, and wish Messrs. Wiley & Putnam would either adjust the account of the African Cruiser, or, at least, permit me to draw on them for a further sum. I care not which they do—so I get some cash.

I hope you will go on with the project of the Juvenile Series of books;—there seems to me to be a vacancy in that department, just now. I have had in my head, this long time, the idea of some stories to be taken out of the cold moonshine of classical mythology, and modernized, or perhap gothicized, so that they may be felt by children of these days. For instance, the story of Midas seems admirable for the purpose—so does that of Pandora, with her box—and a multitude of others.[3] I know I could make a very pretty volume of such materials. Tell me more definitely about the plan of your series, if you conclude to go on with it.

My office (the duties of it being chiefly performable by deputy) will allow me as much time for literature as can be profitably applied. I mean to leave off Magazine writing altogether, and try histories, biographies, and all such stuff.

I sent you, some time ago, a notice of "Typee," which I like uncommonly well. Whenever you choose to send me any numbers of your series, I will notice them, for better or worse, in the Democratic paper of this town.[4]

*   *   *

2. As surveyor for the Salem Custom-House.
3. Hawthorne retold the stories of Midas and Pandora in *The Wonder Book* (Boston: Ticknor and Fields, 1851). Wiley and Putnam went out of business in 1848.
4. Melville's *Typee* was published by Wiley and Putnam in March 1846. Hawthorne wrote an anonymous "notice" or review for the *Salem Advertiser*. For a reprint, see *American Literature* 5 (1934): 327–41, or CE 23: 235–36.

To R. W. Griswold, Philadelphia[†]

West Newton, Dec. 15th. 1851.

My dear Sir,

As regards the proposition for twelve short tales,[1] I shall not be able to accept it; because experience has taught me that the thought and trouble, expended on that kind of production, is vastly greater, in proportion, than what is required for a long story.

I doubt whether my romances would succeed in the serial mode of publication; lacking, as they certainly do, the variety of interest and character which seem to have made the success of other works, so published. The reader would inevitably be tired to death of the one prominent idea, if presented to him under different aspects for a twelvemonth together. The effect of such a story, it appears to me, depends on its being read continuously. If, on completion of another work, it should seem fairly and naturally divisible into serial portions, I will think further of your proposal.

I have by me a story which I wrote just before leaving Lenox, and which I thought of sending to Dr. Bailey of the National Era, who has offered me $100 for an article.[2] But, being somewhat grotesque in its character, and therefore not quite adapted to the grave and sedate character of that Journal, I hesitate about so doing, and will send it to the International, should you wish it at the price above-mentioned.[3] The story would make between twenty and thirty of such pages as Ticknor's editions of my books—hardly long enough, I think, to be broken into two articles for your magazine; but you might please yourself on that point. I cannot afford it for less than $100, and would not write another for the same price.

Very truly Yours,
Nath Hawthorne.

---

† Reprinted by permission of The Ohio State University Press.
1. Rufus W. Griswold (1815–57), editor of International Monthly Magazine, 1850–52, had invited Hawthorne to write either a series of monthly tales or a serialized romance for the magazine.
2. Gamaliel Bailey (1807–1859), editor of the weekly National Era. In December 1851, Harriet Beecher Stowe's Uncle Tom's Cabin was being serialized in the National Era.
3. Griswold paid the price and "Feathertop" was published in the International in two parts in February and March 1852.

To James T. Fields, Boston[†]

U.S. Consulate,
Liverpool, April 13th '54

Dear Fields,

I am very glad that the "Mosses" have come into the hands of our firm; and I return the copy sent me, after a careful revision.[1] When I wrote those dreamy sketches, I little thought that I should ever prepare an edition for the press amidst the bustling life of a Liverpool consul. Upon my honor, I am not quite sure that I entirely comprehend my own meaning in some of these blasted allegories; but I remember that I always had a meaning—or, at least, thought I had. I am a good deal changed since those times; and to tell you the truth, my past self is not very much to my taste, as I see myself in this book. Yet certainly there is more in it than the public generally gave me credit for, at the time it was written. But I don't think myself worthy of very much more credit than I got. It has been a very disagreeable task to read the book.

The story of "Rappaccini's Daughter" was published in the Democratic Review about the year 1844; and it was prefaced by some remarks on the celebrated French author (a certain M. de l'Aubepine) from whose works it was translated. I left out this preface, when the story was republished; but I wish you would turn to it in the Democratic, and see whether it is worth while to insert it in the new edition. I leave it altogether to your judgement.[2]

* * *

We shall begin to look for you now by every steamer from Boston. You must make up your mind to spend a good while with us before going to see your London friends.

Did you read the article on your De Quincy in the last Westminster?[3] It was written by Mr. H. A. Bright of this city, who was in America a year or two ago. The article is pretty well, but does nothing like adequate justice to De Quincy; and in fact no Englishman cares a pin for him. We are ten times as good readers and critics as

---

† Reprinted by permission of The Ohio State University Press.
1. James T. Fields (1817–1881) was Hawthorne's editor starting in 1849, and his publisher along with William D. Ticknor (1810–1864). Ticknor and Fields bought the plates of *Mosses from an Old Manse* (1846) from George Putnam (of the publishers Wiley and Putnam) in March 1854, and Fields immediately made plans for a new edition. He sent a copy of the 1846 edition for corrections and revisions to Hawthorne in England.
2. Fields did restore Aubépine's preface, and it appeared before "Rappaccini's Daughter" in the 1854 edition of *Mosses*.
3. An article on the English author Thomas de Quincey in the *Westminster Review* of London. Ticknor and Fields were De Quincey's publishers in America.

they. By the by, I hear horrible stories about De Quincy's morality, in times past.

Is not Whipple[4] coming here soon?

Truly Yours,
Nath Hawthorne.

FROM THE AMERICAN NOTEBOOKS[†]

Hawthorne used his notebooks for several purposes: to jot down ideas and information for stories he might later compose, to keep a diary of his observations and experiences, and—more rarely—to reflect on his life or on life in general. The earliest notebook entries that have come down to us date from 1835. The "American notebooks" end in 1853, when he left with his wife and three children for England. The early notebooks contain a much higher proportion of ideas for stories than do the later ones. After Hawthorne married Sophia Peabody in 1842, he tended to become more of a diarist. Often he and Sophia kept journals together.

This section is meant not only to provide specific background for the tales collected in the Norton Critical Edition but also to give readers something of the flavor of the American notebooks when read at large. We trust that some will enjoy the selection as a single unit, while others will consult it as it suits their needs. It is presented chronologically, with the result that outlines for plots, narratives from diaries, and general reflections appear side by side. Hawthorne gives exact dates when he is writing a diary but does not date his fragmentary notations for fiction; they come before us as precise but timeless plots on a page. Nevertheless, the selection as a whole reflects the changing character of his mind. Between 1835 and 1838, the notebooks sometimes exhibit an intense preoccupation with sin, isolation, and celibacy, as if the writer were feeling the strain of his anonymous years in Salem, that thirteen-year period during which some of his greatest tales disappeared into print like pebbles into a pond. On the other hand, Hawthorne is buoyant and cheerfully observant in his diary of a trip to western Massachusetts in the summer of 1838, as he often is when recording his trips and outings. The reader will find

---

4. Edwin P. Whipple (1819–1886), literary critic and friend and associate of Fields and Hawthorne.
† Reprinted by permission of The Ohio State University Press. The entries for 1835–37 and 1839–41, as well as the first two and last two entries for 1838, are from the so-called lost notebook, pp. 123–224 of *Miscellaneous Prose and Verse*, edited by Thomas Woodson, Claude M. Simpson, and L. Neal Smith, CE 23. The remaining entries for 1838 and all the entries for 1842–53 are from *The American Notebooks*, edited by Claude M. Simpson, CE 8.

here a good portion of this Berkshire diary, both because it is lively in itself and because Hawthorne used it later in "Ethan Brand." When Hawthorne drew close to Sophia Peabody in late 1838, his notebooks reflect his incipient happiness, and after his marriage to her in 1842, he shows repeatedly that he is grateful for what his wife and family have brought into his life. Yet throughout the American notebooks and in the notebooks written in Europe as well, he remains a brooder, preoccupied with the illusoriness of thought, the transience of experience, the temptations as well as the pleasures of art, and the virtues of ordinary people oblivious to his gifts.

The selection of notebooks is drawn from *The American Notebooks,* edited by Claude M. Simpson (CE 8) and from the so-called lost notebook, included in *Miscellaneous Prose and Verse* (CE 23). (The manuscript of the lost notebook is known to have been in possession of the Hawthorne family in 1866, but disappeared until 1976, when Barbara Mouffe of Boulder, Colorado, found it in an antique cabinet belonging to her family.) For the story of the recovery of what Hawthorne himself wrote in his notebooks, insofar as it is recoverable, the reader should consult Simpson's preface and commentary. Briefly, Sophia Hawthorne, for reasons she considered honorable, tampered with the text, scissoring out bits of it and inking out or erasing other passages she thought her husband would have deemed improper. Then she revised and deleted discreetly when she transcribed parts of the manuscript for publication in 1866–68. Fortunately, the Centenary Edition now contains a remarkably accurate transcription of all that survives of the American notebooks.

1835

A story, the hero of which is to be represented as naturally capable of deep and strong passion, and looking forward to the time when he shall feel passionate love, which is to be the great event of his existence. But it so chances that he never falls in love, and at length gives up the expectation of so doing, and marries calmly, yet somewhat sadly, with sentiments merely of esteem for his bride. The lady might be one who had loved him early in life, but whom then, in his expectation of passionate love, he had scorned.

The story of a man cold and hard-hearted, and acknowledging no brotherhood with mankind. At his death, these might try to dig him a grave, but, at a little space beneath the ground, strike upon a rock, as if the earth refused to receive her unnatural son into her bosom. Then they would put him into an old sepulchre, where the corpses and coffins were all turned to dust, and he would be alone. Then the body would petrify, and he having died in some characteristic act and expression, he would seem, through endless ages of death, to repel society as in life; and none would be buried in that tomb forever.[1]

A person to be writing a tale, and to find that it shapes itself against his intentions; that the characters act otherwise than he thought; that unforeseen events occur; and a catastrophe which he strives in vain to avert. It might shadow forth his own fate—he having made himself one of the personages.[2]

1836

Four precepts;—to break off custom—to shake off spirits ill-disposed—to meditate on youth—to do nothing against a man's genius.

To picture the predicament of worldly people, if admitted to Paradise.

In this dismal and squalid chamber, FAME was won.[3]

Those who are very difficult in choosing wives, seem as they would take none of Nature's ready-made articles, but want a woman manufactured purposely to their order.

A man, to escape detection for some offence, immures a woman whom he has loved in some cavern or other secret place. He gradually becomes cruel to her; and feels a loathing delight in his cruelty. She comes to hate him; and loses all her intellect and sensibility, except this hatred. They show an example how the damned, who have partaken of guilt, shall mutually wreak vengeance hereafter. In the catastrophe, the hidden person is discovered.

An essay on the misery of being always under a masque—A veil may sometimes be needful, but never a masque. Instances of people who wear masques, in all classes of society, and never take it off even in the most familiar moments—though sometimes it may chance to slip aside.

There is a fund of evil in every human heart, which may remain latent, perhaps through the whole of life; but circumstances may arouse it to activity. To imagine such circumstances. A woman tempted

1. Cf. "The Man of Adamant."
2. In Hawthorne's *Blithedale Romance* (1852), Miles Coverdale imagines his life at Blithedale as if it were a romance, then finds himself caught up as a participant-spectator in an unexpected tragedy.
3. In her transcription, Mrs. Hawthorne deleted the words "and squalid." Hawthorne's chamber was in his mother's house on Herbert Street, Salem.

to be false to her husband, apparently through mere whim—a young man to feel an instinctive thirst for blood, and to commit murder; this appetite may be traced in the popularity of criminal trials—   The appetite might be observed first in a child, and then traced upwards, manifesting itself in crimes suited to every stage of life.

What would a man do, if he were compelled to live always in the sultry heat of society, and could never bathe himself in cool solitude.

A girl's lover to be slain and buried in her flower garden; and the earth leveled over him. That particular spot (which she happens to plant with some peculiar variety of flowers) produces them of admirable splendor, beauty, and perfume; and she delights, with an indescribable impulse, to wear them in her bosom, and have them to perfume her chamber. Thus the classic fantasies would be realized, of dead people transformed to flowers.[4]

Objects seen by a magic lantern, reversed. A street, or other location, might be presented, where there would be opportunity to bring forward all objects of worldly interest; and thus much pleasant satire might be the result.[5]

1837

A man tries to be happy in love; he cannot sincerely give his heart, and the affair seems like a dream;—in domestic life, the same;—in politics, a seeming patriot; but still he is sincere, and all seems like a theatre.

Man's finest workmanship, the closer you observe it, the more imperfections it shows:—as, in a piece of polished steel, a microscope will discover a rough surface.—   Whereas, what may look coarse and rough in Nature's workmanship, will show an infinitely minute perfection, the closer you look into it.

A person to be in the possession of something as perfect as mortal man has a right to demand; he tries to make it better, and ruins it entirely:— * * *

A person to spend all his life and splendid talents in trying to achieve something naturally impossible—as to make a conquest over nature—[6]

---

4. The transformations of Hyacinth and Narcissus into flowers are described in Ovid's *Metamorphoses*, one of Hawthorne's favorite classics. The idea of an animated garden reappears in "Rappaccini's Daughter."
5. Cf. the moving puppet show in Hawthorne's "Main-street (1849)."
6. Cf. "The Birthmark" and "Rappaccini's Daughter."

1838
July 4

In the old burial-ground, Charter St. a slate grave-stone, carved round the borders, to the memory of "Col. John Hathorne, Esq." who died in 1717. This was the witch-judge. The stone is sunk deep into the earth, and leans forward, and the grass grows very long around it; and what with the moss, it was rather difficult to make out the date &c. Other Hathornes lie buried in a range with him, on either side.

A perception, for a moment, of one's mental and moral self, as if it were another person—the observant faculty being separated, and looking intently at the qualities of the character. There is a surprise, when this happens—this getting out of one's self, and then the observer sees how queer a fellow he is

July 29 [*from Hawthorne's journal of his trip*
to Western Massachusetts]

Remarkable characters:—a disagreeable figure, waning from middle-age, clad in a pair of tow homespun pantaloons[7] and very dirty shirt, bare-foot, and with one of his feet maimed by an axe; also, an arm amputated two or three inches below the elbow. His beard of a week's growth, grim and grisly, with a general effect of black;—altogether a filthy and disgusting object. Yet he has the signs of having been a handsome man in his idea; though now such a beastly figure that, probably, no living thing but his great dog could touch him without an effort. Coming to the stoop, where several persons were sitting * * * he sat himself down on the lower step * * *, and began to talk; and the conversation being turned upon his bare feet, by one of the company, he related the story of his losing his toes by the glancing aside of an axe, and with what grim fortitude he bore it. Thence he made a transition to the loss of his arm; and setting his teeth and drawing in his breath, said that the pain was dreadful; but this, too, he seems to have borne like an Indian; and a person testified to his fortitude by saying that he did not suppose that there was any feeling in him, from observing how he bore it. The man spoke of the pain of cutting the muscles, and the particular agony at one moment, while the bone was being sawed asunder; and there was a strange expression of remembered agony, as he shrugged his half limb, and described the matter. Afterwards, in reply to a question of mine whether he still seemed to feel the hand that had been amputated, he

7. A pair of pants made of light coarse cloth of flax or hemp.

answered that he did, always—and baring the stump, he moved the
severed muscles, saying "there is the thumb, there is the forefinger
&c." Then he talked to me about phrenology, of which he seems a
firm believer and skilful practitioner, telling how he had hit upon the
true characters of many people. There was a great deal of sense and
acuteness in his talk, and something of elevation in his expression;
perhaps a studied elevation—and a sort of courtesy in his manner;
but his sense had something out-of-the way in it; something wild,
and ruined, and desperate, in his talk, though I can hardly say what
it was. There was something of the gentleman and man of intellect in
his deep degradation; and a pleasure in intellectual pursuits, and an
acuteness and trained judgment, which bespoke a mind once strong
and cultivated. "My study is man," said he. And looking at me "I do
not know your name," said he, "but there is something of the hawk-
eye about you too."

Another character—a blacksmith of fifty or upwards; a corpulent
figure, big in the belly, and enormous in the backsides; yet there is
such an appearance of strength and robustness in his frame, that
his corpulence appears very proper and necessary to him. A pound
of flesh could not be spared from his abundance, any more than
from the leanest man; and he walks about briskly, without any panting, or symptom of labor and pain in his motion. He has a round
jolly face, always mirthful and humorous, and shrewd—and the air
of a man well to do, and well-respected, yet not caring much about
the opinions of men, because his independence is sufficient to itself.
Nobody would take him for other than a man of some importance in
the community, though his summer dress is a tow cloth pair of pantaloons, a shirt not of the cleanest, open at the breast, and the
sleeves rolled up at the elbows, and a straw hat. There is not such a
vast difference between this costume and that of lawyer Haynes,
above-mentioned—yet never was there a greater diversity of appearance than between these two men; and a glance at them, would be
sufficient to mark the difference. The blacksmith loves his glass,
and comes to the tavern for it, whenever it seems good to him, not
calling for it slily and shyly, but marching sturdily to the bar, or calling across the room for it to be prepared. He speaks with great bitterness against the new license law, and vows if it be not repealed by fair
means, it shall be by violence, and that he will be as ready to cock his
rifle for such a cause as for any other. On this subject his talk is really
fierce; but as to all other matters he is good-natured, and good-
hearted, fond of joke, and shaking his jolly sides with frequent laughter. His conversation has much strong, unlettered sense, imbued with
humor, as everybody's talk is, in New-England. He takes a queer position sometimes—queer for his figure, particularly—straddling across
a chair, facing the back, with his arms resting thereon, and his chin

on them, for the benefit of conversing closely with some one. When he has spent as much time in the bar-room, or under the stoop, as he chooses to spare, he gets up at once and goes off with a brisk, vigorous pace. He owns a mill, and seems to be well to do in the world. I know no man who seems more like a man—more indescribably human—than this sturdy blacksmith.

July 31

[AN IDEA FOR A STORY]

A steam engine in a factory to be supposed to possess a malignant spirit; it catches one man's arm, and pulls it off; seizes another by the coat-tails; and almost grapples him bodily;—catches a girl by the hair, and scalps her;—and finally draws a man, and crushes him to death.

August 31

A ride, on Tuesday, to Shelburne Falls, * * * The first house, after reaching the summit, is a small, homely tavern, kept by P. Witt. We left our horse in the shed; and entering the little unpainted barroom, we heard a voice, in a strange outlandish accent, explaining a diorama. It was an old man, with a full, gray-bearded countenance; and Mr. Leach exclaimed "Ah here's the old Dutchman again!" And he answered "Yes, Captain, here's the old Dutchman;"— tho' by the way, he is a German, and travels the country with this diorama, in a wagon; and had recently been at South Adams, and was now returning from Saratoga Springs. We looked through the glass orifices of his machine, while he exhibited a succession of the very worst scratchings and daubings that can be imagined—worn out, too, and full of cracks and wrinkles, besmeared with tobacco smoke, and every otherwise dilapidated. There were none in a later fashion than thirty years since, except some figures that had been cut from tailors' show-bills. There were views of cities and edifices in Europe, and ruins,—and of Napoleon's battles and Nelson's seafights; in the midst of which would be seen a gigantic, brown, hairy hand—the Hand of Destiny—pointing at the principal points of the conflict, while the old Dutchman explained. He gave considerable dramatic effect to his descriptions, but his accent and intonation cannot be written. He seemed to take an interest and pride in his exhibition; yet when the utter and ludicrous miserability thereof made us laugh, he joined in the joke very readily. When the last picture had been exhibited, he caused a country boor, who stood gaping beside the machine to put his head within it, and thrust his tongue out. The head becoming gigantic, a singular effect was produced.

The old Dutchman's exhibition over, a great dog—apparently an elderly dog—suddenly made himself the object of notice, evidently in rivalship of the Dutchman. He had seemed to be a good-natured, quiet kind of dog, offering his head to be patted by those kindly disposed towards him. This great, old dog, suddenly and of his own motion, began to run round after his own not very long tail, with the utmost eagerness; and catching hold of it, he growled furiously at it, and still continued to circle round, growling and snarling, with increasing rage, as if one half of his body were at deadly enmity with the other. Faster and faster went he round and roundabout, growling still fiercer, till at last he ceased in a state of utter exhaustion; but no sooner had his exhibition finished, than he became the same mild, quiet, sensible old dog as before; and no one could have suspected him of such nonsense as getting enraged with his own tail. He was first taught this trick by attaching a bell to the end of his tail; but he now commences entirely of his own accord, and I really believe feels vain at the attention he excites.

It was chill and bleak on the mountain-top, and a fire was burning in the bar-room. The old Dutchman bestowed on everybody the title of Captain—perhaps because such a title has a great chance of suiting an American.

September 7

Mr. Leach and I took a walk by moonlight, last evening, on the road that leads over the mountain. Remote from houses, far up on the hill side, we found a lime kiln burning near the road side; and approaching it, a watcher started from the ground, where he had been lying at his length. There are several of these lime-kilns in this vicinity; they are built circular with stones, like a round tower, eighteen or twenty feet high; having a hillock heaped around a considerable of their circumference, so that the marble may be brought and thrown in by cart loads at the top. At the bottom there is a door-way large enough to admit a man in a stooping posture. Thus an edifice of great solidity is composed, which will endure for centuries, unless needless pains are taken to tear it down. * * * In the one we saw last night, a hard wood fire was burning merrily beneath the superincumbent marble—the kiln being heaped full; and shortly after we came, the man (a dark, black-bearded, figure in shirt-sleeves) opened the iron door, through the chinks of which the fire was gleaming, and thrust in huge logs of wood, and stirred the immense coals with a long pole; and showed us the glowing lime-stone,—the lower layer of it. The glow of the fire was powerful, at the distance of several yards from the open door. He talked very sociably with us,—being doubtless glad to have two visitors to vary his solitary night-watch; for it would not do for him to get asleep; since the fire should be refreshed as often as every twenty minutes. We ascended the hillock to the top of the kiln; and the marble was red-hot and burning with a bluish lambent flame, quivering up, sometimes, nearly a yard high, and resembling the flame of anthracite coal—only, the marble being in larger fragments, the flame was higher. The kiln was perhaps six or eight feet across. Four hundred bushels of marble were then in a state of combustion. * * * We talked with the man about whether he would run across the top of the intensely burning kiln for a thousand dollars, barefooted; and he said he would for ten;—he said that the lime had been burning 48 hours, and would be finished in 36 more, and cooled sufficiently to handle in 12 more. He liked the business of watching it better by night than day; because the days were often hot; but such a mild and beautiful night as the last was just right. [* * *][8] Here a poet might make verses, with moonlight in them—and a gleam of fierce firelight flickering through them. . . .

[In Salem, later in 1838]

S.A.P.—taking my likeness, I said that such changes would come over my face, that she would not know me when we met again in Heaven. "See if I dont!" said she, smiling. There was the most peculiar and beautiful humor in the point itself, and in her manner, that can be imagined.[9]

1839

Letters in the shape of figures of men &c. At a distance the words composed by the letters were alone distinguishable. Close at hand, the figures alone were seen, and not distinguished as letters. Thus things may have a positive, a relative, and a composite meaning, when seen at the proper distance &.

Selfishness is one of the qualities most apt to inspire love. This might be thought out at great length.

A person to be the death of his beloved, in trying to raise her to more than mortal perfection; yet there should be comfort to him, for having aimed so highly and holily.[1]

---

8. One and one-half lines of Hawthorne's manuscript were here inked out by his wife.
9. S.A.P. is Sophia Peabody, who became engaged to Hawthorne in 1839 and married him in 1842. "Likeness": portrait; Sophia was a gifted and assiduous amateur artist.
1. Cf. "The Birthmark."

1840

To make a story out of a scarecrow—giving it queer attributes. From different points of view, it should appear to change sex, being an old man or woman, a gunner, a farmer, the Old Nick &c.[2]

1841

To represent a man as spending life and the intensest labor, in the accomplishment of some mechanical trifle—as in making a miniature coach to be drawn by fleas, or a dinner service to be put into a cherrystone.[3]

A bonfire to be made of the gallows and of all symbols of evil, such as bands, gun carriages, &c &c &c.[4]

The love of prosperity is a consequence of the necessity of Death. If a man were sure of living forever, he would not care about his offspring.

1842

It seems a greater pity that an accomplished worker with the hand should perish prematurely, than a person of great intellect, because intellectual arts may be cultivated in the next world, but not physical ones.

August 22

I took a walk through the woods, yesterday afternoon, to Mr. Emerson's, with a book which Margaret Fuller had left behind her, after a call on Saturday eve. * * *

After leaving the book at Mr. Emerson's, I returned through the woods, and entering Sleepy Hollow, I perceived a lady reclining near the path which bends along its verge. It was Margaret herself. She had been there the whole afternoon, meditating or reading; for she had a book in her hand, with some strange title, which I did not understand and have forgotten. She said that nobody had broken her solitude, and was just giving utterance to a theory that no inhabitant of Concord ever visited Sleepy Hollow, when we saw a whole group of people entering the sacred precincts. Most of them followed a

2. The first hint of "Feathertop."
3. Cf., perhaps, "The Artist of the Beautiful."
4. An idea taken up in "Earth's Holocaust."

path that led them remote from us; but an old man passed near us, and smiled to see Margaret lying on the ground, and me sitting by her side. He made some remark about the beauty of the afternoon, and withdrew himself into the shadow of the wood. Then we talked about Autumn—and about the pleasures of getting lost in the woods—and about the crows, whose voices Margaret had heard— and about the experiences of early childhood, whose influence remains upon the character after the collection of them has passed away—and about the sight of mountains from a distance, and the view from their summits—and about other matters of high and low philosophy. In the midst of our talk, we heard footsteps above us, on the high bank; and while the intruder was still hidden among the trees, he called to Margaret, of whom he had gotten a glimpse. Then he emerged from the green shade; and, behold, it was Mr. Emerson, who, in spite of his clerical consecration, had found no better way of spending the Sabbath than to ramble among the woods.[5] He appeared to have had a pleasant time; for he said that there were Muses in the woods to-day, and whispers to be heard in the breezes. It being now nearly six o'clock, we separated, Mr. Emerson and Margaret towards his house, and I towards mine, where my little wife was very busy getting tea. * * *

August 30

In the afternoon, Mr. Emerson called, bringing Mr. Frost, the col-league and successor of Dr. Ripley. He is a good sort of hum-drum parson enough, and well fitted to increase the stock of manuscript sermons of which there must be a fearful quantity already in the world. I find that my respect for clerical people, as such, and my faith in the utility of their office, decreases daily. We certainly do need a new revelation—a new system—for there seems to be no life in the old one. Mr. Frost, however, is probably one of the best and most use-ful of his class; because no suspicion of the necessity of his profes-sion, constituted as it now is, to mankind, and of his own usefulness and success in it, has hitherto disturbed him; and therefore he labors with faith and confidence, as ministers did a hundred years ago, when they had really something to do in the world.[6]

---

5. Emerson was an ordained Unitarian minister but no longer practiced in 1842, skipping church when he chose to.
6. Hawthorne and his wife had recently moved to the Old Manse in Concord. Mr. Frost is Barzillai Frost, minister of the Concord Unitarian Church. Emerson in his journals pri-vately excoriated Frost for his blandness. Dr. Ripley is Ezra Ripley, minister in Concord and tenant of the Old Manse for fifty years before his death in 1841.

1843
March 31

On the 9th of this month, we left home on a visit to Boston and Salem—at least, my wife stopt at the former place, and I went to the latter, where I resumed all my bachelor habits for nearly a fortnight, leading the same life in which ten years of my youth flitted away like a dream. But how much changed was I!—at last, I had caught hold of a reality, which never could be taken from me. It was good thus to get apart from my happiness, for the sake of contemplating it.

When the reformation of the world is complete, a fire shall be made of the gallows; and the Hangman shall come and sit down by it, in solitude and despair. To him shall come the Last Thief, the Last Prostitute, the Last Drunkard, and other representatives of past crime and vice; and they shall hold a dismal merry-making, quaffing the contents of the Drunkard's last Brandy Bottle.[7]

The human Heart to be allegorized as a cavern; at the entrance there is sunshine, and flowers growing about it. You step within, but a short distance, and begin to find yourself surrounded with a terrible gloom, and monsters of divers kinds; it seems like Hell itself. You are bewildered, and wander long without hope. At last a light strikes upon you. You press towards it yon, and find yourself in a region that seems, in some sort, to reproduce the flowers and sunny beauty of the entrance, but all perfect. These are the depths of the heart, or of human nature, bright and peaceful; the gloom and terror may lie deep; but deeper still is this eternal beauty.

Madame Calderon de la B (in Life in Mexico)[8] speaks of persons who have been inoculated with the venom of rattlesnakes, by pricking them in various places with the tooth. These persons are thus secured forever after against the bite of any venomous reptile. They have the power of calling snakes, and feel great pleasure in playing with and handling them. Their own bite becomes poisonous to people not inoculated in the same manner. Thus a part of the serpent's nature appears to be transfused into them.

An examination of wits and poets at a police-court; and they to be sentenced by the Judge to various penalties, as fines, the house of

7. Cf. "Earth's Holocaust."
8. Madame Calderón de la Barca was a Scottish lady married to a Spaniard. Her *Life in Mexico During a Residence of Two Years in That Country* (1843) supplied several hints for "Rappaccini's Daughter."

correction, whipping &c, according to the moral offences of which they were guilty.

The print in blood of a naked foot to be traced through the street of a town.

To write a dream, which shall resemble the real course of a dream, with all its inconsistency, its strange transformations, which are all taken as a matter of course, its eccentricities and aimlessness—with nevertheless a leading idea running through the whole. Up to this old age of the world, no such thing ever has been written.

1844

The search of an investigator for the Unpardonable Sin;—he at last finds it in his own heart and practice.

The trees reflected in the river;—they are unconscious of a spiritual world so near them. So are we.

The life of a woman, who, by the old colony law, was condemned always to wear the letter A, sewed on her garment, in token of her having committed adultery.

The Unpardonable Sin might consist in a want of love and reverence for the Human Soul; in consequence of which, the investigator pried into its dark depths, not with a hope or purpose of making it better, but from a cold philosophical curosity,—content that it should be wicked in whatever kind or degree, and only desiring to study it out. Would not this, in other words, be the separation of the intellect from the heart?[9]

To represent the influence which Dead Men have among living affairs;—for instance, a Dead Man controls the disposition of wealth; a Dead Man sits on the judgment-seat, and the living judges do but repeat his decisions; Dead Men's opinions in all things control the living truth; we believe in Dead Men's religion; we laugh at Dead Men's jokes; we cry at Dead Men's pathos; everywhere and in all matters, Dead Men tyrannize inexorably over us.

People who write about themselves and their feelings, as Byron did, may be said to serve up their own hearts, duly spiced, and

9. Cf. "Ethan Brand."

with brain-sauce out of their own heads, as a repast for the public.[1]

To make literal pictures of figurative expressions;—for instance, he burst into tears—a man suddenly turned into a shower of briny drops. An explosion of laughter—a man blowing up, and his fragments flying about on all sides. He cast his eyes upon the ground—a man standing eyeless, with his eyes on the ground, staring up at him in wonderment &c &c &c.

1848
March 19[2]

¼ of 8 o'clock. I have taken a walk round Buffum's corner, and returning, after some half an hour's absence, find Julian gone to bed. He sat up in his mother's lap, called for milk, "ice" (rice) and "'arter" (water)—asked to see the stars, which could not well be, as it is a cloudy night—and so finally took his departure. Thus ends the day of these two children—one of them four years old; the other, some months less than two. But the days and the years melt away so rapidly, that I hardly know whether they are still little children at their parents' knees, or already a maiden and a youth—a woman and a man. This present life has hardly substance and tangibility enough to be the image of eternity;—the future too soon becomes the present, which, before we can grasp it, looks back upon us as the past;—it must, I think, be only the image of an image. Our next state of existence, we may hope, will be more real—that is to say, it may be only one remove from a reality. But, as yet, we dwell in the shadow cast by Time, which is itself the shadow cast by Eternity.

1849

A modern magician to make the semblance of a human being, with two laths for legs, a pumpkin for a head &c—of the rudest and most meagre materials. Then a tailor helps him to finish his work, and transforms this scarecrow into quite a fashionable figure. N.B. R.S.R. At the end of the story, after deceiving the world for a long time, the spell should be broken; and the gray dandy be discovered to be nothing but a suit of clothes, with these few sticks inside of it. All through his seeming existence as a human being, there shall be

---

1. In "The Old Manse," Hawthorne writes that *he* does not so serve up his heart to the public. He is critical of Byron also in "Earth's Holocaust."
2. Part of a diary kept jointly by Hawthorne and Sophia focusing on their children Una and Julian. In 1848 the family lived in Salem, where Hawthorne worked at the Custom-House.

some characteristics, some tokens, that, to the man of close obser-vation and insight, betray him to be a mere thing of laths and clothes, without heart, soul, or intellect. And so this wretched old thing shall become the symbol of a large class.[3]

1853
June

I burned great heaps of old letters and other papers, a little while ago, preparatory to going to England. Among them were hundreds of Sophia's maiden letters—the world has no more such; and now they are all ashes. What a trustful guardian of secret matters fire is! What should we do without Fire and Death?

---

3. Cf. "Feathertop." R.S.R. is Richard S. Rogers, one of the Whigs who conspired to remove Hawthorne from the Salem Custom-House in 1849. Sophia Hawthorne characterized him as "the illustrious and highly intellectual Richard S. Rogers, who never had an idea in his life" (quoted in Arlin Turner, *Nathaniel Hawthorne: A Biography* [New York: Oxford University Press, 1980], 180).

CRITICISM

Early Criticism

Hawthorne received a gratifying measure of critical recognition and understanding even in his lifetime. From *Twice-told Tales* on, his books drew praise from most of his numerous reviewers. In the 1850s, he was often regarded, especially in England, as the preeminent American writer of fiction, finer than Cooper, bolder than Irving, more moral than Poe. Yet during his earlier career he was in danger of being damned with faint praise and relegated to insignificance as a gentle dreamer with a fine style, a "feminine" delicacy of observation, "quiet humor," and an occasional flight of "wild" or "strange" imagination. These are more or less the terms with which Longfellow sought to rescue his college classmate from obscurity and make him respectable, and the terms stuck like burrs to Hawthorne's name, until he made them seem somewhat silly in *The Scarlet Letter*.

All the more valuable, then, are the two most serious contemporary reviews of Hawthorne's tales, those by Poe and Melville. Poe's attack on Hawthorne's allegory, didacticism, and indirection in his 1847 review may arise in part from his irritation at Bostonians in general, and at Hawthorne's friends Longfellow and Emerson in particular, as well as from his resentment at Hawthorne's blithe dismissal of Poe himself as a critic. But Poe writes from conviction as well as with prejudice. He had come to believe in the basic rightness of popular taste, if properly appealed to. From Poe's standpoint Hawthorne's disposition to write for a restricted audience with a willfully refined point of view was as bad as his fondness for allegory. Poe's intelligently argued essay forces us even today to think through more exactly our appreciation of "Young Goodman Brown," for example, a story Poe singled out for condemnation. Melville's praise of Hawthorne's "blackness, ten times black" and his celebration of his writing as archetypically American may be in part vicarious expressions of Melville's own literary ambitions; but Melville was also fighting the usual critical tendency to stereotype Hawthorne as safe and genteel. Moreover, Melville's piece in its own right is one of the most fervent and thoughtful statements ever made concerning the situation of an American writer.

Hawthorne was responsive to any criticism that took him seriously. To Longfellow, whose long appreciation appeared in the *North American Review* (the most respectable oracle of opinion in New England) and who did more than anyone else to make him known, Hawthorne wrote a graceful letter of thanks that helped animate a friendship of signal importance to both men. To Poe, Hawthorne sent a presentation copy of *Mosses from an Old Manse* acknowledging Poe's earlier enthusiasm for *Twice-told Tales:*

> I have read your occasional notices of my productions with great interest—not so much because your judgment was, upon the whole, favorable, as because it seemed to be given in earnest. I care for nothing but the truth; and shall always much more readily accept a harsh truth, in regard to my writings, than a sugared falsehood.[1]

Yet Hawthorne added, "I admire you rather as a writer of Tales than as a critic upon them," an opinion he had already made evident in one of his magazine sketches, "The Hall of Fantasy."[2] Poe's response to this qualified tribute was to inflict "harsh truth" in abundance on his New England rival in "Tale-Writing—Nathaniel Hawthorne." And Hawthorne seems to have felt sharply the force of Poe's criticism. In his 1851 preface to *Twice-told Tales*, he almost transcribes Poe's charge that his books have been written "to himself and his particular friends alone." He condemned his own tendency to allegory not only publicly in this preface but privately—and with vigor—in his notorious 1854 letter to Fields stigmatizing the "blasted allegories" in *Mosses*. With Melville, Hawthorne showed his courteous sympathy with a kindred mind, even if he was too modest or cautious to agree entirely with the supposed "Virginian." He wrote to Melville's editor, Evert Duyckinck that he had read the review

> with very great pleasure. The writer has a truly generous heart; nor do I think it necessary to appropriate the whole magnificence of his encomium, any more than to devour everything on the table, when a host of noble hospitality spreads a banquet before me. But he is no common man, and, next to deserving his praise, it is good to have beguiled or bewitched such a man into praising me more than I deserve.[3]

I have also included a selection from Margaret Fuller's review of *Mosses from an Old Manse* in the 1846 *New-York Daily Tribune*. Fuller saw a good deal of Hawthorne during the time he and Sophia lived in Concord at the Old Manse. She was imaginatively infatuated with him, while he tried to maintain a distance from her, and their complex relationship may have made it hard for her to write about his work incisively, as she does, for example, in *Tribune* reviews of Melville's *Typee* and Douglass's *Narrative of a Slave*. Nevertheless, with her formidable critical intelligence she has an accurate appreciation of his strengths, and the stories she singles out for praise tend to be the ones that have lasted.

---

1. Hawthorne, *The Letters, 1843–1853* CE, 16:168.
2. "Mr. Poe had gained ready admittance [to the Hall of Fantasy] for the sake of his imagination, but was threatened with ejectment, as belonging to the obnoxious class of critics" (CE 10:636). Hawthorne cut these comments when he revised "The Hall of Fantasy" for *Mosses from an Old Manse*, but Poe almost surely read them in the *Pioneer* in 1843, a magazine to which he himself contributed.
3. Hawthorne, *The Letters, 1843–1853*, CE 16:362.

Henry James's short critical biography contains the most important later nineteenth-century commentary on Hawthorne and is the starting point for twentieth-century readings and reevaluations. James, like Poe and Melville, was stimulated by Hawthorne to define his own aims implicitly, even while he was engaged in evoking the qualities of his American predecessor. Hawthorne, however admirable in his life and work, was for the young James a quintessentially provincial writer, just what he himself did not want to be. James's Hawthorne is remote from Melville's—from the power of blackness, the far roar of Niagara, and the sane madness of vital truth. James had no inclination to associate Hawthorne with such extravagant ideas. He wanted his representative New-Englander to be virtuous and innocent, not savage or Shakespearean. Yet given James's limiting conception of Hawthorne, his comments on the stories are sympathetic and extremely perceptive. They are a useful corrective for all those who would burden Hawthorne with more than his rightful share of Puritanic gloom.

HENRY WADSWORTH LONGFELLOW

Hawthorne's *Twice-told Tales*†

When a new star rises in the heavens, people gaze after it for a season with the naked eye, and with such telescopes as they may find. In the stream of thought, which flows so peacefully deep and clear, through the pages of this book, we see the bright reflection of a spiritual star, after which men will be fain to gaze "with the naked eye, and with the spyglasses of criticism." This star is but newly risen; and ere long the observations of numerous star-gazers, perched up on arm-chairs and editors' tables, will inform the world of its magnitude and its place in the heaven of poetry, whether it be in the paw of the Great Bear, or on the forehead of Pegasus, or on the strings of the Lyre, or in the wing of the Eagle.[1] Our own observations are as follows.

To this little work we would say, "Live ever, sweet, sweet book." It comes from the hand of a man of genius. Every thing about it has the freshness of morning and of May. These flowers and green leaves of poetry have not the dust of the highway upon them. They have been gathered fresh from the secret places of a peaceful and gentle heart. There flow deep waters, silent, calm, and cool; and the green trees

---

† From an unsigned review of *Twice-told Tales* (1837), *North American Review* 45 (July 1837) 59–73. Longfellow and Hawthorne were classmates at Bowdoin in the 1820s. By 1837, Longfellow was professor of foreign languages at Harvard and an established author, though not yet a famous one. All notes are the editor's.

1. Constellations, here representing poetic qualities—rough power, dynamic inspiration, musical grace, lofty majesty.

look into them, and "God's blue heaven." The book, though in prose, is written nevertheless by a poet. He looks upon all things in the spirit of love, and with lively sympathies; for to him external form is but the representation of internal being, all things having a life, an end and aim. The true poet is a friendly man. He takes to his arms even cold and inanimate things, and rejoices in his heart, as did St. Bernard of old, when he kissed his Bride of *Snow*.[2] To his eye all things are beautiful and holy; all are objects of feeling and of song, from the great hierarchy of the silent, saint-like stairs that rule the night, down to the little flowers which are "stars in the firmament of the earth." * * *

There are some honest people into whose hearts "Nature cannot find the way." They have no imagination by which to invest the ruder forms of earthly things with poetry. They are like Wordsworth's Peter Bell;

> "A primrose by a river's brim,
> A yellow primrose was to him,
> And it was nothing more."[3]

But it is one of the high attributes of the poetic mind, to feel a universal sympathy with Nature, both in the material world and in the soul of man. It identifies itself likewise with every object of its sympathy, giving it new sensation and poetic life, whatever that object may be, whether man, bird, beast, flower, or star. As to the pure mind all things are pure, so to the poetic mind all things are poetical. To such souls no age and no country can be utterly dull and prosaic. They make unto themselves their age and country; dwelling in the universal mind of man, and in the universal forms of things. Of such is the author of this book.

* * *

The Twice-told Tales are so called, we presume, from having been first published in various annuals and magazines, and now collected together, and told a second time in a volume by themselves. And a very delightful volume do they make; one of those, which excite in you a feeling of personal interest for the author. A calm, thoughtful face seems to be looking at you from every page; with now a pleasant smile, and now a shade of sadness stealing over its features.

---

2. According to legend, St. Francis of Assisi (ca. 1182–1226), not St. Bernard of Clairvaux (ca. 1090–1153), went out into the moonlight and made a snow wife and three snow children to combat his lustful impulses. When he "embraced his Bride of Snow," he felt peaceful. Longfellow correctly writes of St. Francis and his Bride of Snow two years later in *Hyperion* (1839).
3. Wordsworth, "Peter-Bell: A Tale," lines 248–50. Peter Bell is a brutish boor who eventually learns to sympathize imaginatively with his fellow creatures.

Sometimes, though not often, it glares wildly at you, with a strange and painful expression, as, in the German romance, the bronze knocker of the Archivarius Lindhorst makes up faces at the Student Anselmus.[4]

One of the most prominent characteristics of these tales is, that they are national in their character. The author has wisely chosen his themes among the traditions of New England; the dusty legends of "the good Old Colony times, when we lived under a king." This is the right material for story. It seems as natural to make tales out of old tumble-down traditions, as canes and snuff-boxes out of old steeples, or trees planted by great men. The puritanical times begin to look romantic in the distance. * * * Truly, many quaint and quiet customs, many comic scenes and strange adventures, many wild and wondrous things, fit for humorous tale and soft, pathetic story, lie all about us here in New England. * * *

Another characteristic of this writer is the exceeding beauty of his style. It is as clear as running waters are. Indeed he uses words as mere stepping-stones, upon which, with a free and youthful bound, his spirit crosses and recrosses the bright and rushing stream of thought. Some writers of the present day have introduced a kind of Gothic architecture into their style. All is fantastic, vast, and wondrous in the outward form, and within is mysterious twilight, and the swelling sound of an organ, and a voice chanting hymns in Latin, which need a translation for many of the crowd. To this we do not object. Let the priest chant in what language he will, so long as he understands his own mass-book. But if he wishes the world to listen and be edified, he will do well to choose a language that is generally understood.

And now let us give some specimens of the bright, poetic style we praise so highly.[5]

* * *

These extracts are sufficient to show the beautiful and simple style of the book before us, its vein of pleasant philosophy, and the quiet humor, which is to the face of a book what a smile is to the face of man. In speaking in terms of such high praise as we have done, we have given utterance not alone to our own feelings, but we trust to those of all gentle readers of the Twice-told Tales. Like children we say, "Tell us more."

---

4. In E. T. A. Hoffmann's "The Golden Pot," the Student Anselmus confronts a bewitched doorknocker that makes twisted faces at him when he approaches the Archivist Lindhorst's house to seek employment. Longfellow points to the element of uncanny fantasy in some of Hawthorne's work.
5. Longfellow gives examples of Hawthorne's writing from lighter pieces, such as "The Vision of the Fountain" and "A Rill from the Town Pump."

EDGAR ALLAN POE

[*Twice-told Tales*, Second Edition]†

* * *

Of Mr. Hawthorne's Tales we would say, emphatically, that they belong to the highest region of Art—an Art subservient to genius of a very lofty order. We had supposed, with good reason for so supposing, that he had been thrust into his present position by one of the impudent *cliques* which beset our literature, and whose pretensions it is our full purpose to expose at the earliest opportunity; but we have been most agreeably mistaken. We know of few compositions which the critic can more honestly commend then these "Twice-told Tales." As Americans, we feel proud of the book.

Mr. Hawthorne's distinctive trait is invention, creation, imagination, originality—a trait which, in the literature of fiction, is positively worth all the rest. But the nature of originality, so far as regards its manifestation in letters, is but imperfectly understood. The inventive or original mind as frequently displays itself in novelty of *tone* as in novelty of matter. Mr. Hawthorne is original at *all* points.

It would be a matter of some difficulty to designate the best of these tales; we repeat that, without exception they are beautiful. "Wakefield" is remarkable for the skill with which an old idea—a well-known incident—is worked up or discussed. A man of whims conceives the purpose of quitting his wife and residing *incognito*, for twenty years, in her immediate neighborhood. Something of this kind actually happened in London. The force of Mr. Hawthorne's tale lies in the analysis of the motives which must or might have impelled the husband to such folly, in the first instance, with the possible causes of his perseverance. Upon this thesis a sketch of singular power has been constructed.

* * *

"The Minister's Black Veil" is a masterly composition of which the sole defect is that to the rabble its exquisite skill will be *caviare*. The *obvious* meaning of this article will be found to smother its insinuated one. The *moral* put into the mouth of the dying minister will be supposed to convey the *true* import of the narrative; and that a crime of dark dye, (having reference to the "young lady") has

---

† From an unsigned review of *Twice-told Tales* (1842), *Graham's Magazine* 20 (May 1842): 298–300. This is Poe's second notice of Hawthorne, and the most favorable of the five he published.

been committed, is a point which only minds congenial with that of the author will perceive.

* * *

In the way of objection we have scarcely a word to say of these tales. There is, perhaps, a somewhat too general or prevalent *tone*—a tone of melancholy and mysticism. The subjects are insufficiently varied. There is not so much of *versatility* evinced as we might well be warranted in expecting from the high powers of Mr. Hawthorne. But beyond these trivial exceptions we have really none to make. The style is purity itself. Force abounds. High imagination gleams from every page. Mr. Hawthorne is a man of the truest genius. We only regret that the limits of our Magazine will not permit us to pay him that full tribute of commendation, which, under other circumstances, we should be so eager to pay.

EDGAR ALLAN POE

Tale-Writing—Nathaniel Hawthorne[†]

TWICE-TOLD TALES. By Nathaniel Hawthorne. James Munroe & Co., Boston. 1842
MOSSES FROM AN OLD MANSE. By Nathaniel Hawthorne. Wiley & Putnam, New York. 1846.

In the preface to my sketches of New York Literati, while speaking of the broad distinction between the seeming public and real private opinion respecting our authors, I thus alluded to Nathaniel Hawthorne:—

> "For example, Mr. Hawthorne, the author of 'Twice-told Tales,' is scarcely recognized by the press or by the public, and when noticed at all, is noticed merely to be damned by faint praise. Now, my own opinion of him is, that although his walk is limited and he is fairly to be charged with mannerism, treating all subjects in a similar tone of dreamy *innuendo*, yet in this walk he evinces extraordinary genius, having no rival either in America or elsewhere; and this opinion I have never heard gainsaid by any one literary person in the country. That this opinion, however, is a spoken and not a written one, is referable to the facts, first, that Mr. Hawthorne *is* a poor man, and, secondly, that he *is not* an ubiquitous quack."[1]

† From *Godey's Lady's Book* 35 (November 1847): 252–56. All notes are the editor's.
1. Poe quotes from his own "Author's Introduction" to "The Literati of New York City," *Godey's Lady's Book* 32 (May 1846): 194–201.

The reputation of the author of "Twice-told Tales" has been confined, indeed, until very lately, to literary society; and I have not been wrong, perhaps, in citing him as *the* example, *par excellence*, in this country, of the privately-admired and publicly-unappreciated man of genius. * * *

Beyond doubt, this inappreciation of him on the part of the public arose chiefly from the two causes to which I have referred— from the facts that he is neither a man of wealth nor a quack;—but these are insufficient to account for the whole effect. No small portion of it is attributable to the very marked idiosyncrasy of Mr. Hawthorne himself. In one sense, and in great measure, to be peculiar is to be original, and than the true originality there is no higher literary virtue. This true or commendable originality, however, implies not the uniform, but the continuous peculiarity—a peculiarity springing from ever-active vigor of fancy—better still if from ever-present force of imagination, giving its own hue, its own character to everything it touches, and, especially *self impelled to touch everything.*

It is often said, inconsiderately, that very original writers always fail in popularity—that such and such persons are too original to be comprehended by the mass. "Too peculiar," should be the phrase, "too idiosyncratic." It is, in fact, the excitable, undisciplined and child-like popular mind which most keenly feels the original. * * *

The fact is, that if Mr. Hawthorne were really original, he could not fail of making himself felt by the public. But the fact is, he is *not* original in any sense. Those who speak of him as original, mean nothing more than that he differs in his manner or tone, and in his choice of subjects, from any author of their acquaintance—their acquaintance not extending to the German Tieck,[2] whose manner, in *some* of his works, is absolutely identical with that *habitual* to Hawthorne. * * *

* * * The critic (unacquainted with Tieck) who reads a single tale or essay by Hawthorne, may be justified in thinking him original; but the tone, or manner, or choice of subject, which induces in this critic the sense of the new, will—if not in a second tale, at least in a third and all subsequent ones—not only fail of inducing it, but bring about an exactly antagonistic impression. In concluding a volume and more especially in concluding all the volumes of the author, the critic will abandon his first design of calling him "original," and content himself with styling him "peculiar."

2. Ludwig Tieck (1773–1853), tale writer and an important playwright, critic, and novelist in the German Romantic movement. Though Hawthorne once tried to read Tieck in German, he seems not to have paid much attention to him. An affinity between the two writers was also noticed by other contemporaries, though not with Poe's histrionic assertiveness.

*   *   *

The "peculiarity" or sameness, or monotone of Hawthorne, would, in its mere character of "peculiarity," and without reference to what *is* the peculiarity, suffice to deprive him of all chance of popular appreciation. But at his failure to be appreciated, we can, *of course*, no longer wonder, when we find him monotonous at decidedly the worst of all possible points—at that point which, having the least concern with Nature, is the farthest removed from the popular intellect, from the popular sentiment and from the popular taste. I allude to the strain of allegory which completely overwhelms the greater number of his subjects, and which in some measure interferes with the direct conduct of absolutely all.

In defence of allegory, (however, or for whatever object, employed,) there is scarcely one respectable word to be said. * * * The deepest emotion aroused within us by the happiest allegory, *as* allegory, is a very, very imperfectly satisfied sense of the writer's ingenuity in overcoming a difficulty we should have preferred his not having attempted to overcome. * * * If allegory ever establishes a fact, it is by dint of overturning a fiction. Where the suggested meaning runs through the obvious one in a *very* profound under-current, so as never to interfere with the upper one without our own volition, so as never to show itself unless *called* to the surface, there only, for the proper uses of fictitious narrative, is it available at all. Under the best circumstances, it must always interfere with that unity of effect which, to the artist, is worth all the allegory in the world. Its vital injury, however, is rendered to the most vitally important point in fiction—that of earnestness or verisimilitude. That "The Pilgrim's Progress" is a ludicrously over-rated book, owing its seeming popularity to one or two of those accidents in critical literature which by the critical are sufficiently well understood, is a matter upon which no two thinking people disagree; but the pleasure derivable from it, in any sense, will be found in the direct ratio of the reader's capacity to smother its true purpose, in the direct ratio of his ability to keep the allegory out of sight, or of his inability to comprehend it. Of allegory properly handled, judiciously subdued, seen only as a shadow or by suggestive glimpses, and making its nearest approach to truth in a not obtrusive and therefore not unpleasant *appositeness*, the "Undine" of De La Motte Fouque[3] is the best, and undoubtedly a very remarkable specimen.

---

3. Friedrich, Baron de La Motte-Fouqué (1777–1843), author of *Undine*, a romantic tale of a mermaid who loved a German knight but left him and disappeared among the waters when he was unfaithful to her.

The obvious causes, however, which have prevented Mr. Hawthorne's *popularity*, do not suffice to condemn him in the eyes of the few who belong properly to books, and to whom books, perhaps, do not quite so properly belong. These few estimate an author, not as do the public, altogether by what he does, but in great measure—indeed, even in the greatest measure—by what he evinces a capability of doing. In this view, Hawthorne stands among literary people in America much in the same light as did Coleridge[4] in England. The few, also, through a certain warping of the taste, which long pondering upon books as books merely never fails to induce, are not in condition to view the errors of a scholar as errors altogether. At any time these gentlemen are prone to think the public not right rather than an educated author wrong. But the simple truth is, that the writer who aims at impressing the people, is *always* wrong when he fails in forcing that people to receive the impression. How far Mr. Hawthorne has addressed the people at all, is, of course, not a question for me to decide. His books afford strong internal evidence of having been written to himself and his particular friends alone.

* * *

I must defer to the better opportunity of a volume now in hand, a full discussion of his individual pieces, and hasten to conclude this paper with a summary of his merits and demerits.

He is peculiar and *not* original—unless in those detailed fancies and detached thoughts which his want of general originality will deprive of the appreciation due to them, in preventing them forever reaching the *public* eye. He is infinitely too fond of allegory, and can never hope for popularity so long as he persists in it. This he will not do, for allegory is at war with the whole tone of his nature, which disports itself never so well as when escaping from the mysticism of his Goodman Browns and White Old Maids into the hearty, genial, but still Indian-summer sunshine of his Wakefields and Little Annie's Rambles. Indeed, *his* spirit of "metaphor run-mad" is clearly imbibed from the phalanx and phalanstery atmosphere[5] in which he has been so long struggling for breath. He has not half the material for the exclusiveness of authorship that he possesses for its universality. He has the purest style, the finest taste, the most available

---

4. Samuel Taylor Coleridge (1772–1834), English poet and philosopher, promised more than he performed. Yet he achieved a distinct reputation in his lifetime partly because his genius was so evident in his writings and conversation.
5. I.e., the atmosphere of New England transcendentalism. Poe did not take kindly to the genial account of Emerson and company in "The Old Manse." "Phalanx" and "phalanstery" refer to the community at Brook Farm, where Hawthorne lived for six months in 1841.

scholarship, the most delicate humor, the most touching pathos, the most radiant imagination, the most consummate ingenuity; and with these varied good qualities he has done *well* as a mystic. But is there any one of these qualities which should prevent his doing doubly as well in a career of honest, upright, sensible, prehensible, and comprehensible things? Let him mend his pen, get a bottle of visible ink, come out from the Old Manse, cut Mr. Alcott, hang (if possible) the editor of "The Dial," and throw out of the window to the pigs all his odd numbers of "The North American Review."[6]

MARGARET FULLER

[Hawthorne's *Mosses from an Old Manse*][†]

We have been seated here the last ten minutes, pen in hand, thinking what we can possibly say about this book that will not be either superfluous or impertinent.

Superfluous, because the attractions of Hawthorne's writings cannot fail of one and the same effect on all persons who possess the common sympathies of men. To all who are still happy in some groundwork of unperverted Nature, the delicate, simple, human tenderness, unsought, unbought and therefore precious morality, the tranquil elegance and playfulness, the humor which never breaks the impression of sweetness and dignity, do an inevitable message which requires no comment of the critic to make its meaning clear. Impertinent, because the influence of this mind, like that of some loveliest aspects of Nature, is to induce silence from a feeling of repose. We do not think of any thing particularly worth saying about this that has been so fitly and pleasantly said.

Yet it seems *un*fit that we, in our office of chronicler of intellectual advents and apparitions, should omit to render open and audible honor to one whom we have long delighted to honor. It may be, too, that this slight notice of ours may awaken the attention of those distant or busy who might not otherwise search for the volume, which comes betimes in the leafy month of June.

---

6. A conservative Boston journal. Amos Bronson Alcott (1799–1888); a notoriously vague transcendentalist. *The Dial*, a transcendentalist journal—its editor had been Emerson.

† Nathaniel Hawthorne. *Mosses from an Old Manse*. New York: Wiley & Putnam, 1846. In *New-York Daily Tribune*, 22 June 1846, p. 1; title supplied. Reprinted in *Margaret Fuller: Essays on American Life and Letters*, ed. Joel Myerson (New Haven: College University Press, 1978), 371–74.

So we will give a slight account of it. * * * Though Hawthorne
has now a standard reputation, both for the qualities we have mentioned and the beauty of the style in which they are embodied, yet
we believe he has not been very widely read. This is only because
his works have not been published in the way to insure extensive
circulation in this new, hurrying world of ours. The immense extent
of country over which the reading (still very small in proportion to
the mere working) community is scattered, the rushing and push-
ing of our life at this electrical stage of development, leave no work
a chance to be speedily and largely known that is not trumpeted
and placarded. * * * Under the auspices of Wiley and Putnam,
Hawthorne will have a chance to collect all his own public about
him, and that be felt as a presence which before was only a rumor.

The volume before us shares the charms of Hawthorne's earlier
tales; the only difference being that his range of subjects is a little
wider. There is the same gentle and sincere companionship with
Nature, the same delicate but fearless scrutiny of the secrets of the
heart, the same serene independence of petty and artificial restrictions, whether on opinions or conduct, the same familiar, yet pensive sense of the spiritual or demoniacal influences that haunt the
palpable life and common walks of men, not by many apprehended
except in results. * * *

The introduction to the "Mosses," in which the old Manse, its
inhabitants and visitants are portrayed, is written with even more
than his usual charm of placid grace and many strokes of his admirable good sense. Those who are not, like ourselves, familiar with the
scene and its denizens, will still perceive how true that picture must
be; those of us who are thus familiar will best know how to prize the
record of objects and influences unique in our country and time.

"The Birth Mark" and "Rappaccini's Daughter" embody truths of
profound importance in shapes of aerial elegance. In these, as here
and there in all these pieces, shines the loveliest ideal of love and
the beauty of feminine purity, (by which we mean no mere acts or
abstinences, but perfect single truth felt and done in gentleness)
which is its root.

"The Celestial Railroad," for its wit, wisdom, and the graceful
adroitness with which the natural and material objects are interwoven with the allegories, has already won its meed of admiration.—
"Fire-worship" is a most charming essay for its domestic sweetness
and thoughtful life. "Goodman Brown" is [a] disclosure * * * of the
secrets of the breast. Who has not known such a trial that is capable
indeed of sincere aspiration toward that only good, that infinite
essence, which men call God. Who has not known the hour when
even that best-beloved image cherished as the one precious symbol

left, in the range of human nature, believed to be still pure gold when all the rest have turned to clay, shows, in severe ordeal, the symptoms of alloy. Oh hour of anguish, when the old familiar faces grow dark and dim in the lurid light—when the gods of the hearth, honored in childhood, adored in youth, crumble, and nothing, nothing is left which the daily earthly feelings can embrace—can cherish with unbroken Faith! Yet some survive that trial more happily than young Goodman Brown. They are those who have not sought it—have never of their own accord walked forth with the Tempter into the dim shades of Doubt. Mrs. Bull-Frog is an excellent humorous picture of what is called to be "content at last with substantial realities"!! The "Artist of the Beautiful" presents in a form that is, indeed, beautiful, the opposite view as to what *are* the substantial realities of life. Let each man choose between them according to his kind: Had Hawthorne written "Roger Malvin's Burial" alone, we should be pervaded with the sense of the poetry and religion of his soul.

As a critic, the style of Hawthorne, faithful to his mind, shows repose, a great reserve of strength, a slow secure movement. Though a very refined, he is also a very clear writer, showing * * * a placid grace, and an indolent command of language.

And now, beside the full, calm yet romantic stream of his mind, we will rest. It has refreshment for the weary, islets of fascination no less than dark recesses and shadows for the imaginative, pure reflections for the pure of heart and eye, and, like the Concord he so well describes, many exquisite lilies for him who knows how to get at them.

HERMAN MELVILLE

Hawthorne and His Mosses†

By a Virginian Spending July in Vermont[1]

A papered chamber in a fine old farm-house—a mile from any other dwelling, and dipped to the eaves in foliage—surrounded by mountains, old woods, and Indian ponds,—this, surely, is the place to write of Hawthorne. Some charm is in this northern air, for love and duty seem both impelling to the task. A man of a deep and noble nature has seized me in this seclusion. His wild, witch voice rings through me; or, in softer cadences, I seem to hear it in the songs of the hill-side birds, that sing in the larch trees at my window.

Would that all excellent books were foundlings, without father or mother, that so it might be, we could glorify them, without including their ostensible authors. Nor would any true man take exception to this;—least of all, he who writes,—"When the Artist rises high enough to achieve the Beautiful, the symbol by which he makes it perceptible to mortal senses becomes of little value in his eyes, while his spirit possesses itself in the enjoyment of the reality."[2]

But more than this. I know not what would be the right name to put on the title-page of an excellent book, but this I feel, that the names of all fine authors are fictitious ones, far more so than that of Junius,[3]—simply standing, as they do, for the mystical, ever-eluding Spirit of all Beauty, which ubiquitously possesses men of

† First published in the *Literary World* (*LW*), August 17 and 24, 1850. This text, edited by Harrison Hayford and Hershel Parker, is reprinted from the *Piazza Tales*, volume 9 of *The Writings of Herman Melville* (Evanston and Chicago: Northwestern University Press and The Newberry Library, 1987), pp. 239–53 (NN). It is based on Melville's manuscript rather than on the *Literary World*. The manuscript, in the Duyckinck Collection of the New York Public Library, is a fair copy made by Melville's wife, Elizabeth Shaw Melville. Evert Duyckinck, the editor of the *Literary World*, corrected and toned down Melville's essay slightly for publication. In the footnotes I draw freely on Hershel Parker's notes to the essay both in *The Norton Anthology of American Literature*, 2 vols. (New York: Norton, 1979), 1: 2056–70, and in the NCE of *Moby-Dick* (New York: Norton, 2002), pp. 370–88. All notes not marked *Parker* are my own.

1. A fictitious persona, adopted by Melville partly to stress Hawthorne's national appeal. Melville was a New Yorker, with strong family ties to New England. He wrote the review while visiting relatives in Pittsfield, Massachusetts, not far from Hawthorne's residence in Lenox, and later that year he settled in Pittsfield. He had met and befriended Hawthorne on August 5, at a cheerful all-day party for local and visiting literary celebrities. But for several weeks Hawthorne was ignorant of Melville's authorship of the review; "the Virginian" was at first a mystery-man to Hawthorne and his wife. Melville's fresh enthusiasm for Hawthorne's writing was enhanced by his interest in his new neighbor.
2. From the ending of "The Artist of the Beautiful." Melville adapted the wording of this and other quotations slightly. [*Parker*]
3. Pseudonym of unidentified British author of famous political satires (1769–72), now thought to have been Sir Philip Francis. [*Parker*]

genius. Purely imaginative as this fancy may appear, it nevertheless seems to receive some warranty from the fact, that on a personal interview no great author has ever come up to the idea of his reader. But that dust of which our bodies are composed, how can it fitly express the nobler intelligences among us? With reverence be it spoken, that not even in the case of one deemed more than man, not even in our Saviour, did his visible frame betoken anything of the augustness of the nature within. Else, how could those Jewish eyewitnesses fail to see heaven in his glance.

It is curious, how a man may travel along a country road, and yet miss the grandest, or sweetest of prospects, by reason of an intervening hedge, so like all other hedges, as in no way to hint of the wide landscape beyond. So has it been with me concerning the enchanting landscape in the soul of this Hawthorne, this most excellent Man of Mosses. His "Old Manse" has been written now four years, but I never read it till a day or two since. I had seen it in the book-stores—heard of it often—even had it recommended to me by a tasteful friend, as a rare, quiet book, perhaps too deserving of popularity to be popular. But there are so many books called "excellent", and so much unpopular merit, that amid the thick stir of other things, the hint of my tasteful friend was disregarded; and for four years the Mosses on the old Manse never refreshed me with their perennial green. It may be, however, that all this while, the book, like wine, was only improving in flavor and body. At any rate, it so chanced that this long procrastination eventuated in a happy result. At breakfast the other day, a mountain girl, a cousin of mine,[4] who for the last two weeks has every morning helped me to strawberries and raspberries,—which, like the roses and pearls in the fairy-tale, seemed to fall into the saucer from those strawberry-beds her cheeks,—this delightful creature, this charming Cherry says to me—"I see you spend your mornings in the hay-mow; and yesterday I found there 'Dwight's Travels in New England"[5] Now I have something far better than that,—something more congenial to our summer on these hills. Take these raspberries, and then I will give you some moss."—"Moss!" said I.—"Yes, and you must take it to the barn with you, and good-bye to 'Dwight'".

With that she left me, and soon returned with a volume, verdantly bound, and garnished with a curious frontispiece in green,—nothing less, than a fragment of real moss cunningly pressed to a fly-leaf.— "Why this," said I spilling my raspberries, "this is the 'Mosses from an Old Manse'". "Yes" said cousin Cherry "yes, it is that flowery

4. In fact, Melville's elderly Aunt Mary Melville gave him the book in mid-July.
5. Timothy Dwight's *Travels in New-England and New-York* (1821–22). Dwight (1752–1817) was president of Yale, a public representative of Federalist-Puritan New England, and a literal-minded chronicler compared to Hawthorne and Melville.

Hawthorne."—"Hawthorne and Mosses" said I "no more: it is morning: it is July in the country: and I am off for the barn".

Stretched on that new mown clover, the hill-side breeze blowing over me through the wide barn door, and soothed by the hum of the bees in the meadows around, how magically stole over me this Mossy Man! and how amply, how bountifully, did he redeem that delicious promise to his guests in the Old Manse, of whom it is written— "Others could give them pleasure, or amusement, or instruction— these could be picked up anywhere—but it was for me to give them rest. Rest, in a life of trouble! What better could be done for weary and world-worn spirits? what better could be done for anybody, who came within our magic circle, than to throw the spell of a magic spirit over him?"[6]—So all that day, half-buried in the new clover, I watched this Hawthorne's "Assyrian dawn, and Paphian sunset and moonrise, from the summit of our Eastern Hill."[7]

The soft ravishments of the man spun me round about in a web of dreams, and when the book was closed, when the spell was over, this wizard "dismissed me with but misty reminiscences, as if I had been dreaming of him".[8]

What a mild moonlight of contemplative humor bathes that Old Manse!—the rich and rare distilment of a spicy and slowly-oozing heart. No rollicking rudeness, no gross fun fed on fat dinners, and bred in the lees of wine,—but a humor so spiritually gentle, so high, so deep, and yet so richly relishable, that it were hardly inappropriate in an angel. It is the very religion of mirth; for nothing so human but it may be advanced to that. The orchard of the Old Manse seems the visible type of the fine mind that has described it. Those twisted, and contorted old trees, "that stretch out their crooked branches, and take such hold of the imagination, that we remember them as humorists, and odd-fellows." And then, as surrounded by these grotesque forms, and hushed in the noon-day repose of this Hawthorne's spell, how aptly might the still fall of his ruddy thoughts into your soul be symbolized by "the thump of a great apple, in the stillest afternoon, falling without a breath of wind, from the mere necessity of perfect ripeness"! For no less ripe than ruddy are the apples of the thoughts and fancies in this sweet Man of Mosses.

"Buds and Bird-voices"—What a delicious thing is that!—"Will the world ever be so decayed, that Spring may not renew its greenness?"—And the "Fire-Worship". Was ever the hearth so glorified into an altar before? The mere title of that piece is better than any common work in fifty folio volumes. How exquisite is this:—

6. From "The Old Manse." Hawthorne wrote "tranquil spirit."
7. Also from "The Old Manse." Hawthorne paraphrases Emerson's *Nature* here, though Melville seems not to have known it. See p. 296, n. 3.
8. From "The Old Manse," as are the quotations in the following paragraph.

"Nor did it lessen the charm of his soft, familiar courtesy and help-fulness, that the mighty spirit, were opportunity offered him, would run riot through the peaceful house, wrap its inmates in his terri-ble embrace, and leave nothing of them save their whitened bones. This possibility of mad destruction only made his domestic kind-ness the more beautiful and touching. It was so sweet of him, being endowed with such power, to dwell, day after day, and one long, lonesome night after another, on the dusky hearth, only now and then betraying his wild nature, by thrusting his red tongue out of the chimney-top! True, he had done much mischief in the world, and was pretty certain to do more, but his warm heart atoned for all. He was kindly to the race of man."

But he has still other apples, not quite so ruddy, though full as ripe;—apples, that have been left to wither on the tree, after the pleasant autumn gathering is past. The sketch of "The Old Apple Dealer" is conceived in the subtlest spirit of sadness; he whose "sub-dued and nerveless boyhood prefigured his abortive prime, which, likewise, contained within itself the prophecy and image of his lean and torpid age". Such touches as are in this piece can not proceed from any common heart. They argue such a depth of tenderness, such a boundless sympathy with all forms of being, such an omni-present love, that we must needs say, that this Hawthorne is here almost alone in his generation,—at least, in the artistic manifesta-tion of these things. Still more. Such touches as these,—and many, very many similar ones, all through his chapters—furnish clews, whereby we enter a little way into the intricate, profound heart where they originated. And we see, that suffering, some time or other and in some shape or other,—this only can enable any man to depict it in others. All over him, Hawthorne's melancholy rests like an Indian Summer, which though bathing a whole country in one softness, still reveals the distinctive hue of every towering hill, and each far-winding vale.

But it is the least part of genius that attracts admiration. Where Hawthorne is known, he seems to be deemed a pleasant writer, with a pleasant style,—a sequestered, harmless man, from whom any deep and weighty thing would hardly be anticipated:—a man who means no meanings. But there is no man, in whom humor and love, like mountain peaks, soar to such a rapt height, as to receive the irradiations of the upper skies;—there is no man in whom humor and love are developed in that high form called genius; no such man can exist without also possessing, as the indispensable complement of these, a great, deep intellect, which drops down into the universe like a plummet. Or, love and humor are only the eyes, through which such an intellect views this world. The great beauty in such a mind is but the product of its strength. What, to all readers, can be more charming than the piece entitled "Monsieur du Miroir"; and to a reader at all capable of fully fathoming it, what, at the same time, can possess more mystical depth of meaning?—Yes, there he sits, and looks at me,—this "shape of mystery", this "identical Monsieur du Miroir".—"Methinks I should tremble now, were his wizard power of gliding through all impediments in search of me, to place him suddenly before my eyes".

How profound, nay appalling, is the moral evolved by the "Earth's Holocaust"; where—beginning with the hollow follies and affectations of the world,—all vanities and empty theories and forms, are, one after another, and by an admirably graduated, growing comprehensiveness, thrown into the allegorical fire, till, at length, nothing is left but the all-engendering heart of man; which remaining still unconsumed, the great conflagration is nought.

Of a piece with this, is the "Intelligence Office", a wondrous symbolizing of the secret workings in men's souls. There are other sketches, still more charged with ponderous import.

"The Christmas Banquet", and "The Bosom Serpent" would be fine subjects for a curious and elaborate analysis, touching the conjectural parts of the mind, that produced them. For spite of all the Indian-summer sunlight on the hither side of Hawthorne's soul, the other side—like the dark half of the physical sphere—is shrouded in a blackness, ten times black. But this darkness but gives more effect to the ever-moving dawn, that forever advances through it, and circumnavigates his world. Whether Hawthorne has simply availed himself of this mystical blackness as a means to the wondrous effects he makes it to produce in his lights and shades; or whether there really lurks in him, perhaps unknown to himself, a touch of Puritanic gloom,—this, I cannot altogether tell. Certain it is, however, that this great power of blackness in him derives its force from its appeals to that Calvinistic sense of Innate Depravity and Original Sin, from whose visitations, in some shape or other, no deeply thinking mind is always and wholly free. For, in certain moods, no man can weigh this world, without throwing in something, somehow like Original Sin, to strike the uneven balance. At all events, perhaps no writer has ever wielded this terrific thought with greater terror than this same harmless Hawthorne. Still more: this black conceit pervades him, through and through. You may be witched by his sunlight,—transported by the bright gildings in the skies he builds over you;—but there is the blackness of darkness beyond; and even his bright gildings but fringe, and play upon the edges of thunder-clouds.—In one word, the world is mistaken in this Nathaniel Hawthorne. He himself must often have smiled at its absurd misconception of him. He is immeasurably deeper than the plummet of the mere critic. For it is not the brain that can test such a man; it is only the heart. You cannot come to know greatness by inspecting it; there is no glimpse to be caught of it, except by intuition; you need not ring it, you but touch it, and you find it is gold.

Now it is that blackness in Hawthorne, of which I have spoken, that so fixes and fascinates me. It may be, nevertheless, that it is too largely developed in him. Perhaps he does not give us a ray of his light for every shade of his dark. But however this may be, this blackness it is that furnishes the infinite obscure of his back-ground,— that back-ground, against which Shakespeare plays his grandest conceits, the things that have made for Shakespeare his loftiest, but most circumscribed renown, as the profoundest of thinkers. For by philosophers Shakespeare is not adored as the great man of tragedy and comedy.—"Off with his head! so much for Buckingham!"[9] this sort of rant, interlined by another hand, brings down the house,—those mistaken souls, who dream of Shakespeare as a mere man of Richard-the-Third humps, and Macbeth daggers. But it is those deep far-away things in him; those occasional flashings-forth of the intuitive Truth in him; those short, quick probings at the very axis of reality;—these are the things that make Shakespeare, Shakespeare. Through the mouths of the dark characters of Hamlet, Timon, Lear, and Iago, he craftily says, or sometimes insinuates the things, which we feel to be so terrifically true, that it were all but madness for any good man, in his own proper character, to utter, or even hint of them. Tormented into desperation, Lear the frantic King tears off the mask, and speaks the sane madness of vital truth, But, as I before said, it is the least part of genius that attracts admiration. And so, much of the blind, unbridled admiration that has been heaped upon Shakespeare, has been lavished upon the least part of him. And few of his endless commentators and critics seem to have remembered, or even perceived, that the immediate products of a great mind are not so great, as that undeveloped, (and sometimes undevelopable) yet dimly-discernable greatness, to which these immediate products are but the infallible indices. In Shakespeare's tomb lies infinitely more than Shakspeare[1] ever wrote. And if I magnify Shakespeare, it is not so much for what he did do, as for what he did not do, or refrained from doing. For in this world of lies, Truth is forced to fly like a scared white doe in the woodlands; and only by cunning glimpses will she reveal herself, as in Shakespeare and

---

9. Famous line added to Shakespeare's *Richard III* by Colley Cibber (1671–1757) in his 18th-century stage version of the play.
1. An acceptable variant spelling then, and Melville's own spelling here (and sometimes elsewhere), even though "Shakespeare" is Mrs. Melville's consistent spelling, which he let stand twice in this passage, all through the essay, and used himself four times in revising her fair copy. The NN editors do not emend such spellings (see "Spencer" at p. 383 and "Marlow" at p. 384). [*Parker*]

other masters of the great Art of Telling the Truth,—even though it be covertly, and by snatches.

But if this view of the all-popular Shakespeare be seldom taken by his readers, and if very few who extol him, have ever read him deeply, or, perhaps, only have seen him on the tricky stage, (which alone made, and is still making him his mere mob renown)—if few men have time, or patience, or palate, for the spiritual truth as it is in that great genius;—it is, then, no matter of surprise that in a contemporaneous age, Nathaniel Hawthorne is a man, as yet, almost utterly mistaken among men. Here and there, in some quiet arm-chair in the noisy town, or some deep nook among the noiseless mountains, he may be appreciated for something of what he is. But unlike Shakespeare, who was forced to the contrary course by cir-cumstances, Hawthorne (either from simple disinclination, or else from inaptitude) refrains from all the popularizing noise and show of broad farce, and blood-besmeared tragedy; content with the still, rich utterances of a great intellect in repose, and which sends few thoughts into circulation, except they be arterialized at his large warm lungs, and expanded in his honest heart.

Nor need you fix upon that blackness in him, if it suit you not. Nor, indeed, will all readers discern it, for it is, mostly, insinuated to those who may best understand it, and account for it; it is not obtruded upon every one alike.

Some may start to read of Shakespeare and Hawthorne on the same page. They may say, that if an illustration were needed, a lesser light might have sufficed to elucidate this Hawthorne, this small man of yesterday. But I am not, willingly, one of those, who, as touching Shakespeare at least, exemplify the maxim of Rochefoucault,[2] that "we exalt the reputation of some, in order to depress that of others";—who, to teach all noble-souled aspirants that there is no hope for them, pronounce Shakespeare absolutely unapproachable. But Shakespeare has been approached. There are minds that have gone as far as Shakespeare into the universe. And hardly a mortal man, who, at some time or other, has not felt as great thoughts in him as any you will find in Hamlet. We must not inferentially malign mankind for the sake of any one man, whoever he may be. This is too cheap a pur-chase of contentment for conscious mediocrity to make. Besides, this absolute and unconditional adoration of Shakespeare has grown to be a part of our Anglo Saxon superstitions. The Thirty Nine articles[3] are now Forty. Intolerance has come to exist in this matter. You must

2. François de la Rochefoucauld (1613–1680), French moralist noted for his acerbic *Moral Reflections & Maxims* with their dim view of human nature. [*Parker*]
3. Articles of faith issued in 1551 and 1553 by the Church of England, acceptance of which is obligatory for its clergy. The phrase came to refer to any such basic list of beliefs. [*Parker*]

believe in Shakespeare's unapproachability, or quit the country. But what sort of a belief is this for an American, a man who is bound to carry republican progressiveness into Literature, as well as into Life? Believe me, my friends that Shakespeares are this day being born on the banks of the Ohio.[4] And the day will come, when you shall say who reads a book by an Englishman that is a modern?[5] The great mistake seems to be, that even with those Americans who look forward to the coming of a great literary genius among us, they somehow fancy he will come in the costume of Queen Elizabeth's day,—be a writer of dramas founded upon old English history, or the tales of Boccaccio.[6] Whereas, great geniuses are parts of the times; they themselves are the times; and possess a correspondent coloring. It is of a piece with the Jews, who while their Shiloh[7] was meekly walking in their streets, were still praying for his magnificent coming; looking for him in a chariot, who was already among them on an ass. Nor must we forget, that, in his own life-time, Shakespeare was not Shakespeare, but only Master William Shakespeare of the shrewd, thriving, business firm of Condell, Shakespeare & Co., proprietors of the Globe Theatre in London; and by a courtly author, of the name of Greene,[8] was hooted at, as an "upstart crow" beautified "with other birds' feathers". For, mark it well, imitation is often the first charge brought against real originality. Why this is so, there is not space to set forth here. You must have plenty of sea-room to tell the Truth in; especially, when it seems to have an aspect of newness, as America did in 1492, though it was then just as old, and perhaps older than Asia, only those sagacious philosophers, the common sailors, had never seen it before; swearing it was all water and moonshine there.

Now, I do not say that Nathaniel of Salem is a greater than William of Avon, or as great. But the difference between the two men is by no means immeasurable. Not a very great deal more, and Nathaniel were verily William.

This, too, I mean, that if Shakespeare has not been equalled, he is sure to be surpassed, and surpassed by an American born now or yet to be born.[9] For it will never do for us who in most other things

---

4. Melville, surely at Duyckinck's urging, toned this down to "that men not very much inferior to Shakespeare are being born on the banks of the Ohio." [Parker]
5. Reference to a famous insult by Sydney Smith, a Scottish critic, in the Edinburgh Review 33 (January 1820): "In the four quarters of the globe, who reads an American book? Or goes to an American play? Or looks at an American picture or statue?" [Parker]
6. Tales in the Decameron (1349–51) of Giovanni Boccaccio (1313–1375). [Parker]
7. From Genesis 49.10, a messiah or expected great leader, most often applied to Jesus. [Parker]
8. Robert Greene made these slurs against the young Shakespeare in Groatsworth of Wit Bought with a Million Repentance (1592). [Parker]
9. Duyckinck almost certainly was the one who toned the passage down to read "if Shakespeare has not been equalled, give the world time, and he is sure to be surpassed, in one hemisphere or the other." [Parker]

out-do as well as out-brag the world, it will not do for us to fold our hands and say, In the highest department advance there is none. Nor will it at all do to say, that the world is getting grey and grizzled now, and has lost that fresh charm which she wore of old, and by virtue of which the great poets of past times made themselves what we esteem them to be. Not so. The world is as young today, as when it was created; and this Vermont morning dew is as wet to my feet, as Eden's dew to Adam's. Nor has Nature been all over ransacked by our progenitors, so that no new charms and mysteries remain for this latter generation to find. Far from it. The trillionth part has not yet been said; and all that has been said, but multiplies the avenues to what remains to be said. It is not so much paucity, as superabundance of material that seems to incapacitate modern authors.

Let America then prize and cherish her writers; yea, let her glorify them. They are not so many in number, as to exhaust her goodwill. And while she has good kith and kin of her own, to take to her bosom, let her not lavish her embraces upon the household of an alien. For believe it or not England, after all, is, in many things, an alien to us. China has more bowels of real love for us than she. But even were there no Hawthorne, no Emerson, no Whittier, no Irving, no Bryant, no Dana, no Cooper, no Willis (not the author of the "Dashes", but the author of the "Belfry Pigeon")[1]—were there none of these, and others of like calibre among us, nevertheless, let America first praise mediocrity even, in her own children, before she praises (for everywhere, merit demands acknowledgment from every one) the best excellence in the children of any other land. Let her own authors, I say, have the priority of appreciation. I was much pleased with a hot-headed Carolina cousin of mine, who once said,—"If there were no other American to stand by, in Literature,—why, then, I would stand by Pop Emmons[2] and his 'Fredoniad,' and till a better epic came along, swear it was not very far behind the Iliad." Take away the words, and in spirit he was sound.

Not that American genius needs patronage in order to expand. For that explosive sort of stuff will expand though screwed up in a vice, and burst it, though it were triple steel. It is for the nation's sake, and not for her authors' sake, that I would have America be heedful of

---

1. Melville's journalist friend Nathaniel Parker Willis (1806–1857) wrote *Dashes at Life with a Free Pencil* (1845) and the poem "The Belfry Pigeon" (1831). [*Parker*]
2. "Pop" Emmons is a result of Melville's confusion. As a child he was taken for walks on the Boston Common where a local orator, William (Pop) Emmons kept a concessionaire's stand at which he sold what the Portland *Daily Advertiser* on November 14, 1851, recalled as "a delectable beverage known in those days as 'egg pop,'" hence the soubriquet "Pop Emmons." In the stand Emmons also kept for sale copies of his patriotic orations, which he would willingly repeat. When Melville later saw the four-volume nationalistic epic poem about naval battles in the war of 1812 *The Fredoniad* he assumed it was by the man he remembered, but the poem was actually by Pop Emmons's brother Richard Emmons. [*Parker*]

the increasing greatness among her writers. For how great the shame, if other nations should be before her, in crowning her heroes of the pen. But this is almost the case now. American authors have received more just and discriminating praise (however loftily and ridiculously given, in certain cases) even from some Englishmen, than from their own countrymen. There are hardly five critics in America; and several of them are asleep. As for patronage, it is the American author who now patronizes his country, and not his country him. And if at times some among them appeal to the people for more recognition, it is not always with selfish motives, but patriotic ones.

It is true, that but few of them as yet have evinced that decide originality which merits great praise. But that graceful writer,[3] who perhaps of all Americans has received the most plaudits from his own country for his productions,—that very popular and amiable writer, however good, and self-reliant in many things, perhaps owes his chief reputation to the self-acknowledged imitation of a foreign model, and to the studied avoidance of all topics but smooth ones. But it is better to fail in originality, than to succeed in imitation. He who has never failed somewhere, that man can not be great. Failure is the true test of greatness. And if it be said, that continual success is a proof that a man wisely knows his powers,—it is only to be added, that, in that case, he knows them to be small. Let us believe it, then, once for all, that there is no hope for us in these smooth pleasing writers that know their powers. Without malice, but to speak the plain fact, they but furnish an appendix to Goldsmith, and other English authors. And we want no American Goldsmiths;[4] nay, we want no American Miltons. It were the vilest thing you could say of a true American author, that he were an American Tompkins.[5] Call him an American, and have done; for you can not say a nobler thing of him.—But it is not meant that all American writers should studiously cleave to nationality in their writings: only this, no American writer should write like an Englishman, or a Frenchman; let him write like a man, for then he will be sure to write like an American. Let us away with this Bostonian[6] leaven of literary flunkeyism towards England. If either must play the flunkey in this thing, let England do it, not us. And the time is not far off when

3. Washington Irving. Hawthorne was sometimes coupled with Irving as another graceful and amiable writer.
4. Irving was often called the American Goldsmith [*Parker*]. Oliver Goldsmith (1730–1774) was an Irish-born English author of poems, plays, sketches, and a novel, *The Vicar of Wakefield*. His writings are notable for their good humor, gracefulness, and tender sentimentality.
5. Melville means "any Tom, Dick, or Harry," an "American Anybody." [*Parker*]
6. Melville canceled this word, probably under Duyckinck's pressure, which was restored by the NN editors. [*Parker*]

circumstances may force her to it.[7] While we are rapidly preparing for that political supremacy among the nations, which prophetically awaits us at the close of the present century; in a literary point of view, we are deplorably unprepared for it; and we seem studious to remain so. Hitherto, reasons might have existed why this should be; but no good reason exists now. And all that is requisite to amendment in this matter, is simply this: that, while freely acknowledging all excellence, everywhere, we should refrain from unduly lauding foreign writers and, at the same time, duly recognize the meritorious writers that are our own;—those writers, who breathe that unshackled, democratic spirit of Christianity in all things, which now takes the practical lead in this world, though at the same time led by ourselves—us Americans. Let us boldly contemn all imitation, though it comes to us graceful and fragrant as the morning; and foster all originality, though, at first, it be crabbed and ugly as our own pine knots. And if any of our authors fail, or seem to fail, then, in the words of my enthusiastic Carolina cousin, let us clap him on the shoulder, and back him against all Europe for his second round; The truth is, that in our point of view, this matter of a national literature has come to such a pass with us, that in some sense we must turn bullies, else the day is lost, or superiority so far beyond us, that we can hardly say it will ever be ours.

And now, my countrymen, as an excellent author, of your own flesh and blood,—an unimitating, and, perhaps, in his way, an inimitable man—whom better can I commend to you, in the first place, than Nathaniel Hawthorne. He is one of the new, and far better generation of your writers. The smell of your beeches and hemlocks is upon him; your own broad praries are in his soul; and if you travel away inland into his deep and noble nature, you will hear the far roar of his Niagara. Give not over to future generations the glad duty of acknowledging him for what he is. Take that joy to your self, in your own generation; and so shall he feel those grateful impulses in him, that may possibly prompt him to the full flower of some still greater achievement in your eyes. And by confessing him, you thereby confess others; you brace the whole brotherhood. For genius, all over the world, stands hand in hand, and one shock of recognition runs the whole circle round.

In treating of Hawthorne, or rather of Hawthorne in his writings (for I never saw the man[8] and in the chances of a quiet plantation life, remote from his haunts, perhaps never shall) in treating of his works, I say, I have thus far omitted all mention of his "Twice Told

---

7. The NN editors restore this prophetic sentence, which Melville canceled, apparently under Duyckinck's influence. [*Parker*]
8. In fact, Melville had met Hawthorne just before writing the essay. [*Parker*]

Tales", and "Scarlet Letter". Both are excellent; but full of such manifold, strange and diffusive beauties, that time would all but fail me, to point the half of them out. But there are things in those two books, which, had they been written in England a century ago, Nathaniel Hawthorne had utterly displaced many of the bright names we now revere on authority. But I am content to leave Hawthorne to himself, and to the infallible finding of posterity; and however great may be the praise I have bestowed upon him, I feel, that in so doing, I have more served and honored myself, than him. For, at bottom, great excellence is praise enough to itself; but the feeling of a sincere and appreciative love and admiration towards it, this is relieved by utterance; and warm, honest praise ever leaves a pleasant flavor in the mouth; and it is an honorable thing to confess to what is honorable in others.

But I cannot leave my subject yet. No man can read a fine author, and relish him to his very bones, while he reads, without subsequently fancying to himself some ideal image of the man and his mind. And if you rightly look for it, you will almost always find that the author himself has somewhere furnished you with his own picture.—For poets (whether in prose or verse), being painters of Nature, are like their brethren of the pencil, the true portrait-painters, who, in the multitude of likenesses to be sketched, do not invariably omit their own; and in all high instances, they paint them without any vanity, though, at times, with a lurking something, that would take several pages to properly define.

I submit it, then, to those best acquainted with the man personally, whether the following is not Nathaniel Hawthorne;—and to himself, whether something involved in it does not express the temper of his mind,—that lasting temper of all true, candid men—a seeker, not a finder yet:—

> "A man now entered, in neglected attire, with the aspect of a thinker, but somewhat too rough-hewn and brawny for a scholar. His face was full of sturdy vigor, with some finer and keener attribute beneath; though harsh at first, it was tempered with the glow of a large, warm heart, which had force enough to heat his powerful intellect through and through. He advanced to the Intelligencer, and looked at him with a glance of such stern sincerity, that perhaps few secrets were beyond its scope.
>
> "'I seek for Truth', said he."[9]

• • •

9. From "The Intelligence Office," an office where various types imagined by Hawthorne seek employment, information, and missing articles both physical and spiritual.

Twenty four hours have elapsed since writing the foregoing. I have just returned from the hay mow, charged more and more with love and admiration of Hawthorne. For I have just been gleaning through the Mosses, picking up many things here and there that had previously escaped me. And I found that but to glean after this man, is better than to be in at the harvest of others. To be frank (though, perhaps, rather foolish) notwithstanding what I wrote yesterday of these Mosses, I had not then culled them all; but had, nevertheless, been sufficiently sensible of the subtle essence, in them, as to write as I did. To what infinite height of loving wonder and admiration I may yet be borne, when by repeatedly banquetting on these Mosses, I shall have thoroughly incorporated their whole stuff into my being,—that, I can not tell. But already I feel that this Hawthorne has dropped germinous seeds into my soul. He expands and deepens down, the more I contemplate him; and further, and further, shoots his strong New-England roots into the hot soil of my Southern soul.

By careful reference to the "Table of Contents", I now find, that I have gone through all the sketches; but that when I yesterday wrote, I had not all read two particular pieces, to which I now desire to call special attention,—"A Select Party", and "Young Goodman Brown". Here, be it said to all those whom this poor fugitive scrawl of mine may tempt to the perusal of the "Mosses," that they must on no account suffer themselves to be trifled with, disappointed, or deceived by the triviality of many of the titles to these Sketches. For in more than one instance, the title utterly belies the piece. It is as if rustic demijohns containing the very best and costliest of Falernian and Tokay, were labelled "Cider", "Perry," and "Elderberry wine". The truth seems to be, that like many other geniuses, this Man of Mosses takes great delight in hoodwinking the world,—at least, with respect to himself. Personally, I doubt not, that he rather prefers to be generally esteemed but a so-so sort of author; being willing to reserve the thorough and acute appreciation of what he is, to that party most qualified to judge—that is, to himself. Besides, at the bottom of their natures, men like Hawthorne, in many things, deem the plaudits of the public such strong presumptive evidence of mediocrity in the object of them, that it would in some degree render them doubtful of their own powers, did they hear much and vociferous braying concerning them in the public pastures. True, I have been braying myself (if you please to be witty enough, to have it so) but then I claim to be the first that has so brayed in this particular matter; and therefore, while pleading guilty to the charge still claim all the merit due to originality.

But with whatever motive, playful or profound, Nathaniel Hawthorne has chosen to entitle his pieces in the manner he has, it is certain, that some of them are directly calculated to deceive—egregiously deceive, the superficial skimmer of pages. To be downright and candid once more, let me cheerfully say, that two of these titles did dolefully dupe no less an eagle-eyed reader than myself; and that, too, after I had been impressed with a sense of the great depth and breadth of this American man. "Who in the name of thunder" (as the country-people say in this neighborhood) "who in the name of thunder", would anticipate any marvel in a piece entitled "Young Goodman Brown"? You would of course suppose that it was a simple little tale, intended as a supplement to "Goody Two Shoes".[1] Whereas, it is deep as Dante; nor can you finish it, without addressing the author in his own words—"It is yours to penetrate, in every bosom, the deep mystery of sin". And with Young Goodman, too, in allegorical pursuit of his Puritan wife, you cry out in your anguish,—

> "'Faith!' shouted Goodman Brown, in a voice of agony and desperation; and the echoes of the forest mocked him, crying—'Faith! Faith!' as if bewildered wretches were seeking her all through the wilderness."

Now this same piece, entitled "Young Goodman Brown", is one of the two that I had not all read yesterday; and I allude to it now, because it is, in itself, such a strong positive illustration of that blackness in Hawthorne, which I had assumed from the mere occasional shadows of it, as revealed in several of the other sketches. But had I previously perused "Young Goodman Brown", I should have been at no pains to draw the conclusion, which I came to, at a time, when I was ignorant that the book contained one such direct and unqualified manifestation of it.

The other piece of the two referred to, is entitled "A Select Party", which, in my first simplicity upon originally taking hold of the book, I fancied must treat of some pumpkin-pie party in Old Salem, or some chowder party on Cape Cod. Whereas, by all the gods of Peedee![2] it is the sweetest and sublimest thing that has been written since Spencer[3] wrote. Nay, there is nothing in Spencer that surpasses it perhaps, nothing that equals it. And the test is this: read any canto in "The Faery Queen", and then read "A Select Party", and decide which pleases you the most,—that is, if you are qualified to judge. Do not be frightened at this; for when Spencer was alive, he was thought of very much as Hawthorne is now,—was generally accounted just such a "gentle" harmless man. It may be, that to common eyes, the sublimity of Hawthorne seems lost in his sweetness,—as perhaps in

---

1. A nursery tale, attributed to Goldsmith. [*Parker*]
2. Melville substituted "Peedee" for his original "Greece." Peedee is a river in the Carolinas. [*Parker*]
3. Edmund Spenser (1552?–1599) whose allegorical *Faerie Queene* (1590, 1596) was favorite reading of both Hawthorne and Melville. [*Parker*]

this same "Select Party" of his; for whom, he has builded so august a dome of sunset clouds, and served them on richer plate, than Belshazzar's when he banquetted his lords in Babylon.[4]

But my chief business now, is to point out a particular page in this piece, having reference to an honored guest, who under the name of "The Master Genius" but in the guise of "a young man of poor attire, with no insignia of rank or acknowledged eminence", is introduced to the Man of Fancy, who is the giver of the feast. Now the page having reference to this "Master Genius", so happily expresses much of what I yesterday wrote, touching the coming of the literary Shiloh of America, that I cannot but be charmed by the coincidence; especially, when it shows such a parity of ideas, at least in this one point, between a man like Hawthorne and a man like me.

And here, let me throw out another conceit of mine touching this American Shiloh, or "Master Genius", as Hawthorne calls him. May it not be, that this commanding mind has not been, is not, and never will be, individually developed in any one man? And would it, indeed, appear so unreasonable to suppose, that this great fullness and overflowing may be, or may be destined to be, shared by a plurality of men of genius? Surely, to take the very greatest example on record, Shakespeare cannot be regarded as in himself the concretion of all the genius of his time; nor as so immeasurably beyond Marlow, Webster, Ford, Beaumont, Jonson, that those great men can be said to share none of his power? For one, I conceive that there were dramatists in Elizabeth's day, between whom and Shakespeare the distance was by no means great. Let anyone, hitherto little acquainted with those neglected old authors, for the first time read them thoroughly, or even read Charles Lamb's[5] Specimens of them, and he will be amazed at the wondrous ability of those Anaks of men, and shocked at this renewed example of the fact, that Fortune has more to do with fame than merit,—though, without merit, lasting fame there can be none.

Nevertheless, it would argue too illy of my country were this maxim to hold good concerning Nathaniel Hawthorne, a man, who already, in some few minds, has shed "such a light, as never illuminates the earth, save when a great heart burns as the household fire of a grand intellect."

The words are his,—in the "Select Party"; and they are a magnificent setting to a coincident sentiment of my own, but ramblingly expressed yesterday, in reference to himself. Gainsay it who will, as I now write, I am Posterity speaking by proxy—and after times will

---

4. The "great feast" Belshazzar, king of Babylon (6th century B.C.E.), gave "to a thousand of his lords" (Daniel 5.1). [*Parker*]
5. Editor of *Specimens of the English Dramatic Poets Who Lived about the Time of Shakespeare* (1808). "Anaks": giants (Joshua 11:21). [*Parker*]

make it more than good, when I declare—that the American, who up to the present day, has evinced, in Literature, the largest brain with the largest heart, that man is Nathaniel Hawthorne. Moreover, that whatever Nathaniel Hawthorne may hereafter write, "The Mosses from an Old Manse" will be ultimately accounted his masterpiece. For there is a sure, though a secret sign in some works which prove the culmination of the powers (only the developable ones, however) that produced them. But I am by no means desirous of the glory of a prophet. I pray Heaven that Hawthorne may *yet* prove me an impostor in this prediction. Especially, as I somehow cling to the strange fancy, that, in all men, hiddenly reside certain wondrous, occult properties—as in some plants and minerals—which by some happy but very rare accident (as bronze was discovered by the melting of the iron and brass in the burning of Corinth)[6] may chance to be called forth here on earth; not entirely waiting for their better discovery in the more congenial, blessed atmosphere of heaven.

Once more—for it is hard to be finite upon an infinite subject, and all subjects are infinite. By some people, this entire scrawl of mine may be esteemed altogether unnecessary, inasmuch, "as years ago" (they may say) "we found out the rich and rare stuff in this Hawthorne, whom you now parade forth, as if only *yourself* were the discoverer of this Portuguese diamond[7] in our Literature".— But even granting all this; and adding to it, the assumption that the books of Hawthorne have sold by the five-thousand,—what does that signify?—They should be sold by the hundred-thousand; and read by the million; and admired by every one who is capable of admiration.

HENRY JAMES

Early Writings[†]

* * *

No portrait of Hawthorne at this period[1] is at all exact which fails to insist upon the constant struggle which must have gone on between his shyness and his desire to know something of life; between what may be called his evasive and his inquisitive tendencies. I suppose it is no injustice to Hawthorne to say that on the whole his shyness

---

6. Greek city plundered and burned by the Romans in 146 B.C.E. [*Parker*]
7. A diamond cut according to an elaborate system and prized for its splendor and finish. [*Parker*]
† From *Hawthorne* (London, 1879), chap. 3:55–66. All notes are the editor's.
1. The 1830s and the early 1840s.

always prevailed; and yet, obviously, the struggle was constantly there. He says of his *Twice-Told Tales*, in the preface, "They are not the talk of a secluded man with his own mind and heart (had it been so they could hardly have failed to be more deeply and permanently valuable,) but his attempts, and very imperfectly successful ones, to open an intercourse with the world." We are speaking here of small things, it must be remembered—of little attempts, little sketches, a little world. But everything is relative, and this smallness of scale must not render less apparent the interesting character of Hawthorne's efforts. As for the *Twice-Told Tales* themselves, they are an old story now; every one knows them a little, and those who admire them particularly have read them a great many times. The writer of this sketch belongs to the latter class, and he has been trying to forget his familiarity with them, and ask himself what impression they would have made upon him at the time they appeared, in the first bloom of their freshness, and before the particular Hawthorne-quality, as it may be called, had become an established, a recognised and valued, fact. Certainly, I am inclined to think, if one had encountered these delicate, dusky flowers in the blossomless garden of American journalism, one would have plucked them with a very tender hand; one would have felt that here was something essentially fresh and new; here, in no extraordinary force or abundance, but in a degree distinctly appreciable, was an original element in literature. When I think of it, I almost envy Hawthorne's earliest readers; the sensation of opening upon *The Great Carbuncle, The Seven Vagabonds,* or *The Threefold Destiny* in an American annual of forty years ago, must have been highly agreeable.

Among these shorter things (it is better to speak of the whole collection, including the *Snow Image,* and the *Mosses from an Old Manse* at once) there are three sorts of tales, each one of which has an original stamp. There are, to begin with, the stories of fantasy and allegory—those among which the three I have just mentioned would be numbered, and which on the whole, are the most original. This is the group to which such little masterpieces as *Malvin's Burial, Rappacini's Daughter,* and *Young Goodman Brown* also belong—these two last perhaps representing the highest point that Hawthorne reached in this direction. Then there are the little tales of New England history, which are scarcely less admirable, and of which *The Grey Champion, The Maypole of Merry Mount,* and the four beautiful *Legends of the Province House,* as they are called, are the most successful specimens. Lastly come the slender sketches of actual scenes and of the objects and manners about him, by means of which, more particularly, he endeavoured "to open an intercourse with the world," and which, in spite of their slenderness, have an infinite grace and charm. Among these things *A Rill from the Town Pump, The Village Uncle, The Toll-Gatherer's Day,* the *Chippings with a Chisel,* may most naturally be mentioned. As we turn over these volumes we feel that the pieces that spring most directly from his fancy, constitute, as I have said (putting his four novels aside), his most substantial claim to our attention. It would be a mistake to insist too much upon them; Hawthorne was himself the first to recognise that. "These fitful sketches," he says in the preface to the *Mosses from an Old Manse,* "with so little of external life about them, yet claiming no profundity of purpose—so reserved even while they sometimes seem so frank—often but half in earnest, and never, even when most so, expressing satisfactorily the thoughts which they profess to image—such trifles, I truly feel, afford no solid basis for a literary reputation." This is very becomingly uttered; but it may be said, partly in answer to it, and partly in confirmation, that the valuable element in these things was not what Hawthorne put into them consciously, but what passed into them without his being able to measure it—the element of simple genius, the quality of imagination. This is the real charm of Hawthorne's writing—this purity and spontaneity and naturalness of fancy. For the rest, it is interesting to see how it borrowed a particular colour from the other faculties that lay near it—how the imagination, in this capital son of the old Puritans, reflected the hue of the more purely moral part, of the dusky, overshadowed conscience. The conscience, by no fault of its own, in every genuine offshoot of that sombre lineage, lay under the shadow of the sense of *sin.* This darkening cloud was no essential part of the nature of the individual; it stood fixed in the general moral heaven under which he grew up and looked at life. It projected from above, from outside, a black patch over his spirit, and it was for him to do what he could with the black patch. There were all sorts of possible ways of dealing with it; they depended upon the personal temperament. Some natures would let it lie as it fell, and contrive to be tolerably comfortable beneath it. Others would groan and sweat and suffer; but the dusky blight would remain, and their lives would be lives of misery. Here and there an individual, irritated beyond endurance, would throw it off in anger, plunging probably into what would be deemed deeper abysses of depravity. Hawthorne's way was the best, for he contrived, by an exquisite process, best known to himself, to transmute this heavy moral burden into the very substance of the imagination, to make it evaporate in the light and charming fumes of artistic production. But Hawthorne, of course, was exceptionally fortunate; he had his genius to help him. Nothing is more curious and interesting than this almost exclusively *imported* character of the sense of sin in Hawthorne's mind; it seems to exist there merely for an artistic or literary purpose. He had ample cognizance of the Puritan conscience; it was his natural heritage; it was reproduced in him; looking into his soul, he found it there. But his relation to it was only, as one may say, intellectual; it was not moral and theological. He played with it and used it as a pigment; he treated it, as the metaphysicians say, objectively. He was not discomposed, disturbed, haunted by it, in the manner of its usual and regular victims, who had not the little postern door of fancy to slip through, to the other side of the wall. It was, indeed, to his imaginative vision, the great fact of man's nature; the light element that had been mingled with his own composition always clung to this rugged prominence of moral responsibility, like the mist that hovers about the mountain. It was a necessary condition for a man of Hawthorne's stock that if his imagination should take licence to amuse itself, it should at least select this grim precinct of the Puritan morality for its play-ground. He speaks of the dark disapproval with which his old ancestors, in the case of their coming to life, would see him trifling himself away as a story-teller. But how far more darkly would they have frowned could they have understood that he had converted the very principle of their own being into one of his toys!

It will be seen that I am far from being struck with the justice of that view of the author of the *Twice-Told Tales*, which is so happily expressed by the French critic to whom I alluded at an earlier stage of this essay. To speak of Hawthorne, as M. Emile Montégut does, as a *romancier pessimiste*,[2] seems to me very much beside the mark. He is no more a pessimist than an optimist, though he is certainly not much of either. He does not pretend to conclude, or to have a philosophy of human nature; indeed, I should even say that at bottom he does not take human nature as hard as he may seem to do. "His bitterness," says M. Montégut, "is without abatement, and his bad opinion of man is without compensation. . . . His little tales have the air of confessions which the soul makes to itself; they are so many little slaps which the author applies to our face." This, it seems to me, is to exaggerate almost immeasurably the reach of Hawthorne's relish of gloomy subjects. What pleased him in such subjects was their picturesqueness, their rich duskiness of colour, their chiaroscuro; but they were not the expression of a hopeless, or even of a predominantly melancholy, feeling about the human soul. Such at least is my own impression. He is to a considerable degree ironical—this is part of his charm—part even, one may say, of his brightness; but he is neither bitter nor cynical—he is rarely even what I should call tragical.

2. Emile Montégut, "*Un Romancier Pessimiste en Amérique*," *Revue des Deux Mondes* (August 1, 1860): 668–703.

There have certainly been story-tellers of a gayer and lighter spirit; there have been observers more humorous, more hilarious—though on the whole Hawthorne's observation has a smile in it oftener than may at first appear; but there has rarely been an observer more serene, less agitated by what he sees and less disposed to call things deeply into question. * * * "This marked love of cases of conscience," says M. Montégut, "this taciturn, scornful cast of mind, this habit of seeing sin everywhere and hell always gaping open, this dusky gaze bent always upon a damned world and a nature draped in mourning, these lonely conversations of the imagination with the conscience, this pitiless analysis resulting from a perpetual examination of one's self, and from the tortures of a heart closed before men and open to God—all these elements of the Puritan character have passed into Mr. Hawthorne, or to speak more justly, have *filtered* into him, through a long succession of generations." This is a very pretty and very vivid account of Hawthorne, superficially considered; and it is just such a view of the case as would commend itself most easily and most naturally to a hasty critic. It is all true indeed, with a difference; Hawthorne was all that M. Montégut says, *minus* the conviction. The old Puritan moral sense, the consciousness of sin and hell, of the fearful nature of our responsibilities and the savage character of our Taskmaster—these things had been lodged in the mind of a man of Fancy, whose fancy had straightway begun to take liberties and play tricks with them—to judge them (Heaven forgive him!) from the poetic and aesthetic point of view, the point of view of entertainment and irony. This absence of conviction makes the difference; but the difference is great.

* * *

As a general thing I should characterise the more metaphysical of our author's short stories as graceful and felicitous conceits. They seem to me to be qualified in this manner by the very fact that they belong to the province of allegory. Hawthorne, in his metaphysical moods, is nothing if not allegorical, and allegory, to my sense, is quite one of the lighter exercises of the imagination. Many excellent judges, I know, have a great stomach for it; they delight in symbols and correspondences, in seeing a story told as if it were another and a very different story. I frankly confess that I have as a general thing but little enjoyment of it and that it has never seemed to me to be, as it were, a first-rate literary form. It has produced assuredly some first-rate works; and Hawthorne in his younger years had been a great reader and devotee of Bunyan and Spenser, the great masters of allegory. But it is apt to spoil two good things—a story and a moral, a meaning and a form; and the taste for it is responsible for a large part of the forcible-feeble writing that has been inflicted upon the world. The only cases in which it is endurable is when it is extremely spontaneous, when the analogy presents itself with eager promptitude. When it shows signs of having been groped and fumbled for, the needful illusion is of course absent and the failure complete. Then the machinery alone is visible, and the end to which it operates becomes a matter of indifference. There was but little literary criticism in the United States at the time Hawthorne's earlier works were published; but among the reviewers Edgar Poe perhaps held the scales the highest. He at any rate rattled them loudest, and pretended, more than any one else, to conduct the weighing-process on scientific principles. Very remarkable was this process of Edgar Poe's, and very extraordinary were his principles; but he had the advantage of being a man of genius, and his intelligence was frequently great. His collection of critical sketches of the American writers flourishing in what M. Taine[3] would call his *milieu* and *moment*, is very curious and interesting reading, and it has one quality which ought to keep it from ever being completely forgotten. It is probably the most complete and exquisite specimen of *provincialism* ever prepared for the edification of men. Poe's judgments are pretentious, spiteful, vulgar; but they contain a great deal of sense and discrimination as well, and here and there, sometimes at frequent intervals, we find a phrase of happy insight imbedded in a patch of the most fatuous pedantry. He wrote a chapter upon Hawthorne, and spoke of him on the whole very kindly; and his estimate is of sufficient value to make it noticeable that he should express lively disapproval of the large part allotted to allegory in his tales— in defence of which, he says, "however, or for whatever object employed, there is scarcely one respectable word to be said. * * * The deepest emotion," he goes on, "aroused within us by the happiest allegory *as* allegory, is a very, *very* imperfectly satisfied sense of the writer's ingenuity in overcoming a difficulty we should have preferred his not having attempted to overcome * * * ;" and Poe has furthermore the courage to remark that the *Pilgrim's Progress* is a "ludicrously over-rated book." Certainly, as a general thing, we are struck with the ingenuity and felicity of Hawthorne's analogies and correspondences; the idea appears to have made itself at home in them easily. Nothing could be better in this respect than *The Snow-Image* (a little masterpiece), or *The Great Carbuncle*, or *Doctor Heidegger's Experiment*, or *Rappacini's Daughter*. But in such things as *The Birth-Mark* and *The Bosom-Serpent*, we are struck with something stiff and mechanical, slightly incongruous, as if the kernel had

---

3. Hippolyte Taine (1828–1893), French critic and historian.

not assimilated its envelope. But these are matters of light impression, and there would be a want of tact in pretending to discriminate too closely among things which all, in one way or another, have a charm. The charm—the great charm—is that they are glimpses of a great field, of the whole deep mystery of man's soul and conscience. They are moral, and their interest is moral; they deal with something more than the mere accidents and conventionalities, the surface occurrences of life. The fine thing in Hawthorne is that he cared for the deeper psychology, and that, in his way, he tried to become familiar with it. This natural, yet fanciful familiarity with it, this air, on the author's part of being a confirmed *habitué* of a region of mysteries and subtleties, constitutes the originality of his tales. And then they have the further merit of seeming, for what they are, to spring up so freely and lightly. The author has all the ease, indeed, of a regular dweller in the moral, psychological realm; he goes to and fro in it, as a man who knows his way. His tread is a light and modest one, but he keeps the key in his pocket.

His little historical stories all seem to me admirable; they are so good that you may re-read them many times. They are not numerous, and they are very short; but they are full of a vivid and delightful sense of the New England past; they have, moreover, the distinction, little tales of a dozen and fifteen pages as they are, of being the only successful attempts at historical fiction that have been made in the United States. Hawthorne was at home in the early New England history; he had thumbed its records and he had breathed its air, in whatever odd receptacles this somewhat pungent compound still lurked. He was fond of it, and he was proud of it, as any New Englander must be, measuring the part of that handful of half-starved fanatics who formed his earliest precursors, in laying the foundations of a mighty empire. Hungry for the picturesque as he always was, and not finding any very copious provision of it around him, he turned back into the two preceding centuries, with the earnest determination that the primitive annals of Massachusetts should at least *appear* picturesque. His fancy, which was always alive, played a little with the somewhat meagre and angular facts of the colonial period and forthwith converted a great many of them into impressive legends and pictures. There is a little infusion of colour, a little vagueness about certain details, but it is very gracefully and discreetly done, and realities are kept in view sufficiently to make us feel that if we are reading romance, it is romance that rather supplements than contradicts history. The early annals of New England were not fertile in legend, but Hawthorne laid his hands upon everything that would serve his purpose, and in two or three cases his version of the story has a great deal of beauty. *The*

Grey Champion is a sketch of less than eight pages, but the little figures stand up in the tale as stoutly, at the least, as if they were
propped up on half-a-dozen chapters by a dryer annalist, and the
whole thing has the merit of those cabinet pictures in which the artist has been able to make his persons look the size of life. * * *

Modern Criticism

Hawthorne's tales generated a great deal of interest in the years after World War II, both because during this period American literature came into its own as a subject worthy of study and because the tales lend themselves well to precise literary and historical analysis. While the critics of the 1950s and 1960s tended to look for structural elements intrinsic to the tales as literature, for irony and complexity in Hawthorne's language, and for symbolism in his expression of themes, critics since then have sometimes been attracted to approaches that are not so strictly or exclusively literary. Hawthorne has been studied by feminists and new historicists, by Freudians and post-Freudians, and by philosophical poststructuralists, to name a few of these approaches. In my selection, I have made an effort to include modern criticism from numerous different perspectives.

An excerpt from Q. D. Leavis's seminal essay of 1951 opens the section. Leavis reawakened interest in Hawthorne's exact and poetic use of language and revealed the thematic drama at work in his imagination of his country's past. Her essay is still an eloquent introduction to Hawthorne. Leavis's interpretation of "My Kinsman, Major Molineux" is challenged by John P. McWilliams Jr.; the reader may choose between them. McWilliams and Michael J. Colacurcio base their work on thorough studies of Hawthorne's use of history. Colacurcio in particular shows just how aware Hawthorne was of the effects of Puritan doctrines and assumptions on representative New Englanders like Goodman Brown. Frederick Crews and Robert Heilman, on the other hand, are more literary than historical in their interests. Both are close readers of texts, the first with a Freudian and the second with a Christian slant on Hawthorne. Jorge Luis Borges's appreciation of Hawthorne is the tribute of one incantatory dreamer of fictions to another. Nina Baym, alone among our critics, focuses on a phase of Hawthorne's development. She sees him gradually gathering courage in the face of a repressive conception of culture he had imposed on himself. Leo Marx suggests how "Ethan Brand" may be in part a response to nascent industrialism in New England. The excerpt from Sharon Cameron is drawn from a book in which she studies how Hawthorne's and Melville's characters are frustrated by ordinary bodily existence and seek exemption from it or willful connections with spheres beyond it.

I have added three new pieces for this edition: a selection from J. Hillis Miller's *Hawthorne and History: Defacing It*, all of Judith Fetterley's "Women Beware Science: Hawthorne's 'The Birthmark,'" and a selection from Martin Bidney's "Fire, Flutter, Fall, and Scatter: A Structure in the Epiphanies of Hawthorne's Tales." Miller's and Bidney's essays are too long to be included whole; interested readers might well seek them out in their original publications. Miller's essay is an exemplary piece of criticism stemming from "deconstruction," a school of thought that highlights the contingent character of language and metaphorical thinking and casts doubt on efforts to arrive at final meanings. He gives a provocative reading of "The Minister's Black Veil" while raising questions about the practice of historical criticism more generally. Fetterley's is a pioneering instance of feminist literary criticism drawn from her book *The Resisting Reader*. One of the established critical texts she resists is Heilman's "Hawthorne's 'The Birthmark,'" included here. According to Fetterley, Heilman glosses over the violence done by a male character to a woman in "The Birthmark." The reader is welcome to judge their quarrel. Bidney's essay is an arresting example of "phenomenological" criticism. He seeks to reveal a pattern of sensuous phenomena or imagery that appears in most of Hawthorne's short fiction. This pattern takes hold of Hawthorne's imagination and empowers his tales even when it works against what appear to be his conscious moral intentions. Bidney gives a new focus to Hawthorne's imaginative obsessions while leaving ample room for discussion and disagreement in his treatment of individual stories.

Thus I have sought not a consensus but a spectrum of opinions and approaches. Fortunately, Hawthorne cannot be bound to one school of thought or exhausted by one style of reading. Nina Baym once testified to "the remarkable 'openness' of Hawthorne, his adaptability to an enormous range of critical modes. Interpretation in general is dedicated to the task of 'closing' an author, eliminating or at least limiting the range of statements which may be acceptably made about him. A criticism which acknowledged Hawthorne's openness instead of accepting it only as a challenge to be surmounted, and which devoted itself to the cause of that openness, would be revolutionary indeed."[1] Because critics in the very act of arguing have always taken partial positions, it may be the informed contemporary reader who can best initiate that silent revolution.

---

1. Nina Baym, "Hawthorne," *American Literary Scholarship: An Annual, 1970,* edited by J. Albert Robbins (Durham, NC: Duke University Press, 1972), 21.

Q. D. LEAVIS

Hawthorne as Poet†

For an English person to offer an opinion on Hawthorne, much more an evaluation of his *oeuvre*, must be felt in America to be an impertinence. But the excuse that would justify writing on Hawthorne in an English context—that he is, except as author of one "Puritanical" novel, unread and unrecognized, will, it seems to me, serve here too if somewhat modified. To me, a tremendous admirer of long standing of much of Hawthorne's work, it appears that the essential nature of his achievement has not been isolated and established critically. * * * I should like to present my own reading of his work, if only to get endorsement from others. In England one can never assume an intelligent knowledge of Hawthorne in the professional world of letters. * * * But what is one to conclude when faced with the account of Hawthorne in that admirable American work *The American People* (1949) by Professor H. B. Parkes? Here Hawthorne is characterized as

> a man of low emotional pressure who adopted throughout his life the role of an observer. Remaining always aloof from the world around him, he was able to record what he felt with a remarkable balance and detachment. * * * But since he lacked the compulsive drive of the writer who is himself the victim of conflict and must find a way of salvation, his work lacked force and energy. Carefully and delicately constructed, it was devoid of color and drama and almost passionless. Hawthorne's obsessing personal problem was his sense of isolation. He came to regard isolation as almost the root of all evil, and made it the theme of many of his stories. But Hawthorne's treatment of the subject was always too conscious and deliberate; he expressed it allegorically and not in symbols; and consequently he was unable to say anything about it that enlarges our understanding either of human nature or of the society in which Hawthorne lived.

This is in effect the account of Hawthorne that has always been in currency. * * * Even Henry James, whose monograph on Hawthorne is felt, and was clearly intended, to be the tribute of an artist to the predecessor from whom he inherits, even James demurs at what he calls "allegory, quite one of the lighter exercises of the

† From Q. D. Leavis, "Hawthorne as Poet," part 1, *Sewanee Review* 59 (spring 1951): 179–205. Copyright © 1951, 1979 by the University of the South. Reprinted by permission of the editor.

imagination."[1] * * * But when James wrote "Hawthorne is perpetually looking for images which shall place themselves in picturesque correspondence with the spiritual facts with which he is concerned, and of course the search is of the very essence of poetry," he admits, however inadequately, that Hawthorne's intention is a poetic one, nothing less. Similarly, in general acceptance Hawthorne is a "delicate" writer, but when he is praised for his "delicacy" it is intended to stamp his art as something minor. I should prefer to have the purity of his writing noted instead. Nor is the epithet "charming," selected by Henry James, appropriate.

The account, as endorsed by Mr. Parkes, contrives to be unjust to Hawthorne's object and to ignore the very nature of his art. Hawthorne's less interesting work bulks large, no doubt, but it is easily cut free from what is his essential contribution to American literature. The essential Hawthorne—and he seems to me a great genius, the creator of a literary tradition as well as a wonderfully original and accomplished artist—is the author of *Young Goodman Brown*, *The Maypole of Merry Mount*, *My Kinsman Major Molineux*, *The Snow-Image*, *The Blithedale Romance*, *The Scarlet Letter*, and of a number of sketches and less pregnant stories associated with these works such as *The Gray Champion*, *Main Street*, *Old News*, *Endicott of the Red Cross*, *The Artist of the Beautiful*. This work is not comparable with the productions of the eighteenth-century "allegorical" essayists nor is it in the manner of Spenser, Milton, or Bunyan—whom of course it can be seen he has not merely studied but assimilated. The first batch of works I specified is essentially dramatic, its use of language is poetic, and it is symbolic, and richly so, as is the dramatic poet's. In fact I should suggest that Hawthorne can have gone to school with no one but Shakespeare for his inspiration and model.[2] Mr. Wilson Knight's approach to Shakespeare's tragedies—each play an expanded metaphor—is a cue for the method of rightly apprehending these works of Hawthorne's, where the "symbol" is the thing itself, with no separable paraphrasable meaning as in an allegory: the language is directly evocative. Rereading this work, one is certainly not conscious of a limited and devitalized talent employing a simple-minded pedestrian technique; one is constantly struck by fresh subtleties of organization, of intention, expression and feeling, of original psychological insight and a new minting of terms to convey it, as well as of a predominantly dramatic construction. * * *

---

1. For a selection from James's *Hawthorne*, see p. 385, in this volume [*Editor's note*].
2. I find support for this in "Our Old Home": "Shakespeare has surface beneath surface, to an immeasurable depth. . . . There is no exhausting the various interpretation of his symbols."

The aspect of Hawthorne that I want to stress as the important one, decisive for American literature, and to be found most convincingly in the works I specified, is this: that he was the critic and interpreter of American cultural history and thereby the finder and creator of a literary tradition from which sprang Henry James on the one hand and Melville on the other. I find it impossible to follow Mr. Parkes's argument[3] that "what is lacking in [Hawthorne's] framework of experience is any sense of society as a kind of organic whole to which the individual belongs and in which he has his appointed place. And lacking the notion of social continuity and tradition, [he] lacks also the corresponding metaphysical conception of the natural universe as an ordered unity which harmonizes with human ideals."[4] It is precisely those problems, the relation of the individual to society, the way in which a distinctively American society developed and how it came to have a tradition of its own, the relation of the creative writer to the earlier nineteenth-century American community, and his function and how he could contrive to exercise it—the exploration of these questions and the communication in literary art of his findings—that are his claim to importance. It is true that he is most successful in treating pre-Revolutionary America, but that, after all, is, as he saw it, the decisive period. * * * As I see it, Hawthorne's sense of being part of the contemporary America could be expressed only in concern for its evolution—he needed to see how it had come about and by discovering what America had, culturally speaking, started from and with, to find what choices had faced his countrymen and what they had had to sacrifice in order to create that distinctive "organic whole." He was very conscious of the nature of his work; he asserted that to be the function of every great writer, as when in *The Old Manse* he wrote: "A work of genius is but the newspaper of a century, or perchance of a hundred centuries." * * * And he prepared himself for the task by study, though Providence had furnished him with an eminently usable private Past, in the history of his own family, which epitomized the earlier phases of New England history; this vividly stylized the social history of Colonial America, provided him with a personal mythology, and gave him an emotional stake in the past, a private key to tradition. We know that his first pieces which he later burnt in despair of getting published

---

3. "Poe, Hawthorne, Melville: An Essay in Sociological Criticism," *Partisan Review*, Feb. 1949.

4. This naïve demand should be measured against this passage from *Hawthorne's Last Phase* (E. H. Davidson, 1949): "The rare springtime beauty of the English scene struck him more forcibly than it could the ordinary tourist, for it represented to him the perfect balance between man and nature. This balance was conspicuously absent in the untamed forests of the U.S., where man was busily engaged in subduing nature and dominating a continent. 'It is only an American who can feel it.' Hawthorne wrote."

were called *Seven Tales of My Native Land*. Though he was the very
opposite of a Dreiser (whom Mr. Parkes backs in contrast) yet I
should choose to describe Hawthorne as a sociological novelist in
effect, employing a poetic technique which communicates instead of
stating his findings. The just comparison with *The Scarlet Letter* is
not *The Pilgrim's Progress* but *Anna Karenina*, which in theme and
technique it seems to me astonishingly to resemble. This brings up
again the objection cited above that "Remaining always aloof from
the world around him, he was able to record what he felt with a
remarkable balance and detachment, but lacked the compulsive
drive of the writer who is himself the victim of conflict and must find
a way of salvation." There is disguised here a romantic assumption
about the Artist. We surely recognize, equally in the Shakespeare of
the great tragedies and *Measure for Measure*, in Henry James in his
novels and *nouvelles*, and in the Tolstoy of *Anna* (as opposed to the
Tolstoy of *Resurrection*) that "remarkable balance and detachment"
which is indispensable to the greatest achievement of literary art.
Like these artists Hawthorne in his best work is offering in dramatic
form an analysis of a complex situation in which he sides with no one
party but is imaginatively present in each, having created each to
represent a facet of the total experience he is concerned to communicate. The analysis and the synthesis help us to find our own "way
of salvation" (not a form of words I should have chosen). Tolstoy *was*
in many respects Levin, as we know, but *Anna Karenina* the novel is
not presented through Levin's eyes, and could not have been written
by Levin. To analyze the way in which Hawthorne actually works as
a writer is the only safe way to come at the nature of his creation, to
make sure we are taking what he has written and neither overlooking
it nor fathering on the author some misreading of our own or of inert
traditional acceptance. * * *

The Maypole of Merry Mount is an early work bearing obvious signs
of immaturity but it also shows great originality, and it is a root
work, proving that Hawthorne had laid the foundations of much
later successes, notably *The Scarlet Letter* and *The Blithedale
Romance*, in his beginnings almost. It proves also that he decided
in his youth on his characteristic technique. We notice that it is
essentially a poetic technique: the opening is almost too deliberately poetic in rhythm and word-order. But once the convention has
been established in the first two paragraphs, he relaxes and proceeds
less artificially. We are, or should be, struck in this early piece by
the mastery Hawthorne achieves in a new form of prose art, by the
skill with which he manages to convey ironic inflexions and to control transitions from one layer of meaning to another, and by which
he turns, as it was to become his great distinction to do, history

into myth and anecdote into parable. The essential if not the greatest Hawthorne had so soon found himself.

The tale originally had a sub-title: "A Parable," and in a few prefa-
tory sentences Hawthorne wrote that "the curious history of the
early settlement of Mount Wollaston, or Merry Mount" furnishes
"an admirable foundation for a philosophic romance"—we see his
decision to take for his own from the start the associations of
"romance" and not of "novel" or some such term suggesting a dis-
ingenuous connection between fiction and daily life. He continued:
"In the slight sketch here attempted the facts, recorded on the
grave pages of our New England annalists, have wrought themselves, almost spontaneously, into a sort of allegory." If an allegory
(unfortunate word), it is a "sort" that no experience of *The Faerie
Queen* and *The Pilgrim's Progress* can prepare us for. Its distinctive
quality is its use of symbols to convey meaning, and a boldness of
imagination and stylization which while drawing on life does not
hesitate to rearrange facts and even violate history in that interest.
The outline of the historically insignificant Merry Mount affair,
whether as recorded by the Puritan historian Governor Bradford or
so very differently by the protagonist Thomas Merton in his entertaining *New England Canaan*, was a godsend to Hawthorne, who
saw in it a means of precipitating his own reactions to his forefathers' choice. While Hawthorne's imagination was historical in a
large sense, he was never an imaginative recreator of the romantic
past, a historical novelist: he had always from the first very clearly
in view the *criticism* of the past. The past was his peculiar concern
since it was the source of his present. He always works through the
external forms of a society to its essence and its origin. He felt that
the significance of early America lay in the conflict between the
Puritans who became New England and thus America, and the non-
Puritans who were, to him, merely the English in America and whom
he partly with triumph but partly also with anguish sees as being cast
out (here is a source of conflict). He saw this process as a symbolic
recurring struggle, an endless drama that he recorded in a series of
works—*The Maypole, My Kinsman Major Molineux, Endicott of the
Red Cross, The Gray Champion, The Scarlet Letter, The Blithedale
Romance*, among others—that together form something that it would
not be fanciful to describe as a ritual drama reminding us of, for
instance, the Norse Edda. If his artistic medium is primitive, his
intention is not. It is a kind of spiritual and cultural casting-up of
accounts: what was lost and what gained, what sacrificed to create
what? he is perpetually asking, and showing.

Perhaps the American Puritans * * * were more intensively intolerant than those who remained at home, or perhaps the persecut-
ing aspect of their way of life was peculiarly present to Hawthorne

because of the witch-hanging judge and the Quaker-whipping Major among his ancestors. But the essential truth Hawthorne rightly seized on, that the decisive minority set themselves in absolute hostility to the immemorial culture of the English folk with its Catholic and ultimately pagan roots, preserved in song and dance, festivals and superstitions, and especially the rites and dramatic practices of which the May-Day ceremonies were the key. Morton did rear a Maypole at Merry Mount and the fanatic Governor Endicott did indeed (but only after Morton had been seized and shipped home) visit the settlement and have the abominable tree cut down. Moreover the early theologians and historians had dramatized in their writings the elements of the scene in scriptural and theological terms. But this theological myth Hawthorne adapted to convey subtle and often ironic meanings, just as he freely adapts the historical facts. Morton was actually as well as ideally a High Churchman of good birth, a Royalist and deliberately anti-Puritan, but the object of his settlement was profitable trading with the Indians. Having none of the Puritans' conviction of the damned state of the savages, he made friends with them. Thus Hawthorne could make these settlers embody the old way of living as opposed to the new. He starts with the Maypole as the symbol of the pagan religion for "what chiefly characterized the colonists of Merry Mount was their veneration for the Maypole. It has made their true history a poet's tale." A living tree, "venerated" for it is the center of life and changes with the seasons, it is now on the festival of Midsummer's Eve hung with roses, "some that had been gathered in the sunniest spots of the forest and others, of still richer blush, which the colonists had reared from English seed." Here we have the earliest use of one of Hawthorne's chief symbols, the rose, and we notice that the native wild rose and the cultivated rose carried as seed from England (with generations of grafting and cultivation behind it) are in process of being mingled at Merry Mount. Round the tree the worshippers of the natural religion are figured with extraordinary vitality of imagination: "Gothic monsters, though perhaps of Grecian ancestry," the animal-masked figures of mythology and primitive art (man as wolf, bear, stag and he-goat); "And, almost as wondrous, stood a real bear of the dark forest, lending each of his fore-paws to the grasp of a human hand, and as ready for the dance as any in that circle. His inferior nature rose half-way to meet his companions as they stooped"; "the Salvage Man, well known in heraldry, hairy as a baboon and girdled with green leaves"; Indians real and counterfeit. The harmony between man and beast and nature that was once recognized by a religious ritual could hardly be more poetically conjured up. Then the youth and maiden who represent the May Lord and Lady are shown; they are about to be permanently as well as ritually married, by an English priest who wears also "a chaplet of the native vine-leaves." Later on he is named by Endicott as "Blackstone," though Hawthorne protects himself against the fact that the historic Blaxton had nothing to do with Merry Mount by an equivocal footnote: Blackstone here represents a poetic license which Hawthorne is perfectly justified in taking. Blackstone, who is similarly imported into *The Scarlet Letter* in a key passage, was actually not a High Churchman nor "a clerk of Oxford" as he declares in *The Maypole*, but like most New England divines a Cambridge man and anti-Episcopalian. But he must be of Oxford because Hawthorne needs him to represent Catholicism and Royalism, to complete the culture-complex of Merry Mount, which has been shown in every other respect to be ancient, harmonious and traditional, a chain of life from the dim past, from the tree and animal upwards, all tolerated and respected as part of the natural and right order. The reader is expected to take the reference to the historical Blaxton, who like Endicott and Ann Hutchinson, among others, become in Hawthorne's art cultural heroes. How eminently adapted for Hawthorne's purpose he was is seen in this account by the historian of *The Colonial Period of American History*:

> The Rev. William Blaxton, M.A. Emmanuel College, Cambridge, removed to the western slope of Shawmut peninsula [Beacon Hill] where, near an excellent spring, he built a house, planted an orchard, raised apples, and cultivated a vegetable garden. Leaving Boston in 1635, disillusioned because of the intolerance of the Puritan magistrates, he went southward saying as he departed, "I came from England because I did not like the Lord Bishops, but I cannot join with you because I would not be under the Lord Brethren" He too wanted to worship God in his own way.

He represents, among other things, the crowning, the unPuritan virtue of tolerance, one of Hawthorne's main positives. Without what he stands for the dance and drama round the Maypole and the whole pagan year-cycle of "hereditary pastimes" would be negligible in comparison with the Christian culture even of the Puritans.

Meanwhile a bank of Puritans in hiding are watching the scene. To them the masquers and their comrades are like "those devils and ruined souls with whom their superstitions peopled the black wilderness." For

> Unfortunately there were men in the new world, of a sterner faith than these Maypole worshippers. Not far from Merry Mount was a settlement of Puritans, most dismal wretches, who said their prayers before daylight, and then wrought in the forest or the cornfield, till evening made it prayer time again.

This, to judge by the "most dismal wretches," is to be discounted by the reader as probably the prejudiced view of the Maypole worshippers, just as to the Puritans the others appear to be "the crew of Comus." But if so persuaded, we are brought up short by a characteristic taut statement about the Puritans, shocking both in its literal and allegorical implications, that immediately follows: "Their weapons were always at hand to shoot down the straggling savage." At Merry Mount we have seen a life where the "savage," without and within the human breast, is accepted as part of life. Hawthorne continues in the same tone:

> When they met in conclave, it was never to keep up the old English mirth, but to hear sermons three hours long, or to proclaim bounties on the heads of wolves and the scalps of Indians. Their festivals were fast days, and their chief pastime the singing of psalms. Woe to the youth or maiden who did but dream of a dance! The selectman nodded to the constable; and there sat the light-heeled reprobate in the stock; or if he danced, it was round the whipping-post, which might be termed the Puritan Maypole.

The practices of the Puritan are described as being a horrible parody of those of the Maypole worshipers, a deliberate offense against the spirit of Life. The force of the cunning phrase "to proclaim bounties on the heads of wolves and the scalps of Indians," charged with a sense of the inhumanity that leveled the Indian with the wolf, should not be overlooked.

* * * We find ourselves then inescapably faced by Hawthorne with the question: And what did the Puritans worship? We are left in no doubt as to Hawthorne's answer: Force. Hawthorne had realized that religion is a matter of symbols, and his choice of appropriate symbols is not at all simple-minded. The Maypole worshipers are not, it turns out, to be accepted without qualification. They have another symbolic quality attached to them, they are "silken"— "Sworn triflers of a life-time, they would not venture among the sober truths of life, not even to be truly blest." Everyone was "gay" at Merry Mount, but what really was "the quality of their mirth"? "Once, it is said, they were seen following a flower-decked corpse, with merriment and festive music, to his grave. But did the dead man laugh?" * * * The term for the Puritans corresponding to "silken" for the settlers is "iron." We find it immediately after the passage quoted above where their practices are described as systematically inhumane. A party comes "toiling through the difficult woods, each with a horse-load of iron armour to burden his footsteps." A little later they are "men of iron," and when they surround and overpower the Maypole-worshipers their leader is revealed as

iron all through: "So stern was the energy of his aspect, that the whole man, visage, frame and soul, seemed wrought of iron, gifted with life and thought, yet all of one substance with his headpiece and breast-plate. It was the Puritan of Puritans; it was Endicott himself." He cuts down the Maypole with his sword, which he rests on while deciding the fate of the May Lord and Lady, and "with his own gauntleted hand" he finally crowns them with the wreath of mingled roses from the ruin of the Maypole. The associations of iron are all brought into play, suggesting the rigid system which burdens life, the metal that makes man militant and ultimately inhuman, and it is spiritually the sign of heaviness and gloom, opposed in every way to the associations of lightness—silken, sunny, gay, and mirthful, used for the followers of the old way of life. * * *

The Puritans' religion is expressed in their rites—acts of persecution, oppression and cruelty. Endicott and his followers pass sentence on "the heathen crew." Their tame bear is to be shot—"I suspect witchcraft in the beast," says the leader, and even the "long glossy curls" on the May Lord's head must be cut. "Crop it forthwith, and that in the true pumpkin-shell fashion"—the brutal denial of personal dignity and natural comeliness is indicated with striking economy. The language of Bunyan is made to sound very differently in these mouths; Hawthorne, a master of language, has many such resources at his command. But Hawthorne's total meaning is very complex and his last word is not by any means a simple condemnation. While the Merry Mount way of life embodies something essential that is lacking in the Puritans', making theirs appear ugly and inhuman, yet Hawthorne's point is that in the New World the old way could be only an imported artifice; New England, he deeply felt, could never be a mere reproduction of the Old. The fairies, as John Wilson says in *The Scarlet Letter*, were left behind in old England with Catholicism. And Hawthorne implies that the outlook of Merry Mount is not consonant with the realities of life in the New World, or the new phrase of the world anywhere perhaps. The Puritans may be odious but they have a secret which is a better thing than the religion of nature and humanity. The May Lord and Lady, at Endicott's command, leave their Paradise—the reference to Adam and Eve driven from the Garden is unmistakable, as others to Milton in this tale—and there is a general suggestion that the "choice" imposed on New England is like that made by Adam and Eve, they sacrifice bliss for something more arduous and better worth having. Hawthorne has no doubt that the May Lord and Lady enter into a finer bond in Christian marriage than they could otherwise have known as symbolic figures in a fertility rite. Nevertheless though their future is "blessed" it is not pleasant or gracious. Hawthorne felt acutely the wrong the Lord Brethren had done to the Blaxtons, typified by the doings of an Endicott. The close parallel between the Merry Mount drama and the corresponding conflict in Milton's poem between the Brothers and the followers of Comus must be intentional—there are explicit references—and intended by Hawthorne as a criticism of Milton's presentment of the case. Virtue and Vice are a simple-minded division in Milton's *Comus*, however his symbolism may be interpreted. In Hawthorne's view that contest was quite other than a matter of Right and Wrong; his Puritans are an ironic comment on Milton's cause and case. Hawthorne's rendering shows two partial truths or qualified goods set in regrettable opposition. What Hawthorne implies is that it was a disaster for New England that they could not be reconciled. Hawthorne is both subtler and wiser than Milton, and his poem, unlike Milton's, is really dramatic and embodies a genuine cultural and spiritual conflict. Milton is a Puritan and Hawthorne is not; to Hawthorne, Milton is a man of iron. Hawthorne is seen explicitly the unwilling heir of the Puritans, and their indignant critic, in a fine passage in *Main Street* which ends "Let us thank God for having given us such ancestors; and let each successive generation thank him not less fervently, for being one step further from them in the march of ages."

* * *

In his introduction to a volume of tales brought out in 1851 but mostly written much earlier Hawthorne, then in his prime as an artist, with *The Scarlet Letter* a year behind him, confessed that he was "disposed to quarrel with the earlier sketches," most of all "because they come so nearly up to the standard of the best that I can achieve now." As one of the earlier sketches in his collection was *My Kinsman Major Molineux* (1831), he might justly have felt that he was never to achieve anything better.

* * * This remarkable tale might have been less commonly overlooked or misunderstood if it had had a sub-title, such as Hawthorne often provided by way of a hint. It could do with some such explanatory sub-title as "America Comes of Age." But though if a naturalistic story is looked for the reader would be left merely puzzled, the tale lends itself readily to comprehension as a poetic parable in dramatic form, and the opening paragraph as usual clearly explains the situation and furnishes the required clue. We are in the age which was preparing the colonies for the War of Independence and we are made to take part in a dramatic precipitation of, or prophetic forecast of, the rejection of England that was to occur in fact much later.

The actual tale begins by describing a country-bred youth coming to town, starting with the significant sentence: "It was near nine o'clock of a moonlight evening, when a boat crossed the ferry

with a single passenger." The sturdy pious youth Robin, the son of
the typical farmer-clergyman, represents the young America; he has
left his home in the village in the woods and crossing by the *ferry,
alone, at nightfall,* reaches the little metropolis of a New England
port—that is, the contemporary scene where the historic future
will be decided. He arrives poor but hopeful, confidently anticipat-
ing help in making his fortune from "my kinsman Major Molineux,"
the reiteration of the phrase being an important contribution to the
total effect. The kinsman is Hawthorne's and ours (if we are Americans) as well as Robin's, and his name suggests both his military
and aristocratic status. Robin explains much later in the tale that
his father and the Major are brother's sons—that is, one brother
had stayed in England and the other left to colonize New England.
Their children, the next generation, represented by Robin's father
and the Major, had kept on friendly terms and the rich Major, representative in New England of the British civil and military rule
and keeping "great pomp," was in a position to patronize his poor
country cousin. We do not get this straightforward account in the
tale, of course, we have to unravel it for ourselves, for the presentation of the theme is entirely dramatic and we have to identify our
consciousness with the protagonist Robin. The essential information is revealed only when we have ourselves experienced for some
time the same bewilderment as poor Robin, who cannot understand why his request to be directed to the house of his kinsman is
met by the various types of citizen with suspicion, with contempt,
with anger, with disgust, with sneers, or with laughter. In fact,
Robin has arrived at a critical moment in his kinsman's history.
The colonists—with considerable skill and economy Hawthorne
represents all ranks and classes of the states in this dream-town—
have secretly planned to throw off British rule, or at any rate to rid
themselves of Major Molineux, a symbolic action which, performed
in the street outside the church at midnight and before the innocent
eyes of the mystified youth, takes the form of something between a
pageant and a ritual drama, disguised in the emotional logic of a
dream. As a dream it has a far greater emotional pull than actuality
could have. Hawthorne never anywhere surpassed this tale (written
when he was not more than twenty-seven) in dramatic power, in
control of tone, pace, and tension, and in something more wonderful, the creation of a suspension between the fullest consciousness
of meaning and the emotional incoherence of dreaming. How this
is achieved and for what purpose can be seen only by a careful
examination of the last half of the tale, but I will quote as sparingly
as possible.

Until this point, precisely the middle of the work, no departure
from the everyday normal has been necessary, though we have

been wrought to a state of exasperation which is ready for working on. And Hawthorne now introduces another note:

> He now roamed desperately, and at random, through the town, almost ready to believe that a spell was on him, like that by which a wizard of his country had once kept three pursuers wandering, a whole winter night, within twenty paces of the cottage which they sought. The streets lay before him, strange and desolate, and the lights were extinguished in almost every house. Twice, however, little parties of men, among whom Robin distinguished individuals in outlandish attire, came hurrying along; but though on both occasions they paused to address him, such intercourse did not at all enlighten his perplexity. They did but utter a few words in some language of which Robin knew nothing, and perceiving his inability to answer, bestowed a curse upon him in plain English, and hastened away. Finally, the lad determined to knock at the door of every mansion, trusting that perseverance would overcome the fatality that had hitherto thwarted him. Firm in this resolve, he was passing beneath the walls of a church, which formed the corner of two streets, when, as he turned into the shade of its steeple, he encountered a bulky stranger, muffled in a cloak. The man was proceeding with the speed of earnest business, but Robin planted himself full before him, holding the oak cudgel with both hands across his body, as a bar to further passage.
>
> "Halt, honest man, and answer me a question," said he, very resolutely. "Tell me, this instant, whereabouts is the dwelling of my kinsman, Major Molineux!"
>
> . . . The stranger, instead of attempting to force his passage, stepped back into the moonlight, unmuffled his face, and stared full into that of Robin.
>
> "Watch here an hour, and Major Molineux will pass by," said he.
>
> Robin gazed with dismay and astonishment on the unprecedented physiognomy of the speaker. The forehead with its double prominence, the broad hooked nose, the shaggy eyebrow, and fiery eyes, were those which he had noticed at the inn, but the man's complexion had undergone a singular, or, more properly, a two-fold change. One side of the face blazed an intense red, while the other was black as midnight, the division line being in the broad bridge of the nose; and a mouth which seemed to extend from ear to ear was black or red, in contrast to the color of the cheek. The effect was as if two individual devils, a fiend of fire and a fiend of darknes, had united themselves to form this infernal visage. The stranger grinned in Robin's face, muffled his parti-colored features, and was out of sight in a moment.

The stranger, whose unearthly appearance we were prepared for by the "individuals in outlandish attire" speaking in a code—for as we realize later they were obviously conspirators demanding from Robin a password he could not furnish, but they help to increase the nightmare atmosphere—is shown by his face to be something more than a man in disguise. The tension is being screwed up to the pitch needed for the approaching climax of the drama: this is not a man like the others but a Janus-like fiend of fire and darkness, that is, we presently learn, "war personified" in its dual aspects of Death and Destruction. But it is not just a personification, it is a symbol with emotional repercussions which passes through a series of suggestive forms. The account of its features at first: "The forehead with its double prominence, the broad hooked nose" etc. suggests Punch and so also the grotesque associations of puppet-show farce. The division of the face into black and red implies the conventional get-up of the jester, and indeed he "grinned in Robin's face" before he "muffled his parti-colored features." At this point Robin, carrying the reader with him, having "consumed a few moments in philosophical speculation upon the species of man who had just left him," is able to "settle this point shrewdly, rationally and satisfactorily." He and we are of course deceived in our complacency. He falls into a drowse by sending his thoughts "to imagine how that evening of ambiguity and weariness had been spent in his father's household." This actually completes his bewilderment—"Am I here or there?" he cries, "But still his mind kept vibrating between fancy and reality."

Now, so prepared, we hear the murmur that becomes a confused medley of voices and shouts as it approaches, turning into "frequent bursts from many instruments of discord, and a wild and confused laughter filled up the intervals." "The antipodes of music" heralds "a mighty stream of people" led by a single horseman whom Robin recognizes as the eerie stranger in a fresh avatar. With the "rough music" that in Old England was traditionally used to drive undesirable characters out of the community, by the red glare of torches and with "War personified" as their leader, the citizens of America, with Indians in their train and cheered on by their women, are symbolically if proleptically casting out the English ruler. The nightmare impression reaches its climax: "In his train were wild figures in the Indian dress, and many fantastic shapes without a model, giving the whole march a visionary air, as if a dream had broken forth from some feverish brain, and were sweeping visibly through the midnight streets. . . . 'The double-faced fellow has his eye upon me' muttered Robin, with an indefinite but uncomfortable idea that he was himself to bear a part in the pageantry."

It seems indeed that the pageant has been brought to this place for Robin's benefit.

A moment more, and the leader thundered a command to halt: the trumpets vomited a horrid breath, and then held their peace; the shouts and laughter of the people died away, and there remained only a universal hum, allied to silence. Right before Robin's eyes was an uncovered cart. There the torches blazed the brightest, there the moon shone out like day, and there, in tar-and-feather dignity, sat his kinsman Major Molineux!

He was an elderly man, of large and majestic person, and strong, square features, betokening a steady soul; but steady as it was, his enemies had found means to shake it. His face was pale as death, and far more ghastly; the broad forehead was contracted in his agony, so that his eyebrows formed one griz-zled line; his eyes were red and wild, and the foam hung white upon his quivering lip. His whole frame was agitated by a quick and continual tremor, which his pride strove to quell, even in those circumstances of overwhelming humiliation. But perhaps the bitterest pang of all was when his eyes met those of Robin; for he evidently knew him on the instant, as the youth stood witnessing the foul disgrace of a head grown gray in honor. They stared at each other in silence, and Robin's knees shook, and his hair bristled, with a mixture of pity and terror.

The pageant is thus seen to represent a tragedy and is felt by us as such; it arouses in Robin the appropriate blend of emotions—the classical "pity and terror." But Hawthorne has by some inspiration—for how could he have known except intuitively of the origins of tragedy in ritual drama?—gone back to the type of action that fathered Tragedy. Just as the "War personified" suggests an idol or a human representative of the god, so does the other terrible figure "in tar-and-feathery dignity" in the cart. We seem to be spectators at that most primitive of all dramatic representations, the conquest of the old king by the new.

If the story had ended here, on this note, it would have been remarkable enough, but Hawthorne has an almost incredible con-summation to follow. I mean incredible in being so subtly achieved with such mastery of tone. From being a spectator at a tragedy, Robin has to fulfill his premonitions of having "to bear a part in the pageantry" himself. He is drawn into the emotional vortex and comes to share the reactions of the participants. He has felt intimately the dreadful degradation of his English kinsman, but now he is seized with the excitement of the victors, his fellow-countrymen, and sees their triumph as his own—"a perception of tremendous ridicule in the whole scene affected him with a sort of mental inebriety." Drunk with success the whole town roars in a frenzy of laughter, and Rob-in's shout joins theirs and is the loudest. Then in a sudden calm that follows this orgy "the procession resumed its march. On they went, like fiends that throng in mockery around some dead potentate, mighty no more, but majestic still in his agony." We are left in the silent street, brought back into the world of problems in which the tale opened. Robin still has to settle with reality and decide his future, the future of his generation. He asks to be shown the way back to the ferry: "I begin to grow weary of a town life" he says to the townsman who has stayed behind to note his reactions. But his new friend replies: "Some few days hence, if you wish it, I will speed you on your journey. Or, if you prefer to remain with us, perhaps as you are a shrewd youth, you may rise in the world without the help of your kinsman, Major Molineux."

Hawthorne has been blamed for failing to provide a "solution" and for not being optimistic as a good American should be, but it seems to me that here, as in *The Maypole*, he ends in reasonable, sober hopefulness for the future of life. Provided we recognize the facts and fully comprehend the positions, we can cope with it, if not master it, he implies. Declining to be, perhaps incapable of being, a naturalistic novelist, he was true to his best perceptions of his genius when he did the work of a dramatic poet, the interpreter and radical critic of the society which had produced him and for whose benefit he expressed his insight in a unique literature.

JOHN P. McWILLIAMS JR.

Hawthorne and the Puritan Revolution of 1776[†]

By the 1830's, the untainted glory of the American Revolution had become an indisputable article of national faith. Although orators and political journalists felt free to argue whether the Constitution represented the glorious end of all necessary political change, or merely provided the procedural framework for further change, the merits of the War for Independence were not to be seriously questioned.[1] The two accounts of the Revolution most thoroughly known to nineteenth-century readers, Mason Weems's *Life of Washington* (1800) and Bancroft's *History of the United States* (1834–74), agree in crucial assertions. Both present the Revolution as the watershed of human history, an event in which Divine Providence had revealed the virtues of Liberty and Democracy by blessing a

---

† From John P. McWilliams Jr., "'Thoroughgoing Democrat' and 'Modern Tory': Haw-thorne and the Puritan Revolution of 1776," *Studies in Romanticism* 15 (fall 1976): 549–71. Reprinted by permission of the Trustees of Boston University.
1. See Rush Welter, *The Mind of America* 1820–1860 (New York: Columbia University Press, 1975), pp. 3–25.

defensive rebellion with success and a nation with prosperity. Both demonstrate the merits of revolution by association of character. To prove that rifles were fired only to secure man's natural and legal rights, Weems and Bancroft cast the revolutionaries as two different types of the disinterested patriot: the rational gentleman reluctantly agreeing to public leadership for the sake of Liberty, and the yeoman farmer bluntly asserting his right to property, legal equality and self-determination.[2] Bancroft and Weems show us that, for at least four generations after 1787, the Revolution continued to exemplify the model virtues of the American polity and the American character.

There were, however, problems in this complacent rendering of history. It slighted such troubling facts as the conduct of popular crowds, the demagoguery of popular leaders and the plight of American loyalists. It justified the deeds of the past by proclaiming the successes of the present. And it assumed that Americans could be motivated only by the nobility of abstract ideals, not by profit, security or a need to prove one's manliness under trial.

*   *   *

Weems and Bancroft, writing two generations apart, adopt entirely different but equally specious strategies for dealing with pre-Revolutionary agitation and the transition in national character between Puritan and yeoman. Weems simply skips over political and economic issues of the 1760's in order to create pseudo-Homeric battles replete with tributes to Liberty, Republicanism and the character of Washington. Bancroft, however, attempts a chronological history which would unravel the skein of Progress while upholding the nobility of both Revolutionary and Puritan fathers. The Puritans, he repeatedly proclaims, had actually sown all the seeds of the Revolution. The signing of the Mayflower Compact had been "the birth of constitutional liberty," after which Pilgrims and Puritans, who believed in "liberty of conscience," had "scattered the seminal principles of republican freedom and national independence." When by 1776 the entire American folk began "the political regeneration of the world," Bancroft needs only to state that the Revolution, "prepared by glorious forerunners, grew naturally and necessarily out of the series of past events by the formative principle of a living belief." In the context of so reassuring a providential design, Puritan proceedings against heretics and witches are revealed to have been "no more than a train of mists hovering, of an autumn morning, over the

---

2. Mason L. Weems. *The Life of Washington*, ed. M. Cunliffe (1809; rpt. Cambridge, Mass.: Harvard University Press, 1962), pp. 128, 187–202; George Bancroft, *The History of the United States of America*, 5th ed. (Boston: Little, Brown, 1861), VII, 294–296, 384–403.

channel of a fine river, that diffused freshness and fertility wherever it wound.'[3] Any later instances of overzealous rebellion, such as the burning of Lieutenant Governor Hutchinson's house or the seizure of British goods, could be excused as measures necessary to the conquest of luxury, avarice and tyranny. Fortunately, by the time Bancroft had completed his historical volumes on the Revolution, romancers such as Cooper, Hawthorne and Melville had written fictions which were more true to historical fact.

Hawthorne's interest in regional history and the ancestral origins of character inevitably led him to be concerned with these issues. And yet, although the Revolution served as a recurrent setting and subject for his writings from 1830 to 1840, his portrayal of it has never been considered in depth, nor have the appropriate works been brought together for comparative study. To understand Hawthorne's fictional recreations of the era, familiarity with his explicit historical judgments in lesser known works such as *Grandfather's Chair* and "Old News"[4] is essential. We need to distinguish, more carefully than previous critics have done, between Hawthorne's approval of revolutionary motives and his distaste for revolutionary events. Even the much discussed historical dimension of "My Kinsman, Major Molineux" cannot be fully appreciated until the story is placed in the context of all his writings concerned with the Revolutionary era.

* * *

In his journalism and minor sketches, Hawthorne was capable of rehearsing the most familiar of contemporary pieties about the character of Revolutionary leaders. His George Washington has the Weems stamp of glacial dignity, his General Lincoln is an American Cincinnatus, and his Boston Tea Party is an unpremeditated uprising of an entire folk against injustices.[5] Like Cooper and Melville, Hawthorne praises the Revolutionary fathers as "men of an heroic age," then regrets that they are "now so utterly departed, as not even to touch upon the passing generation."[6]

To dismiss such statements as hackwork or pandering to popular clichés is not justifiable. The biographical and written record shows Hawthorne's desire to believe that such tenets of Revolutionary mythology had been historically accurate. Patriotic certitudes are,

3. Bancroft, *History of the United States*, quotations from, in order, vol. I (4th ed., 1838), 310. 322; vol VII (5th ed., 1861), 23; vol. I (4th ed., 1838), 463.
4. A series of three historical sketches of 18th-century New England, first published in the *New England Magazine* in 1835. *The Whole History of Grandfather's Chair* (Boston, 1841) is Hawthorne's retelling of New England history for children [*Editor's note*].
5. *Hawthorne as Editor*, ed. Arlin Turner (1941); rpt. Port Washington, N.Y.: Kennikat Press, 1972), pp. 20, 23, 97.
6. "A Book of Autographs," in *The Snow-Image and Uncollected Tales*, ed. J. D. Crowley. Vol. XI of the Centenary Edition (Columbus: Ohio State University Press, 1974), p. 373.

however, only one thread in a cross-woven web of responses. Hawthorne's disapproval of British political tyranny coexists with his fearful scorn for revolutionary mobs. Commendable ideals of political independence and individual liberty, he suspects, had ended all too frequently in senseless violence. Nor does Hawthorne's approval of the new republican political institutions preclude his fondness for the social graces of the old aristocratic Province. His writings on the Revolutionary era are of historical interest because of the complexity, not the uniformity, of their author's responses. He sought to justify the Revolution without historical inaccuracy and without a comforting exclusion of the loyalist point of view.

* * *

Because *Grandfather's Chair* is a history written without falsification but for children, Hawthorne's difficulties in justifying the Revolution emerge more clearly than in his fiction. By tracing "a distinct and unbroken thread of authentic history," Hawthorne tries to show that an underlying continuity of character made the Revolution possible.[7] That continuity, however, is not one of Progress but of decline preceding recovery. Historical developments from 1690 to 1763 show how "the iron race of Puritans . . . has now given place to quite a different set of men" (71). While a virtually independent theocracy has devolved into an imperial province, stern simplicity has given way to aristocratic pomp. The new era, Hawthorne regrets, is ruled by "ambitious politicians, soldiers and adventurers, having no pretension to that high religious and moral principle, which gave to our first Epoch a character of the truest and loftiest romance" (72). Significantly, it is a sudden thirst for military glory which shows how "the old moral and religous character of New England was in danger of being utterly lost" (96).

The great merit of the Revolution, Hawthorne insists, is that it brought about a rebirth of seventeenth-century Puritanism in the American character: "No sooner did England offer wrong to the colonies, than the descendants of the early settlers proved that they had the same kind of temper as their forefathers. The moment before, New England appeared like a humble and loyal subject of the crown; the next instant, she showed the grim, dark features of an old king-

---

7. *Grandfather's Chair*, in *True Stories From History and Biography*, ed. R. H. Pearce, Vol. VI of the Centenary Edition (1972), p. 5. The word "authentic," even when applied to the historicism of all of Hawthorne's Revolutionary writing, seems a characteristically modest claim. Between 1828 and 1840 Hawthorne withdrew the following books from the Salem Athenaeum: five volumes of Franklin's *Works*, three volumes of Hamilton's *Works*, two volumes of Jefferson's *Memoirs*, Sparks's *Life of Washington*, Tucker's *Life of Jefferson*, Hutchinson's *History of the Colony and Province of Massachusetts Bay*, and various State Department papers on the Revolutionary era. See Marion L. Kesselring, *Hawthorne's Reading: 1828–1850* (1949; rpt. Folcroft, Pa.: Folcroft Press, 1969), pp. 43–64.

resisting Puritan" (151). This definition of revolutionary heroics is one which few contemporary democrats (or Democrats) could have shared. Superficially, Hawthorne may resemble Bancroft in portraying the Revolution as an expression of the Puritan temper, but where Bancroft detects progress, Hawthorne detects only restoration. Bancroft's Puritan Revolutionaries are heirs to British ideals of constitutional liberty and republicanism; they do not show the "grim, dark features" of old Puritan king-killers. For Hawthorne, the revival of the Puritan spirit restricts the meaning of the term "liberty" to independence from the king and to representation of the select Freemen in legislative bodies. Liberty is not a question of natural rights, nor of any vaporous Spirit of Democracy. It is precisely the same spirit of aggressive resistance, of rigid devotion to the principle of independence, which Hawthorne had hymned at the conclusion of both "Endicott and the Red Cross" and "The Gray Champion." In those stories, however, acts of king-resisting could be interpreted as types of the Revolution only by acknowledging the underside of Puritan character. The implacable strength of John Endicott had enabled him to defy Charles the First; it also led him brutally to punish all the deviants of Salem.[8]

To substantiate the patriotic sentiment in *Grandfather's Chair*, Hawthorne had to find important events in Revolutionary history which could display the rebirth of king resisting integrity without the taint of sadism or self-righteousness. Fidelity to the historical facts of three crucial incidents forced Hawthorne to acknowledge, however, that the Puritan must be resurrected *in toto*. "The Hutchinson Mob," "The Boston Massacre" and "The Boston Tea Party" all suggest that great principles are being unwittingly acted out by thoughtless mobs. In none of the three is Hawthorne able to dramatize his contention that the patriots displayed a resurgence of Puritan self-control. If any quality of Hawthorne's Puritans resurfaces in the crowd, it is the sudden and decisive brutality of a John Endicott.

The spectacle of mob violence arouses Hawthorne's sympathy for the plight of the loyalist official caught between monarchical loyalties, fondness for his colonial birthright, and an official obligation to serve both king and colonist. Hawthorne may exult over Hutchinson's complacent illusions about the coming of a landed nobility, but as soon as the mob gathers Hutchinson is seen as a principled gentleman who has refused to descend to demagoguery. When young Charlie exclaims that all Tories should have been tarred and

---

8. I am indebted to Michael Bell's comments upon Endicott as Hawthorne's representative Puritan (*Hawthorne and the Historical Romance of New England* [Princeton, N.J.: Princeton University Press, 1972], pp. 53–60).

feathered (like Major Molineux), Grandfather rebukes him and asks, "Can you not respect that principle of loyalty, which made the royalists give up country, friends, fortune, everything, rather than be false to their king?" (177–78). Hawthorne's three extensive treatments of the Revolution all end by concentrating on the dilemma of the loyalist. The last sketch of *Grandfather's Chair* is "The Tory's Farewell"; the last sketeh of "Old News" is "The Old Tory"; the last of the four "Legends"[9] is "Old Esther Dudley." In all three sketches, Hawthorne's desire to arouse sympathy for the plight of the loyalist stops just short of his explicitly adopting, in politics and in narrative technique, the "Tory" point of view.

* * *

Knowledge of the complexities of Hawthorne's response to the Revolution will clarify the historical aspects of "My Kinsman, Major Molineux," the first and certainly the finest of Hawthorne's eighteenth-century tales. The most common historical interpretation remains that of Q. D. Leavis, who claimed the tale could be subtitled "America Comes of Age." Robin Molineux, representative of Young America, having learned the necessity of casting off British political authority, rises to manhood by joining in the laughter at his uncle, a disgraced royalist father figure.[1] Because the tale is seen as a rite of maturity for an American naif, the act of rebellion in the story, seldom closely examined, somehow has seemed justified. The popular agitation of the era is thus viewed merely as the means by which an increasingly shrewd youth learns to rise in the world and to free himself from the past.[2]

This interpretation resembles the fictive John Hancock's view of the Revolution, but not Hawthorne's.[3] Hoping to provide a corrective, Roy Harvey Pearce has argued that Robin's debatable growth into maturity must have been brought about, if at all, through com-

9. I.e., "Legends of the Province House" (1838–39), four stories set in Boston during the Revolutionary period [*Editor's note*].
1. Q. D. Leavis, "Hawthorne As Poet," *Sewanee Review*, 59 (1951), 200. [For Leavis's commentary on "My Kinsman, Major Molineux," see p. 395, in this volume—*Editor*.]
2. Q. D. Leavis, "Hawthorne As Poet," 200–205. The following comments illustrate the persistence of Leavis's interpretation. Daniel Hoffman: "Robin has cast off the remaining dependence of his immaturity" (*Form and Fable in American Fiction*, p. 122); Richard Chase: "the legend of a youth who achieves manhood through searching for a spiritual father" (PR, 16 [1949], 98); Roy Male: "Robin's coming of age . . . applies to the awakening of our national consciousness . . . Robin becomes a symbol of young Colonial America beginning to break free from its provincial Puritanism and its dependence upon the wealth of England" (*Hawthorne's Tragic Vision* (Austin: University of Texas Press, 1957], p. 52); Julian Smith: Both Robin and Ben Franklin "out of their humiliation learn the lesson of self-reliance" ("Coming of Age in America: Young Ben Franklin and Robin Molineux," AQ, 17 (1965), 551).
3. John Hancock is presented as an unreflective opportunist and optimist in "Old Esther Dudley," the last of Hawthorne's "Legends of the Province House"—at least as McWilliams interprets the tale [*Editor's note*].

plicity in an act of historical guilt[4] Any critic familiar with such pieces as "The Hutchinson Mob" or "Old News" must assent to Pearce's conclusion. Before accepting the political value of Robin's maturing, one should also recall that Hawthorne's later writings were to associate the achieving of revolution with the strength of old Puritans, not the good will of country youth. Robin's vicarious complicity in guilt should lead to two further questions about the historicity of the tale. If Robin's growth is not real, what justification for rebellion does the tale suggest? Secondly, does Robin's persistent innocence, like Hancock's, have any cultural significance?

The first paragraph of "My Kinsman, Major Molineux" establishes the same sympathetic understanding for the plight of the Provincial official which we find in *Grandfather's Chair*. Caught between King and people, four of the six governors were imprisoned, driven out by force, or hounded to death by "continual bickerings" or "popular insurrection." When the Provincial government attempted "softening" British regulations to maintain peace, the people "usually rewarded the rulers with slender gratitude." "Inferior members of the court party," such as Major Molineux, "led scarcely a more desirable life." The word Hawthorne chooses to describe the temper of the people on the evening of the tale is "inflammation."

Through accumulation of consistent detail, "My Kinsman, Major Molineux" portrays the viciousness of patriotic mobs and the injustices done to loyalists. Not one word in the story suggests that Major Molineux is anything but an "elderly man, of large and majestic person, and strong, square features, betokening a steady soul." The tarring and feathering of the Major is precisely what Hawthorne says it is—"the foul disgrace of a head that had grown gray in honor." The phrases describing the procession form one coherent judgment: "counterfeited pomp," "senseless uproar," and "friends that throng in mockery round some dead potentate." A reader who recalls how John Hancock "trod upon humbled Royalty" might note Hawthorne's reference to the patriotic procession "trampling all on an old man's heart."

The memorable figure with the half-red, half-black face has been made the symbol of various kinds of psychic deviltries in man or repressed fears in Robin, none of which Hawthorne mentions. Surely it is of some importance that the figure is revealed actually to be the leader of the popular procession, and that Hawthorne likens him to "war personified." With his shaggy eyebrows, glaring eyes, and a face half-incendiary, half-deathlike, the leader just might resemble all

---

4. "Guilt is the price which Hawthorne makes Robin pay for his freedom" (Roy Harvey Pearce, "Robin Molineux on the Analyst's Couch," *Criticism*, I [1959], 87). See also Pearce's "Hawthorne and the Sense of the Past; or, The Immortality of Major Molineux," *ELH*, 31 (1954), 327–349.

the animal violence and crazed belligerence Hawthorne was repeatedly to associate with the Revolutionary War.

As the reader begins "My Kinsman, Major Molineux," he must make an astute guess after close scrutiny of the first paragraph, or he will continue to find his sense of political reality being inverted. Because Hawthorne seems to adopt Robin's point of view, pre-Revolutionary Boston is assumed to be an ordered and loyal town where an uncle's status will be recognized. Unlike Robin, however, a perceptive reader soon senses that the people Robin meets, whom he persists in believing to be loyal, are conspiring to commit some unknown act. A pattern quickly develops in which the townspeople ridicule Robin, threaten him with various punishments, and take delight in keeping him confounded. This pattern is, of course, a necessary device for maintaining the impact of the climactic procession, but it also affects the reader's political presumptions. Insidious traits which Hawthorne's contemporaries would have ascribed to Tories are associated with makers of rebellion. Clichés about colonial grievances never appear, but a display of mob sadism does. In the entire tale, only the first half of the second sentence ("The people looked with most jealous scrutiny to the exercise of power which did not emanate from themselves") intimates that a political principle might have inspired the revolt.

Hawthorne's revolutionaries are not young men needing to come of age. Frederick Crews's statement, "Hawthorne, like Tom Paine, sees revolution itself in terms of filial revolt,"[5] is true of Paine, but not of Hawthorne. Robin may be young and dependent upon father figures, but he displays no will to rebel. The revolutionaries in the tale are the figures Robin meets in the barber's shop, tavern, streets and procession. Like the Puritan revolutionaries in "Howe's Masquerade," "Edward Randolph's Portrait," and *Grandfather's Chair*, they are elderly, decisive and self-assured. They do not, however, exhibit the Puritan piety and integrity which Hawthorne was to claim for the Revolutionaries. In this tale, piety and integrity are qualities associated either with the Major or, by Robin, with his father, a "clergyman" in the seventeenth-century tradition, fond of "old thanksgivings" and of "old supplications," who lives in the country, and who is the cousin of Major Molineux.

The tarring and feathering of the Major has been slighted or rationalized because it has seemed the necessary means to Robin's maturity. Yet Hawthorne never confirms that Robin has changed or learned anything. When the leader of the procession, already likened

5. Frederick Crews, *The Sins of the Fathers: Hawthorne's Psychological Themes* (New York: Oxford University Press, 1966), p. 78.

to "war personified," fixes his eye meaningfully upon Robin, Robin turns away, sensing no hint of the future. The condemnations of the Major's foul disgrace are written by Hawthorne, not spoken by Robin. Robin's joining into the common laughter may express no recognition of historical irony, and no repressed delight in disgracing father figures. Hawthorne, after all, wrote only "the contagion was spreading among the multitude, when, all at once, it seized upon Robin." In context, the word "contagion" suggests that the widespread scorn for loyalists is a disease, while the statement as a whole emphasizes Robin's passivity, not his awareness.

The ending of the tale, evidence of Robin's maturing to so many critics, can more plausibly be regarded as evidence of his persistent naiveté. Robin says merely that he wishes to go to the ferry because he is "weary of a town life"—a response quite inadequate to his night's experience. Because Robin seems never to have understood where he has been, or what he has seen, his readiness to return to rural innocence is ironically apt. It is only the old gentleman who suggests that Robin stay and gain success through independence: "Some few days hence, if you continue to wish it, I will speed you on your journey. Or, if you prefer to remain with us, perhaps, as you are a shrewd youth, you may rise in the world, without the help of your kinsman, Major Molineux." A regard for syntax shows Hawthorne's equivocation here. The statement presents two alternatives, each of which contains a conditional clause. Moreover, the second alternative, which is the one at issue, contains two further qualifications ("perhaps" and "you may rise"). Because the old gentleman knows Robin to be anything but shrewd, his words may show Hawthorne's desire to deflate Franklinian assurances about young men rising through self-help in pre-Revolutionary American cities.

The assumption that it is Robin Molineux who represents Young America is equally arbitrary. Are we to assume that Robin represents America simply because he is young, innocent and from the country, like other American Adams? Should not Hawthorne's view of Young America in the pre-Revolutionary era be sought, not in Robin Molineux, but in the crafty old tacticians who are acting out a revolt before our eyes? Critics who accept the premise that Robin must bear a national identity are not likely to recognize that Robin Molineux is not only a character in historical time, but the narrative voice through which a presumably historical occurrence is seen. Thus Robin also serves as a device, a means for measuring the reader's insight into aspects of human and historical experience. Hawthorne may even have intended Robin to embody the attitudes of many contemporary patriots, of those readers who, even when confronted with the violence and demagoguery of the Revolution, prove unwilling or unable to recognize them.

As romancer and historian, Hawthorne was able to dramatize only a part of his contention that Revolutionary violence had been redeemed by its nobility of purpose. Because the brutalities of Revolutionary history seemed more real than any political abstraction, his revolutionaries could be nobly motivated only when they were said to possess Puritan traits idealized beyond the author's custom. When seen in action, however, Hawthorne's Revolutionary Puritan exhibits the single-minded self-righteousness and colorless sobriety of his seventeenth-century prototype. While the worthy motives of the Revolution thus looked only toward the past, the true merit of the Revolution, which could not include such superficial achievements as the Constitution, westward expansion or prosperity, remained perplexingly difficult to specify. If John Hancock was a representative new American, his ideas seemed as simplistic as Holgrave's, and he might act with as little discrimination as the reformers in "Earth's Holocaust."

Throughout the patriotic hectoring of the Jacksonian era, Hawthorne had preserved a disturbingly complex view of the Revolution. Accepting the premise that the revolutionaries of 1776 must resemble the Puritans of 1640, he provided a continuity to colonial history which did not totally neglect the darker side of king-killing absolutism. His insistence on judging by deed rather than catchword, on revealing the character which creates law, rather than vice versa, is courageously atypical in an age and country which often sought external proof for its rising glory.

FREDERICK C. CREWS

The Logic of Compulsion[†]

> "It don't make no difference whether you do right or wrong, a person's conscience ain't got no sense and just goes for him *anyway*."
> —*Huckleberry Finn*

One further story from Hawthorne's unpublished "Provincial Tales" requires our close interest, both because it has been generally misunderstood and because, once understood, it merits a high place among his fiction. In addition, "Roger Malvin's Burial" offers a classic instance of the way Hawthorne undermines questions of conscious moral choice with demonstrations of psychological necessity. As Harry Levin puts it, "Hawthorne was well aware that the sense

† From Frederick C. Crews, *The Sins of the Fathers: Hawthorne's Psychological Themes* (New York: Oxford University Press, 1966), 80–95. Reprinted by permission of Oxford University Press.

of sin is more ultimately related to inhibition than to indulgence; that the most exquisite consciences are the ones that suffer most; the guilt is a by-product of that very compunction which aims at goodness and acknowledges higher laws; and that lesser evils seem blacker to the innocent than to the experienced."[1] In previous chapters we have tried to define, not only the customary form that "exquisite conscience" takes in Hawthorne's tales, but also the primitive resentment and ambition that bring such conscience into operation. The plot of "Roger Malvin's Burial" makes sense in no other terms than these—and in these it is precisely, indeed shockingly, logical.

The story goes as follows. Roger Malvin, an old Indian-fighter who has been seriously wounded and finds himself unable to survive the homeward journey through a forest, persuades his young companion, Reuben Bourne, to leave him to die. Reuben will thereby gain a chance to survive, whereas to remain would simply mean two deaths instead of one. After promising to return some day to bury his old friend, Reuben departs and is eventually rescued by a search party. Though he marries Roger's daughter Dorcas, he is unable to explain to her that he left her father alive, preferring to let her imagine that he has already been buried. Reuben's public character and fortunes soon begin to go awry, until finally he is forced to take his wife and adolescent son off into the wilderness to seek a new life. Yet his steps bring him, not to the intended destination, but to the clearing where he left Roger Malvin many years before. There, detecting what might be a deer behind some undergrowth, he fires his musket, only to discover that he has killed his son Cyrus on the very spot where Roger died. The story ends, nonetheless, on an affirmative and extremely pious note: "Then Reuben's heart was stricken, and the tears gushed out like water from a rock. The vow that the wounded youth had made the blighted man had come to redeem. His sin was expiated,—the curse was gone from him; and in the hour when he had shed blood dearer to him than his own, a prayer, the first for years, went up to Heaven from the lips of Reuben Bourne."

Such language naturally leads us to interpret "Roger Malvin's Burial" as a parable of atonement, for Reuben's act of manslaughter has melted his heart and enabled him to beg God for forgiveness. But forgiveness for what? It is unclear whether Reuben has atoned merely for not burying Roger or for some other failing, and critics disagree as to what he has done wrong. In Harry Levin's view, Reuben is "innocent" of Roger Malvin's death and only "inadvertently guilty" of

---

1. Harry Levin, *The Power of Blackness* (New York, 1960), p. 40. For another valuable formulation of Hawthorne's reduction of religious problems to psychological ones, see Melvin W. Askew, "Hawthorne, the Fall, and the Psychology of Maturity," *American Literature*, XXXIV (November 1962), 335–43.

his son's. Mark Van Doren, on the other hand, holds Reuben accountable for both the desertion of Roger and the hypocrisy of silence
toward Dorcas: "he has committed a sin and he has failed to confess it when he could." A third interpretation is that of Arlin Turner,
who finds that Hawthorne "relieves Reuben Bourne of any guilt for
abandoning Malvin" but shows the ill effects of his failure to be
honest with Dorcas. The only point of general agreement is that the
slaying of Reuben's son Cyrus is accidental. For Van Doren it is
"Fate" that engineers the final catastrophe, and that event strikes
Levin as "one of those coincidences that seem to lay bare the design
of the universe.[2]

All of these opinions, including the unquestioned one about
Cyrus's death, miss the essence of Hawthorne's story by not recognizing a difference between the feeling of guilt and the state of being
guilty. Turner, to be sure, makes the point that Reuben's guilt is subjective, but in regard to the desertion scene he apparently confuses a
moral absolving of Reuben by Hawthorne with an absence of guilty
feeling on Reuben's part. We can see, however, in this scene and
throughout the story, that Hawthorne is concerned *only* with subjective guilt as Reuben's conscience manufactures it, independently
of the moral "sinfulness" or "innocence" of his outward deeds. That
this is so at the end of the tale is obvious, for how could we take seriously the religious notion that a man can make his peace with the
Christian God by shooting his innocent son? It is clear that Reuben
has not performed a Christian expiation but simply rid himself of his
burden of guilty feeling. It can be shown, furthermore, that this
guilty feeling was never generated by a committed sin or crime in
the first place. Once we have recognized this, the task of deciding
whether Reuben has been morally absolved becomes pointless, and
Reuben's own theory that his steps have been led by "a supernatural
power" appears in its true light—as a delusion fostered by, and serving to cloak, a process of unconscious compulsion that is evidenced
in great detail.[3]

Everyone agrees that Reuben feels guilty after misleading Dorcas,
and it seems quite evident that Reuben's behavior in that scene is
governed by an inner discomfort over his having left Roger Malvin
behind. But why should Reuben feel this discomfort? The scene of

2. See *The Power of Blackness*, p. 55; Mark Van Doren, *Nathaniel Hawthorne* (New York,
1949), p. 80; and Arlin Turner, *Nathaniel Hawthorne: An Introduction and Interpretation* (New York, 1961), p. 31.
3. The argument that follows has been anticipated in part by various studies. See Waggoner, *Hawthorne*, pp. 90–98: Richard P. Adams, "Hawthorne's *Provincial Tales*," *New
England Quarterly*, XXX (March 1957), 39–57; Louis B. Salomon, "Hawthorne and His
Father: A Conjecture," *Literature and Psychology*, XIII (Winter 1963), 12–17; and Agnes
McNeill Donohue, "'From Whose Bourn No Traveler Returns': A Reading of 'Roger Malvin's Burial,'" *Nineteenth-Century Fiction*, XVIII (June 1963), 1–19.

desertion is presented in such a way as to put every justification on Reuben's side; Roger's arguments have persuaded not only Reuben but most of the tale's critics to feel that there is only one reasonable decision to be made. Why, then, does Reuben find it so difficult to explain the true circumstances to Dorcas? The answer seems to be that in some deep way Reuben feels more responsible for Roger's death than he actually is. "By a certain association of ideas," as Hawthorne says of him later, "he at times almost imagined himself a murderer."

How could Reuben feel himself even remotely to be Roger's murderer? If there is no factual basis for the self-accusation, perhaps there is a psychological basis. The charge seems, indeed, to be true in fantasy if not true in fact, for Reuben shows definite signs of looking forward to deserting Roger in spite of his comradely feeling for him. When Roger adduces the point that Dorcas must not be left desolate, Reuben feels reminded "that there were other and less questionable duties than that of sharing the fate of a man whom his death could not benefit. Nor," adds Hawthorne significantly, "can it be affirmed that no selfish feeling strove to enter Reuben's heart, though the consciousness made him more earnestly resist his companion's entreaties." This would seem to be the source of all Reuben's trouble. It is obviously advantageous as well as reasonable for him to go on without Roger, since he faces a prospect of married bliss if he survives. The contrast between Roger's altruism and his own self-seeking motives is painful to his conscience; his personal claims must strive for recognition, and Reuben feels a need to counterattack them with a redoubled commitment to remain with Roger. "He felt as if it were both sin and folly to think of happiness at such a moment." Thus we see that his feelings of guilt have already set in before he has made a final decision to leave. He feels guilty, not for anything he has done, but for thoughts of happiness—a happiness that will be bought at the price of a man's life.

The more closely we look at the scene of desertion, the more ironical Hawthorne's view of Reuben's mental struggle appears. The mention of Dorcas marks a turning-point between a series of melodramatic, self-sacrificing protestations of faithfulness and a new tone of puzzlement, self-doubt, and finally insincerity. Reuben is no longer really combating Roger's wishes after this point, but posing objections that he knows Roger will easily refute. "How terrible to wait the slow approach of death in this solitude!" But a brave man, answers Roger, knows how to die. "And your daughter,—how shall I dare to meet her eye?" The question is already how *shall* I, not how *would* I! When this too has been answered, Reuben needs only to be assured of the possibility of his returning with a rescue party. "No merely selfish motive, nor even the desolate condition of Dorcas, could have induced him to desert his companion at such a moment—but his wishes seized on the thought that Malvin's life might be preserved, and his sanguine nature heightened almost to certainty the remote possibility of procuring human aid." There follows a grim comedy in which Roger pretends to see a similarity between the present case and another one, twenty years previously, that turned out well, and Reuben fatuously allows himself to be convinced. Hawthorne leaves no doubt that Reuben is semi-deliberately deceiving himself in order to silence his conscience. "This example, powerful in affecting Reuben's decision, was aided, unconsciously to himself, by the hidden strength of many another motive." When he finally does leave, the act is presented as a triumph of these other motives over his human sympathy: "His generous nature would fain have delayed him, at whatever risk, till the dying scene were past; but the desire of existence and the hope of happiness had strengthened in his heart, and he was unable to resist them."

These citations from the story's first scene make it evident that Hawthorne, by having Reuben's self-seeking wishes concur with a morally legitimate but painful decision, has set in bold relief the purely psychological problem of guilt. Unlike his critics, Hawthorne does not dwell on the moral defensibility of Reuben's leaving: rather, he demonstrates how this act appears to Reuben as a fulfillment of his egoistic wishes, so that he is already beginning to punish himself *as if* he had positively brought about Roger's death. * * * Hawthorne has anticipated Freud's discovery that (in Freud's terminology) the superego takes revenge for unfulfilled death-wishes as well as for actual murder.[4] Indeed, Hawthorne's whole rendering of Reuben's mind is based on what we would now call psychoanalytic principles. Some of Reuben's motives, as we have seen, operate "unconsciously to himself," which is to say that they have been repressed; and once this repression has circumvented conscious moral control, Reuben becomes a classic example of the man who, because he can neither overcome his thoughts nor admit them into consciousness, becomes their victim. The real reason for his inability to state the outward facts of the case to Dorcas is that these facts have become associated with the unbearable fantasy that he has murdered his friend. Guilty feeling leads to a hypocrisy, which in turn provides further reinforcement of guilt; "and Reuben, while reason told him that he had done

---

4. I do not mean, however, that Reuben actively wills Roger's death at any point. The link between his prospective happiness and Roger's imminent, already inevitable death is originally a fortuitous irony of circumstance and nothing more. But Reuben's punctilious conscience turns this link into one of causality; he will no longer be able to contemplate his own welfare without imagining, quite falsely, that he has bought it with Roger Malvin's blood.

right, experienced in no small degree the mental horrors which punish the perpetrator of undiscovered crime."

One other inconspicuous, but absolutely decisive, element in the scene of desertion remains to be mentioned, namely, that the relationship between Roger and Reuben is that of a father to a son. Roger repeatedly calls him "my boy" and "my son," and at a certain point he turns this language to an argumentative use: "I have loved you like a father, Reuben; and at a time like this I should have something of a father's authority." Reuben's reply is curious: "And because you have been a father to me, should I therefore leave you to perish and to lie unburied in the wilderness?" From a strictly Freudian point of view the answer to this rhetorical question could be *yes*; the "son" feels murderous impulses toward the "father" simply because he *is* the father, i.e., the sexual rival. It is questionable whether Hawthorne's thinking has gone quite this far. Yet it remains true that Reuben, in leaving Roger to die, will get to have Dorcas's affections all to himself, and we cannot say that such a consideration is not among the "many another motive" for his departure. The "father's authority" of which Roger ingenuously speaks is going to be left behind in the forest. In terms of the unconscious role he has assumed in relation to Roger, Reuben must think of himself not simply as a murderer but as a patricide.

This conclusion needs, of course, much further confirmation in order to be persuasive. Yet we may pause here to say that everything we have found in other tales—the violent and sometimes historically unfounded hatred against figures of authority, the crippling sense of guilt for unspecified criminal thoughts, and even a fairly plain fantasy of patricide in "Alice Doane's Appeal"—leads us to believe that Hawthorne was capable of taking the father-son symbolism as a basis for unconscious motivation. Nor can we quite avoid seeing that the complement to patricide, namely incest, lurks in the background of "Roger Malvin's Burial." If Roger is to be seen as Reuben's father, Dorcas becomes his sister. Without pressing this argument further, we may observe that Dorcas's later feeling for her son—"my beautiful young hunter!"—does not dispel the characteristic Hawthornian atmosphere of over-intimacy in this tale.

But let us return to less tenuous evidence. Reuben, who henceforth is occupied in "defending himself against an imaginary accusation," gradually turns his interest to his son Cyrus. "The boy was loved by his father with a deep and silent strength, as if whatever was good and happy in his own nature had been transferred to his child, carrying his affections with it. Even Dorcas, though loving and beloved, was far less dear to him; for Reuben's secret thoughts and insulated emotions had gradually made him a selfish man, and he could no longer love deeply except where he saw or imagined some reflection or likeness of his own mind. In Cyrus he recognized what he had himself been in other days . . ." Reuben has, in a word, projected himself into his son. And what is to be the conclusive deed of "Roger Malvin's Burial"? Reuben, who harbors an accusation of having murdered a "father" and who cannot bring this accusation up to the rational criticism of consciousness, shoots and kills the boy who has come to stand for himself. In killing Cyrus he is destroying the "guilty" side of himself, and hence avenging Roger Malvin's death in an appallingly primitive way. The blood of a "father" rests on the "son," who disburdens himself of it by becoming a father and slaying his son. This is the terrible logic of Hawthorne's tale.

Thus I would maintain, in opposition to the generally held view, that the slaying of Cyrus is not at all the hunting accident it appears to be. It is a sacrificial murder dictated by Reuben's unconscious charge of patricide and by his inability to bring the charge directly against himself. He has become the accusing Roger at the same time that he has projected his own guilty self into Cyrus. These unconscious stratagems are his means of dealing with the contradictory repressed wishes (the desire to atone and the unwillingness to accept blame) that have transformed him into an irritable, moody, and misanthropic man over the course of the years. The killing of Cyrus, by canceling Reuben's imaginary blood-debt, frees his whole mind at last for the task of making peace with God; yet this religious achievement becomes possible, as Hawthorne stresses in the closing sentence, only "in the hour when he had shed blood dearer to him than his own."

There are two main obstacles to the theory that Reuben's shooting his son is intentional. One is that Reuben has no idea that his target is Cyrus instead of a deer; he simply fires at a noise and a motion in the distance. Secondly, there is the possibility that not Reuben but God is responsible for bringing the tale to its catastrophe. The final paragraph, after all, speaks of the lifting of a curse, and Roger Malvin has imposed a religious vow on Reuben to "return to this wild rock, and lay my bones in the grave, and say a prayer over them." Both Roger and Reuben are religious men, and Reuben "trusted that it was Heaven's intent to afford him an opportunity of expiating his sin." Perhaps we are meant to read the story in divine rather than psychological terms.

The answer to this latter point is provided by Hawthorne in a single sentence describing Reuben in the final scene: "Unable to penetrate to the secret place of his soul where his motives lay hidden, he believed that a supernatural voice had called him onward, and that a supernatural power had obstructed his retreat." No one who ponders these words can imagine that Hawthorne's famous ambiguity between natural and supernatural causality is really sustained in "Roger Malvin's Burial." As for the other objection, it is certainly true that Reuben shows no conscious awareness that he is firing at his son. But does this make the act wholly unintentional? Before investigating the actual shooting we must see just what Hawthorne means by intention. His theory is evidently somewhat deeper than that of our law courts, which would surely have acquitted Reuben in a trial for murder. "Roger Malvin's Burial" discriminates from the first between surface intentions and buried ones, between outward tokens of generous concern and inward selfishness, between total ignorance and a knowledge that is temporarily unavailable to consciousness. For this last distinction we may point to the statement that Reuben cannot choose to return and bury Roger because he does not know how to find his way back: "his remembrance of every portion of his travel thence was indistinct, and the latter part had left no impression upon his mind." Yet we have just seen that Reuben will be guided by "his motives," residing in a "secret place of his soul." Furthermore, he has always "had a strange impression that, were he to make the trial, he would be led straight to Malvin's bones." We can only conclude that knowledge of the route he took in that traumatic flight from the deserted comrade has been repressed, not lost; when Reuben finally gives himself over to the guidance of his unconscious he is led infallibly back to the scene.

In order to see the killing of Cyrus in its true light we must scrutinize Reuben's prior behavior. Although Cyrus reminds him again and again that he is taking the family in a different direction from the announced one, Reuben keeps resuming his original course after each correction. His thoughts are obviously dwelling on something other than the relocation of his home. "His quick and wandering glances were sent forward, apparently in search of enemies lurking behind the tree trunks; and, seeing nothing there, he would cast his eyes backwards as if in fear of some pursuer." Reuben would appear to be projecting his self-accusations into multiple exterior threats to himself. The internalized Roger Malvin—the Roger Malvin created by Reuben's unwarranted self-accusation of murder—is evidently redoubling his demand to be avenged as the anniversary of his death draws near. When the fifth day's encampment is made, Dorcas reminds Reuben of the date. "'The twelfth of May! I should remember it well,' muttered he, while many thoughts occasioned a momentary confusion in his mind. 'Where am I? Whither am I wandering? Where did I leave him?'" Among those "many thoughts" that have suddenly been jolted into consciousness are probably the answers to all three of Reuben's questions. Dorcas has accidentally brought to the surface, though only for a moment, Reuben's feeling that he is on a deliberate mission.

Is this mission simply to bury Roger's bones? Evidently something further is involved, for in reply to Dorcas's next words, praising Reuben for having loyally stayed with Roger to the end, Reuben pleads, "Pray Heaven, Dorcas, . . . pray Heaven that neither of us three dies solitary and lies unburied in this howling wilderness!" And on this foreboding note he hastens away at once. It seems to me obvious that Reuben's terribly sincere "prayer" is a response to his own unconscious urge to commit the sacrificial killing—an urge that has been screwed to the sticking place by Dorcas's unwitting irony. Like all men in the grip of a destructive obsession, Reuben hopes desperately that his own deep wishes will be thwarted; yet he rushes off in the next moment, and a few minutes later Cyrus will be dead.

We have, then, an abundance of evidence to show that one side of Reuben's nature, the compulsive side, has gained mastery over his conscious intentions. The evidence continues to accumulate as the moment of the shooting draws nearer. Reuben is assaulted by "many strange reflections" that keep him from governing his steps in the supposed hunt for a deer; "and, straying onward rather like a sleep walker than a hunter, it was attributable to no care of his own that his devious course kept him in the vicinity of the encampment." No *conscious* care, that is, for Reuben has a very good compulsive reason for his movements. Cyrus has previously set out on another deer hunt, "promising not to quit *the vicinity of the encampment*" (my italics). Surely Hawthorne's repetition of these five words within the space of two pages is meant to strike our attention. Without quite realizing what he is doing, Reuben is stalking his son. His conscious thoughts are straying vaguely over the puzzle of his having reached this spot on this date, and he arrives at a conscious interpretation— explicitly rejected by Hawthorne, as we have already seen—that "it was Heaven's intent to afford him an opportunity of expiating his sin." The consciously accepted "sin" is that of leaving Roger Malvin unburied, but while Reuben busies himself with this lesser anxiety he is going about the business of squaring his deeper unconscious debt. Here is the deed itself:

> From these thoughts he was aroused by a rustling in the forest at some distance from the spot to which he had wandered. Perceiving the motion of some object behind a thick veil of undergrowth, he fired, with the instinct of a hunter and the aim of a practised marksman. A low moan, which told his success, and by which even animals can express their dying agony, was unheeded by Reuben Bourne. What were the recollections now breaking upon him?

These are brilliantly suggestive lines. Reuben is supposedly deer-hunting, but Hawthorne leaves no implication that Reuben thinks he has spotted a deer; he fires at a "rustling" and a "motion." To say that he does this with a hunter's instinct is slyly ironical, for of course a good hunter does not shoot at ambiguous noises, particularly in "the vicinity of the encampment"! The moan that would tell Reuben of his ironic "success," if he were sufficiently in command of himself to heed it, is said to be one "by which *even* animals can express their dying agony"—a hint that animals have not been his primary target. And finally, the question at the end serves to put the blame for Cyrus's death where it properly belongs. The repressed "recollections" of the original scene are now free to become wholly conscious because the guilt-compulsion that protected them has finally completed its work.

If this argument is correct, the various interpretations of "Roger Malvin's Burial" in terms of religious symbolism must be regarded with suspicion. It is true, for example, that three of the four major characters' names are Biblical, but it is doubtful that this entitles us to say that Reuben achieves "salvation" through Cyrus.[5] Even the Abraham-Isaac parallel, which seems more prominent than any other, must be taken in an ironic spirit, for Reuben's "sacrifice" of his son is dictated not by God but by self-loathing. The story's ending is heretical, to put it mildly: Reuben's alleged redemption has been achieved through murder, while the guilt from which he has thereby freed himself stemmed from an imaginary crime.[6] The real murder is unrepented yet—indeed, Reuben shows little concern for his dead son—while the fantasy-murder brings forth tears and prayer.[7] The Biblical allusions suggesting a possible redemption serve the purpose of placing in relief the merely pathological nature of the case at hand. For the idea of divine care is cruelly mocked by a plot in which all exhortations to Heaven spring from self-delusion, and in which the "redeemer" performs his redemptive function by unintentionally stopping a musket ball.

---

5. See W. R. Thompson, "The Biblical Sources of Hawthorne's 'Roger Malvin's Burial,'" *PMLA*, LXXVII (March 1962), 92–6. The fourth principal name appears to be historical rather than Biblical. Two survivors of Lovewell's (or Lovell's) Fight in the Penobscot War, as Hawthorne knew, were Eleanor and David Melvin. See G. Harrison Orians, "The Source of Hawthorne's 'Roger Malvin's Burial,'" *American Literature*, X (November 1938), 313–18, and David S. Lovejoy, "Lovewell's Fight and Hawthorne's 'Roger Malvin's Burial,'" *A Casebook on the Hawthorne Question*, ed. Agnes McNeill Donohue (New York, 1963), pp. 89–92.
6. It is significant that although Reuben consciously thinks that his expiation will consist of burying Roger's bones, the actual release of his guilt-feeling comes about through the killing of Cyrus. There is no mention of burial at the end, yet the "atonement" is indeed complete; it is atonement for the imagined murder of Roger, not for the broken vow to bury him.
7. We can judge the abnormality of Reuben's reaction by contrasting it with that of Dorcas: "With one wild shriek, that seemed to force its way from the sufferer's inmost soul, she sank insensible by the side of her dead boy."

The other symbols in Hawthorne's story ought likewise to be considered in relationship to its essential savagery. The most conspicuous symbol is, of course, the oak sapling upon which Reuben places
a bloodstained handkerchief, partly as a signal of rescue for Roger
and partly to symbolize his own vow to return. When he does return
the tree has grown into "luxuriant life," with "an excess of vegetation" on the trunk, but its "very topmost bough was withered, sapless,
and utterly dead." This branch, which is the one that formerly bore
the emblem of the vow, falls in fragments upon the *tableau vivant*
of the living and dead at the very end. The symbolic meaning is, if
anything, too obvious. The sapling is Reuben, whose innocent young
life has been "bent" (he bends the sapling downward to affix the
handkerchief to it) to a sworn purpose and to a secret self-reproach;
Reuben grows as the tree grows, becoming mature in outward
respects but blasted at the top, in his soul or mind; and when the
withered bough crumbles we are doubtless meant to conclude that
the guilt has been canceled and that a possibility now exists for
more normal development. I would call particular attention, however, to the *excessive* vegetation and *luxuriant* lower branches. Luxuriance in Hawthorne almost always has something sick about it, and
the word "excess" speaks for itself. I would surmise that these aspects
of the tree represent the compensatory elements in Reuben's character, the gradual accretion of defenses against the tormenting thoughts
that he has been fighting down for years. His peace of mind is partly
restored at the end of the tale, but he will never again be the simple
person we met in the beginning.

Finally, let us consider the symbolic value of the forest itself. Reuben's initiation into guilt, like Young Goodman Brown's and Arthur
Dimmesdale's, occurs in the forest, and it is in the forest that he will
bring forth what his guilty feelings have hatched. "He was," as Hawthorne says of Reuben's desire to seek a new home, "to throw sunlight into some deep recess of the forest." The forest is of course
his own mind, in which is deeply buried a secret spot, a trauma, to
which he will have to return. He thinks he does not know the way
back, he resists the opportunity to go, but ultimately he is overruled
by the strength of what he has repressed. Self-knowledge is knowledge of what is almost inaccessibly remote, and Reuben will not be
free until he has reached this point and released what lies imprisoned
there. The tale of compulsion is fittingly climaxed in "a region of
which savage beasts and savage men were as yet the sole possessors"—
the mental region of Hawthorne's best insight and highest art.

MICHAEL J. COLACURCIO

Visible Sanctity and Specter Evidence: The Moral World of Hawthorne's "Young Goodman Brown"†

* * *

At the beginning of his fateful excursion into the forest, Goodman Brown is a more than tolerably naive young man. We scarcely need to observe his dismay at hearing (and then seeing) communicants and tavern-haunters, saints and sinners, mixed together to sense his initial assumption that the orderly divisions of the Puritan Community embody Moral Reality. More particularly, his initial attitude toward his wife is so naive as to be condescending: "Say thy prayers, dear Faith, and go to bed at dusk, and no harm will come to thee." On the face of things this is too easy; and the reader of "Fancy's Show Box" knows that, on the contrary, "In the solitude of a midnight chamber . . . the soul may pollute itself with those crimes we are accustomed to deem altogether carnal" (I, 250).[1] But such naivete is far from his worst trait. Whatever may be the truth about the moral character of Brown's pink-ribboned wife, and whatever may be our own working assumptions about the relation between faith and salvation, we are expected to worry about this Goodman's belief that "after this one night" he can cling to the skirts of Faith and "follow her to heaven." Even before we get any sense of the sorts of self-indulgence that may become available to Goodman Brown, we know that this sort of temporizing with one's eternal salvation is likely to be risky.

---

† From Michael J. Colacurcio, "Visible Sanctity and Specter Evidence: The Moral World of Hawthorne's 'Young Goodman Brown,'" *Essex Institute Historical Collections* 110 (1974): 263–76, 278–85, 287–91. The essay has been reprinted in adapted form in Colacurcio's *The Province of Piety: Moral History in Hawthorne's Early Tales* (Cambridge: Harvard University Press, 1984), 283–313. Reprinted by permission of The Phillips Library at the Peabody Essex Museum.

    About half of Colacurcio's essay is included in this edition. Colacurcio takes as his starting point David Levin's "Shadows of Doubt: Specter Evidence in Hawthorne's 'Young Goodman Brown,'" *American Literature* 34 (1962): 344–52. Like Levin, Colacurcio insists that we must begin by reading the story literally and historically as an account of a young man living in Salem Village in the 1690s who goes into the forest at night to meet the devil and is tempted by the devil to imagine that all his relations and neighbors are evil. The devil conducts his temptation by staging a spectral drama in which the human figures Brown sees are not real persons but specters conjured up by diabolical power. Brown is left thereafter in desperate and gloomy doubt for the rest of his life and trusts neither his neighbors nor his wife, his "Faith." Colacurcio sides with Levin against Paul J. Hurley, who argues that Brown's trip to the forest is a projection of his disordered imagination and that his conversations with the devil are interior monologues. (See Hurley's "Young Goodman Brown's 'Heart of Darkness,'" *American Literature* 37 [1966]: 410–19.)

1. All references to Hawthorne's works not included in this Norton edition are from the Riverside Edition of *The Complete Works of Nathaniel Hawthorne* (Boston, 1883) and will be identified by volume and page number in the text [*Editor's note*].

Actually, as it turns out, Goodman Brown is already in a state of "bad faith": there has already been some sort of devilish prearrangement concerning his nocturnal outing; he knows at the outset that he is going off to "keep covenant" with the Powers of Darkness. His "excellent resolve for the future" may be temporarily successful in allowing him to feel "justified in making more haste on his present evil purpose," but the rationalization is as transparent to the psychologist as the risk is to the theologian; it is not likely to stand much testing. And, as an external sign of his compromised internal condition, he has *already* begun to be suspicious of others, even those in whose virtue he is most accustomed naively to trust. Accordingly, his wife's understandable plea that he stay with her, to quiet her fears, on this "of all nights of the year," draws a nervously revealing response: "Dost thou doubt me already, and we but three months married?" Now October 31 *is* a good night for Puritans to stay home,[2] and there is not the slightest evidence to suggest that Faith doubts her husband in any way. Brown's attitude is clearly some sort of guilty projection: his own will-to-evil is *already* causing him to begin the transfer of his own moral obliquity to others.

Clearly, then, much more is at stake than simple naivete, or the much-discussed innocence of the archetypal American hero. Studied closely, Brown's situation is not much like that of Robin Molineux. And well before the analyst has much evidence of oedipal anxiety to work on, any decent theologian (Puritan or otherwise) is constrained to conclude that Goodman Brown is deeply involved in that particular sort of bad faith which used to be called "presumption." He is assuming his own final perseverance, even as he deliberately embarks on a journey which he knows is directed diametrically away from the normal pursuit of salvation. The point is not trivial: to understand the "unpardonable" gravity of his initial moral assumptions is to be protected from being more tender-minded about the terrifying results of his experience than Hawthorne's tough and tight-lipped conclusion asks us to be. No especially severe morality is required to see that, from one very significant point of view, Goodman Brown deserves whatever happens.

Given the unflinching and unpardoning outcome, of a story that is already well under way when we first began to hear about it, we ought to find ourselves wondering how Goodman Brown has got himself *already* so far involved in the "unpardonable sin" of presumption. If everything seems to follow from, or indeed to be contained

---

2. The story never actually *tells* us what night "of all nights" we are dealing with, but I see no reason to quarrel with the conjecture of Daniel Hoffman; see *Form and Fable in American Fiction* (New York, 1961), p. 150.

in, the initial situation of the story, perhaps that initial situation itself deserves very careful attention. We need to proceed with care: on the one hand, it is very easy to distort and make nonsense out of Hawthorne's delicate ethical formulae by going behind the donnée of his initial premises; on the other hand, his stories are often packed with clues about exactly "where," morally speaking, we really are. And "Young Goodman Brown" does not leave us entirely without such clues.

If Brown is "but three months married" to Faith, then it is absolutely necessary to regard him as a recent convert to the high mysteries of the Puritan religion. * * * But evidently the situation is not quite simple, for we swiftly learn that this good man's father and grandfather have been faithful Puritans before him; and that he himself has been duly catechized, in his youth, by the dutiful Goody Cloyse. At the first glance there may seem to be some sort of confusion in the allegory: can Goodman Brown be, at once, a new convert *and* an heir to a redoubtable saintly ancestry and a formidable Christian nurture? The solution to this apparent difficulty, as well as the key to Goodman Brown's presumptuous psychology, lies in the implicit but clear and precise Puritan background of the story, in the subtly emphasized fact that Young Goodman Brown is a *third-generation* Puritan.

Thus even before we encounter any enchantments, we are forced to realize that Hawthorne's reading in Mather's *Magnalia* has been extremely perceptive and that his use of a particular Puritan world is entirely functional; for Goodman Brown is quite evidently the product (victim, as it turns out) of the Half-Way Covenant, that bold compromise by which the Puritans tried to salvage their theory of "visible sanctity," of a church composed of fully professed saints, in the face of changing historical conditions.[3] Externally, at least, Goodman Brown's status is perfectly standard, indeed inevitable: as a third-generation Puritan he would have been spending the years of his minority in the half-way situation defined by the compromise of 1662.[4] Grandson of an original saint, son of a professing member, he

---

3. In my view, Hawthorne's ability to write YGB was as fundamentally dependent on his reading of Books Four and Five of the *Magnalia*—together with Cotton Mather's *Parentator*—as on any of the proven witchcraft sources, including Mather's own *Wonders of the Invisible World*. We know, from Kesselring, that Hawthorne read the *Magnalia* as early as 1827. And we strongly suspect, from the evidence of *Grandfather's Chair* (IV, 511–514), that it was a book he kept rereading, one that made as deep an impression on his mind as did *The Faerie Queene*. * * *

4. The year in which the so-called Half-Way Covenant was adopted by the Massachusetts church. The original leaders of New England Congregationalism insisted that believers had to make a public profession of their personal experience of religious conversion before they could be admitted to communion. In other words, only "visible saints" could take communion; infant baptism was not enough. In 1662, the church decided hence-

has been reared, like virtually everyone else in his generation, in the half-way condition of presumptive but not yet professed or tested sainthood. Obviously he has had something to do with the community of visible saints because the promises of the new covenant are made with "the seed" of saints as well as with the saints themselves; but just as obviously he has not (until very recently) been a full, "communing" member because he had not been capable of that fully voluntary confession of conversion and profession of committed sainthood which alone could redeem the New England Way from the crassest sort of tribalism.

Original sin might well be transmitted by the simple act of physical generation. So also, * * * a saint might fairly expect baptism for his seed, and baptism ought to have some gracious significance. But in the last analysis the new birth had to be truly "spiritual" in every sense; thus "sanctifying grace" could come neither biologically nor by infant ritual. And so, as the New England theology gradually clarified itself, that troubled third generation of Puritans simply had to *wait*: in the *expectation* of full, visible sainthood *eventually*, they all attended church, were duly catechized and nurtured, were thoroughly indoctrinated (and threatened) by jeremiads into the proper respect for the ancestral appearances of saintliness. And eventually some, however few, were admitted into that most guarded and holy of holies—full, "communing" membership.[5] Into this ultimate earthly state, Goodman Brown has but newly entered. After years of "preparation" and presumptive but not proven sainthood Goodman Brown has, we must infer, finally received official certification by the public representatives of the Communion of Saints. In an ultimate theological sense, which in his world is by no means trivial, Brown has finally arrived. And this fact can scarcely be unrelated to the terrible ease of his moral premises.

Goodman Brown's assurance is not, one should hasten to stress, orthodox. The expounders of the Puritan system never tired of emphasizing that (despite Calvin's stress on the "comfort" the saint might find in a predestinarian system) one's assurance could never be complete: indeed too great (or, at any rate, too easy) an assurance should certainly mean that one's experience of gracious regeneration

---

forth to allow children of the saints to take communion but to deny these children full membership in the church until they had made a profession of faith. This compromise instituted the Half-Way Covenant [*Editor's note*].

5. "Revisionist" interpretation of the precise significance of the Half-Way Covenant begins with Chapter Four of Edmund S. Morgan's *Visible Saints* (New York, 1963). After that moment of clarity, things have once again grown confused, but two other books seem essential: for the theology, Norman Pettit, *The Heart Prepared* (New Haven, Conn., 1966), esp. pp. 158–216; and for the sociology and ecclesiology, Robert G. Pope, *The Half-Way Covenant* (Princeton, N.J., 1969).

was illusory. But Hawthorne was no mere "expounder" of the system, and he seems to have sensed that all such warnings would not alter the basic psychology of the situation: * * * whenever one declared oneself a saint and had that weighty claim accepted by the community, the basic declaration and the social fact might well tend to loom larger, psychologically, than any attendant (fussy) qualifications about continuing uncertainty, or about the sole importance of God's free grace in the process, or about the continuing need for watchfulness and sanctification; and by providing a formalized schema of waiting or probation out of which many persons never moved, the Half-Way Covenant may well have served to increase this basic psychological tendency. Although the new dispensation served to broaden the base of baptized membership in the Puritan churches, it left the inner circle of full communicants as small as ever, and seemed, if anything, to heighten the significance of that *sanctum sanctorum*.

When one moved, then, from the lamented and berated coolness of half-way membership into the warmth of full communion, the event could have no small significance. And one perfectly likely (though by no means "approved") meaning of such an experience is implied in the moral posture of Goodman Brown as recent-convert. After all protective distinctions have been made, the doctrine of election, especially in the context of third-generation Puritanism, which Hawthorne so delicately evokes, is likely to mean the sin of presumption. Hawthorne seems to say it all in the first scene when he tells us that "Goodman Brown *felt himself justified*." To Cotton Mather, no doubt; to Edward Taylor; or to any other approved theorist of latter-day Puritan conversion psychology, Brown would be an example of the bold hypocrite, outrageously presuming on grace: no really converted person ever *would* behave in such a manner. We can view him that way if we choose. To Hawthorne himself, however, he is only the enduring natural man whose naturally self-regarding instincts have been treacherously reinforced by the psychological implications of doctrine.

Now all of this is merely the story's background, implied by the setting and compressed context, and helping us to place the sociologically and doctrinally precise point of Goodman Brown's departure. If the analysis seems somewhat technical, we may well recall that, as early as the sketch of "Dr. Bullivant," Hawthorne had been intensely interested in the mentality of declining Puritanism; and here he associates the experience of Goodman Brown not only with the context of the witchcraft (the most dramatic problem of Puritan third-generation declension) but also with the pervasive moral quality of that mentality. No one can read Hawthorne's known sources without sensing that with the death of the original saints, whose experience in England and in "coming out" to America made their stance of sainthood seem natural and believable, the problem of continuing an order of visible saints became disproportionate, even obsessive. The rest, perhaps, is Hawthorne's own speculation; but surely it is apt. No Arminian critic of Calvinism ever fails to warn that the doctrine of election protects the sovereignty of God only at the risk of human smugness, over-confidence, self-indulgence, antinomianism. The Calvinist doctrine of election looks very much like the traditional sin of presumption. And nowhere, Hawthorne cogently suggests, was the danger greater than in declining New England, in those exasperating days when the Puritan churches turned nearly all their attention to the continuance of churches constituted of God's visible saints. Obviously Goodman Brown's experience is not to be taken as a model of "Augustinian Piety." And even if his career does not represent any sort of statistical Puritan "average," he is a representative, latter-day Puritan nevertheless, following a highly probable moral logic. The general situation is indeed as Roy Harvey Pearce has suggested: "granting the Puritan faith . . . it is inevitable that Young Goodman Brown should have envisaged his loss of faith as he did and as a consequence have been destroyed as a person."[6]

Accordingly, his situation will not bear immediate psychoanalytic translation or complete reduction. *Of course* Goodman Brown will prove anxious about his relation to his father, and to "his father before him"; this is an inevitable fact of Puritan life in the 1670's, 80's, and 90's, where, as Perry Miller has remarked, the spokesmen for the failing Puritan Way "called for such a veneration of progenitors as is hardly to be matched outside China."[7] It is *their* reputed level of piety which has, we are asked to imagine, been repeatedly used to mark the level of Goodman Brown's own declension. In a very real sense it is into the community of *their* putative sanctity that he has so recently been admitted. The perception that the Puritan world "in declension" was bound to be fraught with oedipal anxiety belongs as obviously to the order of history as to the order of psychoanalysis. And the suspicion that in such a world a son, however naive, might be all too likely to make certain diabolical discoveries about his venerable progenitors belongs to the order of common sense. Together these insights add up to something like the figure of Young Goodman Brown, the moral adolescent who, after years of spiritual (as well as sexual) anxiety, has newly achieved what his ancestors defined as "Faith"; and who is now, from the absolutely

---

6. "Romance and the Study of History," in *Hawthorne Centenary Essays* (Columbus, Ohio, 1964), p. 233.
7. *The New England Mind: From Colony to Province* (Cambridge, Mass., 1953), p. 135.

"inamissable"[8] safety of that position, about to check out the reality of the dark world he has escaped.

The moral progress of Young Goodman Brown, from the presumption of his own salvation by Faith, together with a naive but thin confidence in the simple goodness of familiar saints; through a state of melodramatic despair; and on to the enduring suspicion that outside of his own will "there is no good on earth," represents a triumph of compression unequaled in Hawthorne's art. Robin Molineux's "evening of weariness and ambiguity" is, by comparison, tediously drawn out. Here things happen almost too fast, and only with a sense of the special Puritan character of Brown's beginning can we accurately trace his path.

Brown enters the forest convinced that he can always return to the Bosom of Faith; his nice pink-ribboned little wife and his familiar place in a stable and salutary community of saints will always be there. It may be that neither his marriage nor his conversion has, after three months proved quite so enduringly satisfactory or perpetually climactic as could be hoped; but both have provided him with the assurance needed by one who would press beyond the limits of socialized sex or religion. Recalling the typological significance of marital union in "The May-pole of Merry Mount," or of its absence in "The Man of Adamant," we can see the danger of Brown's presumptive confidence. But the full significance of his presumption lies in his feeling that he can now explore the dimension of diabolical evil with impunity. Having joined the ranks of the safe and socially sanctioned he can, he believes, have a little taste of witchcraft, which is simply, as Cotton Mather says, human depravity *par excellence*: without the grace of Faith, "we should every one of us be a *Dog* and a *Witch* too."[9] An intriguing proposition. Now that he is finally sure which side he is on, he can afford to see how the other moral half lives.

The most significant fact about Brown's naive acceptance of the appearance of sanctity in his fellow saints is the swiftness with which it disappears. Based on the normal, approved, social, presumably "real" manifestations of goodness, it is destroyed by extraordinary, private, "spectral" intimations of badness. His ancestors have been "a race of honest men"; Goody Cloyse "taught him his catechism in his youth"; the Minister and the Deacon are pillars of the religious community, sentries who stand guard at the "wall" which surrounds the "garden" of true grace, models of converted holiness

8. "Inamissable" faith cannot be lost by the believer because it comes from God [*Editors's note*].
9. *Memorable Providences, Relating to Witchcrafts and Possessions*, quoted from David Levin, ed., *What Happened in Salem?* (New York, 1960), p. 102. * * *

whose experiences are the standard by which those of new applicants for communion are judged. All this is evidentially certain: it is visible; it makes the Puritan world go round. But what if these same figures of sanctity are reported, or even "seen" to perform other actions? What if a grandfather is reputed to have had devilish motives in lashing a Quaker woman (half naked) through the streets? or the teacher of catechism is seen to conjure the Devil? or the sternly inhibiting elders are heard to smack their lips over a "goodly young woman" about to be taken into a quite different communion? Surely this contradiction of evidences will prove unsettling to a young man who has the habit of believing the moral world is adequately defined as the mirror-image opposition between the covenants and communions of God and Satan, and that these ultimate differences can be discovered with enough certainty to guarantee the organization of society. Only some very special, as yet undreamed species of faith could rescue him from such a contradiction of evidences.

Ultimately, of course, Goodman Brown passes through a phase of distraught, despairing confusion into a more or less settled state of faithless desolation. But more remarkable, almost, is the equanimity with which he at first accepts the Devil's "revelations." He jokes about the moral secrets of his saintly ancestors: funny he had never heard any such family secrets before; no, on second thought he guesses they *would* keep their forest activities a secret, since we Puritans are "a people of prayer and good works to boot, and abide no such wickedness." * * * He is * * * being rather too easily ironical about his worthy forebears. And if he is, in the next moment, truly amazed to hear the Devil claim such an impressively general acquaintance among the important personages of New England, still he responds less by doubting or discounting the Devil's claim to near-sovereignty than by writing it off as irrelevant to his own moral condition: "Howbeit, I have nothing to do with the council; they have their own ways, and are no rule for a simple husbandman like me." This social deference might be a species of humility; except that Goody Cloyse, with whom his moral connection *has* been direct and important, whose "rule" has been quite literally his own rule, can be dismissed just as easily: "What if a wretched old woman do choose to go to the devil when I thought she was going to heaven; is that any reason why I should quit my dear Faith and go after her?"

Now clearly all of Goodman Brown's responses are still too easy. Even before the Devil has introduced his most convincing, most visible evidence; even when it is all a matter of mere rumor, Goodman Brown has been quite willing to accept the Devil's "doubtful" informations at something like their face value; he believes their truth and merely denies their relevance. * * * Brown's habitual, doctrinally ingrained sense of the relative fewness of the visibly elect is growing more and more keen. Firmly possessed of the distinction between the inner circle of proven saints and all outer circles of the many "others," he seems willing to reduce the circumference of that inmost circle *almost* to its single-point limit. *I* and *my* Faith: it all comes down to that naive center. But since he has already deceived and abandoned his wife (and, in doing so, vitiated his faith through presumption), even this two-term protestation rings false. The Devil really has not very much difficulty with this Easy-Faith of a Young Goodman Brown. "With heaven above and Faith below, I will yet stand firm against the devil!", so our self-assured young man roundly declaims, after consigning the rest of his world to perdition. But a murmur of spectral voices and a flutter of spectral ribbons later and his "Faith is gone." It could hardly have turned out otherwise.

And yet the swiftness and seeming inevitability of Goodman Brown's reduction to despair depend for their believability on more than his naive and presumptuous understanding of faith as a sort of private haven. "Young Goodman Brown" is, no less than "Rappaccini's Daughter," a story about Faith and Evidence; and so there is also, just as crucially, the question of his evidences to be considered. Explicitly, of course, Hawthorne raises the question only at the very end of the story, and then in a completely non-technical way: "Had Young Goodman Brown fallen asleep in the forest and only dreamed a wild dream of a witch-meeting?" Was his evidence, therefore, only "subjective," a species of that diseased fantasy to which the nineteenth century universally ascribed the witchcraft "delusions"? As David Levin has amply and carefully shown, however, the evidence or "reality" question is built into the story everywhere in a very precise seventeenth-century way. Not only are we apprised from the outset that Goodman Brown is speaking to the Father of Lies, so that scandalous rumor and innuendo may be even *less* trustworthy than usual, even in a notoriously quarrelsome Puritan small town; but everywhere the persons seen by Brown are referred to as "shapes" or "figures" or "appearances." People appear and disappear in the most magical sorts of ways, and no one is substantial enough to cast a shadow. It is all, quite demonstrably, a technical case of specter evidence. And this is precisely why Hawthorne's seemingly casual answer to the dream-or-not question ("Be it so if you will") is neither a coy evasion nor a profound "ambiguity." It simply does not matter: obviously not in terms of practical consequences, since the psycho-moral response is certain and terrible, whatever the nature of the stimulus; and not in terms of epistemological assumptions either, since the choice lies (as Levin put it) "between a dream and a reality that is unquestionably spectral."

It is really distressing to see a critic claim that Levin has tried to make all the stories' challenging moral problems go away by blaming everything on "infernal powers"; and that, *really*, Goodman Brown's "visions' are the product of his suspicion and distrust, not the Devil's wiles." The point is surely that in Hawthorne's psychological schema Brown's suspicion and distrust and the Devil's wiles are not different.[1]

Hawthorne "believed in" the Devil even less than did Spenser, who had long before deliberately conflated Archimago's magic powers with the Red Cross Knight's suppressed desires; and as Hawthorne conned the lesson of Spenser's faith-protagonist, and then defined the problem in "Alice Doane's Appeal," specter evidence became *nothing but* the necessary historical "figure" for guilty, projective dreams or fantasies. "Literally," in the seventeenth century, Brown "sees specters" that *seem* to reveal the diabolical commitment of the persons to whom they belong; but this seeming is highly untrustworthy, and Brown's inferences are illegitimate. "Allegorically," as we interpret Brown's twilight or limit-experiences; as we try, with Hawthorne, to imagine what sort of reality might lie behind the widespread but ultimately superstitious belief that people have detachable specters which may or may not require a pact with the Devil to detach, we can only conclude that specter evidence is projective fantasy.[2]

Once again, as so often is the case in a Hawthorne "allegory," history itself provided the "figurative" term: specter evidence was simply there, a given; Hawthorne had merely to imagine what it really (psychologically and morally) meant. And if we really understand this perfectly historical but almost antiallegorical process, we can see how fundamentally wrongheaded is the assumption that Hawthorne merely "used history" as costume or as convenient setting for his timeless themes. Hawthorne's problem in "Young Goodman Brown" was not to find an appropriate historical delusion which might validly enfigure Man's persistent tendency to project his own moral uneasiness onto others; it was, rather, to discover the sorts of reality (some of them transient, some of them permanent) which made the belief in specter evidence possible at *any* point in human experience. As is the case with "The Gentle Boy," "Young Goodman Brown" is primarily a moment in which there is brought to bear on an actual, complex historical situation all the imaginative sympathy

1. See Levin, "Shadows," p. 352; and Hurley, "Brown's 'Heart of Darkness,'" p. 411.
2. For a suggestive account of how guilty projection might have worked in the actual, outward world of witch accusations in seventeenth-century New England, see John Demos, "Underlying Themes in the Witchcraft of Seventeenth-Century New England," *American Historical Review*, 75 (1970), 1311–1326.

and psychological acumen at the command of the artist. That, I think, we are constrained to call *history as history*. It is good history because the artist in question was one who constantly monitored his own, and speculated about all other mental life.

The doctrine of specters as a specific form of superstition is actually not very complicated, though the story is immeasurably enriched for the reader who is familiar with the witchcraft sources, and who can thus sense the full historic reality of Goodman Brown's problem as a classic case of seventeenth-century religious epistemology. Perhaps we need not linger over all the wonderful ramifications of the problem about whether God would or would not permit Satan to manipulate the spectral form of a person who had *not* entered the Devil's own covenant. * * * But if the ramifications are teasing, still the crux is simple. To imagine the epistemological heart of Goodman Brown's problem, Hawthorne probably needed no more than a single interrogative suggestion from Increase Mather's *Illustrious Providences*: "Suppose the devil saith, these people are witches, must the just, therefore, condemn them?"[3]

* * * It is hard to imagine a clearer posing of the question which faces Goodman Brown. Whether we are thinking of the Devil's verbal slanders, or the spectral sounds and sights of the forest, or those famous now-you-see-them, now-you-don't pink ribbons, the case is essentially the same. For granting that the Devil is, from time to time, permitted to impersonate saints without their consent; and granting that in these days of his last desperate assault against the purity of Faith in the New World he would do so if ever he could; then, "literally," there is no evidential difference between the Devil's general and urbane innuendoes about all the Great and Holy of New England and Goodman Brown's actually "seeing" Goody Cloyse, or Deacon Gookin, or his parents, or Faith, with or without her ribbons. Nasty small-town rumor, simplistic tricks of "materialization" such as even Pharaoh's Magi could perform, spectral simulation: in all these instances, Goodman Brown's vaunted "insights" into Mankind's Total and Unredeemed Depravity depend on a diabolical communication.

* * *

Probably, if we find such speculations interesting, the Devil is telling the truth when he implicates Brown's ancestors in persecution and sadistic cruelty: these are, after all, the sins of Hawthorne's own fathers, and of the fathers of many others among his historically naive generation; doubtless the Father of Lies is well practiced in the

---

3. *An Essay for the Recording of Illustrious Providence* (Boston, 1684), p. 200. * * *

meretricious rhetorical art of universalizing the Half Truth. Probably the Devil exaggerates when he claims that nearly all of the deacons, selectmen, and general court representatives in New England owe him their covenanted allegiance. (Hawthorne would have been, I imagine, less disturbed than some liberal modern historians to learn that, for all the historian can discover, there was indeed some real enough witchcraft at the bottom of the Salem hysteria; but his statistical reservations about the size of Satan's consciously enlisted army would have been as wary as his doctrinal reservations about the Totality of human depravity.) And presumably the Devil's use of the specific "specters" of Goody Cloyse, Deacon Gookin, and Faith is pure deceit: he conjures their shapes without their contractual permission in order to test (destroy, as it lamentably turns out) the naive and compromised faith of Goodman Brown. A cheap trick, perhaps, but not without a certain diabolical cleverness; and not, in this case, ineffective. Young Calvinist Brown may think that * * * the final perseverance of the Elect is certain and "indefectable." But Satan evidently knows better: even fully communing Saints can be had. Or, if the Calvinist Fathers of Dort[4] were correct, if the gracious gift of a true faith cannot indeed be lost, then at least there is the diabolical pleasure of hazing the "presumptive" saint whose faith only seemed true and whose salvation was all too easily assumed. In any case, the extreme result of this new communicant's presumptive bad faith is his willingness to accept spectral (whether diabolical or traumatic) intimations of evil as more authoritative than the ordinary social appearances of goodness.

Once we realize how fundamentally Goodman Brown's moral discoveries depend on the spirit (and the place) in which he asks his questions, we are inevitably led to wonder about the validity of the questions themselves. Clearly it is "impertinent" (in Levin's language) to ask whether the people represented to Brown in the forest are "really" evil: questions concerning the nature and extent of human depravity may not, in themselves, lie "beyond the limits of fiction"; but surely the true, ultimate condition of Goody Cloyse is a question whose answer lies beyond the proper limits of *this story*, which is "not about the evil of other people but about Brown's doubt, his discovery of the *possibility* of universal evil."[5] And there is reason to believe, further, that certain forms of the depravity-question are themselves illegitimate. Posed in certain terms, they may be the Devil's own questions.

---

4. At the Synod of Dort, in 1618–19, orthodox Dutch Calvinists reaffirmed their doctrines, including the doctrine that God's free grace, once given to his elect, could not be lost—- i.e., once a saint, always a saint [*Editor's note*].
5. Levin, "Shadows of Doubt," p. 351. * * *

From Hawthorne's frankly Arminian, though by no means Pela-
gian, point of view, Goodman Brown is habitually making simple
judgments about settled moral realities in a world where only the
most flickering sorts of appearances are available as evidence. And
he is asking about spiritual "essences" where probably only a process exists. In one very important sense the private evidence of the
forest is no more "spectral" than was all the previous communal
evidence in favor of the saintliness of the now-exposed hypocrites.
Hawthorne repeatedly joked about the separation between his own
real and spectral selves; and as the author of "The Christmas Banquet" he perfectly agreed with the Emersonian dictum that "souls
never touch." Further, he made it unmistakably clear in "Fancy's
Show Box" (which ought to be read as a gloss on "Young Goodman
Brown," revealing Hawthorne's *own* doctrine of depravity) that
stains upon the soul are simply not visible. Moral or spiritual status
is, accordingly, an invincibly interior and a radically *in*visible quality. Any outward representation of a person's absolutely private
moral intentionality, of his voluntary allegiance to God or Satan,
of his "state" with reference to the "grace" of "faith" (even if this
is not a process of constant, "ambivalent" fluctuation) is a mere
simulacrum—a specter. Giving the epistemology of Berkeley or Kant
a distinctive moral twist (which Jeremy Taylor could have appreciated better than Emerson), Hawthorne means to suggest that all
moral knowledge of others exists in us as phenomena, or idea, or
appearance merely; the moral essence, like the Lockean substance
or the Kantian *ding an sich*, remains an *ignotum x*. True, for certain fairly important social uses, we must assume that a person's
statements and bodily actions correspond to his own intention,
that he and not some devil is in control of his bodily form. But this
is only a working premise. It should not be taken as an accurate
rendition of Reality. * * *
  In a sense, therefore, any answer to questions concerning an individual's absolute moral condition will be in terms of spectral evidence. Probably the truth lies with the Arminians and Pragmatists
and Existentialists: man makes himself; he has a moral history but
no moral essence, not at birth and not by rebirth; his whole life is
a journey which may or may not lead to the goal, and a series of
choices in which any one choice may undo the moral import (though
not, of course, all the psychological results) of any other. The "sides"
in such a world would be impossible to define. But even if there were
sides, ineluctably defined by ineffable divine decree, who could ever
discover them? Accordingly, Goodman Brown's mental organization
(and, by implication, the Puritan ecclesiology) dissolves into moral
chaos because in every instance he must choose between the show
of social appearance and the specter of diabolical simulation and

suggestion. In every case evidence counters evidence, where, Hawthorne implies, only faith can be salutary.

* * *

Ultimately, evidence fails. Finally, in a way Goodman Brown had little expected and is totally unprepared to accept or even comprehend, everything does depend on Faith. The individual can judge his own moral case. Imperfectly, no doubt, but with some legitimacy; for besides the Searcher of Hearts only he has access to the evidence of his own intentions, which are (according to Jeremy Taylor) related to his words and actions as the soul to the body. In every other case, moral judgment is irreducibly a species of faith. Morally speaking, we can observe specters flirting with the Devil, but (even if such a thing is possible), we cannot observe a soul fix itself in an evil state.

That certain people in a Puritan world might *wish* so to fix themselves, we can easily imagine: the case recorded by Winthrop, of the woman who murdered her child so that she could now be "sure she would be damned," is full of terrible instruction; and doubtless there were many more unrecorded cases of persons for whom "a guilty identity was better than none."[6] Especially in the latter days of Puritanism, when so many people lived out whole lives of spiritual tension in a half-way status, the temptations must have been both strong and various: simply to get the whole business settled; or manfully to accept the highly probable import of one's unremitting sinfulness (and perhaps to enjoy some sense of true significance in this world); or even to join the Devil's party out of sheer rebellion against such singularly infelicitous figures of Covenant authority as Cotton Mather. Thus for every village hag who practiced some crude form of image magic or evil eye to frighten her neighbors into a frenzy of self-destruction, there must have been dozens of more robust souls who saw their appropriate moral hypothesis quite clearly: "If I am the devil's child, I will live then from the devil." But obviously such intentions are reversible: above all else the Puritans tried to obtain repentant confessions from accused witches, to bring them back from the Deviant to the Normative Covenant.[7] This might strain their predestinarian logic, but not perhaps unduly. One could be as wrong about one's reprobation as about one's election: in

6. The formula is one which Frederick Crews applies to Hawthorne himself, in his relation to his hated Puritan "fathers" (see Frederick C. Crews, *The Sins of the Fathers: Hawthorne's Psychological Themes* ([New York, 1966], p. 38); but it applies a little more appropriately to Puritan Witches than to our blue-eyed Nathaniel. For Winthrop's account of the child-murderer, see his *Journal* (1790: rpt. New York, 1908), 1. 230. ° ° °
7. The Puritan Covenant of Grace, in which a believing Christian surrenders himself or herself to God. The Deviant Covenant is the contract a rebel or a witch makes with the devil. [*Editor's note*].

either theological case, one "consented" but did not, himself, make the really efficacious choice; and in psychological practice, a wild, desperate, overly wilful embracing of unconditional and irrevocable reprobation is probably no easier to protect from doubt or change of mood than the astonished and relieved acceptance of one's election. Certainly Goodman Brown ultimately draws back—from one of the most blasphemous declarations of despair in all literature.

But this is getting slightly ahead of the immediate question, which concerns the relation of faith and evidence to the serious moral judgement of others. * * * In an ultimate sense, * * * it is true that Brown does not hold a fixed and final conviction that his wife is in league with the devil. But practically there is not much question. Hawthorne did not need the will-to-believe analysis of William James to tell him that theoretical doubts have a way of solving themselves in practice, in accordance with the individual's deepest suspicions: and at this level Brown's ideas are quite clear. He hears an "anthem of sin" when the congregation sings a holy psalm; he scowls while his family prays; he shrinks at midnight from the bosom of Faith; and he dies in an aura which even Puritans recognize as one of inordinate moral gloom.

To be sure, he does not die in precisely the same state of "despair" that sent him raging through the forest, challenging the Devil, burning to meet him on his own ground. At that moment his despair is universal: "there is no good on earth: and sin is but a name." At that moment it includes himself, indeed it applies to himself preeminently: "Come witch, come wizard, come Indian powwow, come devil himself, and here comes Goodman Brown. You may as well fear him as he fear you." At that moment only does the element of hesitancy * * * disappear from his mental state; and as it disappears Brown becomes guilty not only of some sort of cosmic blasphemy but also of that personal and technical sort of "despair" which, in its utter abandonment of the possibility of personal redemption, constitutes the second of traditional Christianity's two unpardonable sins—the other, its obverse, being the presumption with which Brown began. But as we have said, this lurid, melodramatic phase subsides: his call upon Faith to "resist" is, in part, his way of taking back his own overly wilful self-abandonment. And thus, as he was initially not entirely certain he wanted to sneak off into the forest at all, so he is finally not convinced that he himself is a lost soul. Nevertheless neither his crucial refusal of baptism nor his returning ambivalence can now save him from some sort of moral gloom for which there may be no neatly prepared theological name, but which the story exists to define. Indeed Goodman Brown's final (exorcised) state may be his worst of all.

Having begun by assuming that all visible sanctity was real sanctity, and by presuming his own final perseverance in faith; having next despaired of *all* goodness; he ends by doubting the existence of any ultimate goodness but his own. There is, it seems to me, no other way to account for the way Goodman Brown spends the rest of his life. Evidently he clings to the precious knowledge that he, at least, resisted the wicked one's final invitation to diabolical communion; accordingly, the lurid satisfactions of Satan's anti-Covenant are not available to him. But neither are the sweet delights of the Communion of Saints. He knows he resisted the "last, last crime" of witchcraft, but his deepest suspicion seems to be that Faith did not resist. Or if that seems too strong a formulation for sentimental readers, he cannot make his faith in Faith prevail. Without such a prevailing faith, he is left outside the bounds of all communion: his own unbartered soul is the only certain locus of goodness in a world otherwise altogether blasted.

* * *

For finally, once Goodman Brown's search for evidences has ended in nightmare, his enduring doubt and suspicion prove to be only an abiding "faith" in the probability of evil. Lacking conclusive evidence, he yet suspects—"believes," I think we may say—the worst of Faith. His doubt of goodness is equally a faith in evil. The Judgement of Charity (which the wariest of the Puritans always insisted was the proper rule in estimating the presence of grace and by which they almost undid their basic premises) might construe even Faith's actual presence in the forest in some lenient way; charity ought to be willing to believe that a wife would refuse a Devil at least as soon as a husband would. But bad faith precludes such charity. What determines Brown's practical disbelief in Faith and in all "other" goodness is the subconscious effort of his own dark (if ambivalent) reasons for being in the forest, reinforced no doubt by the violence of his blasphemous nihilism; the total personality, it turns out, is less supple and flexible than the "will." Brown's initial easy-faith in his own election, which makes everything else possible, is based on the evidence of his acceptance (finally!) into a community of professing, visible saints. His final gloomy-faith in the reprobation of the rest of his world is based on the suppression and outward projection of his own continuing fallenness. Goodman Brown believes the Devil's spectral evidence because ultimately it coincides with his own guilty projections; indeed the "levels" of the "allegory" collapse so perfectly that the spectral evidence produced by the Devil's most potent magic becomes indistinguishable from the bad dream of a man in bad faith. Goodman Brown's supposedly "inamissable" faith has, to paraphrase

Poe, indeed "flown away." And whether "In a vision, or in none, /Is it therefore the less gone?" The note of finalty seems cruel, but so, apparently, are the pitfalls of visible sanctity for a Young Calvinist Saint.

Hawthorne will return to the question of faith and evidence, most significantly in "Rappaccini's Daughter" at the climax of his second or "Old Manse" period. There the "vile empiric" will turn out to be not any scientific experimenter or positivist, but the Brown-like Giovanni Guasconti, who loses his Dantesque Beatrice for many of the same reasons Goodman Brown loses his Spenserian Faith. By then, Hawthorne's fictional arguments will have caught up with contemporaneous religious questions. * * * But in the early and middle 1830's, Hawthorne is not yet writing "The History of His Own Time." His outlook is still dominated, and his most serious concerns are still unified, by his wide and perceptive readings in seventeenth-century Puritanism; the subjects of his most penetrating analyses are still Puritans trapped by the moral definitions of their historical world. As with "The Gentle Boy," "Young Goodman Brown" unarguably demonstrates that (however we choose to define "history as history") Hawthorne's most powerful early stories grew directly out of an authentic and creative encounter with the Puritan mind.

* * *

"Young Goodman Brown" is * * * a dazzling achievement of the historical imagination, and its greatness cannot be accounted for without close and continuous reference to its insight into the psychology of religion in New England, especially in its most "troubled" period. From one point of view, "Young Goodman Brown" may well be "Freud Anticipated"; from another it unquestionably is "Spenser Applied." But it applies the Spenserian teaching to New England's problems of spectral evidence and visible sanctity as certainly and as precisely as "The Maypole of Merrymount" applies the Miltonic doctrines of mythic innocence and historic fall to the problem of America's imaginative (and political) state; or, later, as surely as "The Celestial Railroad" would apply Bunyan; or "Rappaccini's Daughter," Dante; or "Ethan Brand," Goethe, to problems which had a specific American context and quiddity. And if "Young Goodman Brown" is one of Hawthorne's more stunning anticipations of Freudian themes, it *discovers* these themes in the historical record, not only in the painfully obvious testimony of men who were lewdly tempted at night by the "specter" of the local prostitute, but also in that painfully distressing record of the moral identity crisis which two generations of Saints had inevitably if inadvertently prepared for a third. Granted the "enthusiastic" decision of the 1630's to depart from all previous Reformation practice and require virtual "proof" of sainthood for full membership in Congregations of Visible Saints; and granted the existence of scores of diaries and spiritual autobiographies from the first and second generations of New England saints, documents written "Of Providence, For Posterity," solemnly charging the son "to know and love the great and most high god . . . of his father"; granted these, the piteous and fearful experience of Puritanism's third generation was indeed inevitable.[8] And Hawthorne has enfigured it all, with classic economy and without misplaced romantic sympathy, in the tragic career of Young Goodman Brown.

* * * In this, though not in every instance, Hawthorne is a writer of *psycho-historical* fiction; as such, and with the full authority of Scott behind him, he has gone straight to the task of creating a doctrinally adequate and dramatically believable version of "how it might have felt" to live in the moral climate of Puritanism's most troubled years. The imaginative insight which lies behind "Young Goodman Brown" may stand as a significant part of Hawthorne's reasons for being so "fervently" glad to have been born beyond the temporal limits of the Puritan world. Hawthorne was, to be sure, far from unique in preferring the moral climate of the 1830's to that of the 1690's. * * * But no one else in Hawthorne's generation was able to dramatize with such compelling clarity, and with so firm a grasp of the psychological implications of doctrine, what the older system might have meant to a representative individual conscience.

*   *   *

JORGE LUIS BORGES

Nathaniel Hawthorne[†]

I shall begin the history of American literature with the history of a metaphor; or rather, with some examples of that metaphor. I don't know who invented it; perhaps it is a mistake to suppose that meta-

---

8. The solemn charge quoted is from Thomas Shepard to his son, on the first page of his *Autobiography*. That particular document may stand as typical of the way first-generation Puritans created spiritual trauma and oedipal strife for their descendants; see *Publications of the Colonial Society of Massachusetts*, 27 (1932), 357–392.

† From Jorge Luis Borges, *Other Inquisitions: 1937–1952*, trans. Ruth L. C. Simms (Austin: University of Texas Press, 1964), 47–65. Borges's piece on Hawthorne is the text of a lecture given at the Colegio Libre de Estudios Superiores in Buenos Aires in March 1949. © 1964, renewed 1993. Reprinted by permission of the University of Texas Press.

phors can be invented. The real ones, those that formulate intimate connections between one image and another, have always existed; those we can still invent are the false ones, which are not worth inventing. The metaphor I am speaking of is the one that compares dreams to a theatrical performance. * * * Luis de Góngora made it a part of the sonnet "Varia imaginación," where we read:

> A dream is a playwright
> Clothed in beautiful shadows
> In a theatre fashioned on the wind.

In the eighteenth century Addison will say it more precisely. When the soul dreams (he writes) it is the theatre, the actors, and the audience. Long before, the Persian Omar Khayyām had written that the history of the world is a play that God—the multiform God of the pantheists—contrives, enacts, and beholds to entertain his eternity; long afterward, Jung the Swiss in charming and doubtless accurate volumes compares literary inventions to oneiric inventions, literature to dreams.

If literature is a dream (a controlled and deliberate dream, but fundamentally a dream) then Góngora's verses would be an appropriate epigraph to this story about American literature, and a look at Hawthorne, the dreamer, would be a good beginning. There are other American writers before him—Fenimore Cooper, a sort of Eduardo Gutiérrez infinitely inferior to Eduardo Gutiérrez; Washington Irving, a contriver of pleasant Spanish fantasies—but we can skip over them without any consequence.

Hawthorne was born in 1804 in the port of Salem, which suffered, even then, from two traits that were anomalous in America: it was a very old, but poor, city; it was a city in decadence. Hawthorne lived in that old and decaying city with the honest biblical name until 1836; he loved it with the sad love inspired by persons who do not love us, or by failures, illness, and manias; essentially it is not untrue to say that he never left his birthplace. Fifty years later, in London or Rome, he continued to live in his Puritan town of Salem; for example, when he denounced sculptors (remember that this was in the nineteenth century) for making nude statues. * * *

* * *

Hawthorne was tall, handsome, lean, dark. He walked with the rocking gait of a seaman. At that time children's literature did not exist (fortunately for boys and girls!). Hawthorne had read *Pilgrim's Progress* at the age of six; the first book he bought with his own money was *The Faërie Queene*; two allegories. Also, * * * he read the Bible; perhaps the same Bible that the first Hawthorne, William Hathorne, brought from England with a sword in 1630. I have used the word "allegories"; the word is important, perhaps imprudent or indiscreet, to use when speaking of the work of Hawthorne. It is common knowledge that Edgar Allan Poe accused Hawthorne of allegorizing and that Poe deemed both the activity and the genre indefensible. * * *

The best refutation of allegories I know is Croce's; the best vindication, Chesterton's. Croce says that the allegory is a tiresome pleonasm, a collection of useless repetitions which shows us (for example) Dante led by Virgil and Beatrice and then explains to us, or gives us to understand, that Dante is the soul, Virgil is philosophy or reason or natural intelligence, and Beatrice is theology or grace. According to Croce's argument (the example is not his), Dante's first step was to think: "Reason and faith bring about the salvation of souls" or "Philosophy and theology lead us to heaven" and then, for *reason* or *philosophy* he substituted *Virgil* and for *faith* or *theology* he put *Beatrice*, all of which became a kind of masquerade. By that derogatory definition an allegory would be a puzzle, more extensive, boring, and unpleasant than other puzzles. It would be a barbaric or puerile genre, an aesthetic sport. Croce wrote that refutation in 1907; Chesterton had already refuted him in 1904 without Croce's knowing it. How vast and uncommunicative is the world of literature!

The page from Chesterton to which I refer is part of a monograph on the artist Watts, who was famous in England at the end of the nineteenth century and was accused, like Hawthorne, of allegorism. Chesterton admits that Watts has produced allegories, but he denies that the genre is censurable. He reasons that reality is interminably rich and that the language of men does not exhaust that vertiginous treasure. He writes:

> Man knows that there are in the soul tints more bewildering, more numberless, and more nameless than the colours of an autumn forest; . . . Yet he seriously believes that these things can every one of them, in all their tones and semi-tones, in all their blends and unions, be accurately represented by an arbitrary system of grunts and squeals. He believes that an ordinary civilized stockbroker can really produce out of his own inside noises which denote all the mysteries of memory and all the agonies of desire.

Later Chesterton infers that various languages can somehow correspond to the ungraspable reality, and among them are allegories and fables.

In other words, Beatrice is not an emblem of faith, a belabored and arbitrary synonym of the word *faith*. The truth is that something— a peculiar sentiment, an intimate process, a series of analogous states—exists in the world that can be indicated by two symbols:

one, quite insignificant, the sound of the word *faith*; the other, Beatrice, the glorious Beatrice who descended from Heaven and left her footprints in Hell to save Dante. I don't know whether Chesterton's thesis is valid; I do know that the less an allegory can be reduced to a plan, to a cold set of abstractions, the better it is. * * * When an abstract man, a reasoner, also wants to be imaginative, or to pass as such, then the allegory denounced by Croce occurs. * * * A famous example of that ailment is the case of José Ortega y Gasset, whose good thought is obstructed by difficult and adventitious metaphors; many times this is true of Hawthorne. Outside of that, the two writers are antagonistic. Ortega can reason, well or badly, but he cannot imagine; Hawthorne was a man of continual and curious imagination; but he was refractory, so to speak, to reason. I am not saying he was stupid; I say that he thought in images, in intuitions, as women usually think, not with a dialectical mechanism.

One aesthetic error debased him: the Puritan desire to make a fable out of each imagining induced him to add morals and sometimes to falsify and to deform them. The notebooks in which he jotted down ideas for plots have been preserved; in one of them, dated 1836, he wrote: "A snake taken into a man's stomach and nourished there from fifteen years to thirty-five, tormenting him most horribly." That is enough, but Hawthorne considers himself obliged to add: "A type of envy or some other evil passion." Another example, this time from 1838: "A series of strange, mysterious, dreadful events to occur, wholly destructive of a person's happiness. He to impute them to various persons and causes, but ultimately finds that he is himself the sole agent. Moral, that our welfare depends on ourselves." Another, from the same year: "A person, while awake and in the business of life, to think highly of another, and place perfect confidence in him, but to be troubled with dreams in which this seeming friend appears to act the part of a most deadly enemy. Finally it is discovered that the dream-character is the true one. The explanation would be—the soul's instinctive perception." Better are those pure fantasies that do not look for a justification or moral and that seem to have no other substance than an obscure terror. Again, from 1838: "The situation of a man in the midst of a crowd, yet as completely in the power of another, life and all, as if they two were in the deepest solitude." The following, which Hawthorne noted five years later, is a variation of the above: "Some man of powerful character to command a person, morally subjected to him, to perform some act. The commanding person to suddenly die; and, for all the rest of his life, the subjected one continues to perform that act." (I don't know how Hawthorne would have written that story. I don't know if he would have decided that the act performed should be trivial or slightly horrible or fantastic or perhaps humiliating.) This one also has slavery—subjection to another—as its theme: "A rich man left by will his mansion and estate to a poor couple. They remove into it, and find there a darksome servant, whom they are forbidden by will to turn away. He becomes a torment to them; and, in the finale, he turns out to be the former master of the estate." I shall mention two more sketches, rather curious ones; their theme, not unknown to Pirandello or André Gide, is the coincidence or the confusion of the aesthetic plane and the common plane, of art and reality. The first one: "Two persons to be expecting some occurrence, and watching for the two principal actors in it, and to find that the occurrence is even then passing, and that they themselves are the two actors." The other is more complex: "A person to be writing a tale, and to find that it shapes itself against his intentions; that the characters act otherwise than he thought; that unforeseen events occur; and a catastrophe comes which he strives in vain to avert. It might shadow forth his own fate—he having made himself one of the personages." These games, these momentary confluences of the imaginative world and the real world—the world we pretend is real when we read—are; or seem to us, modern. * * * Hawthorne liked those contacts of the imaginary and the real, those reflections and duplications of art; and in the sketches I have mentioned we observe that he leaned toward the pantheistic notion that one man is the others, that one man is all men.

Something more serious than duplications and pantheism is seen in the sketches, something more serious for a man who aspires to be a novelist, I mean. It is that, in general, situations were Hawthorne's stimulus, Hawthorne's point of departure—situations, not characters. Hawthorne first imagined, perhaps unwittingly, a situation and then sought the characters to embody it. I am not a novelist, but I suspect that few novelists have proceeded in that fashion. * * * That method can produce, or tolerate, admirable stories because their brevity makes the plot more visible than the actors, but not admirable novels, where the general form (if there is one) is visible only at the end and a single badly invented character can contaminate the others with unreality. From the foregoing statement it will be inferred that Hawthorne's stories are better than Hawthorne's novels. I believe that is true. The twenty-four chapters of *The Scarlet Letter* abound in memorable passages, written in good and sensitive prose, but none of them has moved me like the singular story of "Wakefield" in the *Twice-Told Tales*.

Hawthorne had read in a newspaper, or pretended for literary reasons that he had read in a newspaper, the case of an Englishman who left his wife without cause, took lodgings in the next street and there, without anyone's suspecting it, remained hidden for twenty years. During that long period he spent all his days across from his house or watched it from the corner, and many times he caught a glimpse of his wife. When they had given him up for dead, when his wife had been resigned to widowhood for a long time, the man opened the door of his house one day and walked in—simply, as if he had been away only a few hours. (To the day of his death he was an exemplary husband.) Hawthorne read about the curious case uneasily and tried to understand it, to imagine it. He pondered on the subject; "Wakefield" is the conjectural story of that exile. The interpretations of the riddle can be infinite; let us look at Hawthorne's.

He imagines Wakefield to be a calm man, timidly vain, selfish, given to childish mysteries and the keeping of insignificant secrets; a dispassionate man of great imaginative and mental poverty, but capable of long, leisurely, inconclusive, and vague meditations; a constant husband, by virtue of his laziness. One October evening Wakefield bids farewell to his wife, He tells her—we must not forget we are at the beginning of the nineteenth century—that he is going to take the stagecoach and will return, at the latest, within a few days. His wife, who knows he is addicted to inoffensive mysteries, does not ask the reason for the trip. Wakefield is wearing boots, a rain hat, and an overcoat; he carries an umbrella and a valise. Wakefield—and this surprises me—does not yet know what will happen. He goes out, more or less firm in his decision to disturb or to surprise his wife by being away from home for a whole week. He goes out, closes the front door, then half opens it, and, for a moment, smiles. Years later his wife will remember that last smile. She will imagine him in a coffin with the smile frozen on his face, or in paradise, in glory, smiling with cunning and tranquility. Everyone will believe he has died but she will remember that smile and think that perhaps she is not a widow.

Going by a roundabout way, Wakefield reaches the lodging place where he has made arrangements to stay. He makes himself comfortable by the fireplace and smiles; he is one street away from his house and has arrived at the end of his journey. He doubts; he congratulates himself; he finds it incredible to be there already; he fears that he may have been observed and that someone may inform on him. Almost repentant, he goes to bed, stretches out his arms in the vast emptiness and says aloud: "I will not sleep alone another night." The next morning he awakens earlier than usual and asks himself, in amazement, what he is going to do. He knows that he has some purpose, but he has difficulty defining it. Finally he realizes that his purpose is to discover the effect that one week of widowhood will have on the virtuous Mrs. Wakefield. * * * Obsessed, he lets time pass; before he had thought, "I shall return in a few days," but now he thinks, "in a few weeks." And so ten years pass. For a long time he has not known that his conduct is strange. With all the lukewarm affection of which his heart is capable. Wakefield continues to love his wife, while she is forgetting him. One Sunday morning the two meet in the street amid the crowds of London. * * * Face to face, the two look into each other's eyes. The crowd separates them, and soon they are lost within it. Wakefield hurries to his lodgings, bolts the door, and throws himself on the bed where he is seized by a fit of sobbing. For an instant he sees the miserable oddity of his life. "Wakefield, Wakefield! You are mad!" he says to himself.

Perhaps he is. In the center of London he has severed his ties with the world. Without having died, he has renounced his place and his privileges among living men. Mentally he continues to live with his wife in his home. He does not know, or almost never knows, that he is a different person. He keeps saying, "I shall soon go back," and he does not realize that he has been repeating these words for twenty years. In his memory the twenty years of solitude seem to be an interlude, a mere parenthesis. One afternoon, an afternoon like other afternoons, like the thousands of previous afternoons, Wakefield looks at his house. He sees that they have lighted the fire in the second-floor bedroom; grotesquely, the flames project Mrs. Wakefield's shadow on the ceiling. Rain begins to fall, and Wakefield feels a gust of cold air. Why should he get wet when his house, his home, is there. He walks heavily up the steps and opens the door. The crafty smile we already know is hovering, ghostlike, on his face. At last Wakefield has returned. Hawthorne does not tell us of his subsequent fate, but lets us guess that he was already dead, in a sense. I quote the final words: "Amid the seeming confusion of our mysterious world, individuals are so nicely adjusted to a system, and systems to one another, and to a whole, that by stepping aside for a moment a man exposes himself to a fearful risk of losing his place for ever. Like Wakefield, he may become, as it were, the Outcast of the Universe."

In that brief and ominous parable, which dates from 1835, we have already entered the world of Herman Melville, of Kafka—a world of enigmatic punishments and indecipherable sins. You may say that there is nothing strange about that, since Kafka's world is Judaism, and Hawthorne's, the wrath and punishments of the Old Testament. That is a just observation, but it applies only to ethics, and the horrible story of Wakefield and many stories by Kafka are united not only by a common ethic but also by a common rhetoric. For example, the protagonist's profound *triviality*, which contrasts with the magnitude of his perdition and delivers him, even more helpless, to the Furies. There is the murky background against which the nightmare is etched. Hawthorne invokes a romantic past in other stories, but the scene of this tale is middle-class London, whose crowds serve, moreover, to conceal the hero.

Here, without any discredit to Hawthorne, I should like to insert an observation. The circumstance, the strange circumstance, of perceiving in a story written by Hawthorne at the beginning of the nineteenth century the same quality that distinguishes the stories Kafka wrote at the beginning of the twentieth must not cause us to forget that Hawthorne's particular quality has been created, or determined, by Kafka. "Wakefield" prefigures Franz Kafka, but Kafka modifies and refines the reading of "Wakefield." The debt is mutual; a great writer creates his precursors. He creates and somehow justifies them. What, for example, would Marlowe be without Shakespeare?

The translator and critic Malcolm Cowley sees in "Wakefield" an allegory of Nathaniel Hawthorne's curious life of reclusion. Schopenhauer has written the famous words to the effect that no act, no thought, no illness is involuntary; if there is any truth in that opinion, it would be valid to conjecture that Nathaniel Hawthorne left the society of other human beings for many years so that the singular story of Wakefield would exist in the universe, whose purpose may be variety. If Kafka had written that story, Wakefield would never have returned to his home; Hawthorne lets him return, but his return is no less lamentable or less atrocious than is his long absence.

*   *   *

Like Stevenson, also the son of Puritans, Hawthorne never ceased to feel that the task of the writer was frivolous or, what is worse, even sinful. In the preface to *The Scarlet Letter* he imagines that the shadows of his forefathers are watching him write his novel. It is a curious passage. "What is he?" says one ancient shadow to the other. "A writer of storybooks! What kind of a business in life—what mode of glorifying God, or being serviceable to mankind in his day and generation—may that be? Why, the degenerate fellow might as well have been a fiddler!" The passage is curious, because it is in the nature of a confidence and reveals intimate scruples. It harks back to the ancient dispute between ethics and aesthetics or, if you prefer, theology and aesthetics. One early example of this dispute was in the Holy Scriptures and forbade men to adore idols. Another example, by Plato, was in the *Republic*, Book X; "God creates the Archetype (the original idea) of the table; the carpenter makes an imitation of the Archetype; the painter, an imitation of the imitation." Another is by Mohammed, who declared that every representation of a living thing will appear before the Lord on the day of the Last Judgment. The angels will order the artisan to animate what he has made; he will fail to do so and they will cast him into Hell for a certain length of time. * * *

Nathaniel Hawthorne solved that difficulty (which is not a mere illusion). His solution was to compose moralities and fables; he made or tried to make art a function of the conscience. * * * The fact that Hawthorne pursued, or tolerated, a moral purpose does not invalidate, cannot invalidate his work. In the course of a lifetime dedicated less to living than to reading, I have been able to verify repeatedly that aims and literary theories are nothing but stimuli; the finished work frequently ignores and even contradicts them. If the writer has something of value within him, no aim, however trite or erroneous it may be, will succeed in affecting his work irreparably. An author may suffer from absurd prejudices, but it will be impossible for his work to be absurd if it is genuine, if it responds to a genuine vision. Around 1916 the novelists of England and France believed (or thought they believed) that all Germans were devils; but they presented them as human beings in their novels. In Hawthorne the germinal vision was always true; what is false, what is ultimately false, are the moralities he added in the last paragraph or the characters he conceived, or assembled, in order to represent that vision. The characters in *The Scarlet Letter*—especially Hester Prynne, the heroine—are more independent, more autonomous, than those in his other stories; they are more like the inhabitants of most novels and not mere projections of Hawthorne, thinly disguised. This objectivity, this relative and partial objectivity, is perhaps the reason why two such acute (and dissimilar) writers as Henry James and Ludwig Lewisohn called *The Scarlet Letter* Hawthorne's masterpiece, his definitive testimony. But I would venture to differ with those two authorities. If a person longs for objectivity, if he hungers and thirsts for objectivity, let him look for it in Joseph Conrad or Tolstoi; if a person looks for the peculiar flavor of Nathaniel Hawthorne, he will be less apt to find it in the laborious novels than on some random page or in the trifling and pathetic stories. I don't know exactly how to justify my difference of opinion; in the three American novels and *The Marble Faun* I see only a series of situations, planned with professional skill to affect the reader, not a spontaneous and lively activity of the imagination. The imagination (I repeat) has planned the general plot and the digressions, not the weaving together of the episodes and the psychology—we have to call it by some name—of the actors.

* * *

I have quoted several fragments from the journal Hawthorne kept to entertain his long hours of solitude; I have given brief résumés of two stories; now I shall quote a page from *The Marble Faun* so that you may read Hawthorne's own words. The subject is that abyss or well that opened up, according to Latin historians, in the center of the Forum; a Roman, armed and on horseback, threw himself into its blind depths to propitiate the gods. Hawthorne's text reads as follows:

> "Let us settle it," said Kenyon, "that this is precisely the spot where the chasm opened, into which Curtius precipitated his good steed and himself. Imagine the great, dusky gap, impenetrably deep, and with half-shaped monsters and hideous faces looming upward out of it, to the vast affright of the good citizens who peeped over the brim! Within it, beyond a question, there were prophetic visions,—intimations of all the future calamities of Rome,—shades of Goths, and Gauls, and even of the French soldiers of today. It was a pity to close it up so soon! I would give much for a peep into such a chasm."
>
> "I fancy," remarked Miriam, "that every person takes a peep into it in moments of gloom and despondency; that is to say, in his moments of deepest insight.
>
> "The chasm was merely one of the orifices of that pit of blackness that lies beneath us, everywhere. The firmest substance of human happiness is but a thin crust spread over it, with just reality enough to bear up the illusive stage-scenery amid which we tread. It needs no earthquake to open the chasm. A footstep, a little heavier than ordinary, will serve; and we must step very daintily, not to break through the crust at any moment. By and by, we inevitably sink! It was a foolish piece of heroism in Curtius to precipitate himself there, in advance; for all Rome, you see, has been swallowed up in that gulf, in spite of him. The Palace of the Caesars has gone down thither, with a hollow, rumbling sound of its fragments! All the temples have tumbled into it; and thousands of statues have been thrown after! All the armies and the triumphs have marched into the great chasm, with their martial music playing, as they stepped over the brink . . ."

From the standpoint of reason, of mere reason—which should not interfere with art—the fervent passage I have quoted is indefensible. The fissure that opened in the middle of the Forum is too many things. In the course of a single paragraph it is the crevice mentioned by Latin historians and it is also the mouth of Hell "with half-shaped monsters and hideous faces"; it is the essential horror of human life; it is Time, which devours statues and armies, and Eternity, which embraces all time. It is a multiple symbol, a symbol that is capable of many, perhaps incompatible, values. Such values can be offensive to reason, to logical understanding, but not to dreams, which have their singular and secret algebra, and in whose ambiguous realm one thing may be many. Hawthorne's world is the world of dreams. Once he planned to write a dream, "which shall resemble the real course of a dream, with all its inconsistency, its eccentricities and aimlessness," and he was amazed that no one had ever done such a thing before. The same journal in which he wrote about that strange plan—which our "modern" literature tries vainly to achieve and which, perhaps, has only been achieved by Lewis Carroll—contains his notes on thousands of trivial impressions, small concrete details (the movement of a hen, the shadow of a branch on the wall); they fill six volumes and their inexplicable abundance is the consternation of all his biographers. "They read like a series of very pleasant, though rather dullish and decidedly formal, letters, addressed to himself by a man who, having suspicions that they might be opened in the post, should have determined to insert nothing compromising." Henry James wrote that, with obvious perplexity. I believe that Nathaniel Hawthorne recorded those trivialities over the years to show himself that he was real, to free himself, somehow, from the impression of unreality, of ghostliness, that usually visited him.

One day in 1840 he wrote:

> Here I sit in my old accustomed chamber, where I used to sit in days gone by . . . Here I have written many tales—many that have been burned to ashes, many that have doubtless deserved the same fate. This claims to be called a haunted chamber, for thousands upon thousands of visions have appeared to me in it; and some few of them have become visible to the world . . . And sometimes it seemed to me as if I were already in the grave, with only life enough to be chilled and benumbed. But oftener I was happy . . . And now I begin to understand why I was imprisoned so many years in this lonely chamber, and why I could never break through the viewless bolts and bars; for if I had sooner made my escape into the world, I should have grown hard and rough, and been covered with earthly dust, and my heart might/ have become callous . . . Indeed, we are but shadows . . ."[1]

In the lines I have just quoted, Hawthorne mentions "thousands upon thousands of visions." Perhaps this is not an exaggeration; the twelve volumes of Hawthorne's complete works include more than

---

1. Actually a revised version of part of a letter Hawthorne wrote to his betrothed, Sophia Peabody. Sophia rewrote the letter after Hawthorne's death for inclusion in *Passages from the American Notebooks* (1868–69), the text Borges follows. The text of the original letter is reprinted on p. 330 in this volume [*Editor's note*].

a hundred stories, and those are only a few of the very many he out-lined in his journal. * * * Miss Margaret Fuller, who knew him in the Utopian community of Brook Farm, wrote later, "Of that ocean we have had only a few drops," and Emerson, who was also a friend of his, thought Hawthorne had never given his full measure. Haw-thorne married in 1842, when he was thirty-eight; until that time his life had been almost purely imaginative, mental. He worked in the Boston customhouse; he served as United States consul at Liverpool; he lived in Florence, Rome, and London. But his reality was always the filmy twilight, or lunar world, of the fantastic imagination.

At the beginning of this essay I mentioned the doctrine of the psychologist Jung, who compared literary inventions to oneiric inventions, or literature to dreams. That doctrine does not seem to be applicable to the literatures written in the Spanish language, which deal in dictionaries and rhetoric, not fantasy. On the other hand, it does pertain to the literature of North America, which (like the literatures of England or Germany) tends more toward inven-tion than transcription, more toward creation than observation. Perhaps that is the reason for the curious veneration North Ameri-cans render to realistic works, which induces them to postulate, for example, that Maupassant is more important than Hugo. It is within the power of a North American writer to be Hugo, but not, without violence, Maupassant. In comparison with the literature of the United States, which has produced several men of genius and has had its influence felt in England and France, our Argentine litera-ture may possibly seem somewhat provincial. Nevertheless, in the nineteenth century we produced some admirable works of realism—by Echeverría, Ascasubi, Hernandez, and the forgotten Eduardo Gutiérrez—the North Americans have not surpassed (perhaps have not equaled) them to this day. Someone will object that Faulkner is no less brutal than our Gaucho writers. True, but his brutality is of the hallucinatory sort—the infernal, not the terrestrial sort of bru-tality. It is the kind that issues from dreams, the kind inaugurated by Hawthorne.

Hawthorne died on May 18, 1864, in the mountains of New Hampshire. His death was tranquil and it was mysterious, because it occurred in his sleep. Nothing keeps us from imagining that he died while dreaming and we can even invent the story that he dreamed—the last of an infinite series—and the manner in which death completed or erased it. Perhaps I shall write it some day; I shall try to redeem this deficient and too digressive essay with an acceptable story.

* * *

458

SHARON CAMERON

The Self Outside Itself:
"Wakefield" and "The Ambitious Guest"†

Allegory, as we generally understand it, implies a split or separation, whether this be between an icon and what it represents, or between the particular aspect of a tale and some other level of significance recoverable in a detached sphere. One crucial difference between all non-literal language and Hawthorne's allegory in particular is that the latter not only renders the object in question nonbodily—as, for example, metaphor would—it also partializes that object. In addition, at least for the Hawthorne of the tales, the "object" in question is often a human self. Allegory in the tales partializes the self for the explicit purpose of making divisions visible that would otherwise be experienced as internal, with the effect that discrepancy is displaced from within the self to an exterior realm. This is the case in "Young Goodman Brown," a tale of a man in search of an "outside" that will give form to what he fears so that, rooting guilt from his heart, he can *see* evil rather then feel it. It is the case in "The Birth-mark" where a man, to exorcise mortality, to extract its manifestation from the skin of a beautiful woman, simultaneously kills her. It is the case in "The Minister's Black Veil," which takes the split between the body and the soul (between what is corporeal and what is not) and makes the split material. It is the case in "The Prophetic Pictures," in which a man and woman are painted only to come to look progressively like the artist's renditions of them. In each of these tales, a self apparently imagines that could it find something inhuman and exterior to it that would represent it as an essence, this object would eliminate the schisms that would otherwise be internal.

It is toward the replication of life—life divorced from bodily person and even from representative corporeal essence—after which the artist of the beautiful and Drowne with his wooden image so arduously strain. So in the latter tale, we are told of the newly-created figure who walks the sea-coast town:

> On the whole, there was something so airy and yet so real in the figure, and withal so perfectly did it represent Drowne's image, that people knew not whether to suppose the magic wood ethe-

---

† From Sharon Cameron, *The Corporeal Self: Allegories of the Body in Melville and Hawthorne* (Baltimore: Johns Hopkins University Press, 1981), 111–14, 128–31. © 1981 The Johns Hopkins University Press. Reprinted by permission of The Johns Hopkins University Press. The excerpt has been slightly revised for this edition. An underlying assumption of Cameron's work is that the concept of bodily or corporeal identity lies at the heart of the two authors she considers and of the American literary tradition in general.

realized into a spirit, or warmed and softened into an actual woman.

For a moment the wood is the woman, or the other way around. But "'is it alive?'" Annie, in "The Artist of the Beautiful," asks of the butterfly Owen Warland has made. And Robert Danforth, the ultimate man of sense, pays the image the ultimate compliment and criticism solidified into a single statement: "'Well, that does beat all nature!'" he marvels, mesmerized by the creation. The theme of noncorporeal form imbued with life wholly self-sufficient will never again be as delicately rendered as it is in "The Artist of the Beautiful" and in "Drowne's Wooden Image." Behind the tales of bodily projection or aesthetic recreation are other tales which directly address the question of why man would want life in his image—in his image rather than in himself.

The substitution of image for self is made explicitly in "The Ambitious Guest!" In this tale a young man travelling through the Notch of the White Hills on his way to Vermont stops to rest for a night in a cottage located at the slope of a mountain so steep that "the stones would often rumble down its sides, and startle [the inhabitants] at midnight." The secret of the young man's life, as he reveals it to the family that houses him for the night, is his yearning not to be forgotten. For while he tells us that he could bear to live an unacknowledged life, he could not bear the thought of dying without commemoration. The problem with this ambition, and in fact its very essence, is that it has yet to find an object. "'Were I to vanish from the earth to-morrow,'" he confesses, "'none would know so much of me as you. . . . But, I cannot die until I have achieved my destiny. Then, let Death come! I shall have built my monument!'" Monuments thus conceived are to memorialize the self—by what means is immaterial—and in fact it is no accident that the young man focuses on the certainty of the monument rather than on what it is to represent or on how it is to be achieved. In this respect, without an object, the monument has a status comparable to that of the Idea in "The Hall of Fantasy" which, unfleshed out, will nonetheless prefigure all. A monument is displaced from life. It is not made of life's accomplishments but rather stands outside of them, freezing them to static form. The young man himself acknowledges the discrepancy between desire for such a monument as it materializes in his mind and the way in which this desire parodies, by rendering contentless as well as frozen, the life it is memorializing:

> "You think my ambition as nonsensical as if I were to freeze myself to death on the top of Mount Washington, only that people might spy at me from the country round-about. And truly, that would be a noble pedestal for a man's statue!"

As the young man talks, others confess to comparable dreams. The father imagines owning a house at the bottom of the mountain, imagines how his tombstone would be situated in the open for all to pass and see. The children wish to take a drink from "the basin of the Flume"—near impossible since it tumbles over a precipice deep inside the mountains. The grandmother wishes that when she dies a mirror could be held to her face, for she explains that there is an old legend·insisting that the dead will never rest in peace "'if anything were amiss with a corpse, if only the ruff were not smooth, or the cap did not sit right.'" The daughter entertains wishes that issue from "lonesomeness," whose remedy, though unspecified, would probably have as its object this, or some similar, young man. But when he tries to prod her to speak ("'Shall I put these feelings into words?'" he provocatively asks) she rebukes him thus: "'They would not be a girl's feelings any longer, if they could be put into words.'"

The idea of putting feelings into words, of moving the cottage to a visible place, of arriving at a mountain stream rumored to be inaccessible, of imagining that death itself will immobilize the body while leaving the corpse's eyes open, and still able to ascertain the bodily world, are hopes which however different harp on the same theme. In each case they translate life into material, that is, into visible form. Thus in the minds of others, as in the mind of the ambitious guest, the desire for being is replaced by the desire for its palpability—for existence outside the body, yet (much as the grandmother depicts it) accessible to its scrutiny. Life from within its vital boundaries is not so much paltry—something wanting in achievement—as it is excruciatingly unclear, that which is felt rather than seen, intuited but lacking the coherent shape a monument would bequeath to it. Although the young man claims that he does not mind whether he is known in his lifetime so long as a monument stands for him after his death, the unspoken part of the wish is that he cannot be known in life, since life, by definition, does not clarify itself accordingly. In this connection, the young girl's refusal to allow the guest to articulate her dreams ("'They would not be a girl's feelings any longer, if they could be put into words'") lies at the heart of the tale. Translate feeling into form (whether of words or of monuments) and you replace by externalizing it. The tale focuses on the desire for such externalization, and plays upon the knowledge the reader has from the beginning[1] that in death the body is destroyed

---

1. Neal Frank Doubleday (*Hawthorne's Early Tales: A Critical Study* [Durham. North Carolina: Duke University Press, 1972], pp. 141–5) points out that Hawthorne was working with a plot—the death of a particular family in a mountain slide—which his audience would have known. Hence the outcome of the wish and its attendant irony is implicit from the tale's beginning. But it is implicit before the end in the tale's *internal* evidence, too. Thus when the young man tells the family he would like to be frozen to a statue on

rather than made either visible or complete. As the young man muses on the fact that "Old and young, we dream of graves and monuments," his dream—their communal dream—instantly comes true. The tale's focus, however, is not on the irony implicit in the instant gratification of the wish, nor on the fact that the guest who most passionately desires the monument not only fails to receive it but has his very existence called into question ("Others denied that there were sufficient grounds . . . to suppose that a stranger had been received into the cottage [that] night"). The tale's emphasis is rather on the human desire to exchange life itself for an embodied meaning, on what prompts the desire for such an exchange when it is not simply construed as "vanity" or ordinary ambition.

The feared mountain slide rumbles above their heads and begins its descent toward the cottage. As the initial instinct of each was to convert life to commemorative emblem so the communal instinct now is to run outside the cottage and to seek safety in "a sort of barrier [that has] been reared" without. "Alas!" we are told by the narrator, "they had quitted their security, and fled right into the pathway of destruction." The house remains intact. Had they stayed inside, they would have been preserved. For to be, by definition, is to reside within, to feel rather than see the forms our lives have taken. "'As yet, I have done nothing,'" the youth initially claimed, unabashed by the discrepancy between the monument and the undone, as well as unspecified thing for which it will some day stand. As I suggested earlier, however, this discrepancy is not accidental. It rather defines the difference between a monument and a life. If we dream of graves and monuments, of images of ourselves hewn in marble or other stone, this is not so much a consequence of vanity as it is of despair that we cannot see our lives, will not know them from without, as for example the grandmother wishes to do— wishes to have the mirror held to her dead face to ascertain that all is in order, that all *has* an order she could in life, at best, plan. "'I want one of you,'" she says to her children, "'—when your mother is drest, and in the coffin—to hold a looking-glass over my face. Who knows but I may take a glimpse at myself, and see whether all's right?'" If the monument could *be* the body (the idea of the statue frozen on Mount Washington), or if the monument could be *in* the bodily apparel (as the grandmother hopes the death garments will clothe the body-monument inside of them), we might embody, as well as dream, the palpable shape for which the idea of a monument stands. "Their bodies were never found," Hawthorne tells us of the

---

the summit of Mt. Washington, the young girl chides him: "'It is better to sit here, by this fire . . . though nobody thinks about us.'" Better to be alive in our bodies than dead out of them.

whole crew. What does survive is the house—a vacated body of sorts—the life from which they fled. They could have survived in their bodies, but that survival would have been cluttered by what Hawthorne calls "tokens," those things in fact left "by which those, who had known the family, were made to shed a tear for each." Even in death what represents the self are things fragmented from life, made in its piecemeal image.

*　*　*

In "Wakefield" a man, for apparently no reason, vacates his life to look at it. This tale epitomizes the self-abandonment about which I have been speaking: for in the process of looking at his life, Wakefield loses it. Unlike the characters in "The Ambitious Guest," however, Wakefield remains alive. We are told he is one of the living dead. In this tale Hawthorne is showing us what happens when characters receive the absention from their lives they think they have wanted and simultaneously remain alive to appreciate the consequence. We are told: "The man, under pretence of going a journey, took lodgings in the next street to his own house . . . and without the shadow of a reason for such self-banishment, dwelt upwards for twenty years." His house, his life, his wife are attachments to his being which he delusively thinks he can regard from the outside while he still retains possession of them. Wakefield, curiously, has no motivation, "no suspicion of what is before him." In "the self-banished Wakefield," the man banished from himself and banished by himself, the split within the man generates the secondary split between the man and his life. If in "The Ambitious Guest" we saw life imagined outside the body, so in "Wakefield" we see the body imagined outside the life. Yet Wakefield's action is not aberrant. The narrator tells us: "We know, each for himself, that none of us would perpetrate such a folly, yet feel as if some other might." If this is a tale which dramatizes the imp of the perverse, then, it does so by suggesting that perversity is imbued in human nature itself. It is something done by another or which we attribute to an other, because it comes so naturally to our own minds that it does not seem improbable. In thought if not in deed—that other is ourselves. And this is exactly what Wakefield attempts to make of his own life—an other which is yet himself. Wakefield's action cannot be explained in terms of character—since except for "a peculiar sort of vanity" and "a little strangeness" (epithets amorphous enough to define us all), Wakefield has no character. He is a man almost deprived of a life before he determines to further dispense with it. In fact the tale transforms its focus from the question Wakefield would ask—can one watch one's life from outside of it?—to the question Hawthorne would make him ask—if one *is* outside one's life is there anything left to watch?

After the first night away, when Wakefield has executed his plan, has not returned home, we are told "It is accomplished. Wakefield is another man." And as he ruminates on Mrs. Wakefield, who, as much as himself, is the object of the capricious experiment, he determines, "He will not go back until she be frightened half to death." Will not go back until her existence records the estrangement of his. For what excites Wakefield from his customary torpor is feeling (whether of grief or anguish) felt on his account. He wants feeling to be outside of him, to be felt *for* rather than by him. And such an insistent wish to be "another man," to "step aside for a moment" (when that expression refers to one's life), and so to expose oneself "to a fearful risk of losing [one's] place forever," to vanish, to "give up one's place . . . without being admitted to the dead," is the predicament of the man who would exchange life for memorialization. Thus as Wakefield leaves, he smiles at his wife—an expression incidental and momentary.

> But, long afterwards, when she has been more years a widow than a wife, that smile recurs, and flickers across all her reminiscences of Wakefield's visage. In her many musings, she surrounds the original smile with a multitude of fantasies, which make it strange and awful; as, for instance, if she imagines him in a coffin, that parting look is frozen on his pale features; or, if she dreams of him in Heaven, still his blessed spirit wears a quiet and crafty smile. Yet, for its sake, when all others have given him up for dead, she sometimes doubts whether she is a widow.

Thus images taken from life but frozen into the mind's interpretation of them replace life itself. The smile replaces the man, as the man has replaced himself. Or rather the displacement which more accurately describes Wakefield's departure from his life turns into a conversion of the man into a synecdoche, a memorial that signifies the human totality that was. In fact, when, after a ten-year separation, Wakefield bumps into his wife and they stand "face to face, staring into each other's eyes," he has the anonymity he thought he wanted—she does not recognize the man. No longer lover or husband, he is in fact another man.

After Wakefield's first night away, the narrator addresses him:

> Poor Wakefield! Little knowest thou thine own insignificance in this great world! No mortal eye but mine has traced thee. Go quietly to thy bed, foolish man; and, on the morrow, if thou wilt be wise, get thee home to good Mrs. Wakefield, and tell her the truth. Remove not thyself, even for a little week, from thy place in her chaste bosom. Were she, for a single moment, to deem thee dead, or lost, or lastingly divided from her, thou wouldst

be woefully conscious of a change in thy true wife, forever after. It is perilous to make a chasm in human affections; not that they gape so long and wide—but so quickly close again!

What makes Wakefield a tale of terror is that the exemption from the self of which Hawthorne's characters so frequently dream is not difficult to achieve. It is in fact easy to achieve. We achieve it all the time: Hawthorne insists Wakefield is an ordinary man. He is called "feebleminded" and "insignifican[t]"; we are told he is not "perplexed with Originality." Being "other" to ourselves—as if dead to ourselves—we are simultaneously dead to those around us. We do not matter in this world. We have no designated "place" outside the bodies that are our lives. Unless we keep the ground we walk on we will be converted from life into static image. This is what Hawthorne's characters dream they want—the grandmother in "The Ambitious Guest" able to see her appearance in the world, to see the smile on the coffined face.

J. HILLIS MILLER

Defacing It: Hawthorne and History†

* * *

"The Minister's Black Veil" depends on a remarkable *donnée*, remarkable in its simplicity and profundity. It is a profundity that is all on the surface, or is accomplished by a change in marks all on the surface. The good Reverend Mr Hooper appears one Sunday at the door of his house to conduct the morning church service with "but one thing remarkable in his appearance." [1] He is wearing a black veil. He has covered over all but two of those features by which we ordinarily interpret a person's mind and feelings through his or her face. Hooper has replaced his face with another kind of mark. He has veiled his face.

No certain explanation is ever given, by the narrator, by Mr Hooper, or in any other way, of the reason or reasons he does this. His act is not related by him to his vocation as a minister, nor given explicit scriptural precedent, nor justified by other institutional precedents within his church, nor explained by a claim that he has been commanded to wear the black veil by God, or by his conscience, or

† From J. Hillis Miller, *Hawthorne and History: Defacing It* (Oxford, Basil Blackwell, 1991), 66–106. Reprinted by permission.
1. Roy Harvey Pearce, ed., *Tales and Sketches* by Nathaniel Hawthorne (New York: The Library of America, 1982), 372.

by any other sort of message from on high or from out of this world. Such a message might have authorized him to wear the black veil as a sign transmitting that message, however enigmatically, to his community. Such explicit justifications for strange behavior by a claim to having a special mission or election are a familiar part of the history of Christianity, for example in the New England Puritanism that is the explicit historical reference of the story. Nor have they vanished today, when, for example, a TV Evangelist claims that "God will call him home" unless his followers donate several million dollars to his cause before such and such a day. Such explicit justifications are conspicuously absent from anything Hooper or the narrator or anyone else says about the reasons Hooper dons the black veil. In fact no explicit justification or explanation is ever given. This absence is itself a major clue to the right reading of the story.

Nor does the black veil itself, unlike the letter A in *The Scarlet Letter*, contain in itself any easily readable clues to its own meaning: "Swathed about his forehead, and hanging down over his face, so low as to be shaken by his breath, Mr Hooper had on a black veil. On a nearer view, it seemed to consist of two folds of crape, which entirely concealed his features, except the mouth and chin, but probably did not intercept his sight, farther than to give a darkened aspect to all living and inanimate things." "A" stands for adultery, but black is more ambiguous. Certainly the story never says, in so many words, "Black stands for so and so". Black as such, moreover, is more the absence of signification than a clearly identifiable sign. The black veil is blank, featureless, except for its fold. It is remarkable in its absence of marks. What difference does it make that the veil is black rather than white or red? The reader is left to guess, primarily on the basis of universal associations of black with night-time, the absence of light, evil, death.

*   *   *

"The Minister's Black Veil" is a little like the parables of Jesus in the form modern biblical scholars tell us they were almost certainly presented by Jesus himself, that is, as enigmatic stories entirely lacking explicit interpretation. The latter were almost certainly added by the gospel-makers when they wrote down the story of Jesus's life a generation later. In the case of Hawthorne's story, though everyone involved – the narrator, Hooper's parishioners, Hooper himself, and the reader – are fascinated by the black veil and by the question of its meaning, no other than hypothetical explanations are ever given, even by Hooper himself. He tells his fiancée Elizabeth that "this veil is a type and a symbol", but when she asks in effect the natural next question, "Type and symbol of what?" or rather, to be specific, asks, "What grievous affliction hath befallen you . . . that you should thus darken your eyes for ever?," he answers only in riddles and enigmas. He speaks in terms of "if" and "perhaps": "If it be a sign of mourning, . . . I, perhaps, like most other mortals, have sorrows dark enough to be typified by a black veil. . . . If I hide my face for sorrow, there is cause enough . . . and if I cover it for secret sin, what mortal might not do the same?"

*   *   *

The black veil covers all of Hooper's face but his mouth and chin. Much is made of the "sad smile" that dimly glimmers beneath the Reverend Hooper's black veil. That smile is another sign, another textual clue to be read, but it too has no certain meaning. A sad smile is an oxymoron. It is neither happy nor sad, but both at once. A smile detached from the rest of the features of a human face is fundamentally ambiguous. It is not open to certain interpretation. It may mean this or it may mean that. It may mean Hooper is happy or it may mean he is sad. It is impossible to tell, since the meaning of a smile depends on its configuration with the other features of the face. These are in the Reverend Hooper's case invisible. He is in this like the Cheshire cat in *Alice in Wonderland*. That cat, you will remember, vanishes bit by bit until only its disembodied smile remains. "I have seen a cat without a smile", says Alice, "but never a smile without a cat." The good Reverend Mr Hooper has a smile without a face.

*   *   *

"The Minister's Black Veil" * * * opens with a celebration of the happy openness and reciprocity of the Milford community. Everyone's face is open to his neighbour's face on this bright sunshiny Sunday at churchtime: "The old people of the village came stooping along the street. Children, with bright faces, tript merrily beside their parents, or mimicked a graver gait, in the conscious dignity of their Sunday clothes. Spruce bachelors looked sidelong at the pretty maidens, and fancied that the Sabbath sunshine made them prettier than on weekdays." All the generations are here together with open faces in the sunshine: old folks, parents, children, courting unmarried citizens, that is, bachelors and maidens preparing for the marriages leading to new children with bright faces. It is almost as if the kingdom of heaven were already here on earth. It is almost as if the good people of Milford could already see not through a glass darkly but face to face.

Mr Hooper's appearance in his black veil at the door of his house for the short walk to preside over the Sunday service is a devastating eclipse of all that sunshine openness. It interrupts the universal process, necessary to all human society – community life, family life, and face to face "interpersonal" relations – whereby each of us interprets the countenances of those around us as signs of those persons' selfhoods. When the parson appears in his black veil, his soul, his thoughts, or his feelings, may no longer be read from his face. There is no way to tell whether he is happy, or whether he has a secret sorrow or sin. It is impossible to be sure the same person is in there, or any person at all. It may be a stranger's visage, product of some diabolical shifting or displacement: "'Are you sure it is our parson?' inquired Goodman Gray of the sexton . . . 'I can't really feel as if good Mr Hooper's face was behind that piece of crape,' said the sexton"; "They longed for a breath of wind to blow aside the veil, almost believing that a stranger's visage would be discovered, though the form, gesture, and voice were those of Mr Hooper." Something worse even than a stranger, a ghost or a demon, may be hidden behind the veil: "He has changed himself into something awful, only by hiding his face"; "The black veil, though it covers only our pastor's face, throws its influence over his whole person, and makes him ghostlike from head to foot."

* * *

Hooper's veil also interrupts the process whereby each of us interprets himself in the same way, for example when we look in the mirror: "That is me there facing me from within the glass, the self I am for myself and the self I am for other people." If the black veil makes Hooper "awful" to his neighbours, he also becomes awful to himself. His attempt to wish happiness to the couple he has just married is broken when "catching a glimpse of his figure in the looking-glass, the black veil involved his own spirit in the horror with which it overwhelmed all others. His frame shuddered—his lips grew white—he spilt the untasted wine upon the carpet—and rushed forth into the darkness." Later the narrator tells the reader that Hooper felt "that a preternatural horror was interwoven with the threads of the black crape. In truth, his own antipathy to the veil was known to be so great, that he never willingly passed before a mirror, nor stooped to drink at a still fountain, lest, in its peaceful bosom, he should be affrighted by himself." The black veil hides Hooper from himself, as he thinks he has access to that self by looking at his own face in the mirror.

* * *

Hooper's veil also interrupts an important way in which we sustain our sense of ourselves. This is the way other people whose faces we can see look us in the face with signs of recognition. These looks affirm that we are familiar to those around us. This leads us to believe that we are who we think we are. One of the most disquieting effects of Hooper's wearing of the black veil is the way it puts in doubt his parishioners' sense of themselves. This has depended to a considerable degree on their feeling that they live under the benign fatherly eye of the good Reverend Mr Hooper. Now they cannot be sure whether he is looking at them or not, or indeed whether it is still Hooper at all behind the veil. "Lift the veil but once", implores Elizabeth, Hooper's fiancée, "and look me in the face." Our sense of ourselves is determined in part by the fact that others look us in the face and affirm our sense of our own selfhood. The other who looks me and my neighbours in the face plays the role of the all-illuminating sun, or of God himself. The look of the paternal other brings each of us into visible or externalized existence and keeps us there by responding to our faces, smiles, frowns, and speech as valid signs that there is something behind our faces, that is, our real selves. The veiled face of the other is a terrifying or "awful" threat to that.

Hooper's appearance in his black veil interrupts even the way in which we interpret a dead body as the effigy of that person. A dead body is normally taken as the model or form of that person's departed soul, for example in the case of recumbent statues on tombs in medieval churches. We want to look the dead in the face, as in the ceremony of viewing the corpse, both to be sure that the dead are really dead and as a way of forming an image of what the dead must still be like in the realm of death to which they have now crossed over. The custom of viewing the dead is a way of personifying death, giving it a face, and thereby giving ourselves the courage to face it.

All the interchanges and transactions of ordinary social life – birth, courtship, marriage, going to church, discussions among citizens of matters of interest to the community, the ritual acceptance of death, and so on – depend on accepting the face as a trustworthy sign of the subjectivity within, readable as an index to that subjectivity by those who know how to read. All these transactions are interrupted, inhibited, or suspended when Hooper appears in his veil.

The effects on the community of Milford of this interruption are catastrophic. Everything presupposed by the cheerful picture of social harmony sketched in the opening paragraph breaks down. Hooper preaches from behind his black veil a sermon on "secret sin", the sin we would hide from our neighbours, from ourselves, and from God. The sermon causes the hearts of Hooper's parishioners to quake. When they leave the church they have been transformed, at least in the narrator's description, from faces open to one another in the sunlight into mouths without faces or into solitary selves, veiled in secret meditation: "Some gathered in little circles, huddled closely together, with their mouths all whispering in the centre; some went homeward alone, wrapt in silent meditation."

The story thereafter is a series of episodes in which one by one the normal activities of the community are shown to be disabled, transformed, or suspended by Hooper's wearing the black veil: a funeral service, a wedding, consultation with the minister by members of his congregation, Hooper's open interchange with his fiancée, his customary evening walk to the graveyard, his power as a preacher, his own deathbed scene, even the thought of him after his death by those who survive him. Once the minister puts on his black veil there is no more open discussion, no more courtship, no more marrying or giving in marriage, or, rather, marriages become indistinguishable from funerals, and funerals cease to be an institutionalized acceptance of the fact that the dead are really dead.

* * *

Just why does the simple act of wearing the black veil cause all this devastation in the little community of Milford? The catastrophic effect seems outrageously incommensurate with its trivial cause. The wearing of the veil, I answer, suspends two of the basic assumptions that make society possible: the assumption that a person's face is the sign of his selfhood and the accompanying presumption that this sign can in one way or another be read. A whole series of presuppositions accompany those assumptions: the presupposition that there are natural as opposed to arbitrary signs, in this case the face; the presupposition that the face as exterior and visible natural sign refers to an interior, non-linguistic entity, the consciousness, subjectivity, soul, or selfhood of the person who presents that face to the world; the presupposition that the procedure whereby we read a person's selfhood by his or her face is paradigmatic for sign-reading in general. The reading of person by face can then be universally extended to the reading of all natural and supernatural entities, all entities not persons – the absent, the inanimate, the dead. This reading would be expressed by those most basic of tropes, prosopopoeia and apostrophe,[2] as in Wordsworth's opening address in "The Boy of Winander": "There was a boy: ye knew him well, ye cliffs / And islands of Winander!" It is all very well to say that of course we know that reading a personality by a face is a precarious dependence on an unreliable trope, but we go on knowing, choosing, and deciding in daily life as if this were not the case. Hawthorne's story shows that if the originary figure of reading self by face is put in question, then the whole set of assumptions making individual and social life possible are suspended.

---

2. A rhetorical figure in which a writer addresses a person or thing. "Prosopopoeia" or personification, a rhetorical figure or trope giving personal existence to an inanimate thing [Editor's note].

When he puts on the black veil the Reverend Hooper is as if he were already dead. Or, rather, he seems already to have withdrawn to that realm where signs cannot reach, for which "death" is one name. Or, rather, it is as if the simple act of putting on the black veil had revealed the unverifiable possibility that each of us already dwells in that realm, both as we are for other people and even as we are for ourselves. The black veil reveals in these effects the possibility that unveiling, apocalyptic or otherwise, is impossible.

The most literal and direct effect of the veil is to suspend for Hooper's parishioners access to his subjectivity. His "figure" becomes ambiguous, disquietingly attractive, fascinating, just because his face has become invisible. This is expressed by a regular distinction between "face" and "figure" that Hawthorne borrows from common parlance: "Strangers came long distances to attend services at his church, with the mere idle purpose of gazing at his figure, because it was forbidden them to behold his face."

Hooper's last words, "I look around me, and, lo! on every visage a Black Veil," assert that the face itself is a veil. Hooper's corpse mouldering in the earth, still veiled, is a veiled veil, a veil on top of a veil. There is no reason to assume that even the most extravagant series of unveilings would ever reach anything but another veil. Death, as Paul de Man says, is "a displaced name for a linguistic predicament".[3] This is the predicament of never being able to name the realities we most want to name – the self, nature, God, the realm beyond the borders of life—except in that unverifiable trope called a catachresis.[4] Catachresis often takes the form of a prosopopoeia, as in "face of a mountain" or "eye of a storm". Such a trope defaces or disfigures in the very act whereby it ascribes a face to what has none.

Hawthorne gives striking typological expression to this predicament in his image of the veiled face as a veil behind a veil. The black veil is literally a de-facement or disfigurement. It deprives Hooper of the face whereby his neighbours assume they know him. However one wishes to describe it generically, as allegorical personification, or as parabolic realism, or as apocalyptic prophecy, the veil as type or symbol de-faces that for which it stands. At the same time the veil disfigures its referent in another way. The veil between us and that for which it is a type and a symbol is an enigmatic sign that appears to give access to what it stands for while forbidding the one who confronts it to move behind it by any effort of hermeneutic interpretation. If Hooper's face behind the veil, like that of all his neigh-

---

3. Paul de Man, "Autobiography as De-Facement", *The Rhetoric of Romanticism* (New York: Columbia University Press, 1984), 81.
4. A figure of speech that strains credulity and is literally impossible, as in Hamlet's "To take arms against a sea of troubles" [*Editor's note*].

bours, is yet another veil, then it can be said that the real face too is
not a valid sign but another de-facement. The face de-faces . . . it.

Systematic narrative and figurative notations in the story of the
things that are covered by a black veil extend the meaning of veiling
to cover the whole repertoire of those entities that are the outside
grounding of social life: nature, God, death, or the realm we shall
enter after death. It is as if the inaccessibility of what the black veil
covers makes it spread out to include not just Hooper's face as the
sign of his selfhood but the whole array of things that are the threatening exterior of social life, while at the same time presumed to be
its secure foundation.

When Hooper's subjectivity becomes inaccessible by way of his
face, his veil covers a kind of floating location of the unlocatable.
The spectator's speculations about what may be behind the veil drifts
from consciousness to the place of death, to God, to nature. Hawthorne's story implicitly recognizes that prosopopoeia is the primary
means by which mankind names and tames all that is outside the
human. We give nature, God, or death a human face in order to give
ourselves the illusion that we can have access to them, understand
them, appropriate them as the grounds of our social intercourse. But
Hooper's wearing the black veil, by suspending that primary "literal"
prosopopoeia whereby we interpret a person's facial features as the
signs of his or her selfhood, suspends also those extensions of prosopopoeia that are ordinarily so taken for granted as not even to be
recognizable as tropes, for example when we call nature "she".

When Hooper is affrighted by his own face in the mirror during
the wedding service, he rushes forth into the darkness: "For the
Earth, too, had on her Black Veil." "Dying sinners" shudder when
Hooper puts his veiled face near their own, "such were the terrors of
the black veil, even when Death had bared his visage." In his deathbed speech Hooper speaks of the way man now does "vainly shrink
from the eye of his Creator." All these prosopopoeias—Earth as a
woman, Death as man, God as possessing an all-seeing eye—
discreetly signalled by capitals, by pronouns, or by the projection on
what is not human of parts of the human body, are so inextricably
woven into everyday speech as to be almost invisible. They are
almost effaced or "dead" metaphors. Of course we speak of the
earth as "she". Of course we speak of being face to face with death,
or of being under the eye of God. How could we speak at all of
these things otherwise? Such universal tropes become visible only
when they are suspended. Prosopopoeia is essential to allegory, as
in the capitalizations of Earth, Death, and Creator here. How could
there be allegory without abstractions personified and capitalized,

"Orgoglio" in Spenser, or "Caritas" and the rest in Giotto's Allegory of the Virtues and Vices at Padua? Prosopopoeia is the catachrestic trope that covers our ignorance of nature, death, and God. Prosopopoeia makes everything we say of these, like what we say of the human heart, an allegory. They are allegorical in the sense of being simultaneously an unveiling (speaking of Mother Earth opens up the possibility of incorporating nature into our discourse), and a veiling (speaking of Mother Earth covers over the otherness of nature by ascribing to it a spurious similarity to ourselves).

Much is at stake in being able to go on seeing these effaced prosopopoeias as valid. At stake is our ability to go on living with a modest sense of security as mortals in an alien and threatening universe. At stake also is even our sense of ourselves *as* selves, since to question those ubiquitous personifications of nature, God, and death is, by a reciprocal putting in question, to suspend that "literal" prosopopoeia whereby a human face, our own or that of another, is an index to a self behind the face. It is no wonder the good citizens of Milford are appalled.

* * *

The veil is the type and symbol of the fact that all signs are potentially unreadable, or that the reading of them is potentially unverifiable. If the reader has no access to what lies behind a sign but another sign, then all reading of signs cannot be sure whether or not it is in error. Reading would then be a perpetual wandering or displacement that can never be checked against anything except another sign. If the artwork should be, in Kant's formulation, the indispensable bridge between epistemology and ethics, from knowledge to justified action, Hawthorne's story, it can be said, puts all its readers together on that bridge, stuck there without entrance or egress, able to go neither forward nor backward, neither back to certain knowledge of what the story means nor forward to conscientious ethical or political action in the real world.

This situation is intolerable. To live is to act, to need to act, and to need to act with a sense that we are justified in what we do. We would do anything to escape from this situation or to persuade ourselves that we are not in it. "The Minister's Black Veil" presents the reader with a full repertoire of the ways this attempt can be made. All critical essays on the story are so many more attempts to put something verifiable behind the veil, to make the veil the type and symbol of something definite one can confront directly, face to face, *through* the veil, by means of the veil. Each of these attempts proffers an hypothesis about the meaning of the veil. Each proposes or posits some entity there. This is followed, in each case, by unsuccessful attempts to verify this hypothesis, or by an implicit recognition in the act of positing the hypothesis that it is intrinsically unverifiable.

* * *

If, after death, good Mr Hooper's face "mouldered beneath the Black Veil," this suggests the inextricable involvement of the inaccessibility of death in the ideological system of veiling. It confirms that death is indeed a displaced name for a linguistic predicament, the predicament of being able to posit or project names freely, in primal personifying apostrophes, but unable to validate those names by any direct experience of what is named. The positing itself erects a barrier or veil. Such naming is pre-mimetic or pre-representational, that is, it does not point toward anything that can be directly experienced. At the same time such naming forbids ever entering a representational or mimetic domain where words can be matched with things known directly, prior to language. The face is a defacing, as the *pro* ("in front of, before") in *prosopon* or *prosopopoeia* suggests. *Prosopon* means face *or* mask, the face as mask put in front of an unfathomable enigma. The figure of the face as that which is "in front" of something behind is present still in all our English words in "front": "confront", "affront", "frontal", and "front" itself. These come from Latin *frons:*"forehead", "brow". The title of Hardy's "In Front of the Landscape", for example, is already a covert prosopopoeia, as is a colloquial phrase like "the front of the house". The most disquieting effect of Hooper's veil, as the story makes clear in Hooper's last speech, is to show that the face itself is already an impenetrable veil. A veiled face is a veil over a veil, a veiling of what is already veiled.

* * *

As I began my discussion of the story by saying, Hooper nowhere claims that his authority for wearing the veil is some special mission, election, or calling that has commanded him to do so as witness to some peculiar insight mediated to his congregation by means of the veil. He is conspicuously silent where he might speak out, by saying "God commanded me to do it", or "A still small voice told me to do it", or even, "The devil made me do it". He just does it. Though Hooper becomes an awesome power in the New England church, a famous preacher who strikes religious terror into the hearts of all who hear him, that church dispatches a representative to his deathbed to try (unsuccessfully) to persuade Hooper to remove the veil before he dies. His stubborn refusal is seen as a scandal by his church.

Moreover, the traditional theological terminology of Hooper's refusal (in the words "mystery" and "obscurely typifies") is displaced to name the linguistic predicament I have identified. The emphasis is on that particular form of this predicament so fascinating to Hawthorne: the incommensurability of solitary consciousness and any language whatsoever that "may be understood and felt by anybody, who will give himself the trouble to read it." The logic of Hooper's formulation turns on "when" and "then". *When* each of us does not hide his inmost heart from God, from those closest to him, even from himself, or as Hooper has put it in his initial sermon after he dons the Black Veil, when we no longer cover "those sad mysteries which we hide from our nearest and dearest, and would fain conceal from our own consciousness, even forgetting that the Omniscient can detect them," *then* "deem me a monster, for the symbol beneath which I have lived, and die!" The now of that "then", however, has not yet come. In this life it remains the imminence of a perpetual "not quite yet" within which "every visage" is a Black Veil, as impenetrable as Hooper's literal veil of crape. Within the time of waiting for that perpetually deferred uncovering, Hooper is not a monster, or not yet a monster, unless all others are monsters too, though it *would* be monstrous to wear the black veil still, after the universal unveiling at the apocalypse.

*   *   *

Hooper dies not only still veiled, but still with "a faint smile lingering on the lips." This dimly glimmering smile is the sign of his characteristic irony, meaning by irony a perpetual suspension of definite meaning. Hooper's smile accompanies the unresolvable ambiguity of the veil itself and of everything that is said about it, by the narrator, by the people of Milford, and by Hooper himself, however desperate all of these are to put an end to that ambiguity by saying something definite and verifiable about the meaning of the veil. Hooper's neighbours, the narrator, and the readers of the story are driven to extravagant unverifiable hypotheses by the juxtaposition of that faint smile and the surmounting blank black veil, marked only by its fold. I suggested earlier that the fold in the veil may perhaps be related to the twice-telling of this tale and to the way a secondary parabolic meaning is superimposed on the primary literal meaning. It would be just as plausible to relate the folding to the double meaning of irony. The two signs, the dim smile without a face and the folded veil above it, would then mean the same thing or would double one another. They would be the type and symbol of the radical undecidability of all ironic expression, even of that form of ironic expression that is not verbal but facial. Irony keeps its own counsel. It responds to our interrogations only with a further ironic smile or with an ominously permissive, "Of course, if you say so".

Insofar as Hooper's sin is the sin of irony, it is appropriate that the story should end with his death, since death and irony have a secret and unsettling alliance. Though Hooper, unlike Socrates, is not put to death for being an ironist, in both cases irony is shown to be lethal. It is deadly both for the ironist and for those on whom the irony is inflicted. Irony puts both the ironist and his victims in proximity to death, but it ironically survives the death of the ironist to go on through perhaps centuries of human history effecting its deadly work of the suspension of that definite meaning for which we all long and which we all think we ought to have. The putting to death of Socrates did not put an end to the effect of Socrates's irony, as the citizens of Athens may have hoped. Quite the contrary, as any good reader of the Platonic dialogues knows. And the citizens of Milford, like the narrator, who in his last sentence places the events he has been telling at a firm historical distance ("The grass of many years has sprung up and withered on that grave"), are still haunted by the memory of Hooper's smile and by the image of his face mouldering beneath the veil.

The attempt by the characters and by the narrator to put an end to painful hermeneutic suspension is continued by all the commentaries on Hawthorne's story that propose some definite explanation of it. One example would be an explanation in terms of history: "The Minister's Black Veil" is a representation by Hawthorne of the historical situation of New England Puritanism surviving into a Franklinian society. Another explanation would appeal to the psychology of the author: "The Minister's Black Veil" expresses Hawthorne's obsession with the theme of secret sin or guilt. Another explanation would be based on inter-textual analogies: "The Minister's Black Veil" is to be read in terms of its echoes of similar themes and figures in other works by Hawthorne, for example the motif of the veil in *The Blithedale Romance* and *The Marble Faun*, or the motif of secret sexual transgression in *The Scarlet Letter*, or the theme of unpardonable sin in "Ethan Brand". D. A. Miller's Foucauldian interpretation of the story,[5] * * * argues that the story is made definite in meaning when it is placed in the context of nineteenth-century ideas about sexual secrets. My reading differs in principle from all these in being an unveiling and putting in question of the ideology of unveiling that inveigles Hooper, his community,

---

5. D. A. Miller associates Hooper's black veil with the repressive 19th-century culture in which Hawthorne developed and wrote. J. Hillis Miller discusses D. A. Miller's ideas on pp. 79–82 of *Hawthorne and History* [Editor's note].

and most readers of the story into believing that there must be something definite behind the veil – both Hooper's veil and the veil of the text as the words on the page – and that our business as readers is to identify it.

"The Minister's Black Veil", both the veil itself, *in* the story, and the text of the story in the sense of the materiality of the letter, the words there on the page, patiently endures all these positings and projections of meaning, but it does not unequivocally endorse any of them. It offers itself to be read. If there is a veil in the text that all those inside the story want desperately to pierce or to lift so they can name once and for all what is behind it, for readers of "The Minister's Black Veil", here and now in 1990, the text itself is a veil we would pierce or lift. This desire to establish a definitive meaning for the black veil by relating it to something behind it for which it stands is an example of the hermeneutic desire as such. This desire would put a stop to the endless drifting of interpretation by saying, once and for all, "The veil means so and so". The reader shares this desire with Hooper's congregation, with his fiancée, with Hooper himself. This might be expressed by saying that the story is an allegory of the reader's own situation in reading it. If this hermeneutic desire could be appeased, then example could be a confirmation of theory, or a means of adjusting it so it could be confirmed. Allegory and realism would then be reconciled, since the realistic story would be the unambiguous carrier of a definite allegorical meaning. Language and history would be brought to touch one another, merge, overlap.

This happy reconciliation, this crossing over by means of parable into the land of parable, behind the veil, does not in this case occur. One remembers Lewis Carroll's poem of "The Walrus and the Carpenter". To the final interrogation of the oysters, "answer came there none, / Which was not surprising since / They'd eaten every one." Of all our interrogations of the veil of "The Minister's Black Veil", as of the interrogations of the veil itself within the story, it can be said "answer came there none". This is not because the text is a self-consuming artifact that eats itself up through some internal contradiction or undecidability. Rather, the attempt to turn the opacity of parabolic symbol into transparent concept is the eating up of the text. The text says what it says, if it says anything, in the way parable does, that is, by way of opaque symbols that resist translation into perspicuous concepts: To say of the veil it is a symbol of sin, it is sorrow, it is madness, it is New England Puritanism in a Franklinian culture, or it is the cover for sexual secrets is to receive no response from the text.

The text remains silent. It gives no answer to our questions, though it endures being translated into the unverifiable concepts which eat it up. Such translations make the story disappear from the page and become those blank pages in the sunlight Hawthorne feared all his works were. To alter the metaphor again: "The Minister's Black Veil", like Bartleby in Melville's story, answers to all our demands: "I should prefer not to." Like Bartleby's phrase, with its conditional "should", its gently indecisive "prefer", both inhibiting the "not" from being the negative of some positive and thereby something we can make part of some dialectical reasoning, "The Minister's Black Veil" is neither positive nor negative. It is patiently neutral. It says neither yes nor no to whatever hypotheses about it the reader proposes. The text offers neither confirmation nor disconfirmation of any speculative formulation about its meaning.

In this the text is like the black veil itself. The performative efficacy of "The Minister's Black Veil" lies in this similarity. It works. Like the veil, the story is a strange kind of efficacious speech act. It is a way of doing things with proffered signs. But it does to undo, to take away foundation or authority from anything any reader can say of it.

*   *   *

<h1 style="text-align:center">ROBERT B. HEILMAN</h1>

<h2 style="text-align:center">Hawthorne's "The Birthmark": Science as Religion[†]</h2>

Hawthorne's "The Birthmark" has been called, not inappropriately, a parable. The "truth" which it aims to set forth can be disengaged from the narrative: in a rational attempt to "perfect" nature man may destroy the organic life from which the imperfection is inseparable. But * * * it is necessary to guard against an oversimplification of what the story says, to guard particularly against converting even a parabolic drama into melodrama. Aylmer, the overweening scientist, resembles less the villain than the tragic hero: in his catastrophic attempt to improve on human actuality there is not only pride and a deficient sense of reality but also disinterested aspiration. The story does not advocate total resignation or a flat acquiescence in the immediate state of affairs. Despite its firm expository conclusion, "The Birthmark" hardly advocates at all; it enters the neighborhood of greatness because it has a great theme, but is not tempted into pat answers. The theme which Hawthorne explores may be defined as the problem of mediating between irrational passivity and a hyper-rational reorganization of life. Failure in this problem, as in others,

[†] From Robert B. Heilman. "Hawthorne's 'The Birthmark': Science as Religion," *The South Atlantic Quarterly* 48 (October 1949): 575–83. Copyright © 1949 by Duke University Press. All rights reserved. Reprinted by permission of the publisher.

may coincide with urgent good will; this is the formulation of the tragic actor which Hawthorne adopts, in contrast with the tragic structure in which an evil or perverted will is joined to saving qualities such as the capacity for repentance. But Hawthorne makes a more precise definition of the tragic error—one which is worth a brief examination.

This definition is made implicitly in the language of the story—language which may be either literal or figurative but in either case has influential overtones. What we find recurrently in "The Birthmark," and therefore insistently asking to be taken into account, is the terminology and imagery of religion. Specifically religious problems are not overtly introduced into the story, but the language of religion is there so unfailingly that, like iterative imagery in drama and poetry, it must be closely inspected if a final reading of the story is to be complete. What it does is create a story that transcends the parabolic: the foreground parable concerns man's relations with nature, but the immanent story is about man's conceptions of evil. The further we trace the implications of language, the less simple we discover Hawthorne's tale to be.

The scientific progress of Aylmer's day, we are told, "seemed to open paths into the region of *miracle*"; scientists are called *votaries*; Aylmer may have shared their "*faith* in man's ultimate control over Nature." The subjects of their study are called *secrets*, but also, repeatedly, *mysteries*; at the end, the "*mysterious* symbol had passed away," but it had been inseparable from the very "*mystery* of life." When Georgiana's and Aylmer's union has been virtually identified with the scientific effort to remove the birthmark, Georgiana thinks of Aylmer's devotion to her—to the perfected her—as "*holy* love." What is made clear by such terms, which function precisely like poetic images, is that science itself has become religion, able to provide an ultimate account of reality and therefore to exact complete human dedication. It has become religion not only for Aylmer but also for Georgiana—". . . she *prayed* that, for a single moment, she might satisfy his highest and deepest conception." Indeed, her taking of Aylmer's final potion, which is to effect her transformation, is recorded in terms which make it virtually a Christian act. The drink is "bright enough to be the draught of *immortality*"; to Georgiana it is "like water from a *heavenly* fountain," and it will allay "a feverish thirst that had parched me for many days." Since Biblical language makes frequent use of metaphors of thirst to express spiritual yearnings, it is difficult not to read in such a passage a reminiscence of John 4:14—". . . whosoever drinketh of the waters that I shall give him shall never thirst; but the water that I shall give him shall be in him a well of water springing up into everlasting life."

The question, of course, is whether Georgiana's draught is really heavenly and has the power to allay the thirst that from the soul doth rise; whether, in other words, the auspices under which she drinks are spiritual principles. The irony of her illusion is subtly carried on by her blunt command, "Give me the goblet." At one level the analogy with communion is amplified; but *goblet* also has a metaphorical value, and we are inevitably reminded of the cup which is an ordeal: ". . . the cup which my Father hath given me, shall I not drink it?" Georgiana has overcome her dread and has come to conceive of herself, at least in part, as a sacrifice. The end is the secular salvation of mortal man.

The cup has been given by Aylmer. The language-pattern of the story indicates that in the religion of science Aylmer is less priest than God. The votaries believed, Hawthorne records, that the scientist would "lay his hands on the *secret of creative force* and perhaps *make new worlds for himself.*" The word *wonders* is used repeatedly to describe what Aylmer and other scientists achieved. Aylmer, though he speaks jokingly, does apply the term *sorcerer* to himself; a laboratory exploit of his is *magical*; he is confident that he can "draw a *magic* circle around her within which no evil might intrude." He could make, he intimates, "an *immortal* nostrum"; he has created an "elixir of *immortality*"; the potion which he prepares for Georgiana may be the draught "of *immortal* happiness or misery." Aylmer has given to the problems offered by the birthmark such deep thought that he feels almost able "to *create* a being less perfect" than Georgiana. He is sure that he can make her cheek *faultless*. And then he makes an allusion which contributes importantly to this part of the meaning: "Even Pygmalion, when his sculptured woman assumed life, felt not greater ecstasy than mine will be." Formally, Aylmer rarely fails to exhibit a consciousness of human limitations; but still he cannot discipline that part of himself which aspires to infinite power. At the conclusion of the experiment he exclaims spontaneously, "By *Heaven!* it is well nigh gone!" What is this Heaven? Has a superhuman power aided him? Or has his power itself seemed to go beyond the terrestrial? A minute later he lets "the light of *natural* day" enter the room, and Aminadab, "the *earthly* mass," chuckles grossly. It is as though Aylmer has descended for a moment into another kind of reality from that which is proper to him. Indeed, he distinguishes two kinds of force which he declares have been at work: "Matter and spirit—*earth and heaven*—have both done their part in this!" But the question is whether Aylmer really accepts the dualism to which his words give expression.

In fact, we have almost a parody of the Father who gives the bitter cup to drink. Aylmer, as we have seen, is virtually translated into the godhead: His *"sorcerer's* book," Georgiana insists to him, "has made me *worship* you more than ever." The confusion of values has spread to Georgiana. Aylmer's own confusion is shown further in his paradoxical inclination to adore as well as create: "the spectral hand wrote mortality where he would fain have *worshiped.*" Yet later, in a context which shows that his evaluation is moral, he assures her, "You are fit for heaven without tasting death!" Perhaps, then, she ought to be almost suitable for adoration, and the hand itself should seem a negligible flaw. Yet over it Aylmer is almost hysterical, while, as we shall see, he is blind to more serious flaws closer to home.

That Aylmer is a confused man has always been plain to readers of the story. But, when we examine it in detail, we discover that the language of the story defines his confusion very precisely—defines it as the mistaking of science for religion. The essential story, I have said, is about man's conception of evil: Aylmer does not, in the long run, regard evil as real. Without actually denying its reality, Aylmer in effect simplifies and attenuates it by treating it as manageable, subject to human control, indeed removable. Aylmer's religion reverses the Christian sense of the reality of evil—a reality which can ultimately be dealt with only by divine grace. Aylmer is a romantic perfectibilitarian, who suffers from a dangerous fastidiousness in the presence of complex actuality. "You are perfect!" he assures Georgiana—as she is dying. He believes in perfectibility without retaining the modifying concept of damnability. Man's confidence in his ability to deal with evil by some physical or psychological or social surgery makes him an earthly god: in his presumption he proposes to establish a heaven on earth. Thus, like Aylmer, man becomes committed to a hyperrational—that is, a shallowly grounded—reorganization of life. Hawthorne brilliantly summarizes the metaphysics of the scientific religion in Aylmer's explication of the series of steps in his rehabilitation of Georgiana. He tells her, "I have already administered agents powerful enough to change your entire physical system. Only one thing remains to be tried." ". . . to change your entire physical system" is, in this cosmology, the equivalent of regeneration or conversion. Aylmer's faith becomes, in effect: improve the body, and you save the soul.

Hawthorne repeatedly underlines the error of Aylmer's ways. His confusion of values shows in the fact that his husbandly love can have strength only "by intertwining itself with his love of science." The birthmark which he proposes to remove is "fairy," "mysterious," "magic"—terms which indicate how much more is at stake than Aylmer suspects at his most acute. He accepts uncritically Georgiana's assurance that from his hand she is willing "to take a dose of poison," an ironic anticipation of the way in which his elixir actually does work. He demands complete "trust" and is angry when, following him into the laboratory, she throws "the blight of that fatal birthmark over my labors"—his own word, *blight*, having a summary accuracy of which he is ironically innocent. Aylmer accepts entirely his wife's passionate exclamation that if the birthmark is not removed "we shall both go mad!" What the reader must see in this madness is a simple inability to accept the facts of life. It is precisely this inability of which Hawthorne, throughout the story, keeps reminding us, almost overwhelmingly.

Hawthorne could hardly have found a better symbol than the birthmark, which speaks of the imperfection born with man, with man as a race. Here is original sin in fine imaginative form. Aylmer does not altogether fail to see what is involved; he is not crudely stupid; but his sense of power leads him to undervalue the penalties of life. His tragedy is that he lacks the tragic sense; he is, we may say, a characteristic modern, the exponent of an age which has deified science and regards it as an irresistibly utopianizing force. His tragic flaw is to fail to see the tragic flaw in humanity. Hawthorne never lets the reader forget the deep significance of the "human hand" which scars Georgiana. He comments ironically on the lovers who hoped to see "one living specimen of ideal loveliness without the semblance of a flaw," a suggestion of a common attitude for which Aylmer speaks. The birthmark is a "symbol of imperfection," "the spectral hand that wrote mortality," the "sole token of human imperfection." This "fatal flaw of humanity"—the terms are virtually Christian—implies that all the productions of nature are "temporary and finite" and that "their perfection must be wrought by toil and pain." For spiritual discipline Aylmer wants to substitute magic—not quite pushbutton magic perhaps, but still a shortcut, a kind of prestidigitation. It is not that he is ignorant in a gross way; he sees much, but his premises stop him at the threshold of wisdom. He recognizes that the blemish on Georgiana's face is a "mark of earthly imperfection"; he even selects it "as the symbol of his wife's liability to sin, sorrow, decay, and death." The frequency of images of death in the story is a thematic reminder of the reality from which Aylmer doggedly turns away. Although here he actually puts his finger upon the realities which the mature man must come to terms with, his faith leads him to feel, as we have seen, "that he could draw a magic circle round her within which no evil might intrude." Evil is manageable: the symbol itself has become the reality.

What we finally come to is the problem of spirit, and the test of Aylmer's creed is the kind of spiritual values it embodies. We hear repeatedly about Aylmer's spirit and his interest in the spiritual. He had "attempted to fathom," we learn, "the very process by which Nature assimilates all her precious influences from earth and air, and from the *spiritual* world, to create and foster man, her master-piece." Aminadab represents "man's physical nature"; in Aylmer we see "the *spiritual* element." Georgiana is almost convinced "that her husband possessed sway over the *spiritual* world." As she reads his record of experiments, the author, apparently speaking for her, com-ments: "He handled physical details as if there were nothing beyond them; yet *spiritualized* them all, and redeemed himself from materi-alism by his strong and eager aspiration towards the *infinite*. In his grasp the veriest clod of earth assumed a *soul*." His failures are those of "the *spirit* burdened with clay and working in matter"; "his *spirit* was ever on the march, ever ascending"—the spirit, one is tempted to say, of progress. But as a result of this spiritual yearning of his, another's "angelic spirit" leaves on its "heavenward flight."

At the end Hawthorne, distinguishing "mortal" and "celestial," reaffirms a dualism which he has insisted upon throughout the story and which, as various words of theirs make clear, is formally assented to also by Georgiana and Aylmer. But the first defect of Aylmer's reli-gion, as the drama makes clear, is that in practice he does not accept dualism at all: for him, spirit is not distinct from matter but is the perfecting of matter. The material stigma that shocks him he is said, just once, to regard as symbol; but his efforts at amelioration are directed wholly at the symbol, not at its antecedent substance. Aylmer is actually symptom-doctoring and is unaware that the locus of the disease is elsewhere. His creed is secular and monistic. All the talk about spirit is an ironic commentary upon his essential lack of insight into real problems of spirit.

The story specifies what level of spiritual comprehension Aylmer does reach. He aspires, and his aspiration is presented with a good deal of sympathy, as is just; as between aspiration and passivity, the choice is, in the main, clear; but a judgment must be made between one kind of aspiration and another. So the question becomes: how, and toward what, does Aylmer actually aspire: Does he, for instance, aspire toward better insight? Toward charity? Toward wisdom? Or is it not rather that his aspiration is inextricably involved with the exercise of power? "There is no taint of imperfection on thy spirit," he tells Georgiana. Why? Because Georgiana has just indicated an unreserved willingness to accept his potion; her faith in him is total. He is not content with her perfection of "spirit." For him, immense knowledge is a means of doing things, of achieving physi-cal, visible ends. We see in him no evidence of concern with the quality of his own life, or perception, or thought.

In this man of science divine discontent is with others; as Geor-giana puts it, his love "would accept nothing less than perfection nor miserably make itself contented with an earthlier nature than he had dreamed of." It is of course Georgiana who shall be "all perfect." The romantic scientist has no thought of the problem of perfecting himself; indeed, his spiritual perception is very close to that of uplift and do-good-ism. He begs the real problem of spirit and is fanatical about the shortcomings of the world. Hawthorne is very acute in analyzing further the especial quality of Aylmer's outward-bound perfectionism and in discerning in it a core of intense fastidiousness. This hypersensitivity rushes in, indeed, at the very moment at which Aylmer fleetingly achieves a kind of wholeness of response to Georgiana, an acceptance of her which implies a spiritual modification of himself. "Yet once, by a strange and unaccountable impulse, he pressed it [the birthmark] with his lips." Here is virtually a redefinition of his love. But immediately his fastidiousness reasserts itself and gives the parting tone to the action: "His *spirit* recoiled, however, in the very act. . . ." That is his spirit: a primary awareness of the flaws of others and of the demand which they appear to make for remedy from without.

The heir of Prometheus kills his beneficiary, not by conferring a single blessing, but by endeavoring to eradicate the imperfections humanity is heir to. Upon this aspiration to divinity Hawthorne comments in his account of Aylmer's library, of the works of "these antique naturalists" who "perhaps imagined themselves to have acquired from the investigation of Nature a power above Nature, and from physics a sway over the spiritual world." Hawthorne has already remarked that the "great creative Mother . . . is yet severely careful to keep her own secrets." What Hawthorne has done, really, is to blueprint the course of science in modern imagination, to dramatize its persuasive faith in its omnipotence, and thus its taking on the colors of religion.

This very formulation commits Hawthorne to a critique—a critique which he makes by disclosing the false spirituality of Aylmer. It is the false spirituality of power conjoined with fastidiousness, of physical improvement, of external remedy, of *ad hoc* prescriptions, of reform: Aylmer's surgery is a fine symbol for a familiar code. Yet the code would have only an innocuous life in a museum-case if it did not gain converts. Thus we have Georgiana's very important role in the story: she is less the innocent victim than the fascinated sharer in magic who conspires in her own doom. Georgiana, the woman killed with kindness by the man who would be god, is really humanity—with its share of the heroic, its common sense, which enables it to question heroes, and yet its capacity for being beguiled, for combining good intention, devotion, and destructive delusion. In the marriage of science and humanity we see the inevitably catastrophic interaction of a mechanical perfectionism and the "birthmark of mortality." Science has no way of coming to terms with human imperfection, and humanity, tutored by science, can no longer accept its liability to sin and death.

Ironically, it is Georgiana who cuts off, or at least helps cut off, a final path of spiritual rectification for Aylmer. "Do not *repent*," she says, "that . . . you have rejected the best earth could offer." Not only is Aylmer's definition of "the best" inadequate, but he is encouraged in a hardening of spirit which precludes his entering upon a reconsideration of values. His religion offers no way of dealing with his pride. And his pride—with its intense demand that the world submit itself to his limited criteria—gives us another definition of the spiritual defect of this man who is so convinced that spirit is his concern. When Georgiana confesses her desire to worship him more fully, he scarcely bothers to be deprecatory: "Ah, wait for this one success, . . . then *worship* me if you will. I shall deem myself hardly unworthy of it." These are the ultimate marks of his moral infatuation.

The critical problem in "The Birthmark" has to do with the kind of mistake Aylmer makes. Hawthorne's language tells us, subtly but insistently, that Aylmer has apotheosized science; and the images and drama together define the spiritual shortcoming of this new revelation—its belief in the eradicability of evil, its Faustian proneness to love power, its incapacity to bring about renunciation or self-examination, its pride. I once thought that Hawthorne had stopped short of the proper goal of the story by not including the next phase of Aylmer's experience—the phase in which, if the tragic view of Aylmer were to prevail, Aylmer would entertain the Furies. But the summation of Aylmer's defects is that he cannot see the Furies. The story stops where it must.

JUDITH FETTERLEY

Women Beware Science: "The Birthmark"†

The scientist Aylmer in Nathaniel Hawthorne's "The Birthmark" provides another stage in the psychological history of the American protagonist. Aylmer is Irving's Rip and Anderson's boy discovered in that middle age which Rip evades and the boy rejects.[1] Aylmer is squarely confronted with the realities of marriage, sex, and women.

† From Judith Fetterley, *The Resisting Reader: A Feminist Approach to American Fiction* (Bloomington: Indiana University Press, 1978), 22–33. Reprinted with permission of Indiana University Press.
1. Fetterly discusses Washington Irving's "Rip Van Winkle" and Sherwood Anderson's "I Want to Know Why" earlier in *The Resisting Reader* [Editor's Note].

There are compensations, however, for as an adult he has access to a complex set of mechanisms for accomplishing the great American dream of eliminating women. It is testimony at once to Hawthorne's ambivalence, his seeking to cover with one hand what he uncovers with the other, and to the pervasive sexism of our culture that most readers would describe "The Birthmark" as a story of failure rather than as the success story it really is—the demonstration of how to murder your wife and get away with it. It is, of course, possible to read "The Birthmark" as a story of misguided idealism, a tale of the unhappy consequences of man's nevertheless worthy passion for perfecting and transcending nature; and this is the reading usually given it.[2] This reading, however, ignores the significance of the form idealism takes in the story. It is not irrelevant that "The Birthmark" is about a man's desire to perfect his wife, nor is it accidental that the consequence of this idealism is the wife's death. In fact, "The Birthmark" provides a brilliant analysis of the sexual politics of idealization and a brilliant exposure of the mechanisms whereby hatred can be disguised as love, neurosis can be disguised as science, murder can be disguised as idealization, and success can be disguised as failure. Thus, Hawthorne's insistence in his story on

2. See, for example, Cleanth Brooks and Robert Penn Warren, *Understanding Fiction* (New York: Appleton-Century-Croft, 1943), pp. 103–106: "We are not, of course, to conceive of Aylmer as a monster, a man who would experiment on his own wife for his own greater glory. Hawthorne does not mean to suggest that Aylmer is depraved and heartless. . . . Aylmer has not realized that perfection is something never achieved on earth and in terms of mortality"; Richard Harter Fogle, *Hawthorne's Fiction: The Light and The Dark*, rev. ed. (Norman, Okla.: University of Oklahoma Press, 1964), pp. 117–81; Robert Heilman, "Hawthorne's 'The Birthmark': Science as Religion," *South Atlantic Quarterly* 48 (1949), 575–83: "Aylmer, the overweening scientist, resembles less the villain than the tragic hero: in his catastrophic attempt to improve on human actuality there is not only pride and a deficient sense of reality but also disinterested aspiration"; F. O. Matthiessen, *American Renaissance* (New York: Oxford University Press, 1941), pp. 253–55; Arlin Turner, *Nathaniel Hawthorne* (New York: Holt, Rinehart, and Winston, 1961), pp. 88, 98, 132. * * * The major variation in these readings occurs as a result of the degree to which individual critics see Hawthorne as critical of Aylmer. Still, those who see Hawthorne as critical locate the source of his criticism in Aylmer's idealistic pursuit of perfection—e.g., Millicent Bell, *Hawthorne's View of the Artist* (New York: State University of New York, 1962), pp. 182–85: "Hawthorne, with his powerful Christian sense of the inextricable mixture of evil in the human compound, regards Aylmer as a dangerous perfectibilitarian." * * * Even Simon Lesser, *Fiction and the Unconscious* (1957; rpt. New York: Vintage-Random, 1962), pp. 87–90 and pp. 94–98, who is clearly aware of the sexual implications of the story, subsumes his analysis under the reading of misguided idealism and in so doing provides a fine instance of phallic criticism in action: "The ultimate purpose of Hawthorne's attempt to present Aylmer in balanced perspective is to quiet our fears so that the wishes which motivate his experiment, which are also urgent, can be given their opportunity. Aylmer's sincerity and idealism give us a sense of kinship with him. We see that the plan takes shape gradually in his mind, almost against his conscious intention. We are reassured by the fact that he loves Georgiana and feels confident that his attempt to remove the birthmark will succeed. Thus at the same time that we recoil we can identify with Aylmer and through him act out some of our secret desires." * * * The one significant dissenting view is offered by Frederick Crews, *The Sins of the Fathers* (New York: Oxford University Press, 1966), whose scattered comments on the story focus on the specific form of Aylmer's idealism and its implications for his secret motives.

the metaphor of disguise serves as both warning and clue to a feminist reading.

Even a brief outline is suggestive. A man, dedicated to the pursuit of science, puts aside his passion in order to marry a beautiful woman. Shortly after the marriage he discovers that he is deeply troubled by a tiny birthmark on her left cheek. Of negligible importance to him before marriage, the birthmark now assumes the proportions of an obsession. He reads it as a sign of the inevitable imperfection of all things in nature and sees in it a challenge to man's ability to transcend nature. So nearly perfect as she is, he would have her be completely perfect. In pursuit of this lofty aim, he secludes her in chambers that he has converted for the purpose, subjects her to a series of influences, and finally presents her with a potion which, as she drinks it, removes at last the hated birthmark but kills her in the process. At the end of the story Georgiana is both perfect and dead.

One cannot imagine this story in reverse—that is, a woman's discovering an obsessive need to perfect her husband and deciding to perform experiments on him—nor can one imagine the story being about a man's conceiving such an obsession for another man. It is woman, and specifically woman as wife, who elicits the obsession with imperfection and the compulsion to achieve perfection, just as it is man, and specifically man as husband, who is thus obsessed and compelled. In addition, it is clear from the summary that the imagined perfection is purely physical. Aylmer is not concerned with the quality of Georgiana's character or with the state of her soul, for he considers her "fit for heaven without tasting death." Rather, he is absorbed in her physical appearance, and perfection for him is equivalent to physical beauty. Georgiana is an exemplum of woman as beautiful object, reduced to and defined by her body. And finally, the conjunction of perfection and nonexistence, while reminding us of Anderson's story in which the good girl is the one you never see, develops what is only implicit in that story: namely, that the only good woman is a dead one and that the motive underlying the desire to perfect is the need to eliminate. "The Birthmark" demonstrates the fact that the idealization of women has its source in a profound hostility toward women and that it is at once a disguise for this hostility and the fullest expression of it.

The emotion that generates the drama of "The Birthmark" is revulsion. Aylmer is moved not by the vision of Georgiana's potential perfection but by his horror at her present condition. His revulsion for the birthmark is insistent: he can't bear to see it or touch it; he has nightmares about it; he has to get it out. Until she is "fixed," he can hardly bear the sight of her and must hide her away in secluded chambers which he visits only intermittently, so great is his fear of contamination. Aylmer's compulsion to perfect Georgiana is a result of his horrified perception of what she actually is, and all his lofty talk about wanting her to be perfect so that just this once the potential of Nature will be fulfilled is but a cover for his central emotion of revulsion. But Aylmer is a creature of disguise and illusion. In order to persuade this beautiful woman to become his wife, he "left his laboratory to the care of an assistant, cleared his fine countenance from the furnace smoke, washed the stains of acid from his fingers." Best not to let her know who he really is or what he really feels, lest she might say before the marriage instead of after, "You cannot love what shocks you!" In the chambers where Aylmer secludes Georgiana, "airy figures, absolutely bodiless ideas, and forms of unsubstantial beauty" come disguised as substance in an illusion so nearly perfect as to "warrant the belief that her husband possessed sway over the spiritual world." While Aylmer does not really possess sway over the spiritual world, he certainly controls Georgiana and he does so in great part because of his mastery of the art of illusion.

If the motive force for Aylmer's action in the story is repulsion, it is the birthmark that is the symbolic location of all that repels him. And it is important that the birthmark is just that: a birth *mark*, that is, something physical; and a *birth* mark, that is, something not acquired but inherent, one of Georgiana's givens, in fact equivalent to her.[3] The close connection between Georgiana and her birthmark is continually emphasized. As her emotions change, so does the birthmark, fading or deepening in response to her feelings and providing a precise clue to her state of mind. Similarly, when her senses are aroused, stroked by the influences that pervade her chamber, the birthmark throbs sympathetically. In his efforts to get rid of the birthmark Aylmer has "administered agents powerful enough to do aught except change your entire physical system," and these have failed. The object of Aylmer's obsessive revulsion, then, is Georgiana's "physical system," and what defines this particular system is the fact that it is female. It is Georgiana's female physiology, which is to say her sexuality, that is the object of Aylmer's relentless attack. The link between Georgiana's birthmark and her sexuality is implicit in the birthmark's role as her emotional barometer, but one specific characteristic of the birthmark makes the connection explicit: the

3. In the conventional reading of the story Georgiana's birthmark is seen as the symbol of original sin—see, for example, Heilman, p. 579; Bell, p. 185. But what this reading ignores are, of course, the implications of the fact that the symbol of original sin is female and that the story only "works" because men have the power to project that definition onto women.

hand which shaped Georgiana's birth has left its mark on her in *blood*. The birthmark is redolent with references to the particular nature of female sexuality; we hardly need Aylmer's insistence on seclusion, with its reminiscences of the treatment of women when they are "unclean," to point us in this direction. What repels Aylmer is Georgiana's sexuality; what is imperfect in her is the fact that she is female; and what perfection means is elimination.

In Hawthorne's analysis the idealization of women stems from a vision of them as hideous and unnatural; it is a form of compensation, an attempt to bring them up to the level of nature. To symbolize female physiology as a blemish, a deformity, a birthmark suggests that women are in need of some such redemption. Indeed, "The Birthmark" is a parable of woman's relation to the cult of female beauty, a cult whose political function is to remind women that they are, in their natural state, unacceptable, imperfect, monstrous. Una Stannard in "The Mask of Beauty" has done a brilliant job of analyzing the implications of this cult:

> Every day, in every way, the billion-dollar beauty business tells women they are monsters in disguise. Every ad for bras tells a woman that her breasts need lifting, every ad for padded bras that what she's got isn't big enough, every ad for girdles that her belly sags and her hips are too wide, every ad for high heels that her legs need propping, every ad for cosmetics that her skin is too dry, too oily, too pale, or too ruddy, or her lips are not bright enough, or her lashes not long enough, every ad for deodorants and perfumes that her natural odors all need disguising, every ad for hair dye, curlers, and permanents that the hair she was born with is the wrong color or too straight or too curly, and lately ads for wigs tell her that she would be better off covering up nature's mistake completely. In this culture women are told they are the fair sex, but at the same time that their "beauty" needs lifting, shaping, dyeing, painting, curling, padding. Women are really being told that "the beauty" is a beast.[4]

The dynamics of idealization are beautifully contained in an analogy which Hawthorne, in typical fashion, remarks on casually: "But it would be as reasonable to say that one of those small blue stains which sometimes occur in the purest statuary marble would convert the Eve of Powers to a monster." This comparison, despite its apparent protest against just such a conclusion, implies that where women are concerned it doesn't take much to convert purity into monstrosity; Eve herself is a classic example of the ease with which such a

---

4. Vivian Gornick and Barbara Moran, eds., *Women in Sexist Society* (New York: Signet, 1972), p. 192.

transition can occur. And the transition is easy because the presentation of woman's image in marble is essentially an attempt to disguise and cover a monstrous reality. Thus, the slightest flaw will have an immense effect, for it serves as a reminder of the reality that produces the continual need to cast Eve in the form of purest marble and women in the molds of idealization.

In exploring the sources of men's compulsion to idealize women Hawthorne is writing a story about the sickness of men, not a story about the flawed and imperfect nature of women. There is a hint of the nature of Aylmer's ailment in the description of his relation to "mother" Nature, a suggestion that his revulsion for Georgiana has its root in part in a jealousy of the power which her sexuality represents and a frustration in the face of its impenetrable mystery. Aylmer's scientific aspirations have as their ultimate goal the desire to create human life, but "the latter pursuit, however, Aylmer had long laid aside in unwilling recognition of the truth—against which all seekers sooner or later stumble—that our great creative Mother, while she amuses us with apparently working in the broadest sunshine, is yet severely careful to keep her own secrets, and, in spite of her pretended openness, shows us nothing but results. She permits us, indeed, to mar, but seldom to mend, and, like a jealous patentee, on no account to make." This passage is striking for its undercurrent of jealousy, hostility, and frustration toward a specifically female force. In the vision of Nature as playing with man, deluding him into thinking he can acquire her power, and then at the last minute closing him off and allowing him only the role of one who mars, Hawthorne provides another version of woman as enemy, the force that interposes between man and the accomplishment of his deepest desires. Yet Hawthorne locates the source of this attitude in man's jealousy of woman's having something he does not and his rage at being excluded from participating in it.

Out of Aylmer's jealousy at feeling less than Nature and thus less than woman—for if Nature is woman, woman is also Nature and has, by virtue of her biology, a power he does not—comes his obsessional program for perfecting Georgiana. Believing he is less, he has to convince himself he is more: "and then, most beloved, what will be my triumph when I shall have corrected what Nature left imperfect in her fairest work! Even Pygmalion, when his sculptured woman assumed life, felt not greater ecstasy than mine will be." What a triumph indeed to upstage and outdo Nature and make himself superior to her. The function of the fantasy that underlies the myth of Pygmalion, as it underlies the myth of Genesis (making Adam, in the words of Mary Daly, "the first among history's unmarried pregnant males"[5]), is obvious from the reality which it seeks to invert. Such myths are powerful image builders, salving man's injured ego by convincing him that he is not only equal to but better than woman, for he creates in spite of, against, and finally better than nature. Yet Aylmer's failure here is as certain as the failure of his other "experiments," for the sickness which he carries within him makes him able only to destroy, not to create.

If Georgiana is envied and hated because she represents what is different from Aylmer and reminds him of what he is not and cannot be, she is feared for her similarity to him and for the fact that she represents aspects of himself that he finds intolerable. Georgiana is as much a reminder to Aylmer of what he is as of what he is not. This apparently contradictory pattern of double-duty is understandable in the light of feminist analyses of female characters in literature, who frequently function this way. Mirrors for men, they serve to indicate the involutions of the male psyche with which literature is primarily concerned, and their characters and identities shift accordingly. They are projections, not people; and thus coherence of characterization is a concept that often makes sense only when applied to the male characters of a particular work. Hawthorne's tale is a classic example of the woman as mirror, for, despite Aylmer's belief that his response to Georgiana is an objective concern for the intellectual and spiritual problem she presents, it is obvious that his reaction to her is intensely subjective. "Shocks you, my husband?" queries Georgiana, thus neatly exposing his mask, for one is not shocked by objective perceptions. Indeed, Aylmer views Georgiana's existence as a personal insult and threat to him, which, of course, it is, because what he sees in her is that part of himself he cannot tolerate. By the desire she elicits in him to marry her and possess her birthmark, she forces him to confront his own earthiness and "imperfection."

But it is precisely to avoid such a confrontation that Aylmer has fled to the kingdom of science, where he can project himself as a "type of the spiritual element." Unlike Georgiana, in whom the physical and the spiritual are complexly intertwined, Aylmer is hopelessly alienated from himself. Through the figure of Aminadab, the shaggy creature of clay, Hawthorne presents sharply the image of Aylmer's alienation. Aminadab symbolizes that earthly, physical, erotic self

5. Mary Daly, *Beyond God the Father: Toward a Philosophy of Women's Liberation* (Boston: Beacon, 1973), 195. It is useful to compare Daly's analysis of "Male Mothers" with Mary Ellmann's discussion of the "imagined motherhood of the male" in *Thinking About Women* (New York: Harcourt Brace Jovanovich, 1968), pp. 15ff. It is obvious that this myth is prevalent in patriarchal culture, and it would seem reasonable to suggest that the patterns of co-optation noticed in "Rip Van Winkle" and "I Want to Know Why" are minor manifestations of it. *An American Dream* provides a major manifestation, in fact a tour de force, of the myth of male motherhood.

that has been split off from Aylmer, that he refuses to recognize as part of himself, and that has become monstrous and grotesque as a result: "With his vast strength, his shaggy hair, his smoky aspect, and the indescribable earthiness that incrusted him, he seemed to represent man's physical nature; while Aylmer's slender figure, and pale, intellectual face, were no less apt a type of the spiritual element." Aminadab's allegorical function is obvious and so is his connection to Aylmer, for while Aylmer may project himself as objective, intellectual, and scientific and while he may pretend to be totally unrelated to the creature whom he keeps locked up in his dark room to do his dirty work, he cannot function without him. It is Aminadab, after all, who fires the furnace for Aylmer's experiments; physicality provides the energy for Aylmer's "science" just as revulsion generates his investment in idealization. Aylmer is, despite his pretenses to the contrary, a highly emotional man: his scientific interests tend suspiciously toward fires and volcanoes; he is given to intense emotional outbursts; and his obsession with his wife's birthmark is a feeling so profound as to disrupt his entire life. Unable to accept himself for what he is, Aylmer constructs a mythology of science and adopts the character of a scientist to disguise his true nature and to hide his real motives, from himself as well as others. As a consequence, he acquires a way of acting out these motives without in fact having to be aware of them. One might describe "The Birthmark" as an exposé of science because it demonstrates the ease with which science can be invoked to conceal highly subjective motives. "The Birthmark" is an exposure of the realities that underlie the scientist's posture of objectivity and rationality and the claims of science to operate in an amoral and value-free world. Pale Aylmer, the intellectual scientist, is a mask for the brutish, earthy, soot-smeared Aminadab, just as the mythology of scientific research and objectivity finally masks murder, disguising Georgiana's death as just one more experiment that failed.

Hawthorne's attitude toward men and their fantasies is more critical than either Irving's or Anderson's. One responds to Aylmer not with pity but with horror. For, unlike Irving and Anderson, Hawthorne has not omitted from his treatment of men an image of the consequences of their ailments for the women who are involved with them. The result of Aylmer's massive self-deception is to live in an unreal world, a world filled with illusions, semblances, and appearances, one which admits of no sunlight and makes no contact with anything outside itself and at whose center is a laboratory, the physical correlative of his utter solipsism. Nevertheless, Hawthorne makes it clear that Aylmer has got someone locked up in that laboratory with him. While "The Birthmark" is by no means explicitly feminist, since Hawthorne seems as eager to be misread and to conceal as he is to be read and to reveal, still it is impossible to read his story without being aware that Georgiana is completely in Aylmer's power. For the subject is finally power. Aylmer is able to project himself onto Georgiana and to work out his obsession through her because as woman and as wife she is his possession and in his power; and because as man he has access to the language and structures of that science which provides the mechanisms for such a process and legitimizes it. In addition, since the power of definition and the authority to make those definitions stick is vested in men, Aylmer can endow his illusions with the weight of spiritual aspiration and universal truth.

The implicit feminism in "The Birthmark" is considerable. On one level the story is a study of sexual politics, of the powerlessness of women and of the psychology which results from that powerlessness. Hawthorne dramatizes the fact that woman's identity is a product of men's responses to her: "It must not be concealed, however, that the impression wrought by this fairy sign manual varied exceedingly, according to the difference of temperament in the beholders." To those who love Georgiana, her birthmark is evidence of her beauty; to those who envy or hate her, it is an object of disgust. It is Aylmer's repugnance for the birthmark that makes Georgiana blanch, thus causing the mark to emerge as a sharply-defined blemish against the whiteness of her cheek. Clearly, the birthmark takes on its character from the eye of the beholder. And just as clearly Georgiana's attitude toward her birthmark varies in response to different observers and definers. Her self-image derives from internalizing the attitudes toward her of the man or men around her. Since what surrounds Georgiana is an obsessional attraction expressed as a total revulsion, the result is not surprising: continual self-consciousness that leads to a pervasive sense of shame and a self-hatred that terminates in an utter readiness to be killed. "The Birthmark" demonstrates the consequences to women of being trapped in the laboratory of man's mind, the object of unrelenting scrutiny, examination, and experimentation.

In addition, "The Birthmark" reveals an implicit understanding of the consequences for women of a linguistic system in which the word "man" refers to both male people and all people. Because of the conventions of this system, Aylmer is able to equate his peculiarly male needs with the needs of all human beings, men and women. And since Aylmer can present his compulsion to idealize and perfect Georgiana as a human aspiration, Georgiana is forced to identify with it. Yet to identify with his aspiration is in fact to identify with his hatred of her and his need to eliminate her. Georgiana's situation is a fictional version of the experience that women undergo when they read a story like "Rip Van Winkle." Under the influence of Aylmer's mind, in the laboratory where she is subjected to his subliminal messages, Georgiana is co-opted into a view of herself as flawed and comes to hate herself as an impediment to Aylmer's aspiration; eventually she wishes to be dead rather than to remain alive as an irritant to him and as a reminder of his failure. And as she identifies with him in her attitude toward herself, so she comes to worship him for his hatred of her and for his refusal to tolerate her existence. The process of projection is neatly reversed: he locates in her everything he cannot accept in himself, and she attributes to him all that is good and then worships in him the image of her own humanity.

Through the system of sexual politics that is Aylmer's compensation for growing up, Hawthorne shows how men gain power over women, the power to create and kill, to "mar," "mend," and "make," without ever having to relinquish their image as "nice guys." Under such a system there need be very few power struggles, because women are programmed to deny the validity of their own perceptions and responses and to accept male illusions as truth. Georgiana does faint when she first enters Aylmer's laboratory and sees it for one second with her own eyes; she is also aware that Aylmer is filling her chamber with appearances, not realities; and she is finally aware that his scientific record is in his own terms one of continual failure. Yet so perfect is the program that she comes to respect him even more for these failures and to aspire to be yet another of them.

Hawthorne's unrelenting emphasis on "seems" and his complex use of the metaphors and structures of disguise imply that women are being deceived and destroyed by man's system. And perhaps the most vicious part of this system is its definition of what constitutes nobility in women: "Drink, then, thou lofty creature," exclaims Aylmer with "fervid admiration" as he hands Georgiana the cup that will kill her. Loftiness in women is directly equivalent to the willingness with which they die at the hands of their husbands, and since such loftiness is the only thing about Georgiana which does elicit admiration from Aylmer, it is no wonder she is willing. Georgiana plays well the one role allowed her, yet one might be justified in suggesting that Hawthorne grants her at the end a slight touch of the satisfaction of revenge: "'My poor Aylmer,' she repeated, with a more than human tenderness, you have aimed loftily; you have done nobly. Do not repent that with so high and pure a feeling, you have rejected the best the earth could offer.'" Since dying is the only option, best to make the most of it.

NINA BAYM

[The Tales of the Manse Period]†

* * * We find only six fictions written in the Manse period. These are "The Antique Ring," "Egotism; or, the Bosom Serpent," "The Birthmark," "Rappaccini's Daughter," "The Artist of the Beautiful," and "Drowne's Wooden Image." It is difficult to find consistency of matter or manner in the group. But except for "The Antique Ring," which is a gothic fiction set in a satiric frame, these stories are among the most interesting and puzzling in Hawthorne's canon. All of them are characterized by an intervening, prosy narrator; but this narrator's commentary is often inadequate to and sometimes even incompatible with the narrative and symbolic content of the fiction. It seems most unlikely that Hawthorne was experimenting with the device of an obtuse narrator, for such a procedure would implicitly undermine the position of the speaker in the Manse sketches;[1] nevertheless, the persona of the Manse does become obtuse when he is pressed into service as a narrator of fiction. The material escapes his attempts to control it.

In at least one case Hawthorne appears to recognize this fact, for he presents the story as though not the persona, but another author, were the creator. "Rappaccini's Daughter" begins with an introduction in which the persona takes the role of the translator and critic of the fiction composed by the French writer M. de l'Aubépine (French for Hawthorne). This author, he says, "must necessarily find himself without an audience" because "if not too refined, he is at all events too remote, too shadowy and unsubstantial in his modes of development, to suit the taste of the [multitude], and yet too popular to satisfy the spiritual or metaphysical requisitions of the [transcendentalists]." But despite his failure in popularity, M. de l'Aubépine "is voluminous; he continues to write and publish with as much praiseworthy and indefatigable prolixity, as if his efforts were crowned with the brilliant success that so justly attends those of Eugene Sue." A list of more than fourteen of his books is cited, including a three-volume "Le Voyage Céleste à Chemin de Fer" and a five-volume "L'Artiste du Beau, ou le Papillon Mécanique."

---

† From Nina Baym, *The Shape of Hawthorne's Career* (Ithaca, NY: Cornell University Press, 1976), 105–12. Copyright © 1976 by Cornell University. Used by permission of the publisher. This selection is from chapter 3, "The Manse Decade, 1840–1849." Baym prefers Hawthorne's long romances to his stories, and her argument here prepares the reader for what she calls his "major phase."

1. I.e., the sketches in *Mosses from an Old Manse* that are presented from the standpoint of the author [*Editor's note*].

How is one to take this facetious introduction? Obviously, its ironies refer to certain objective truths, touching on Hawthorne's dissatisfaction with the meagerness of both his audience and his output. But at the same time the analysis is just the sort of well-meaning but imperceptive commentary that a critic like Oliver Wendell Holmes or James Russell Lowell might impose on a romantic or visionary author. The split between Hawthorne the Manse persona and Aubépine the writer of fiction exposes the shortcomings of both, and makes especially clear the underlying discomfort that Hawthorne experienced with his Manse voice because of its inhospitality to fiction.

Aubépine, however, is not a perfect narrator for "Rappaccini's Daughter," for this is one of the richest stories in the canon, at once a visionary tale and a commentary on the visionary imagination, calling for a narrator firmly based in the camps of both the real and the ideal. The story may even be too rich, in the sense that it is susceptible of a number of partial explanations but seems to evade any single wholly satisfactory reading. It offers itself as an allegory of faith, an allegory of science, and an allegory of sex all at once. At first it proceeds along the familiar Hawthorne track. Young Giovanni is another obsessed protagonist who brings harm to himself and others by persisting in his delusion, which is that the beautiful Beatrice has been made poisonous, like a deadly plant, by her father's experiments and that she is poisoning him. This delusion is the product, we are made to think, of Giovanni's basically cynical and shallow mind. But at a certain point it becomes absolutely clear that Giovanni is not deluded; Beatrice really is poisonous. Still, the narrator continues to scold Giovanni, and the design of the plot exposes him as terribly in error, for his attempt to cure Beatrice has the effect of killing her.

This plot becomes less puzzling if the story is read as an allegory of faith. The question is not Giovanni's delusion but his belief. Had he believed in Beatrice, she would not have been poisonous. The statement that Hawthorne is making about faith is not merely that one must persist without evidence. It is far more extreme—one must persist in belief *despite* evidence. If this is one meaning of "Rappaccini's Daughter," then it is antithetical to the familiar Hawthorne story of visionary delusion, for it urges Giovanni to reject the corrective influence of his senses and hold instead to his intuitions. Although it is not likely that Hawthorne intended this story to refer to any particular doctrinal question, given his lack of interest in theological niceties, "Rappaccini's Daughter" is a story with which Christian critics have felt especially comfortable, because the kind of idealism it endorses is certainly compatible with orthodox belief.

If "Rappaccini's Daughter" makes an uncharacteristic defense of the visionary imagination, it appears to do so at the expense of science, the alternative world view. Rappaccini, Baglioni, and Giovanni are all nineteenth-century scientists of a sort, their approach to life determined by their premise that sensory evidence is real. But as a criticism of science the story comes full circle, for these scientists are not men of reason but visionary fanatics after all.[2] They are criticized not for their rationality but for their delusion that they are rational. They believe that they have detached their minds from their emotions, while all the time it is their emotions that determine their behavior: Giovanni is governed by his lust, Baglioni by his rivalry with Rappaccini, and Rappaccini by his wish to put his daughter beyond the reach of ordinary human experience.

The story is also an allegory of sex, and because writing about sex is so rare in Hawthorne's time this may be its most interesting aspect to a modern reader. It is evident in many ways that Beatrice's poison is her sexuality, particularly in the image of the deadly erotic flower with which she is identified. Her attraction for Giovanni is largely sexual, and he fears that attraction because it suggests that Beatrice has power over him. Thus, "poison" may be seen as a symbol for the power of sex. The interpretative dilemma is whether this sex is real and good or horrible but (fortunately) delusory. When Hawthorne writes that "all this ugly mystery was but an earthly illusion, and . . . whatever mist of evil might seem to have gathered over her, the real Beatrice was a heavenly angel," does he mean that in essence Beatrice was free of the "ugly mystery" of sex; or that properly seen, sex is not an ugly mystery? The question is not resolved, and rightly not, because Giovanni is a type of the sexually confused Victorian male, struggling between his wish to accept sex as a beneficent part of life and his strong conviction that it is unnatural and evil.

Given these multiple meanings, one must conclude that no persona Hawthorne had yet developed in his career was adequate to tell the tale. It would have been better presented unmediated by a narrative voice, like the earliest stories. In fact, however, it is heavy with authorial interpolation. One might suspect also that the short form was becoming a confinement, for although one may celebrate the richness and complexity of "Rappaccini's Daughter," one may also feel that its method represents a kind of shorthand notation for what by rights could have been a much longer, and correspondingly richer (even though perhaps less suggestive), work. There is a better fit in "Egotism; or, the Bosom Serpent" and "The Birth-mark" between teller and tale, largely because these are simpler fictions. They are both pure, undigressive stories about the obsessional imagination and lend themselves to unitary interpretations. "Egotism," which substitutes for a specific *idée fixe* the conventional notion of a serpent

---

2. M. D. Uroff has pointed out this lack of scientific objectivity in "The Doctors in 'Rappaccini's Daughter,'" *Nineteenth-Century Fiction*, 27 (1972), 61–70.

in the breast, is clearly an allegory, paradigmatic of all Hawthorne's other stories of estranged protagonists. In "Egotism," as in most of the stories of this type, the cure for the hero's disease rests in a loving woman who connects—or can connect, if he accepts her—the lonely male with the social order and gives him a chance to develop his own capacities for altruism and love. The figure of the woman is highly idealized.

In "The Birth-mark" Hawthorne examines more specifically than he had done before the sexual problems that underlie the protagonist's social alienation, as well as the sexual reasons for his inability to take the help offered by the woman. Critics have found adumbrations of the motif of rejection of the female in such stories as "Roger Malvin's Burial," "Young Goodman Brown," and "The Minister's Black Veil,"[3] but this is the first instance in which Hawthorne identifies the male obsession overtly with a revulsion against women and specifically with a revulsion against her physical nature. "Rappaccini's Daughter" was written almost two years after "The Birth-mark"; its treatment of the sexual theme is more ambiguous because the earlier story states simply that sex is good and that Aylmer's revulsion is perverse. His idealism is nothing more than a rationalized distaste for sexuality.

Another woman-hater is Owen Warland, the protagonist in "The Artist of the Beautiful." In this story the narrator and the narrative flatly contradict each other, demonstrating again the inadequacy of the Manse voice for fiction. When the narrator brings the tale to a close with the assurance that "when the artist rose high enough to achieve the Beautiful, the symbol by which he made it perceptible to mortal senses became of little value in his eyes, while his spirit possessed itself in the enjoyment of the Reality," he claims a dignity for Owen Warland that the story will not support. The conflict here is directly related to Hawthorne's own literary dilemma, for if Owen's audience is faulted for its indifference to his art, so is he faulted for devoting himself to the realization of ideas that have so little connection to the life around him.

Indeed, in scene after scene Hawthorne shows that Warland's impulse to attain the beautiful springs not from a desire to enrich life but from the need to escape it. To Danforth's strength, to Hovenden's acuity, even to Annie's warmth, he responds with fear. The ideal that takes shape is a mechanical miniature, exquisite to be sure, but lifeless and depthless: a fragile, cold bauble. In a literal sense, the miniature that he produces represents the belittling of imagination. The heart of this story lies neither in the pathetic situ-

---

3. Especially, of course, Frederick C. Crews in *The Sins of the Fathers* (New York: Oxford University Press, 1965).

ation of the unappreciated artist nor in his ultimate triumphant indifference to reputation. At the core of "The Artist of the Beautiful" is Hawthorne's recognition of how inadequate a figure Owen is for the vocation he has chosen, how timid and shrunken his conception of art. The narrative belies the narrator's claim for Owen's artistic stature and calls for another kind of artistry than his.

"Drowne's Wooden Image," the story Hawthorne wrote immediately before "The Artist of the Beautiful," proposes passion as the source of a truly great art. More than any other work of the Manse period, this story looks ahead to the long romances. Comfortably situated in a port town as a carver of ship's figureheads, Drowne is a mechanic and businessman rather than an artist. He turns out crude but serviceable figureheads in a prompt and efficient manner. He aspires to no artistic heights and has no conception of his medium—wood—as other than material. Is he lacking that sense of nonmaterial essence, that devotion to the exquisite, exemplified in Owen Warland? Perhaps, but Drowne's lack of spirituality is not his shortcoming as an artist; what he needs is a powerful emotion. When he falls in love with the beautiful woman he has been asked to represent in a figurehead, his art is transformed. Wood becomes an expressive form, fluid to his emotions as it never was to his tools. The completed figure is almost frighteningly real, exhibiting a skill far beyond Drowne's ordinary capabilities. Beauty combines with force, idea with material, purpose with craft. Such art needs no justification, is beyond apologies and manifestos. Such art convinces by its very existence; it does not so much please as conquer its audience.

Nothing before in Hawthorne's work resembles this concept of art and the artist. It shares little with the sensitive gentleman of *Twice-told Tales* or the cosmopolitan man of letters writing from the Old Manse. * * * It requires an exertion and dedication beyond anything that has been demanded of Hawthorne's author figures; it taxes the whole range of the artist's emotions and experience and channels his whole existence into the creation of his work. The artist lives at the intersection of his imaginative life and his work; no other considerations matter.

This is the idea against which Hawthorne is measuring Owen Warland; and in comparison to this idea he would also have to judge his own work thin and superficial. One can only speculate about the cumulative dissatisfactions that generated this sudden expression of romantic feeling. It seems a reaction to long years of working within an idea of authorship that failed to satisfy him. Hawthorne had curtailed his powers in order to please an imagined audience, and an audience had materialized; but the exchange was uneven. He had given up more than he had received. "Drowne's Wooden Image" points the way to a vision of art as a fully serious, absorbing enterprise, and to the artist as an independent person responsible only to his art and to himself. Of course, Drowne receives far greater recognition for this self-reflexive work than for all the obedient productions of his studio. This was to be precisely Hawthorne's experience in *The Scarlet Letter*. Unique among Hawthorne's writings at this time, "Drowne's Wooden Image" is not a proclamation or a declaration of independence, but it is an augur of the future.

* * *

LEO MARX

["Ethan Brand"]†

Hawthorne and Melville match the machine-in-the-garden motif to a darker view of life than Thoreau's. In their work, the design also conveys a sense of the widening gap between the facts and the ideals of American life, but the implications are more ominous. A nice illustration is Hawthorne's "Ethan Brand" (1850). * * * On the surface, at least, there is no indication that "Ethan Brand" embodies a significant response to the transformation of life associated with machine power. In fact, Hawthorne conceived of this fable as a variant of the Faust legend. Four years before writing it, in 1844, he had entered his *donnée* in his notebook. * * * "The search of an investigator for the Unpardonable Sin:—he at last finds it in his own heart and practice." And then, again, on the same page:

> The Unpardonable Sin might consist in a want of love and reverence for the Human Soul; in consequence of which, the investigator pried into its dark depths, not with a hope or purpose of making it better, but from a cold philosophical curiosity,— content that it should be wicked in what ever kind or degree, and only desiring to study it out. Would not this, in other words, be the separation of the intellect from the heart?[1]

† From Leo Marx, *The Machine in the Garden: Technology and the Pastoral Ideal in America* (New York: Oxford University Press, 1967), 265–77. Reprinted by permission of the *Massachusetts Review*. Drawing on a broad range of sources, Marx develops the thesis of his book, that Americans throughout their history have tended to imagine ideal pastoral spaces free of social conflict, where technology is either deliberately excluded or brought in as if it had no transforming effect. The impulse to idealize a trouble-free American nature, and to imagine that one can live an undisturbed life in it, Marx labels "sentimental pastoralism." Responsible artists, such as Thoreau, Melville, and Hawthorne, dramatized the intrusion of the machine in the garden and treated sentimental pastoralism ironically, even if they had their own complex pastoral ideas.
1. Hawthorne, *The American Notebooks*, ed. Randall Stewart, New Haven, 1932, p. 106.

The tale is set on a lonely hillside in the Berkshires. Bartram, a doltish lime-burner, is sitting with his son at nightfall watching his kiln. They hear a roar of laughter—a chilling, mirthless laugh— and it frightens the child. We learn that the kiln formerly had belonged to one Ethan Brand, who, after gazing too long into the fire, had become possessed. A monomaniacal compulsion to seize an absolute truth had taken hold of him, and he had conducted a world-wide search for the Unpardonable Sin. He now appears, and with his bitter, self-mocking laugh announces the successful completion of his quest. He has found the worst of all sins in his own heart. An ironic circularity invests Brand's fate. Not only has he sought throughout the world for what was closest to himself, but, as it turns out, the Unpardonable Sin resides in the very principle for which he undertook the quest: the desire for knowledge as an end in itself.

At his father's behest, meanwhile, the boy has gone off to tell the "jolly fellows" in the tavern of Brand's return. Soon a whole shift-less regiment of drunks and derelicts appears on the mountain. Several of these worthies greet Brand and earnestly invite him to share their bottle, but he coldly rejects them. A series of minor incidents (a dog madly chasing its tail, as in *Faust*) underscores the tragic irony of Brand's life. After the crowd leaves and Bartram and his son have gone off to sleep, Brand sits alone beside the kiln review-ing his melancholy career. The compulsive quest has been a "suc-cess" in more than one sense. Not only has he found what he was seeking, but the search had been a means of education: Brand has become a world-renowned scholar. But he also recognizes that he has been transformed in the process. Once a simple man, capable of tenderness and pity, he is now an unfeeling, monomaniacal "fiend" who has lost his hold upon "the magnetic chain of humanity." With a cry of despair he throws himself into the fire. The next morning Bar-tram and his boy awake to a magnificent dawn. * * * The mood of anxiety and gloom has been dispelled. As the boy suggests, the very sky and mountains seem to be rejoicing in Brand's disappearance. In the kiln they find his skeleton, converted into lime, though the shape of a human heart (was it made of marble?) remains visible between the ribs.

Taken by itself, the fable reveals no link between Brand's fate and Hawthorne's attitude toward industrialization. On the other hand, certain facts about the genesis of the story are suggestive. For many of the details, especially the setting and the portraits of several minor characters, Hawthorne drew upon notes he had made during a vacation journey in the Berkshires in 1838.[2] At that time a small-

---

2. For a selection from Hawthorne's Berkshire notebooks, see p. 344, in this volume [*Edi-tor's note*].

scale industrial revolution was under way in the area. Textile production was increasing at a rapid rate, and near North Adams
Hawthorne's stage-coach passed several new factories, ". . . the
machinery whizzing, and girls looking out of the windows. . . ."
Apparently fascinated by the sight, he took elaborate notes:

> There are several factories in different parts of North-Adams,
> along the banks of a stream, a wild highland rivulet, which,
> however, does vast work of a civilized nature. It is strange to see
> such a rough and untamed stream as it looks to be, so tamed
> down to the purposes of man, and making cottons, woolens
> &c—sawing boards, marbles, and giving employment to so
> many men and girls; and there is a sort of picturesqueness in
> finding these factories, supremely artificial establishments, in
> the midst of such wild scenery. For now the stream will be flow-
> ing through a rude forest, with the trees erect and dark, as when
> the Indians fished there; and it brawls, and tumbles, and eddies,
> over its rock-strewn current. Perhaps there is a precipice hun-
> dreds of feet high, beside it, down which, by heavy rains or the
> melting of snows, great pine-trees have slid or tumbled headlong,
> and lie at the bottom or half-way down; while their brethren
> seem to be gazing at their fall from the summit, and anticipating
> a like fate. And taking a turn in the road, behold these factories
> and their range of boarding-houses, with the girls looking out of
> the window as aforesaid. And perhaps the wild scenery is all
> around the very site of the factory, and mingles its impression
> strangely with those opposite ones.[3]

The scene impresses Hawthorne with the sudden, violent character of change. In a single stroke a rude forest is being supplanted by
"supremely artificial establishments," and all of nature seems poised,
like the majestic pines, at the abyss. * * * Hawthorne traveled in the
area for several days, and his observations, random sketches of places
and people (including several "remarkable characters" who reappear
in "Ethan Brand"), convey his sense of unreality and disorientation.
One of the most revealing is this idea for a story:

> A steam engine in a factory to be supposed to possess a malig-
> nant spirit; it catches one man's arm, and pulls it off; seizes
> another by the coat-tails, and almost grapples him bodily;—
> catches a girl by the hair, and scalps her;—and finally draws a
> man, and crushes him to death.[4]

So far as we know, Hawthorne never developed this idea. And when
he mined his Berkshire notes for "Ethan Brand," some ten years later,

3. *American Notebooks*, pp. 34–35.
4. *American Notebooks*, p. 42.

he passed over most of the economic and social data he had recorded. The factories do not appear in the story. Nor does it contain any explicit reference to the changing conditions of life—to industrialization. And yet there are more important ways in which the presence of the "machine" makes itself felt in the tale.

A sense of loss, anxiety, and dislocation overshadows the world of "Ethan Brand." Initially, Hawthorne invests this feeling in his account of the lonesome lives of lime-burners and of the desolate, Gothic landscape. We are told that many of the kilns in this tract of country have been "long deserted," and that the wild flowers growing in the chinks make them look like "relics of antiquity."[5] A similar air of obsolescence clings to the villagers who climb the hillside to see Brand. All three selected for special mention are broken, unfulfilled men. One, formerly a successful doctor with a rare gift of healing, has become an alcoholic; another, "a wilted and smoke-dried man," representative of a vocation "once ubiquitous . . . now almost extinct," is the stage-agent; and a third, who also has known better days, is a lawyer who has come to be "but the fragment of a human being, a part of one foot having been chopped off by an axe, and an entire hand torn away by the devilish grip of a steam-engine." All of these people, along with a Wandering Jew and a forlorn old man searching for his lost daughter, are victims of change. Like the monomaniac Brand, whose "bleak and terrible loneliness" the young boy recognizes, each in his way is a maimed, alienated man. The center of the story is Brand's "cold philosophical curiosity," a disorder which finally results in a fatal "separation of the intellect from the heart."

But what is the cause of Brand's alienation? Of the two explanations Hawthorne provides, the first is mythic. According to local legend, Brand's intellectual obsession emanated from the fire. We learn that he "had been accustomed to evoke a fiend from the hot furnace of the limekiln," and that together they spent many nights evolving the idea of the quest. But the fiend, who may have been Satan himself, always retreated through the "iron door" of the furnace at the first glimmer of sunlight. Hawthorne manifestly borrows this image of fire, and the conventional contrast between fire

5. Ethan's kiln, later called a "furnace," is a link in a chain of virtually free association. It connects Hawthorne's response to the factories with his feelings about science and, more specifically, the revolutionary steam technology of the age. That the association transcends ordinary common-sense perception is indicated, for one thing, by the fact that the actual mills he saw near North Adams were operated by water—not steam—power. For another, the kilns in the tale serve as a curiously blended token of advancing technology and a mode of production rendered obsolete by that advance. The process of combining opposite meanings in a single image is akin to the "condensation" Freud discovers in dream symbols. The technological symbolism of "Ethan Brand" foreshadows the extraordinary fusion, in the whaling lore of *Moby-Dick*, of the most primitive hunting methods with advanced technical skills.

and sun, from the literary tradition he knows best. The opposition between Satanic fire and life-giving sun, light of divine truth and righteousness, is a recurrent device in the work of Dante, Spenser, Milton, and Bunyan. The association of fire with technology, which goes back to Prometheus and Vulcan, also forms a part of the Christian myth. Before the fall, according to Milton, there was no need of technology. The garden contained only such tools "as art yet rude, / Guiltless of fire had formed." After the expulsion, however, Adam and Eve were grateful for the gift of fire.[6]

But if the contrast between fire and sun was conventional, it also was particularly meaningful to an age that called itself the "Age of Steam." * * * And it can be shown that Hawthorne uses the same images, words, and phrases to describe the fire in "Ethan Brand" that he uses elsewhere for direct reference to industrialization. A whole cluster of images surrounding the word "iron," including "fire," "smoke," "furnace," and "forge," serves to blend his feelings about his own age with the culture's dominant religious and literary tradition. As the Berkshire notes suggest, moreover, the introduction of industrial power in the American setting imparts a peculiar intensity to the dialectic of art versus nature. In this case the fire-sun antithesis provides the symbolic frame for the entire story: "Ethan Brand" begins at sundown and ends at dawn. During the long night the action centers upon the kiln, or "furnace," which replaces the sun as the origin of warmth, light, and (indirectly) sustenance. The fire imagery aligns Ethan's fate simultaneously with the Christian doctrine of sin and with the scientific-industrial revolution. Only when the fire has been extinguished does Hawthorne introduce a vision of the garden.

That fire is a surrogate for the "machine" * * * becomes more apparent as the story nears its climax. In describing Ethan's reflections while he sits alone beside the kiln, Hawthorne supplies a second (historical) explanation for his fall. This version makes the protagonist an embodiment of a changing America. It recalls the view of history put forward by Jefferson when, speaking of the War of 1812, he had awarded the British enemy the "consolation of Satan" for helping to transform a peaceable, agricultural nation into a military and manufacturing one. Now Ethan Brand (an archetypal Yankee name joined to an image of burning and infamy) sees it all clearly. Once, when "the dark forest had whispered to him," he had been "a simple and loving man." He had felt tenderness and sympathy for mankind. But then—here is the point, presumably, when the fiend had emerged from the fire—he had begun, with the highest humanitarian motives, "to contemplate those ideas which afterwards

6. *Paradise Lost*, IX, 391–92 and X, 1060–93.

became the inspiration of his life." In this telling Hawthorne aban-
dons the language of myth. Alluding to neither fiend nor fire, he now
attributes Ethan's obsession to a "vast intellectual development,
which . . . disturbed the counterpoise between his mind and heart."
With the weakening of his moral nature he had become "a cold
observer, looking on mankind as the subject of his experiment." In
other words, Ethan is at once an agent and a victim of scientific
empiricism or "mechanism." * * * The Unpardonable Sin is the great
sin of the Enlightenment—the idea of knowledge as an end in itself.
Now he recognizes the destructiveness of the idea. Lonely, desperate, alienated from nature and mankind, he plunges to his death in
the kiln.

During the night the fire goes out, and this is the scene when
Bartram and his son arise at daybreak:

> The early sunshine was already pouring its gold upon the
> mountain-tops, and though the valleys were still in shadow, they
> smiled cheerfully in the promise of the bright day that was has-
> tening onward. The village, completely shut in by hills, which
> swelled away gently about it, looked as if it had rested peace-
> fully in the hollow of the great hand of Providence. Every dwell-
> ing was distinctly visible; the little spires of the two churches
> pointed upwards, and caught a fore-glimmering of brightness
> from the sun-gilt skies upon their gilded weather-cocks. The
> tavern was astir, and the figure of the old, smoke-dried stage-
> agent, cigar in mouth, was seen beneath the stoop. Old Gray-
> lock was glorified with a golden cloud upon his head. Scattered
> likewise over the breasts of the surrounding mountains, there
> were heaps of hoary mist, in fantastic shapes, some of them far
> down into the valley, others high up towards the summits, and
> still others, of the same family of mist or cloud, hovering in the
> gold radiance of the upper atmosphere. Stepping from one to
> another of the clouds that rested on the hills, and thence to the
> loftier brotherhood that sailed in air, it seemed almost as if a
> mortal man might thus ascend into the heavenly regions. Earth
> was so mingled with sky that it was a day-dream to look at it.
>   To supply that charm of the familiar and homely, which
> Nature so readily adopts into a scene like this, the stage-coach
> was rattling down the mountain-road, and the driver sounded
> his horn, while Echo caught up the notes, and intertwined
> them into a rich and varied and elaborate harmony, of which
> the original performer could lay claim to little share. The great
> hills played a concert among themselves, each contributing a
> strain of airy sweetness.

The immediate effect of this radiant prospect is to heighten the
sense of evil surrounding Ethan Brand and his quest. It all too abun-

dantly represents the American Eden from which he has fallen. * * *
Instead of fire and smoke, there is perfect sunlit visibility; instead of
anxiety and gloom, the countryside is invested with order, peace, and
permanence, and the image of a stepladder into the heavens projects
the harmony between man and nature beyond nature. No traces of
the "machine" remain. Having referred to the imminent disappearance of the stagecoach, Hawthorne now restores that picturesque
vehicle to its proper place in the New England landscape. Like the
coming of spring at the end of *Walden*, this eighteenth-century tableau figures a "realization of the Golden Age." With the elimination
of Ethan Brand and everything that he represents, Hawthorne
seems to be saying, the pastoral ideal has been realized.

But it is apparent that the perceptive reader is not expected to take
this grand picture of the morning sun "pouring its gold" upon the
land entirely at face value. For a moment, to be sure, Hawthorne may
seem to be inviting the obvious response. But the florid, unabashedly
trite language should make us wary. What Melville said of other
aspects of Hawthorne's stories may be applied to his narrative voice:
it seems to have been "directly calculated to deceive—egregiously
deceive—the superficial skimmer of pages." One has only to sample
the fiction in contemporary magazines, especially the ladies books
for which he often wrote, to see how perfectly Hawthorne has caught
the sickly sweet, credulous tone of sentimental pastoralism. In fact,
he has assembled a splendid exhibit of bucolic clichés. They are all
here, the gold laid on thick, the hills swelling gently, the heaps of
hoary mist on breasts of mountains, the charms that "Nature . . .
adopts into a scene like this"—"it was a day-dream to look at it"—
and, dominating the whole glorious panorama, the rich, varied, elaborate harmony of Echo. Removed from its dramatic context this set
piece reads like parody: "The great hills played a concert among
themselves, each contributing a strain of airy sweetness."[7]

But what, then, is the relation between the subtle meretricious-
ness of the pastoral moment and the suicide of Ethan Brand? That
Hawthorne means the juxtaposition to be ironic is evident. On the
basis of the tale alone, however, it is difficult to know what the irony
signifies. Perhaps because the author himself was uncertain, or
because he wanted it to work both ways, the ending is unusually
muted. For that matter the entire story gives an impression of con-
stricted thought. Of all Hawthorne's well-known stories, "Ethan
Brand" is the least polished: the action is spasmodic; the texture
jagged; the irony severely understated; the conclusion elliptical. In

---

7. For a discussion of the cultural climate evoked by Hawthorne's sentimental pastoralism,
see E. Douglas Branch, *The Sentimental Years, 1836–1860*, New York, 1934, and Herbert R. Brown, *The Sentimental Novel in America, 1789–1860*, Durham, N.C., 1940.

places one can see where passages from the notebooks have been imperfectly joined. Yet the story is crammed with unrealized power— fairly bursting with it, like the synopsis of a Wagnerian libretto. Perhaps this is because it was written at a turning point in Hawthorne's career, when he was about to shift from the short story to the novel-length romance. In fact, there are good reasons for thinking that it was intended as a longer work. (He gave it the subtitle, "A Chapter from an Abortive Romance.") At any rate, the constrained, fettered manner reflects Hawthorne's state of mind at the time. In 1848, apparently referring to "Ethan Brand," he told a New York editor: "At last, by main strength, I have wrenched and torn an idea out of my miserable brain; or rather, the fragment of an idea, like a tooth ill-drawn, and leaving the roots to torture me."[8]

The meaning of Hawthorne's complex version of pastoral is to be found among the torn roots of his ideas. In writing "Ethan Brand," he had left behind the manifestly topical content of his 1838 Berkshire notes, but he had transferred certain ideas and emotions once attached to that material to other themes and images. Although the striking sight of factories in the wilderness does not appear in the tale, Hawthorne's feelings about it do. Ethan is destroyed by the fires of change associated with factories, and nothing confirms this fact as forcibly as the meretricious idyllic vision that follows his death. Having observed the illusoriness of the middle landscape ideal in reality (the wilderness is to be supplanted by factories, not gardens), Hawthorne now accomplishes its restoration in fiction. Needless to say, the restoration is ironic. As the hollow rhetoric indicates, this stock eighteenth-century tableau serves as an oblique comment upon the fate of the Yankee hero. It says that the dream of pastoral harmony will be easy to realize as soon as the Faustian drive of mankind—the Brand element—has been extirpated. Nor is the perfervid idiom of sentimental pastoralism the only clue to the irony. It is reinforced by such details as the histrionic stagecoach, a vehicle supplied, absurdly enough, by "Nature." To fulfill the pastoral hope, in other words, nothing less is required than a reversal of history. "Ethan Brand" conveys Hawthorne's inchoate sense of the doom awaiting the self-contained village culture, not the institutions alone, but the whole quasi-religious ideology that rests, finally, upon the hope that Americans will subordinate their burning desire for knowledge, wealth, and power to the pursuit of rural happiness. Hence the pretty picture that accompanies Ethan's death. "The village, completely shut in by hills, which swelled away gently about it,

---

8. From a letter to Charles W. Webber, December 14, 1848. Webber had invited Hawthorne to contribute to his projected magazine, *The American Review*. See Hawthorne, *The Letters, 1843–1853*, CE 16:251–52 [*Editor's note*].

looked as if it had rested peacefully in the hollow of the great hand of Providence."

MARTIN BIDNEY

Fire, Flutter, Fall, and Scatter: A Structure in the Epiphanies of Hawthorne's Tales[†]

Lyrical epiphanies are typically the creative center, the imaginative climax, of Nathaniel Hawthorne's tales. But although his imagery has been clarified in various ways, no one has yet attempted to define a pattern that can unite Hawthorne's focal visionary moments and show its implications.[1] Hawthorne's epiphany pattern shows a form and dynamism of experience deeply rooted in this prose poet's psyche. My method of analysis, a systematized, supplemented refashioning of Gaston Bachelard's phenomenology of elemental reverie (to be explained shortly), focuses on the form of the epiphanic experience as given in the texts of the tales. That formal structure, though richly varied, can be summed up as a cluster of four image-motifs; fire, flutter, fall, and scatter. It is a "descendental" moment of passionate, though always ambivalent, fullness yielding to sudden disintegration.

With an inevitability suggesting unconscious origins, this vivid pattern of oneiric force repeatedly overwhelms, first with joy and then with disillusionment, Hawthorne's habitual, conscious concern with subtle moral distinctions. A Hawthorne epiphany, involving a scenario of startling and rapid collapse, brings in the motif cluster with a dreamlike insistence; the image pattern can arise apropos of nearly anything, and it may be seen by anyone, regardless of supposed moral standing. The narrator-persona may experience it, or else a major or minor character or a group or crowd. Mad scientist or guileless merrymaker, devoted craftsman or Faustian criminal— ministering maiden, ambitious youth, royalist or rebel—any perceiver or imaginer may see, undergo, or precipitate the fall and scattering. * * * The epiphanic descents and dispersals vary in mood

---

[†] From *Texas Studies in Literature and Language* 50 (2008): 58–89. Copyright © 2008 by the University of Texas Press. All rights reserved. I have abridged the essay and especially the notes, while seeking to maintain the tenor and complexity of Bidney's thinking— *Editor.*

1. I have not found the word "epiphany" or its variants in the title of any study of the short stories published in the last forty years, Richard Harter Fogle pioneered systematic image study in *Hawthorne's Fiction: The Light and the Dark* (Norman: University of Oklahoma Press, 1952) but limits his symbolic readings to a "broadly Christian scheme which contains heaven, earth, and hell" (p. 5).

and meaning—tragic or tragicomic, madly triumphant, whimsical, absurd, nightmarish, retributive—but all feel as fateful and unexplainable as being in a dream. An epiphany of Hawthornean hallucinatory power resembles a waking dream, arising as by dream logic. The epiphanic motif cluster is a pattern that morphs, as in the dream realm of Morpheus, from character to group to narrator within the body, or corpus, of the tales.

A dream-rooted motif pattern which, as I hope to show, can give an often hallucinatory intensity to a striking abundance of short story epiphanies must be regarded as rooted in Hawthorne's most intimate self, more intimate than his copious and complex moral pronouncements, ranging from the charmingly casual to the serious or somber. In his landmark essay, "Our Hawthorne," Lionel Trilling contrasted Henry James's portrayal of Hawthorne as playing with moral notions in a spirit of graceful artistic freedom to what Trilling considered the more modern view of Hawthorne as darkly Kafkaesque, an evoker of subliminal chthonic depths where no morality reigns. Trilling finds some truth in both of these differing appraisals. But I would also underline a similarity implicit in Trilling's description of his "James" and "Kafka" Hawthornes: they share an indifference to moral questions considered for their own sake.[2] My study will suggest that the yielding of discursive moral allegory to fateful oneiric epiphany is a large-scale phenomenon: only by a wide-ranging portrayal of Hawthorne's epiphanic achievement can one sense how pervasively the obsessional visionary pattern appears to sweep aside, to overwhelm, his delicately balanced moralizing (often equivocal, but sometimes more sharply defined: we are to sympathize with birth-marked Georgiana, to deplore Ethan Brand). My exhibits will show that these oneiric epiphanies, with their independently vivid, unconsciously rooted power, are in themselves wholly amoral, something that fatefully happens alike to the just and the unjust, the thoughtful and the heedless, or simply to the chance

2. Trilling notes that the darkness of Kafkan sensibility had not yet saturated our thinking deeply enough to motivate either Austin Warren (1938) or Newton Arvin (1946) to regard the darkly enigmatic "My Kinsman, Major Molineux" as worth including in their selected editions of Hawthorne. But just as, in a Kafka novel, the characters' "spiritual life" has "no discernible connection with morality," so likewise: "It is questions that Hawthorne leaves us with. It is, really, not at all clear why Young Goodman Brown must live out his life in sullenness because he refuses to sign the Devil's pact; nor is it clear why Robin must join the violent mob in laughter at his kinsman before he is his own master, and indeed it is not clear why being his own master is a wholly admirable condition." Thus, Hawthorne "takes somber moral principles and makes them into toys—we have but to give to the idea of play the consideration it deserves to see that Henry James's description of his activity is not so deficient in justice as it seems." A whimsically or willfully riddling refusal to reach a "moral" despite often (bluntly or subtly) misleading allegorical talk is, for Trilling, what relates Hawthorne most convincingly to James's analysis and Kafka's practice; see Lionel Trilling, "Our Hawthorne," *Hawthorne Centenary Essays*, ed. Roy Harvey Pearce (Columbus: Ohio State University Press, 1964), pp. 443, 450, 456–57.

observer. And if it can be suggested, through a sufficiently broad and evocative survey, that Hawthorne in his best tales is—perhaps primarily—an epiphanist of intense power, we may well need to shift our sense of his most "intimate" poetic priorities.

The method of analysis to be used here is an amplified and systematized remaking of Gaston Bachelard's phenomenology of elemental reverie, as worked out in my *Patterns of Epiphany* (1997) and subsequent studies.[3] Bachelard's "reveries" are, in this view, equatable to anglophone critics' "epiphanies," and his emphasis on elements (earth, water, air, and fire) in such revelatory moments is equally central to my approach here. My method, like Bachelard's, is phenomenological literary criticism, focused on structures of experience perceived by the reader of the literary work. But unlike Bachelard, whose analyses tend to characterize groups of writers in an attempt to establish types of shared responses to a given natural element, I focus always on the individual author, seeking to establish features that will distinguish his or her recurrent epiphany pattern from that of any other writer. This is important because one can view the distinctive epiphany pattern of an author as that person's unique and irreplaceable contribution to the legacy of human epiphanic perception.

I define an epiphany from two standpoints: subjective and objective. Considered subjectively, it is a literarily represented moment that the reader feels to be emotionally intense, mysterious (not rationally accountable), and expansive (meaning more than such a brief moment would seem to warrant). Such an epiphany may be described by a character directly or in free indirect discourse, or by a lyric poet or dramatist in any sort of literarily constructed voice. I have suggested that epiphany patterns have unconscious roots, but as presented in literary works they are, in varying degrees, processed consciously by the writer, and what I analyze is the epiphany as perceived by the attentive reader of the text. Part of the origin of the writerly experience perceived by the reader may be unconscious and thus powerfully dreamlike, but conscious processing alters and recrafts the material in all kinds of secondary elaborations and evolving variants—with

---

3. See my *Patterns of Epiphany: From Wordsworth to Tolstoy, Pater, and Barrett Browning* (Carbondale: Southern Illinois University Press, 1997), pp. 1–21, for methodological theory treated in a context of Morris Beja, Robert Langbaum, Ashton Nichols, and, in particular, Bachelard. See also my "Failed Verticals, Failed Horizontals, Unreachable Circles of Light: Philip Larkin's Epiphanies," *Moment of Moment: Aspects of the Literary Epiphany*, ed. Wim Tigges (Amsterdam and Atlanta: Rodopi Press, 1999), pp. 353–74; "The Aestheticist Epiphanies of J. D. Salinger: Bright Hued Circles, Spheres, and Patches; 'Elemental' Joy and Pain," *Style* 34 (2000), 117–31; "'Controlled Panic': Mastering the Terrors of Dissolution and Isolation in Elizabeth Bishop's Epiphanies," *Style* 34 (2000), 487–511; "The Secretive-Playful Epiphanies of Robert Frost: Solitude, Companionship, and the Ambivalent Imagination," *Papers on Language and Literature* 53 (2002), 270–94; [and other works].

suppressions and amplifications, too. We never get dream content "raw." Conscious or semiconscious attitudes reshape the presentation of epiphanic materials in an endless variety of moods—satiric, sardonic, parodistic, elegiac, nostalgic, tragicomic.

* * *

The locating of a "paradigm" epiphany for a writer is an especially valuable methodological step, for if we can find an epiphany that clearly manifests the maximum richness of recurrent features, we can then more easily spot less complete variants of the pattern.

In Hawthorne's epiphanies, intimately interrelated motion patterns are central to the structure of fire, flutter, fall, and scatter. Though there is no "required" temporal ordering, the first two components mentioned are somewhat likelier to come early than the last two. We see many forms of fire-related light: glowing, flush, blazing, sparkling, flashing, glittering, shining, radiance. Closely bound up with this, simultaneous or quickly following it, is a fitfulness, fluttering, flitting, quivering, tremor or trembling, shivering, tottering, shuddering. The important component of a fall leads to, or itself involves, a dispersal, sprinkling, scattering, shattering, tattering, fragmenting, crumbling, melting, or corrosion into, or sweeping away of, a multitude of dead or sundered objects. Because Hawthornean descendental motion frequently involves a transformation through two or more elements, they are intimately bound up with the motion. The upper glow is often fiery, the fluttering aery, and the fall and scattering windy, watery, or earthy, while the objects scattered may be related to water or earth.

* * *

The high object that, glows or flashes may be a fire: burning tree, torch, bonfire. Or it may be rounded: face, flower, heart. A color related to hearts, flowers, flushed faces, and flames is red, along with its compounds: pink, purple, orange. (Golden, silver, and white light relate to sun, moon, and stars.) The flashing or redly glowing object may be angular or squarish: flaming pyramid, flag or banner, handkerchief, or a rocky elevation with burning trees at its four comers. Fiery gems and jewels are prominent. An aery thing that flutters may be a feather or veil, or the spirit of May. Fire, too, trembles or quivers in fitful flickerings. Flashing may combine with fluttering (in a butterfly). A human body may shudder; body parts and expressions may quiver or tremble—a heart or a breath; an eyelid or a smile. A mountain may quake before an avalanche; an insect flits, with shivering wings.

     * * * [A] prominent epiphanic shape is that of the recurring smile, a mild upward curve of the lip-line contrasting to all the downward motions. Sometimes the smile is varied as laughter. * * * An impulse to smiling self-parody often mitigates potential tragedy in Hawthornean epiphanic presentations.

* * *

I

The "banner-staff" epiphany in "The May-Pole of Merry Mount" is the best orienting paradigm for Hawthorne's epiphanic achievement. Here we have not only the four most notable motion-centered components but also the fully developed supplementary features of hearts, flowers, faces, ribbons, and the glorious maypole itself. The descendental epiphany is more than a personal loss, it is a cultural one; in fact, nature herself appears darkened by the substitution of Puritan Endicott's whipping post for the colorfully glowing maypole, so that by story's end we no longer view the natural brightness of "May, or her mirthful spirit" as she had fluttered or "flitted, with a dreamlike smile" (9: 54)[4]—the epiphanic tremor and the epiphanic smile. The "venerated emblem" or maypole is a "pine tree" from whose top "streamed a silken banner, colored like the rainbow," and decorated all over with "ribbons" and with the "flowery splendor" of a "Golden Age" (9: 55). Abundant are the heart- and sun-colors of red, purple, and gold: the May queen and her betrothed, "the two airiest forms" ever found in a solider place than a "purple and golden cloud"—he with a "gilded staff," both of them with bright "roses" that "glowed" in their hair—felt the beginning of a descendental epiphany when "[n]o sooner had their hearts glowed with real passion" than "down came a little shower of withering rose leaves from the May-Pole" (9: 56–58). The glowing banner-staff is linked to flames and flowers—to "bonfires" and "garlands" thrown "into the flame" on St. John's Eve, to summer "roses of the deepest blush," to the "red and yellow gorgeousness" of autumn, to the "cold sunshine" of winter (9: 60). Yet all this multifarious heart-fire, rosy redness, solar and floral radiance must fall and be dispersed as Endicott assaults the maypole with his paternal sword:

> It groaned with a dismal sound; it showered leaves and rose-buds upon the remorseless enthusiast, and finally, with all its green boughs, and ribbons, and flowers, symbolic of departed pleasures, down fell the banner-staff of Merry Mount. As it sank, tradition says, the evening sky grew darker, and the woods threw forth a more sombre shadow. (9: 63)

---

4. All citations (volume and page numbers in parentheses) refer to *The Centenary Edition of the Works of Nathaniel Hawthorne*, ed. William Charvat and others (Columbus: Ohio State University Press, 1962–94).

As the "glow" of the youthful pair is "chastened" while the maypole falls and the sun of the revelry sets, Endicott, who "smile[s]" (a faint echo of the epiphany-theme, for admittedly he "almost sighed"), decrees that the "youth's hair be cut" (9: 66), a final castratory scattering (as if maypole severing weren't enough) to serve as coda to the epiphanic dispersal of killed-off joys. Yet Hawthorne will not let us rest with the simple notion of a fall from Eden, or a banishment from the Tree of Life. Instead, he shadows the maypole with ambivalence. The Lord and Lady of the May were actually being married by the festival's English priest, who by the "riot of his rolling eye, and the pagan decorations of his holy garb," seemed "the wildest monster there, and the very Comus" of the "crew" of revelers in animal disguises—"some already transformed to brutes, some midway between man and beast, and the others rioting in the flow of tipsey jollity that foreran the change" (9: 56–57). If the Golden Age banner-staff implies polymorphous (or theriomorphic) perversity, it is in some sense fated to be outgrown.[5]

"Rappaccini's Daughter," a tale of the fire-fall epiphany of innocent Beatrice, daughter of a crazed, blamable experimenter, is comparably, baroquely rich in Hawthornean epiphanic motifs. The fiery flower theme comes back from "May-Pole," and a fatal descent of the poisonous vapors the mad scientist has infused into that flower-source varies the epiphany theme of scattered flame. Right at the start, the "ruin" of a "wofully shattered" marble fountain in Beatrice Rappaccini's garden sounds the theme of fall and scattering. Her suitor Giovanni hearing her voice, thinks of "deep hues of purple or crimson (10: 94–97), for he sees the woman as herself a blood-hued heart-flower, "the human sister of those vegetable ones"; "[f]lower and maiden" are "fraught with some strange peril in either shape" (10: 97–98). Giovanni may be charged with arbitrarily linking Beatrice to the demonism that a clearer moral thinker would ascribe to her father alone, but his epiphanic rhetoric lends a pervasively ominous mood to his perceptions. The Gothic atmosphere accents the Hawthornean ambivalence of enchanting-portentous fires and flowers.

As Giovanni sees her "glistening" ringlets "intermingled" with the "gemlike flowers" of a shrub, and as Beatrice places a gem-bloom

5. During the time of his Freudian allegiance Frederick C. Crews, in a formulation still worth considering, described the plot of this tale as "profoundly typical of Hawthorne's plots throughout his career: inadmissible fantasies are unleashed in an inhibited, decadent form and then further checked by a resurgence of authority"; see his Sins of the Fathers: Hawthorne's Psychological Themes (New York: Oxford University Press, 1966), p. 25. Though the formulation may not do full justice to the visionary appeal of the passionate-maternal flushed faces and fiery flowers, there is nonetheless real merit to Crews's idea. I have sought to amplify it above by supplementing the Freudian censored id with the Lacanian unrecapturable Imaginary.

"beside" her "heart," beautifully building up the epiphanic theme cluster of gem-glow-heart-flower, the crucial descent-to-a-sprinkling occurs in three stages. First, a "small orange-colored" reptile passes by, and "a drop or two of moisture from the broken stem of the flower descend[s] upon the lizard's head"; "contorted," the creature dies (10: 102–03). Next, as the epiphany gathers force and the fluttering or tremor-theme is added, we behold the death of a "beautiful insect" which "lingered in the air" and "fluttered about her head" until "its bright wings shivered" (10: 103). As the epiphany culminates, the final stage of fluttering-and-scattering occurs: a "swarm of insects," seen "flitting" in the "fatal" garden, "circled round Giovanni's head": he "sent forth a breath among them, and *smiled bitterly* at Beatrice as at least a score of the insects fell dead upon the ground" (10: 125; emphasis added). Beatrice now knows the full capacity of her "father's fatal science" (10: 128) to transmit from purple-red, heart-hued gem-flowers to humans the power to scatter death. Remarkably, the recurrent Hawthornean epiphanic smile can still appear on her crazed father's face as the insects die. Sensual hues and objects of passionate beauty have diffused multiple deaths. Beatrice, too, dies, for her suitor's medicinal antidote is fatal to one contaminated with its antibody ("as poison had been life, so the powerful antidote was death" [10: 127–28]). The victim, not the fanatical "scientist" perpetrator, dies in this amoral scenario.

In the highly ambivalent epiphany of "The Birth Mark," a mad scientist tale like "Rappaccini's Daughter," guileless Georgiana's handlike facial mark is a glowing, flower-hued heart-fire resulting in horrible falls and fragmentations. Like Beatrice, Georgiana will suffer death by a mad male's hubristic science, a favorite Hawthornean plot-scheme for generating amoral epiphanies of retribution sadly visited upon victims. The mark is a "token of the magic endowments" that gave Georgiana "sway over all hearts," and whenever she blushed the mark gradually "vanished amid the triumphant rush of blood that bathed the whole cheek with its brilliant glow" (10: 37–38). But to her crazed husband's eyes, rather than glowing the ruddy radiance seemed "flickering" by the wood-fire; in a still more dreadful variant of the epiphanic fluttering or shivering motif, he even looks at the brilliant blood-glow with a "convulsive shudder" (10: 39, 44). Aylmer's curative treatment of his wife's flaw makes her fatal touch, "as by the agency of fire," disintegrate a flower with a "blight" that turns it "coal-black." Next he takes her "portrait" by "rays of light striking upon a polished plate of metal"; horrified to see a hand replace the cheek in the picture, Aylmer "snatched the metallic plate and threw it into a jar of corrosive acid" (10: 45), disintegrating her shining face as he had made her touch corrode flowers. Corrosive disintegration is an exceptionally malign and horrid form of Hawthornean

fragmenting and dispersal. In the epiphanic climax of elixir drinking, as Georgiana's senses are "closing over" her "spirit" like "leaves
around the heart of a rose at sunset" (dazzling but falling heart-
flower-fire!), Aylmer watches the glow change to a threefold flutter: "a
slight irregularity of breath, a quiver of the eyelid, a hardly perceptible tremor through the frame" (10: 54). A "faint smile flit[s] over her
lips" as she dies, and the "disastrous brilliancy" of the birthmark's
"blaze" (10: 55) perishes as Aylmer's helper laughs. The epiphanic
smile is ironic, the epiphanic laugh demonic. Georgiana's special
beauty was her disfiguration; it was as fiery as the crazed cure.
Ambivalence was there from the beginning, and it is intensified in
the tragic end.

The protagonist in "The Artist of the Beautiful" is not so Gothi-
cally possessed as Aylmer, yet his idealized firebright epiphany
embodies the source of its own destruction, his self-centered idealism. The mechanical butterfly created by a rather childlike, self-
absorbed seeker of the Ideal, a fluttering, incandescent apparition to
be scattered to sparkling fragments in the central epiphany, begins
as a gemlike flame: "firelight glimmered around this wonder—the
candles gleamed upon it, but it glistened apparently by its own radiance, and illuminated" the hand where it rested "with a white gleam
like that of precious stones" (10: 470). In the climax, the glowing
gemlike fire-creature trembles before its doom-descent:

> With a wavering movement, and emitting a tremulous radiance,
> the butterfly struggled, as it were, towards the infant, and was
> about to alight upon his finger; but, while it still hovered in the
> air, the little child of strength . . . made a snatch at the marvel-
> lous insect and compressed it in his hand. [As his wife screamed
> and his father-in-law laughed, the] blacksmith, by main force,
> unclosed the infant's hand, and found within the palm a small
> heap of glittering fragments, whence the mystery of beauty had
> fled forever. (10: 475)

Fire, fluttering, descent, and fragmentation; Hawthorne's descendentalism could not be more powerfully, pithily expressed. But no
stern morality is enforced: the so sadly deprived idealistic artist is
narcissistic but not felt to be evil.[6] Rather, there was always an
ambivalence at the core of the artist's epiphanic project; the child's
instinctive violence that it called forth arose from the same heedless
narcissism that first animated the artist to make it.

---

6. Admittedly, we see in Owen a limiting "absorption with ingenuity for its own sake, pre-
ciousness." One notes here "Hawthorne's process of balancing attributes as he works
toward his highly qualified, severely challenged endorsement of the artist," says John
Caldwell Stubbs, The Pursuit of Form: A Study of Hawthorne and the Romance (Urbana:
University of Illinois Press, 1970), pp. 58, 60. * * *

The moral indifference of the all-pervading Hawthornean descendentalism becomes particularly clear when we juxtapose "The Artist of the Beautiful" to "Ethan Brand": the artist of the beautiful sought an ethereal ideal, while Brand is a would-be Faustian criminal, but the Hawthornean epiphanic fall and dispersal comes equally to seekers of supernal beauty and of ultimate evil. The fragmenting and scattering of Brand's satanically exalted self-image are adumbrated in the first paragraph as Bartram the lime-burner's son plays with "scattered fragments of marble" at the kiln (11: 83). The crazed Brand, whose surname means a burning stick, embodies the fire-heart-flower theme: "regardless of the fierce glare that reddened upon his face," he tells of having looked "into many a human heart that was seven times hotter with sinful passion than yonder furnace is with fire," but even that offense paled beside what "grew within" his "own breast"—the "bright and gorgeous flower" of the "Unpardonable Sin" he had sought and found (11: 89–90, 99). Epiphanic tremors next begin as the burning "fragments" of marble send up "spouts of blue flame" that "quivered aloft and danced madly" and an airlike hot "breath" arises; as the "wild and ghastly light" plays over his face, he jumps "into the gulf" (11: 99–100). Bartram "lift[s]" his pole—an epiphanic emblem recalling the fallen eponymous maypole—and as he lets it "fall upon" the "snow-white" skeleton with its marmoreally white heart, "the relics of Ethan Brand" are "crumbled into fragments" (11: 102). As the pole falls, the once fiery heart-flower is fragmented, its parts dispersed.[7]

* * *

[In]"Feathertop" [the title character] is as lifelike a scarecrow as ever was seen," in whose artificial body the "most important item" is an epiphanic pole, not a maypole this time but Mother Rigby's "broomstick" (10: 223–24). Linked to blood, heart, and fire is the creature's "plum-colored coat" with its "round hole" where possibly "the hot heart of some former wearer had scorched it through and through" (10: 225). Connected to aery fluttering are silk stockings "as unsubstantial as a dream" and "the longest tail-feather of a rooster" decorating the hat-top; the scarecrow even manages the requisite epiphanic "grin" (10: 225–26). Air turns more aery, fire more intensely flaming as the witch sends Feathertop out to a party at the Gookins': he gets the breath of "life" from smoking the "vapor" of her "pipe"; as he takes her "staff" it becomes a bright "gold-headed cane";

---

7. Lightening the moralism of Ethan's retribution and leavening it with "black humor" is the fact that even though he has sought to deny both the community and Mother Earth, his corpse enriches the community with "an extra half bushel of good lime" and will probably enrich the earth as fertilizer, notes Charles Swann, *Nathaniel Hawthorne: Tradition and Revolution* (Cambridge: Cambridge University Press, 1991), pp. 61–62.

and the "star on Feathertop's breast," now "all a-blaze," has "scintillated actual flames" (10: 234–41). But however "unutterable" the "splendor" with which his "star, his embroidery, his buckles, glowed," as soon as the attractive hostess Polly Gookin sees him in a mirror she collapses "insensible" (10: 243–44).

The theme of descent-and-scattering reaches a climax when the traumatized Feathertop, so shocked by her reaction that he vows to "exist no longer," sinks in turn "upon the floor, a medley of straw and tattered garments," while the narrator moralizes that the pained lover may have scattered his resources too readily: why are "thousands of coxcombs" who are "made up of just such a jumble of worn-out, forgotten, and good-for-nothing trash, as he was" (10: 245), saved from descent and dispersal? But Feathertop, Mother Rigby explains, had "too much heart" to compete in a "heartless world" (10: 246). Gleaming creatures with too much heart must fall into an epiphany of fragments, reduced to a jumble of tatters and trash.[8] Though fanciful and half-jocular, the epiphany is not for children; the misery of "May-Pole" has, so to speak, infected it. The resulting ambivalence is felt as uncomfortable; it is a "problem" fairy tale.

*   *   *

It may be diverting to end this part on a whimsical note: the brief, quirky vision of "Wakefield" helps to show, with its unexpected comic note, the emotional variety of Hawthorne's epiphanic effects. Donning a wig "of reddish hair" that may remind one of a clown, Wakefield, the wife-abandoning recluse, at first is relieved whenever he escapes detection: "Right glad is his heart" when he reaches "the coal-fire" of his new lodgings (9: 135). But when this heart-fire theme comes back with force in the "twentieth year" of Wakefield's self-imposed reclusion, it quickly leads to a multiple fluttering or tremor (glimmer, fitful flash), then to a fall and sprinkling:

> Wakefield discerns, through the parlor-windows of the second floor, the red glow, and the glimmer and fitful flash, of a comfortable fire. On the ceiling appears a grotesque shadow of good Mrs. Wakefield . . . which dances, moreover, with the up-flickering and down-sinking blaze, almost too merrily for the shade of an elderly widow. At this instant, a shower chances to fall, and is driven, by the unmannerly gust, full into Wakefield's face and bosom. (9:139)

8. This fairytale not only shows surprising epiphanic power, it is also, like "Wakefield," one of Hawthorne's subtlest pieces of metafictional playing with points of view; see Ellen E. Westbrook, "Exposing the Verisimilar: Hawthorne's 'Wakefield' and 'Feathertop,'" *Arizona Quarterly* 45 (winter 1989), pp. 1–23.

Rather than stand "shivering," he assumes an epiphanic "crafty smile" and enters; but we do "not follow" this "Outcast of the Universe" any further (9: 139–40). Perhaps the dispersal of chill drops has waked him from the field of dreams. For a purported universal outcast, the momentary retribution was brief and comical: the goal of the tale is to offer not a moral lesson but a *divertissement* with a quick and vivid shorthand epiphany.

II

In this final section I look at epiphanies that manifest the paradigm structure less completely than do those so far considered, yet are still memorable and striking. In epiphanies of this group, one or more of the formal components (fire, flutter, fall, or scatter) is lacking or attenuated. The biggest subgroup of epiphanies with an incomplete pattern contains those with the scatter-motif absent or only implied. Two less common categories lack respectively the vivid fire and the explicit fall. Yet the epiphanies we will examine are not necessarily to be devalued for their typological incompleteness. True, it may point at times to a partial weakening of vision. But the lack of one or another formal component can also heighten the imaginative drama of an epiphany by adding more mystery, intensifying our puzzlement or piquing our curiosity. We will see this happen in such visionary triumphs as "The Minister's Black Veil" and "Young Goodman Brown."

"My Kinsman, Major Molineux," where a surreal, grotesque epiphany of cosmic proportions is amorally visited upon a confused, hapless youth, attenuates the scatter-theme, yet abounds in oneiric power. Fires fill young Robin's epiphany of a procession. It begins with the "redder light" that "disturbed the moonbeams" and with the "dense multitude of torches" concealing "by their glare whatever object they illuminated"; and it culminates with those torches blazing "their brightest" before the "tar-and-feathery dignity" of the Major (11: 227–28), who proves hardly to be the prestigious citizen Robin had pictured as his likely patron. Epiphanic flutterings, too, are everywhere, starting with the torch-fires themselves, whose "unsteady brightness" forms "a veil" Robin cannot see through; yet soon he notices that the "foam" hangs "white" on Molineux's "quivering lip," and that his "whole frame" is "agitated by a quick, and continual tremor" (11: 228–29). The procession's leader, "war personified," bears a "drawn sword," varying the epiphanic horizontal-rod motif. And when "the procession resume[s] its march," the Major's persecutors appear as "fiends" hellishly "trampling on an old man's heart" (11: 230). The motif of a smashed and fallen heart is clear, but what is fragmented or scattered? Only a stream of fiendish

laughter is broken into bits: "there sailed over the heads of the multitude a great, broad laugh, broken in the midst by two deep sepulchral hems; thus—'Haw, haw, haw—hem, hem—haw, haw, haw,
haw!'" (11: 229). Yet the metaphoric dispersal takes on cosmic range:
not only does it appear to blend with the laughter of all who had
derided Robin that night, but Earth echoes it, and even the "Man in
the Moon hear[s] the far bellow" (11: 230).[9] A valid variant of the
Hawthornean epiphanic smile, the punctuated laugh yet seems a
rather attenuated scatter. It's almost as if Robin were trying to laugh
off his own hellish dream of a fevered, rabid father figure, mistak-
enly idealized and perhaps, more troublingly, unconsciously hated
and contemned.

☼　☼　☼

Though no scatter is depicted in the epiphany of "Drowne's Wooden
Image," we feel a high-blazing magical heart-life whose amorally
inflicted, undeserved descent darkens the world. Drowne, an artist
of the beautiful in the form of a ship-prow image carver, a "modern
Pygmalion in the person of a Yankee mechanic," quietly but epiph-
anically "smile[s]" when complimented on the skillful construction
of his beloved image for the "Cynosure" or North Star, betokening
stellar fire (10: 311–12, 306). When the image apparently comes to
life, a portentous shifty tremor is added to the heart-fire-flower
glow: with many a "rich flower upon her head," a "broad gold" neck-
chain that "glistened," a face with a "brilliant depth of complexion,"
she makes her shining progress "with garments fluttering" in the
breeze and with a "continually shifting" expression of "mirthful
mischief" recalling the shifting "gleam upon a bubbling fountain"
(10: 316–17). The epiphanic "fluttering" or tremor perilously intensi-
fies as she is "observed to flutter" her "pearl and ebony fan" with "such
vehement rapidity" that it remains "broken in her hand" (10: 317).
The pearls perhaps remain unscattered, but "traces" of the artisan's
sprinkled "tears" appear on his "visage" when, seeming to awaken
from "a kind of dream," he finds his Galatea is but wood: "'The world
looks darker now that she has vanished,' said some of the young men"
(10: 318). Drowne's heart-fire is sunken, his stellar world-sun dark.

　　"Endicott and the Red Cross" presents a short but strong (scatterless) epiphany of a fire-red emblem cut down by a puritan crusader
recalling those who dashed the epiphanic maypole, though once
again fanatical zealotry, no matter how glorified by imaginative

---

9. Michael J. Colacurcio's historic-contextual reading is psychologically astute also as he
notes the ironic frustrations Robin encounters in seeking a "more tolerant surrogate for
the loving but strict, ministerial father he has left behind"; see *The Province of Piety;
Moral History in Hawthorne's Early Tales* (Cambridge: Harvard University Press, 1984),
p. 131.

courage, is no moral ideal to the urbane Hawthorne. Indeed, this
red-cross slasher is himself a fire-heart, though his own pride
remains unhumbled: shining splendor and heart's blood combine in
his "highly polished," "glittering steel" breastplate depicting the
scene of a prayer-house, with the "blood" of a wolf's head, claimed
for bounty, "still plashing on the door-step" (9: 434). When he hears
of the hoisting of an English flag with a red cross that he considers
idolatrously papistical, "blood glow[s] through" Endicott's "manly
countenance," the breastplate itself appearing "red hot, with the
angry fire of the bosom which it covered" (9: 437), a fine collocation
of heart, fire, and the banner-theme of "May-Pole." The flutter and
smile components enter as a "sad and quiet smile flit[s]" over the face
of mild Roger Williams (9: 439). The pole theme is varied as Endicott, "brandishing his sword," "thrust it through the cloth" and "rent
the Red Cross completely out of the banner. He then waved the tattered ensign above his head" (9: 440). Though the redness of the
cloth is torn out, it is not scattered; the tattering results from the
cutting away only of the central emblem. A scattering may be
implied, though, by the fact that wolf-blood still seems "plashing" on
the prayer-house doorsteps of the awe-inspiring breastplate.

The effective (scatterless) epiphany of "The Grey Champion"
resembles that of "Endicott and the Red Cross," in that both are historically retrospective portrayals of single-minded visionaries, quix-
otic yet intense. The equally fantastical and zealous protagonist of
"The Grey Champion" is less fiery than Endicott—probably because
he is only the ghost of a Puritan past—but as he leads a crowd who
rage over the royal annulment of the Massachusetts Bay charter, he
must face a wall of flames in the form of soldiers "with shouldered
matchlocks, and matches burning, so as to present a row of fires in
the dusk" (9: 12). As he emerges from that dusk, with "but a staff in
his hand, to assist the tremulous gait of age," the theme of tremor
accompanies the epiphanic staff. As the champion approaches holding the staff before him, the British commander, beholding the
crowd "burning" with "hot lurid wrath," orders retreat, and then the
spectral form "fade[s] from their eyes, melting slowly into the hues of
twilight," into "empty space" (9: 17). This melting away (not quite a
scatter) of a trembling vision from hot eye-fires is a moving descendental epiphany, bringing sadness after a moment of seeming
victory.

*   *   *

"Roger Malvin's Burial" is * * * deprived of a vital fire where it is
sorely needed. That lack helps account for the strong pathos of its
climactic dark epiphany when the fluttering of a bloodied handkerchief signals the descent, from the topmost tree-bough, of fragments

scattering over the bones of a man who had been culpably abandoned. Roger's friend Reuben had gone for help when Roger was
dying and had promised to return; his unexpiated failure to keep
that promise may seem to be the tragic flaw leading, in horridly
disproportionate retribution, to his unwitting shooting of his son
on returning to the gravesite eighteen years later. The identifying
"banner" Reuben had originally affixed to an oak sapling's branch
to help him find Roger's death-site was a "handkerchief" made
"bloody" by an arm wound Reuben had incurred (10: 343–44, 346).
With the hope of "expiating his sin" and thus letting "sunlight into
the sepulcher of his heart" to kindle a heart-glow (10: 356), Reuben
returns to the now fully grown oak. But no sunlight will enter, no
fire will arise in that heart.

Reuben begins to "tremble" as he remembers "how the little banner has fluttered" on the bough—a twofold epiphanic tremor—for a
"blight" has "withered" the now "dead" branch (10: 357). His wife
mirrors the motif of tremulous fluttering (combined with the only
briefly mentioned fire theme) as she begins to "tremble" by the "glowing fire" when she hears a shot (10: 358). Learning that Reuben has
accidentally killed their son, with a "wild shriek" she falls "insensible" by the dead boy's side: "At that moment the withered topmost
bough of the oak loosened itself in the stilly air, and fell in soft, light
fragments" upon the mourners and upon Roger Malvin's bones (10:
360). Though Reuben's "sin was expiated" (10: 360), the penance
required was grotesque. It has the irrational horror of tragedy, not of
a moral tale.

In "The Minister's Black Veil," Hawthorne masters a notable
challenge: although, instead of shining fire, a diametrically opposed
black veil (remarkable for its aporetic[1] amorality) is the title-topic,
he nonetheless stirs up a masterly flutter-fall-scatter-smile epiphany
in two stages. Each part also offers spectral intimations of the absent
fire, as if to remind us of what the enigmatic minister has possibly,
perhaps vainly, sought. A glow, though always faint is persistent—in
gleams, glimmers, trembling flickers: "A sad smile gleamed faintly
from beneath" Mr. Hooper's "black veil, and flickered about his
mouth, glimmering" (9: 41). In the first stage of the tale's great
epiphany, expectations of fire-gleam arise as Hooper, at a wedding,
offers good wishes with the "pleasantry that ought to have brightened the features of the guests, like a cheerful gleam from the

---

1. J. Hillis Miller's searching treatment of the story as centered upon the aporetic epiphany
of the veil (see *Hawthorne and History: Defacing It* [Oxford: Basil Blackwell, 1991], pp.
66–103) does not deal with the motif cluster analyzed here but leads me to ask, regarding
Hawthorne's epiphanies generally, whether they may not all tend toward (moral) deconstruction. Indeed, all epiphanies—intense, mysterious, disproportionately expansive in
meaning—deconstructively challenge categories.

hearth" (9: 43). Cheer is needed, for strong epiphanic tremors have already begun: "the bride's cold fingers quivered in the tremulous hand of the bridegroom" (9: 43). Then, as Hooper raises the wine glass and sees his own form in the mirror, his "frame shuddered— his lips grew white—he spilt the untasted wine upon the carpet— and rushed forth into the darkness" (9: 44): shuddering, fall, droplet-dispersal, dark.

The second stage, the deathbed scene, begins with faint glimmers, faint smiles, and more tremulous shudders. Hooper "raise[s] himself in bed" and sits trembling or "shivering," his "faint, sad smile" still appearing "to glimmer" with vague light. Yet he feels that his flutter- ing veil has allowed him, paradoxically but sincerely, to show "his inmost heart" (9: 52), for his deepest conviction is that on "every vis- age" an enigmatic "Black Veil" is placed; thus, the enigma of his glimmering smile betokens his heartfelt belief. Yet when he explains this, a great scattering occurs, the sudden mutual dispersal of his hearers as Hooper falls. "While his auditors shrank from one another, in mutual affright. Father Hooper fell back upon his pillow, a veiled corpse, with a faint smile lingering on the lips" (9: 52). Heart, glim- mer, shiver, fall, scatter, smile: a two-stage epiphany is complete in the only form Hooper can offer. But though the glimmers are desper- ately faint, the odd Hawthornean epiphanic smile accompanies them to the last. The vision cannot be called tragic, with its intimations of so peculiar a peace.

I conclude with the central vision of "Young Goodman Brown," an exhibit whose enigmatic fascination can be helpfully contextual- ized when we see it as a Hawthornean epiphany with no explicit indication of a "fall." As some of the ardent "votaries" in "The May- Pole of Merry Mount" had called the maypole "their religion, or their altar" (9: 60), so in the dire-bright witches' sabbath or *Walpur- gisnacht* epiphany shown to Brown we may see that glowing festal emblem of fiery passion transformed and multiplied, with "a rock resembling an altar or a pulpit, and surrounded by four blazing pines, their tops aflame, their stems untouched, like candles at an evening meeting," and with a "mass of foliage that had overgrown the summit of the rock" all "on fire," each "pendent twig and leafy festoon" in "a blaze" (10: 84). Rather than see an undifferentiated mass of incandescent heat, we view each individual twig and leaf outlined and surrounded in fire—something never seen in nature. Like the burning candle-tops of trees otherwise intact, this is magi- cal, supernatural fire, corresponding, in its ambivalence, to the equivocal mood expressed by the town's many watchful and epiph- anically tremulous faces "quivering to-and-fro, *between gloom and splendor*" (10: 84–85; emphasis added). The final phrase is telling. This fire is as glorious and resplendent as it is gloomy and menacing, a typically ambivalent instance of the always terror-based Burkean "sublime,"[2] as in the Miltonic Pandemonium of John Martin or the Dantesque Inferno of Gustave Doré.

Does one "fall" from such a moment? It isn't shown that Goodman does. True, as a "cry of grief, rage and terror" is "drowned" and "fades" into "far-off laughter," Goodman Brown notices that the "pink ribbon" worn by his wife Faith has "fluttered lightly down through the air and caught on the branch of a tree" (10: 88). As the unhappy cry is drowned, so too the bannerlike ribbon (recalling "Burial" or "May-Pole") flutters down—another tremor to add to that of the quivering faces. As Goodman vainly summons Faith to resist seduction, a dark ghostly figure confirms him in his feeling of "a loathful brotherhood, by the sympathy of all that was wicked in his heart"; he learns that it will be his special endowment to know everyone's "secret deeds," to "penetrate, in every bosom, the deep mystery of sin, the fountain of all wicked arts" (10: 86–87). Then the epiphany moves to a final scatter, a sprinkle:

> he found himself amid calm night and solitude, listening to a roar of the wind which died heavily away through the forest. He staggered against the rock, and felt it chill and damp, while a hanging twig, that had been all on fire, besprinkled his cheek with the coldest dew. (10: 88)

The aspersions this horrid epiphany scattered on Goodman's love and "Faith" took the light from his heart; his kinfolk "carved no hopeful verse upon his tombstone; for his dying hour was gloom" (10: 90). A cry was drowned, and a ribbon fell—but did Goodman?

Whether Goodman has "fallen" or not is the question to help us interpret what "moral" the epiphany may or may not reveal. Here "loathful brotherhood" is the key phrase. Goodman understands his kinship with the community under the aspect of loathsomeness. It's easy to view his subsequent universal disgust with sinful humans as a projection of what he doesn't want to admit he shares with them. If he has sublimated the newly revealed fiery passion (to him, demonic wickedness) by massively projecting it onto everyone else in town, he has not fallen but risen in his own esteem. To "sublimate" is to make a passionate ("fiery") feeling rise as something different and purer (such as moral indignation). The superego rises with its purified progeny; the crestfallen id subsides. Moral betterment, or pathology? One

2. "The keystone of Burke's aesthetic is emotion, and the foundation of his theory of sublimity is the emotion of terror." Edmund Burke helped "to spread the cult of romantic terror throughout the literature of the era that just precedes the rise of romantic art." See Samuel H. Monk, *The Sublime: A Study of Critical Theories in XVIII-Century England* (Ann Arbor: University of Michigan Press, 1960), pp. 87, 100.

can see Hawthorne smile as he samples the hundreds of articles written on this tale.[3]

The combined effect of the best epiphanies in Hawthorne's tales is rather like that of a meteor shower. A flower-gem-fire-heart-glow, then a flitting-tremor-flutter, a descent, a scatter. Ambivalence is there, always, from the start. Transcendent hopes are dashed, and often with a smile—of whimsy, madness, crafty glee, or sad bemusement. Observing the relentless recurrence of Hawthorne's epiphanic pattern will surely make us think anew about his fascination with the subtleties and difficulties of moral allegorizing and his peculiar persistence in the attempt. For at the most intense, inclusive moments of his imagining, Hawthorne sees the same descendental scattering revealed to nearly everyone on every moral or amoral level. Perhaps the same fate finds us all: an ambivalent and scattered splendor.

3. "'Young Goodman Brown' is Hawthorne's most successful story" because here he is most "free" from the "editorializing" that mars other works, says Robert E. Moosberger, "The Woe That Is Madness: Goodman Brown and the Face of the Fire," *The Nathaniel Hawthorne Journal* 1973, ed. C. E. Frazer Clark Jr., p. 177. By 1976 it had generated "over 400" studies, but, reading a survey of these and others, one is struck by the simplistic debate as to whether Brown is "good" or "evil," or—still normatively dogmatizing—whether he attains "maturity" or not; see Lea Bertani Vozar Newman, *A Reader's Guide to the Short Stories of Nathaniel Hawthorne* (Boston: G. K. Hall, 1979), pp. 341–48. Michael Tritt appears correct in claiming he is the first to maintain, in "'Young Goodman Brown' and the Psychology of Projection," *Studies in Short Fiction* 23 (1986), 113–17, the thesis that Brown projects his self-loathing onto society.

Nathaniel Hawthorne:
A Chronology

1804	Born July 4, the only son and second child of Nathaniel Hathorne, a sea captain, and Elizabeth Manning Hathorne.
1808	Father dies of yellow fever in Dutch Guiana (Surinam). The boy Nathaniel, his mother, and his two sisters Elizabeth and Louisa are taken in by the Manning clan.
1813–14	Suffers from mysterious lameness for fourteen months.
1816–19	Lives during some of this period in Raymond, Maine, where the Mannings owned land near Sebago Lake at the edge of what was then wilderness. For the time being, Elizabeth Hathorne plans to settle with her family in Raymond.
1819–21	Nathaniel returns to Salem to prepare for college while his mother and older sister "Ebe" remain in Raymond.
1821–25	Studies at Bowdoin College, Brunswick, Maine. Two of his classmates were Henry Wadsworth Longfellow, the writer, and Franklin Pierce, later fourteenth president of the United States. Adds *w* to his name.
1825–39	Lives in Salem in mother's house on Herbert Street. Makes occasional summer trips to different parts of New England and once at least through New York to Niagara Falls.
1825–30	Intensive study of New England history. Wide reading during the first years of his career as a writer.
1828	Anonymously publishes *Fanshawe*, a melodramatic romance set in a country college town. Later, Hawthorne repented of *Fanshawe* and seems to have burned all the copies he could lay his hands on.
1829	Corresponds with Samuel Goodrich about his early tales. Goodrich, who found great promise in *Fanshawe*, was editor of *The Token*, an annual Christmas gift-book containing short essays, fiction, and poetry.

1830   Earliest sketch, "Sights from a Steeple," published anonymously in October in *The Token*. Earliest tale, "The Hollow of the Three Hills," published in November in *The Salem Gazette*.

1831   First major tales: "My Kinsman, Major Molineux," "Roger Malvin's Burial," and "The Gentle Boy." All published in *The Token*.

1830–39   Publishes over seventy tales and sketches in various magazines and *The Token*.

1834   Finishes the manuscript of "The Story Teller," a collection of tales linked together by a frame narrative. This ambitious work was never published as a whole, and the manuscript itself has disappeared.

1836   Edits the *American Magazine of Useful and Entertaining Knowledge* and writes most of the copy for it, living for eight months in Boston.

1837   *Twice-told Tales* appears, its publication secretly guaranteed against failure by Hawthorne's classmate, Horatio Bridge. Longfellow writes a laudatory review, and he and Hawthorne renew their friendship. Late in 1837, Hawthorne meets Sophia Peabody.

1839   Engaged to marry Sophia Peabody.

1839–40   Inspector in the Boston Custom-House.

1840–41   Publishes *Grandfather's Chair*, a history of New England retold as a frame narrative for children.

1841   Invests in the Brook Farm Community in West Roxbury, Massachusetts, and lives at Brook Farm from April to November. The life of a farmer-idealist did not suit Hawthorne, however. In the mid-1840s he sued to recover his investment, but though he won the case he never got his money back.

1842   *Twice-told Tales*, second (enlarged) edition.

1842   Marries Sophia Peabody and moves to the Old Manse in Concord, Massachusetts. While at the Old Manse Hawthorne deepens his acquaintance with the Transcendentalists: Emerson, Thoreau, Fuller, Channing, and others.

1842–45   Writes and publishes some twenty tales and sketches while living at the Old Manse.

1844   Daughter Una born.

1845   The Hawthornes move back to Salem. Their financial circumstances, never easy, are now more difficult than usual.

1846   Publishes *Mosses from an Old Manse*. Son Julian born.

1846–49 Surveyor of Customs at the port of Salem. Hawthorne obtained this appointment through his political connections in the Democratic Party.

1846–48 Writes occasional criticism for the *Salem Advertiser*, including reviews of Melville's *Typee* and Longfellow's "Evangeline."

1849 Dismissed from his position in the Custom-House in June, following the Whig election victory in 1848. Hawthorne regarded his dismissal as unfair and took revenge on his political adversaries in "The Custom-House," the introduction to *The Scarlet Letter*. Mother dies, July. Hawthorne begins *The Scarlet Letter*, apparently in September.

1850 Publishes *The Scarlet Letter*. Moves to Lenox, in western Massachusetts. Later that year Herman Melville buys a farm in Pittsfield, within fifteen miles of the Hawthornes.

1851 Publishes *The House of the Seven Gables*. Publishes *The Snow Image and Other Twice-told Tales*. Writes and publishes "Feathertop," his last tale. Publishes *The Wonder Book*, a collection of classical myths retold for children and his most successful children's book. Daughter Rose born in May. Hawthorne family moves to West Newton, in eastern Massachusetts, in November.

1852 Publishes *The Blithedale Romance*, a novel based in part on his experience at Brook Farm. Publishes a campaign biography of Franklin Pierce. Pierce elected president of the United States, November. Hawthorne buys the Wayside, a home for his family in Concord, Massachusetts.

1853 Publishes *Tanglewood Tales*, another collection of classical myths for children. Obtains post as U.S. consul in Liverpool, England. The Hawthornes move to England in July.

1853–57 Consul in Liverpool.

1854 *Mosses from an Old Manse*, second edition.

1857–59 Lives in Rome and Florence, Italy.

1859 Returns to England to complete *The Marble Faun*.

1860 Publishes *The Marble Faun*, his last novel. Returns to the United States and to the Wayside in Concord.

1862 Publishes "Chiefly about War Matters," a reflective, ironic essay on the Civil War.

1863 Publishes *Our Old Home*, a book of reflections on his experience in England.

1864   Leaves home for a last journey, apparently knowing that he is dying. Dies May 19, in the company of Franklin Pierce, in Plymouth, New Hampshire.

Selected Bibliography

I. HAWTHORNE'S WRITINGS

Charvat, William, Roy Harvey Pearce, Claude M. Simpson, Fredson Bowers, Matthew J. Bruccoli, L. Neal Smith, and Thomas Woodson, eds. *The Centenary Edition of the Works of Nathaniel Hawthorne*. 23 vols. Columbus: Ohio State University Press, 1962–94. Especially: vol 6, *True Stories from History and Biography*, 1972. Intro. Roy Harvey Pearce; vol. 8, *The American Notebooks*, 1972. Ed. Claude M. Simpson; vol. 9, *Twice-told Tales*, 1974; vol. 10, *Mosses from an Old Manse*, 1974; vol. 11, *The Snow-Image and Uncollected Tales*, 1974; vols. 9, 10, and 11 have historical commentaries by J. Donald Crowley and textual commentaries by Fredson Bowers: vol. 15, *The Letters, 1813–1843*, 1984; vol. 16, *The Letters, 1843–1853*, 1985. Ed. Thomas Woodson, L. Neal Smith, and Norman Holmes Pearson; vol. 23, *Miscellaneous Prose and Verse*, 1994. Ed. Thomas Woodson, Claude M. Simpson, and L. Neal Smith.
Love Letters of Nathaniel Hawthorne, 1839–1863. 1907. Foreward by C. E. Frazer Clark Jr. Washington, D.C: NCR/Microcard Editions, 1972.
Turner, Arlin, ed. *Hawthorne as Editor: Selections from His Writings in the American Magazine of Useful and Entertaining Knowledge*. Baton Rouge: Louisiana State University Press, 1941.

II. BIBLIOGRAPHIES, GUIDES

American Literary Scholarship. Durham: Duke University Press, annually since 1963. One chapter in each volume surveys and evaluates the year's work on Hawthorne.
Clark, C. E. Frazer Jr. *Nathaniel Hawthorne: A Descriptive Bibliography*. Pittsburgh, University of Pittsburgh Press, 1978. A list and description of virtually all publications of Hawthorne's writings. Illustrated.
Gale, Robert L. *A Nathaniel Hawthorne Encyclopedia*. Westport, CT: Greenwood, 1991.
Idol, John L. Jr., and Buford Jones, eds. *Nathaniel Hawthorne: The Contemporary Reviews*. New York: Cambridge University Press, 1994.
Nathaniel Hawthorne Review. A journal sponsored by the Nathaniel Hawthorne Society since 1975 that publishes annotated bibliographies periodically, usually every fall, as well as essays, book reviews, and other material pertaining to Hawthorne. A recent bibliography appears in *Nathaniel Hawthorne Review* 36.2 (2010): 121–33.
Newman, Lea Bertani Vozar. *A Reader's Guide to the Short Stories of Nathaniel Hawthorne*. Boston: G. K. Hall, 1979. Factual and bibliographical essays on fifty-four stories, supplemented by a bibliography.

III. BIOGRAPHIES, MEMOIRS

Bosco, Ronald A. and Jillmarie Murphy. *Hawthorne in His Own Time: A Biographical Chronicle of His Life, Drawn from Recollections Interviews, and*

Memoirs by Family, Friends, and Associates. Iowa City: University of Iowa Press, 2007.

Bridge, Horatio. *Personal Recollections of Nathaniel Hawthorne*. New York, 1893.

Capper, Charles. *Margaret Fuller: An American Romantic Life*. Volume II: *The Public Years*. New York: Oxford University Press, 2007.

Conway, Moncure. *Life of Nathaniel Hawthorne*. New York, 1890.

Erlich, Gloria C. *Family Themes in Hawthorne's Fiction: The Tenacious Web*. New Brunswick, NJ: Rutgers University Press, 1984.

Gollin, Rita K. "'The Animal Department of Our Nature.'" *Nathaniel Hawthorne Review* 30 (2004): 145–65.

Hawthorne, Julian. *Nathaniel Hawthorne and His Wife: A Biography*. 2 vols. Cambridge, MA, 1884–85.

Herbert, T. Walter. *Dearest Beloved: The Hawthornes and the Making of the Middle-Class Family*. Berkeley: University of California Press, 1993.

James, Henry. *Hawthorne*. London, 1879.

La Plante, Eve. *American Jezebel: The Uncommon Life of Anne Hutchinson, the Woman Who Defied the Puritans*. New York: HarperCollins, 2004.

Marshall, Megan. *The Peabody Sisters: Three Women Who Ignited American Romanticism*. Boston and New York: Houghton-Mifflin, 2005.

Mellow, James R. *Nathaniel Hawthorne in His Times*. Boston: Houghton Mifflin, 1980.

Moore, Margaret B. *The Salem World of Nathaniel Hawthorne*. Columbia and London: University of Missouri Press, 1998.

Miller, Edwin Haviland. *Salem Is My Dwelling Place: A Life of Nathaniel Hawthorne*. Iowa City: University of Iowa Press, 1991.

Parker, Hershel. *Herman Melville: A Biography*. Volume I, 1819–1851. Baltimore and London: The Johns Hopkins University Press, 1996.

Turner, Arlin. *Nathaniel Hawthorne: A Biography*. New York: Oxford University Press, 1980.

Valenti, Patricia Dunlavy. *Sophia Peabody Hawthorne: A Life*. Volume 1: *1809–1847*. Columbia and London: University of Missouri Press, 2004.

Van Doren, Mark. *Nathaniel Hawthorne*. New York: W. Sloane, 1949.

Wineapple, Brenda. *Hawthorne: A Life*. New York: Knopf, 2003.

———. "Hawthorne and Melville: or, The Ambiguities." In *Hawthorne and Melville: Writing a Relationship*. Ed. Jana L. Argersinger and Leland S. Person. Athens and London: University of Georgia Press, 2008.

IV. GENERAL STUDIES AND HISTORICAL BACKGROUNDS

Baym, Nina. *Novels, Readers, and Reviewers: Responses to Fiction in Antebellum America*. Ithaca, NY: Cornell University Press, 1984.

Bercovitch, Sacvan. *The American Jeremiad*. Madison: University of Wisconsin Press, 1978.

———, ed. *The Cambridge History of American Literature*. Volume 2: *1820–1865*. New York: Cambridge University Press, 1995. Includes "Conditions of Literary Vocation," by Michael Davitt Bell, pp. 9–124; "The Literature of Expansion and Race," by Eric J. Sundquist, pp. 125–328; "The Transcendentalists," by Barbara Packer, pp. 329–604; and "Narrative Forms," by Jonathan Arac, pp. 605–777.

———. "How the Puritans Won the American Revolution." *Massachusetts Review* 17 (1976): 597–630.

Brodhead, Richard H. *Cultures of Letters: Scenes of Reading and Writing in Nineteenth-Century America*. Chicago: University of Chicago Press, 1993.

Brown, Gillian. *Domestic Individualism: Imagining Self in Nineteenth-Century America*. Berkeley: University of California Press, 1990.

Buell, Lawrence. *Literary Transcendentalism: Style and Vision in the American Renaissance*. Ithaca, NY: Cornell University Press, 1973.

———. *New England Literary Culture: From Revolution through Renaissance*. New York: Cambridge University Press, 1986.

Charvat, William. *Literary Publishing in America, 1790–1850*. Philadelphia: University of Pennsylvania Press, 1959.

———. *The Origins of American Critical Thought*. Philadelphia: University of Pennsylvania Press, 1936.

Crane, Gregg D. *Race, Citizenship, and Law in American Literature*. Cambridge: Cambridge University Press, 2002.

Davis, Theo. *Formalism, Experience, and the Making of American Literature in the Nineteenth Century*. Cambridge: Cambridge University Press, 2007.

Dekker, George. *The American Historical Romance*. Cambridge: Cambridge University Press, 1987.

Douglas, Ann. *The Feminization of American Culture*. New York: Knopf, 1977.

Feidelson, Charles. *Symbolism and American Literature*. Chicago: University of Chicago Press, 1953.

Fisher, Philip. *Hard Facts: Setting and Form in the American Novel*. New York: Oxford University Press, 1985.

Fussell, Edwin S. *Frontier: American Literature and the American West*. Princeton, NJ: Princeton University Press, 1965.

Gilmore, Michael T. *American Romanticism and the Marketplace*. Chicago: University of Chicago Press, 1985.

Goddu, Teresa A. *Gothic America: Narrative, History, and Nation*. New York: Columbia University Press, 1997.

Halttunen, Karen. *Confidence Men and Painted Women: A Study of Middle-Class Culture in America, 1830–1870*. New Haven, CT: Yale University Press, 1982.

Hatch, Nathan O. *The Democratization of American Christianity*. New Haven, CT: Yale University Press, 1989.

Hoffman, Daniel G. *Form and Fable in American Fiction*. New York: Oxford University Press, 1961.

Howe, Daniel Walker. *What Hath God Wrought: The Transformation of America, 1815–1848*. New York: Oxford University Press, 2007.

Irwin, John. "The Symbol of the Hieroglyphics in the American Renaissance." *American Quarterly* 26 (1974): 103–26.

———. *American Hieroglyphics: The Symbol of the Egyptian Hieroglyphics in the American Renaissance*. New Haven, CT: Yale University Press, 1980.

Kasson, Joy S. "Narratives of the Female Body: *The Greek Slave*." In *The Culture of Sentiment: Race, Gender, and Sentimentality in Nineteenth-Century America* (172–90). Ed. Shirley Samuels. New York: Oxford University Press, 1992.

Lang, Amy Schrager. *Prophetic Woman: Anne Hutchinson and the Problem of Dissent in the Literature of New England*. Berkeley: University of California Press, 1987.

Larson, Kerry. *Imagining Equality in Nineteenth-Century American Literature*. Cambridge: Cambridge University Press, 2008.

Levin, David. *History as Romantic Art: Bancroft, Prescott, Motley, and Parkman*. Stanford, CA: Stanford University Press, 1959.

Levine, Robert S. *Dislocating Race and Nation: Episodes in Nineteenth-Century Literary Nationalism*. Chapel Hill: University of North Carolina Press, 2008.

Martin, Terence. *The Instructed Vision: Scottish Common Sense Philosophy and the Origins of American Fiction*. Bloomington: Indiana University Press, 1961.

Matthiessen, F. O. *American Renaissance: Art and Expression in the Age of Emerson and Whitman*. New York: Oxford University Press, 1941.

McGill, Meredith L. *American Literature and the Culture of Reprinting, 1834–1853*. Philadelphia: University of Pennsylvania Press, 2003.

McWilliams, John P. Jr. *New England's Crises and Cultural Memory: Literature, Politics, History, Religion, 1620–1860*. Cambridge: Cambridge University Press, 2004.

Miller, Perry. *Errand into the Wilderness*. Cambridge: Harvard University Press, 1956.

————. *The Raven and the Whale: The War of Words and Wits in the Era of Poe and Melville.* New York: Harcourt Brace, 1956.

————, ed. *The Transcendentalists: An Anthology.* Cambridge: Harvard University Press, 1950.

Packer, Barbara. "The Transcendentalists." In Bercovitch, ed., *Cambridge History.* Rprnt. Athens: University of Georgia Press, 2007.

Poirier, Richard. *A World Elsewhere: The Place of Style in American Literature.* New York: Oxford University Press, 1966.

Reynolds, David S. *Beneath the American Renaissance: The Subversive Imagination in the Age of Emerson and Melville.* New York: Knopf, 1988.

Smith, Henry Nash. *Democracy and the Novel: Popular Resistance to Classic American Writers.* New York: Oxford University Press, 1978.

Tocqueville, Alexis de. *Democracy in America.* Trans. Henry Reeve, 2 vols. New York: Vintage Books, 1945. [Originally published 1838–40.]

Tomkins, Jane. *Sensational Designs: The Cultural Work of American Fiction, 1790–1860.* New York: Oxford University Press, 1985.

Wilentz, Sean. *The Rise of American Democracy: Jefferson to Lincoln.* New York: Norton, 2005.

Zboray, Ronald J., and Mary Saracino Zboray. *Everyday Ideas: Socioliterary Experience among Antebellum New Englanders.* Knoxville: University of Tennessee Press, 2006.

V. STUDIES OF HAWTHORNE

Adams, Richard P. "Hawthorne's *Provincial Tales.*" *New England Quarterly* 30 (1957): 39–57.

————. "Hawthorne: The Old Manse Period." *Tulane Studies in English* 8 (1958): 115–51.

Adkins, Nelson F. "The Early Projected Works of Nathaniel Hawthorne." *Papers of the Bibliographical Society of America* 39 (1945): 119–45.

Bales, Kent. "Hawthorne's Prefaces and Romantic Perspectivism." *Emerson Society Quarterly* 23 (1977): 69–88.

Baym, Nina. "Revisiting Hawthorne's Feminism." *Nathaniel Hawthorne Review* 30 (2004): 32–55.

————. *The Shape of Hawthorne's Career.* Ithaca, NY: Cornell University Press, 1976.

Bell, Michael Davitt, *Hawthorne and the Historical Romance of New England.* Princeton, NJ: Princeton University Press, 1971.

Bell, Millicent. ed. *Hawthorne and the Real: Bicentennial Essays.* Columbus: Ohio State University Press, 2005.

————. *Hawthorne's View of the Artist.* New York: New York State University Press, 1962.

Berlant, Lauren. *The Anatomy of National Fantasy: Hawthorne Utopia, and Everyday Life.* Chicago: University of Chicago Press, 1991.

Brodhead, Richard. *Hawthorne, Melville, and the Novel.* Chicago: University of Chicago Press, 1976.

————. *The School of Hawthorne.* New York: Oxford University Press, 1986.

Cameron, Sharon. *The Corporeal Self: Allegories of the Body in Melville and Hawthorne.* Baltimore and London: Johns Hopkins University Press, 1981.

Christopherson, Bill. "Agnostic Tendencies in Hawthorne's Short Fiction." *American Literature* 72 (2000): 594–624.

Colacurcio, Michael J. *The Province of Piety: Moral History in Hawthorne's Early Tales.* Cambridge: Harvard University Press, 1984.

Crews, Frederick C. *The Sins of the Fathers: Hawthorne's Psychological Themes.* New York: Oxford University Press, 1966.

Crowley, J. Donald, ed. *Hawthorne: The Critical Heritage.* New York: Barnes & Noble, 1970.

Dauber, Kenneth. *Rediscovering Hawthorne*. Princeton, NJ: Princeton University Press, 1977.

Davis, Clark. *Hawthorne's Shyness: Ethics, Politics and the Question of Engagement*. Baltimore and London: Johns Hopkins University Press, 2004.

Doubleday, Neal Frank. *Hawthorne's Early Tales: A Critical Study*. Durham, NC: Duke University Press, 1972.

Dryden, Edgar A. *Nathaniel Hawthorne: The Poetics of Enchantment*. Ithaca, NY: Cornell University Press, 1977.

Fogle, Richard Harter, *Hawthorne's Fiction: The Light and the Dark*. Rev. ed. Norman: Oklahoma University Press, 1964.

Kesselring, M. L. "Hawthorne's Reading, 1828–1850." *Bulletin of the New York Public Library* 53 (1949): 55–71, 121–38, 173–94.

McWilliams, John P. Jr. *Hawthorne, Melville, and the American Character: A Looking-Glass Business*. Cambridge: Cambridge University Press, 1984.

Male, Roy R. *Hawthorne's Tragic Vision*. Austin: University of Texas Press, 1957.

Marks, Alfred H. "German Romantic Irony in Hawthorne's Tales." *Symposium* 7 (1953): 274–305.

Martin, Terence. *Nathaniel Hawthorne*. New York: Twayne, 1965.

Milder, Robert. "Hawthorne's Winter Dreams." *Nineteenth-Century Fiction* 54 (1999): 165–201.

———. "The Other Hawthorne." *New England Quarterly* 81 (2008): 559–95.

Millington, Richard H. *Practicing Romance: Narrative Form and Cultural Engagement in Hawthorne's Fiction*. Princeton, NJ: Princeton University Press, 1992.

———, ed. *The Cambridge Companion to Nathaniel Hawthorne*. Cambridge: Cambridge University Press, 2004. See especially Joel Pfister, "Hawthorne as Cultural Theorist, 35–59; T. Walter Herbert, "Hawthorne and American Masculinity, 60–78; Alison Easton, "Hawthorne and the Question of Women," 79–98; and Kristie Hamilton, "Hawthorne, Modernity, and the Literary Sketch," 99 120.

Mitchell, Thomas R. *Hawthorne's Fuller Mystery*. Amherst: University of Massachusetts Press, 1998.

Newberry, Frederick. *Hawthorne's Divided Loyalties: England and America in His Works*. Rutherford, NJ: Farleigh Dickinson University Press, 1987.

Pearce, Roy Harvey, ed. *Hawthorne Centenary Essays*. Columbus: Ohio State University Press, 1964.

Person, Leland S. *Aesthetic Headaches: Women and a Masculine Poetics in Poe, Melville, and Hawthorne*. Athens: University of Georgia Press, 1988.

———. *The Cambridge Introduction to Nathaniel Hawthorne*. New York: Cambridge University Press, 2006.

Pfister, Joel. *The Production of Personal Life: Class Gender, and the Psychological in Hawthorne's Fiction*. Stanford, CA: Stanford University Press, 1991.

Reynolds, Larry. *Devils and Rebels: The Making of Hawthorne's Damn Politics*. Ann Arbor: University of Michigan Press, 2008.

———. *A Historical Guide to Nathaniel Hawthorne*. New York: Oxford University Press, 2001.

Shaw, Peter. "Hawthorne's Ritual Typology of the American Revolution." *Prospects* 3 (1977): 69–88.

Trollope, Anthony. "The Genius of Nathaniel Hawthorne." *North American Review* 129 (1879): 203–22.

Ullén, Magnus. *The Half-Vanished Structure: Hawthorne's Allegorical Dialectics*. Bern: Peter Lang, 2004.

Waggoner, Hyatt Howe. *Hawthorne: A Critical Study*. Rev. ed. Cambridge: Harvard University Press, 1963.

Warren, Robert Penn. "Hawthorne Revisited: Some Remarks on Hellfiredness." *Sewanee Review* 81 (1973): 75–111.

Woodson, Thomas. "Hawthorne and the Author's Immortal Fame," *Nathaniel Hawthorne Review* 30 (2004): 56–91.
Wright, John W. "Borges and Hawthorne." In *Prose for Borges*. Ed. Charles Newman. Evanston, IL: Northwestern University Press, 1974: 286–307.

VI. STUDIES OF INDIVIDUAL TALES AND PREFACES

"The Artist of the Beautiful"

Bell, Millicent. *Hawthorne's View of the Artist* (94–113).
Liebman, Sheldon W. "Hawthorne's Romanticism: 'The Artist of the Beautiful.'" *Emerson Society Quarterly* 22 (1976): 85–95.
Pfister, Joel, "The Cultural Job of Industrial-Era Soulmaking." From his "Hawthorne as Cultural Theorist." In *The Cambridge Companion to Nathaniel Hawthorne* (47–54). Ed. Richard H. Millington.
Urban, David V. "Evasions of the Finite in Hawthorne's 'Artist of the Beautiful.'" *Christianity and Literature* 54:3 (2005): 343–58.

"The Birthmark"

Micklus, Robert. "Hawthorne's Jeckyll and Hyde: The Aminadab in Aylmer." *Literature and Psychology* 29 (1979): 148–59.
Pfister, Joel. *The Production of Personal Life* (13–51).
Van Leer, David M. "Aylmer's Library: Transcendental Alchemy in Hawthorne's 'The Birthmark.'" *American Transcendental Quarterly* 25 (1975): 211–20.

"The Celestial Rail-road"

Weinstein, Cindy. "Easy Rider / Easy Reader." In *The Literature of Labor and the Labor of Literature: Allegory in Nineteenth-Century American Fiction* (55–69). New York: Cambridge University Press, 1995.

"Drowne's Wooden Image"

Newberry, Frederick. "Fantasy, Reality, and Audience in Hawthorne's 'Drowne's Wooden Image.'" *Studies in the Novel* 23 (1991): 28–45.

"Endicott and the Red Cross"

Doubleday, Neal Frank. *Hawthorne's Early Tales* (101–08).
Nickel, John. "Hawthorne's Demystification of History in 'Endicott and the Red Cross.'" *Texas Studies in Literature and Language* 42 (2000): 347–62.

"Ethan Brand"

Cameron, Sharon. *The Corporeal Self* (88–102).
Fogle, Richard Harter. *Hawthorne's Fiction* (41–58).
Martin, Terence. *Nathaniel Hawthorne* (98–103).

"Feathertop"

Westbrook, Ellen E. "Exposing the Verisimilar: Hawthorne's 'Wakefield' and 'Feathertop.'" *Arizona Quarterly* 45 (1989): 1–23.
Wright, John W. "A Feathertop Kit." In *Nathaniel Hawthorne's Tales* (439–54). Ed. James McIntosh. New York: Norton, 1987.

"The Gentle Boy"

Colacurcio, Michael J. *The Province of Piety* (160–202).
Crews, Frederick. *The Sins of the Fathers* (61–72).
Doubleday, Neal Frank. *Hawthorne's Early Tales* (159–70).

Gross, Seymour. "Hawthorne's Revisions of 'The Gentle Boy.'" *American Lit-erature* 26 (1954): 196–208.
Miller, Edwin Haviland. "'Wounded Love': Nathaniel Hawthorne's 'The Gentle Boy.'" *Nathaniel Hawthorne Journal* 1978: 47–54.

"The May-Pole of Merry Mount"

Colacurcio, Michael J. *The Province of Piety* (251–82).
Doubleday, Neal Frank. *Hawthorne's Early Tales* (92–101).
McWilliams, John P., Jr. "Fictions of Merry Mount." *Arizona Quarterly* 29 (1977): 3–30.
Vickery, John P. "The Golden Bough at Merry Mount." *Nineteenth-Century Fiction* 12 (1957): 203–14.

"The Minister's Black Veil"

Boone, N. S. "'The Minister's Black Veil' and Hawthorne's Ethical Refusal of Responsibility: A Levinasian Parable." *Renascence* 57 (2005): 165–79.
Brumm, Ursula. *American Thought and Religious Typology* (118–21), Trans. John Hoaglund. New Brunswick, NJ: Rutgers University Press, 1970.
Carnochan, W. B. "'The Minister's Black Veil': Symbol, Meaning, and the Context of Hawthorne's Art." *Nineteenth-Century Fiction* 24 (1969): 182–93.
Colacurcio, Michael J. *The Province of Piety* (314–85).
Davis, Theo. *Formalism, Experience, and the Making of American Literature in the Nineteenth Century* (74–77).
Martin, Terence. *Nathaniel Hawthorne* (72–77).
Reese, James B. "Mr. Hooper's Vow." *Emerson Society Quarterly* 21 (1975): 93–102.

"My Kinsman, Major Molineux"

Hoffman, Daniel G. *Form and Fable in American Fiction* (113–25).
Pearce, Roy Harvey. "Hawthorne and the Sense of the Past, or, The Immortality of Major Molineux." In *Historicism Once More: Problems and Occasions for the American Scholar.* (137–74) Princeton, NJ: Princeton University Press, 1969.
———. "Robin Molineux on the Analyst's Couch: A Note on the Limits of Psychoanalytic Criticism." In *Historicism Once More* (96–106).
Shaw, Peter. "Fathers, Sons, and the Ambiguities of Revolution in 'My Kinsman, Major Molineux.'" *New England Quarterly* 49 (1976): 559–76.
Trilling, Lionel. *The Experience of Literature: A Reader with Commentaries* (438–40). New York: Holt, Rinehart and Winston, 1967.

"The Old Manse"

Baym, Nina. *The Shape of Hawthorne's Career* (113–16).
Cox, James. "The Scarlet Letter: Through The Old Manse and The Custom House." *Virginia Quarterly Review* 51 (1975): 432–47.
Person, Leland S. Jr. "Hawthorne's Bliss of Paternity: Sophia's Absence from 'The Old Manse.'" *Studies in the Novel* 23 (1991): 28–45.
Reynolds, Larry J. "Hawthorne and Emerson in 'The Old Manse.'" *Studies in the Novel* 23 (1991): 60–80.
Willoughby, John C. "The Old Manse Revisited: Some Analogies for Art." *New England Quarterly* 46 (1973): 45–61.

"Rappaccini's Daughter"

Adams, Richard P. "Hawthorne: The Old Manse Period" (139–51).
Bensick, Carol Marie. *La Nouvelle Béatrice: Renaissance and Romance in "Rappaccini's Daughter."* New Brunswick, NJ: Rutgers University Press, 1985.

Cook, Jonathan. "The Biographical Background to 'Rappaccini's Daughter.'" *Nathaniel Hawthorne Review* 31 (2005): 34–73.
Crews, Frederick C. *The Sins of the Fathers* (117–35).
Karlow, Martin. "'Rappaccini's Daughter' and the Art of Dreaming." *University of Hartford Studies in Literature* 13 (1981): 122–38.
Martin, Terence. *Nathaniel Hawthorne* (93–98).
Uroff, M. D. "The Doctors in 'Rappaccini's Daughter.'" *Nineteenth-Century Fiction* 27 (1972): 61–70.

"Roger Malvin's Burial"

Cameron, Sharon. *The Corporeal Self* (137–44).
Colacurcio, Michael J. *The Province of Piety* (107–30).
Daly, Robert S. "History and Chivalric Myth in 'Roger Malvin's Burial.'" *Essex Institute Historical Collections* 109 (1973): 99–115.
Levin, David. "Modern Misjudgments of Racial Imperialism in Hawthorne and Parkman." *Yearbook of English Studies* 13 (1983): 145–58.
McIntosh, James. "Nature and Frontier in 'Roger Malvin's Burial.'" *American Literature* 60 (1988): 188–204.
Millington, Richard H. *Practicing Romance* (15–25).
Person, Leland S. "Hawthorne's Early Tales: Male Authorship, Domestic Violence, and Female Readers." In *Hawthorne and the Real* (125–43). Ed. Millicent Bell.
Scheick, William J. "The Hieroglyphic Rock in Hawthorne's 'Roger Malvin's Burial.'" *Emerson Society Quarterly* 24 (1978): 72–76.

"Wakefield"

Chibka, Robert L. "Hawthorne's Tale Told Twice: A Reading of 'Wakefield.'" *Emerson Society Quarterly* 28 (1982): 220–32.
Weinstein, Arnold. "Hawthorne's 'Wakefield' and the Art of Self-Possession." *Nobody's Home: Speech, Self, and Place* (13–26). New York: Oxford University Press, 1993.

"Young Goodman Brown"

Abel, Darrell. "Black Glove and Pink Ribbon: Hawthorne's Metonymic Symbols." *New England Quarterly* 42 (1969): 163–80.
Clark, James W., Jr. "Hawthorne's Use of Evidence in 'Young Goodman Brown.'" *Essex Institute Historical Collections* 111 (1975): 12–34.
Levin, David. "Shadows of Doubt: Specter Evidence in Hawthorne's 'Young Goodman Brown.'" *American Literature* 34 (1962): 344–52.
Levy, Leo B. "The Problem of Faith in 'Young Goodman Brown.'" *Journal of English and Germanic Philology* 74 (1975): 375–87.
Liebman, Sheldon W. "The Reader in 'Young Goodman Brown.'" *Nathaniel Hawthorne Journal* 5 1975: 156–69.
Magee, Bruce R. "Faith and Fantasy in 'Young Goodman Brown.'" *Nathaniel Hawthorne Review* 29 (2003): 1–24.